Praise for Randy Lee Eickhoff and *The Fourth Horseman*

"Poisoned by the violence of the war, Doc Holliday carried Death with him as a constant companion and slowly destroyed himself even as he was destroying others. Randy Lee Eickhoff sees him as a metaphor for the Old West, for it too had its few blazing moments in the sun, then faded away with the inevitability of a Greek tragedy."

—Elmer Kelton

"Besides his fine research, Randy Lee Eickhoff has looked deep into the sad, strange soul of Doc Holliday and found truth."

—Win Blevins, Spur Award–winning author of *Stone Song*

"Doc Holliday, friend of Wyatt Earp, emerges as a sharply defined, tragic character in Eickhoff's fifth book. . . . Bad whiskey, bad women, and bad luck carry Doc to his own destruction, but not before he squares accounts with some of the West's worst hombres in this engaging and morally ambiguous tale."

—*Publishers Weekly*

"*The Fourth Horseman* is a definitive volume on Doc Holliday—and a milestone in the literature of the American heartland."

Kathleen O'Neal Gear,
rs of *People of the Mist*

inest writer of suspense

—Clive Cussler

Forge Books by Randy Lee Eickhoff

The Raid
The Feast
The Fourth Horseman
Bowie (with Leonard C. Lewis)
*Fallon's Wake**
*The Sorrows**

Other Works

FICTION

A Hand to Execute
The Gombeen Man

NONFICTION

Exiled
*forthcoming

THE FOURTH HORSEMAN

Randy Lee Eickhoff

A TOM DOHERTY ASSOCIATES BOOK
NEW YORK

This is a work of fiction. All the characters and events portrayed in this book are either products of the author's imagination or are used fictitiously.

THE FOURTH HORSEMAN

Copyright © 1998 by Randy Lee Eickhoff

A Forge Book
Published by Tom Doherty Associates, LLC
175 Fifth Avenue
New York, NY 10010

Forge® is a registered trademark of Tom Doherty Associates, LLC.

ISBN 0-812-57183-5
Library of Congress Catalog Card Number: 97-40371

First edition: February 1998
First mass market edition: November 1999

Printed in the United States of America

0 9 8 7 6 5 4 3 2 1

for
Kip Lane Eickhoff

ACKNOWLEDGMENTS

A work of this size may be an individual's own vision, but the author still owes a large debt of gratitude to many people. I would like to thank Leon Metz for the generous loan of his library, much of which has been piled in my own for well over a year; Dale L. Walker for his constant encouragement; Jory Sherman and Richard S. Wheeler for daring to go where I follow; Carlos Fuentes whose own works gave me the idea for the novel's voice; and my agent, Jacques de Spoelberch, who kept the work honest with his constant questioning, and Robert Gleason, my editor.

And they rode upon the earth,
The Four Horsemen of the Apocalypse
And among them we knew their names:
Conquest, Pestilence, War, and Death.
But the most feared among them was He
Who was fourth and rode the pale horse.

PROLOGUE

. . . *Mattie* . . .

    . . . *Cast aside your veil and fall with me, now, into the dark, moonless deep, out of the depths of memory, into the frosty November of our lives. . . . Let us share, finally, what we planned, what has been forbidden us by your vows and my sickness, the worm turning in my chest, eating my life from me. . . .*

    . . . *And here comes the good Father approaching my bedside, his robe spreading its vulture wings, to gather me into the bosom of a god who forsook me long ago as I foresook him . . . saving even your memory from the sin of my thought that might mar your spirit, your soul (do nuns keep their sex? or is that taken from them when they take the veil?). . . . His words spread dust upon my body . . . Will I feel the cold of a wintery grave? . . . Or will the last thoughts of your arms, your white arms holding me tightly, the tremor of your lips brushing mine, will these thoughts warm me in death? . . .*

". . . in nomine Patre, et Fili, et spiritus sanctus . . ."

. . . I know the rote well . . . useless words designed to comfort a dying man. . . . But I take no comfort in them. . . . But now, the final confession, the final words, the act of contrition. . . . For a moment, a brief moment, you will have to forgive me, dear Mattie, as I step back into the world I knew to prepare myself for . . . what? . . . I do not know. . . .

". . . And so we shuffle into the final chapter, Father Downey . . .

". . . illusion. . . ."

one

CONQUEST

1

"JOHN HENRY!"

The voice bellowed out from Father's library, curled around the magnolia trees in the front yard, streaked down past the stable, and finally found me playing with Sam, a son of one of Father's former nigras, down by the old slave cabins at the beginning of the long grove of pecan trees. I cringed. I knew that tone: Father had been a major with Fannin's Avengers during the Mexican War and the Twenty-seventh Georgia Infantry in the Confederate Army, and his military coldness carried over to the family when he was angry—almost a constant state with him since we had moved from Griffin (in the piedmont region of Georgia following my sister's death and Sherman's march to the sea) to Valdosta, where he had established himself as a lawyer and planter. I wondered what I had done this time as I took my jackknife back from Sam, forfeiting our game of mumblety-peg, and ran as fast as I could for the house. If I didn't show before the third calling of my name, I would feel Father's wrath through his razor strap on my backside and Father was heavy-handed.

"John Henry!"

My chest burned as I scrambled up the back porch past the lilac bushes and raced down the hall, my feet clattering on the freshly waxed boards. Lizie, one of our house servants, flattened herself against the floral papered wall muttering, "Lawd, run, child, run!" as I sped past, sliding recklessly around the doorjamb just as Father was gathering his voice for the third cry.

"Yes, Father?" I panted, trying to stand straight. My knees shook from my frantic efforts to get to him before the final call, and I concentrated desperately upon keeping them stiff.

Father thought that trembling was a mark of weakness, and the scornful lashing of his tongue cut almost as deeply as the razor strap.

He gave me his level gaze; I quailed inward, striving to keep my fear from showing upon my face. The early afternoon cast deep golden rays through slatted shades, but already he wore a claw-hammer white coat with matching trousers and a gold brocade waistcoat for the evening. I couldn't see his feet, but I knew his balmorals had been highly polished by his personal nigra. He looked with disdain at the coarse butternut cotton shirt I wore against the heat and my gray trousers and shook his head. I never could dress to please him.

He pointed a manicured finger to the bookshelves on my right. My gaze obediently followed his nicotine-stained forefinger, clutching a thick cigar between it and his middle finger.

"Where," he said softly, "is that book?"

"Which one, Father?" I asked, stalling for time.

"Don't be a fool," he said stiffly. "The one that belongs in the place where there is none: Swift's *Gulliver's Travels*."

He stood, towering above the gleaming mahogany of his desk. The tips of his fingers rested on the green felt pad in front of him: a recognized pose mirrored in the oil painting of him above the fireplace, except in the painting he wore his uniform. The walnut paneling glowed with a soft richness and reflected the brass fittings of the whale-oil lamps on the walls. The chairs in the room were black walnut spool-turned except for the Beltner chair he used behind his desk.

"What have I told you about borrowing things without asking?"

"Not to, sir," I said. I concentrated on the broken veins spreading across the deep pores of his ruddy cheeks and nose. I had discovered that if I kept my eyes there, he would think I was meeting his blue-eyed stare. For years I had been playing this game as his stare seemed to burn its way through my eyes to the back of my brain, reading my thoughts there. I had feared his stare since I couldn't remember. No, I do.

Once he stepped on a toy of mine—I think it was a wooden locomotive one of our bondsmen had carved—and his heavy hand flashed out, striking my cheek and sending me reeling against the wall, his heavy signet ring splitting my cheek. I was two or three, perhaps. Usually his bursts of temper spent themselves upon my back. I carried a large, keloid weal there from one of his more enthusiastic punishments when I knocked over a bottle of wine he had opened for dinner while reaching for a fresh watermelon pickle Lizie had put up during her June canning.

Suddenly the pit of my stomach lurched, then a coldness settled in it and began to creep up my chest. I shifted my gaze and stared into his eyes. My brain seethed, and hateful words began to form themselves in my throat.

"And?" he continued, his voice lowering dangerously. A recklessness began to burn within me. I threw my head back and stood straighter, surprising myself when I met his eyes direct. I opened my mouth to speak, but a voice interrupted me.

"For heaven's sake, Henry, I took the book," Mother said from behind my shoulder as she swept into the room in front of me, her crinoline and skirt brushing my legs. She paused to lick her hand and press down a tuft of hair on my head. A faint scent of lemon verbena slipped down her wrist. Her quiet, black eyes stared warmly for a moment into mine, then hardened as she turned to Father.

"You came home late last night, and I took the book to help pass the time while I waited for you. Honestly, you wouldn't condemn a lawyer for accusing someone without giving him a moment to explain in court; don't you think you owe your son the same courtesy?"

"You know his habit, Alice," Father said sternly. "If he is innocent, why doesn't he come out and say it?"

"Have you given him a chance?" she challenged.

Father glared at her, but Mother calmly met his anger. He lifted his hand from the pad, clasping the velvet lapel of his white coat, shifting his shoulders back. It was the pose he held when he was finished with the moment and had decided to move on to something else. A muscle fluttered in my chest.

"Very well," he said. He looked at me. "You may go."

I didn't move. An eyebrow quirked, and he frowned at me.

"You may go," he said, emphasizing his words. Mother sensed the anger and turned quickly to me.

"Go on, now," she said softly. I hesitated. Her eyes softened with pleading. "You need to practice the Mozart concerto. It's not quite ready yet."

The rage left me, and I turned, stumbling a bit on the rug as I stepped away from the door. I took a step down the hall, then leaned against the wall across from the deacon's bench used by people to clean their shoes when it rained. I felt feverish, hot and cold, my lungs still aching from my sprint.

"Henry, you have to stop bullying that boy," Mother said.

Father snorted at her words.

"Alice, it would be best if you stayed out of the matters between us. You had him for the first ten years. You played your game of house with him: teaching him the piano, reading to him. But now it is time he learned how to be a man."

"He's just a boy!"

"At the end, the boys were fighting the war," Father said quietly. "Have you forgotten the cadets who routed one of Sherman's troops near Atlanta?"

"The war is over," Mother said. "It is time to let boys be boys again."

"That time will never return, Alice. There is no time for boys to be boys anymore. The war has killed our youth. They have to learn to be men. If your brother was here, he would agree with me."

"Thomas isn't here and well you know it," she answered.

"And you can thank Sherman for that," Father said icily. "He is the one who tore up the railroad tracks, leaving our boys to come home from Appomattox and Savannah on foot. It takes time to walk that far, Alice. It takes time."

"You could do something about that," she said.

"What would you have me do, Alice?"

"Go after him."

"I'm too busy. I have a law practice and the planting of the new scuppernong vines for the vineyard I'm planning. I'm also trying to introduce the pod pepper, the wanderer. I simply do not have the time, Alice, despite what you may think. I have a life to rebuild here, and I have the means to do it. You remember what it was like when I came back in 'sixty-two after Malvern Hill. I was sick and we were broke. We were almost ruined! Why, if I hadn't bought this property in Valdosta when the Savannah & Gulf Railroad came through, I don't know what we would have done. We have been mighty lucky, and I don't intend to take time off to go galli-vanting over the country on some fool's errand. Romantic nonsense!"

I knew that tone of voice; it was dismissal. I scurried down the hall and into the salon before Mother came out and caught me listening. Although she was my protector, she took a dim view of eavesdropping.

I slid open the door and stepped inside, pausing for a moment. The salon had been furnished with balloon-shaped rosewood chairs standing beside cartouche-shaped tables. A medallion-backed sofa stood facing the piano. I loved the room. Here, we played games when my cousin visited: Copenhagen, Fox and Goose, Consequences, Pencil, Change Partners. Mattie and I used to ask each other riddles, each trying to outdo the other, and sing songs. She sang, that is, in a high soprano while I accompanied her on the piano. Now I stepped to the piano and slipped onto the bench, fumbling with the music propped on the stand. I ran my fingers over the keys, playing a chromatic scale to loosen them, then rolled into the concerto Mother had decided I would play at her next soirée. I sensed Mother entering the room behind me, but I ignored her, concentrating on the music, letting it wash over me, soothe me. When I finished, she came behind me and affectionately smoothed my hair.

"You're too angry, John," she said. "Mozart should be played lightly, delicately. You sound as if you're trying to drive the keys through the sound board."

"I hate him, Mother," I said, leaning over the keyboard, avoiding her eyes.

"Shh. Now, you don't mean that. He's your father."

"An accident," I said. "I didn't pick him. And I don't think he would have picked me if he would have had a choice."

"I know. I know," she sighed. She turned her head, coughing gently into a handkerchief she took from her sleeve.

"Why did you marry him, Mother? Surely there were others."

She smiled wryly. Her blue eyes looked off into the distance of memory.

"Oh my, yes, there were others. But Papa decided that the major was the better choice for me."

"You should have chosen the one you wanted," I said.

"Why, John Henry! You know that's the way of things. It is a father's duty to select the husband for his daughter."

"That isn't right," I argued. "I can understand the nigras being treated like that, but why a white woman?"

She sighed and fondly tweaked my nose. Tiny beads of perspiration dotted her upper lip. Her eyes looked bright and moist.

"Now don't mind about that. You can't change things that have become the ways. You need to get back to work on that concerto. And remember this time: lightly, delicately."

Obediently, I turned and began working my way through the concerto again. She sat on a small chair beside me, humming along as I played, lightly tapping the underside of my wrists, raising them so my hands would curve over the keys. After a while, I sensed the tapping of her foot out of time. I glanced at her, noticing her pinched nostrils, the lines etching themselves at the corners of her lips and eyes. She smiled, patted my shoulder, and rose and left. I knew where she was going: to her room where she kept laudanum and a bottle of sherry, her medicine against mysterious ailments that seemed to afflict her in the afternoons.

"Where are you going?"

The voice startled me, and I fumbled at the keys a moment before stopping. I turned on the bench and saw Father standing in the doorway, blocking Mother from leaving.

"I'm feeling faint, Henry," she said lowly. "I'm going to my room."

"To your bottle, you mean. I think you'd better lay off that stuff," he said.

"You drink your toddies!" I burst out.

Silence fell in the room. Father looked over Mother's head at me, and I saw the anger in his eyes. My heart thudded in my chest.

"What did you say, boy?" he asked quietly. I had heard that tone of voice once before when a nigra—Sam's father—had sassed him out in the grove. When Father was finished, the nigra had to be taken to his cabin until the veterinarian could come and treat him with Dr. Flint's Quaker Bitters and jalap. Once I would have quailed at that tone, but now I could feel the rage moving through me, creeping up my chest into my throat.

"Leave her alone," I said. My words rang clearly in the room. He flushed and started around Mother. She reached out and grabbed his hand, throwing herself in front of him.

"John Henry! Go to your room!" she commanded. I hesitated, then slipped out the other door.

"Get back here, boy!" Father yelled angrily. I heard a gasp, then a thud.

"Oh, you brute!"

I turned back to the room. Father was kneeling beside her, concern showing on his face. She saw me standing in the doorway and waved her hand at me behind Father's back. I turned and ran down the hall. Swiftly, I mounted the stairs to my room and fell on the bed, trying to make myself stop panting for air. The air seemed thicker, heavier than it had been in the past. I took a deep breath and held it for a moment, then slowly let it trickle from my lips. I glanced at the small, plain table beside my bed: *Gulliver's Travels* rested there, a dried primrose, given me by Mattie, marking my place. I lifted the book from the table, my fingers caressing the leather of its spine, tracing the letters stamped in gold. Tears came to my eyes as I remembered Father's words to me. I felt their cut deeply and swallowed against the thick ball rising in my throat, the prelude to tears.

I didn't know why he hated me so, but I knew he hated me

as much as he hated the Yankees who had torn our country apart. When I looked into his eyes, I saw no feeling there: only coldness and aloofness. When he drank he was worse, his words taking on an extra edge, his criticism homing in on what was precious to me at the moment.

I tried to be what he wanted, but other things besides hunting and farming were more important to me. I didn't fit into the preconceived mold he had for me, into his world. And he couldn't understand mine. Not, I reflected sourly, that I had a world since the war.

The door opened, and Mother stepped into my room. She saw the book in my hands and smiled tiredly. She crossed to the bed and sat beside me. Her breath came in tiny gasps from having climbed the stairs. She nodded at the book.

"I think you'd better let me have that," she said.

Soundlessly, I handed it to her. She smiled and opened it to the pages I had marked with the primrose.

"Now, quickly: Tell me what I have been reading."

"It's not fair," I said, the words bursting from me. "It's not as if I was stealing the book."

She hushed me, placing a soft finger across my lips.

"I know. I know. But you must remember to ask, John. That's all. You know he'll let you borrow the books if you only ask."

"After he gives me his lecture on responsibility," I said, pushing my head back against the softness of my pillow, sulking. "And when I return it, I get his lecture on promptness. Everything is a lecture with him."

She sighed and smoothed my hair. She frowned and pressed her palm against my forehead. Concern touched her eyes.

"Are you well? You feel warm."

"Tired," I confessed. "That's all."

"Well," she said, rising. "You rest. I'll return the book for you." She bent and pressed her lips against my cheek, then straightened, took a deep breath, and crossed to the door.

"Mother?"

She turned and smiled, waiting.

"When will Uncle Thomas return from the war?"

A tiny frown line appeared between her eyes. "Soon, John. Soon. I hope."

She left, closing the door silently behind her. I rolled over on my side and stared through my window. A lone hawk climbed high in the sky, spiraling in lazy circles. Clouds marched by above him. I closed my eyes.

And slept.

2

The night opened into a large, black, airless sarcophagus as hot as a forge, fetid as an abandoned outhouse, and through the darkness a form moved, large pustules dripping yellow pus from its face, hair hanging in lank strands along hollow cheeks, eyes jellied stones, and it stretched its rotting hand with black fingernails toward me, slowly reaching, touching my cheek. . . .

Father!

I awoke. Streams of late afternoon sunlight, filtered through the panes of my window, painted bars across my ceiling. I sat up and swung my feet off the counterpane to the floor. I felt dizzy and gripped the edge of the bed until the dizziness passed.

Angry voices slipped up to my window from below. Curious, I rose and walked to the window and looked out. Father stood on the gravel below, his white suit contrasting with the gray rock. In front of him stood a heavyset man who mopped his florid face repeatedly with a large handkerchief the size of a small tablecloth. An equally large nigra wearing a yellow suit and derby hat too small for his kinky head sat watchfully on the seat behind him. Curious, I slipped the catch and pushed the window open. The movement caught the man's eye, and he glanced up. His blue-washed eyes, red with drink, stared into mine for a moment, then returned again to Father's.

"This isn't the Boutain place," Father said slowly. He tapped a riding whip lightly against his right leg. To one who didn't know him, his words sounded soft and apologetic, but I knew that tone and the heat behind the words ready to explode.

The man leered at him and looked over his shoulder at the nigra waiting watchfully in the buggy. He shook his head and turned back to Father.

"Yes, that's what all you people say," he said arrogantly. The words rasped upon my ears in his northern twang. "It ain't the right place. I've come to the wrong house. Whatever. Truth of the matter is that the place *is* the right place and taxes are still owed on it. This here,"—he paused as he slipped a limp piece of paper out of an inside pocket and waved it aloft, declaiming like Cicero—"gives me the right to move you out of here and seize your property. You will see that I have paid the taxes and the filing fees. I have bought your place, Mr. Boutain. That's all there is to it. Clean and simple."

"Things with you white trash are seldom simple and never clean," Father said. "Get off my land."

"Ah, ah." He wagged a fat finger in front of Father's nose. *"My* land."

"My name," Father said, emphasizing each word, "is Major Henry Holliday. Not Boutain. Now, will you get off our land?"

"Well, if you ain't Boutain, then just where in hell is *his* land?" the man asked.

"Find out for yourself, damn it!" Father exploded. His hand flashed up, the stock of the whip jabbing itself into the man's belly. Father followed him as he backed away from the whip's prodding. "Now get the hell off my land and don't come back. If you do, I'll file a suit in court charging you with harassment and trespass."

"A *northern* court," the man sneered, but he backed away

anyway and clambered into the buggy. The nigra edged around, his hand sliding inside his coat.

"Your hand better come out empty, boy," Father said dangerously. His left hand slid behind his back.

"That's enough, Nat!" the white man said sharply. I knew his concern: He was in the line of fire. The white man then did an odd thing: He reached over and patted the nigra on his knee. Reluctantly, the nigra slowly brought his hand out and held it up empty to Father. His thick lips split in a yellow-toothed grin.

"We be back if we find out you name Boutain," the nigra said. "If it be, then I kick you white trash ass off personally."

The white man snapped the buggy whip sharp against the horse's back. It leaped forward and he sawed on the reins, jerking its head in a sharp turn that almost tipped over the buggy. Gravel spurted away from the wheels as it lurched down the lane, gathering speed. Father stood, watching it disappear around the pecan trees, then shook his shoulders in anger and slapped the whip hard against his leg. He turned back to our house, his eyes sliding up the white columns to meet mine gazing down at him. For a moment anger flared in them, then settled into smoldering coals. He nodded curtly and mounted the steps below the balcony, disappearing from view.

A soft knock came at the door behind me. I pulled the shutter closed and turned.

"Come in!" I called.

The door opened and Lizie entered, balancing a tray on one hand. She crossed to the small table beside my bed and slid the tray onto it. I glanced at the blue plates on it: collard greens, a pork chop, buttered potato, fresh corn pone, and a glass of buttermilk, with brown betty for dessert. She caught my eye and grinned, her teeth startling white against the gleaming ebony of her face.

"Y'Mama thought you would eat better up here," she said, the words rolling out through a rich alto that seemed to burst the walls of the colored Baptist church on Sundays. "Lawd, y'*know* better than to try you Papa like that. He whip you good."

"Thanks, Lizie," I said. I gave her a smile. "You take good care of me. What would I ever do without you?"

"Git y'self whopped, that's sure," she said sternly. Then she smiled and tucked a napkin in my collar. "Now y'eat everything on this plate, you hear? I means *ev'thing,* young John. Including the collards."

"I don't like collards," I complained.

"Y'need the greens," she said firmly. She picked up my fork, filled it with collards, and stabbed it toward my mouth. I opened my mouth in self-defense, and she deftly slipped the fork into it.

"There," she said with satisfaction. "Now, y'swaller that."

I chewed convulsively twice and swallowed and made a face, reaching for the buttermilk to chase the mild vinegary taste out of my mouth.

"Was Father disappointed that I'm not there for supper?"

"That man! 'Course he is. Y'know how he gets," she said, rolling her eyes toward the open doorway. She lowered her voice. "Y'momma puts him right, never you fear. But she's worried terrible now. Terrible." She shook her head.

"What about?" I asked around a mouthful of potato. I washed it down with another gulp of buttermilk. Lizie frowned.

"Y'chew you food, now. Gulping will give you the belly-ache for sure and then Ah'll have to dose you with the Hostetter's Bitters." She nodded approvingly as I chewed a bit of meat. It was mostly gristle.

" 'Bout y'Uncle Thomas. He's not home yet, and that gots her worried."

"And Father won't go after him," I finished. I pushed myself back from the plate. "I don't want any more. I'm full."

She scowled and started to say something, but I pulled the napkin from my neck, wiped my mouth, and dropped the napkin over the plate. She glared at me, then picked up the tray and started for the door.

"Boy don't eat enough to keep a bird alive," she muttered. She paused at the door and looked back at me. "It sure would help around here if Mr. McKey was back. Give y'momma a bit of help with y'daddy." She sighed. "Lawd willing, maybe soon."

She left, pulling the door shut behind her. I lay back on my bed, clasping my hands beneath my head. I stared out the window, watching the red streaks slowly retreat behind the advancing black. The faint outline of the full moon showed white, slowly turning to orange.

Hunter's moon, I thought absently. Then I again heard Lizie's words and wished Uncle Thomas was home, too, bitterly thinking, If Uncle Thomas was here, then Father would spend more time in town and leave the running of the farm to him. But Father won't go after him. That wouldn't be right. After all, a man's got to make his own way in the world; nobody will give him anything. I can repeat that lecture verbatim. I can repeat all his lectures verbatim.

An idea slipped across my mind on bat wings and disappeared. I frowned, groping for it, finding it, bringing it back: If Father won't go after him, why don't you?

Startled, I sat up quickly in bed, automatically clutching the side of the bed against the expected dizziness. Go after Uncle Thomas? What an absurd idea! And how would I get there?

Father's stallion is in the stable, and the mare that pulls Mother's cabriolet when she goes to the Presbyterian Church outside Valdosta. You could take both horses and go after him yourself.

But . . .

You could take one of Father's pistols!

I rose and crossed to the window and stared out into the twilight. A whippoorwill sounded in the distance, his voice rising solemnly, lonely, through the scale. I looked down at the old slave cabins dimly showing through the limbs of the trees. Sam's door was open, light spilling out into the night. One of the men was singing in a rich bass, the old spiritual rolling out, chasing the devil from the night. I turned and caught a glimpse of myself in the mirror above my bureau. Thin, gaunt, some might say, with high cheekbones and ash-blond hair. My eyes were startling blue in the white of my face.

Why not? It might make Father mad.

A wild recklessness fell over me, and my blood lurched within me, burning with a fierce resolution. I stepped to the wardrobe in the corner, stripping my clothes from my body and leaving them where they fell on the floor. I dressed in the black suit I wore to church and sat down on the floor to tug on my Wellington boots cobbled out of soft leather that came to the knee. I rose and quietly settled my feet in them, moving my toes around to try and stretch the leather a bit more. I had not worn them in nearly a year after falling from Sarah, the dainty mare I was given to ride, and now they seemed a bit small for my feet.

I've grown, I thought wonderingly, forcing away the memory of Father screaming at me as I lay on the ground, the breath knocked out of me after I fell from Sarah's back. I crossed back to the mirror to stare again at the face there. A faint downy line showed over my upper lip. I stroked it curiously, feeling its softness. I had seen it before, but not in this light and not with tonight's meaning behind it. I turned from the mirror and left the room, moving quietly on the balls of my feet down the stairs. My heart hammered in my chest as I thought dreaded thoughts of discovery and Father pulling me by my ear into the back anteroom where he kept a razor strap hidden in the cupboard. Unwilling pictures kept flashing in my mind. . . .

"Drive that damn devil from you, boy! You hear me?"

And the strap moving like wispy shadows up and down, snicking tiny cuts in my back, barking and biting. I smell the oil soap used to clean the wood of the table I'm bent over and see the thick cords of the woven rug beneath the table and the colors faded where the sun strikes them day by day. I smell the dust, and the smell sets me to coughing and I feel that my lungs will never draw a full breath without the pain being etched into my back with a leather stylus. I clench my teeth and concentrate on the ruby drops spattering in flagellant fury on the floor. . . .

I stepped down from the stairs and crept close to the wall, trying to stay on the hall runner that deadens the sound my boot heels would make on the pegged-pine floor.

Cautiously I eased my head around the door frame and glanced into the dining room with its floral wallpaper and picture by Currier and Ives: "The United States Army Leaving the Gulf Squadron—9th March, 1847," as drawn by J. M. Ladd. Father sat at the head of the table, filling his wineglass from the half-full bottle behind him. The light from the camphene lamps spread a golden light over the heavy black walnut and mahogany furniture and shone through the burgundy, turning it to crimson, and I knew he would be at the table another half hour until the wine was finished before going to the study to have a cigar and brandy. Mother sat patiently at the foot of the table, shaking her head when he raised the bottle questioningly.

I tiptoed down the hall to the study, carefully sliding the door open. I stepped into the room. A fire flickered gently in the fireplace, casting teasing shadows across the spines of the books. I glanced at the place where Father had pointed earlier; *Gulliver's Travels* had been returned to its place. I crossed over the green Oriental rug to the cupboard at the end of the room where Father kept his guns. I tugged on the door; it was locked. I swore softly to myself and went to Father's desk, quietly slipping the center drawer open. The key lay on a pile of papers. I took it and started to close the drawer, then caught sight of a small chamois bag. I pulled the drawer open and picked up the bag. Coins clinked against each other. I hesitated, then dropped the bag into my coat pocket. I had started to push the drawer shut again when my eye fell upon a sheet of paper bearing the Army, Confederate States of America logo. I picked it up and glanced at it; it was Father's discharge from the army. I started to read it, then heard chairs scraping in the dining room. I stuffed the letter into my pocket and pushed the drawer shut. It scraped across the runner, and my heart stopped for a moment. I strained, listening in the dark, but did not hear Father's heavy heels coming down the hallway. My blood throbbed in my head, and I sti-

fled an impulse to cough as I moved back to the cupboard.
Father's Navy Colt .36-caliber pistol lay on a shelf beside his
army holster and belt with the CSA buckle. I tried to buckle
it around my waist, but the belt was too big. I took off my
coat, lengthened the belt, then slipped it around my shoulders
like a bandolier and replaced my coat. The holster snuggled
under my arm. I tucked the flap back under the holster, feeling the butt cold against my chest. A warm wave rolled over
me, soothing, strangely familiar. I reached under my coat,
and the Colt slipped easily from the holster. My hand curved
around the butt. I slipped it back into the holster and reached
again onto the shelf, dropping a small bag of caps and balls
into my other coat pocket. I slipped a small flask of powder
from the shelf and placed it in my inside breast pocket. One
thing about me Father could not criticize: I was a natural
shot. I remembered the amazement on his face when he
decided to teach me to load and shoot the Navy Colt and I
had placed the second five shots in the bull after the first shot
went wide. That was the one time Father did not criticize me.

I shook away my musings and locked the cupboard,
replaced the key in Father's desk, then stole quietly out of the
study and down the hallway, pausing to remove Father's
inverness from a hook.

Lizie looked up from the sawbuck table as I entered the
kitchen. Light from the kitchen fire shone off her black face
and reflected off the pans hanging from iron hooks. Her eyebrows raised at my suit and the inverness folded over my
arm. I held my forefinger against my lips, silencing the question bubbling up inside her.

"I'm going after Uncle Thomas," I said softly.

"What? Y'poor little fool! Y'can't do that! The road's full
of scalawags and riffraff just waiting for a little jacknips like
you! No sir! Y'ain't gonna go!"

"Be quiet," I ordered. Her face screwed up indignantly like
it did before the War when I had sassed her in the kitchen
when she was cooking. Words of admonishment seemed to
wait on her lips to drop down hard on me, scolding me for
my impertinence. She started to say something, then took

another look at me and fell silent, her face folding into that impassive mask the nigras wore in front of the overseer when he gave them orders before departing for the fields. Her eyes became curious, then hurt, then guarded.

"Don't tell Mother or Father anything until tomorrow morning. Understand?" I listened to the new authority in my voice and waited, half fearful, half wishing, that she would refuse and scold me for taking on airs. But she didn't, and when she didn't, I knew that something had passed between us that I didn't understand but that had changed our relationship. She nodded.

"I mean that, now, Lizie." She nodded again. I started past her, but she stopped me, placing her hand on my arm. Tears filled her large brown eyes.

"Y'be careful, now, hear?" she said softly. Her eyes were brown and moist. I nodded, patted her hand, then impulsively kissed her cheek. Her hand flew to her cheek as if it was scalded.

"Remember," I cautioned.

She nodded, and I stepped out into the cool night.

Cicadas sang in the trees. A mourning dove called, startling itself into silence. I breathed deeply of the fragrant blossoms as I walked softly down through the trees to the stables. Night air moved damply against my face. The stable door creaked against a rusty hinge as I opened it. Ares, Father's big black stallion, stirred restlessly in his stall, nickering softly at my presence. Sarah, my mare, snorted and twisted in her stall, thrusting her blaze-marked head over the wall of her stall to see what had bothered Father's horse.

"Easy, Ares," I murmured softly. I crossed to his stall and slowly raised my hand to stroke his velvet nose. He tossed his head away from my hand, his hooves shuffling in the thick straw. His eyes gleamed in the darkness of the stable, rolling at the shadows behind me. I stiffened, my hand creeping under my suit to clutch the Navy Colt. I took a step to the side and crouched as Sam walked out of the shadows.

"What y'think you doing, Mr. John?" Sam asked. "Y'know that horse only let your daddy ride him."

His ebony face gleamed faintly in the dark of the stable as he came to my side. He looked disapprovingly at me. I could smell the stale wood smoke on his clothes and the musky scent of his sweat. I straightened and let my hand slip from the Navy Colt.

"I'm going after Uncle Thomas, Sam," I said. I crossed to the tack room and took Father's saddle and bridle from their wooden pegs on the wall.

"You saddle Sarah," I said. I draped the saddle over Ares's stall and slid in beside him. He jerked his head away from me as I tried to slip the bridle over his head. I reached up and grabbed an ear, twisting it to hold his head in place as I firmly placed the bit against his mouth and pushed.

"No, sir," Sam protested. "Ah ain't gonna help you kill yourself. No, sir."

Ares pushed his mighty chest against me, pinning me against the wall. I struggled to slip out away from him. He pushed harder against me, and I flipped the reins of the bridle around his head and pulled back on them with my free hand, twisting his head away from me. He grumbled and followed the pull of the reins. I lay my head against his gleaming black flank and panted.

"Here, gimme that," Sam said solicitously, reaching for the reins. "Ah'll take care of him while you go back to the house."

I slapped his hands away and stepped out of Ares's stall. I threw my head back and glared at Sam. He held his hands in front of him, frowning at me like a child whose hand had been caught in the cookie jar. An eyebrow quivered, then he drew away, his eyes white in the darkness.

"Damn you, do as you're told," I said softly. "Now, you saddle Sarah and do it properly, you hear me?"

He stared hard at me for a long moment, his face slowly closing up into the mask most black people presented to whites. Suddenly I knew that our boyhood was behind us. I had become the white man and he the nigra. There would be no more games of mumblety-peg, no more sneaking out of the house for midnight hunts along the Withlacoochee River.

For a moment I felt a great emptiness, a loss. Then the exhilaration of the moment returned and I could almost taste the
excitement. I breathed deeply, smelling the rich manure of
the stable, the musty hay, the sour oat bran in the bin near the
front. Sam watched for a moment, then silently turned to the
tack room and fetched Sarah's saddle and bridle and walked
past without looking at me to her stall.

I lifted Ares's saddle from the stall and turned to place it
across his wide·back. He shrugged and the saddle started to
slip. I stepped back, doubled my fist, and struck him on the
wide bone of his nose.

"Enough! Stand!" I said, echoing Father's words.

His eyes, brown like walnuts, moved wildly and his
hooves shuffled against the straw-strewn floor of his stall,
but he stood still, muscles trembling beneath his satin coat. I
placed the saddle on his back and drew the cinch tightly
before leading him out of the stall. Sam waited for me,
Sarah's reins held loosely in his hands.

"I'm sorry, Sam," I said. "But this is something I have to
do for Mother."

He nodded silently and handed me the reins. He watched
impassively as I mounted Ares. I felt the big horse stiffen
under me and pulled back tightly on the reins, holding his
head up high to keep him from arching his back and throwing
me. He sidled toward the stable door. I ducked my head as
we moved out into the night, then touched him lightly with
my spurs, still keeping him from ducking his head between
his legs and tossing me over his head. He snorted and hopped
a little before settling into a stiff jog down the lane toward
the highway. Sarah stepped into a dainty trot beside us.

The moon moved like a ghostly galleon dancing behind
the clouds as we emerged onto the highway. I pulled Ares's
head toward the north, and he obediently settled into a lope,
reluctantly resigning himself to the pressure of the bit. Miles
disappeared beneath the hooves of the horses as we moved
steadily north. Now and then, a small campfire flickered in
the night beneath the black, crooked arms of old oaks, and
dark forms sat up outside Sibley tents to watch us pass. Gray

streamers of Spanish moss hung from the branches of oak and hickory trees, occasionally startling Ares when a stray breeze stirred them into spectral life beside the road. I kept nervously touching the Navy Colt beneath my arm, taking comfort from its presence whenever Ares danced sideways. We crossed a small creek, hooves thundering on the planks of the bridge. A small fog bank drifted across the road and the tendrils damply caressed my cheeks. A small breeze wafted across a swale of broomstraw, bringing the smell of rotting straw with it.

Then the miles turned into monotony, and the rhythm of Ares's gait dulled my senses into lethargy. I still touched the Colt, but more from a newly formed habit than from need. Morning found us well on our way toward Savannah. I slowed Ares to a walk. His hooves kicked up tiny clouds of dust on the road. Near a small creek close to Pearson, I found a mossy hummock beneath a yard-wide oak and dismounted, walking stiffly to loosen the muscles in my legs. I tied Sarah and Ares to a small elm in a patch of grass close by and stretched out on the hummock to rest. A mockingbird sang and a bee buzzed inquisitively around my face before streaking off. Somewhere, a squirrel scolded a blue jay. The sun was warm on my face, and I closed my eyes, not meaning to sleep, but the miles had drained the excitement away and the sun the tension. I dozed.

The sun stood high when I awoke, thirsty and slightly feverish. I sat up, panting to control the dizziness that momentarily darkened the world in front of my eyes. I stood, leaning against the gnarled oak tree, contemplating the creek in front of me. Then I heard the slow trickle of water across the glade behind me. I crossed and found a spring bubbling gently up through the center of an old, virid moss-covered stump, its edges blackened with age, beneath a chestnut tree. I scooped some water in my hand and bent my head, cautiously sipping: It tasted sweet, and I thrust my face in its coldness, drinking deeply while it cooled my fevered brow.

A warbler sang deep in the dusty bracken beyond the

trees. I lay down beneath the chestnut tree. Paper crinkled in my pocket. I reached inside and pulled out Father's discharge, badly wrinkled. I smoothed it out and read:

> I certify that I have carefully examined Major H. B. Holliday of the 27th Reg. Ga. Vol. and find him suffering with Chronic Diarrhea and general disability. He has been in the above mentioned condition ever since the return of our Army from Yorktown and consequently has been all that time either absent from the Rgt. under Med. treatment or recuperating in town from nostalgia. I doubt his prospect for recovery in the Army. I therefore respectfully recommend that his resignation be accepted.

Stunned, I lay back against the soft hummock. Father, discharged for runny shit. The man I thought to be a hero wasn't what he had been pretending. It was the first time my illusions were shattered—or maybe they were shattered before, when I discovered that my family was deficient in the love I saw in other families. But now I knew what had happened: Father had suddenly lost his nerve. That was why he refused to go after Uncle Thomas.

Ares snorted behind me, and I straightened and turned to find a large black man grinning and standing between me and the horses. My stomach knotted with fear. A smaller, ragged nigra stood behind him, clutching the reins in one dusty hand. I blinked in confusion for a moment, then weariness disappeared as Ares restlessly stamped his feet.

"It the sweet-gum in the stump that makes the water taste sweet. Didja know that, boy?" the big one said.

I shook my head.

"You long way from home, aintcha, boy?" the nigra said.

I swallowed, looking from one to the other. They grinned, recognizing my fear. I looked into their eyes and saw . . . contempt. And cruel power. My legs began to tremble and I had a burning need to pee. Suddenly I hated them for what they were making me become.

"That's my business. Now be off on your own," I replied. My voice sounded shrill to my ears. Did they notice?

"That ain't nice, now, boy," he said, the grin slipping a bit from his face.

"We gots as much right to this road as you now. The man in Washernton done give us that right. Now, what you got that we could use?"

He drew a large clasp knife from a pocket and opened it, waving it gently in front of me. Light glinted from its edge. I looked past him to the skinny black holding the horses. He grinned at me, and I knew that nothing I said would turn them from their intentions. The big nigra in front of me made a sudden movement to come closer, and I turned my attention to him.

"Now, boy," he said. The smile had slipped from his face. His eyes were black and shining with excitement. Tiny bubbles of spit appeared at the corners of his mouth.

I slipped my hand beneath my coat and the Navy Colt slid easily from its holster, surprising even me as I pulled it free and pointed it at him. His eyes widened, and he took three steps back from me, nearly falling into the creek. I stepped quickly to the side, facing the skinny one holding the reins of Sarah and Ares. Rage boiled up from my stomach, spilling into my throat. I felt light-headed, and the day suddenly became brighter, like crystal. Colors edged themselves into brilliant hues, greens and golds. Tiny dust motes danced in the sunlight shining through the leaves of the chestnut tree. I breathed deeply and smelled fear for the first time. Mine and theirs. My mouth felt dry. I swallowed, trying to clear the tightness at the back of my throat. I held on to the grip with both hands and rocked the hammer back with the joint of my thumb. The barrel wavered for a second, then steadied. What next? I wondered. What would Uncle Thomas do?

"What you planning on doing with that pistol, boy?" the big nigra said, and I could hear the nervousness in his voice. My blood sang and a recklessness ran through me. I shook with excitement as I realized that I only had to press gently with my forefinger to send them to hell.

And they knew it.

I could tell from their eyes and the way the big one licked his thick lips, his pink tongue sliding out like a thick dog's tongue. The skinny one took a nervous shuffle to his left. I laughed.

"Now, you goddamn nigras," I said. "You want me? Well, I'm your huckleberry. You—" I motioned to the nigra holding the horses. He flinched as the barrel of my pistol centered on him. "Tie those reins to that oak."

He hesitated, and I raised the Navy Colt, sighting down the barrel.

"I'll blow your nappy head off in a minute," I warned.

He bobbed his head and quickly ran the reins across a low branch, then stepped clear, working sideways to join his partner, trying to slither behind him. I took a deep breath, trying to relax the pounding in my temples. I considered the two in front of me: They wore ragged coats over butternut work-shirts. Their gray cotton pants were shapeless and coated with dried mud. The large one had cut the sides of his brogues open to relax the tension against his bunions. The small one's toes peeped from his brogues where the sole had parted from the leather uppers. Each had a haversack slung over his shoulder.

"Watcha gonna do?" he asked softly. His eyes were round with fear. I motioned at the large one.

"Toss that knife in the creek," I ordered. He hesitated, stared into my eyes, then hastily flipped the knife over into the leaf-dappled water. "Now, get back to that road and head south." They moved silently to the road. "Faster," I said, raising my voice.

They broke into a jog, their haversacks flopping on their rumps. The small one glanced over his shoulder. I raised the pistol, sighting. He broke into a dead run, his feet slapping dust clouds from the road. The large one lumbered after him. I watched until they disappeared around a curve, then lowered the hammer on the Navy Colt and slid it back into the holster under my arm. I leaned back against a gnarled bole of the oak and took a handkerchief from an inside pocket of my

coat and dabbed my forehead. My legs began to shake. My
fingers trembled and I tasted something brassy at the back of
my throat. Something moved in my chest, forcing me to
cough. I drew a deep, shaky breath, then walked to Ares. He
allowed me to stroke his nose, then tossed his head impatiently. I laughed.

"Thanks," I said. He bobbed his head as if he knew what I
was saying. Sarah nudged my arm, and I gave her a quick
pat, then untied both and swung up on Ares's back.

"Well," I said as Ares pricked his ears. "Let's get going.
We've got a fair lot of miles to travel yet."

He moved off impatiently onto the road. I turned him
north, and he shook his head with the joy of movement, then
settled into a ground-gaining trot. Sarah came up next to us,
and we moved off into the heat of the day. My eyes felt
scratchy and puffy, but the weariness had fled, and I could
feel my soul merging with the big black stallion as I settled
easily into the saddle, swaying to the metronomic beat of
hooves.

3

Dust rose from the road, choking me and covering the black
sheen of Ares with a fine, gray silt. The sun pounded down,
and, a mile or so back, a throbbing pain had begun between
my shoulder blades from the constant beat of Ares' hooves.
Beside me gentle Sarah trotted patiently, her nose close to
Ares's flank. It had been four days, and I knew that we were
close to Savannah, but just how close I had no idea. Time had
eclipsed itself, the seconds and minutes and hours merging
into only now.

I began to see the silliness of leaving to search for Uncle
Thomas. To find one man in the confusion following Lee's

surrender, to think that I would be able to stumble across him. Mere chance, I said to myself. You, John Henry Holliday, are a fool. Idle dreaming, romantic nature. Too many novels with chance happenings and contrived endings. Practicality is needed, not youthful dreaming. Remember what Father said? Fools live in dreams.

Snatches of verse swept through my mind, then flitted away on the wings of an errant raven. The road had been empty, but ahead I could see a business buggy bearing down on me, drawn by an impatient chestnut that tossed its head, mouthing angrily at the bit in its mouth.

I guided Ares to the side of the road to make room, but the business buggy swung over, pushing me relentlessly to the edge. I drew rein, waiting for it to pass, but it halted beside me. Nervous perspiration popped out on my forehead as I recognized the man who had confronted Father five days ago: beefy and red-faced, wearing a long white duster and a bowler hat tilted rakishly to one side. Beside him sat the same nigra, this time in a shiny green suit, his collar wings jammed tightly against black jowls. A string tie had been loosely knotted around his neck. His face was damp with perspiration and the sleeve of his jacket dark from where he had continually wiped it across his face. The nigra grinned insolently at me. I took the reins in my left hand and lightly rested my right hand on my left wrist, within easy reach of the Navy Colt. My fingers twitched from nervousness. Ares snorted. Sarah pushed her nose gently against the back of my thigh.

"Morning," the white man called, setting the brake on the business buggy. His shrewd eyes swept over Ares and Sarah, then me. A small smile of contempt touched his eyes.

"Past that by a few hours, I reckon, sir," I answered politely. I kept my eyes on the nigra, feeling instinctively that if anything was to come it would come from him.

"Yes, I guess you're right," the white man said. I knew him then: a carpetbagger down to rake over the ashes of the South and claim as much land as he could from delinquent taxes. The nigra was his bodyguard, one of those protected by the Freemen's Bureau who took great pleasure in the South's defeat.

"Nice horses," he said, nodding admiringly at Ares and Sarah. "Especially the black."

"He is," I replied.

"I don't suppose you'd be willing to sell him?"

"Not mine to sell, sir," I answered. "He belongs to my father."

"I see," he said musingly. He glanced at the nigra beside him, then back to me. "What's your name, boy?"

Annoyance slipped into me. *Boy!* I felt my lips tighten in their smile, fixing it to my cheeks.

"That's my concern," I said. His eyebrows raised at my short retort.

"That don't seem very friendly, boy. I don't need no sass from some spit not dry behind the ears," he said softly. "Might be we have to learn you some manners."

I could feel the rage building inside of me. The day became clear and sharp. Tiny lights danced and shimmered at the corners of my eyes. I straightened, dropping my left hand down onto my saddle. I kept my right hand close by my coat.

"I meant no disrespect, sir. All I want is to get on down that road," I said tightly, forcing myself to be polite. I didn't want any trouble. At least no trouble like this. "Fact is, I'm looking for my uncle. He should have been home a long while ago. My mother's sick and needs him." I tried to sound meek, but I sensed they could feel the anger behind my words.

"Maybe. But you know what I think? I think you're part of that white southern trash who still thinks they own the world."

My anger flared and I turned Ares a bit so my right side was toward them. My leg muscles flexed and unflexed against Ares' sides. I could feel his muscles respond, his head coming up, ears pointing forward, waiting.

"I expect you think you know us pretty well, sir," I said softly. I nodded at the nigra. "But I know your type, too. You come down here to gnaw on our bones and take along former cotton-choppers to do your dirty work for you."

He flushed, his red face turning the color of old liver. He looked at Ares again and nodded, making up his mind.

"Know what I think, boy? I think you're one of the Smith boys from over around Surrency way, and I think your daddy sent you out with those horses to avoid having them taken for tax money. What you think about that?"

"I think you'd best be on your way, and I'll go mine," I said.

"And," he said, fumbling inside the duster, "I think we'll just take them horses until we can determine who you are. Hell, for all I know you might have stolen them. This here's my authorization."

The nigra made a move to get out of the carriage, hoisting himself up with his beefy hands. He froze as the Navy Colt slid shakily into my hands.

"Sit back down, you damn nigra!" I said, my voice squeaking with anger and nervousness.

"What . . ." The words rose to a squawk in the white man's throat.

"Now see here, boy," he said sternly, but his eyes showed sudden fear. "My name's Buford Tyler and I'm duly authorized by the court as the tax official for these here parts!"

"Bring your hand out from your coat," I said.

His eyes narrowed, and somehow, I don't know how, I knew what he was going to try. I rolled back the hammer on the Navy Colt with the ball of my thumb and took up the slack in the trigger. I caught the glimpse of metal as his hand cleared the lapel of his coat, and I jerked the trigger convulsively, automatically thumbing the hammer back again. The .36 ball tore off part of his ear. He clapped his hand against his head and screamed as he fell back against the cushion of the business buggy. His pistol fell out of the buggy, smacked the wheel, and dropped into the dust. The nigra reached behind his neck. A knife flickered, and this time I remembered to squeeze the trigger, holding low to accommodate the kick of the pistol. The knife fell to the road as the nigra clutched his stomach and rolled against the white man. The chestnut reared and spooked, laying his ears flat. He ripped the reins from the white man's fingers as he galloped away.

Ares nervously danced sideways. Automatically, I checked him, pulling hard against the bit in his mouth. He stood still, his black skin rippling with tension.

"Easy, now," I said, speaking softly. I put the pistol back in its holster and gently patted his neck. "It's over now. Easy."

He tossed his head, eager to move away, and I lifted him to a trot, pointing him down the road. A wild joy ran through my veins. I slid the pistol back into its holster and leaned back in the saddle, breathing deeply. I laughed and suddenly a song bubbled from my lips:

> "Early one morning as I was a-walking
>   I spied a young maiden alone in a dell"

Ares's ears perked, and I laughed again.

We rounded a curve and ahead I saw a group of men wearing Confederate gray trudging along the road. I slowed Ares to a walk, scanning their faces as I drew near. They were surly and unshaved, their eyes bloodshot from the heat and the dust, lips cracked from the walks between water.

"John?"

The question stopped me. I drew rein and looked at the group. A lone man stood, facing me. There was something familiar about his face, but through the stubble of beard and dust caking him from head to foot, I couldn't identify him.

"That you, John?"

The voice, low and soft, stirred memories. I dismounted and looked closely at him, noting the tarnished braid of his coat, the dark spots where his rank had been ripped away. His knee peeped through a hole in his pants. The brim of his cavalry hat had been broken and slouched against the back of his neck and folded over to shade his eyes against the glaring sun.

"Uncle Thomas?" I asked hesitantly.

He looked up and down the road, his brow carving deep furrows through the dust caking it. He nodded his head, puzzled.

"Where's your daddy?" he asked. I shrugged.

"Home, I reckon," I said.

Disbelief widened his eyes. He looked at the dust covering me, at Ares and Sarah patiently cropping grass at the side of the road.

"What are you doing here alone? It ain't safe for a thirteen-year-old boy to be out with horses these days." He shifted his haversack from one shoulder to the next.

"Looking for you," I replied, ignoring his comment. "Besides, you're only ten years older than me."

"Ten years is a lifetime nowadays. What was your daddy thinking, sending you this way?" He shook his head in disgust. "The Major sure had his mind elsewheres when he did that."

"I did it," I said coolly. "He didn't know."

His eyes swept up to hold mine.

"Mother needs you and Father couldn't come. So I did."

"Well, I'll be damned," he said softly. A smile tugged at his lips. "My own paladin."

I handed him Sarah's reins. He looked at them, then at Ares. A glint of humor appeared in his eyes, but he took the pony's reins without a word, adjusted the stirrups, and mounted. Sarah grunted from his weight and stamped her feet. He soothed her with his hand, running it down her mane. I swung Ares and touched him lightly with my spurs, turning him back the way we had come. Uncle Thomas's legs hung down comically from Sarah's sides. He moved up beside me.

"Is everything all right at home?" he asked. I shook my head. The smile disappeared from his lips and the corners of his mouth drew down, carving deep lines into his gaunt cheeks.

"No, sir. We have nigra troops stationed in Valdosta now, and the courthouse has been taken over by the carpetbaggers and their scalawag friends. Father spends a lot of time in court, trying to keep them from taking over the farms around the town. He keeps telling everyone to think logically. He wins a few cases, but things are getting worse. The Yankees just keep raising the taxes on the land they want."

"What are they doing with the taxes?"

"Nobody knows," I said.

Uncle Thomas nodded, his lips drawing down in an angry line. We rounded a curve. Up ahead, I could see the business buggy over-turned beside the road, the chestnut trembling in the traces. The nigra lay curled into a fetal ball in the ditch while the white man sat on the dirt, his back against the business buggy, his legs sprawled open in front of him. He whimpered as he held a blood-stained handkerchief to his ear. Blood made a dark streak on his dirty duster. He squinted his eyes against the sun's glare as he looked up at us. He swore as he recognized me.

"Looks like you have a bit of trouble," Uncle Thomas said. Tyler spat, his spittle rolling into tiny balls in the dust. He nodded at me.

"Ask that boy there," he grunted. "The little son of a bitch!"

Uncle Thomas raised an eyebrow as he turned to me.

"They tried to take Ares and Sarah," I answered.

His face hardened as he faced the white man. He looked past him to the nigra rolled into a ball.

"He dead?"

Tyler nodded his head and winced from a sudden start of pain.

"That boy's gonna pay for this," he said through clenched teeth.

"I don't think so," Uncle Thomas answered. "You tried to rob him, and he just defended himself."

"We'll see about that when we get him back to Jesup and the law there!" the man said.

"With your Reconstruction sheriff and Reconstruction judges? Yes, I suppose he would be found guilty. But . . ."

Uncle Thomas dismounted and took a large clasp knife

from his pocket. He opened it and stepped toward the man. The man's eyes widened.

"What are you going to do?" he demanded hoarsely. "Don't!"

Uncle Thomas looked contemptuously at him and crossed to the nigra. Cautiously, he rolled him over and looked at the wound. The nigra whimpered when he saw Uncle Thomas.

"Don't be hurtin' me, massa," he said. "I shot and shot good by that devil-boy."

"You're not hurt much," Uncle Thomas said after prying the nigra's hands away from his wound. "Leastways you won't be if you get to a doctor soon. The ball just cut a hole through some of your fat and went out your side. Couldn't have touched anything vital under all that blubber."

He stepped away from the nigra and eyed the chestnut. He crossed to it, speaking softly. The chestnut's eyes rolled with fear. With four quick slices, Uncle Thomas severed the reins, cutting the horse free. He looped the reins over the horse's head and led him clear of the traces. He patted the chestnut's neck, soothing him.

"This horse hasn't been broke for harness," he said. "He's a hunter. Where'd you get him?"

"Tax seizure," the man said. "Over by Braxley." He winced against another start of pain. "You gotta help us!"

"I see," Uncle Thomas said slowly. He made up his mind and took the reins firmly in his hand.

"Let's just say he evens the score for what you tried to do to this boy," he said.

"My God, man! You can't leave us here." The man looked, wildly up and down the road. Dust sifted from the weeds. He sneezed and groaned. "There's highwaymen around! We won't stand a chance!"

"No more than what you were planning for the boy," Uncle Thomas said. He remounted Sarah. "This'll slow you down some, I'm thinking."

He nudged Sarah with his heels. She trotted away from the

carriage, the chestnut trailing behind her. I pushed Ares up beside Uncle Thomas. He glanced over at me.

"That man right? You shoot him and that nigra?"

I opened my coat, showing him Father's Navy Colt nestled in its holster beneath my arm. He nodded his head admiringly.

"You took a big chance, John."

"Not so big," I said. "No one expects a boy like me to have a pistol. That gives me a little advantage."

"You've been lucky so far," he said. "There are some hard men out here now who would take that pistol away from you and leave you where we left those vultures."

"Maybe," I said.

He looked long and hard at me, then turned his attention to the road ahead of us. He asked about Mother, and I told him that she had been getting sicker over the past few months. His face tightened at this, and tiny muscles bunched hard at the corners of his jaw. He glanced down at the old Confederate coat. It had been patched several times, neatly, but patched. The once-gold braid wrapping proudly around the sleeves and collar seemed tarnished and green, although one could still see where his captain's rank had been. The peak of his hat had a tiny hole in it, the brim broken and flopping over his forehead to shade his eyes. I remembered the dapper Uncle Thomas who used to visit us at Griffin before we moved to Valdosta after Father was mustered out of the Confederate Army. I felt saddened at the turn in his fortune.

Night fell full upon us before we found a catslide house turned into a tavern tucked off the side of the road. Sun had burned the porch posts slate-gray while heavy moss grew down the shake shingles where the sun's rays didn't touch. We heard fiddle music long before we saw the dim lights glowing orange through the oiled parchment covering the windows. Uncle Thomas tied Ares and Sarah to a post rammed into the ground in place of a hitching rail, and together we entered the tavern.

The music stopped as soon as the door swung open on heavy leather hinges and seven pairs of suspicious eyes turned warily toward us, measuring, contemplating. My nose crinkled at the smell of unwashed bodies and onions. The bark had been peeled away from the log walls, leaving them gleaming like dirty bones in the dim light. Cobwebs dangled in strands from the rafters. Greasy smoke hung over the room. A bare plank table, scoured gray and stained with sock-eye gravy, ran down the center of the room over the dirt-packed floor to a river-stoned fireplace at the far end where chunks of venison and beef hung over a spit, dripping onto the hot coals of the fire. Plain pottery tankards, their lips chipped, rested close by the men's hands on the table. The fiddler, hollow-cheeked, skeletal, wispy hair sticking up like thatch, perched on a high chair in the corner, his instrument tucked low on his cadaverous chest instead of under his chin. The innkeeper bustled toward us, wiping his hands on a dirty apron as he approached. His hair hung in lanky tendrils down his collar and above a porky face.

"Well, sirs, an' what can I be doing for y'all?" he said. He scratched deeply into his long black beard with a dirty fingernail.

"We are looking for rooms for the night," Uncle Thomas said.

The innkeeper shrewdly sized him up, noting the patched Confederate coat, the shoes rundown at the heel. An eyebrow quirked as he briefly considered then dismissed me.

"Times are hard," he said. "The charges gots to be paid in advance of yer stay."

Tiny muscles bunched tightly under Uncle Thomas's jaw. His lips drew down tightly.

"We are gentlemen, sir," he said to the insult. The innkeeper appeared nonplussed at his words.

"Not many of 'em left anymores," he said. "Leastways that I can find. All the gentlemens I knows got that shot outta them in the war. Now theys nothin' more than white trash if they ain't got the coin to pay for their wares."

A deep red began filling Uncle Thomas's face, rising from beneath his collar. I watched as the muscles bunched under his shoulders and up along his neck.

"No matter," I said hastily. I reached into the pocket of my coat and took out Father's purse. Coins jangled heavily as I removed a five-dollar gold piece and held it out to the innkeeper. His eyes gleamed as they followed the purse's path back to my pocket. I handed the piece to him. He took it and bit hard on it with stumpy black teeth, then checked it closely.

"That should be enough, I would think," I said.

"Oh, you would, would yuh?" he said. Heavy black eyebrows wiggled like caterpillars over his piggish eyes. "Well, Ah reckon we can let y'all have a bite and bed for that. But not breakfast," he cautioned, waving a thick forefinger at us. "That'll cost yuh extry."

"We'll consider it then," Uncle Thomas said.

"Now would save yuh the trouble," he said. Uncle Thomas stared levelly at him until the man shrugged, turning away.

"Suit yourselves, then," he said surly. "Have a sit and I'll bring yer drinks directly."

"Water will do," Uncle Thomas said. The innkeeper turned, glowering at him.

"The ale's best this side of Savannah," he said. "Made it myself. And you're refusin'?' "

"Water," Uncle Thomas said sternly. "I don't drink and the boy's too young."

The innkeeper turned away disgustedly and shuffled off to the corner, where he dipped two mugs into a small barrel and returned, slamming them on the plank table in front of us. The others turned away as we sat, murmuring softly among themselves. The fiddler began "Lorena" lowly, drawing the bow gently across the strings, bending the notes with supple fingers. One of the men at the table looked over at us.

"Come far?" he said, raising his head from his platter. Gravy dripped off his beard. Blackheads spotted his forehead and nose.

"Enough," Uncle Thomas said. He took a bowl and ladled some suppawn into it from a crock on the table and handed it to me, then filled another for himself. I looked at the white mush and grimaced.

"Yer son," he said, nodding at me.

"Nephew," Uncle Thomas said, giving me a small grin.

"Seems a bit wet to be out this time of night. You a long ways from home, Ah'll bet."

"Would you, now," Uncle Thomas said easily. He took a spoonful of suppawn and nearly gagged. He swallowed and hastily reached for his cup of water.

"Ahuh," the other said. "I would. And Ah take it you're a gamin' man."

"You take it wrong. Who can afford gambling now what with the carpetbaggers and scalawags running around?" I said.

He raised an eyebrow and nodded at me.

"Seems like yer nephew gots to learn when he should be quiet," he said. "A man might take those words personal."

"A lot of people have a lot to learn now that Lee's surrendered," Uncle Thomas said quietly. He pushed the bowl of suppawn from him and lifted his mug of water, sipping.

"What's that supposed to mean?" the man said suspiciously, hunching forward on the table as if to rise.

"Whatever you want it to," Uncle Thomas said. His hands slipped off the table. The other noted their movement, his jaws moving as he considered his options. Then he forced a smile and settled back down on the bench.

"Hell," he said. "Ain't no sense gettin' worked up over such a little thing. Maybe we'll have a hand or two of cards later. Like gentlemen?" he added slyly. The others laughed loudly.

"We may have trouble," Uncle Thomas said quietly behind the mug as he raised it to his lips. "You shouldn't have showed your purse openly like that."

"Sorry. I didn't think," I said, copying his motions and sipping the water.

"You couldn't have known," he said. He fell quiet as the innkeeper approached with two platters heaped with burnt meat. Gravy slopped over the sides of the platters as he plunked them down in front of us and added a dirty fork and knife.

"If yuh want more, help yourselfs," he grumbled, nodding

at the meat on the fire. "Gravy's in the tun on the fire at the right. Yer pallet's in the corner there." He pointed at the corner farthest from the fire.

I pulled a clean handkerchief from a pocket as he turned away, and scrubbed the dried food off my fork tines. Uncle Thomas poured a little water over his and rubbed it clean on the sleeve of his coat.

"After you eat, you better get some sleep," he said as I yawned deeply.

"I wish you would stop treating me like a child," I said.

He laughed.

"I guess I still think of you playing with the nigra boys around the place," he said. "I didn't know you had grown up."

I winced from the sudden memory only a few short days before.

"We all change," I said, looking at him with new eyes. Deep lines sat around his eyes and brow where they had been smooth before. Silver streaked his hair as if touched from an artist's palette.

I cut a small chunk of meat and ate, chewing carefully: the meat was tough and stringy and after a few bites I pushed the platter aside. Uncle Thomas looked quizzically at me.

"I've had enough," I said.

"You didn't eat much," he said reprovingly. "It's not much, but it's better than nothing." A bitter grin touched the corners of his eyes. "A lot of times I ate worse and was glad to have it."

"I haven't," I said. "And I've eaten all I want."

I felt very tired and yawned deeply again, politely covering my mouth with my hand. A man saw my movement and sniggered, nudging his partner and pointing at me. They all laughed and turned away, imitating my gesture. I ignored them and crossed to my pallet. I looked with distaste at the moldy straw poking out of the dirty cover drawn over the tick. I lay down and rolled on my side away from the room, slipping my hand under my coat and grasping the Navy Colt. For a moment, I listened to the strident chirruping of a myriad of black crickets in the night. Then the heat radiating from the fire, and the hum of the voices and the quiet fiddle-bow coupled to lull me to sleep. Just before the darkness slipped over me, I heard Uncle Thomas refuse an invitation to join the men for a few hands of cards. Then I sensed him lying down beside me.

My eyes opened automatically to the darkened room. I lay still, trying half-fearfully to identify what had awakened me. Then I heard a soft rustling noise and turned my head. The bearded man who had had words with Uncle Thomas stood on the balls of his feet, outlined as a huge black beast against the red glow of the fireplace behind him. Fear bunched brass-ily in my mouth as Lizie's stories of dark incubuses and Dambullah and his walking dead, stories from the black continent of her ancestors, fluttered into the room on dark wings. Tiny lights danced off the long-bladed Bowie knife he clutched in his right hand. He saw my movement, and his lips pulled back wolfishly as he crouched to spring.

I rolled to my back, the Navy Colt sliding out of my coat, the hammer locking back loudly with the movement. He froze.

"You think yuh kin handle that thing, boy?" he said.

The fear slid away with the arrogance of his words, leaving cold anger behind. I sat up, steadying the Colt on my knee.

"I'm your huckleberry," I said, holding the sight steady on his chest. Sudden concern slipped over his face as he stared into my eyes. His eyes wavered, then fell, then came up defiantly and his muscles tensed.

"Drop it," Uncle Thomas said to him from my side. He rose, carefully stepping away from the barrel of my pistol.

The man glared sullenly at him as Uncle Thomas produced a small pepperbox pistol from a pocket and cocked it, raising it level with the man's face.

"I'd just as soon kill you. The choice is yours," he said softly. "If I miss, and I won't, the boy'll kill you certain. He's already earned his spurs."

The man's eyes widened. He grunted. His fingers opened, and the knife fell to the floor. Uncle Thomas stepped to a hurricane lantern hanging from an iron hook on the wall and struck a match, lighting it. A weak yellow glow cut through the gloom, stirring the others.

"Innkeeper!" Uncle Thomas called. The others started to rise, then froze as the tableau registered on them. I swung the revolver in their general direction, trying to watch all at once.

"Here, what's going on? What are you doing with those pistols on my guests?" the innkeeper blustered. Uncle Thomas shot him a withering glance.

"And of course, you had no idea of his plan to murder us in our beds," he said scathingly.

The innkeeper's heavy brows furrowed deeply. His eyes shifted away, then slid back as he drew himself up.

"Murder? This here's a respectable inn," he said.

"This inn has seen more than one suspicious death, I'm thinking. I know of inns on the Natchez Trace I'd feel safer in," Uncle Thomas said grimly. "Let's have no more of your foolishness. If you're not behind this business, you knew about it."

"What're yuh gonna do?" the innkeeper asked, his eyes narrowing watchfully.

"Hanging's too good for you, but it's what you probably deserve. I won't hang you," Uncle Thomas said grimly as the innkeeper drew away, "but it'll be a long time before you entertain here again. Outside, John. Saddle the horses and bring them to the front."

I slipped out the door and hurried to the lean-to doubling as a stable. Ares snorted indignantly as I slipped in beside him and ran the bridle up over his nose, forcing the bit between his teeth. I glanced over my shoulder and through the door into the tavern as I heaved the saddle up on his back, cinching it tightly. Uncle Thomas took the hurricane lantern from its iron hook and smashed it against the wall. Flames licked hungrily at the dried timbers as the innkeeper roared with anger and raced to the water barrel. Uncle Thomas slipped out the door as the others leaped from their blankets and tried to stem the racing flames by swinging their blankets at the fire. But the blankets only fanned the fire, sending it out of control before the innkeeper could return with the first bucket of water.

"The horses! Quick!" Uncle Thomas ordered.

But I had already saddled them, placing his saddle on the chestnut we had taken from the carpetbagger. Ares rolled his eyes at the flames beginning to snap above the roof and moved fearfully, trying to tear the reins from my hand. Uncle Thomas fired his pepperbox through the doorway. Someone screamed. I handed the chestnut's reins to him and swung up on Ares's back, firmly gripping Sarah's reins in my left hand, leaving my right free to fire if necessary. Uncle Thomas drummed his heels against the chestnut's flanks. A strange, ululating yell burst from his lips as he lifted the chestnut into a quick gallop. Ares took the bit in his mouth and followed close on the chestnut's heels as he thundered down the road away from the inn. Behind us, flames roared to the sky as we galloped away down the road, snaking whitely between the oaks stretching their black, twisted arms hung with gray Spanish moss to the night and the bloodred hunter's moon looming over our shoulders.

4

Father stood impatiently between the two columns on the front porch as we rode up the lane between the old oaks to the house on the knoll. He wore a white frock coat and trousers, a crease stiffly ironed down each leg. His tie had been carefully knotted around his stiff collar, the ends tucked neatly beneath his white brocade vest. Mother, dressed in black velvet as if in mourning, sat in a wicker chair beside him, a blanket covering her lap. She looked pale and thin, her eyes large and luminescent, dark hollows surrounding them. Father's face was a controlled mask of fury, his eyes hard and glinting like washed agate, his lips a hard, straight line.

We reined to a halt in front of him and slumped in our saddles. Ares bowed his head and wearily pawed the ground in front of him. Sarah dropped her head and nuzzled the grass. Only the chestnut Uncle Thomas rode seemed to have life left in him, nervously dancing for a moment before standing still, ears pricked forward, sensing the sudden tension in the air between Father and Uncle Thomas and me. Dust covered us, making my coat as gray as Uncle Thomas's.

"Thank God!" Mother said. She made to rise, then fell back weakly in the chair. "We thought you had been killed."

"Thomas," Father said. He nodded curtly. "You're looking tolerable."

"Henry," Uncle Thomas said stiffly. His eyes softened as they went to Mother. "Hello, Alice."

"Thomas. I have worried so much. I thought . . ." She bit her lip, fighting back tears and tried to rise again. Uncle Thomas quickly dismounted and reached her side in a few quick strides.

"I'm home now," he said. "Don't worry." He smiled down at her then looked up at me. "John has taken very good care of me." He glanced over at Father. "You should be proud of him."

Father gave him a hard look, then motioned to Sam, standing by the edge of the house.

"Take the horses and care for them," he ordered. "You," he said to me, "can go to the study. I will meet with you there in a few minutes."

I dismounted, silently handing the reins to Sam, who avoided my eyes as he took them from me. He collected the reins of the chestnut and Sarah and, clucking softly to them, led them away down the knoll toward the stable.

"Henry—" Mother began, but he cut her off with a quick motion. She fell silent as Uncle Thomas rose from his knees beside her to face him.

"I don't know what you've got planned, Henry," he said quietly. "But I owe a lot to John. He did a man's work these past couple of weeks."

"Would a man have crept off in the dead of the night like a

sneak thief?" Father said. He looked up at me. "You're little more than that, boy. Where's the money you took?"

Silently, I reached into the pocket of my coat and removed the purse, considerably lighter now than when I had taken it from his desk. I handed it to him. He weighed it in his hand, then dropped it into a side pocket of his frock coat.

"And the rest?" he asked quietly.

"I spent it on expenses getting here," I said, holding his eyes with mine. An icy calmness descended over me. I straightened my shoulders, forcing the ache from them. He made a gesture of dismissal with his hand.

"Go to the study. I'll be there in a few minutes, and we'll talk about this recent behavior problem of yours," he said.

"And there I'll get a beating? No, I don't think so. Never again. Not now. I've seen what you've seen and I didn't run from it."

Father's eyes tightened. A white band of anger appeared around his mouth. His head tilted back, nostrils flaring.

"Henry—" Uncle Thomas said tightly, taking a step forward. But I interrupted him.

"I want a bath first, and a change of clothes. I'll meet you there then," I said calmly.

They froze, staring at me. Mother's hands fluttered nervously as she darted glances between Father and myself. I held Father's eyes, watching the tiny coals of anger burn behind them. He stepped down off the porch and reached me in two strides, his open hand slapping me, hard, across my cheek. He started a backswing, then froze. I heard Mother gasp from her chair. Father's eyes left mine, slowly descending to where the Navy Colt pressed against his stomach.

"John," Uncle Thomas said as Father backed away. I looked up at him, confused.

"Put it away," he said softly.

I looked up into Father's eyes, seeing something there I had never seen before: Grudging respect? A wariness? I couldn't be certain, but suddenly I knew that something had happened between us that was rewriting our relationship. I had crossed some invisible bridge and burned it behind me, closing one part of our relationship without knowing it.

Father turned on his heel and disappeared into the house. I felt Uncle Thomas's hand on mine, gently pushing the revolver down and taking it from my fingers. He patted me on the shoulder, and I looked up at him.

"Go get cleaned up now. Your father will be waiting for you in the study," he said soothingly.

I nodded and stumbled up onto the porch. I paused beside Mother, looking down into her tear-filled eyes. I bent and awkwardly kissed her. Her hands clutched for a moment at my shoulders, then slowly released me.

"I'm sorry, Mother," I said.

She waved her hand in the air while blotting the tears from her eye with a handkerchief she had taken from her sleeve. A faint hint of lemon wafted gently to me.

"It's all right," she said. Her eyes were sad.

An ache lifted from my stomach into my throat. I swallowed against it and pressed her hand between mine.

"Times," she said. "These times." She looked at Uncle Thomas and held her other hand out to him. He took it, turning it gently in his sun-browned hands, pressing gently on her palm with callused fingers.

"Ah, these times. There is no time left for children to be children," she said sadly. "Our world is gone now, Thomas. There is nothing left to us but memories, and those memories . . ." She fell silent for a long moment, then leaned back in her chair, a dreamy smile upon her lips.

"Can you smell the lilacs, Thomas?"

We looked at each other: The lilac bushes had yet to bloom, a few leaves showing on the wooden branches and twigs only.

"This is my favorite time of year, you know. Papa usually sets our first reception when the magnolia blooms, but I know that time is not far off when the lilacs begin to flower. That's when we begin the guest list. Oh, we'll invite the judge and his wife, although she is a horrid gossip and seldom has anything good to say about anyone, and the Griffins and Ralstons and Howell Bird. Then there's the Williams and Myddletons . . ."

Her voice trailed off, and she began rocking gently back and forth in her chair, the sound creaking against the morning, lost in a time where I could not go. I gently released my hand and looked at Uncle Thomas.

"I had no idea," he said. His eyes were moist.

"Nor did I," I answered.

"Has she been seeing a doctor?"

I nodded. "He's been giving her laudanum for her spells. She and Father have had quite a few fights over that. And the Methodist minister, N. B. Ousley. Did you ever meet him?"

He shook his head. "No. Methodist? When did she begin attending Methodist services? We have always been Presbyterian."

"Right after Father returned from the War," I answered. "I think she wrote to you about it."

"I never received it. I seldom received any correspondence," he said regretfully. "Especially after Sherman decided to cut a swath through Georgia," he added bitterly.

"She was worried about you, too," I said.

He nodded, holding her hand tightly in his own.

"I know," he said thickly. "I know."

He handed the Navy Colt to me. I slid it back into its holster and left them there: Uncle Thomas remembering the past few years, regretting the present; Mother even farther back in time, to my grandfather's house along Indian Creek in Pike County, remembering the gentleness of those times. Either way, it was a time not for me.

I climbed the stairs to my room. The curtains had been drawn back by Lizie, and fresh clothes had been laid out on my bed. Down the hall, I could hear Lizie filling the tin bathtub in the room between Mother's and Father's. I looked at myself in the mirror. A stranger stared back, with red-rimmed eyes and dusty, unruly hair. A thick patina of dust lay over my shoulders and covered my coat and trousers. My boots were scuffed and badly in need of polishing. I shrugged out of my coat and dropped it on the floor. My shirt was stained from perspiration, large yellow circles showing under my arms and along where the belt and holster for Father's Navy Colt hung. The shoulders had almost separated themselves. I slipped it off over my head and tossed it on the bed and crossed to the bootjack to pull off my boots. One stocking had a hole in the heel. I grimaced and quickly stripped, wrapping myself in a robe before heading down the hall to my bath.

Lizie was waiting for me inside the room when I entered. The tin tub had been partially filled and a washcloth and bar of Mother's Pears Soap laid out for my use. She looked at me, her eyes white and moist in the black ebony of her face. I gave her a smile and she sniffed.

"Hello, Lizie," I said. "Thank you for preparing the bath for me."

"An' just who else was gonna do for you?" she said. "Wash youself good now, you heah me? Or Ah will just have to get that old lye soap from the kitchen and scrub good behind you ears."

"Yes, Lizie," I said.

"Now you just get yourself in that tub, heah? Well, what you waiting on? Water ain't gettin' no hotter with you standing there."

"I would like a little privacy, Lizie," I said.

"Now, John Henry, Ah've changed y'didies more than Ah can count. Ain't nuthin' about you Ah haint seen many a times."

"I don't wear didies anymore, Lizie. It's been a long time since I have."

She looked searchingly into my eyes. Her face grew long, and her lower lip trembled a bit. She reached out a heavy hand and clumsily patted my shoulder, lifting a corner of her apron with the other hand to wipe away a tear.

"Yessuh, Ah guess you don't." She crossed to the door, then turned to look at me and gave a start.

"What's the matter, Lizie?" I asked, crossing to her.

She shrank from me and put her hands up reflexively.

"Don' you come near!" she said.

I stopped, puzzled. A look of fear crossed her face.

"Lizie?"

"There's another one with y'John Henry," she said, looking away. Her fingers twisted in an odd gesture like a pagan blessing on herself to whatever gods her black soul remembered.

I glanced around the room: We were alone.

"Another what?" I asked.

"Lawd, Ah sees him standing right besides you. All dressed in black." She took a deep, shuddering breath. "Y'now one of the counted ones, John Henry. One of the counted ones. Ah'll tell y'daddy you be down directly."

She left, slamming the door behind her. I opened the door and watched as she ran down the hall and clambered down the stairs. I closed the door, perplexed, then sighed and shrugged out of the robe and gently lowered myself into the tub, stretching back as much as I could, relaxing as the warm water worked the knots from my muscles. I held my breath and slid under the water. I rose, blowing water from my face, then picked up the Pears and worked the soap into my hair and over my face. I felt bristles under my hands when I ran my palms down my jaws, and I glanced up at the washstand in the corner where Father's razor lay next to his shaving mug.

Father stood when I entered the study, my hair still damp from my bath, my face smarting from my first clumsy shave with his razor. I wore one of his boiled shirts, the collar a bit too large for my neck, but I had knotted a tie around it. He glanced at it and picked up a glass of bourbon from his desk, sipping it. I handed him the Navy Colt, holstered, the belt wrapped around it. I stood in front of the desk, waiting. He laid the Navy Colt on the desk, then nodded at the chair across from him. I sat down, leaning back gratefully into its softness.

"Thomas told me pretty much what happened," he said. He placed the glass on the desk in front of him and sat, leaning back in his chair, drumming his fingers gently upon the desk.

"What made you do it?" he asked. I shrugged.

"It seemed the thing to do at the time," I said. "It *needed* to be done. And you couldn't do it."

He sighed, picked up his drink, then put it down again.

"Yes," he said. For the first time, he looked away from me at his picture on the wall. "Yes, you're right. I couldn't do it. Not anymore." He bowed his head and studied his hands for a long moment, then raised his head and faced me squarely.

"The War changed a lot of us, John," he said. "I guess I've been trying not to see that. Maybe I didn't want to see that."

He dropped his eyes to his desk. He toyed absently with the glass paperweight and a silver letter opener, turning the point reflectively in his palm. I slumped down in my chair, watching, waiting. Finally, he cleared his throat, looking up.

"It's not that I didn't want to go after Thomas, it's just that . . . I couldn't. This war . . ."

He took a deep breath, letting it out slowly while his knuckles tightened whitely around the handle of the letter opener.

"The War was a big mistake," he said quietly. "I thought that it was my duty to do what Georgia and the South asked. The nigras were only a part of it at the beginning—it was all the sanctions the factories in the North were putting on us, other things. The damned Abolitionists and northern colporteurs made it all into a slavery issue. Took the honor from it. You have no idea, John, what it was like to travel in the North just before the War and have people there know you for a Southerner. I was called everything you can imagine: nigra-beater, rapist, murderer, other names I can't repeat. And now when I go into town and have to deal with the Freedmen's Bureau nigras and the colored soldiers stationed there, deal with their contempt and the carpetbaggers and scalawags, well, it takes everything I've got. When people find out you were a soldier in an unpopular war, you are hated, reviled, and treated with contempt—almost as if you are something they scraped off the bottom of their shoes after stumbling off the street. D'you understand what I'm trying to say?"

I nodded. Relief flickered in his eyes. He poured a glass of bourbon and drained half of it.

"Later, I discovered that the whole thing was a mistake and the South . . . Well, we couldn't win. And I became . . . I knew . . . I knew that it was useless to hang on to the bitter end. A man needs pride, but stubborn pride against common sense is the mark of the fool. So I left the army with as much dignity as I could muster and came home." He waved his hand around the room. "This is . . . sanctuary. Here, I don't have to answer to anyone. Here, I can get my strength back up to make another trip into town to defend another one like myself when the Freedmen's Bureau brings him to the Lowndes County Courthouse against a northern judge. It takes all I've got to do that, John."

He shook his head in despair.

"And," he added softly, "the Yankees have placed a nigra garrison of occupation at the corner of South Patterson Street and West Hill Avenue, just a few short blocks away from that house I bought from the Howells to keep the Yankees from getting it for taxes. I couldn't go after Thomas. I had to stay here and keep the damn nigras from everybody's throat." He sighed. "I'm trying to forget the War, John. Thomas keeps reminding me of it."

"And," I said, breaking in, "he made it all the way through the War."

Surprise touched his eyes, and his lips twisted into a bitter smile.

"That too," he said softly.

I reached into my pocket and removed the crumbled piece of paper that held the reasons for his discharge from the Confederate Army I had found in his desk drawer when I took the gold. His eyes widened as he took it from my fingers and slowly unwrapped it. He glanced at it, his lips tightening.

"I never thought you were a saint, Father. But Mother needed Thomas. At least she needed to know what had happened to him."

"Don't condemn me, John. Not until you've heard grapeshot whistling overhead from the Napoleons, cutting through the branches and trees, and watched living bodies dance and jerk as minié balls rip into them."

"Maybe you should have tried to let us understand that instead of shutting us away from it," I said. He smiled ruefully.

"I guess I was trying to make everything the way it was before the War. I'm sorry, John."

I nodded. He swallowed another large draught of bourbon.

"I guess," he said, "we'd better start rethinking what our future is going to be."

I waited, knowing he had come to some decision.

"We, some of the other fortunate individuals the War has managed to leave semi-intact, have contacted Samuel Varnedoe over in Thomasville to come to Valdosta and open a private school, the Valdosta Institute, in town so our children will receive the education they need. The institute will be at the corner of Varnedoe and River Streets. He has agreed to our request and will be bringing his two daughters with him to help teach: Miss Matilda and Miss Sallie Lou. It will not be an easy curriculum, but it will be one that will prepare our people not only in the old ways, but in the ways that they will need in the future. You need to attend it, John. You need to learn how to live in our new world."

"I'd rather not," I said.

His brows raised in surprise, then he smiled faintly.

"What do you want?"

"What we've got," I answered. "Mother needs me."

"She has Thomas now. He can mind her while you get on with your life, John. Why do you think I've kept you here all along instead of sending you away to school? I've known what Alice has needed all along."

"Then why did you get mad every time I took a book from here if my schooling means so much to you?" I demanded.

"Why did you keep doing it?" he asked.

"Because . . ." I shook my head and leaned back in my chair.

"Because I forbade it, you kept coming after them," he finished for me. "You've always been like that, John. Every time I've told you that you couldn't do something, you've gone ahead and done it. You're contrary, John."

I tried again.

"You could bring Mr. Simon back out here. He could tutor."

"John," he said quietly, placing the glass on his desk. "The day of the gentleman has passed. Even gentlemen have to make their own way in the world now. The land no longer is enough to support us. We've overspent and overused the land. You need to learn how the other half lives because you're going to have to live with them."

"Never!" I said hotly.

"You have no choice," he said grimly.

"Damn Yankees," I said darkly.

"Things are going to be a bit tight for a while as we rebuild," he said. "And it's going to take a long time to bring us back up on parity with the North. If," he added, "we can ever manage to do that. Frankly, I don't think we can. Too much has been taken from us."

His face darkened.

"You'll have to learn to live like a tradesman or a professional man, John, but never forget that you were once raised to be a gentleman."

He pointed to the andirons standing in front of the fire in the fireplace. I twisted my head to look at them, remembering when Sam's uncle had made them in his forge before the war, hammering them out of red-hot iron as I helped pump the billows. Terrible figures, riding deadly horses. Sam's uncle had modeled them on the description of the apocalypse from the Book of Revelation.

"Look at them," he said. "They have trampled our country to dust. The four horsemen of the apocalypse: Conquest, Pestilence, War, Death."

I looked at the firelight flickering redly through the hollows of their eyes and the grinning mouth in the skull face of the fourth horseman. I shuddered and turned away.

"Our world's gone, John," Father whispered. "All gone."

He stood, signifying our meeting was over. I remained seated. He frowned.

"Was there something else?"

I cleared my throat.

"About what happened out front, Father," I began. He waved his hand in dismissal.

"You're becoming a man, John. I guess I wasn't ready to treat you as one. I'm sorry that you had to grow up so quickly. There's a lot of fun that you will not experience, now. I guess we've robbed that from you, too."

"It wasn't your fault," I started.

"Oh, yes, it is. At least, a part of it is. We're all guilty of being a part of everything."

"You know, the funniest thing happened upstairs," I said, trying to lighten the mood. "Lizie all of a sudden thought she saw someone else in the room."

He raised an eyebrow.

"Was the light behind you?" he asked.

"Yes." His face whitened, and he forced a laugh.

"Superstitious stuff," he said shakily. "She thought she saw Baron Sameda beside you. You know how these nigras get with their superstitions."

He picked up the pistol, weighed it in his hand, then reached across the desk, handing it to me.

"I have a feeling you're going to need this, John," he said. "I hope I'm wrong, but . . ."

A far-off look came into his eyes. He picked up the bottle of bourbon and refilled his glass. He turned and walked to the French windows behind his desk and stood, looking out.

There wasn't anything else for me to say. I rose and left the room, taking the pistol with me, quietly closing the door behind me, feeling a part of me staying behind in the study, waiting for the chance to sneak a book from the shelves. Suddenly, I felt very lonely.

5

The tang of the longleaf pine trees along the streets and in the forest around Valdosta filled my mouth as I moved slowly through the warmth of the sun toward the Valdosta Institute, feeling the heat of the sun baking my shoulders beneath my long coat and soaking my white shirt beneath it. When I had awakened three hours earlier, I had felt the promise of the day filtering in through the starched lace curtains of my bedroom in the house on Savannah Street Father had bought from Stephen Martin to keep it from being sold for taxes to one of the carpetbaggers who were daily greedily snatching up every piece of land and property they could lay their fingers upon.

The past eighteen months had been hard, what with the curriculum Mr. Varnedoe had imposed upon us. The day of the gentleman may have passed, but Mr. Varnedoe grimly made us aware that a gentleman was still needed in the country to counter the crude ways of the nigra troops who had been stationed only a couple of blocks from the institute's doors. The nigras didn't waste much time making sure that all the white people knew they were no longer slaves. They spent most of their time in saloons where once they were forbidden entrance, arrogantly accosting the white women while they were shopping. If a white man came to the assistance of the women, the nigras would arrest him for disturbing the peace. Relations quickly became strained in Valdosta, with the white men trying to avoid the nigras as much as possible and yet provide protection for their wives and children. Tension was high in the town, and one could feel smoldering anger threatening to burst forth in violence.

"The South may have lost the War, gentlemen, but we

have not lost ourselves and our dignity. Someday you may find a need for what you are going to be taught here," Mr. Varnedoe constantly reminded us.

Our curriculum stressed mathematics, rhetoric, English composition, history, logic, physics and chemistry, economics, geography, astronomy, and the Classics: Greek, Latin, considerable French, including *Don Quixote* and the *Chanson de Roland*. But my favorite was *Roman de la Rose*. I even read parts of it to Mattie, Uncle Robert's daughter from Father's side, who visited us from time to time when Uncle Robert came to Valdosta from Jonesboro to visit Father. She had stayed several months with us during the war in 1864. Mattie and I became very close, very close . . .

"Morning, John," Ben Hawkins said, falling in beside me.

"Morning," I answered. I grinned at him. "You get those two chapters on Caesar translated for today?"

He made a face, shaking his head.

"No. I was about to make you a special offer," he said. "That is, if you've finished?"

"Finished around eleven," I answered. "And you know the answer to that."

"How about a dollar?"

"No."

"You and your damn honor," he sighed. "It gets in the way of sound business."

"I don't know about that being sound business," I answered. "Seems pretty dubious to me."

He sighed and walked along beside me as we turned the corner to cross past where the nigra garrison was stationed in town and past the courthouse.

"I'd rather be squirrel hunting out along the Withlacoochee. I hate to waste the day," he grumbled.

I laughed. Ben would figure and plot and plan until he had convinced himself that he was justified in skipping classes. I was about the only friend he had in town, his parents being Yankees and all who had moved down after the War to open the bank.

"What do you think, John?" he asked slyly. "Want to join me?"

Before I could answer, the door of Drago's Saloon burst open and a group of black soldiers staggered out, stumbling into us.

"Watch where yer goin', boy!" a nigra sergeant said. A shiver crossed down my spine as I thought I recognized the nigra I had shot a year earlier. Then I noticed the small differences that made him a near twin. I shrugged and tried to move around him, but he stepped back in my way, frowning insolently. His companions laughed and nudged each other, grinning at me.

"Y'speak when you spoken to, boy, you hear me? Didn't y'mammy give you any manners? Ah thought a gentleman's supposed to tip his hat and say his hellos when another greeted him."

"Only when he meets another gentleman," I said icily.

"Hear that, Rafe," one of his friends laughed. "Y'must not be a gentlemans!"

The sergeant's face darkened with anger at my words. He stepped closer, and I could smell the corn liquor on his breath, the stale sweat from the wool of his Yankee uniform overdue for a wash.

"Damn me if Ah'm taking any more lip from white trash," he said. He nudged my chest with a thick black forefinger. "Y'hear me, boy?"

"I hear you. And you can keep your damn hands to yourself," I said in measured tones. His lips spread in a thick grin.

"What's the matter? Think the color will rub off'n you?"

"Let it go, John," Ben said uneasily.

"Wouldn't make any difference," I said, ignoring him. The nigra's eyes grew hard behind the jaundiced yellow. "You'd still be a nigra if you were all white."

His yellow eyes flashed with anger. He balled his hand into a fist and struck me, knocking me back against the wall of Drago's Saloon. My head rang from the blow. My books fell from my hands. I caught a glimpse of Ben, his face white

with fear, edging away from me. The rage began to bubble
up from deep inside. My hands curled into fists, and I stepped
away from the wall, sliding around on the balls of my feet. I
knew that he would beat me, but suddenly, I no longer cared.

"I'm your huckleberry," I said softly.

His eyes widened as I slid forward. Then an animal pleasure fell over them at the prospect of a hunt. Much the same,
I imagine, that a wolf feels when encountering a sick doe.

"Watch yerself, Rafe," one of the others called and snickered. "He looks like a real pug-a-list to me!" The others
laughed with him. Rafe turned his head and laughed, pointing a thick forefinger at them.

I took the opportunity to stab a fist toward his face. He
leaned back nonchalantly at the hips, and I quickly stepped in
and threw my right, splitting his lip and spraying blood over
his face. His face grew tight with rage. He took a step toward
me, his hands swelling into rock-hard fists.

"That's enough!" a voice commanded icily from the street.

Automatically, we looked out at Uncle Thomas sitting on
his chestnut, his hands folded in front of him. But his eyes
were cold with anger, staring at the nigras.

"Your mother needs you, John," he said. I heard a catch in
his throat.

"What's wrong?" I asked, my pulse quickening as I bent to
retrieve my books.

"She's taken a turn for the worse. The doctor's with her
now," he said despondently.

I handed my books to Ben and turned toward the livery
stable.

"We ain't done with this!" the sergeant hollered after me.

I ignored him and strode rapidly down the street. Uncle
Thomas pulled up beside me.

"Take it easy, John," he warned in a low voice. "You'd be
better off forgetting about him. The damn nigras have been
getting more and more impossible to live with since the
Freedmen's Bureau was established and the courts filled with
those damn Yankees ruling in favor of them on everything.

They're trying to make up for a couple hundred years of slavery in a couple of years."

I paid no attention to him, stepping into the cool darkness of the stables. Ares recognized me, pushing affectionately at my arm. I paused to stroke his velvet nose, then hurriedly saddled and led him from the stall. Uncle Thomas waited while I mounted, then wordlessly, we galloped from the town, heading south along the Old Plantation Road.

My heart lurched in my chest and a coldness settled in my stomach as Uncle Thomas and I galloped up to the front porch. Father stood waiting for us, his face drawn and tight, dark smudges under his eyes. His tie looked like blackened, wilted kale. I swung down and tossed the reins to Sam as I climbed the steps to stand next to Father.

"It's not good, John," he said gruffly.

"Is she . . ." I left the sentence unfinished.

"Dr. Sullivan and Reverend Ousley are with her now," he said.

Thomas made a strangling noise in his throat and pushed past us, into the house. The screen door slapped shut behind him, loud in the sudden silence. A mourning dove sounded from the pecan trees. Somewhere a dog howled. I shivered.

"I thought she was better," I said.

"She was." He started to explain further, then paused, looking at the smoke curling up from his cigar.

"Well? What happened?" I demanded impatiently. He sighed and looked out in the distance over the pecan trees he'd planted in the new orchard last spring.

"She went to the Methodist church yesterday. . . . You knew she'd changed churches, didn't you?" I nodded my head. "She'd lost faith in the Presbyterian minister. He's a different one, the Reverend David Comfort, always going on about the woman's duty to her husband and how she's to blame for our downfall, sneaking off to sin with the serpent and all."

"Father!" I said abruptly.

He gave me a startled look, then resignedly drew deeply on his cigar, allowing the smoke to dribble from his lips.

"Sorry, John. Lately I've been having trouble staying focused upon anything."

"What happened?" I asked in exasperation.

"After church, she and Mrs. Watkins decided to walk over to visit the Widow Haskins for a glass of lemonade. . . . The Widow's been ailing some lately, you know, her arthritis, I think." I nodded. "Well, as they walked along South Patterson Street, some of those damn nigra bluebellies accosted them outside Barnes Drug Store."

I drew a deep, shaky breath. The day seemed brighter, images sharply outlined, casual details suddenly important: the cufflinks on Father's shirt, the knot in his tie slightly askew, dried mud still clinging to the boot scraper, the dust hanging in the air, the smell of bay rum from the lotion Father had splashed on his cheeks after shaving, paint beginning to blister from the walls.

"What did they do?" I asked quietly.

Father glanced at me, started to speak, then his voice froze and he looked away.

"Let it be, John," he said. "There's nothing you can do about it."

"There's the law. . . ."

"They are the law. Leastways, they have the power to make the law whatever they want."

"That doesn't give them the right to molest women," I said hotly.

"Yes, it does."

His words chilled me. He looked with distaste at the cigar in his hand, grimaced, and threw it onto the gravel in front of the porch. He rubbed his hand tiredly over his face, pinching the bridge of his nose hard between his eyes.

"You have no idea of what they are capable . . . of what they have done. Last week, five nigra soldiers caught Bill Jenning's wife out in the field . . . you don't know him; he's a sharecropper over by Three Points . . . and they raped and sodomized her. The court refused to even hear the charges. There are no just causes anymore, John—only death."

Dizziness swept over me. I leaned against one of the pillars of the porch for support.

"Go on," I said thickly.

"Her son witnessed it." He shuddered. "One of them even . . . the boy . . ." He drew a deep, shaky breath. "Judge Samuels said it was only the word of a boy, a *southern* boy against five colored men. Naturally, he had been taught to hate the nigras and would lie against them. He threw the case out of court for lack of evidence. Those damn nigras laughed at all the white folks there, taunting and jeering at them as they swaggered out of court as if they owned it."

He paused, looking listlessly at the cigar smoldering on the ground. "I reckon they do."

I barely heard his last words. I turned and stumbled blindly into the house and made my way upstairs. Dr. Sullivan and the man I took to be Reverend Ousley stood outside Mother's door. They wore identical black suits, but Dr. Sullivan had a brocaded vest stretched across his paunch while Reverend Ousley wore a matching vest with his suit. Deep creases lined Dr. Sullivan's rubicund face and a wreath of white hair circled his bald dome. The Reverend Ousley was thin and pale, his eyes black and gentle beneath a high forehead topped with close-cut hair carefully combed. I started into her room, then stopped and looked at Dr. Sullivan.

"Is she. . . ." I swallowed against the sudden lump in my throat. He solemnly nodded.

"Did those damned nigras . . ." I clenched my hands as the rage began bubbling up inside me. He understood my unfinished question and hesitated before answering.

"No, John, they didn't harm her. *Physically*," he emphasized.

I blindly reached out and grasped the doorjamb, steadying myself.

"The nigras surrounded them and pushed them back and forth, calling them white trash." He hesitated again, then continued.

"Other things. Saying they would do things to them like they did to Mrs. Jennings. Mrs. Watkins struck one of them with her parasol and cut him above the eye. He slapped her and knocked her down. Your mama tried to run for help and another one grabbed her and tore her dress. He tried to . . . kiss her. That's when some of the martial troops arrived and broke it up. They took the nigras back to the garrison."

"And Mother?"

"Reverend Ousley brought her home." He nodded at the man standing next to him. "She's been sinking ever since. It's almost as if—" he paused. His lips tightened, and he frowned, his eyes growing distant. "It's almost as if she has lost the will to live anymore. Like she knows her time in this world is over. The past is gone now, and she's seen nothing for herself in the future. Nothing she wants, anyway, to go on living."

I nodded, looking past him to the minister.

"Thank you for taking care of her, Reverend."

"You're welcome," he said in a low but vibrant voice, subdued for the occasion, but I sensed the power lying in wait behind it, the power to drive out demons and call down the wrath of the Lord. "I just wish I could do more."

The words were the type that come automatically to most people's lips at times like this, but in his case I instinctively believed him. There seemed to be a truth about him missing in most people, and I could see why Mother had taken to going to the Methodist church instead of the Presbyterian church where she and Father had been married and where I had been baptized.

"Has Mother been going to your church for very long?" I asked.

"Not long," he said, "but long enough. She no longer sees through a glass darkly, as Paul puts it." He smiled gently at my raised eyebrow.

"She has prepared herself," he gently explained, motioning to the room.

I nodded and turned to enter the room. The canopied mahogany bed stood just in front of me. To my right were her matching bureau and wardrobe, to my left, a small vanity table with a marble top upon which lay a copy of *Godey's Ladies Book, Lippincott's Magazine,* and *Harper's Monthly Magazine.* On top of them lay Nathaniel Hawthorne's *The House of the Seven Gables* and *The Scarlet Letter.* A small divan with a serpentine back stood in front of the French windows opening out onto a small balcony, a "widow's walk." A thick, Turkish carpet covered most of the floor.

Mother lay in bed, eyes closed. Her ash-blond hair which I shared, lay spread in soft waves, framing her white face against her pillow. Uncle Thomas knelt by her side, holding her hand. He rose as I entered and silently stood back as I approached the bed and gently sat on its edge.

Her eyes fluttered open as my weight shifted the mattress. Puzzlement shone from her eyes for a moment, then they cleared, and she reached for my hands, her fingers moving feebly against my palm. I took the hand in both of mine and held it tightly. She coughed, long and racking, the effort shaking her thin shoulders.

"I'm sorry, John," she whispered.

"For what?" I asked.

"For bringing you into this world," she said.

A lone tear trickled down her cheek. I wiped it away. Beneath the wetness, her skin felt dry, like parchment.

"There is no friendship in the world anymore. It's become a lonely, lonely place. The War's made it so."

"Don't talk so," I said awkwardly. "There's more to the world than here."

"Then find it, John," she said fiercely. Her hands clawed at mine. "Find it."

She gripped my hand hard, straining to pull herself upward. I gently pushed her back against the pillow.

"I will," I promised.

She relaxed and her eyes fluttered weakly. She opened them, staring at me. Tears moistened them.

"Are you still practicing the Mozart, John?"

"Chopin now, Mother," I said. She nodded, her eyes closing.

"Chopin. That's nice." She breathed gently for a moment, then her eyes opened again, clear and bright.

"I'm afraid for you, John," she said. "I'm sorry." Her eyes closed. "But, Chopin is nice."

Slowly, her breathing stopped. She gave a last sigh, then lay still, her hand opening slightly in mine. Tears burned my eyes, falling softly to my lips.

"Mother?"

I pressed her hand hard, trying to squeeze life back into her. A great hollowness grew within me. I shook from a sudden chill as something seemed to lift from me on feathery wings and soar into the empty air above us.

"Mama?"

Uncle Thomas pressed my shoulders gently.

"She's gone, John," he said. His voice cracked.

He took her hands from mine and folded them carefully across her breast. He brushed her hair back from her forehead, then reached into his pocket and removed a small, silver penknife. Carefully, he cut off two ringlets, wrapped them tightly around his forefinger, pressing the curl in. He slipped one into his vest pocket, hesitated, then took his watch out of the other pocket and unclipped the chain from his vest. He opened the back of the watch and carefully placed the curl inside, closing it. He wound the watch, then opened the clock face and handed it to me. Chopin's "Opus No. 1 in B-flat Minor" tinkled musically. I looked at the picture of Mother pressed in the outer lid.

"I want you to have this," he said.

"It's your watch," I said dully.

"Not anymore. Alice gave it to me before the War. We were very close then." His voice clicked in his throat. He turned away. "I think you have more need of it now."

"Thank you," I said. I closed the cover of the watch and the chimes stopped. Lacking a vest, I slipped it into the inside breast pocket of my coat.

"That was always one of her favorite songs before the War," he said.

"I know," I said, looking at Mother. My eyes burned again, and I felt the tears again running down my cheeks.

"You have to let her go, John," he said softly.

I didn't answer. He hesitated a moment, then turned and went to the door, summoning Dr. Sullivan and Reverend Ousley. I heard them enter as if from a distance. Vaguely, I became aware of them, shadowy forms, as they moved around me. Dr. Sullivan gently lifted Mother's wrist, feeling for a pulse, but it was an automatic gesture only: She was gone and he knew it. He placed her hand back on the coverlet and carefully drew the sheet up over her face.

Reverend Ousley's hands tugged gently on my arm, and I let him lead me from the bed and turn me toward the door.

"I'm sorry, John," Dr. Sullivan said behind me.

I nodded numbly and let Reverend Ousley lead me from the room. We started down the stairs and met Father on his way up. He paused, staring at us.

"Is she . . ."

"Yes," I answered.

He slumped against the banister and passed his hand over his face as if rubbing away memory.

"Well. At last, it's over," he said softly.

"We'll take care of everything, Henry. Do you want burial through my church?" Reverend Ousley asked.

Father shrugged. "As good as the next one, I suppose. Yours was the last she attended."

I frowned. His words seemed cold, indifferent to me.

"Yes, it was. We missed you, though," he said pointedly.

"Sorry, Reverend, but there just doesn't seem much point in acknowledging a God who seems to have forgotten His world." He glanced upstairs. "There's just too much pain and suffering in the world for me to believe in a Creator anymore. Attending services just seems a fashionable way for a man to excuse his faults."

"God says—" Reverend Ousley began, but Father cut him off.

"No, *man* says," Father interrupted. "Nowhere do I find

God taking pen in hand and jotting down His thoughts. But I have no intention of debating theology on the staircase now, Reverend. It's not the time nor the place."

"Maybe," Reverend Ousley said quickly, "it is precisely because God loves us that He gives us the gift of suffering. We learn the goodness of life by experiencing its pain. Maybe this is His way of making us perfect: by allowing us to experience the pain so we may know the enormous pleasure of contentment."

"Maybe," Father said tiredly, shaking his head as if hearing the ramblings of a fool. He turned his back and descended the staircase and crossed the foyer to his study. He paused, hand upon the door. "And maybe pigs will fly. But I doubt it." He closed the door firmly behind him. Reverend Ousley's hand gripped my shoulder tightly.

"Pay no attention to him, John," he said. "Your father's in grief."

I wasn't so sure.

The day of Mother's funeral loomed gray and wet, soaking everyone despite a canvas ceiling erected by the graveside and the ladies' parasols, more fashionable than functional. Almost everyone left from the days before the War came: the Varnedoes, Uncle Thomas and Uncle Robert, B. L. Stephens, W. H. Powell and his family, the mayor, M. J. Griffin and the aldermen R. W. Ralston, Howell Bird, J. M. Williams, and R. T. Myddelton and . . . Mattie, staying close beside me as Reverend Ousley worked his way through the passage he had chosen from Isaiah:

> For as the rain cometh down, and the snow from heaven, and returneth not thither, but watereth the earth, and maketh it bring forth and bud, that it may give seed to the sower and bread to the eater, so shall my word be that goeth forth out of my mouth. For ye shall go out with joy and be led forth with peace: the mountains and the hills shall break forth before you into singing, and all the trees of the field shall clap their hands. It shall not

return unto me void, but it shall accomplish that which I please, and it shall prosper in the thing whereto I sent it.

He paused, looking pointedly across the open grave at Father, then continued.

"Ashes to ashes, dust to dust. . . ."

Beside me, Mattie gently pressed my arm. I felt gratified by her intimacy and her gentle expression of grief, not so much for Mother, although she was very fond of her, but for me.

I patted her hand and looked down, smiling. She smiled back, her eyes large and luminous in her flawless face, concerned, yet warm and friendly. I glanced across the grave to Father. He was patting Rachel Martin's arm.

He glanced up and caught my eye. I frowned. He looked uneasily at Miss Martin, then his lips tightened, and his hand slipped over hers as he raised his eyes defiantly to mine.

"Amen," intoned Reverend Ousley.

I bent and picked up a clod of wet earth and dropped it on Mother's coffin. Mattie threw in a small bouquet of fall flowers. Father followed my lead, then thanked Reverend Ousley and turned and left, leading Rachel Martin to his carriage. He handed her into the carriage, then shook hands with Mayor Griffin and the others.

"John."

I turned and found Uncle Thomas standing next to me. His eyes followed mine to Father standing beside the carriage, shifting his weight from foot to foot, impatient to be off. His face tightened, the skin drawing close to his high cheekbones.

"We all handle our grief in different ways," he said.

"Yes," I answered, turning back to him. "And some of us not at all."

He took my hand and pressed it.

"See you back at the house?" he asked.

I nodded. He tugged the brim of his hat as he smiled at Mattie and turned and stepped his way through the mud back to his carriage, trying to avoid the growing puddles.

"We should go, John," Mattie said. "We can do no more for her now except pray."

"You're right, of course," I said. I led her to Uncle Robert's carriage and handed her inside, climbing after her. Uncle Robert glanced at both of us, then turned and patted his wife's knee before clucking to the horses, turning them back toward our house.

I watched the rear of Father's carriage disappear in front of us in the growing rain. A mockingbird sang a sad rain song.

I shook my head, leaning back against the horsehide-covered cushions of the carriage. Strange feelings that I couldn't explain were beginning to work within me.

Night had fallen and Lizie had silently made her way through the house, lighting the camphene lamps that spread a warm, golden light over the heavy walnut and mahogany furniture. Mattie sat beside me on the piano bench, silently turning the pages of the music in front of me as I played, working my way through the last lessons that Mother had given me. I was in the middle of what Uncle Thomas had told me was her favorite, Chopin's "Opus No. 1 in B-flat Minor," when Father entered the room. He stood silently at the corner of my vision, sipping occasionally from a glass dark with bourbon. Mattie glanced at him, then uneasily looked at me, moving restlessly on the bench. I ignored him, concentrating on the music. When finally I finished, he cleared his throat.

"John, I would like to see you in the study," he said.

"I have a guest," I answered. Mattie nudged me.

"Go on," she said softly. "I'll get a wrap and wait for you on the porch."

I rose as she stood and swept gracefully from the room. I looked at Father: He made a small gesture toward the study. I shrugged and crossed the foyer into the dark, book-lined room. He followed, closing the door behind me. He crossed behind his desk and sat, placing his glass at his right elbow and picking up a sheaf of papers lying on the green blotter in front of him.

"We have some business to settle," he said. He nodded at the chair in front of his desk. "You'd better sit down; this may take a while."

"What is it?" I asked.

He detached a sheet and slid it across to me. I picked it up, glancing at it.

"Your mother left you the land around Griffin," he began. "After we moved here, your grandfather died and split the land among all of his children. Alice received an equal share along with her brothers. I've been administering the land since along with Thomas, James, and William's shares and the shares of your aunts Melissa Ella, Eunice Helena, and Margaret Ann. Thomas is going to take over the running of his and William's land while James has deeded over his land to me in order to establish a medical practice in Atlanta. Now, the land isn't worth much. I've got some of the land in cotton—not much, because the market is still down and, frankly, I don't see any recovery in sight yet—but the most I have in sugar cane and corn."

He leaned back in his chair, regarding me.

"That's a tidy sum for these times," he said. "As you are still not of age yet, I will continue on as manager, but I think that you need to learn about crops and diseases and the details of land management and the responsibilities that go along with it. You may not wish to handle the land yourself, but you should know what has to be done even if you lease it out to a sharecropper."

"Responsibilities?" I asked.

He nodded. "Yes, there are those who depend on you to have a decent crop for harvesting. They supplement their income by working the field during harvest time." His lips turned down. "In the old days before the War, the nigras would have done that, but now, well, there are still some nigras that will work the fields, but mostly we have to rely upon white folks."

"I see," I said slowly.

He frowned.

"Is something bothering you?" he asked.

"Yes. Rachel Martin."

His eyes narrowed. Deliberately, he reached for the glass of bourbon, tasted it, then placed it carefully back on his desk.

"That is none of your business," he said.

"You are the one who brought up responsibilities. What about your responsibilities toward Mother?"

"Your mother is dead," he said flatly.

"We still have certain obligations—" I began but stopped when he held up his hand.

"Those days are gone, John. I'm sorry, but that's the fact. We can no longer afford the luxury to live by our emotions. We have to approach life from a standard built upon logic."

"And Rachel Martin is logical?" I asked sardonically.

He looked long and levelly into my eyes before answering.

"Your mother has been dead for a long time, John," he said quietly. "Since the War when I went away we have not . . . there are certain things . . ." He deliberately let his voice trail off. I stared at him, feeling anger beginning to build deep inside of me, working itself to rage.

"I'm sorry," he said gently. "But there it is. I suppose it really began when the Twenty-seventh and I were ordered to Manassas Junction to build a bridge across Occoquan Run. Your mother didn't want me to go. . . . She felt a certain dread that I was going to be killed there. . . . I guess it was at that time that she really realized what war was like. Before, I had managed to shield her from it, but now, now I was gone, she was forced to deal with it herself. At first it was only the little things that bothered her. She couldn't get pins or thread, paper, ink, soap, tea, coffee . . . the little luxuries that had become so important that we took them for granted. Later, after we fought at Williamsburg, Seven Pines, Mechanicsville and Cold Harbor, White Oak Swamp, Malvern Hill . . ."

He paused, his face white and tense with remembering. He gulped his whiskey and wiped his mouth with the palm of his hand before continuing.

"When we returned to Richmond after Malvern Hill, we had lost a full third of our men. One thousand one hundred fifty-one. Do you know how many men that is, John? No, you have no idea. Your mother had to deal with the widows around Griffin. And she did. For a while. Then"—he sighed—"she had a nervous breakdown. That was the main reason I came home, John. Not because of my personal medical history—although that was certainly a contributing factor—but because I had to get her away from Griffin. We came here."

"I don't believe you," I said flatly.

His eyes flared with anger, then he forced a weak smile.

"I understand," he said. "It's much easier to hate me. But that's the truth, John. You yourself said that Alice needed Uncle Thomas and went after him. You didn't know why she needed him, but you recognized the need. And you were right. I thought having Thomas around would just remind her too much of the War. But it helped. Especially after Sherman's men went through and took the food we had stored for the winter, everything that would be of value to them, burning all the rest. We managed to escape that, for the most part, but then refugees came to Valdosta, and we had to support them. Fortunately, the year had been good for us. We had kale and collards during the winter and new turnips came in January and snap beans in the shelter down by the river. But for your mother, that was too late. The poor diet she had lived on earlier had left her weak, too weak."

He turned, staring out the window. "She saw the War in me, John. That was the last time that I . . . visited her rooms. And, why she changed churches; she couldn't stand being constantly reminded of obligations she couldn't . . . perform."

"And Rachel?" I asked. Tears began to burn my eyes.

"Her fiancé was killed at Bull Run," he said. "We were lonely. Together, we were not." His chin lifted defiantly. "We will be married at the end of the year."

I leaped to my feet, the chair crashing back behind me. He turned, startled, toward me, then slid back away from his desk at what he saw in my eyes.

"I hate you!" I said, my words cold and deliberate. "Damn you, Mother needed not only Uncle Thomas, but she needed you. And you were gone!"

"You're only fourteen, John," he said. "When you are older—"

"I'm old enough," I interrupted. I glanced down at the paper balled in my hand and tossed it onto the table and turned to walk from the room.

"John Henry!"

I ignored him, flinging the door open and blindly stumbling across the foyer and out the front door. I ran into the pecan orchard, my arms and legs pumping hard against the rage inside of me until I could run no more. Then I flung myself down and lay with my face against the earth, smelling the sour richness while the tears came coursing down my cheeks and harsh, deep coughs racked my body.

Mattie found me there hours later and dropped to the ground beside me, ignoring the dirt that stained her dress. Gently, she brushed her hand across my forehead, wiping the smudges from it and my cheeks.

"I'm sorry, John," she said.

I grabbed her hand, holding it within mine, pressing my lips against her palm. Her breath caught in her throat. I looked up at her outlined against the gray sky.

"I love you, Mattie," I said.

Gently, she pulled her hand away from mine and looked down.

"I know," she said. She rose and brushed her dress off. "I came to get you. Did you forget that we have church tonight?"

I rolled over on my stomach away from her. I pulled a piece of grass and placed it between my thumbs and forefingers, blowing gently across it, listening to the chirrup I made.

"John Henry!"

I rolled back and looked at her. She bit her lip and looked away.

"Please?"

I tossed the strand of grass away and climbed to my feet, brushing myself off.

"If you give me a kiss," I said.

She turned, standing on tiptoes, and brushed her lips across mine, then slipped from my arms and ran lightly through the grove back to the house. I stood for a moment, feeling the touch of her lips on mine. Slowly, I made my way back to the house, the events only a few hours before still fresh in my mind, but the touch of Mattie's lips upon mine had momentarily taken the bitterness away.

6

Dust hung heavy in the air and the sorghum leaves and tobacco leaves drooped down, nearly touching the red clay where pecan trees had not been planted and longleaf pine did not stand as Uncle Thomas and I leisurely rode along the Withlacoochee River toward our old swimming hole where it bordered Father's leased property. Here and there, huge old oaks or hickory, hung with long streamers of gray Spanish moss, held nests of bluejays and sparrows. Mockingbirds called to each other despite scolding squirrels. Few people planted cotton anymore, as the land was too worn out to produce the amount of cotton needed to make a crop worthwhile. In the fields, women who had never tended fields before moved slowly down the rows, painfully hoeing weeds, their hands blistered and red from manual labor.

True to his word, Father married Rachel Martin at the end of the year. I was conspicuously absent. In bed with a fever, Father said to inquirers. Relations between us had deteriorated to where we simply nodded at each other as we met in the halls of the house. The family did their best to take my mind off Mother: My uncles took me hunting down to the Ocean Pond while their wives cooked special little treats for me, and Mattie constantly asked me to escort her to one dance and soirée after another, usually at the new hotel, Stewart's, which had a ballroom. Those were the magic times when the orchestra played songs like the old haunting love song "Lorena," that had made several Confederate soldiers so homesick they deserted after hearing it, and "Listen to the Mockingbird," "Jeanie With the Light Brown Hair," and Strauss waltzes that allowed us to come closer together.

And coming closer together was something that southern families—at least, my family—needed to do in a world that had deserted them and made them outcasts from their own land. Like the true Scots they were, my clan drew together with Calvinist tenacity to help me over the difficulties of Mother's death.

The times, however, were not meant for mourning any longer. About that, Father had been right: The carpetbaggers had descended in force upon our town and state. A man from Maine ran the post office while another represented us in the Senate; a Vermont man represented us in Congress; the street commissioner came from Pennsylvania, as did our chief of police; a Massachusetts man held the post of revenue commissioner; our jailer was from Philadelphia; and two nigras represented us in the legislature. In fact, Rufus Butler had stolen the election for governor and had packed the state legislature with nigras he had hired to vote as they were told. Taxes had stripped Georgians to the bone. The Freedmen's Bureau no longer even pretended to be judicially correct: Suits against a nigra were thrown out before going to trial. The South had become a powder keg, and everyone went around carrying pistols and rifles. Ladies even had derringers inside their reticules, fashionably made larger to allow easy access to the pistols. Cords had been attached to the reticules, allowing them to be hung from the shoulder, leaving both hands free. Pistol and rifle matches had become extremely popular. Even I no longer went around unarmed; Father's old Navy Colt was tucked constantly under my arm, and Lizie had tailored my coats to fit neatly over the telltale bulge. I needed to arm myself, though: Buford Tyler had just been appointed as a tax collector in our district and, although our paths seldom crossed what with him making his rounds out in the country, we still came in contact enough that a puzzled frown would draw his bushy eyebrows down over his eyes and his fingers would gently probe the stump where his ear had been before I shot it off. Fortunately, I had changed much over the three years since our confrontation—I had grown a mustache or what would try to pass for one, for one thing—but I made it a point of business to distance myself from him politely every time we met, ducking my head bashfully away from him and muttering my excuses like a whipped puppy, playing the part of a broken Southerner to the hilt.

At eighteen, I was roughly five-ten, blond, blue-eyed—the spit of my mother the friends of Father were prone to say when they gathered at the house for their "meetings." I had graduated from the institute in the spring and now was debating what to do. Father kept pushing for me to read law, while Uncle Thomas wanted me to go to Virginia to college. I kept dragging my feet; things had become very serious between Mattie and myself since that first chaste kiss in the pecan grove. A weakness came over me whenever I came near her. I trembled when I touched her and her breath came in quick, little gasps.

"Have you decided yet, John?"

Uncle Thomas's words broke my reverie. I turned in the saddle to face him.

"Not yet," I answered. "I'm still toying around."

"It's July," he warned. "Time to be making a decision." A grin touched his lips. "Unless, of course, you're planning on going into farming."

"That'll be the day," I laughed, lifting Ares's reins. He shook his head and lifted himself into a lethargic trot: He was feeling the sleepy day as well. Uncle Thomas came up beside me and we rode in silence for a little ways.

"How are things between you and Mattie?" he asked casually. I swung my head back to him, eyeing him warily.

"Good," I said noncommittally. He nodded and we rode in silence for a while, then he sighed.

"John," he began, then stopped. A frown settled over his face as he nibbled at his lower lip. I waited, knowing what was coming. At last, he spoke.

"You know that we all wish the best for you. But marriage

at your age in these times, well, that is . . . bad. Oh, I don't doubt your ability to keep her and to make a family, but . . . well, there is the matter of the discrepancy in your ages."

"There's as much between you and Aunt Sarah," I pointed out.

"Yes, but we were older than you at the time," he said sternly.

I laughed. Only ten years separated us. He tried to glare, but the absurdity of his words wore through his stern composure, and he laughed sheepishly at the pomposity of his words.

"Well, I think you are too young for marriage. Now," he emphasized, holding up his hand to forestall my rebuttal, "you need to establish yourself in a future before you contemplate matrimony. Especially in these unsettled times. There are no jobs available at all, and those jobs that do come available come cheaply because unemployment is high and men are willing to work at anything. Hardscrabble farmers are willing to split time with other employment to make ends meet. I believe I can say without reserve that William will not give his consent for Mattie's marriage for at least another four years. In the meantime, why not go to school, John? Hell, make your daddy happy and read for the law. You know he has friends in Atlanta who would be more than willing to have you as a clerk. Your daddy is a well-thought-of man around Georgia, John, whether you like him or not. Why not take advantage of that? Nothing would make him happier. Pick a profession—anything—something you can fall back upon if the land should be lost."

His face darkened. "And that could happen very easily if that bastard in the governor's chair passes many more bond issues through his pet legislature."

"You make the prospect of school seem somewhat a necessity," I said.

A serious look spread over his face. He slipped his fingers through the reins, forcing the chestnut into a canter. I lifted Ares' reins and touched his sides with my heels. Obediently, he stretched his long legs and settled into a matching gait with the chestnut. We rode in silence for a mile or two. At last, Uncle Thomas reined in the chestnut. I turned Ares in close to the chestnut and let the reins slacken, watching him. Ares dropped his fine head and nuzzled the dusty grass. I waited patiently while Uncle Thomas slumped in the saddle, toying with his reins, thoughtfully chewing on his lower lip. A bee flew lazily by, turned to query the lavender scent I had splashed on my cheeks after shaving that morning, then turned and flew away toward an old oak festooned with tatters of Spanish moss hanging like old veils from its gnarled branches. Red fox squirrels scampered on the ground among the twisted roots. A long glade fell away from it down to a strand of longleaf pine. I knew the place well: It was the dueling oak. A lot of gentlemen's blood had been spilled by its roots. Once Father had pointed out its secret when we had passed it in a carriage while riding to services at the Presbyterian church in the early days at Valdosta when we still attended church together.

I remember the words of advice Father gave me, the one set of words that I have always remembered:

"Notice the ground, John, how it slopes from the oak. A smart man will take his position away from the oak because a man firing uphill holds his sight higher. But here the ground is deceiving; it is an optical illusion; it slopes uphill away from the oak. Remember this, John: Appearances are often deceiving. What may seem peaceful and idyllic is often deadly."

And I remembered; sometimes not visually or literally, but, subliminally, I remembered.

"The prospect, John, is no longer in your hands. The Yankees have taken it from you," Uncle Thomas said quietly. "I can't put it any other way: We, the South, your family, need you in a profession that we can use. The War isn't over; it still continues, and people like us are becoming more and more the victims. In the coming years, people won't want to know the truth about us. They'll believe that trash written in the North about how we beat and tortured our nigras."

He stared gloomily at a red squirrel foraging in the tall brome grass near the base of the dueling oak.

"Maybe nobody will ever be able to understand. That is the tragedy of war: No one is ever able to understand the immediate need for it on both sides."

He sighed. The chestnut cropped a few blades of grass, stretching its neck along the road edge. Uncle Thomas's sadness reached across to me. I switched my riding crop at a bumblebee. Mixed emotions ran strong in me: anger, frustration, disappointment—all seething inside. I shuddered and gathered Ares's reins.

"Forget the past," I said roughly. Uncle Thomas raised startled eyes to mine. "The world is only the present. Race you to the river!"

Uncle Thomas brought his riding crop down smartly on the chestnut's flanks. It leaped forward in a gallop. I clapped my heels sharply against Ares' flanks. He reared, then lowered himself into a gallop, his long legs reaching effortlessly forward, pulling in the ground and throwing it away behind.

Despite his early lead, Ares quickly overtook the chestnut and pulled ahead. I gently leaned back on the reins, keeping Ares tantalizingly just ahead of Uncle Thomas.

We thundered across the small plank bridge that spanned Devil's Run just before the creek emptied into the Withlacoochee River. I reined in and waited for Uncle Thomas to bring the chestnut to a halt. The chestnut danced indignantly, snorting his willingness to continue the race despite losing.

"He has heart," I said.

Uncle Thomas nodded. "Yes. Too bad his speed isn't up to his heart. We'd have another Ares."

"There's only one Ares," I said, patting the stallion's neck. He tossed his head, vainly agreeing.

We walked the horses to cool them down the lane bordering Father's pasture to where the Withlacoochee curved back upon itself beneath a stand of old hickory trees, creating a deep pool that we used for swimming. Here the current idled beneath the shade of the trees that gave us the privacy we needed. Bass and catfish lay in the pond, too, and sometimes, after we had finished swimming, we would drop lines into the water and laze away the rest of the day, waiting for the shyness to wear off the fish and drive them hungrily toward our baited hooks. Today, though, given the heat, the cool water was on our minds, not fish.

Suddenly, Ares pricked his ears and jerked his head up, staring ahead. He shied nervously. Moments later, the chestnut nickered softly as we emerged into a glade. Dust rose from the deep grass. A group of nigras stared back at us. Their clothes had been carelessly tossed upon the bank, their weapons casually piled on top of their clothes.

"What the hell?" Uncle Thomas murmured from beside me.

I recognized one of the nigras, the one who had accosted me the day Mother died. He glanced up, noticed us, and swam leisurely to the bank. He climbed out and strolled cockily toward us, his manhood conspicuously swinging like a heavy pendulum.

"What you want here?" he demanded, placing his hands on his hips and arrogantly throwing his head back. Water streamed from his mahogany hide. For a brief moment, I thought of Triton emerging from the waters, then the illusion disappeared as his companions silently climbed from the water behind him. Some spread out behind him like nefarious shadows. A couple moved furtively toward their clothes and weapons.

"To swim," I said softly.

"Swim? Heah?" he scoffed. "You too late, white boy. This here's a colored hole, now. Y'white trash move on somewheres else."

The rage began to swell sharply inside me. The day became clearer, and I saw things with a lucidity normally missing.

"Let's go, John. We don't need trouble with their kind," Uncle Thomas said, swinging the chestnut's head away from them.

I said nothing, for I had spotted Buford Tyler floating on his back, his white marbled belly prominent in the air like Moby Dick's snout. He rolled lethargically onto his stomach and paddled awkwardly to the bank, stepping ashore, water streaming from his catfish belly-white body in a flood. His belly hung down, obscuring his pod and pecker, and he pulled on it, trying to stretch it in conscious length to the nigras' around him. He looked up at us, frowning.

"I don't think so," I said. I took a firm grip on Ares's reins with my left hand, letting my right drop casually next to my belt buckle. Beneath my coat, the Navy Colt hung from my shoulder, the butt just above my belt and canted slightly forward.

"What's this?" he blustered. "What are you doing here?"

"We own this," I said softly. "I think the question is, what are you doing here?"

"Why, what you think we doin' here, boy?" the nigra asked. The others sniggered behind him.

"Don't I know you?" Tyler asked, squinting up at me.

"We've met," I said, adding, "in town."

"Yes, yes," he said impatiently. His hand rose, his fingers tapping softly against his ear stump. "But we met somewhere before. Where? Where?"

"I don't know about that, but you people are trespassing on Holliday property," I said. It wasn't really true: We were only leasing the land at the time, but everyone knew that we were leasing it only until money freed up so we could buy it. His eyes narrowed and he shook his head, placing his hands on his fat hips and spreading his naked legs wide.

"No, I don't think so," he said. He raised a hand and waved it around at the river and trees authoritatively. "This land is currently in tax court, open to the first person who pays the back taxes and provides a deposition of intent to abide by revenue law. Ain't no such thing come across my desk in a long time. Far as I can see, this here land's open to first come. And we're first come."

The nigras laughed at this, two of them slipping off into a personal dance and slapping hands.

"Come on, John," Uncle Thomas said nervously. I ignored him.

"Well," I said carefully, "the law specifies that the lessee of property has equal rights as the owner. We lease this land from—"

He broke in, tossing his head back and smoothing his thinning hair away from his lumpy forehead.

"I don't really care who you are leasing this from," he said. "Fact is, you said what the law states: You have the same rights as those who own this land. Right now, that is in question. So your lease is in question. Now, *you* get the hell out of here because as tax collector for this district, I declare this open land to who comes first."

The nigras laughed at this, and my legs tightened in anger against Ares' sides. He moved closer to them, dancing and snorting angrily. The nigra's eyes narrowed.

"Best y'listen to him, boy. You don't want nothing with me here an' not without more of y'white trash around to help you," he said.

"Y'tell him, Rafe," one of the others sniggered. "Dumb white trash."

"You are trespassing," I said stubbornly. "This is Holliday land, and none of you has a right to be here."

"Holliday," Tyler said disgustedly. "I should have known. You are that son of that no-account lawyer that drags me into court every chance he gets. Right? I'll tell you right," he said, stepping forward and raising his finger. But the nigra put his black hand firmly against Tyler's pudgy chest, stopping him.

"No right?" The nigra pointed at a pile of clothes not far from him. "That there blue coat is all the right Ah need. Y'don't seem to understand, boy! Y'days are gone. This here's our time now. Y'now the niggers 'round here. Now, you turn that fine horse around and head out of here 'fore Ah take you off and keep the horse for myself. Fact, Ah think Ah'll do just that."

He stepped forward and raised his hand for Ares' bridle, then froze as the Navy Colt slid smoothly out from beneath my coat.

"My name is John Henry Holliday," I said softly, anger

making my voice shake. "Not boy. You touch my horse and I'll put a ball through your forehead. Go ahead, you nappy-headed son of a bitch! Make a move for that bridle. Come on!"

Slowly, he backed away, anger darkening his features.

"I thought not. All you're good for is to throw your weight around helpless women and children. Now, all of you, get out of here." I swung the pistol around to include them. "Leave your weapons and clothes where they lay."

"Be damned if Ah will!" one of them exploded.

"You'll be dead if you don't," I warned him.

He sneered and bent to retrieve his rifle. I pulled the hammer of the Colt back with the ball of my thumb. He hesitated, looking up at me, indecision clouding his face.

"Pick it up," Rafe said suddenly. "I know this boy. He the boy of that woman what said we try to do things to her."

He gave me a lewd grin and swaggered to his clothes.

"And nothing never happened, did it, boy? That what the court say. Don't mind one bit what y'momma say. The court the one who decide what do and don't happen. 'Course that don't mean that it won't happen. Y'momma a good-lookin' woman. Most good-lookin'. Maybe Ah come visiting and give y'momma a bit of black to taste. Then she never go back to y'daddy. No sir. That a fact. Most white women, they likes the black man. You white folks try to put the courts on us and what you get? Nothin'! Next time, we do what we want."

"My mother's dead," I said softly. "She never recovered from that day that you black bastards put your hands on her. But I heard about what you nigras did. I just didn't know which one of you bastards was responsible. It's good to know that. What say we open the court, now? I've got justice in my hand."

"I know you!" Tyler suddenly squawked. He pointed a shaking finger at me, his belly quivering with excitement. "You're that fucking white trash what shot my ear off." He turned to the big nigra beside him. "And he's the one who blew that hole in your brother!" He turned and looked accusingly at me, his eyes nearly tearing with the memory. "He died. That hole you put in him got gangrene and he died. That's murder."

"You'll have a hard time proving that," Uncle Thomas said grimly. "Especially after you tried to steal his horse."

"Ain't no witness to that," Tyler said, puffing himself up. "But I can testify as to who shot him." He leered. "I'd say offhand, boy, that your southern ass will be in prison real soon. And they'll know what to do with it there!"

"Maybe," Uncle Thomas drawled. "But I'd be damn careful what I said if I were you." He looked over the naked nigras behind Tyler. "People down here take a dim view of things like this."

"Like what?" he said.

Uncle Thomas leaned over his horse, staring hard into Tyler's eyes. "We've heard about you, Tyler. And we've heard how you aren't very partial to women. Your court can't protect you all the time. There's the night to worry about."

Tyler grew pale. He licked his lips and started to say something, but the nigra standing by the pile of weapons made a sudden grab for his rifle. I waited until he turned and brought it to bear, then shot him in the forehead. The back of his head exploded in a fine red mist, driving him backwards. He fell flat on the grass, pink brains and flesh spreading like a fan behind his head. Ares hopped sideways, then reared as I kept a firm grip on the reins. Through the haze of black powder smoke, I saw Rafe leap for his rifle. He whirled, crouching, rapidly bringing the rifle to bear on me. Ares crow-hopped sideways as the rifle exploded. I felt the wind of the ball pass my head. I snapped a shot at him, holding the sight low to allow for Ares's plunging. A scream followed my shot. Rafe dropped his rifle and fell to the ground, clutching his groin and curling into a fetal ball. Blood seeped through his clenched fingers.

"Stop!" Uncle Thomas shouted.

The nigras froze automatically at his parade-ground command, then glanced at the pistol in his hand and slowly backed away from their clothes and weapons.

"Tend to him," Uncle Thomas ordered, nodding at the moaning Rafe.

"Goddamn!" Tyler said softly, his hands cupping himself beneath his fat belly. "Goddamn!"

His eyes bugged out as two of the soldiers obediently crossed to Rafe and knelt beside him. They pulled his hands away from his groin. One swallowed and looked away.

"Gawd! He done shot his pecker off!" he announced to the others. The other took a soiled neckerchief from the pile of Rafe's clothing and roughly wadded it into place, binding it tight with strips torn from Rafe's uniform blouse.

"No!" Tyler wailed, falling on his knees beside the nigra. "Rafe! Oh God! Rafe!" He clumsily tried to cradle the nigra's head in his arms.

"Now pick him up and get off this land," Uncle Thomas ordered gruffly.

"Our clothes . . ." one began complaining, but Uncle Thomas cut him short.

"They'll be returned to your commanding officer along with an account of your behavior on a gentleman's private land. I daresay he'll have a few words to say to you," he said coldly. He gestured at the dead man. "I'll send a wagon in with him."

Four of the nigras picked Rafe up, balancing him awkwardly on their shoulders. Tyler stood, fussing over him, his hands waving like limp white butterflies in the air. The nigras ignored him and left, stumbling barefoot over the ruts in the lane. At the fork, one turned and defiantly shouted back to us.

"You gonna pay for this! When we git done ain't gonna be a stick standin' on your fine land! Hear me!"

"You'll regret this!" Tyler said furiously. He turned, tears streaming from his eyes. "I promise you this, you little cocksucker! I'll put you and your daddy in the poorhouse before I'm through! Goddamn if I won't!"

I cocked the revolver and, holding high, sent a ball singing over his head. He turned and sprinted around the curve, his white buttocks bouncing obscenely like river scum. He passed the others, who were jogging as quickly as their burden would allow them.

"Well, that wasn't the smartest thing you've ever done, John Henry!" Uncle Thomas said angrily as they disappeared around the bend. Hard lines appeared around his lips.

I holstered the Navy Colt and turned to face him.

"They tried to take Ares," I said quietly. "And you heard what they said about Mother."

"John, there isn't a court in the land will take your word over theirs, and they will lie."

"He was the one who tried to molest Mother," I said. "You remember the day you came to get me in town and those nigras were pushing us around? That was the same one."

His eyes widened, then dropped from mine and stared at the river moving slowly past us.

"That may mean something in your eyes, but the court will use that against you. Premeditation, they'll call it," he said, shaking his head. "But that's a job for the Major. Maybe he can build a case on them harassing the Hollidays. Your mother's case is on file, and we have the word of others in town who saw him push you. Maybe. I don't know."

"Maybe it's time that we did something about taking back our land like the night riders are doing over by Griffin and up around Macon," I said.

"Those are mostly low-type men, John," he said. "Drunken, lawless vagabonds who are taking advantage of us just as much as the carpetbaggers and scalawags."

"At least they aren't simply sitting around and letting these damned Yankees run over us!" I said hotly.

He sighed and looked sadly at me. "You never have admitted that we are a conquered people, John, have you?"

I shook my head. I knew the truth of his words. But deep inside I felt a certain satisfaction, a certain glow of satisfaction for what I had done.

"A man's defeated only when he admits it to himself," I answered. "Like Father has. And you."

He looked startled for a moment, then shook his head as he turned the chestnut back down the path.

"I don't know. Maybe you're right. Right now, though, I think we'd better get away from here. I'll go to see your father and explain what happened. You take the back roads and ride over to William's place at Griffin. They'll be looking for you around here and west. Even if the Federal troops come looking for you there, the night riders will keep them away from you once they find out what you have done. It'll gain us some time. Have you any money?" I nodded. A grim smile played across his lips. "For what it's worth, John, I do understand. Maybe sometimes a man just has to do something wrong like this to remember his manhood."

He turned and spurred away. I listened to the chestnut's hooves thud over the soft ground, carrying a part of me away, until they fell away in the distance. I looked at the dead nigra lying on the dusty grass in the middle of the glade. Blue-bottle flies buzzed around him. Above, a turkey buzzard spiraled in lazy, concentric circles. A woodpecker broke the silence and a blue jay angrily scolded him. A crow cawed and I heard the low, hesitant coos of a least bittern.

I rode Ares down the lane and crossed the Withlacoochee. When we reached the other bank, I lifted him into a canter, riding through the dusty day away from my youth.

two

PESTILENCE

1

Ah, Mattie!

With cornflower blue eyes and the kiss of the sun in her hair!

In the end, it was Mattie who made the difference. Strangely enough, it was the last night we were alone together. The wisteria was still in bloom, and late lilacs poured their scent through the air. The magnolia tree provided a canopy over the terrace of Uncle William's house, dropping soft white and pink petals onto us.

Father had arrived full of his pompous fury, angry over what I had done, angrier still that I had done what he had wanted to do for so long. I knew the strictness in him, but I also felt the deepness of his love although he never said it.

Father never said he loved me, nor Mother.

Reading for the law was no longer possible for Father's friends across the state were of a like kind with him in regards to the Reconstruction and Republicanism the nigras and Northerners were trying to cram down our throats. To place me with one of them would be giving me to the northern courts. Oh, not that they would have done that deliberately, but a time would come after a few glasses of bourbon in one of their clubs when they would proudly claim they had John Henry Holliday on their staff, the same John Henry Holliday who had killed that nigra soldier over Valdosta way for being too uppity, and the Federal troops would clap me in the nearest jail within hours and hang me days later.

No, reading for the law was out. I had to get as far North as possible. It would not be long before I was found at William's place after my long, desperate ride.

Ah, the long nights of that ride and the laying up by day in a true southern man's barn, . . . the hoot owls keeping me company . . . the night hawks flying from the mist rising in the pale moon's glow.

Father had made inquiries, and he and my uncles argued long and hotly about what to do with me while Mattie and I took refuge on the terrace.

"I'm afraid for you, John."

"Don't be. It's done with. There's no changing that."

"That's what makes me afraid. What it has done to you."

"I'll have to go away for a while."

"I know."

"Will you . . ."

I tried to say the words, to ask her to wait for me to return, but her sweet lips touched mine, and I tasted the sadness in their quiver and the sweetness of her breath.

I remember still the lone tear trickling down her pink cheek. I remember the smell of the magnolia and the lone mourning dove crying plaintively from somewhere in the night and the flash lightning that illuminated the darkness in the west. I remember the sounds of Father's voice angrily shouting down my equally angry uncles as they debated what to do with me.

I remember everything about the night and small instances in the night, but now I have difficulty picturing her face as it must have become over the years.

". . . I had no trouble before. . . ."

". . . Father is still there. . . ."

". . . giving me the choice of medical school or college, but four years was too long and . . ."

Uncle William remembered that a distant cousin had graduated from the dental school in Philadelphia off Walnut Street. The faculty might not look too closely into the background of a young Georgia gentleman—especially if he brought his records with him along with a sealed letter from his proctor, and Varnadoe was southern enough to give me that.

But best of all, the school was far enough north to be out of the sphere of southern news, and Philadelphia was large enough to lose oneself in. Dentistry was a profession that was becoming highly respectable among the important families—the *once* important families, you understand, Father—and two years of study would place Mattie at twenty-two, for she was two years older than I.

Old enough, but the plans of men cause the gods great amusement, and Mattie must have had a premonition of what lay ahead for us, for she gave me a gold stickpin upon our parting and asked me to always wear it in remembrance of her.

I have.

We were young and foolish and foolishly romantic as we bade each other good-bye, and I left for Philadelphia to do my penance in school as a gentleman scholar.

2

Professor Strachyam moved below us in the small operating theatre, keeping up a running discourse of dry observations, punctuating his remarks with applications of the new foot-pedal-operated pneumatic drill, which was just replacing the Merry drill for dentistry work. He worked deftly on his patient while we sat on hard, straight-backed chairs in the loft above him, taking notes.

"One must be careful, gentlemen," he said as he peered into his patient's gaping mouth, "not to lose one's concentration or press too hard with the drill. Otherwise, the bit might break off in the tooth or slip off the tooth onto the soft tissue of the patient's mouth."

Dick Sutton leaned close to me and offered in a soft, audible whisper, "The patient will, of course, let you know if you have."

His words came a bare moment ahead of Professor

Strachyam's. "The patient, of course, will be certain to let
you know."

Obediently, the class tittered. It was a tired joke and one
familiar to all of us. The faculty seemed to have a tendency to
share tired and dry puns and jokes among themselves. Sutton
took advantage of the obligatory laughter to whisper again.

"Will you be going to the Arch Street Theatre tonight?"

"I don't know," I said, barely moving my lips, keeping my
eyes on Strachyam. "I should study."

"Belle Boyd will be there, reprising her role as Mazeppa,"
he said.

At that precise moment, Strachyam's eyes flickered up to
us and caught the movement of Sutton's lips.

"And you, Mr. Sutton, can you explain to the class what I
should be doing next?" he asked.

Sutton sat sheepishly back in his chair, his normally red face
flushed even more from being caught not paying attention.

"Well?" Strachyam asked impatiently.

"Ah, I'm afraid not," Sutton said.

"I see," Strachyam said icily. "And you, Mr. Holliday, can
you answer the question?"

"Yes, sir. Swab the area around the tooth and the cavity
itself with oil of clove to deaden the pain if any should be
present," I said.

Strachyam's eyebrows flew upward in mock surprise.

"I see. I take it that was the gist of Mr. Sutton's speaking
to you during the lecture? Asking what I should be doing
next?"

"Something like that, sir," I answered smoothly. "We were
speaking about cavities."

Sutton made a strangled noise in his throat from beside me.

"Yes, Mr. Sutton?" Strachyam asked. His bushy black
eyebrows lowered ominously. "Are you all right?"

"Fine, sir," Sutton gurgled. "Some saliva went down the
wrong pipe."

The patient moved restlessly in the chair beside Strachyam. Although "gas" or nitrous oxide had been discovered

by Horace Wells, a dentist in Hartford, Connecticut, in 1844, many dentists were suspicious of its effects. Most of those who did use it used it mainly during extractions.

"Here now, Doctor," he mumbled through the cotton stuffed between cheek and gum to absorb his saliva. "Kin we gid ong wid dis?"

"Of course," Strachyam said, tearing his eyes away from the two of us. He made a palms-up gesture of helplessness to the gallery. "I'm terribly sorry. I realize you are a busy man."

Another quiet titter ran through the students. Strachyam's patient was not one who would be physically engaged with anything other than where to get the money for his next drink. The college took its "practice" patients from among the poor people who could not afford medical expenses in the Limehouse District of lower Philadelphia.

I didn't laugh; I felt a flash of irritation at the mockery from my fellow students' laughter.

"Sounds like a Dixie boy to me," someone said mockingly from behind me.

I recognized the voice, flushed, and turned in my chair, starting to rise. Sutton grabbed my arm, forcing me down. He had heard the voice, too.

"Forget it, John," he said lowly. "This isn't the time or place."

I heeded his words, leaning back in my chair, smoothing the front of my shirt and straightening my carefully knotted tie, touching Mattie's stickpin. Sutton was right, although I knew the remark had been directed toward me. My peers took cruel delight in playing games with the token Southerner in the class. The City of Brotherly Love excluded Southerners as Reconstruction had unleashed the dogs of war. Southerners were made aware that they had become second-class citizens—ad águsta per angusta—and the Northerners took ecstatic delight in playing games upon all who came from the South. Sneers and lewd suggestions followed the women from the South who hurried along the streets, eyes downcast, making their way to the Union centers where they could pick up their pensions from contemptuous clerks after waiting in long lines for hours. Those who thought that the War had been fought to keep them in the Union found themselves socially cast out of it by the predators who follow all wars: those predatory ones who seized all southern property for themselves. The North was not much better than the South, for the Southerner who went north faced the humiliating arrogance by which he was constantly informed that he had lost the War and had been relegated to the low rung on the social ladder. It was not the ideal position to be in, a Southerner in the North. But the War had left the Southerner with very limited possibilities, and the field of dentistry was an easy choice for us to make in 1870. Father had planned well: I would receive a profession for a very limited investment. In fact, after sixteen months or so at the Pennsylvania College of Dental Surgery in Philadelphia, I would earn the title of "Doctor," which would certainly help disguise me from the young man who had slain the nigra and mutilated another at that swimming hole on the Withlacoochee River.

I found rooms above O. B. Demorat's photo studio at 2 South Eighth Street. Demorat did not seem to mind the presence of a southern gentleman in his house. I spent long hours away from my studies watching him photograph the ladies of quality who visited him during the daytime, and the prostitutes who visited him at night to pose in the nude.

My rooms were spartan but comfortable: a small bed and wardrobe occupying one room along with a chamber set—washstand, ewer and basin, and chamber pot—while a desk and chair, and a small sofa and padded chair, filled the adjoining room. Not much compared to home—the place I knew as home, anyway—but it was adequate for my needs. I seldom entertained, preferring to spend most of my time in my rooms, where I immersed myself in my studies, memorizing the names of the teeth, the bones in the body, the various methods for anchoring fillings, crowns, and bridgework, the tempering of gold foil for fillings, how to make dentures out of a new hard rubber called Vulcanite, numerous formulas for mixing various medications to relieve chronic pain and difficulties that might arise from a careless extraction, although most of these could be dealt with by placing a few drops of laudanum in a glass of wine, the proper dosage needed for quinine and opium properties and products. Unlike the Colton Dental Association and College of Dental Surgery down in Baltimore, the Philadelphia College of Dental Surgery demanded its graduates be as familiar with the human body as if they had attended its sister surgeon college.

When a certain restlessness came upon me, I found myself in the Lower End by the riverfront, the Navy Colt tucked beneath my arm, searching out the gambling halls, where I quickly learned to tell a flash-dancer from a square-rigger. I already knew about the right bower and off-jack from games in Valdosta with my friends. I proved quite adept with the pasteboards, easily augmenting my monthly allowance, which came from one of Father's friends in Atlanta who willingly accepted monies from him and passed them on to me to keep the scalawags from tracing his mail to me.

"Stop your woolgathering," Sutton said, nudging me in the ribs.

"Sorry," I whispered back.

"Oh, come on!" he urged. "Going to see a play won't compromise your little magnolia blossom back home. Besides, it's your southern duty to support one of your heroes, isn't it?"

I laughed and quickly changed the laugh to a cough, drawing a glare from Strachyam. I waved an apology, leaning back in my chair, remembering the stories of the seventeen-year-old girl who had been one of "Stonewall" Jackson's best spies during the War.

The daughter of a storekeeper in Martinsburg, Virginia, Belle was an excellent rider, a dead-shot, and had a figure that left most men gulping for air. But it was her fiery temper that drew men to her. When a Union soldier tried to place the stars and stripes over her home, she faced him down, coolly and competently. The Boyd House was the only residence in Martinsburg that did not have the Union flag fluttering triumphantly over it. Later, when a group of Union soldiers tried to place the flag over the house again, Belle drew a pistol and shot one of them. He died of blood poisoning, and Belle's career was forced upon her. She soon became one of the Union's most wanted spies.

Eventually, however, Belle was captured when she tried to sail for Europe from Richmond aboard a blockade runner. But she managed to become engaged to the Union naval officer commanding the ship before he could make port. She was briefly confined in Boston before making her way to Canada and England. Her fiancé followed after being dishonorably discharged. They were married in England, where he eventually died, leaving Belle destitute. She wrote her memoirs, which became very popular reading in the South, then entered the theatre, playing various roles before dusting off the old play *Mazeppa* and once again scandalizing the nation.

Professor Strachyam quickly finished his work, throwing the sheet off the patient with a flourish.

"Tomorrow, gentlemen," he said, "Professor Walton will lecture on the use of opiate derivatives. I suggest that you make an effort to be here for that. Especially," he said, glaring at Sutton and myself, "some who make it a habit to treat these sessions as social gatherings."

He turned and walked out, leaving his aides to escort the patient from the room.

Behind me, someone started to whistle "Dixie." I whirled and caught Artemis Reese with his lips puckered. Light shone from his oily skin. His black eyes narrowed above his acne-scarred nose. Tiny pustules covered his chin above his soiled tie. My hand flashed out, catching him hard across his cheek, the slap ringing in the room. Movement ceased as our peers turned to watch.

"You may," I said, carefully selecting my words, "choose your seconds."

"A challenge," someone whispered. The word swept through the room and spilled out into the hall, where some had already exited. The doorway filled with curious onlookers. Reese blanched and stepped back from me.

"Dueling's illegal," he said, his rubbery lips trying to lift into a smile and attaining a smirk.

"A coward's answer," I said. A coldness settled in my stomach.

"A typically southern response," he said.

A low laugh came from those around us. Arrogance rose to his eyes at the laughter. His voice raised.

"Always trying to win battles now that the War is over. What's the matter, Holliday, one beating not enough for you?"

The laughter came a bit louder. Instinctively, my hand slipped under my coat for the Navy Colt, but I had stopped wearing it since I had come to Philadelphia. His eyes widened at my gesture, then laughter broke from his lips as I slowly brought my hand out empty. His lips pursed, and the first bar of "Dixie" streamed from them. I balled my fist and swung. His nose broke under my fist, splattering him with his blood. He fell back in his chair, tears springing to his eyes. He fumbled a handkerchief from his breast pocket and pressed it against his nose.

The crowd murmured angrily and started to move toward me, but Sutton stepped to my side. I glanced at him: Lights danced in his eyes at the prospect of a fight.

"Now then, let us begin again," he said. "Reese had it coming, and you all know that. If a man can't back up his play, then he had better watch his words. Fair is fair, after all."

"Shanty Irishman," someone murmured.

"Ah now, will the one who spoke those words be kind enough to step forward?" Sutton challenged. "Or is it a coward he is, like all of you who want to use the others for their shields? Then let us have at it: the two of us against all of you. Is that enough of an advantage? Or should we wait until there are more of you?"

"That was a dirty blow, Holliday," Dan Leigh said, moving forward to help Reese. "You had no call to do that: Reese was only having a bit of fun."

"And so was John here. And as for the rest of you, why then, we'll put this down to a little joke that went a bit too far, shall we?" Sutton said lightly. He grabbed my arm and we pushed our way through the crowd, his bull-like shoulders shoving the others aside.

Silently, the others gave ground as we made our way out into the hall. Together we walked down the cavernous hall, our heels echoing on the wooden floor. Sutton pushed the door open and we stepped outside, blinking in the sudden afternoon sunlight.

"All right," I said as we stood, letting our eyes adjust.

"All right what?" Sutton asked.

"We'll go to see *Mazeppa* tonight," I said.

"Well, John Henry!" he said, clapping me on the shoulder. "I do believe your halo is slipping a little. Welcome to the world of mortals."

A horsecar went by, its bell clanging to warn pedestrians. A light cloud of dust rose in its wake. I coughed, reaching for my handkerchief as spasms gripped my chest.

"That's one of the negative things about being mortal," he continued, taking my books from my hand and tucking them under his arm. "The air is not so pristine down here as that rarefied mixture you're accustomed to breathing."

My retort was lost in another paroxysm of coughing.

I missed the South, the quiet song of the cicadas, the balmy nights, the hot, humid days, the quiet talk and movement of the people. And Mattie. I missed Mattie and wrote to her every chance I got, outlining our plans: the dental practice I would have, the house we would build, our lives. Sometimes I would lie awake for hours, listening to the night, seeing her face in the patterns of shadows on the ceiling. Perhaps Sutton was right; a change might do some good. And a play certainly could do no harm.

3

⟨decorative divider⟩

I kept pressing my handkerchief, lightly scented with lemon verbena, to my lips against the stifling air of the Arch Street Theatre. The audience had quieted as guards brought Belle Boyd, playing the male role of the Cossack hetman raised in the Polish court, before the husband of the lady with whom he had had an affair. Like most of the audience, I had a terrible time looking at Belle and trying to picture a man; her bold figure was clearly outlined by her costume: full breasts straining her tunic, long, shapely legs sharply outlined by her hose, her tiny waist neatly cinched by a broad leather belt that accented her sweeping hips. Her hair had been cut short and bobbed.

"Mazeppa, you will be stripped of your garments and tied to the back of a wild horse, which will be set free to return to the wilds from whence it was captured."

I winced at the stilted language, then leaned forward on my seat as the husband's guards stepped forward, surrounding her. They pushed her to the floor, hiding her from the audience, then suddenly stepped back as she rose to her feet.

The air suddenly left the theatre when everyone inhaled as the nude Belle stood before them. Then I saw that a flesh-colored body garment covered her from graceful neck to her fine-boned ankles. But the garment could not hide the woman beneath it: Her nipples stood out, large, sharp, and clear, and a faint triangular shadow showed between her legs. The guards let her stand exposed to the audience for a long moment before leading a docile pony onstage and strapping her artfully on her back to its back, then leading it off presumably to release it again to the wilds.

Thunderous applause followed her departure. Moments

later, the curtain fell, although no one had heard the closing lines of the play. The cast went through a quick curtain call, then Belle stepped between the curtains. She wore a dressing robe over her costume. Deep dimples curved beside her aquiline nose. A cheer rose from the audience, and flowers streamed onto the stage.

"Come on! Let's go!" Sutton said hoarsely, pulling on my arm.

"Where?" I asked, rising and following in his wake as he pushed through the crowd. Several turned to object, then saw the breadth of Sutton's Irish shoulders straining beneath his coat, and his battered features beneath his bowler, and thought better than to object. We crossed the empty foyer and rushed through the theatre doors, throwing them wide. A large poster of Belle discreetly arranged on the pony to suggest nudity without hiding the woman stood to our left. Sutton paused to rip it down, hurriedly rolling it tightly. Intent on preserving his souvenir, he stepped recklessly out onto the sidewalk. He bumped into a young girl selling flowers as we emerged from the theatre onto Arch Street, knocking her basket from her grip.

"Here now!" she squawked. She dropped to her heels and began to gather the flowers that had spilled from her basket.

"Watch where yer goin'!" she said. "Look at this!" She held up a small bouquet of six red roses. "Who'll buy this?"

Their stems had been bent at a right angle. I laughed: She had been clever, expertly twisting their stems with one quick movement like a magician's sleight of hand. She glared at me, then her gaze wavered as I pulled a dollar from my pocket and held it up.

Her gaze steadied on the silver dollar as I rolled it across my knuckles, the lights of the theatre sparkling off first the seated Liberty then the flying eagle. Loftily, she handed the roses to me, snatching the dollar from my knuckles in exchange.

Sutton tugged impatiently at my arm. "Come on! We don't have time for this bunkum."

"What's the hurry?" I asked.

He pulled me around the corner of the theatre into Sixth Streeth, then down a dark alley. The smell of rotting garbage leaped at us, bludgeoning our nostrils. I gagged. A series of coughs burst from my chest. I quickly drew my handkerchief from my coat pocket and covered my mouth and nose. My foot slipped on the slimy cobblestones, and Sutton's grip tightened, steadying me.

"Here we are!" he exclaimed halfway down the alleyway. He released my arm and pulled open a large, rusting, iron door.

"Where?" I asked.

"Stage entrance," he said.

"We can't go in there!" I protested.

"Sure we can," he said. "The doorman's me cousin."

We stepped into the theatre. To our right, a large bank of thick ropes had been gathered from the darkness high overhead and tied to clamps anchored in the wall. High overhead, various scenes painted on heavy canvas had been hung. Dusty curtains draped the sides of the stage and in back. Men in shirtsleeves brushed past us, their hands filled with props that had been used in the play, following the directions of a stage manager to the laying of them on the right or left prop table. In the far corner stood some of the women still in costume, casually flirting with some gentlemen in evening dress. I noticed a few Yankee uniforms among them as well.

A large, beefy man hurried up to us. Runnels of sweat poured from under his bowler and streamed down his red face. Dark half-moons of perspiration showed under the arms of his collarless shirt. Leather galluses held up a pair of stained, brown pants. His huge feet bulged the leather of his brogans. He held a dead cigar tightly clenched between stained teeth. He beamed, stretching out his hand to Sutton.

"Well, now, I was to giving you up for the dark," he said, the brogue strong in his voice. A cloud of whiskey breath rolled to us.

"And did you think, now, that we'd be forgettin' your kind invitation?" Sutton asked. He threw a punch at the man's chin, and the two of them sparred playfully for a moment, then the man reached out and caught Sutton in a headlock and rubbed his knuckles affectionately over Sutton's scalp.

"Given yer fondness for the poteen, I had me thoughts," he answered. He stared curiously at me. Sutton took his cue.

"My good friend John Henry Holliday," he said formally, pushing away from the man. "This lout is me cousin from me mother's side: Patrick Cavendish."

Sutton grasped his shoulder and squeezed it hard. Paddy winced from the pressure of Sutton's grip. I involuntarily flinched, remembering the iron grip of Paddy and how much strength Sutton must have had in his fingers to cause that stalwart pain.

"Thanks, Paddy," Sutton said. "This is a big favor. I owe you one."

"Aw, go on with yuh," Paddy growled, nudging Sutton's chin with knuckles that would have knocked out a horse. "An' be getting over there before she figures you to be nothing more than a dirty sassenach whose word is no better than an Englishman's."

A group in the corner fell silent as he ceremoniously led us past them to Belle's door. A man in a captain's uniform standing next to a heavyset man with a close-cropped beard and hard bowler gave us a hard look as we passed.

"We may be having a bit of trouble," I whispered to Sutton.

He glanced at them, then his lips lifted scornfully.

"Not much to worry about, I'm thinkin'," he said. I looked again at them, noting the angry looks. A recklessness blossomed inside me. I grinned at them and closed in on Paddy as he discreetly knocked.

"Come in!" a low, vibrant voice called from within.

Obediently, Paddy twisted the knob and shoved the door open, formally announcing, "Miss Boyd, me cousin, Richard Sutton, and his good friend John Henry Holliday. Students."

I stepped in, casually glancing around the room: I noticed a framed front page of the Philadelphia *Echo* that proclaimed "Secesh Cleopatra Caged" and other northern papers: the New York *Herald:* "Village Courtesan Captured"; the Philadelphia *Telegraph:* "Bountiful Belle in Prison"; *Leslie's:*

"Confederate Feminine Desperado in Chains: Mosby's Lover Federal Prisoner." I laughed at their sensationalism. Then my attention was drawn to the woman sitting at the dressing table in front of me.

She rose gracefully from her place before a large, oval mirror to greet us. She had stripped her face of its stage makeup. The eyes, made so huge and luminous onstage with a careful application of kohl, had become frank and appraising. Her nose, perhaps too long by some standards, dropped down to full lips above a long and firm jaw. I stared in surprise at her plain face, yet I felt myself drawn to its plainness, even excited by it. My hands grew moist, my lips dry. A well-defined leg gleamed briefly through a floor-length, Chinese dressing gown with lotus flowers brocaded in gold thread as she rose from the chair. Her large and unbound breasts moved freely beneath the gown while her feet, bare and highly arched, peeped beneath its hem. I drew a deep breath. Musk filled my lungs and at first I thought I smelled her perfume, but then I realized I smelled the scent of the flowers that had been packed into the room from ardent admirers.

"My colors!" she exclaimed. "How thoughtful! How did you know?"

For a moment I felt at a loss for words, then I casually lifted the roses and handed them to her as if I had planned their presentation all along.

"My pleasure, ma'am," I said. Her eyebrows arched as she took them, touching them to her nose and inhaling their fragrance.

"My! A Georgia man! And here in my dressing room! I do declare, I don't know what to say!"

"That I cannot believe," I answered warmly. "I cannot imagine you without a word any more than I can imagine Circe without her charms."

"Ah, a learned one at that," she murmured. Her eyes appraised me over the roses. "You are obviously not Paddy's cousin."

"Now how should I be takin' that, ma'am," Sutton said, doffing his hat. He grinned at her. "Why, I would think that one rebel would be as welcome in the house of another rebel as would a bottle of whiskey to the wee ones."

"And to that, you are welcome, good lad," she said, mimicking his accent. Sutton laughed and kissed her fingers, which she extended to him. "But I have a caution against such easy talkers as yourself."

Sutton placed his hand over his heart and rolled his eyes heavenward, intoning, "Ah, sure, and didn't my sainted Muther say me words would be the best of me yet?"

She laughed and leaned forward, kissing him on his cheek. A flash of annoyance swept over me. I frowned at the feeling as she stepped back, saying, "And for that, I commend you to my dresser, Emily."

She gestured toward a quadroon waiting warily at the side of the room. She was shorter than Belle and less physically endowed, but her features carried none of the thick features of the nigra: she had tiny, shell-like ears, a long, thin nose, and lips full but without nigra bulging. Her skin had a light au' lait shade to it. Only in her eyes could one detect a nigra heritage: large and moist, wary, black. She fastened her eyes on Sutton. He rose graciously to the moment.

"Ah! An' isn't she one that would set the bards to composing," he said. He tossed his head back with a flourish, his eyes closing, declaiming:

> "And while lonely, did Venus appear
> Before my eyes a-waitin' here.
> And to her eyes I gave her praise,
> And drank a toast for all my days."

She giggled and held her hands over her eyes for a moment, than took her hands away from them and gave him a bold look.

"You're a saucy one. A woman will have to be careful around you." She looked meaningfully at Emily. "Real careful," she emphasized.

A tiny grin tugged at the woman's mouth. She looked appraisingly at Sutton. He grinned back at her, sticking his thumbs in the pockets of his flowery waistcoat and rocking back and forth on his heels.

"Will I?" she asked, her voice low and full, but behind the bold words I heard a guarded wariness.

His grin widened.

"Of course not," he said. "And what kind of a man would I be if women could trust me? Why, me mother would disown me for sure, and me father would think the blood of an Englishman ran in me veins."

Belle placed her hands on her hips, tossing her head back and laughing, deeply and heartily, her breasts moving freely beneath the dressing gown. A hunger swept through me, and I breathed deeply, suddenly conscious of the intensity of her scent, the smell of her stage makeup, the flowers, the room. Suddenly, her eyes caught mine, large and bold.

"And you. Can I trust you?" she asked archly. She stepped close to me. Her eyes held mine. Mischievous lights gleamed in their depths.

"Only if I can trust you, Miss Boyd," I said levelly. Her lips curved in a huge smile.

"Well then, if you'll give me a moment to change my clothes, I'll let you buy me dinner," she said. I turned to leave, but she placed her hand on my arm, staying me.

"You may wait here," she said. She nodded at an Oriental screen tucked into a corner. "I'll change there."

She turned away, unbelting her robe. I caught a glimpse of white shoulders as she disappeared behind the screen.

"Emily, bring my gray dress, please. The one with the black ribbon," she called.

"Excuse me," Emily said to Sutton. She gave him a bold, smoky look and took the requested dress from a trunk and crossed behind the screen.

Sutton shook his hands as if shaking water from them and raised his eyebrows heavenward, silently mouthing, Lucky, lucky, lucky.

"Try and act like a gentleman," I whispered sternly.

Sutton grinned and walked to one of the bouquets and plucked a bronze chrysanthemum, settling it in his buttonhole.

"There. Now am I a gentleman?" he asked, his eyes twinkling. His words were overheard by Belle as she and Emily emerged from behind the Oriental screen.

"All men should be," Belle said. "That is their tragedy. No woman can be; that is hers."

"Profound," Sutton murmured. Emily crossed to him. He turned, offering his arm. Daintly, Emily tucked her hand in the crook of his elbow, giving him a half curtsy. He looked at Belle, then me, his eyebrows quirking quizzically.

I smiled and opened the door for them. Belle paused to drape a matching cape around her shoulders and, lacking the hair needed to anchor a bonnet, settled a flat-crowned hat on her head, tilting it rakishly aside.

"Well," she said. "Shall we try Delmonico's?" She gave Sutton a roguish look. "All gentlemen eat there."

Sutton blanched and smiled weakly back at her, but he gallantly tipped his hat in agreement, although Delmonico's would severely shrink his purse.

"Of course," I said smoothly, taking her arm. "Is there any other place?"

"Yes, but I don't know you that well. Yet." A smile curved its way along her lips.

The men chatting with the showgirls gave us dirty looks as we escorted Belle and Emily across the stage wing to the door. I smiled pleasantly at them. One, dressed in a checked suit that marked him as a drummer, flushed and started toward us, but a man in evening clothes stopped him, whispering in his ear. Tiny muscles in his jaw clenched and unclenched as he listened. Reluctantly, he nodded and, giving us a last look, hurried off through the dark theatre. His friend lifted his hat and nodded pleasantly at us before turning back to the group. There seemed something deliberate about his movement. I frowned, trying to place the thought gnawing at the edges of my mind, but I shrugged it off as we left the theatre and made our way down the alley to Sixth Street and turned the corner onto Arch Street.

"I'll get a cab," I said, turning away from Belle. I bumped into a Yankee officer with a peroxide blonde on his arm. Her breasts bubbled from the sudden stop, threatening to roll over the top of her red satin dress. She giggled as she clung to his arm, gathering her balance.

"Watch where you're going!" the officer snapped. Alcohol fumes wafted over me. I recognized the captain who had been standing by the bearded man among the hopefuls outside Belle's door when we had been shown inside.

"I'm terribly sorry," I said. "It was all my fault."

"A southern boy," he said. His eyes narrowed to piggish slits in his flushed face. "Why don't you people stay where you belong? We beat you down there, and now you come up here, trying to crowd your betters off the sidewalk." He looked past me to where the others stood, watching.

"Belle Boyd."

She nodded.

"I've heard about you."

"And what have you heard?" Belle asked. Dangerous lights shone from her eyes.

"That you sold your virtue first for Jackson and later for that damned Mosby."

"And what did you sell yours for?" she asked coolly.

He ignored her, looking at Emily.

"A nigger. You don't have to be with them, you know. You're free."

Emily stiffened at his words, a smooth mask settling over her face, her eyes going as opaque as black river-bottom pebbles.

"Freedom gives one the choice," she said quietly.

"All those dead men for ignorance," he said, shaking his head. He looked at the woman clinging to his arm. "Well, my dear, you see the way of it, do you not?"

She giggled.

A coldness settled in my stomach as I took a step back, fighting the rage threatening to build in me. He was an inch or two shorter than I and twice as heavy, his belly threatening the buttons on his jacket. Silently, a small group of soldiers gathered behind him, spreading out in a semicircle on both sides of me.

"Is there any trouble?" Sutton asked, appearing at my shoulder.

"No, no trouble," I said. "Just another damned Yankee who thinks he owns the world."

"Two of you, eh?" the officer said, swaying a bit on his feet. "Just like southern white trash to horn in on a gentleman's argument."

"Must be an Englishman," Sutton said, turning to me. "They're the only ones I know who make a habit of bandying that word about without living up to its meaning." He gave the officer a long, level look. "They have a hard time realizing the truth of themselves, too."

"And what might that be?" the officer asked. His bushy eyebrows drew down together in a frown, disappearing in a parenthesis over his eyes.

Sutton's mouth opened, but I quickly answered, "That you are an ass."

His face turned beet red with fury. He shook his arm free from the woman, sending her staggering against the building.

"Shit!" she complained. "What's got into you?"

"Your wife?" I asked, raising my eyebrows innocently.

He raised his fist to strike me, but I stepped in close and slapped him hard across his suety cheek. His eyes watered as he took a step backward. A low growl emanated from the throats of the other soldiers around us. I took a small step backward, sliding my hand inside my coat and balling my fist as if gripping a weapon. They froze, their anger straining toward me, being held in check only by the threat of the weapon concealed beneath my coat.

"Tomorrow. Six in the morning. Morgan's Point," I said, naming a notorious wooded island south of Philadelphia in the middle of the Delaware River that had been used for settling gentlemen's differences.

"Dueling's been forbidden," someone said from behind him.

"Just like a Northerner to invent an excuse to avoid a fair fight," I said. I looked at Sutton. "But what do you expect? Obviously, they are not gentlemen."

"Pistols, damn you!" the officer in front of me said thickly.

"Your name? I would like to know the name of the man I'm going to kill," I said. A cough bubbled up from my chest. I smothered it with my handkerchief, again smelling the verbena.

"Captain Jack Crawford," he said thickly. "And as for my seconds . . ."

Three soldiers stepped forward. I recognized them from the group in the theatre.

"I reckon we'll do," one of them said coldly to me. The others nodded.

"And I will second my friend," Sutton said. "John Henry Holliday of Georgia."

"And another?" the spokesman for the group asked.

"I only need one to watch my back against Yankee scum," I answered. I turned and walked away, presenting my back to them. I took Belle's arm, leading her away.

"I think I've lost my appetite," she murmured. "Are you really going to fight Captain Crawford?"

"Of course. If he shows up," I answered.

"Oh, he'll show. He can't afford not to since you struck him in front of witnesses," she said. She turned to Emily. "I don't think that I wish to go out tonight. But that's no reason for you two not to have a good time. I'll have Mr. Holliday escort me to my rooms. Besides," she said, turning to me, her eyes suddenly smoky with hot embers glowing deep within them, "you'll be needing your rest."

"I'll see you around four-thirty?" I said to Sutton. He nodded and took Emily's arm, stepping off the curb onto the slick cobblestones to hail a cab. He handed her into the carriage, then glanced at me.

"Watch yourself. I don't trust them," he warned.

"You're learning," I answered. He nodded gravely and stepped into the carriage after Emily. The driver clucked to the horse and pulled away, leaving us standing alone by the theatre.

"My rooms are over on Fourth and Prune," she said.

Together we set off down Arch Street.

"It isn't your fault. He was just trying to impress the doxy with him," she said and laughed. "Unfortunately, he now finds himself in the type of situation he spent the war trying to avoid. I know the type. Office personnel." She glanced at me out of the corners of her eyes.

"Are you worried?"

"Should I be?" I asked.

"Have you done this before? Blazing, I mean."

I shook my head. "No, not quite."

She waited for me to elaborate, but I didn't.

"Brave words," she said, a touch of sarcasm to her words.

I shrugged.

"I've done a little shooting. I'm not new to a pistol. I'll be all right," I said casually.

She laughed. "Well then, if I don't have to worry about you, perhaps you will join me for a bite to eat?"

I stepped to the curb, looking for a cab.

"What are you doing?" she asked.

"We'll need a cab to catch Dick and Emily," I said.

"I don't think we'll need them, do you?"

Lights danced in her eyes as she stepped close to me, leaning up and pressing her lips to mine. Her lips were warm and soft, and their fullness filled me, and I forgot about Mattie in the recklessness of the moment, feeling Belle's breasts move against my chest, and the curve of her hip under my hand. She drew back, looking at me. A tiny pulse hammered in the hollow of her throat. I knew, then, the secret of Belle Boyd, the reason why she had been so successful as a spy for the South during the War: the excitement of the danger spilled over into the excitement of the bed.

"It's not far," she said, her voice low and husky. "There's a cab just at the corner."

"I thought you had to get to know me better," I said.

"Oh, I think I know you fairly well now," she answered.

"Good," I said. I took her hand and we ran down the street, oblivious to all, secure in the dark and with each other.

4

The early morning rose full of gray mist. I had been up for two hours, watching the lead gray emerge from the smoky dark, when I heard Sutton's knock on my door. I turned from my window and walked to the door, opening it. Despite the hour, Sutton had dressed neatly, his hair combed, and neck and cheeks freshly shaved although his eyes glowed a bit bloodshot. He wore a dark suit and derby, and his shoes had been neatly polished. He carried a walnut case tucked under his arm.

He entered my room and crossed to the table I used as a desk as I closed the door behind him. He placed the case on the table and opened it. Light gleamed dully, ominously, from a pair of oiled dueling pistols resting on green velvet in the mahogany box.

"Will these do? My grandfather liberated them from the home of a landowner who preferred English soil to Ireland's," he said, a touch of pride in his words.

I examined them: They were beautifully matched and balanced, a pair of Manton pistols with a cock that did not have to be pulled back as far as others, thanks to a stiffened main spring. The pistols had V-shaped pans and a spur on each trigger guard for the middle finger. I lifted one: the barrels had been fore-weighted and the walnut grips deeply carved in a checkered pattern to keep the hand from slipping in the excitement of the duel.

"They'll do," I said.

He closed the lid and again tucked the box under his arm. I had a bottle of brandy on my desk next to two tumblers. He crossed and poured a half-measure into each, handing one to me. I took it, toasting him. We drank, then turned the glasses upside down together on the desk. He gave me a level look.

"Ready, then? I have a carriage waiting," he said quietly.

I nodded and swung a cloak around my shoulders to keep off the early morning chill since I wore no coat over my loose shirt. I wanted nothing to interfere with movement.

"Ready," I announced. A slight cough bubbled up from my chest.

He opened the door and stood aside in deference to me. Together we descended the stairs. My landlord waited at the foot of the staircase. He pressed my arm, saying, "Good luck, John."

"Thank you, Mr. Demorat," I said.

He tried a smile, but it fell lopsided from his lips. He slipped a ferrotype into my hand. I glanced at it: it was a picture of Belle in her role of Mazeppa except she wore no body covering at all, obviously posing for Demorat's camera and no others. I looked up sharply. He smiled, spreading his hands, the fingertips stained brown.

"The word is all over Philadelphia," he said. "I thought . . . well, maybe . . . For luck?"

"I appreciate your thoughtfulness," I said, slipping the ferrotype inside my shirt. The iron was cold against my skin, and I shivered. A paroxysm of coughing shook me, and I leaned against the wall until it passed.

"Are you all right?" Demorat asked. I nodded weakly. "You should take a toddy for that: whiskey, lemon and honey, and hot water."

"I'll be fine," I said.

He shook my hand and stepped back inside his studio. Sutton opened the outer door and led the way to the carriage. We stepped in, settling ourselves as the driver spoke softly to the horse. Tendrils of mist clammily stroked my face as the horse clip-clopped along, his hooves echoing eerily off the cobblestones. The day seemed sharply detailed beneath its gray covering: shops starkly outlined, lights glowing orange balls from windows as we passed, the smell of fresh bread from the baker's ovens, yet over all was the damp smell of death in the mist, thick and cloying on the senses.

The fog grew even thicker on Water Street near Penn's Landing. I caught a glimpse of the Blue Anchor Inn just north of Dock Street, and then we drew up at the riverfront. A small boat waited for us at the pier. We settled ourselves in the stern as the burly young man took the oars in large, callused hands, and pointed the prow of the boat upstream, pulling powerfully against the current as we swept downstream and around the bend. The current ran swiftly out of the heart of the fog, bearing us down toward the sea, carrying us back to the beginnings of time when the empty river plowed in a great silence through an impenetrable forest. A fish jumped. I flinched against the splash of his body loud in the silence broken only by water lapping against the hull, the creak of the oars in their locks. The smell of primeval mud rose to my nostrils. In the mist, I imagined I saw flatboats drifting by, buckskinned figures standing guard on their decks, horny hands clutching flintlocks, their eyes probing the dark banks where the unbroken forest reached down to the gray water, searching for Indians, I imagined sandhill cranes lifting long necks as the unfamiliar things floated by, standing as still as statues until they disappeared downriver, blue herons feeding along the bars, uttering surprised "booms" as they spread wide wings and stumbled along the shore, cawing crows circling overhead, robins and catbirds and brown wrens, and deer wading knee-deep in the shallow water. Then the shadows disappeared in the mist, and the pungent smell of mud and sewage brought me back to the present as Morgan's Point seemed to drift toward us out of the mist like the hallowed isle of Avalon. Yet today there would be no awakening of any Arthur from its bloodied soil.

The young man swung the boat into a small cove, steadying us by grabbing the bone-white limb of a dead tree lying on its side in the mud offshore. I stepped off the boat onto the island, inhaling deeply. A sulphurous smell like brimstone rose from the muddy shore of the island, and as I stepped ashore, I felt myself moving into a storm of darkness. The island seemed to breathe in deep, rythmic pants. I felt flushed, but no intense heat struck me, baking me, just gray light flickering through the darkness. Then I felt the pulse of the universe beating in the regularity of my own heart. A small trail crept away from me toward the inner part of the island. A strange exhilaration rolled over me. A mourning dove called. The earth seemed unearthly. Sutton appeared at my shoulder, giving me a strange look.

"Why are you smiling?" he asked.

"Am I?" I asked, surprised.

He shook his head and led the way onto the narrow path leading away from the river's edge. We didn't have far to go: the path quickly opened into a grassy clearing surrounded by old elms and cottonwoods, their bark scabby and gray with age. Captain Crawford and his seconds, all wearing dark blue greatcoats, stood in a small group in the center of the clearing. One was slim, deadly looking, a pencil-thin mustache hanging across his upper lip. The other wore burnsides whiskers and a heavy mustache that concealed his upper lip. His shoulders strained his greatcoat. His eyes were cruel and sunken in beneath a bulging brow. A tall, avuncular man dressed in a long coat and top hat stood beside them.

"Good morning, gentlemen," I said, smiling at them. They looked taken aback by my cheerfulness.

"This is Dr. Gideon Morris," Crawford said, introducing the tall man beside him. "He will serve as referee and surgeon unless you have an objection."

"It wouldn't make any difference if I did, would it?" I said dryly. "He's the only one here without, ah, a seemingly vested interest in the outcome, isn't he?"

Dr. Morris flushed and drew himself erect, looking coldly at me.

"My honor, sir, is impeccable. I assure you I will be fair with my judgment toward both concerned partners. I will remain impartial."

Crawford gave him a quick look, frowned, then smiled.

Sutton raised an eyebrow as he turned to question me silently. I shrugged.

"You'd better be," he murmured from beside me.

A deep flush began to creep up Dr. Morris's hollow cheeks.

"If you have any doubts, young man, then your second should have met with those of Captain Crawford's," he sputtered.

"It doesn't matter; the circumstances of the moment preclude another choice," I said calmly. "You'll do."

For a moment I thought he would leave, but his eyes considered me, then he nodded, straightened his shoulders, and considered the two of us.

"Do either of you wish to issue an apology?" Dr. Morris said.

"No," Crawford said firmly.

"Nor do I," I answered.

"Then, gentlemen, please give me your attention." He took a small book from the capacious pocket of his coat and opened it to a well-marked page.

"This will be conducted in accordance to the guidelines placed down by Joseph Wilson in his *Code of Honor* in eighteen fifty-eight."

He bowed his head, reading:

" 'One: The arms used should be smooth-bore pistols, not exceeding nine inches in length, with flint and steel. Percussion pistols may be mutually used if agreed on, but to object on that account is lawful.

" 'Two: Each second informs the other when he is about to load, and invites his presence, but the seconds rarely attend on such invitation as gentlemen may be safely trusted in this matter.

" 'Three: The second, in presenting the pistol to his friend should never put it in his pistol hand, but should place it in the other, which is grasped midway along the barrel, with the muzzle pointing in the contrary way to that which he is to fire, informing him that his pistol is loaded and ready for use.

Before the word is given, the principal grasps the butt firmly in his pistol hand, and brings its muzzle downward to the fighting position.

" 'Four: The fighting position is with the muzzle down and the barrel from you; for although it may be agreed that you may hold your pistol with the muzzle up, it may be objected to, as you can fire sooner from that position, and consequently have a decided advantage, which might not be claimed, and should not be granted.'

"Is this understood?"

We nodded. He closed the book and thrust it back in his pocket.

"Then please see to it."

For some strange reason, I trusted him. He was cranky and arrogant, but his eyes were honest, and I felt drawn to him. His surgeon's bag rested on the ground beside his feet.

A tiny smile of satisfaction played in Crawford's eyes. He glanced swiftly at his seconds. One stepped forward, carrying a lacquered box. He opened it. I glanced at the pistols: Boutet pistols with gilt stars on blue barrels and the butt at right angles to the frame. I knew without picking them up that they had multigrooved rifling. I held up my hands.

"You will, of course, allow the use of my second's weapons since you have had the choice of referee," I said.

I gestured toward the box in Sutton's hands. He dutifully opened the lid, displaying the pistols to Crawford's seconds. The smile slipped from Crawford's lips. Involuntarily, he glanced from the brace of dueling pistols in his second's hands to Sutton's. Indecision flickered across his face. He hesitated.

"I do not believe that Captain Crawford's pistols are smooth-bore and that is reason enough for my objection, is it not so, Dr. Morris?" I said.

"That is correct," he answered. He gave Crawford a stern look. "You have blazed often enough, Captain Crawford, that you should be familiar with the rules."

Crawford glanced swiftly into my eyes. A reckless gaiety filled me. I smiled at him, feeling the corners of my lips pulling into my cheeks. His eyes wavered, then fell. Dr. Morris looked questioningly at him.

"You may, of course, apologize," he said, his voice rasping in the quiet. "And you," he said, turning to me, "may withdraw with full honor if Captain Crawford refuses your presentation since I can tell your pistols are smooth-bore."

I looked at him in surprise. He smiled faintly.

"I said I would be impartial."

I nodded and looked back at Crawford. "Well?"

"All right," he said brusquely. "Let's get it over with." He made a quick motion. One of his seconds stepped forward, hefting each pistol in turn, examining them closely. He replaced them in their box and turned to Crawford.

"There is no discernible difference: a matched pair," he said grudgingly.

"Then we'll proceed," Dr. Morris said. "Are the seconds ready for loading?"

Both nodded, and Dr. Morris held the box while Sutton and his counterpart loaded each pistol, using the silver thimble to carefully measure the black powder, sharply seating each ball, checking the flints for freshness. At last, satisfied, each nodded, and Dr. Morris closed the box and placed it beside his surgeon's bag.

"Gentlemen, prepare yourselves," he announced gravely.

"This is it," Sutton said quietly as I turned and slipped the cloak from my shoulders, handing it to him. He placed the pistol in my left hand and glanced toward Crawford. "You know, I'm beginning to think that you've been set up."

"What makes you think that?" I asked.

"I don't know. Just a feeling I have. He seems too experienced in this sort of thing," Sutton answered. "*We* never thought of a referee or even to have me meet with his seconds. *And* they never asked for a meeting although they knew that was the proper thing to do. Why didn't they?" He shook his head. "I don't know, John, but the more I think about it, the more I feel this is a sucker's play."

"You never did do well in Logic, did you," I said, trying to turn the moment into humor.

"Doesn't take much logic to see that this whole thing doesn't make sense. Why did Crawford make such a to-do over being jostled on the sidewalk? I don't think we can put it down to drunkenness. Oh, I know he smelled like a whiskey bottle, but his eyes, his eyes said otherwise. I think he just washed his mouth out with whiskey to make us *think* he had been drinking."

"Why?"

"Why?" he repeated, frowning.

"Yes, why?" I answered. "What would be his reason? I'm a Southerner, sure, but what else am I? Nothing. Unless he's xenophobic, he has no reason."

"No, what it means is that we don't *know* if he has a reason or not."

"You may have something there," I said, frowning. Murky thoughts moved sluggishly through my mind. I swore. I had been concentrating so much upon the duel and Belle's charms that I had been neglecting the reason behind it. "Listen, I hate to be a bad sport about it all—" Sutton looked at me questioningly—"but if he should get lucky and you find out that this was a setup, kill him."

A tiny smile stretched his lips thin. "Be happy to."

"Gentlemen, please join me," Dr. Morris said, breaking into our conversation. I frowned and moved with Crawford to the center of the clearing. I searched his eyes, looking for an answer to Sutton's question. Crawford stared back mockingly. Warning bells sounded in my mind. The bumpkin of the night before had disappeared.

Slowly, I hefted the pistol, carefully testing its weight, balancing it, the butt fitting smoothly, familiarly, into my hand. Crawford smiled, but the smile didn't touch his eyes, which remained dark and alert, confident.

"Feeling nervous?" he asked mockingly.

And Father's voice suddenly whispered to me: *Notice the ground, John, how it slopes to the oak. A smart man will take his position away from the oak because a man firing uphill holds his sight higher.*

I glanced at the ground sloping slightly uphill behind Crawford.

"You will place your backs together. I will count the paces. When I reach ten, you may turn and fire. If either of you violates the tenets of the *Code of Honor,* it will become my distasteful task to shoot the offender. Is this understood?"

We nodded.

"Then take your places."

I turned and pivoted around Crawford, facing uphill.

"What the hell?" Crawford said.

"Is there a problem?" Dr. Morris asked.

"I prefer this direction," I said calmly.

"Captain Crawford? Do you object?"

"Ah, the hell with it," Crawford said.

I took a half-step backward until I felt Crawford's shoulders touch mine.

"Ready to die, boy?" Crawford whispered.

"Why are you doing this? You had plenty of chances to avoid making it go this far," I said quietly.

I felt his shrug.

"It's my job. No offense, boy, but it's my job," he answered lowly.

"Cock your weapons," Dr. Morris ordered.

I raised my pistol, pulling back the hammer with my thumb. I heard an answering click behind me. I let the pistol dangle at my side.

"Your job? Seems to me a poor thing to make one's occupation and die for," I said softly.

"I object, Dr. Morris," Sutton said. "My friend's opponent carries his pistol at the ready."

I glanced behind me: Crawford's pistol pointed at the sky from shoulder level.

"This is your last warning, Captain Crawford," Dr. Morris said, anger tingeing his words. "Place your pistol in the fighting position now."

Crawford dropped his arm to his side. The back of his neck showed dull red with anger.

"Mr. Holliday? Are you ready?"

"Ready, Dr. Morris," I said.

"Then we shall commence. One."

I stepped away from Crawford, measuring my stride to Dr. Morris's chant.

His job? Was this all it was? The familiar rage began to build within me. What honor is there in killing another as a job? That is the ultimate lowering of the dignity of a man: butchered to make a Roman holiday.

"Ten."

I turned quickly to my right, moving backward a half-step at the same time while sighting down the long barrel. I saw the sudden puff of smoke from the charge of Crawford's pistol and staggered backward, nearly falling as his bullet struck my chest. Bending over, I grabbed at the stabbing pain in my chest. I took my hand away. No blood. I frowned and looked down the glade at Crawford. Smiling confidently, he had begun to walk toward his seconds.

"One moment!" I called.

He froze in midstride, looking with astonishment to where I still stood. Indecision moved across his features.

"I couldn't have missed!" he said.

"You didn't," I answered coldly. "But I believe I still have a shot."

"But . . ."

"Dr. Morris!" I said sharply.

Dr. Morris turned a grim visage to Crawford.

"Resume your place, Captain Crawford," he said.

"But . . . he's hit!" Crawford said, gesticulating with the pistol.

"Your place, sir!" Dr. Morris snapped, raising his pistol. "Or I shall be forced to shoot."

Crawford moved slowly back to his place, staring down at me. I sighted carefully. Tiny beads of perspiration suddenly broke out on his forehead.

"Who hired you, Crawford?" I asked.

A startled look came into his eyes.

"What?"

"You heard me, sir. Who and why?"

A hard, contemptuous sneer crossed his lips.

"You don't have the nerve to shoot," he said, adding arrogantly, "go to hell."

The rage boiled through me. A cough threatened to burst from my lungs. My pulse throbbed in my temples.

"I'll meet you there," I said, touching the trigger, gently squeezing. A puff of black powder momentarily blinded me, then I watched as Crawford's head snapped back. He swayed, stumbled, then fell loose-jointed onto his back, his arms flung out as if crucified by blades of grass to the dark earth.

"No," Sutton said warningly.

I glanced over: Sutton held a small pistol steadily upon Crawford's seconds, their hands thrust deeply into the pockets of their greatcoats. Dr. Morris looked quickly, then brought his own pistol to bear upon them.

"The duel, gentlemen, is not over until all concerned leave the field. The *Code Duello* will be observed at all times. Do I make myself clear?"

They stared furiously at him, remaining silent.

"Good. Then leave. And take Captain Crawford with you."

"You haven't examined him yet," the burly one said gruffly. Dr. Morris stared unblinking at him.

"And I don't have to," he said. "The bullet took him in the forehead. He was dead before he fell."

The two of them stepped forward angrily, lifting Crawford's body between them. The burly one took the trunk, wrapping his arms around the body like a lover, while the other gathered Crawford's legs. They lurched down the path away from us.

"I'll follow them," Sutton said grimly. He fell in behind them, his pistol held in readiness.

Dr. Morris lowered the hammer on his pistol and opened his surgeon's bag, dropping the pistol inside. He removed a flask and two silver cups, handing one to me.

"You must be very careful, young man," he said, pouring brandy into the cups. He quickly drained his and refilled it. His eyes looked dark and mysterious, tiny lights burning deep within their recesses. I tasted the brandy; it was good and its warmth quickly spread throughout my body. I drank appreciatively.

"This is not over yet," he said.

I frowned. "What do you mean?"

"There is no going back from a killing," Dr. Morris said. "Oh, there'll be those friends of his who will hunt you—if he had any friends—but most importantly, there is something that gets displaced inside of you. There."

He touched my chest. I winced and reached into my shirt, removing the ferrotype of Belle. A large dent had been made by Crawford's ball to the right of her hip.

"I had forgotten," he said. "Better let me have a look at your wound."

"I'm all right," I said. "This caught his ball. I showed him the ferrotype. A small smile touched his lips.

"You have been very lucky," he said.

"I think so," I said. I slipped the ferrotype back inside my shirt.

I frowned and glanced at the spot where Crawford's body had fallen. A small pool of blood showed dark against the green grass, blackening it. Dr. Morris caught the direction of my stare and nodded.

"Killing awakens the primitive inside of you, the beast held back by the belief we have that we are civilized beings," he said. He laughed mirthlessly. His teeth were long and yellow. "We waste a lot of time trying to convince ourselves that we are civilized beings together in a world of dreams. But we are not. We live and dream alone. This wasn't your first, though, was it?"

I looked sharply at him. He laughed mirthlessly again. The woods began to come alive again. For a moment I thought I felt their breath upon my neck, stale and stagnant, like the air in a closed sickroom, and I shivered.

"That was Captain Crawford's tragic mistake," he said. "He'd ridden so long with the fourth horseman that he couldn't see the shadow walking with you. I saw it, though. I think," he added slowly, "that he's found a partner, now, who will do him more good."

He threw his head back, looking up into the distance.

"And I looked, and behold a pale horse: and his name that sat on him was Death, and Hell followed with him."

He looked back at me. His face sobered, and strange lights began to reflect from it.

"You're going to be a very lonely man."

He shivered and pulled his coat tighter around him as a gust of wind skidded across the glade, bending the tall grass and rustling the October leaves of the trees. He again drained the brandy against the cold. A luminescence glowed from his eyes.

"Nobody will even remember this in a few months," I said.

"Maybe. But I doubt it. People always remember killings. They just forget what caused them. When the cause disappears, the murderer gets his name. What did he have against you?"

"He hated Southerners, I guess," I answered.

"Crawford? Politics and logistics meant little to him."

"Did you know him?" I asked curiously.

"Not like you mean. But I knew him. This was the third time I have acted as a referee for him. I suspect he had others. He was a professional, you know."

"Professional?"

"Oh, yes. In certain gentlemanly circles there is a need for people like him—one who redresses the wrongs for those whose honor has been damaged by another."

"What honor is that?"

"None," he admitted. "But those who could afford Crawford's fee define honor on their own terms. Honor becomes a mere excuse to eliminate those who have become a nuisance to them.

"You," he continued, pouring another drink for both of us,

"have apparently become a nuisance to someone powerful enough to arrange your death."

"Me?" I said. "I'm just a dental student at the college."

"You're much more than that to someone. Watch yourself," he added warningly as Sutton hurried up to us.

"They're gone," he said. "Is that brandy?"

I handed the cup to him. He took it and drained it with a flourish, smacking his lips.

"Well, 'tisn't from the old country, but 'twill do nicely, it will. Oh, yes."

A sharp, rasping cough prevented my reply. Dr. Morris gave me a quick look.

"How long have you had that?" he asked.

"Not long," I said. "A damn cold brought on by this filthy weather you all have here in the North. It'll be the death of me yet."

"Maybe," Dr. Morris said, looking significantly at the ground where Crawford had fallen.

"Did I miss something?" Sutton asked, his heavy brow furrowing.

"Only my treatise on the uselessness of man," Dr. Morris said acidly, dropping the cups into his surgeon's bag and closing it with a flourish. "I believe I'll have to share your boat, gentlemen."

He gripped the bag in his long, thin fingers and made his way down the path toward the shore.

"D'you think he's a rummie?" Sutton asked in a low voice.

"No, a philosopher," I said.

"Huh?" Sutton frowned.

"In vino veritas," I said.

"I hate it when you do that," Sutton complained, falling into step beside me. "I feel like a fool."

"The world is full of fools, my friend. The trick is knowing the fools from the foolish."

"There you go again," he muttered. "Next time, be your own damned second and get your fool head blown off."

5

❦

I stepped over a pile of green horse apples lying in Fourth Street outside Belle's door. A pungent smell filled the air. A carriage crossed the corner going down Prune Street, a black-and-white mongrel snapping at the heels of the horse. The mongrel paused to urinate against the rusting wrought-iron fence, watching me warily. It finished and trotted back down the street, pausing to sniff inquisitively at invisible markings on the locust trees made by other dogs trying to carve out territorial boundaries.

I stepped up to Belle's door, lifted the heavy knocker in the shape of a lion's head, and let it fall. I stepped back from the door, waiting. The sky was still leaden, although the morning mist had melted away with the day, leaving the damp behind. Sutton had gone back to his rooms to sleep, but the sweet arms of Morpheus were not what I felt the need for, and I had walked up from Water Street in Southwark after our boat brought us back from Morgan's Point, declining Dr. Morris's offer to join him for breakfast. It had been a long walk, but I felt the need for it, to be among people bustling along the stone streets, smelling the smells coming from Swedish ovens in the brick and stone buildings on Queen Street and the sour mud of Swanson Street, past Sparks's Shot Tower and Old Swede's Church.

Someone moved in the alley across the street. I caught a glimpse of a familiar face, then the door opened behind me, and I turned, smiling.

A strange man stood before me, holding the stem of a champagne glass between thumb and forefinger. A bow tie had been knotted around his celluloid collar. He wore a

short-tailed coat, brown-and-gold-checked, with matching
trousers ending before dully polished shoes covered with
white gaiters. His face was long and thin, spotted with pock-
marks. Deep pouches hung below bright black eyes. Light
refracted from his oily hair combed straight back from his
forehead. A faint hint of limewater came to me.

"Yes?" he asked.

"I was looking for Belle Boyd," I answered hesitantly.

"Your card?"

A flash of annoyance swept over me. The expectations I
had built in my long walk up from the docks began to dissi-
pate along with the mist.

"I do not have a card," I mumbled, thrusting my hands into
my pockets.

A grin flashed across his face, animating it.

"Neither do I," he said, throwing the door open. "You
must be Belle's student. Come on in. I'm Eddie Foy. Afraid
we started without you, but we weren't sure if it was to be a
party or a wake and so we decided to get a little prepared for
either. But it made less sense to sit around waiting so . . . we
began."

"John Henry Holliday. We?" I asked, shaking his hand.

"A small gathering of Belle's friends," he explained, closing the door behind us. He opened the door into Belle's living room. The room fell quiet at our appearance.

A small combination curio cabinet and secretariat stood
against the wall on my left. Tiny tables scattered around the
room held a variety of cut-crystal lamps with fringed shades,
more for decoration than for use as light, as the walls had
been fitted with gas lamps. A phonograph with a big daisy
horn stood in one corner on a marble-top table. Bottles
winked from a table set at the back of the room between the
fireplace and a small, upright piano tucked in an alcove. A
small group stood gathered around it, the men dressed in
dark suits, the ladies in a variety of colors and matching hats
with tiny feathers curling down around their left cheeks in
the latest style.

Belle reclined gracefully on a bottle green couch, strategically placed for dramatic effect and command of the room at the opposite side of the fireplace. She wore a long gray dress and tight bodice that needed no padding. A bolero edged in black hung open. Her short hair had been artfully combed and teased to approximate the full swept-back look of the current fashion. Across from Belle's couch stood a heavy, Sleepy Hollow armchair covered in the same bottle-green fabric that matched the heavy green velvet drapes pulled back and tied away from the window. A slim man with long dark hair combed back away from a high brow and falling in waves down his neck sat in the chair. Slim white hands rested upon the arms of the chair. His somber suit had been freshly pressed; his pearl-gray cravat gleamed with a sateen sheen from beneath a soft white collar with long points that lay down across his chest.

He appeared in command of the room as others moved respectfully in orbit around him. A neatly dressed woman with fine, porcelain features sat beside him, balancing a teacup and saucer on her knee. Belle noticed me and called across the room.

"John! Thank God you're alive!"

The man in the chair winced at the stentorian authority of her voice. She dramatically extended a limp hand in my direction, and I crossed, taking it in mine. I bent to kiss her, but she gracefully presented her cheek instead.

"It is over, then?" she said.

"He . . . missed. I did not. I was lucky," I said. I touched the ferrotype under my shirt.

"Luck may have had something to do with it, but luck is worthless without skill," the man in the chair said. I turned to look at him. Belle rose slightly, introducing us.

"John, I would like you to meet Miss Kitty Molony."

I took Miss Molony's hand in mine and kissed her fingers. She boldly appraised me.

"Quite charming, my dear. You were right," she said to Belle.

"Mind yourself, now, Kitty. I believe Belle has the first rights of refusal," the man said, rising from his chair to clasp my hand.

"This is Edwin Booth," Belle said languidly. A tiny, satisfied smile touched her lips as my face registered my surprise and pleasure. Although I had never seen Booth act, his reputation for portraying Hamlet had made him world famous. After his cousin, John Wilkes Booth, had slain that horse's ass Abraham Lincoln, Booth's composure onstage when the audience had pelted him with rotten vegetables had earned him the admiration of the country. And mine, I confess. I took his hand, shaking it warmly, with more enthusiasm than a gentleman should.

"Mr. Booth! I have been a long admirer of yours," I said. He smiled faintly.

"Indeed? As long as that? Well, then, we shall have to take advantage of that, won't we? I'm here to do three nights of *Hamlet* at the Walnut Street Theatre. I hope you will be my guest?" he said.

"I will come all three nights," I said, adding, "providing that I can obtain tickets." I turned beet red as I realized how beggary I must have sounded. He laughed in appreciation and clapped me familiarly upon my shoulder.

"Then all three nights are yours, my friend," he said magnanimously. "I have a box reserved in my name—that's part of my contract, standard with all houses—and your name shall be placed upon it for the entire run."

"Very good, Edwin. I'm quite confident that Mr. Holliday will be able to provide you with the reviews you so richly deserve," Miss Molony said, sipping daintily from her teacup.

Booth's face darkened for a moment, then cleared as he forced a laugh. "My reviews, my dear, will be impeccable, as usual. I am, after all, Edwin Booth. Yours, on the other hand, may be a bit, shall we say, tenuous unless you can manage Ophelia in a less stilted manner than you did in Boston."

Her teacup rattled upon her saucer as she angrily replaced it, then forced a smile as she dabbed daintily at her lips with a serviette. Her face reddened, and Booth turned back to me, a satisfied half-smile playing across his lips.

"You deserve it, my boy," he said. "Egad, I'm not sure that I would have had the fortitude to stand and let a man have a shot at me."

"I wonder," Belle murmured from her place on the couch. I smiled at her, then graciously turned back to Booth.

"If the papers are to be believed, sir . . ."

"Always a big 'if,' indeed," he murmured.

". . . then I have no doubt that you would have acquitted yourself honorably. I read about your behavior in front of your audience after the, ah, antics of your cousin," I finished.

He gave me a level look, his eyebrows raised in surprise.

"Well, a man with tact as well," he said lowly.

"No tact, sir," I protested mildly. "Honesty."

The room broke into applause, and I turned, looking askance at the rest of those in the room, whom I had forgotten. I blushed. Belle laughed, rising.

"Never mind, my dear," she said, affectionately hugging me. "You *have* behaved honorably. In *both* matters," she added, looking significantly at Miss Molony, who blushed and busied herself with using her serviette to mop up the traces of her tea that had spilled into her saucer.

"I just wish I could share that box with you, but"—she said, turning to Booth—"I have my own production those nights. Sorry, Edwin."

He bowed his head, sweeping his hand from his brow to his waist in a dramatic movement. His eyes sparkled.

"Of course, my dear," he said. He nodded at me. "I'm afraid this young man has a problem, doesn't he? Whether to attend your performance or my opening? A very perplexing situation, young man," he said.

They both looked expectantly at me. For a moment I was confused, then I grinned. They both were waiting for their cue lines, with me as the alternate player in the dramatic entr'acte they had created impromptu. I knew without looking around that the rest of the room was quietly watching, determining my worth of belonging in their select circle. I

felt elated, but I knew that I had to tread cautiously in giving
my evaluation. Should I be magnanimous and refuse Booth's
offer in favor of Belle, or should I refuse Belle and go with
the acknowledged senior member of the troupe?

"Oh," I said, "there is no problem there." I looked at Belle.
"I'm afraid I must attend Mr. Booth's performance, my dear.
I have seen yours, and impeccable though it was, I have
never seen Mr. Booth perform and believe I owe him that
courtesy."

Belle's eyes narrowed to glints, then Foy applauded loudly,
approaching us.

"Well said, sir," he said. "Well said. A most noble gesture
indeed. You have, sir, been born to the purple."

"Oh, shut up, Eddie," Belle said testily.

His eyebrows raised as he glanced back and forth
between us.

"Do I detect a lovers' squabble? Why, Belle . . ."

"Please get me a glass of champagne, Eddie," Belle said,
thrusting a glass at him. He looked startled, then a sheepish
look centered over his face and he took the proffered glass,
turning to the sideboard away from us.

"Of course, Belle, of course," he mumbled.

Booth caught my eye, tiny lines appearing at the corners of
his eyes as his lips turned up. He smiled a cat's smile at
Belle, teasing her with unspoken words. Her lips were tight,
straight lines. A spot of color showed high on each cheekbone below her wide and angry eyes.

"I would have thought that we had become a bit more than
. . . friends," she finished tightly.

I became conscious of the room's quiet, of others watching the exchange between us with relish, and a recklessness
came over me, sweeping caution away. I smiled into her
angry eyes.

"I think we have," I said softly, cajoling her. Her nostrils
widened perceptively as a slight titter ran around the room.
Her eyes narrowed warningly. I laughed and impulsively
reached out, pulling her close. She gasped indignantly and
tried to push away. Booth laughed.

"I believe a bit of discretion is called for," he said soberly. "Therefore, in the name of Aphrodite, I release you from your obligation, sir."

"Oh, go see him!" Belle said sharply. She forced a laugh, then stood on her tiptoes and brushed her lips against mine. "It would be only right. As you have attended my play, it would be only fair for you to see the opposition's (she emphasized the word) to make a fair judgment of the better. We"—she indicated the room with a dramatic gesture—"will be awaiting your review."

The others applauded, and I released her, stepping back. She had managed a minor victory, but in doing so she had opened herself to ridicule, trusting our relationship to give her the victory. But I knew without even attending Booth's performance who was the better actor, which was the better production. The Walnut Street Theatre was the oldest theatre in America and the most prestigious. One acquired a certain accomplissement if one played there, since one would be recognized as among the best in the acting profession. Belle was at best a mediocre actress, her popularity hinging upon her scanty costumes and magnificent figure, statuesque, sensual and erotic rather than artistic. But as far as a comparison with Booth, far better for me to compare the moon with the sun even though I had never seen Booth perform. Although she was beautiful, Belle's charm came from the goddess of love rather than from Melpomene.

"Of course," I said smoothly. "I am known far and wide as a truth-teller."

Her eyes widened slightly at my words, then fell, guarded, as the skin over her high cheekbones tightened. She forced a laugh, but I heard the danger in the laughter, the recklessness that had made her the most celebrated spy for the Confederacy. She waved her hand to include the room. Foy took the opportunity to step forward and press the glass of champagne into it. She lifted it high, toasting me.

"Then we shall meet here a week from now to hear the review of our notable critic: John Henry Holliday, Student."

My face reddened. With a one short word, she had reduced

my status in front of her guests. Booth's eyes narrowed as he contemplated Belle. Miss Molony arched her head back to look down her nose at me.

"Really, Belle," Booth began, but was interrupted by one of her other guests who leaped into the awkward silence that had fallen across the room.

"Give us a song, Eddie!" a man by the window exclaimed. The others quickly took up the cry. Foy grinned lopsidedly and shook his head.

"I need a piano player," he said. "Who will play?"

The others looked at each other, shaking their heads. I waited a minute, then stepped to the piano, pulled the stool out, and sat. Booth's eyebrows arched high over his eyes at my movement.

"You play?" Belle asked in disbelief. I grinned at the astonished look upon her face.

"A bit," I said modestly.

"How about 'The Old Man's Drunk Again'?" Foy asked. He hummed a few bars, waggling his eyebrows expectantly. I smothered a laugh and chorded through the melody.

"Key of G?" he asked hopefully, and I moved up into flats in mid-chord. He grinned, rocked on his heels, tucked his thumbs into his vest pockets, and began a strut up and down the middle of the room as the others hastily slipped back against the wall.

"Where's the old man. . . ."

I followed him through the song, playing an impromptu solo when he slipped into a soft-shoe, rolling the chords up into a flash finish. The others broke into applause, and I waited for Foy to quit his exaggerated bows, then I swung into Stephen Foster's "Beautiful Dreamer," segued into "Old Dog Trey," and ended with "Swanee River," with Foy again working through a soft-shoe in the middle of the song. He finished with a sweeping bow that allowed him to collect a glass of champagne smoothly from the table next to his elbow.

"Very good," Belle said, her eyes shining.

"A true Renaissance man," Booth said softly, his eyes twinkling my way. Miss Molony sniffed, daintily dabbing at her lips with her napkin.

"But these are common songs, of course," she said. "He is the type any visitor to melodrama would know."

The smile slipped from Foy's face as he stiffened. Carefully, he placed the glass of champagne back on the table. His eyes stared coldly at Miss Molony.

"Is there something wrong with melodrama?" he asked.

She gestured airily with her free hand. "Absolutely nothing," she said. "But it's not the legitimate theatre."

"But it pays a few bills," Booth said smoothly. "We, ourselves, have done melodrama in the past when the situation has merited."

She gave him a dirty look. "Perhaps, but still, melodrama is not"—she searched for the words—"c'est dommage."

Foy's brow furrowed, lowering upon his eyes like a thundercloud. I rose from the piano stool, reaching for Foy's champagne glass.

"Nous regrettons, si ça ne vous dérange pas," I said.

She frowned uncertainly.

"Oh," she said, waving her hand again, "that is the way it must be, I suppose."

Someone tittered at her faux pas, and she frowned, trying to recognize the joke, which was quickly whispered around the room. A smile tugged at Booth's lips as he recognized my ploy, and I made a mental note not to play French games with him. He gently shook his head and crossed to the drinks table, pouring a large brandy. I gave an elaborate bow and returned to the piano bench, my fingers gently caressing the keys, finding Chopin's "Opus No. 1 in B-Flat Minor" and sliding into it. Slowly, Mother's presence moved gently into the room, her fingers cold upon the nape of my neck.

And her words came on gentle breaths of air: *wrists up, Johnny. That's better. No, the left hand must be softer here. Watch your tempo. Now, with feeling, with feeling, Johnny, move your soul into the music.*

I felt myself become a part of the music, felt the sadness deep within myself as the nocturne rolled up from deep inside of me, moving smoothly up my chest and down my arms, my fingers becoming one with the keys. And then I was finished, my hands relaxing slowly from the keys into my lap. The room remained silent for a long moment, then I felt Booth's hand upon my shoulder.

"A fine accounting," he said quietly. "Don't you think, Kitty? Belle?"

His words had a touch of irony to them, and I knew he had made them for my benefit and Foy's. For that, I was grateful. I started to thank him, but a coughing spell bent me over the keyboard. Something seemed to be trying to tear itself loose in my chest. A glass was thrust into my hand.

"Here. Drink this," Foy commanded. His concerned eyes stared deeply into mine. I nodded my thanks. I took a deep drink, then choked as the whiskey burned the back of my throat. Then the whiskey warmth flooded through me, working its way up my chest, easing the cough. I drew a deep breath and took another cautious sip.

"Thank you," I said lowly. Perspiration broke out upon my forehead, and I became cold and clammy. I took my handkerchief from an inside pocket of my coat and wiped my brow.

"Well," Miss Molony said, "it appears that our *southern* Apollo has feet of clay."

"Shut up, Kitty, or I shall arrange for you to dress with the supernumeraries," Booth said. She flushed and indignantly puffed up like a turkey waving his wattles in front of a mate. He ignored her and turned solicitously to me. "Is there anything we can do?" Foy gave him a puzzled look. I shook my head.

"No, I don't think so," I said. "Really, I need . . ."

A spasm shook my frame. I doubled over, hacking dryly into my handkerchief, which I'd taken from an inside pocket.

"Eddie," he said, but I waved him off.

"Really, I need to go home," I said. "I have been up a long time and, well, frankly, although this is a most pleasurable gathering, I am quite fatigued. The river fog did not agree with me." I coughed again to give emphasis to my words, the cough was not engineered out of politeness but rather an upheaving of my lungs that bent me double.

"Are you sure?" Booth asked quietly, leaning close so that we might not be overheard by others.

"No," I said softly. "I'm not. But, please, sir, let me retire with dignity." A paroxysm of coughing doubled me over. I thought for a moment that the blood vessels in my face would burst.

"Very well," he said softly. "Should I call a cab?"

I shook my head. "No, sir. Please. I shall manage."

"Very well," he said hesitantly. "But I want to hear from you. Do you understand?"

I looked up at him, still coughing, trying to smile. He read my thoughts.

"Not as a parent. A friend," he amended.

I nodded.

"Then, Eddie, would you . . ." He left the remainder unsaid, but Eddie knew his intent and nodded slightly so the others in the room wouldn't see his concern.

"Of course, Edwin. I would be most happy," he said.

"Very well," Edwin said softly, then raised his voice. "Then I will expect to see you after my performance. Backstage. I'm looking forward to it, John."

He thrust his hand forward, stepping between us and the others in the party so they wouldn't see the weakness of my handshake. I drew a deep, shaky breath, holding it as long as I could, then let it out. I felt steadier.

"Excuse me," I said. "I think I'd better go."

"Please, not upon our account," Booth said smoothly, casting a hard look at Miss Molony to convey the fault was hers. I almost smiled at his theatrical gesture.

"No, no," I said. "I'm just a bit . . . tired. That's all."

"Are you all right?" Foy asked, his face a mask of concern.

I nodded and managed a smile. "Perhaps I'll see you later."

"I'm at Fox's New American Theatre over at Chestnut and

Tenth," he said. "I would be very pleased if you would care to take in my show. It's not legitimate theatre,"—he gave a sharp look at Miss Molony, who had the grace to turn faintly red—"but I think we can entertain you. And," his voice dropped conspiratorially, "since I have the same arrangement as Edwin, I can do no less than offer you the same courtesy. Except," he added triumphantly with a sly glance at Booth, "*I* am performing more than *three* days."

Booth laughed and clapped him on the shoulder. "Well done, Eddie! That's putting us in our places."

"It's what I can do, Edwin," Eddie purred. "You must remember that we are, at the best, melodrama." This last was delivered with a poisonous glance at Miss Molony.

"Thank you," I said. My breath seemed to be stabilizing. I inhaled deeply and let it out slowly.

"I'll do that," I promised. I shook his damp hand and turned to Booth.

"Thank you for your invitation, sir," I said politely. "I'll be happy to attend your show."

"The tickets will be waiting at the box office in your name," he said, offering his hand. It was dry and firm, in contrast to Foy's. Yet I felt more of a kinship with Foy, despite my essay into Chopin. I thanked him and turned to Belle. She rose and tucked her arm into mine, escorting me to the door.

"Will you come around after the show?" she asked as we stepped into the entry. "Whichever you decide to attend?"

"Do you want me to?" I asked, opening the door. She glanced around; we were alone.

"Yes, I do. Very much," she whispered. She rose on tiptoes and kissed me, pressing herself against me. The fire from the night before surged through me and I returned her kiss, holding her hard. She broke away, smiling breathlessly.

"I'll be waiting for you," she said.

The door closed behind me. I stood for a moment, staring at the ornate knocker, then turned and stepped down the steps to the street. I glanced up as I opened the gate and saw a familiar face in the alley across the street. I hesitated. The figure turned and ducked back into the alley.

I started across, then jumped back as a horse and carriage nearly ran me down.

"Watch yer step!" the driver cursed as he pulled the horse sharply around away from me.

I hurried across the street and ran into the alley. A man wearing a bowler and a checked suit disappeared at the alley's end where it opened onto Spruce Street. I stood for a moment, perplexed, wondering where I had seen the man before and why he was watching Belle's home.

6

The dog star was in the nether lip of the crescent moon when I escorted Belle home from the theatre. The wet streets smelled dank, an odor of rotting garbage hanging in the air. Belle spoke little on the way to her rooms, and I knew that she was angry that I had not passed up Booth's *Hamlet* for a continued presence in a box at her play. By the time we reached her street, her silence had angered me and dulled the exuberance I had felt after watching Booth's Hamlet. Exhilarated by Booth's performance, I had dawdled outside his door to visit with him and spent several minutes I couldn't spare congratulating him on his performance. It had been ... magnificent. Words could not do it justice. I felt my soul fly out from my body and merge with his when he delivered the famous soliloquy by simply coming downstage and fixing the audience with his dark, enigmatic eyes and slowly addressing us, *To be ... or not ... to be. That is the question.* ... His words soared through the stilled theatre, carrying us with him through the torments of Hamlet's soul. When he finished and turned to rejoin the play, the audience was moved to thunderous applause, acknowledging his interpretation, his *becoming* Hamlet, until he was forced to turn and accept their adulations, stepping from character to become the player.

But the time spent with Booth had made me late for Belle, and she had long closed her performance, stripped away her makeup, and donned her street clothes before I arrived. The temperament of an actor, I learned, cannot be described in terms of logic; everything out of the actor's sense of order becomes a slight.

We walked and the last few blocks in silence. As I opened the iron gate leading up to her steps, I reached over and pulled her to me, bending to kiss her lips. She pressed her hands against my chest, pushing me away. I laughed.

"Don't. The neighbors . . ." she protested. I released her and stepped back.

"Do you think the neighbors don't know what we are doing when they see me leaving your rooms after the 'respectable' hour?" I asked.

"At least it's not overt," she snapped. "Really, John, you act like an impulsive schoolboy instead—" She paused, and I became a bit angrier.

"Instead of what? One of your polished panderers preening around your heels like lap dogs? Sorry. I thought you preferred honesty to that."

I turned away to leave and caught a flicker of shadow merging with deeper shadows in the alley across the street. Suddenly my anger directed itself away from Belle to the person skulking in the shadows across the street. The evening had been too much for me.

"John," she began, her voice softening.

I turned back and pressed my fingers against her lips, hushing her. I leaned closer, murmuring into her shell-like ear, "There is a man across the street. Follow my lead."

I took her arm and escorted her to the door. Emily had been waiting for us with Sutton and opened the door at the first drop of the knocker.

" 'Bout time," she grumbled. "We've been waitin' on you for over an hour now. As you can see."

I glanced into the living room: the table had been set for a late-night supper, a bottle of champagne cooling in a bucket of ice, dishes covered on the table.

"Really, John," Sutton rejoined, "this is most unkind of you. Why, Emily and I have our own plans for this evening."

"Wait here," I commanded, ignoring them. Sutton's eyes narrowed for a moment, and I hastened to explain. "There's a man watching the house from across the street in the alley. I saw him there before."

"What are you going to do?" Sutton asked.

"Find out what he's after," I said. "You stay here with the ladies. I'll go out the back way and pick him up."

"Sure you don't want me to go with you?" he asked. His hands opened and closed at his sides. I could feel the anxiousness for action flowing from him.

"No, one of us had better stay here," I said. "I think I can manage."

I slipped out the back entrance and paused in the yard to let my eyes adjust themselves to the darkness. When I could see the privy at the end of the yard, I moved cautiously past it, pulling myself up and over the six-foot board fence into the alley on the other side. I paused for a moment as a cough rumbled from my chest, then I trotted down the alley, feeling the air heavy within my lungs, willing myself not to cough. I emerged onto Prune Street. I moved quickly over to Fourth Street and crossed over opposite the side on which Belle lived. I moved down the street to the alley, then flattened myself against the side of the building next to the alley. I took a quick look up and down the street: the hour was late enough that I was alone except for a mongrel nosing ash cans down the street away from us.

I took a deep breath, then carefully slid around the corner of the alley. I spotted him immediately behind a stack of crates he had erected at the mouth of the alley to hide his movements. He wore a green-and-brown-plaid suit with a hard bowler, and I knew he was the same person I had seen in the alley earlier. I took another step and the toe of my boot struck a can, sending it skittering down the brick alley.

He started and turned to flee. I slipped my hand inside my

jacket and drew the Navy Colt I had taken to wearing since my duel with Crawford. He froze as I thumbed back the hammer to full-cock.

"Turn and face the wall," I said. "Raise your arms and lock your fingers over your head."

Slowly, he turned and followed my instructions. I stepped forward and jammed the barrel of the Navy Colt hard into his back. He gasped, and his hands started to come down to grab the pain, but I jabbed him again, and he remembered, his hands sweeping back up and over his head. Carefully, I ran my hands over his body. I found his pistol, a Deringer .41, in a sidepocket of his coat and removed it, placing it in mine. I stepped back.

"All right," I said. "Drop your hands and place them in your pockets. We're going across the street. Act natural," I warned. "You try to run, I'll shoot. I'll shoot low enough that you spend the rest of your life in a chair. Do you understand?" He nodded. I jabbed him with the pistol.

"Let's hear it."

"I understand," he said. His voice was sharp and nasal, rasping on the ear.

"Good," I said. "Let's go."

He dropped his hands and shoved them in his pockets. I held the pistol under my jacket as we moved out of the alley and sauntered across the street like old friends. I opened the gate with my left hand, and he hesitated, his dark eyes darting up and down the street, searching for an escape. I brought my hand out from under my jacket. He glanced down at the pistol, then shrugged and mounted the steps to Belle's door. It opened as soon as he reached the top. Sutton threw out a big hand, seizing him by the collar and dragging him inside. I moved quickly up the stairs and into the hallway.

"Well, well," Sutton said. "And what do we have here?"

"A prowler," I said. "Perhaps one might even label him a Peeping Tom. That'd look right fine in the *Echo,* don't you think?"

"I'm no paddy," he said indignantly.

"Paddy? Anti-Irish, are yuh?" Sutton cuffed him across the head.

He staggered. His bowler fell off, and he winced and clamped his hand hard against his ear, trying to still the ringing inside it. He hunched his shoulder, swinging wildly at Sutton. Sutton grinned contemptuously, grabbed his hand and spun him into the plush chair beside the fireplace. He started to rise, but by then I had the Navy Colt leveled between his eyes. Slowly, he relaxed against the back of the chair, watching warily.

"All right," I said softly. "Suppose you begin by telling us who you are and what you are doing watching Miss Boyd's house?"

He remained silent, his face freezing into an impenetrable mask. He shook his head defiantly. I sighed.

"This is not a way to endear us to you," I said. He shrugged.

"Your name?" I asked again.

"His name is Allan Pinkerton," Belle said from behind me. "He's a detective. Or at least that's what he claims to be."

I turned to face her. She stared coolly and levelly at the man in the chair, her lips slightly turned up in scorn, her hands on her hips, shoulders thrown back. A slight flush colored her cheeks.

"A detective?" I frowned.

His eyebrow quirked. "You remembered, Belle. I'm touched."

"How could I forget?" she said dryly. "You almost succeeded in having me hanged."

"It wasn't for lack of trying," he said. His words were serious, no laughter behind them, and I knew that he did not mean them in a joking manner.

"Would someone please explain?" Sutton asked, frowning and looking from Pinkerton to Belle.

"He was Lincoln's bodyguard during the War," Belle explained. "He also coordinated intelligence gathering of sorts. Not very successfully, though. A lot of things you should have intercepted got through, Allan. *And* you really didn't do a very good job guarding Lincoln, did you?"

A burned-red flush rose under his scraggly beard. His shoulders tensed, and I waved the Navy Colt to draw his

attention to it. He sank back against the cushion of the Sleepy
Hollow chair, his face sullen and drawn.

"He was under the army's supervision by then," he said
sharply. "I had been relieved of his responsibility by then."

"And who taught the army?" Belle said sarcastically.

"What are you doing here?" I asked.

He ignored me. I repeated the question. His eyes flickered
toward mine, then back to Belle's. Anger began to simmer
deep inside, working its way through my body. I motioned
again with the Colt, and his lips rose in a sneer.

"You won't shoot. How would you explain the shooting in
her home?" he said mockingly.

He placed his hands on the arms of the chair and made to
rise. I stepped forward, ramming the barrel of my pistol
against his mouth, cutting his lips and breaking teeth. Blood
spurted from his mouth. He raised his hands to push the pistol away, but I ground the barrel against his mouth, pushing it
in. He gagged, and I backed the barrel out of his mouth a
scant inch.

"John!" Belle said sharply.

"What the hell?" Sutton said. I ignored him.

"Don't think for a minute that I won't shoot," I said softly.
"I'll splatter your brains all over this chair. We'll move your
body down to Water Street and leave it in an alley there for
the rats to eat on until someone finds it. You should be pretty
ripe by then and pretty well gnawed. We won't have to
explain a damn thing about a shooting in here because there
won't be anything to see. No body, no blood, nothing. Now,
let's try one more time," I said softly. "What were you doing
watching Miss Boyd's house?"

His throat worked convulsively as he swallowed against
the steel of the pistol barrel. Blood dripped from his split lip
upon the wilted cotton collar of his shirt. I smelled his fear
beneath the stale cigar smoke clinging to his shoulders like
an invisible mantle. I pushed the pistol barrel deeper into his
mouth. He gagged. I stepped back as his gorge splashed into
his lap, then stepped back through the sour smell of vomit

and rammed the pistol again into his mouth, gouging his soft palate with the pistol sight.

"Dickie and I will drop your body behind a trash heap in an alley off Water Street, where the wharf rats are the largest. How much of you do you think someone will find before the wharf rats get all of you? They like the tongue the best, I'm told. The eyes are also quick to go and the soft parts, the cheeks, the throat, the . . ."

I left the rest unsaid but ripped the pistol from his mouth and rammed it against his groin for emphasis. A small trickle of blood emerged from the corner of his mouth. His eyes watered, tears streaming down into his mustache and beard.

"John, don't!" Belle said sharply.

"You see, even they don't want me to do this. But there is nothing they can do to stop me." I grinned into his eyes. They wavered, and I knew I had him. I slowly rocked the hammer back on the pistol.

"All right," he said lowly. I lowered the pistol to half-cock but kept it pressed against his groin. He swallowed and tried to wipe his lips, but I pressed harder with the pistol when his hands came up off the arms of the chair, and he hastily dropped them back in their place.

"May I have a glass of water?" he asked.

"No," I said.

He nodded, hate staring blackly from his eyes into mine. I gave him a smile that I didn't feel. His eyes widened, and deep inside them, I could see fear lurking, the fear that rises from humiliation.

"All right. I believe that Miss Boyd was involved in the conspiracy to assassinate President Lincoln."

"What?"

Stunned, I lifted the pistol and stepped back away from him. He took the moment to take a handkerchief from his pocket and dab at his lips. He grimaced at the sight of his blood on the handkerchief and glared at me. I automatically lifted the barrel a fraction higher.

"You are insane," I said.

"This is ridiculous!" Emily spouted. "Miss Belle ain't been nowhere near that Booth who killed the President. Why, she wasn't even in the country at the time! She was in England."

"Was she?" His eyes glowed with a hypnotic force as he leaned fractionally forward, staring penetratingly at Belle. I could see why he would be effective in his role as a detective. He would have been extremely intimidating if I hadn't had my pistol bearing upon him.

"I think you were," he said. "I think you had returned to the United States two weeks before. But that I can't prove. I *can* prove, however, that you were in Richmond when John Wilkes Booth, an actor (although not of the stature of his cousin Edwin, I admit) was playing Mercutio in *Romeo and Juliet* in the Bow Street Theatre. I have a record of reservations you made there that night. I also know that you attended two of his performances in Washington while under guard, pending the completion of my investigation of you. Those performances were again *Romeo and Juliet* with Booth playing Romeo this time, and Fainall in *The Way of the World*. You attended a post-play party with your guard as escort after *The Way of the World* in honor of Mrs. Fitzgerald, who was playing opposite Booth.

"Additionally," he continued, warming to his recitation, "you are continually seen in the company of actors and actresses."

"Bankers associate with bankers, doctors with doctors, and lawyers with lawyers," Belle answered heatedly. "I am an actress; I associate with theatre people." She shrugged.

"You also have a preference for southern men," he said, pointedly looking at me.

"This is not very logical," I said quietly. "Miss Boyd is from the South. Given the hospitality of the North these days, I shouldn't wonder she would prefer manners and gentility to rudeness and arrogance. I might add that by your analogy, you would have Edwin Booth associated with his cousin as well."

His grin was all teeth and did not touch his eyes. I doubt if any humor ever touched those eyes; they were cold and dead, coming alive only when he scented bloody prey.

"They did," he said softly, "play a charity theatre engagement prior to the war in Kimball's Opera House in Atlanta. I have every reason to suspect that they maintained their association during the War as well."

Belle laughed. "You are a fool, Pinkerton," she said scornfully. "Edwin was playing a long-running engagement in London during most of the War, and touring the rest of Europe during the rest of it."

"Not entirely," he corrected. "He was in New York in the last year of the War, as was his cousin John Wilkes Booth. I have a copy of the hotel book where John Wilkes stayed, four blocks from the rooms taken by his cousin."

"You're quite a daisy, aren't you? All this is pure speculation," I said. I stepped closer to him. I pointed the pistol a bare few inches from his eyes.

"Now, I'm warning you: The past is over; done with. The War has been fought and lost and won. Lincoln is dead. Now you will stop bothering Miss Boyd or I will go to the *Echo* with this. I wonder how that would look for your detecting business, Pinkerton, if people found out how easily you could be intimidated and how idiotic your ideas are. Either way, Pinkerton, I think you would lose. What do you think?"

He stared stubbornly at me, and I knew with stoic fatalism that he had no intention of dropping his pursuit. I stepped back and motioned with my pistol toward the door.

"Now, get out," I said quietly. He rose and started toward the door. I stepped in front of him, and he halted, warily eyeing me.

"And let it alone," I said softly. I pulled the hammer of the pistol back to full-cock and let him stare into the barrel for a long moment before I lowered the pistol and eased the hammer to rest on a cap. He continued on to the door, then turned and looked back at me.

"My pistol?" he asked.

I shook my head.

"I didn't think so," he said.

He opened the door and left, leaving the door standing wide open. Sutton crossed and closed the door, leaning back against it. He took his handkerchief from a pocket inside his coat and wiped his glistening forehead.

"Whew! For a moment there, John, I thought you were going to kill him," he said.

I slipped the pistol into its holster inside my coat. Belle crossed to the champagne bottle in the ice bucket and opened it, pouring wine into the two glasses resting beside it. She brought one to me. I drank thirstily.

"You *were* only bluffing him, weren't you, John?" he asked.

I smiled.

"Jesus!" he said.

He crossed to the liquor table in the alcove beside the fireplace and poured a glass of whiskey, drinking it down, then pouring another. He turned from the table and considered the room again.

"We are at the mercy of a madman, you know," he said to the others.

Belle shook her head. "I think it's over now."

Her eyes were large and luminous upon mine. Her breasts moved with each deep breath, the color high on her cheekbones. A flush started up the white column of her throat. She pressed her lips together, then licked them, her pink tongue darting out like a cat's. I knew then why Belle Boyd had become the dashing spy of the War.

"I'm not sure," I said. "But for now it's over." I looked at Sutton. "And didn't you and Emily have plans?"

He waved his hand and said, "After this?"

"Why not?" Emily said, taking the hint. She moved to the small closet beside the door and removed a cape, swinging it around her shoulders with a gesture I recognized as Belle's. "I'm still hungry and there's only enough here for two. For *two*," she emphasized when Sutton started to speak.

He looked from one to the other, then said, "Will you be all right alone?"

"Oh, I think we'll manage quite well," Belle said, stepping close to me.

I smelled the musk of her perfume and the woman beneath it. A laugh bubbled up from deep inside me. Automatically, I reached for the clove-scented handkerchief I kept with me and pressed it against my lips before the laughter could turn into a cough.

"Yes," I said. "Oh yes, I think we'll be able to manage nicely."

Like a fool, I didn't knock on wood.

7

The derelict in the dental chair suddenly coughed, sending a fine mist into my face. I cursed, dropped my instruments, and stepped back from the chair, taking a handkerchief from my pocket to wipe off his spittle. He leaned over the side of the chair and spat a glob of blood onto the floor. A thick piece of tissue lay like a dark worm in the spittle. The gallery above me broke out into laughter. Strachyam cast a cold eye at the gallery and it fell suddenly quiet. He turned back to me.

"When you are quite ready, Mr. Holliday. You do have a patient in the chair," he said.

The black stumps of the derelict's teeth leered at me. His unshaven jaw moved in clicks as he said, " 'Ata boy, Doc! You tell 'em to finish up 'ere as I'se got important buzzness waitin' on me."

The gallery tittered again. Strachyam froze it with a glare. Then he nodded at me. I stepped back up to the chair and picked up my instruments, sliding a tiny mirror around and into his mouth and following it with the drill bit, grinding as fast as I could with the foot-operated drill. I breathed shal-

lowly through my mouth to avoid inhaling his fetid breath as
much as I could and quickly finished reaming out the cavity
on the molar upon which I was working and tightly packed it
with gold foil, briefly wondering how long it would be before
he pried it loose for drink. Then I scraped it and stepped
back, handing the mirror to Strachyam. He took it, coolly
bent over the patient and checked my work, then stepped
back and scribbled a note in a sheaf of papers he held. He
looked at a roster, selected a name, then looked up into the
gallery.

"Mr. Reese, you are next," he said.

The man in the chair complained, but Strachyam ignored
him as Reese made his way down to the floor of the operating
theatre. He gingerly took the mirror from the tray beside the
chair and bent over the man. He winced as the man's breath
struck him, then he selected a probe and began feeling his
way around in the man's mouth. I waited as he worked, feeling the grin begin on my face as I pictured him coming close
to the rotted wisdom tooth where I had noticed pustules
forming on the gum. Suddenly, the man howled and vomit
spewed from his mouth, catching Reese in his face. He reeled
back, dragging the probe across the man's lip, cutting it. He
gagged, then bent over, his breakfast splashing on the floor
beside his feet. The gallery howled with laughter as the attendant hastily handed Reese a towel.

Strachyam sighed, and made a mark on the papers in his
hand, then stuffed them into a side pocket of his coat.

"Perhaps we'd better break for lunch," he said. "You may
resume after lunch, Mr. Reese."

"I . . . I don't know if I can," Reese muttered, wiping his
blubbery lips with a handkerchief.

Strachyam's eyebrows raised. "It's your grade, Mr. Reese.
You decide."

"I could use a bite meself, Doc," the man in the chair said.

"I suppose," Strachyam answered. He looked up into the
gallery, caught Sutton's eye, and called him to the floor of
the theatre, handing him a gold piece.

"Take our patient to a light lunch, Mr. Sutton, and return at one-thirty. Oh, Mr. Holliday, will you be so kind as to wait on me in my office?"

" 'Bout time," grunted the man in the chair, tearing off the bib. He heaved himself from the chair, perfunctorily wiping himself down with the towel handed him by the attendant.

"I's knows of a leetle pub not far from here," he began slyly.

"Avoid alcohol, Mr. Sutton," Strachyam said mildly, interrupting. The man's face fell.

"Yes sir," Sutton said, gathering the man's arm and pushing him in front of him.

"Watch yourself," he mumbled out of the corner of his mouth as he passed me. I followed him out the door as Strachyam gave the closing remarks to the class, cautioning them to return promptly at one-thirty to avoid penalizing points.

My heels echoed on the granite floor as I strode down the vaulted corridor to Strachyam's office. I entered the waiting area and took a seat beside the door that led into the sanctum sanctorum and settled myself, studying the dusty portraits of men I did not know hanging from the wall opposite the chair. I didn't have long to wait; Strachyam brusquely entered and crossed to the door to his inner office, curtly bidding me to follow him. He went behind an enormous desk, tossed his papers onto the clutter on top of the desk, then dropped with a sigh into the huge leather-covered chair behind the desk. He fumbled a pipe from a stand beside his humidor and loaded it with burley shag before leaning back and lighting it with a kitchen match. He studied me through a haze of blue smoke for a long moment before speaking.

"It has come to the attention of the college that you are, ah, keeping company with an individual of compromising character," he said sternly, frowning as I took the chair opposite him without waiting for permission to sit. I crossed my legs and leaned back, returning his stare.

"And what character might that be?" I asked.

He worried his pipe stem for a long moment before replying. I could see he was bothered. This was not the way interviews were conducted between professors and students.

Instead of a quavering young man in front of him, one whom he could manipulate with a few chosen words, I was placing him on the defensive.

"A showgirl," he said at last. "A young woman who is currently under investigation for an, ah, conspiracy that reaches into the offices of our government."

"Oh?" I raised my eyebrows and waited politely for him to continue.

"Well? What do you have to say for yourself, sir?" he asked.

"In regards to what?" I answered.

He choked on a bit of smoke, then glared at me. "The showgirl!"

"I am currently escorting an actress to dinner following her show," I said. "But as to a showgirl, I would think that would be someone more along the lines of those who appear dancing the cancan down along the saloons on Water Street, wouldn't you?"

"Don't be impertinent!" he snapped.

"I'm not," I calmly replied. "I'm simply trying to define the parameters of our conversation."

"It has also come to the understanding of the regents that you have been involved in a shooting," he said.

"I believe you are referring to an affair of honor," I said.

"Call it whatever you want, dueling is still illegal," he said.

"Yes, I notice how much honor is absent in the North," I replied. "So much so that I feel the *Echo* might like to know where certain regents and some of the faculty spend their evenings when they are away from their homes."

I almost laughed when his face folded into an impassive mask as he studied me, wondering how much I knew about certain habits of some of the college's advisers, men who could little afford to have such things brought to the public's attention in sanctimonious Philadelphia: Williams and Steadman, who preferred young girls; Manning, who had a penchant for young boys; the parties at The Gull and Anchor pub down off Water Street.

Finally he sighed and leaned forward over his desk, resting his pipe in an ashtray. He pinched the bridge of his nose for a long moment, then steepled his fingers in front of him.

"The regents have directed me to make, ah, 'inquiries' concerning you," he said quietly. "Apparently, someone, I know not who, has approached them with a record of your movements over the past few weeks. I am under the impression that I am to summarily dismiss you following my"— he grimaced at the word—" 'investigation.' However, I think, under the circumstances, I will be able to convince the regents that it would be in their own interests to allow you a second chance."

"You're a peach, sir," I said. He looked sharply to see if I was being sarcastic, then he gave a tiny smile.

"Yes, but, Mr. Holliday, I would be careful not to become too embroiled in any more conspiracies or I shall be forced to terminate your association with this college despite the, ah, behavior of some of our esteemed colleagues."

"Thank you, sir," I said politely, rising. "And I think you can assure your colleagues that certain information will not be finding its way into the hands of the yellow journalists."

"Thank you," he said somberly. "But please, Mr. Holliday, do remember: Nemo liber est qui corpori servit. Nemo malus felix."

"Oh, I'm quite aware of Seneca's postulations," I said. "But I also know my Bacon: Nam et ipsa scientia potestas est."

His eyes rose at my Latin, then a faint smile again crept over his lips. He nodded and said, "Have a good day, Mr. Holliday. And please remember our words: I would hate to lose you so close to graduation."

"I shall, Mr. Strachyam," I said. A cough burst from my lips, and I grabbed hurriedly for my handkerchief, inhaling deeply of the clove scent. I took a hesitant, shallow breath.

"Are you all right, Mr. Holliday?" Strachyam said, rising in concern. I waved away his hand.

"For the moment," I said. "A slight cough, a chill. This damned weather is not conducive to the Southerner. Good day, sir."

He bade me farewell as I walked from his office. I hurried down the corridor for the outside, but the sun failed to warm me and chase the sudden chill from my bones as I leaned weakly against the outside of the building, feeling the weariness creep over me.

8

The knocking continued at my door long after I tried to ignore it. At last I rose to my feet and pulled on a robe while staggering my way across my room and flinging open the door. Belle strode dramatically in to the middle of the room before pausing and looking around with a curled lip. Behind her, Eddie Foy slipped past me, grinning sheepishly.

Belle was dressed all in black: black hat with a black feather sweeping dramatically back like Mosby wore during the War, black skirt draped in thick folds over her generous hips, black sacque jacket, with only a bottle green shirtwaist to relieve it. Her black cape was fixed around her neck with an emerald brooch.

"Do come in," I said. I shut the door, leaning against it, willing the weakness to leave me. I felt cold and damp, my robe already clinging to the perspiration seeping from my body. Eddie looked closely at me, the grin slipping from his face.

"Are you all right?" he asked.

A cough grumbled from my chest. I shook my head, then shrugged. "Who knows?"

"You look like hell," Belle said from center stage. "And as for this . . ." She cast a disdainful hand around her.

"You're welcome," I said. She glared at me, then placed her hands on her hips, impatiently tapping the toe of her boot against the floor. I made my way across the room back to my bed and picked up a water pitcher from a small table there, filling a glass and drinking thirstily. I refilled the glass and sipped, waiting.

"Well?" she said finally.

"Well, what?" I repeated. "It's your visit. What brings you here?"

The words were not entirely to her liking, but they were close enough to the scenario she had arranged in her mind for her to launch into her soliloquy.

"What does he take me for?" she asked beginning to pace back and forth in the middle of the room: four steps then turn, four steps then turn. "What—"

"Sorry," I said, breaking in. "Who?"

"Who what?" she asked, pausing. Confusion flickered briefly in her eyes as I pulled her from her rehearsed speech.

"Who takes you for what?" I said.

"What?" She frowned.

"Belle has a problem," Eddie said, slipping apologetically into the conversation.

"Mrs. Davis has closed my show, effective following this weekend," she said dramatically. She glared at me, and I didn't know if it was anger from the closing of her show or that I had interrupted the scenario she had gone to so much trouble to create.

I frowned.

"Why would she do that? It is the most successful show in Philadelphia this season. There's been a full house every night I've attended."

"There have been rumors—" she began, but Eddie could tell I was in no mood for lengthy discussions and interrupted her, drawing a scathing glare.

"City ordinances," he said. "It's an old ploy. When someone wants to get rid of a certain actor, he arranges for the theatre to be visited repeatedly by city inspectors. No theatre can comply with all the codes and ordinances, so the minor ones are usually overlooked. However . . ." he shrugged.

"When someone wants you out of town or simply wants to

make life difficult for you, they arrange for the inspections,"
I said. "I think I'm beginning to understand."

"Oh, yes. No show, no matter how successful it is, can be
retained without an audience," he said. "The theatre owners
have to let the show go despite its success simply to stay
open. Even a half-house is a paying house. An empty house
is simply lost money."

"Pinkerton!" Belle spat his name as if it was something
foul. "He's behind this!"

"What are you going to do?" I asked. Her shoulders suddenly slumped and the flesh on her face became doughy,
showing her age a good ten years past mine. She gave a limp-
wristed wave.

"Chicago," she said dully. "I guess. Maybe we can get
there and get set up before he knows where we are. He won't
expect us to be in his hometown. We were just starting to
break even, too. Now we'll have to go back in hock just to
move the show. It isn't fair!"

A cough exploded from my lips and my lungs began to
spasm, cough after cough rolling from them, threatening to
tear them from my chest. I gripped the table, willing myself
to stop, but I couldn't.

"Here," Eddie said, thrusting something into my hand.
"Drink this!"

Obediently, I raised the flask and drank deeply, gasping as
the raw whiskey bit deeply. My lungs ceased their spasms.
Cautiously, I took another sip. The room suddenly seemed
brighter, the lines distinct and hard. A strange luminescence
glowed around Belle and Eddie. I noticed the deep craters in
Eddie's forehead and nose, a spot of dried soap behind one
ear. Tiny lines irradiated from Belle's eyes, the flesh under
her eyes appearing puffy. I handed the flask back to Eddie.

"An old actor's trick," he explained. "I usually keep one
filled with whiskey and honey in the wings when I perform."

"It seems to be working," I said, ruefully adding,
"although I can't say I like drinking liquor this early in the
morning."

He shrugged. "Think of it as for medicinal purposes only."

"Ah, yes. Medicinal purposes," I murmured.

"Are you sure you're all right? I have some laudanum," Belle said. I looked back at her; she was sincere, twin lines of apprehension appearing between her eyes.

"For now," I said.

She reached up and cupped my cheek. She rose and softly kissed my lips. Her perfume was spicy and tickled my nose.

"I'm going to miss you," she said. "You've been very good for me."

"But the show must go on," I said.

Her lips turned up in a smile, but her eyes held sadness. She nodded, patting my cheek. Then she gathered herself and walked toward the door, Eddie following dutifully in her trail. She paused at the door as he stepped in front of her to open it.

"Yes, the show must go on. This time, to Chicago. We still have four days, though."

"Yes, four days," I answered.

She nodded and left, followed by Eddie, who sadly shook his head as he closed the door softly behind him. I felt tired and drained. A dull anger floated inside me, but it wasn't the cold fire I had known in the past. This time it seemed the anger of disappointment and regret. The killing anger was not there.

I thought about Belle and all that we had become to each other and all that we had not become. Lovers, yes, but loved, no. Still, I felt an obligation toward her and crossed to my shaving tackle and looked in the mirror hanging on the wall. A stranger looked back, dark bristles along his square jaw-line, and his blue eyes appearing gray from deep hollows. A fine sheen of perspiration coated his forehead, which seemed untouched by sun. I sighed and picked up my shaving mug and began building a lather.

A gust of wind kicked a crumbled newspaper down the street, and I huddled deeper into my chesterfield from its cold, biting teeth. I shivered and felt the edges of a dry cough building in my chest. I pulled the pint of whiskey from my pocket, removed the cork, and drank sparingly. Sutton grabbed it before I could replace it and lowered its contents by a half before returning it. I slid the flask into my pocket and for the tenth time touched the Navy Colt through the hole I had made in the right-hand pocket of the chesterfield's lining, reassuring me of its presence. Cautiously, I moved my feet, startling a mongrel bitch nosing a garbage can a few feet away. She hunkered, growling a warning, then moved away, her swollen dugs dragging across the ground.

"How do you want to take him?" Sutton whispered, his lips close enough to my ear for me to feel the gentle puff of his breath on the back of my neck.

"Surprise," I whispered back. "Catch him offguard just before he crosses the street. But we have to be quick; I don't know if he'll be expecting us, but he'll be expecting something."

"How do you know that?" Sutton asked.

"Because I would. Now be quiet. The object is to surprise him, not let him know we are waiting for him."

I moved softly away from Sutton, edging my way closer to the alley mouth. I slid next to the rough brick wall and removed my hat, looking quickly around the alley down Fourth Street. The wind threw a cloud of dirt in my eyes. I drew back, cursing silently to myself as I rubbed them clear with my handkerchief. I peeked cautiously around again: Moonlight gleamed off the street, turning it into a skeleton's bone, the bare limbs of the locust trees twisting in the wind sighing through them. A rat scampered halfway into the street, paused, then fled the rest of the way across, disappearing into a coal chute. The street was bare of any macs looking for customers for their crib girls; in fact, it was bare of all life except for a cab crossing the block at the end of the street, the cabbie tucked deep into his coat, the collar pushed up like bat wings over his ears.

I pulled back into the alley out of the wind's teeth and removed the bottle from my pocket, sipping at it before catching myself, warning myself that my drinking was already becoming automatic. I replaced the bottle before Sutton could reach for it. I did not feel drunk, but I knew that given a moment, Sutton would soon be bellowing verses of "Dubin Rosin" if I let him have any more drinks, even if only for medicinal purposes. I took my watch from my pocket and opened it. The notes of Chopin's "Opus No. 1 in B-Flat Minor" lifted from my hand, soaring through the night. Mother's image swam mistily before my eyes, and I quickly closed the lid of the watch, cutting the music short. Memory moved restlessly within me: Mother, Mattie . . .

"Here he comes!" Sutton whispered, and I automatically pulled back in the alley beside him. He appeared within minutes at the mouth of the alley, a cheroot in his hand winking like a malevolent orange eye in the darkness as he drew upon it. A breath of wind kicked a little dirt down the street, and he turned automatically away from the stinging granules.

I nudged Sutton. He stepped out from the alley and took Pinkerton by the right arm, sliding his hand high up under his armpit and lifting the slighter man up on his toes. His cigar dropped, striking the stones of the street, sending a shower of sparks sweeping upwards. His left hand swept across his body, fumbling awkwardly at his right coat pocket. I placed the barrel of the Navy Colt in his ear and rocked the hammer back. He froze, the color draining from his face. He twisted, trying to face me. I grinned.

"Good evening, Pinkerton. Remember me? I told you to desist, didn't I?" I made a clucking noise with my tongue. "You are a daisy. What is there that made you persist in your inquiries after you were fairly warned?"

"Holliday," he whispered. "Goddamn you!"

"Probably," I said dryly. "But for now, you are close to making such an arrangement with Him personally. I meant what I said, Pinkerton: You should have left well enough alone."

He swung suddenly with his left forearm, throwing my hand to the sky. His fist struck me high on the cheekbone, driving me back. He spun and lifted a knee, trying for Sutton's groin, but Sutton had had time to turn his hip, blocking the knee. He pivoted on the ball of his foot, bringing his right fist around, lifting at his hips as he drove his fist deep into Pinkerton's stomach. The air left Pinkerton's stomach with a loud *whoosh!* and then the detective was kneeling on the ground, gasping for air, his mouth working like a goldfish's as he tried to force his lungs to work again.

"Are you all right?" Sutton asked. He kept a wary eye on Pinkerton as he would on an injured snake.

I nodded and gingerly touched my cheek beneath my eye. It was already beginning to swell. I became aware that I still had the pistol in my hand and lowered the hammer, storing the pistol back under my arm beneath my coat. I was surprised that I had not accidentally triggered it; Pinkerton had taken a huge gamble. I reached down and patted his pockets, finding a Deringer, the mate to the one I had taken earlier, in his right pocket. I removed it and placed it in my own.

"Get him up and let's get out of here before someone comes," I said.

Sutton stepped behind Pinkerton and gathered his collar in one huge hand and lifted him to his feet. He was breathing a little easier now, but Sutton had taken the fight out of him with the blow to his solar plexus. He stumbled down the alley ahead of us with Sutton propelling him with tiny shoves that kept him off balance. His breathing had returned to normal by the time we reached the other end of the alley. I looked cautiously down both sides of the street, then across at Sutton's cousin, Patrick Cavendish, sitting in the seat of the borrowed cab, the reins to the horse held loosely in his hands. He raised his whip and nodded.

"Right," I said to Sutton. "All clear. Let's go."

"Where are you taking me?" Pinkerton asked as Sutton unceremoniously bundled him across the street. His feet slipped on the bricks, and Sutton swore and lifted him up, practically throwing him into the cab.

"You'll see," I said curtly. I stepped into the cab and thumped the ceiling overhead to draw Paddy's attention.

"Let's go."

Paddy clucked to the horse and we moved away with a jerk, heading down to the waterfront.

"You'll never get away with this," Pinkerton said. I could hear the fear beneath his words. The sour smell of his supper rolled from him. I wrinkled my nose and reached in my pocket for my handkerchief. My fingers touched the tiny bottle, and I pulled it out and gave it to him.

"Drink this," I ordered. He looked at it with misgiving.

"I'll be damned if I will. I'm in no mood for these school-boy games," he said, trying to make himself sound rough, but he sounded like a young boy faced with a gang of taunters. Still, I was in no temper for his posturing. The familiar anger began building inside me. I turned on the street to face him.

"I'm in no mood for your mouth," I answered. "Now, god-damnit, you will drink this, or I will put a bullet in your stomach and pour it in that way!"

"Best do as he says," Sutton said solicitously to Pinkerton. "He's been sick lately and that's put him in a wee temper tonight."

Pinkerton gingerly took the bottle from my fingers and pulled the cork from its lip. He smelled it, and shook his head.

"I think not," he said, sounding as if he was trying to convince himself he was still the master of his destiny.

Sutton didn't wait for my order. He grabbed Pinkerton by the hair, cruelly wrenching his head back. I grabbed the bottle from Pinkerton's fingers as he reached back reflexively. I pulled his small Deringer from my pocket and cocked it, placing the barrel beside his temple.

"Your pistol," I said softly. "They'll be finding your body with your own pistol ball in your head in the morning. Suicide, they'll call it, and who's to know the difference. The choice is yours: the bottle or the ball. Make it."

Tiny muscles quivered at the corners of his jaws. He gave a tiny nod, and I placed the lip of the bottle to his lips and tilted. He swallowed convulsively twice, then a third time, emptying the bottle. I threw it out of the cab. Glass tinkled behind us. Sutton eased up on his hold and Pinkerton leaned forward, his tongue working against the foul taste in his mouth. The rain began beating down with a savage intensity.

"What was it?" he asked. Fear tinged his words.

"Laudanum," I answered.

"What . . . what are you going to do?" he whispered, his eyes suddenly round in his chalky face. His throat suddenly convulsed and I placed the Deringer between his eyes.

"You better keep that down," I said lowly.

He swallowed and swallowed again. Perspiration suddenly dotted his forehead and his eyes looked sickly into mine, begging me wordlessly.

"I'm sick," he moaned.

"You'll live. For a while," I said shortly.

Slowly, he began to relax back against the seat as the opiate worked on him. His breathing slowed, then became regular, and his chin fell forward onto his chest. I left him alone for another minute, then eased his head back against the cab's cushions and rolled back an eyelid. He did not move. I nodded in satisfaction and replaced the Deringer in my pocket.

"He's out," I said.

" 'Bout time," Sutton grunted. "You gave him enough laudanum to knock out a horse." He leaned forward and nudged his cousin.

"Let's go to the studio," he ordered.

" 'Bout high time," Paddy grunted and lifted the reins to encourage the horse to a trot. "An' me out here dog-paddling for me life in all this water."

Within minutes, we pulled up outside O. B. Demorat's photo studio. I stepped from the cab and knocked twice on Demorat's door. He opened it a crack, peering out, then sighed in relief and threw the door open wide.

"I was wondering when you would be coming," he whispered. "The girls are becoming impatient."

I turned and motioned to Sutton and Paddy. They stepped from the cab and, taking Pinkerton between them, brought him across the street and into the studio. Demorat closed the door behind us, locking it. He was pale and nervous, his hands trembling slightly as he shot the bolt. He took a handkerchief from his pocket and mopped the high dome of his forehead.

"Let's get going," I said impatiently. "We want to be through before the laudanum wears off."

Demorat wrinkled his nose at the smell of Pinkerton's wet wool coat and waved his hand at the back of his studio. I led Paddy and Sutton through the office, parting the curtains for them into Demorat's studio. They grunted as they maneuvered the lax body between them through the doorway.

The studio had been hastily remade into an approximation of a seraglio. Demorat's camera had been positioned in front of heavy curtains that had been draped across the ceiling and down the side as a frame. Thick cushions had been heaped liberally around the floor. A hookah sat on a small table, the hoses to the pipes writhing like long snakes away from it. On the cushions rested four ladies from the chorus of the Arch Street Theatre and three young girls, children to two of the ladies dressed in wrappers.

"It's about time!" a red-haired chorine complained. She rose and padded barefooted to an ashtray beyond the camera. She stubbed out the cigarillo she had been smoking and looked angrily at Paddy.

"A favor's a favor," she said, scolding him. "But this will cost you." She placed her hands on her hips. Her wrapper fell open, revealing her naked body beneath. Her breasts were high, the nipples pointing saucily at us.

"Okay, okay," Paddy grumbled. "Is it our fault the man was late himself?"

She stepped forward, eyeing Pinkerton's lax body hanging between Sutton and Paddy. Her nose crinkled and she drew back in disgust.

"He stinks! Are you sure he's out? We'd not be wanting him to be remembering any of us later. He has a long memory, I'm told."

"He's out," I said. I tugged at his coat, slipping it awkwardly from his shoulders. "But let's get moving before he does wake up."

She nodded and turned to the others on the cushions. "All

right, girls. This is the bugger who's been doing the turn on
us! Now's our chance. Let's get on with it."

A blonde with green eyes rose and grinned mischievously
at me as she tantalizingly drew her robe down off her shoulders, spotted with freckles, slowly exposing her white figure.
I grinned and shook my head. She pouted, and winked, then
blew me a kiss as she settled herself with a sigh against the
cushions. She was joined within minutes by the other women
and the young girls, who showed no modesty at all in revealing their pubescent bodies for the camera, budding breasts,
the beginnings of a pubic triangle.

Within minutes, we had Pinkerton stripped and arranged
on the couch. The women and girls draped themselves
around and over him, seductively arranging themselves to
show as much of their nudity and his as possible. Demorat
shook his head and took his place behind the camera.

"We could all be in big trouble if this gets out," he
moaned. He pressed the bulb and the flash powder went off,
illuminating the room. He worked rapidly, switching the
plates and refilling the flash pan.

"If this doesn't work, then we'll all be in prison. You
know that," he said. "Bring your leg down a little more, my
dear," he said to one of the young girls. She obeyed him.
"That's right. Hold it." The flash powder went off again.

"I hope you remember your promise," he said to me.
"They will pose later?"

"Of course we will, honey," the dark-haired one with
huge breasts said. She smiled slowly, teasingly, lifting one
breast gently to point it at the camera. "But that's all, you
understand?"

"I'll be damned!" the red-haired one exclaimed.

"What's the matter?" Sutton asked, alarmed.

She pointed.

"The bugger's beginning to respond! "

Demorat immediately touched off the powder again.

I passed the bottle of whiskey to Paddy, who was sitting
miserably in the driver's seat of the cab, rain dripping off the

brim of his bowler. Pinkerton began to moan. Paddy took a deep drink, then passed the bottle to Sutton, who drained it and tossed it from the cab. I heard the glass break against the cobblestones of Water Street. Music floated wildly up from a saloon down the street from us, bringing with it gay laughter and shouts of merrymakers enjoying the show on the small stage of The Hull. It was a foul-smelling place, and the entertainment was provided by those women who augmented their income in tiny cribs down the alley away from The Hull after dancing the cancan. The Hull was an evilly run saloon not above slipping Mickey Finns to certain customers when ship captains found their crew a bit short for putting out to sea.

Pinkerton's eyes flickered, then he sat up, the heavy robe covering his nakedness slipping off him. He looked in confusion around him for a minute, then suddenly became aware of the cold dampness pebbling his flesh. He looked down at himself in astonishment.

"What . . . where . . . I'm . . ."

He stared at me, memory suddenly flooding back.

"What have you done with my clothes?" he demanded.

"You seem to have lost them," I said. "Probably left them here."

I handed him a small pile of pictures. He scanned the top one, then his eyes widened as he slowly thumbed through them. Demorat had outdone himself. The photographs were artfully produced, Rubenesque, although the models were far from being the type favored by Rubens. But the observer would have little doubt as to what Pinkerton had been indulging in when the photographs had been made.

"This is . . . this is . . . outrageous!" he spluttered.

I took the pile of photographs back away from him before he could throw them from the cab.

"Oh yes," Sutton said, lolling back in his seat. He was smoking one of Pinkerton's cigars, and he blew a thin stream toward the ceiling of the cab.

"I most especially find interesting the one of you and the girls. You really are a naughty man. Depraved."

"What is this?" Pinkerton asked, his eyes narrowing and shifting between Sutton and myself.

"Simple," I said. "You stop your investigation of Miss Boyd and promise to leave her alone, or we will make certain that these photographs appear at the offices of the *Echo* and the district attorney. The young girls are definitely underage, and Philadelphia, as you well know, has certain laws that punish certain standards of behavior. You know how hypocritical they are here." I waved the photographs gently. "I think this would pretty much mean the end of your career, don't you? You'd get at least, oh, a year for indecent behavior. Perhaps more. I don't think a man who has put men in jail would be very safe going to the same jail, do you?"

His eyes looked with loathing into mine. "How much?" he asked thickly.

"I told you; leave Miss Boyd alone," I said.

His lips tightened. For a moment I thought he was going to refuse, but then his shoulders slumped, and he nodded resignedly.

"All right," he said, leaning back against the cushions. "You win."

"You will not bother her or interfere with her again in any way whatsoever?" I said. "You will forget she even exists. You will not attend any of her shows or contact anyone in regards to her?"

"I said I wouldn't," he answered sullenly. He reached for the photographs, but I held them back out of reach.

"Uh-uh," I said. "I think I'll keep these. You see, Mr. Pinkerton, I don't trust you. I'll leave them with a friend—never mind, you won't know who—with instructions to release them to the press and courts if you should at any time interfere with Miss Boyd. Or myself and my friend," I amended, remembering that we, too, were now vulnerable. "There are others, too, that could be released if you should be so lucky as to get hold of these. Those are not even in the city by now."

I lied, but he had no way of knowing if I was lying or not. I could see in his eyes that I had won before he slowly nodded.

"Good," I said. I suddenly pulled the robe off him and opened the door. "Now get out."

He looked at me in confusion, then he looked down at his nakedness. Shame blushed through his face, and he tried to hide himself, cupping his hands in his lap.

"Are you mad?" he said frantically. "My clothes!"

"Let this serve as a reminder to you," I said grimly. "You may be a bit embarrassed, but I don't want you to ever forget this night."

"That I won't," he said dangerously. He glared from me to Sutton. Sutton gave him a sudden shove, and he fell from the cab into the street. He gasped in pain as his hands and knees scraped painfully against the cobblestones of Water Street.

"Drive on," I ordered, and Paddy slapped the reins against the horse, startling it into motion. We moved with a jerk away from Pinkerton, who was sprawled naked in the filthy street, and trotted down the street, pulling away from the waterfront.

"Do you think he will listen to you?" Sutton asked, flipping the cigar out into the night.

"For a while. Until time lets his bravery return," I said.

Suddenly I felt tired, drained of the adrenaline that had been keeping me going. I slumped back against the seat and tiredly massaged my eyes with the balls of my fingers.

"Then he'll think about this and look for a way to get even. But until then he'll leave Belle and ourselves alone. He's smart enough to know that I mean what I said. We've already shown him that. Eventually, though, he'll come after us. Me, at any rate, for he knows my name. He doesn't know yours, although I suppose he could discover it if he wants to search for it. By that time, however, Belle will have earned back the money that he's cost her."

"What are you going to do with the pictures?" he asked. "Give them to Belle?"

"No, if he does try to find them, that will be the first place he'll look. I'll simply destroy them," I said.

"Destroy them? But then you will have lost your leverage with him!" Sutton protested.

I shook my head. "No, he won't know where they are.

That's the best way; he can search all he wants, but he will never find them. But they'll still exist in his mind and that will be enough."

"I hope you're right, John," Sutton said.

"I am," I replied, and rested my head back against the cushion, letting the sway of the cab rock and soothe me as we moved through the rainy streets back into the heart of the city. My chest ached, and I felt feverish, tiny coughs erupting apologetically from my chest. I longed for the warmth of the sun, but the sun had no warmth to it in the North, and I longed again for home and Mattie and to be done with this business in an uncaring city where religious pretension and hypocritical piety were the mark of a man's worth.

9

It was spring, and the pecan trees would be greening up, the magnolia trees would be bursting forth with pink and cream blossoms, and the rosebushes would be dripping heavy with scented buds. In my mind, I could see Mother's lilac bushes heavy with purple outside the back door of our house, and Ares moving restlessly in his stall, hungrily eyeing the mares in the pasture, yearning to stretch his powerful legs forward in a mindless gallop.

And Mattie.

I could see Mattie in her white dress drifting among the magnolia trees, petals falling to grace her shoulders, smell the lavender of her perfume, taste the freshness of her lips, feel the softness of her arms. Perhaps it was more than nostalgia, however, as I had received a letter from her only a short time before, asking if anything was wrong, and why hadn't I written. Her letter was fresh and innocent, anxious for my return, fearful that I might not want her anymore now that I had been away from home. I yearned to write her, to reassure her, but how could I tell her about Belle?

Did I want to tell her about Belle?

Or was my lack in writing due to a secret self within me, one who knew the safety and sweetness of Mattie, yet wanted the danger and sensuality of Belle?

As I lay in my bed, weak with the cough that would not go away, I pondered the question, dreaming of demur Mattie during the day, embracing the naked body of Belle at night, burying myself in Belle's wildness, drinking the intoxicating danger from her lips. Perhaps it would be best if Belle went to Chicago, but that, I knew, was an easy train ride from Philadelphia. I could establish a practice as easily in Chicago as I could in Griffin or Atlanta. What to do?

The night of her last show before she entrained for Chicago, I went to Belle's dressing room as usual. In my pocket, I had a small brooch outlined in pearls that I had paid for with my winnings from an all-night poker game at The Boar's Head off Water Street. A river man with an ugly scar had taken issue when I rose from the table with my winnings and drew a knife, threatening to cut me if I walked out with his money, but a glimpse of one of Pinkerton's Deringers quickly changed his mind.

"He's only one shot," one of the others protested. "Git 'im, Bill!"

"That one shot is me," Bill said, retaking his seat. He squinted up at me through a cloud of cigar smoke. "Don't be comin' back 'ere with those fancy tricks of yours, though. Yer free this time; next time will be my time."

"There are other games," I said, shrugging as I replaced the Deringer in my pocket.

"Think so? Not for a cardsharp after this makes the rounds," he said. The others remained still, watching me. I knew what he had called me and also knew that I had to make a stand, or more than a poker game would be denied me.

"I think you'd better explain yourself," I said quietly.

I could tell that he didn't like what was happening in the room, but he had gone too far to back down now. He glanced

over my frame, and I knew what he was thinking. I had lost a
lot of weight recently and my clothes hung from me like a
scarecrow's. My cheeks were hollow and pale from the lack
of sun. Most importantly, however, I was alone.

He stood, grinning, a gap showing between his front teeth
where someone had knocked them out in a brawl somewhere
down the line. He tossed the deck of cards he had been holding onto the scarred table.

"I'm saying that yer a cheat," he said.

"You scum-sucking pig," I said, feeling the rage building
within me. The room became bright and clear, the tobacco
smoke dissipated. I felt easy and relaxed, standing in front of
him. The others pushed their chairs back away from the
table, watching, waiting.

"Careful, Bill," one of the others said. "He's the one who
did Crawford."

Bill blinked and frowned. "Him? Why, I could break him
in two like a twig. Young scut."

His hands dropped to the table, but I took a step backwards
and to the side, my hand sliding easily under my coat and
removing the Navy Colt. He froze as the hammer locked
back, the barrel centering upon him. Slowly he raised his
hands from the table.

"Now," I said, looking at his friend who had spoken earlier. "Now I have more than one shot. There's one here for
you, too, if you want."

He shook his head. He raised his hands and placed them
on the arms of his chair in plain sight. Bill looked at the pistol and sneered.

"Shoulda known a cardy would have something like this,"
he said scornfully. "Ain't no such thing as a fair fight with
you, is there? Gentleman!" He spat on the floor.

"And you planned a fair fight?" I waved the pistol, outlining his frame. "As you said, you could break me in two.
This"—I lifted the Colt—"is my equalizer. How do you like
the odds now, you son of a bitch?"

The rage finally filled me, and I took one of Pinkerton's
pistols from my left pocket and slid it across the table to him.

I shifted the Navy Colt back into its holster and removed the second of Pinkerton's Deringers and dropped it on the table beside my hand.

"All right. You wanted a fight? I'm your huckleberry. Now it's fair, you goat-pumper! We each got a shot. Go ahead!"

He stared from the table to me. I could see in his eyes that he wanted to grab the pistol, but uncertainty rested there as well. Maybe the man at his left was right, and I was the one who had killed Crawford; maybe I wasn't. But his life might be too much to pay for finding out. I knew what his choice was going to be; I had played poker with him for nearly eight hours.

"Need more of an edge?"

I backed a step away from the table, leaving a good two feet between me and the pistol. The one I had slid over to him rested only eight inches away from his hand. Slowly, he reached out and touched his pistol. I stared calmly into his eyes. Sweat broke out on his forehead. He swallowed. Then he shook his head and backed away from the table, shoving his hands into his pockets.

"No," he mumbled. "No. That pistol ain't loaded. No sir, it's a sucker bet."

I stepped forward and contemptuously picked up the pistol I had slid across to him. I cocked it and fired it at his boot. He jumped back at the explosion, the blood draining from his face, leaving black stubble standing starkly against the white. I dropped the pistol back into my pocket. Someone laughed and the blood rushed back into his face. Calmly, I slid the other pistol across to him.

"Want another draw?" I asked.

His eyes flashed angrily, then he shook his head. I reached across the table and picked up the pistol, dropping it into my pocket.

"You are a liar and a coward and one dirty son of a bitch. I plan on playing other games and if I hear you put the word out on me, I'll find you and kill you. Do you understand? I'll follow the river until I find you. From here to New Orleans, I don't care. I will find you and I will kill you. Gentlemen, it has been a pleasure."

I nodded at the others and turned my back on them. I opened the door and walked from the room, contemptuously leaving the door open behind me.

"Yer lucky, Bill," someone said. "That boy's got a lot of sand in him."

"Shut up!"

"Don't tell me to shut up! Yer the one that walked backward, not me!"

I knocked on Belle's door, fingering the brooch in my pocket. I felt a tickle in my throat and pulled my handkerchief from my pocket and breathed deeply of the cloves. The tickle didn't go away. The door opened and I hastily replaced my handkerchief and took a step into the room.

"Belle . . ." I paused as I noticed another man in the room. He was tall and thin, black hair carefully waved back from his long, angular face. He gave me a strange look as Belle rose from her table and crossed to me, folding her dressing gown securely around her. Her face was tight and controlled, her eyes shining brightly, as they had when I had braced Pinkerton in her rooms and challenged Crawford to the duel.

"John," she said throatily. "I would like you to meet my husband, John Hammond, a former officer in the Black Watch. John, this is John Henry Holliday, a young man who has escorted me at times to dinners and such. He's been most attentive."

"Your husband?" I repeated, stunned. I stared at him briefly for a moment, then quickly recovered, extending my hand.

"I have been looking forward to meeting you, sir."

"Have you?" he asked stiffly. He grasped my hand, shaking it firmly. "Belle's told you then about our marriage? I find that rather difficult to believe." He gave Belle a hard look. I took an instant dislike to him.

"Oh, be certain of it," I said blithely. "As certain as you were in giving your marital state to recent acquaintances you may have met."

His lips pulled down and he tilted his head back, frowning to look at me from lowered lids. I was a bit too tall for him to make that look effective, and he succeeded in only making himself look foolish.

"I'm not certain I follow your, ah, insinuations, young man," he said.

"Oh?" I raised my eyebrows innocently. "I wasn't aware I was making any. Were you? Making any, I mean."

Belle smothered a laugh, then changed the subject. "What did you think of the show, dear?" she asked, addressing me.

"Much improved," Hammond replied, not seeing the direction of her eyes. She made a face behind his back. "Much better than those dreadful times you had at rehearsal. I still say, however, that I do not think the theatre is your métier. You really do not have the talent for that. Oh, you are quite good in what you do, er, in a rather *exotic* way, I suppose, but that is really no endorsement for one who wishes to make one's way by performing, is it?"

Angry glints showed in Belle's eyes. Deliberately she loosened her dressing gown, allowing it to fall open to show the body stocking beneath it. The effect was more sexual than if she had been naked.

"Like this, you mean? Is that where you suggest my talent lies?" she asked icily.

"Belle! We are not alone here!" he said, casting a quick look in my direction, then stepping in front of her to block my view. "What one does onstage is different than that shown in the privacy of one's own rooms. You must realize that!"

"Must I?" she asked. I had heard that tone before and broke in hastily.

"I came to pay my respects, Miss Boyd," I said, stepping around her husband. I took the box containing the brooch from my pocket and handed it to her. "This is in appreciation of the many hours of enjoyment I have had with you. In performance," I added with just the slight hesitation. "I am going to miss your performances and our visits on the rare occasions when you allowed me to serve as your escort."

She opened the box and smiled at the brooch. Then she stepped forward and kissed my cheek. Her husband stiffened at this, but said nothing.

"Thank you, John," she said softly. "I'll always treasure it. Will you be there to see us off tomorrow? One-thirty at the station?"

"Of course," I answered. "What friend would not?"

"Thank you," she said.

I nodded and turned to go, then stopped as she called.

"Oh, wait!" She turned back to her dressing table and took a package from it, handing it to me.

"Happy graduation," she said.

I bowed, taking it from her hand. Then on impulse, I stepped forward and kissed her softly on the lips. She started, then returned the kiss quickly and stepped back.

"Really, sir! You go too far!" her husband said furiously, stepping between us. He raised his hand.

"Don't even think about it," I said quickly, lowly.

He hesitated, and Belle stepped forward, shoving him behind her.

"Oh, don't be an ass, John!" she said to him.

"Such effrontery!" he spluttered.

"And he has already blazed," she said quietly.

"What?"

"And he's still alive," she added. Her full lips curved in a deadly smile.

"What?"

He frowned at me, trying to make sense of what she was telling him. My youth told him I was too young to have accomplished what she claimed, but I could tell from his eyes that he wasn't sure if what she was telling him wasn't the truth. And if that were so, then there might be something there that he had better become aware of before acting. I gave him a wintry smile, then bowed to Belle.

"Thank you, Miss Boyd," I said. "I wish you all the success in Chicago."

"Do you think you might be able to make a performance out there?" she asked.

I shook my head. "No, I do not believe so. I am afraid that from here I shall be returning to Georgia."

"I don't suppose that I could change your mind?" she

asked. Her eyes became moist, but I could not tell if she was acting or truly signaling her regret that our time together was over.

"Perhaps," I said. "If circumstances were not as they are."

Ignoring her husband, she stepped forward and kissed me as lovers kiss, not as chaste friends. There could have been little doubt what we had been when she finally stepped back and away, and I knew in that instance that this appearance of her husband was a last effort on his part to preserve that which had fallen away from him. He may have loved her, but what love she bore him had long since dissipated into air from one cause or another. It did not matter; one cause was as good as another. I knew then that I could have her if I followed her to Chicago; the opportunity was there and stated. But how long would we last together? We were too close to each other, two who would be at each other's throats in a matter of time. We might be able to live apart, but never together except in isolated moments that would allow us our passion.

I stepped back and smiled at her. A lone tear trickled down her cheek and for a moment, I felt the spirit of relenting come upon me. The words came to my lips, but I forced them away and nodded at her husband and left.

"Really, Belle . . ." he began.

"Oh, do shut up, John!" she snapped. "You go on about the smallest things. You are becoming quite tiresome." She pressed the pads of her fingers against her eyes and turned back toward the Oriental screen standing discreetly in the corner.

I smiled as I closed the door gently, but firmly, behind me. I took a deep breath, and coughed. The package was heavy in my hand, and I stepped off to the side, away from the others bustling to and fro, carefully taking the set of *Mazeppa* apart for transporting to Chicago. I opened the package and found a silver flask and silver cup, each engraved in a flowing, copperplate hand:

Nec tecum possum vivere nec sine te
Semper Belle

My vision blurred. I began coughing again. I shook the flask; it was full. I opened it and tasted brandy. I drank deeply.

10

Although I was anxious to return home to Georgia after graduating from the Philadelphia College of Dental Surgery, I felt honor-bound to stop over in Baltimore with Dick Sutton, since he had willingly gone through most of the turmoil of my affair with Belle. Sutton had decided that he would set up practice in Baltimore after his uncle had sent him glowing accounts of the need for proper dentists there despite the presence of two of the most prominent schools of dentistry in the nation. I think Sutton was more interested in the slums past East Baltimore Street than he was in making his fortune in private practice. Irish immigrants had settled in such squalor in the slums that twelve to fourteen lived in one room in tenements that were foster homes to rats as big as the terriers that occasionally hunted them. The immigrants there had little hope for medical help, as the money they needed for medical attention was better spent in putting food in their bellies. For all of Dickie's avowal that he was determined to die a millionaire, I knew he had strong philanthropic tendencies. There would be little money coming into Sutton's pockets from Lower Baltimore.

I toyed with the idea of following his lead, even going so far as to register as a dentist with the city authorities and stepping through the muck and mud of the streets below East Baltimore. For a week, I worked with a dentist in the area who still used the old Merry drill and depended upon healthy swigs of cheap whiskey to help deaden the pain of extractions.

At night, I discovered the back streets of Baltimore to be highly intriguing, especially that area down along the Patapsco estuary where clipper ships rode on the tide and sailed out through Chesapeake Bay to the Atlantic. It was a place of relaxation with scantily clad women dancing the cancan, their plump white legs flashing tantalizingly, and street men sporting wilted flowers in the buttonholes of their plaid suits, trying to rope passersby into their individual dens of iniquity.

During the day, I tried to make myself interested in Sutton's patients, but a continual penetrating dampness had followed me down from Philadelphia. Despite the sultry days, I never felt warm and yearned for the heat of a Georgia summer. At last, I decided that I was not a candidate for sainthood. I bade a fond farewell to Sutton with promises to visit, and took the train back to Griffin.

My heart leaped when I stepped off the car at Griffin and discovered Mattie waiting for me, an angel in white taffeta giving me a chaste kiss in front of her father and mine that awakened the old hungers. With an effort, I restrained myself from folding her into my arms and showering her with ardent kisses.

"Father," I said, stepping forward and presenting my hand. For a moment I thought I saw a tear in his eye as he grasped it in both of his and heartily pressed it.

"Welcome home, John," he said gruffly. He took a handkerchief from an inside pocket and pretended to wipe perspiration from his face. I looked beyond him to my stepmother.

"Rachel," I said formally.

She stepped forward and gave me a perfunctory embrace and kissed my cheek.

"John. You have made all of us very proud," she said. I tried to hear a note of sarcasm in her voice, but there was none. She honestly meant what she had said: I had made her proud as well as Father. Still, I could not help remembering her at Mother's graveside and Father's taking her as a bride a few short months after Mother's burial. I gave her a half smile.

"Thank you," I said politely.

A look of sadness came into her eyes. A half smile curled around her lips, and I knew that she understood my reticence.

She nodded. I felt badly about my treatment of her, but memory was still too painfully close for me to feel differently. Uncle Robert quickly stepped forward into the awkward gap between us, grasping my hand and wringing it painfully.

"Well, boy! Or should I say 'Doctor'? You have acquitted yourself proudly. Welcome home, John Henry. Welcome home!"

Mattie tucked her hand under my arm. Her eyes sparkled with happiness as we walked to the carriages waiting outside the train depot. A nigra, the sleeves of his white shirt held up with garters, his face carefully molded into an impassive mask, carried my trunk and cases to the carriages and lashed them on back. I handed Mattie into the carriage and stepped in behind her. Father climbed in beside us while Rachel followed with Uncle Robert. Father beamed as he settled himself next to me.

"Well, John!" He shook his head and took a cigar from an inside pocket. He carefully cut the end of the cigar and lit it. A cloud of fragrant smoke rolled from his lips around Mattie and me. A cough rumbled from my chest. I felt the nagging awareness that it intended to continue. I slipped the flask from an inside pocket of my coat and took a small swallow of the whiskey. The flask was nearly empty. It had been a long and dusty trip down from Baltimore on the Atlantic Gulf Railroad, the last quarter of the trip through the dry, red-baked fields of Georgia that threw clouds of sifting dust into the former Jim Crow car. The numbing effects of the whiskey wore off every hundred miles or so. Father's eyes narrowed slightly.

"Taken to a drink now and then, I see," he said.

"Medicine. I seem to have picked up a cold," I answered, touching my chest. "The weather up North is not conducive to southern men." I capped the flask and put it away. Father laughed and leaned back against the cushion of the carriage.

"Yes, I would imagine that to be true," he said. He took a mouthful of cigar smoke and choked as he laughed at his words. He coughed and motioned toward me, his hand waving demandingly.

"Let me have some of that," he gasped. Obediently, I took the flask from my pocket and handed it to him. He took a long drink, then coughed again as the raw spirits bit hard against the back of his throat. His eyes watered.

"Well! That'd put a bark in a saint's bite!" he said. "Any germ live through that would have a death grip on a man's soul! You been drinking this steady?"

He glanced at the inscription, then his sharp eyes met mine as he handed it back.

"I told you." I grinned, taking the flask from his hand. "Medicine."

"Oh, yes," he replied, studying me carefully. "Medicine. You've changed, John. You've—" He searched for words, shaking his head.

"It's his mustache," Mattie teased, tweaking it with her long fingers. I grabbed them and kissed them. She blushed and pulled back away from me.

"John, behave yourself!" she chided, then smiled to show that she was not to be taken seriously.

I laughed and leaned back in the carriage, enjoying the warmth of the sun, looking at the familiar road and the red clay fields we passed on the way to Uncle Robert's house. I felt as if my life was drawing inward, becoming a part of the furrowed fields heavy with sorghum and cotton. Nigras moved across the fields, pausing in their work to watch us pass by, their eyes large and white in the blackness of their faces. We moved through Griffin, heading out toward Uncle Robert's house in the country, passing the dusty, shady streets where nigra women balanced bundles of clothes tied up in sheets on their turbaned heads, carrying them without so much as a touch of the hand down to the hollow where the nigras had their own community thanks to Reconstruction.

As the horse moved out again into the dust of the road leading past the fields, I looked over at Father, who had sat silent over the past few miles, smoking his cigar and waiting for me to feel the moment for asking questions.

"Well, Father," I said. "How are things in Valdosta?"

"Interesting that you should ask," Father said. He hawked

and spat over the side of the carriage, using the moment to frame his thoughts.

"It would be for the best if you didn't go back to Valdosta," he said quietly. "Oh, things would probably work out all right in the long run, but every once in a while when one of the nigras gets a bit frisky, some folks get to remembering how you settled that one out on the river. Now don't go to worrying yourself about staying around Griffin. Your uncle just got himself named judge of the circuit court in Clayton County. That means that all cases will have to come before him in this area. That works well for you here."

"But back in Valdosta, I'd be summoned before the Reconstruction court, is that it?" I said dryly.

"That's about it," he said quietly. Knots appeared at the end of his jaw as he clenched his teeth.

"What about an arrest and change of venue for conflicting interests? Couldn't someone manage that here?" I asked.

His eyebrows rose.

"You have been learning more than dental work up there in Philadelphia, I see," he murmured. "Very well. There is the chance of that, but it would be a bit tenuous for a marshal to want to risk arresting a white man and transporting him back to Valdosta to stand trial for the killing of a nigra. Especially if that white man had killed one in self-defense."

He tossed his cigar over the side of the carriage and leaned forward, speaking sotto voce, "There's been a lot of changes since you went away, John. Some of Nathan Bedford Forrest's men—remember the general?—have slipped over from Mississippi to help us start up a little group to give protection to the white folks when the nigras get running a bit wild. Although I don't agree with some of what they've been doing, we have needed some sort of protection since those Yankees have given the nigra free rein in the South. Any white man who brings a complaint against a nigra will have his case thrown out of court and be fined for making false allegations. But the nigra can do pretty much what he wants. Or could have before Forrest's men came here. Lately, they've managed to make Griffin and the county fairly safe for the white folks."

"What about Uncle Robert? How did he get onto the bench?"

"Three weeks ago, two nigras were hanged from that big oak tree in front of the post office. They had tried to rape a white woman while her husband was off in the fields. She managed to get into the barn and up into the loft, where she held them off with a pitchfork until her son happened to get home to chase them away with a shotgun. Those nigras took her son to court for threatening them with a shotgun. The judge, one of those damned Reconstruction appointees, found him guilty of assault with a dangerous weapon and sentenced him to six months in jail and fined him five hundred dollars. No one has that kind of money down here unless it's a carpetbagger or scalawag.

"Well, Forrest's men paid a little call on the judge, and he decided to retire from the bench and head back north. That left a position on the bench open, and Rufus Butler decided that he'd better make a token gesture toward the whites in Georgia before they marched on Atlanta. Frankly, I think one of Forrest's men might have helped with a tiny suggestion at the right moment. No, John," he said grimly, "I don't think anyone in his right mind would try to take you back to Valdosta with Forrest's night riders around. Not for the sake of some nigras. Not anymore, at least. The South's becoming much different. Lincoln's men made sure of that. We can only play the cards that are dealt to us, John. Remember that."

"Damn shame that it's come to this," I said. Mattie reached over to pat my hand.

"You're home now, John," she said. "That's all that matters."

"Right," Father said, clapping his hands together and leaning back in the carriage. "Old Doc Flagg is looking to take a vacation and has offered to take you on a temporary basis."

"He still got his office in the old Merrit building on the

corner of West Solomon and State?" I asked. A cloud of dust rose up from the carriage's wheels. I coughed gently, waving irritably at the dust, trying to keep it from clogging my lungs.

"Oh, yes," Father answered. "And he's still collecting Indian teeth in that old gumdrop jar he keeps on his desk. Remember?"

I laughed and nodded. "And does he still close at three in the afternoon to go fishing?"

"Times haven't changed that much," Father answered as the carriage swung into the road leading to Uncle Robert's place.

A carriage had been drawn across the lane, blocking the path. From the backseat, my old nemesis Buford Tyler grinned. He had grown fatter in my absence, his jowls hanging over his collar like dewlaps on an old hound. He wore a brown checkered suit. In front of the carriage stood Jim Buchanon, the county sheriff, looking unhappy. Beside him stood two nigras in blue uniforms. Another held the reins of the team. I recognized the man in the carriage with Tyler: He had been one of the nigras at the swimming hole.

"Well, Holliday," Tyler said with relish. "It looks like the prodigal son has returned."

"Jim, what is this?" Father asked. Buchanon shook his head.

"Sorry, Major, but this man here says he's gotta warrant for John's arrest. Something to do with . . . aw, hell. You know what it's all about. Ain't a man in these parts don't know what happened."

"You can still back away from this, Jim," Father said.

"Now, Major—" Buchanon began, but Father cut him off.

"No, Jim. Not if you want to live in this county. You try to arrest John here and you know what will happen."

"Sounds like a threat to me, Sheriff," Tyler said. "Maybe you better arrest the old man, too."

"Hold on there," Uncle Robert said, stepping down. He walked between us and stared at Buchanon. He dropped his eyes, turning half away from Uncle Robert's glare. "You got a warrant issued in this county for his arrest? *In this county?*"

he emphasized. "If so, signed by whom? Not by me, and I'm the law around here."

"This is a Valdosta warrant," Tyler said.

"And not recognized in this county," Uncle Robert said angrily. "You have no authority here, Tyler. Neither you nor these tame nigras of yours. Get out of here and don't come back."

"You pathetic piece of white trash," Tyler said, his eyes narrowing until they looked like tiny bits of shot stuck in the suet of his flesh. "Ain't you learned yet that we are the law around here? Your court is just a Jim Crow bunch of non-sense. Ain't a goddamn thing you can do about it. Sheriff, do your duty."

Buchanon made a move toward the carriage, then stopped as Father leaned down and caught his arm. He looked up in surprise and made a movement to jerk his arm free, but Father held it tightly, drawing him close.

"You remember what you swore to, Jim Buchanon!" Father said softly. "You remember that or there won't be a stick of your house standing. You know how they work. You're either with them or you're against them. Work with these scum and everyone will know that you are against them."

"Don't threaten me, Major!" Buchanon said, jerking his arm free. His face paled. "I remember. I remember lots of things."

"Yes," Father said. "And remember that it was the people around here who voted you that badge. People around here, Jim! Not some goddamn northern carpetbagger with his pet nigras! You live around here, Jim!"

Buchanon stared for a long time into Father's eyes. Then he said without looking, "Can I see that warrant again, Mr. Tyler?"

Tyler handed the warrant to a nigra, who stepped forward and silently passed it to Buchanon. He unfolded it, glanced at it, then handed it to Uncle Robert.

"Judge, in your professional capacity, is this a legal document for these parts?" he asked.

Uncle Robert scanned it and shook his head. "No, Sheriff. This has not been cosignetl by me or my designate. It is not a Federal warrant, either. Therefore, these people have no jurisdiction in this county."

"Well," Buchanon said, turning to Tyler. "There you have it, Mr. Tyler. I'm sorry, but you didn't get the proper authorization. Sorry to have troubled you, Major," he said formally.

"Now, just a goddamn minute here!" Tyler said indignantly. "I don't care for your Jim Crow attitude around here!"

"Sheriff!" Father's voice rang out. "These men are trespassing. I want them arrested and held in Griffin until court convenes."

Tyler sputtered indignantly at Father's words, his face darkening with anger. I grinned at him.

"Remember when I shot your ear off a few years ago, Buford?" I said softly. "That's when you tried to steal Father's horse."

"You . . . you . . ." he choked. "That's a lie!"

"No, it isn't," Uncle Thomas said, coming up. "In fact, I'll testify to that. This was the man who tried to steal Ares when John came to find me after the War."

"A horse thief? And a witness?" Uncle Robert said. "Well, now." He rubbed his hands together. "That makes it even more official. Arrest the nigras and this man, Sheriff," he ordered. "We'll sort it all out in the morning."

"Arrest us and them night riders take us from you jail," one of the nigras complained, his eyes rolling whitely in his face.

"I don't think so," Father said. "But I do believe that you will be in jail for a few days. And as for you, Tyler," he added sternly, "I don't think that we'll have to worry about you for a spell."

Buchanon moved among them, taking their arms. He looked up at Tyler. "Am I gonna have to search you?"

"I don't carry any pistol," Tyler said.

"Don't reckon I believe you," Buchanon said. "Reckon I'll have to ask you to get out of that carriage."

Tyler turned and started to slide out of the carriage, then his hand fluttered inside his coat. Uncle Thomas stepped forward and grabbed his arm.

"Don't make another damn fool mistake," he said sharply. "You really think you can get away with that here in Griffin? You'll be dead before you can draw that pistol. And it will all be legal."

Tyler hesitated, then nodded and slumped back against the carriage. Uncle Thomas reached inside his coat and pulled out a small pistol and tossed it to Uncle Robert.

"I'll get you Hollidays for this!" Tyler panted, his eyes rolling wildly. His face turned red, then purple. Suddenly, his lips began to pout like a carp's mouth gasping for air. He grabbed his chest, gave a strangled gasp, and slumped to the ground. Uncle Thomas tried to catch him, but his bulk slipped through his fingers. He knelt swiftly, tearing Tyler's collar from his fleshy throat. Tyler's eyes popped open like a frog's, then glazed and turned upwards toward his lumpy forehead.

"Reckon that's it," Uncle Thomas said, rising. "Don't think you need to open court quite as early, Robert."

"No, it doesn't look like it," Uncle Robert said. He motioned to the nigras and Tyler. "You handle this, hear, Jim? Put those nigras in and guard them! We don't need any night-rider incidents on top of this. Going to be bad enough when I file a report that this man died of . . ."

"Choked to death on his own bile," I suggested. The others looked at me strangely.

"We'll think of something," Uncle Robert said.

"I'll take care of everything, Mr. Holliday," Buchanon said.

Father nodded and directed the driver to move Tyler's carriage out of the way. We continued on up to the house, where a lunch had been laid out on boards placed across two sawhorses under the large double oaks at the end of the lawn. I groaned as my relatives came running toward the carriage to greet me as we rolled to a stop. I looked at their shining faces. I didn't think there was a Holliday or McKey left anywhere in Georgia. I groaned again.

"Shame on you, John Henry!" Mattie whispered. "They've come a long ways to greet you. Why, you are a celebrity to the family, don't you know? Every one around here is proud of what you have done. You have shown them that it's still possible to be something despite what the War has made them."

I couldn't answer as Uncle Thomas reached up and seized my hand, pulling me from the carriage to embrace me.

"Welcome home, boy!" he whispered huskily. "Welcome home! I'm sorry about that bastard back there. I had no idea he was waiting in the lane."

I enthusiastically returned his embrace, choking back the tears.

"It's good to be home," I said. Suddenly, a coughing spell exploded from my chest. I pushed away from Uncle Thomas and groped beneath my coat for the flask. But before I could open it, something gave way in my lungs, and I suddenly tasted copper in my mouth. I spat the mouthful of sputum on the ground and felt my flesh crawl as a bright red splotch appeared with a thick, dark worm in its middle. I knew that the bright red of the blood came from my lungs, and if I had any doubt, there was a piece of me, lying like a worm, upon the ground.

11

Atlanta. I stood outside the train depot and looked with despair over what was to be my new home. Six months had passed since I had returned in triumph to Griffin, but as with Caesar's triumph, my own Ides of March had quickly arrived. My health continued to deteriorate, the coughing attacks coming more frequently and lasting longer, necessitating my use of more and more whiskey. Mattie and I had our first quarrel over that, but even she knew that it was better than the laudanum that left me an inert form for most of the day and made dentistry impossible.

Both of us pretended that what I had expectorated upon my arrival was simply an accident due to poor food I had been served during my travel to the South. Mattie pretended that she did not know that the bright red splash of blood was lung blood, and I went along with her dream. Yet I knew, and she knew, what that splash meant. After old Doc Flagg returned from his long overdue vacation, my move to Atlanta to set up a new practice seemed quite appropriate. I had grown thinner and thinner as my appetite waned, until at last even Father had to agree that something had to be done. My move to Atlanta might be the answer.

We all ignored the significance of that bloody splotch on the hard-baked clay of Georgia. Mattie and, God help me, myself, pretended that my health was not as tenuous as we thought. Hector Morgan, Griffin's veterinarian who also doubled as a doctor, allowed as how I might have a simple case of the northern flu, and suggested Atlanta as a place to effect a cure. I knew, after looking in his eyes, that he was as resigned as was I to what I had. Yet, I hoped. I hoped.

Atlanta had found a new industry: the sick and the tired. Large advertisements and stories about miraculous cures were circulated in the best newspapers, encouraging those who suffered from chronic illnesses to come and enjoy Atlanta's healthful climate.

From where I stood, however, I could not imagine Atlanta to be any more healthful than Griffin. Atlanta was still rebuilding from the War when Sherman had marched his arsonists across Georgia. Blocks of blackened ruins waited patiently for the street crews to demolish them to make way for new buildings after they had finished getting the railroads and the industries back in working form. In 1872, the rolling mills and ironworks were just starting to swing into full production with profits being poured back into the business. Some of the reminders of Sherman's visit had been taken down and some streets had been macadamized, but the War was still visible to those who made their way around Atlanta, and it was still occasionally being refought in the saloons between Southerners and off-duty Federal troops under the command of Colonel Ruger.

I sighed and picked up my valise and stepped down to catch a horsecar on the street railway system that wove intermittently through the town.

Father had arranged rooms for me through an old friend with whom he had read law and served with in Mexico, although I had a cousin whom I called Uncle Philip on the Fitzgerald side of my family who was a medical doctor in Atlanta at the time. I could have stayed with him, he claimed in letters he and Father exchanged, but Father knew that Uncle Philip had a family that was growing and a practice that he was trying to establish and thought it would be best for me to have my own rooms. I was happy about this decision, for I knew Uncle Philip was also finding his way back into the Roman Catholic church, and I had no desire to come under his fervent return to Catholicism. Uncle Philip had, however, made arrangements for me to join in practice with Dr. Arthur C. Ford in his offices at the corner of Alabama and Whitehall Streets, and for that I was grateful.

My rooms were as modest as they had been above Demorat's studio in Philadelphia. A stately mansion house that by some miracle had escaped Sherman's fire had been broken up into apartments by a widow whose husband had been killed at Gettysburg during Pickett's Charge. She was a stately woman who dressed in soft gray, well mannered, but, I could tell from the way her eyes kept wandering over me, feeling the strain of her widow's weeds. Mrs. John Wilson's name—*Call me Charlotte, please, Dr. Holliday*—was prominent among the blue bloods of Atlanta, who did not exclude her from their social life simply because she had fallen on hard times. Everyone in Atlanta was still trying to rise from those hard times and although pretensions were still maintained, the social pecking order dictated by cash on the barrelhead had been discreetly altered to accommodate the new times. I felt her attraction the moment I pressed her damp palm and noticed the blood begin to hammer in the vein in her throat, a long, graceful ivory column upon which the head of a Grecian model had been perched. The parlor had been carpeted in a light blue plush with petit-pointed leaves. A crystal chandelier hung overhead and the room was ringed with marble-topped tables.

After a cup of tea, she showed me to my rooms, fussing around them to make sure I would be comfortable and leaving an open suggestion that she would be available anytime if I had "difficulties."

I took stock of my new lodgings after she was called away by a servant. I had a small living room barely adequate to hold a loveseat and chair and table, a dressing room in which a desk had been placed for my use, and a bedroom with a comfortable bed complete with mosquito curtain for use during the "wet" season. I sighed, and quickly unpacked before taking myself around to Uncle Philip's office to inform him of my arrival.

One look at Uncle Philip's offices was enough to suggest his intentions of moving into the upper echelon of Atlanta society. His offices consisted of a waiting room, a surgery, a consultation room, and a private office. The walls had been painted a soft white with burgundy velvet drapes pulled back in sweeping folds and tied to the sides of the windows opening onto a small rose garden, presumably where patients could stroll while waiting for Uncle Philip's attention. The garden was empty when I arrived: apparently no one was feeling well enough for a stroll through the garden, although I availed myself of it while waiting for Uncle Philip to prescribe laudanum for a dowager suffering from some undetermined "vapors."

Uncle Philip rose when his nurse showed me into his inner office. He grabbed my hand, enthusiastically pumping it.

"Welcome! Welcome, John!" he cried. He wore his hair swept forward to cover a receding hairline. His cheeks were red with health, and lean. His clothes were of a harsh, radical cut, severe lines that suggested the severity of his position in society. He motioned me to a seat near his desk. I took it while he settled himself behind his desk, steepling his fingers and staring intently at me. I recognized the pose and smothered a laugh.

"Now then," he said, gesturing inquisitively at a pitcher of water, its sides beaded with moisture, on a tray by a small table. I shook my head. "Well. What seems to be the problem? Your father said something about coughing up a bit of blood?"

I nodded. "I've had this nagging cough for quite some time," I said politely. "It doesn't seem to want to go away. I thought it was just a bad cold or something that I picked up in Philadelphia."

"Are you taking anything for it?"

"Whenever I have to," I said cautiously. "A little whiskey seems to stay it."

He frowned, leaning back in his chair.

"Be careful," he warned. "Whiskey can easily take control of a man. It would be better if you used something else."

"Well, it is better than laudanum. That leaves me unable to work. And I must work," I said, warming to my subject as he nodded. "After all, a man must work."

"Yes," he said. He leaned back, patting the pads of the fingers of one hand against his lips. "Yes, but there are other things that we might try that would work equally as well. Perhaps even better. Let's take a look."

He rose and stepped around the desk to me. He tapped my jaw impatiently. Obediently, I opened. He leaned forward, using a flat stick to push my tongue down, gazing into the recesses of my throat. He took a stethoscope from the pocket of his coat and motioned for me to remove my coat and shirt. His eyebrows rose as I slipped out of the harness of the holster for the Navy Colt.

"Is that necessary?" he asked.

"In these times, yes, I believe so," I said.

"The romanticism of the youth," he sighed. He impatiently tapped the stethoscope on the palm of his hand as I finished disrobing, then leaned forward, directing me to cough at intervals. Finally, he nodded, and stepped around to his chair.

"I'm sure we can do better than that home remedy you've

been using," he said. He leaned forward and pulled a pad to him. He took a pen from the desk and scribbled furiously with it, the nib scratching loudly on the pad with the vigor of his writing. He handed the sheet to me. I read it: copious draughts of mineral spring water with applications of Stafford's Olive Tar.

"I think that will help get rid of the bug, whatever it is," he said confidently. "I've used this before with some of my patients who have a persistent cough. It's never failed."

"Olive tar?" I said skeptically.

"Be sure that the mineral water is magnetized," he said, shaking his finger warningly. "Otherwise, it is useless except for a rub."

"I see," I said. I folded the prescription carefully and placed it in a pocket of my vest.

"Be certain that you drink a lot of the mineral water," he cautioned, leaning forward and waving a finger at me. "And stay away from whiskey. That will do you no good. It will drag you down to the depths of the poor souls who cannot put a bottle aside. Mind me, now. Stay away from the whiskey! If you find you are having a hard time getting away from it, call me. There are those of us who can help. A little laudanum won't do you any harm, either. I know it interferes with your work, but sometimes we simply have to make sacrifices."

"Of course," I said blandly. "I understand perfectly."

"Good." He rose, signaling that our meeting was over. "Margaret and I would love to have you over for dinner this Sunday. Will twelve o'clock be appropriate? After church, of course."

"I have just arrived," I said dryly. "I have no other appointments."

My sarcasm slipped over his head. Over the next few months, I was to recognize this as a trait of his: Nothing that did not fit into his vision of world order would be acknowledged.

"Then we'll see you at noon," he said, grabbing my hand again while escorting me to the door. "Please be prompt, John."

He waited until I had promised, then gave me a curt nod and closed the door in front of me. I stood for a moment, wondering what to do, then decided to explore Atlanta.

I soon discovered that Atlanta did not offer much in the way of entertainment. Pease and His Wife's saloon seemed to be the popular drinking establishment. The patrons of Pease and His Wife's were more interested in exotic drinks such as White Hats than the simple whiskey and beer of the dives along Water Street in Philadelphia. I wandered down to the Chicago Ale Depot and had a whiskey. I listened to a couple of men arguing about a challenge that had recently appeared in the newspaper. Intrigued by what they said, I bought a copy of the *Atlanta Constitution* and drank an ice cream soda at Thompson's Restaurant while I read it, laughing to see how proper society insisted that gamblers be heavily fined on one hand while conducting a tongue-in-cheek lottery on the other. I was interested to note that several lending libraries were in town and made a mental note to visit them. I also took note of a free mineral spring that the city fathers swore had been proven to be highly beneficial to "consumptives and dyspeptic sufferers." I tossed the paper aside and rose, heading back to my rooms. A cough rumbled from my chest. I felt tired and perspiration began to dot my face. I had had enough of Atlanta.

Back in my room, I had a copy of Chapman's translation of Homer's *Iliad* that I had been reading. I decided to finish it. I had found a strange kinship with Achilles. The morrow would be soon enough for me to visit my benefactor, Dr. Ford. My step quickened as lines of Homer began rolling from memory.

. . . And Ackilles, proud Ackilles, sulked in his tent. . . .

The office I shared with Dr. Ford consisted of three rooms in what one might have called the "business district" of Atlanta—if such a district actually existed in 1872. In reality, the business district, like all the other districts that fell prey to Sherman's arsonists, were in the process of rebuilding. The marketing and manufacturing centers and the shipping areas where cotton and wheat and, in season, melons were held until shipping dates were about six blocks from us at the railroad center. Down the street from us, Kimball's Opera House, a fine old establishment that once was home to some of the best productions of its day, was now the home for the legislature and all the state's business offices, including the post office, while DeGive's Opera House provided the lone entertainment for the aesthetes who occupied box seats regardless of the show.

We had one room designated as a waiting room, one room for working on our patients, and one room we shared as an office for consultations. We took patients in shifts with Ford's niece, Eula, serving as our receptionist and May Ann, a young woman recently graduated from St. Anthony's Academy, working as our nurse.

I joined Ford on the first Monday in August that year. The summer had been a wet one and clouds of mosquitoes rose from the pools like mist when eveningtime came, bringing with them Asiatic flu and an itch that wouldn't go away until it finally drove a man to mad fits. But the sweltering days drummed steadily against foreheads to the rapid beat of a marching band, the temperature rising and creating a thin feverish shimmer of mirage. The air was hot and heavy, weighing down the lungs, soaking clothes within a half block. The dog days, we called them.

Ford was a dour man, a Methodist, with a Masonic emblem dangling prominently from his watch chain, which stretched across his ample middle. He wore a long, black frock coat fitted wide around the middle to accommodate his potbelly, and trousers with thin stripes, strap-bottomed in the old-fashioned manner. He had a single-breasted suit and a five-button vest in a subdued pearl silk. In the office, he wore a long, white laboratory coat cut loose around the arms that he would button across his vest before bending over to peer into a patient's mouth. He was brisk with his patients, working them in and out of the chair with little time given to amenities.

"Don't be dawdling with them," he warned me the first day I reported in for work. "Get them in and out of the chair before they manage to work themselves up to a state of nervousness where they'll vomit all over you. That's the best way. You'll have plenty of time after they're out of the chair to visit if that's your style. Frankly, it's a waste of time and time's money. Besides, most people don't like to visit with dentists while they are visiting them. They'd just as soon leave and put it all behind them."

I nodded. A cough rumbled gently from my throat. He looked closely at me.

"A summer cold? That's the worst kind. You need an asafetida bag." He sniffed and frowned. "Have you been drinking?"

"Medicine," I said, automatically thumping the flask in my coat pocket.

He stared levelly at me for a long minute, then meticulously took off his black coat and carefully hung it on a hanger behind the door to the office. He shrugged into his white coat and glanced into the waiting room. Eula's doughy face broke into a smile, and she shook her head.

"Let me know when she comes in," he said. He closed the door and turned to me. "An old dowager given to elderberry wine and laudanum that she calls her medicine. Be careful. Sometimes that sort of thing gets out of hand."

"I'm careful," I said.

He nodded. "You do that. You comfortable?" I nodded. "Good. If there's anything you need . . ."

But it was the thing that people said when there wasn't anything else to say. I knew there wasn't anything he would do; he had done enough by taking me into practice with him, although he would be getting an extra pair of hands for half the price of dental work he wouldn't have to do. It didn't matter; there wasn't anything he could do for me. There wasn't anything anyone could do for me.

I had no appetite when I showed up at Uncle Philip's house for Sunday dinner, embarrassing his wife by toying with the roast beef and carrots and peas on my plate. Her lips grew tighter and tighter until finally I excused myself, saying that I feared I was coming down with the flu. Uncle Philip saw me solicitously to the door, but it was the last time I was invited to their home.

The coughing returned with a vengeance as the dog days rolled on into autumn, turning the leaves of the trees to deep colors, scarlet and gold, before winter rushed in with a November storm filled with sleet and freezing rain. My cough worsened. Patients began to specify Dr. Ford instead of me, as my coughing bothered them. I don't blame them; it is hard enough to have a stranger looking into one's mouth, let alone one coughing into it. My nights became nightmares in which I awoke in the middle, soaked with perspiration, my sheets a tangled shroud wrapped around me. I began drinking four or five ounces of whiskey in the morning simply to stop coughing and get the energy to move.

Finally, the night came when I awoke coughing, spraying blood over the sheets and blankets of my bed. For a moment I was afraid that I would bleed to death. I grabbed a pint of whiskey and choked it down, gagging as it mixed with blood and sputum before sliding down my throat. Eventually, however, the coughing ceased, and I sank back gratefully upon my bed, exhausted, a weight forcing my chest down while I fought to bring it back up, pumping air into my lungs much like a blacksmith billows his fire.

Charlotte discovered me in the morning when I didn't appear for breakfast, and she summoned Uncle Philip and told Dr. Ford. Both appeared almost at the same time. Uncle Philip examined me carefully, then shook his head, putting his stethoscope back in his bag.

"I'm sorry, John," he said, gently pushing my shoulder. "I'm afraid that there is nothing that we can do for you. I certainly miscalled this one. You have consumption, and it has advanced to a stage where there's nothing left of your lungs."

"Consumption? Miscalled?" I echoed.

Dr. Ford shook his head, turning away. He took a handkerchief the size of a tablecloth from his pocket and noisily blew his nose, trumpeting like a swan. Charlotte made a little click in her throat and brought her shawl up to her mouth as if she was afraid to breathe the same air as I.

It took a moment before what Uncle Philip was saying registered, then I felt the power of his words sink through the frail shell of flesh to my soul. I weakly motioned to the flask beside my bed. Uncle Philip frowned and shook his head. Dr. Ford took it and handed it to me.

"What harm will it do now?" he demanded of Uncle Philip.

"A man can still die with dignity," Uncle Philip retorted, then turned beet red as the impact of his words came home to him. He glanced quickly at me, then away.

"A death is still only a death. How a man dies is immaterial. There is only the man to consider," Dr. Ford said sternly.

"How long?" I whispered numbly.

Uncle Philip shook his head.

"I don't know. Not long. Perhaps four months." He glanced at the bedsheets where my blood had mixed with fragments from my lungs. "Perhaps six at the outside."

"There's nothing you can do? Besides mineral water and olive tar?" I asked sardonically. He flushed at the temper of my words and shook his head.

"We don't know much about consumption," he said, helplessly fluttering his hands. He ran his hands through his hair. "What works for one may not work for another. I do know that a hemorrhage such as this usually indicates that the end isn't far."

"What will happen?" I asked.

He looked away. I pushed myself up on my pillows. The effort brought a fine sheen of perspiration to my body. I reached out and grabbed his hand. He tried to pull away, but I gripped tightly, bringing a grimace to his features.

"One day, or night, you will have a massive hemorrhage. It will be so massive that you will not be able to get rid of the blood. You will," he hesitated, searching for the word. I pressed harder. He gasped and glared at me. "You will drown in your own blood."

I released his hand. He drew back, rubbing his hand gently. Behind him, Charlotte began to cry. I felt the numbness of his words. I thought about what had happened during the short life I had led. I thought about Belle, then Mattie and the plans that we had made: the house that we designed one evening in Father's study when it was raining outside and we could not walk through the pecan groves, the children we would have—two boys and a girl who would look just like Mattie, I had insisted, bringing a blush to her face—our marriage, my practice, everything that young people dream about together down to the design on the shape of our crystal and the books that would line the walls of my study. All gone now, destroyed by an unfeeling God who saw in my being a creature upon whom he could play his omniscient pranks, promising a bright future in glowing and beatific terms, then drawing the dreams away in one powerful sweep, leaving a confused and befuddled human behind who had dared to dream the dreams of a benevolent God.

I wept. Those tears were the last tears of my life. From that moment on, I was dead to the world even if my body refused to follow the rules of circumstance. Father arrived with Uncle Philip the day after Uncle Philip's diagnosis of my massive hemorrhage, bringing with him the papers consigning to me the lands of Mother's will.

"Hello, John," he said, entering after Charlotte brought him up. He glanced around my rooms, nodding to himself. He walked into the room, dropped his valise on the floor, and crossed to my bed. He reached down and grasped my hands in his.

"Philip sent a wire," he explained. Tears shone brightly in his eyes, and I knew then, for the second time in my life, that Father loved me.

"Good of him," I whispered. My words slurred through the whiskey I had drunk since awakening that morning. I reached for the smeared glass at my bed table that still held a quarter-inch of whiskey. My fingers shook so that I couldn't pick it up. Father quickly lifted my head and pressed the glass to my lips. I drained the whiskey in one swallow. He glanced at the empty bottle on the table, then gently lowered me back against my pillow and crossed to his valise, opening it and carelessly throwing its contents aside until he found

the whiskey bottle he had purchased in Valdosta. He brought
the bottle to my bedside, filled the tumbler, and again raised
my head, pressing the glass to my lips. I drank half its contents thirstily. He gently lowered my head to the pillow and
placed the glass upon the table.

"Really, Henry!" Uncle Philip protested. "You are encouraging drunkenness!"

"What harm will it do?" Father answered, withering Uncle
Philip with a hard stare. "Your medicines and prescriptions
have done him no good despite your assurances that you
could help him. Now stay out of this, you damn hypocrite,
until I have finished. Then I will have a few words for you. A
summer cold. Pine tar and mineral water. *Phaugh!*" He
shook his head in disgust.

Uncle Philip flushed and started to respond, but a look into
Father's eyes convinced him of the wisdom of silence. He
withdrew into a corner of the room, pouting, but watching
carefully what transpired between us. He reminded me of a
turkey buzzard waiting for the carcass to die.

"I guess I'm always a disappointment to you, Father," I
whispered.

He smoothed my hair back from my forehead.

"No, John. You may have frustrated me a time or two, but
you have not been a disappointment to me." He cleared his
throat, looking away from me. "I have never told you this,
perhaps I should have, I don't know, but I have never loved
anyone as much as I have loved you. Not even your mother."

"Perhaps you should have told me this before," I said. "It
seems terribly anticlimactic now."

A self-mocking grin twisted his lips. "Perhaps. But it is the
truth. I told your mother this once. It nearly destroyed her."
He looked into my eyes and I felt the truth of his words.
"That was when she began taking the laudanum."

"Perhaps you shouldn't have told her," I whispered.

He shrugged. "What's done is done. You're probably
right. But hindsight gives the farmer a different crop to plant
when the drought takes the first one." He paused. "I can

arrange for Mattie to come. I didn't have time to send a wire. I came straightaway."

I felt a quickening of my pulse for a long moment, then shook my head.

"No, I don't want to see her. Please. It's best this way."

He frowned. "I don't understand. I thought . . ."

"Yes. But I would rather she remember me as I was rather than as what I have become."

"You are still you. Despite this damn consumption, you are still you. You can still"—he began, then broke off when I rolled my head to stare at him.

"Still what, Father? Give her two months before she has to nurse me to the end? Change my sheets? Clean my messes? And if I last four months, what then? Will she hate me because I have forced her into a life that she never considered? No, I think not. Let her find someone else and remember me as I was."

Tears came into Father's eyes and he pressed my shoulder gently, but firmly. "All right, John Henry," he said huskily. "All right. Just as you wish."

He rose and crossed to his valise, then opened it and brought a sheaf of papers back to me. He pulled a chair up next to the bed and sat beside me.

"Now, Philip says you have only a few months. If he knows what he's talking about this time." His eyebrows raised in question as he glanced at Philip, who stiffly nodded.

"But," he emphasized, "I have talked with others who say that if you go out west to a drier climate, say, Texas, for example, you might be able to stretch that to a year or even more."

"Really, Henry! This is . . ." Uncle Philip sputtered.

"Shut up," Father said quietly.

Uncle Philip took a look at Father's face and lapsed into silence, crossing to the window away from the bed and pulling back the curtain to stare out the window onto the street below. Father turned back to me. He wiped the tears from his eyes.

"Now then," he said. "There is hope, as I've said. It seems, given the alternative, that the best thing for you is to give it a try. I've got a thousand in ready cash for you here." He produced a purse and tossed it onto the table beside the bottle of whiskey. "There's money. But it's not enough. We'll have to sell off a part of your inheritance to give you the extra you need to make your way until you find a place to settle."

He picked up a sheaf of papers, selected one, and laid it upon my chest. I picked it up, reading it despite my shaking hand.

"Now," he continued, his voice becoming businesslike, "I propose to sell this one acreage for the money you need for now. I suggest that you give me a power of attorney that will allow me to manage the rest of your estate to earn the money to help you over the time when"—his voice hesitated—"well, you know."

"When I can't help myself," I said. He nodded. I shrugged. I had no choice other than that.

"Then let's do it," I said.

He produced a pen and I signed, my signature a shaky scrawl across the bottom of the pages. He carefully folded them and tucked them away into a breast pocket.

"John—" he began, but I cut him off.

."I know, Father," I said. I reached for his hand, pressing it. Tears came into his eyes, and he cried then for me. I glanced out the window beside my bed; a light snow was falling. I remembered then that it was December, the darkest time of the year, and I was just twenty-one.

Into the void that was once my soul flooded the greatest loneliness I had ever known.

three

WAR

1

And so my western adventure began. I felt as though I had been cast out into Purgatory. Yet even as I watched the passing country with mixed emotions, I felt a certain excitement, an anxiousness to let the adventure begin.

I took the train from Atlanta to Chattanooga and from there to Memphis, taking a berth on one of Kimball's sleeping cars. The car was not filled; only two other berths were taken by salesmen traveling in the same direction as I. One sold farm machinery, while the other was a liquor salesman. I got along the best with the latter, spending most of the twenty-nine-hour trip from Chattanooga to Memphis pleasantly sampling his wares while playing a few hands of poker. By the time we arrived in Memphis, I was a couple of hundred dollars richer, and the farm machinery salesman was angry and frustrated.

We arrived in Memphis two days before Christmas in 1872. I arranged to have Ares sent on ahead on a stock boat while I boarded the *Natchez* for the trip to New Orleans. Ares had been very unhappy about being taken onboard, sending one of the stock handlers flying into the water when the unfortunate man got too close to his hooves and insisted on trying to goad Ares from behind. The man's friend pulled back a whip and started to strike Ares. He quickly changed his mind when I showed him the working end of the Navy Colt and promised to send him to hell minus his head if he ever laid a finger on my horse.

The manager came running down the dock to see what was causing the commotion and when apprised of what I intended, promptly fired the two and hired a young black boy to go with Ares to New Orleans. Ares kept tossing his head and looking back inquisitively at me, nickering with disappointment when I didn't follow him onboard. I promised him sugar and an apple upon arriving in New Orleans and made sure the pickaninny knew how seriously I took Ares's treatment.

Life aboard the *Natchez* was much different from life on the railroad. Everything seemed touched with gilt in rococo grandeur. Ornate gingerbread ran around the salon, which had been heavily covered with Turkish carpet. I had a small cabin to myself with a louvered door that let in a bit more of the cold air than I wanted, but I still enjoyed it more than I had my berth in the Kimball car. In fact, all efforts had been made for the comfort of *Natchez*'s passengers. The food was plentiful, although I had little appetite for it, preferring to sample the bartender's wares as my cough became worse from the damp. The bartender's Brandy Smashes and Stone Fences did little, however, to assuage my cough. I seemed to need straight applications of bourbon from an excellent Kentucky still in Nelson County that was just getting reestablished. From the taste of Evan Williams bourbon, I predicted a long and prosperous run. The professional gamblers waited until the afternoon of the first day before gently suggesting I join them in a game.

Jack Sturtevant had been surreptitiously watching me sip bourbon all morning and reckoned around 3 P.M. that I was primed for pumping. I almost laughed as I watched his careful approach, carrying a tumbler of watered coffee designed to look like whiskey. He wore a pearl gray frock coat with a black velvet collar and a bunch of lace at his chin. His legs were encased in tight-fitting riding breeches with calfskin boots that had never stepped into stirrups gleaming on his feet. A large diamond flashed on the ring finger of his left hand, while a pearl stickpin kept his carefully folded cravat from raveling down his chest and spoiling the starch of the ruffles. His hair was carefully pomaded back and heavily scented with bay rum.

"Good afternoon," he said, his voice carrying a Mississippi drawl. "May I join you?"

"Please," I said. For a lark, I thickened my accent. A slight gleam appeared in his eyes, and I knew that he had me pegged for a bumpkin. I nodded at a chair across from me, refraining from rising like a gentleman. He pulled it out and sat with a sigh, carefully placing his glass at his left hand, well away from me.

"Jack Sturtevant," he said, holding out his hand. I took it; it was soft and dry.

"Dr. John Henry Holliday," I said.

"Georgia?" he asked, raising his eyebrows. I nodded. "Were you with Forrest Jackson by any chance during the War?"

I knew then I was being played with; he was a poor judge of character who could not have ascertained my age within a few years and still have come up short enough to allow me to have been with Jackson unless I was a drummer boy. Of course, he could have been playing on my vanity by pretending to take me for a veteran, but somehow I didn't think so. There was no condescension about him. I shook my head.

"No," I said ruefully. "My father was with the Twenty-seventh Georgia Regiment."

"A fine outfit, sir," he said. "A fine outfit. If you'll pardon me, you appear a bit, ah, young to be a doctor."

Too young to be a doctor and old enough to have fought in the War with Jackson? Perhaps I needed to rethink my estimation of him. I shrugged.

"I just graduated. I'm looking for a place to establish a practice now."

"I see," he said. "I hope you do not take offense, sir."

"Oh no," I said hastily. "I realize my youth is a shortcoming for me, sir. I was fortunate enough to have a father who insisted upon my education."

"That explains it," he answered. "Apparently, your father was a man of means. Not many men your age have had the good fortune to manage an education since the 'troubles.'"

"Yes," I said sadly, deliberately taking a long drink from my glass of whiskey. His eyes sharpened at the intake. I smiled to myself. "Fortunately, we lived in a place that remained untouched by the War. A small place in the back-waters of Georgia."

"You were very fortunate," he said. "I have a small farm east of Nashville, but I'm afraid the cotton market isn't what it was before the War."

I glanced at his hands; they hadn't touched dirt in quite a few years. He sipped from his glass. He tapped his fingers against the green felt of the table and glanced across at a couple of men dressed in frock coats and trousers with broad stripes running down their legs and gaitered to soft, low-heeled boots. He feigned a sudden interest and nodded at the pair.

"What do you say to a game of cards to idle away a little time?" he asked. "Perhaps those gentlemen would be willing to join us."

I looked over at the pair pretending to ignore us and pretended to gnaw my lower lip nervously and indecisively.

"Perhaps a hand or two," I ventured cautiously.

He nodded with satisfaction and rose and crossed to them. He took off his hat and introduced himself, but I could tell from the careful distance they kept between them that they were no strangers. I casually readjusted the set of my coat while remaining in my chair at the table, loosening the Deringer in my right vest pocket and pressing my arm against the Navy Colt tucked in the holster beneath my left arm. Pinkerton's other Deringer was in my left coat pocket. I had felt foolish for a moment when placing the pistols upon my person that morning, but I had caught the way I was appraised by the gamblers in the salon when I had ventured out of my cabin the night before in search of a drink. Now, I grimly told myself, perhaps I wasn't shouting in the dark as much as I had thought.

"Well," Sturtevant said, coming to my table with them. "This is Dr. John Henry Holliday, late of Georgia."

I rose to meet them, offering my hand to the one on my right.

"Dick Wilson," he said, touching my fingers briefly. The

other gripped a bit harder, but I could feel the absence of callus on his palms.

"And I'm Bob Bickman," he said.

"Are you gentlemen going to New Orleans on business?" I asked innocently as they seated themselves.

"Tobacco," Bickman said, placing his glass at his elbow. "I'm trying to open a new market."

"And you, sir?" I asked, looking at Wilson. He gave me a thin smile.

"Lumber," he answered. "I plan on floating a few shipments down if I can find buyers. There's a market for walnut and black oak down there. A new fad for ladies' drawing rooms, I'm told. Thought I would check it out."

"Well," I said brightly. "Maybe we'll be able to help each other out. If I hear of anything, I'll let you know."

"Yes," Sturtevant said, signaling to the black man behind the bar. "We should keep an eye out for each other. One can never know when he'll need friends in New Orleans."

The nigra brought two packs of cards on a silver tray to our table. He gave me an impassive look as Sturtevant made a show of taking the cards from the tray. He showed us the seal on the cards before breaking them open, but I knew that didn't mean anything. Sutton had told a story about one of his uncles in Baltimore who manufactured cards, doubling his business through prearranged contacts with professional gamblers and providing them with marked cards fresh in the deck.

Wilson's left hand slipped inside his vest, and when it emerged with a sheaf of bills, a tiny gold band had been added to his ring finger. I knew what that meant: a "shiner" had been added, a ring set with a tiny mirror or highly polished surface that would reflect the cards dealt. A gambler with a good memory would be able to remember all cards a mark held, arranging his partners' hands to beat what the mark held. I had no doubt as to who was the mark in the game.

"Draw poker?" Sturtevant asked.

We all nodded and he quickly dealt the cards, the paste-boards flitting smoothly from his hand with a practiced twist of his wrist. I fingered the cards as I picked them up, sliding my fingers along their smooth edges to test for pinpricks, finding none. The cards were large, the corners square with no figures or pips in the corners or double-head royalty to indicate their value. I permitted myself a small grin. Gambler cards designed to give the professional an edge when the amateur spread the cards way apart to tell the differences between jacks and kings, or reversed them. The differences were in the feet and how they looked in the various suits. But a gambler who was aware of that also had the edge by using it to his advantage, spreading the cards when he wanted to bluff.

I glanced at my cards, making a conscious effort to spread them, although I knew what I had: two kings, a trey, a deuce, and a four. I was under the gun and opened with a dollar wager. Sturtevant glanced at the others, his eyes lowering fractionally, marking me as a rank amateur to them. Wilson allowed a tiny smile to play along his lips.

"Call," Bickman said, throwing in a dollar.

Wilson raised two dollars and Sturtevant answered him with another dollar raise. I hesitated, pretending to consider my cards, then reluctantly added three more dollars to the pool. Bickman followed.

"Cards?" Sturtevant asked.

"Three, I guess," I said, keeping the pair of kings and dis-carding the others.

Sturtevant slipped three cards off the deck to me. Bickman took one, Wilson two, and Sturtevant one. I glanced at my cards, spreading them as if trying to make them out. I had picked up another king on the draw and a five and six. I smiled and took a sip of whiskey before betting.

"This will cost you, gentlemen," I said. I slipped three dol-lars into the pool.

"I think we are in the presence of a poker player," Bick-man said. "But I can add another dollar to that."

He tossed four dollars onto the pool. Wilson and Sturtevant called. I raised another dollar, and everyone stayed with me. I knew they would; it was considered good form to let the mark win the first few hands to give him confidence, although the pot would be small. The idea was to let him eventually suggest the raising of the stakes after he was convinced lady luck was riding on his side. Although we had not set a limit to our bets, the strategy was a good one to follow.

As I predicted, I won the first three hands. When the deal returned to Sturtevant, the amount of the raises casually rose from two and three dollars to five and six. I was still allowed to win two hands out of every four, however. I drank a bit more whiskey, smothering a cough that threatened to bubble from my chest when Sturtevant lit a cigar and a cloud of blue smoke filtered to me.

"I'm sorry," he said solicitously. "Does my cigar offend you?"

I shook my head. "Oh, no. Frankly, I might have one myself."

"Permit me," he said, offering me one of his cheroots. I took it and clipped the end with a small silver knife he handed to me. I lit it, cautiously rolling the smoke around in my mouth. It was fragrant and light, and I relaxed back against my chair, enjoying it.

"From Cuba," he said. "That's where the best cigars are made."

"I agree," Wilson said. Bickman laughed.

"Afraid I don't partake," he said ruefully. "I don't mind selling tobacco, but I have never been able to use it."

"One of the last refuges of the gentleman," Sturtevant said. "It still gives man a chance to excuse himself from the ladies when it's time to leave."

We laughed politely at the innuendo. I glanced at the cards Wilson had slid across the table to me. I didn't have much: only two treys and nothing to make from an eight, jack, and queen.

Sturtevant bet five dollars. I called and was promptly raised five dollars by Bickman. Wilson raised another five dollars and Sturtevant five more. Suddenly it was fifteen dollars to me. I glanced again at my cards. Out of the corner of my eye, I caught the slight nod that Wilson gave Sturtevant.

"This is getting a bit steep," I protested mildly. Sturtevant laughed.

"You're the big winner," he said, nodding at the pile of money in front of me. "We need to be getting a little of it back."

"If you can," I said with the arrogance of a novice winner. I shoved fifteen dollars out in front of me, hesitated, then added another five to the pool.

"But it will cost you another five to find out if you can," I said.

Sturtevant glanced again at Wilson. His eyebrow raised faintly. I knew this was to be the big pool of the night.

"You are right, Dr. Holliday: this is getting a little expensive, but I'll try for the draw," Bickman said, calling my raise.

Wilson followed his example. Sturtevant smiled and raised me another five. I called, as did the other two. Sturtevant took two cards, dropping his discards in the deadwood to his right. I tossed three cards onto the deadwood. Wilson slid three across to me. Bickman took one, made a face, and threw his entire hand onto the deadwood.

"Nothing," he said in disgust.

Wilson gave him a slight smile and dealt himself two cards, carelessly throwing his two cards to the left of the deadwood, near Sturtevant's hand.

"I'll check," Sturtevant said, looking at me.

I took a quick look: I had been given the other two treys and a king. I promptly bet ten dollars. A smug expression came over Wilson's face. He shook his head and dropped his hand casually on top of the deadwood and toyed absently with it.

"Your ten and ten more," Sturtevant said, shoving twenty dollars out into the center of the table. Wilson's hand slipped off the table into his lap. I knew then that I had the winning hand at the moment in the game.

"Well, since we're all throwing caution to the wind, let's

make that, er, fifty more," I said, laying sixty dollars on top of the pile.

"My, you must be confident," Sturtevant said. He dropped his hand to the side of his coat and pulled out a handkerchief, wiping his forehead and casually dropping it on top of his cards. He reached inside a breast pocket and removed a thin sheaf of bills, quickly counted them, then tossed the sheaf into the center of the table.

"But are you confident enough?" he asked challengingly. "There's three hundred on top of your fifty."

He leaned back in his chair and blew a smoke ring at the ceiling.

I squinted anxiously at my cards and coughed gently, feeling the old recklessness build up inside. A fine sheen of perspiration broke out on my forehead. I became conscious of the sudden quiet in the salon and glanced around at the small crowd that had gathered around our table after Sturtevant's last bet. I gave him a tiny smile.

"Well, Mr. Sturtevant. You are indeed a daisy," I said, letting my Georgia drawl out another inch. "My word, but this has become a most expensive experience for little old me."

He made a throwaway gesture with his cigar in his right hand as he casually picked up his handkerchief and returned it to his right pocket. I glanced at the cards in front of him: They appeared to be the same, but the top card now was aligned with the rest of the cards beneath it where it had edged to the left before he had dropped his handkerchief on top of it.

"All the price of life's lessons," he said airily. The crowd chuckled around us.

"Well, then let's make the lesson most beneficial," I said. I took a wallet from my inside pocket, removed the bills, spread them, and laid them in the center of the table.

"Your three hundred and five hundred more," I said.

The crowd gasped at the size of the pot. Even for a riverboat that was a hefty pool. I could see the greed sparkle inside Wilson's eyes. Sturtevant looked involuntarily at him. He nodded again. I took my watch from my pocket and opened it. Two A.M. Chopin's "Opus No. 1 in B-Flat Minor" tinkled softly.

"A pretty tune," Sturtevant said.

"My mother's favorite," I answered. I closed the watch, returning it to my pocket. "I believe it is your bet, Mr. Sturtevant."

"That is quite a sum," he said, nodding at the pool.

"As you said," I said. "One of life's major experiences. I do believe all of life's experiences should be grabbed, don't you, Mr. Sturtevant? Life is so short that one must certainly experience all that is possible in this world before shuffling off to the next."

A tiny frown pinched his eyebrows. He glanced at his cards to reassure himself. A tiny muscle began to tic in the corner of one eye. I could tell this was not going quite according to his plans. Had he made a mistake in his estimation of me? My behavior now was not of the innocent one he had marked when he had sat down to this game. I reached for my glass of bourbon and finished it, calling to the bartender for another. A satisfied look spread over his face. Obviously, I was drunk. That explained my sudden change in behavior.

"Very well," he said, reaching again into his pocket. He removed another sheaf of bills and tossed them without counting into the center of the table. "Let us see what you have. I call."

"Four treys," I said, opening my hand to the view of the others.

A triumphant smile slid across his face. He spread his cards faceup.

"And four jacks," he said. "I guess the learning experience belongs to you."

He stretched his hands out to gather the pool to him. I leaned forward to stop him with my left hand, hiding my right, which was sliding under my coat and removing the Deringer from my vest pocket.

"No," I said, smiling at him. "I'm calling the hand that you have in your right coat pocket."

A stillness settled over the room. He froze, looking into my eyes, slowly settling back in his chair. He glanced around him at the crowd, then back to me, his face hardening.

"That is pretty serious talk," he said.

I nodded and leaned back, leaving my hand just under the table's edge.

"About as serious as could be," I said. I smiled at him.

"Talk like that can get a person killed," he said.

"Or man accused," I answered.

A thin, sallow-faced man pushed his way through the crowd, stepping to the side between us. His eyes were bright blue, piercing with their intentness. Tiny lines pulled down his lips. He wore a gray frock coat and matching trousers. Two hard-looking men with full beards suddenly appeared on either side of him, pushing the crowd back from him.

"What's going on here?" he asked.

"The young one just accused Jack Sturtevant of cheating," someone said.

I smiled at Sturtevant. "It appears that you are well known here, Mr. Sturtevant. Do they know all about you?" He flushed darkly. His hands twitched on the table in front of him.

"That is very serious, young man," the newcomer said, turning to me. His eyes bore brightly into mine, burning with an inner fire alive and intent.

"I buried a jack in the deadwood," I said, nodding at the pile of cards between Wilson and Sturtevant. The other reached for them, stopping when I continued. "You won't find it there. Best look for it on Mr. Wilson." I nodded to my right. "Or on Mr. Bickman. But it's here.

"It doesn't matter, though," I continued. "We just have to look in his handkerchief in his right pocket. You'll find his hand there. I'll be surprised, though, if it beats mine. Mr. Wilson's shiner will have seen to that."

All eyes dropped to Wilson's hands. He flushed and clenched them into a tight fist. The tiny gold band shone in the light, sending back accusing twinkles.

"Come now, Mr. Wilson. Don't be shy. Open your hand and show us the mirror on the back of your ring."

His hands jerked off the table and into his lap. I shook my head.

"Tch, tch. You really need to work on your technique if you plan on continuing to make your living as a flashdancer," I said.

"You are a lying son of a bitch," he said tightly. "You'll answer for that."

"Don't be so impatient, Mr. Wilson," I said gaily. "Your turn will most certainly come. Right now, it is Mr. Sturtevant's turn. You have been called, sir. What is your answer."

His hand flashed inside his coat, then froze as I brought the Deringer up from beneath the table, aiming casually between his eyes.

"A forty-one caliber makes a nasty hole, Mr. Sturtevant. A nasty hole. Your own mother might not recognize you in your coffin."

His hand slid slowly out from beneath his coat and dropped to the table in front of him. I gave him a tiny smile.

"Now, shall we look into your coat pocket, sir? And if I'm wrong, I offer my most humble apologies, sir." I looked up at the newcomer to our table. "Would you do the honors, sir? Mr. Sturtevant appears to be a bit fidgety. It would be a shame if something other than his hanky and his cards came out of his pocket."

The newcomer stepped around to Sturtevant's side and carefully slid his fingers inside Sturtevant's pocket. He removed a handkerchief and slowly unwrapped it. Five cards fell to the table. He turned them over: a kilter, no card above a nine.

"I do believe that I have won this hand, haven't I, Mr. Sturtevant?" I said. I reached out my hand and pulled the money to my side. He made no move to stop me.

"We will be stopping to take on wood and water soon," the newcomer said. "It would be wise, I believe, if you three would leave the *Natchez*. We take a dim view of cardsharps in the South. Especially this close to Mississippi."

An assenting murmur rose from the crowd. Sturtevant

flushed deep red and started to say something, but Wilson leaped to his feet, his chair turning over with a crash.

"I demand satisfaction!" he said hotly. "This man has called me a cheat!"

"Why, you are what you are, sir," I said, laying the Deringer upon the table and carefully arranging the money in neat piles and storing it in my coat pocket.

"Pistols, sir, if you have the nerve!" he retorted.

"I'm your huckleberry," I said, rising to my feet.

"You'll second me, Sturtevant?" he said, glancing to his left. Sturtevant gave a terse nod.

"And you, sir," I said to the newcomer. "Will you do me the honor?"

"I would be most happy to, Mr. . . .?" He extended his hand to me.

"Holliday, sir," I said, taking his hand. "Dr. John Henry Holliday."

"Forrest. Nathan Bedford Forrest of Mississippi," he said.

A gasp went up around the room. The bearded men moved close beside him. He smiled faintly at them.

"My, ah, 'associates,' " he said. "The times are so uncertain, you know. We have been in Tennessee helping our people to establish branches of our society."

The nigra behind the bar gave us a hard look, then turned quickly away as one of Forrest's associates stared impassively at him.

"I have heard of you, sir," I said, extending my hand. He shook hands firmly. "This is, indeed, an honor. I believe you were in Georgia around Griffin not long ago helping my uncle and others with the problems that have arisen there thanks to the freebooters working under the Freedmen's Bureau?"

"You are that Holliday? My compliments, sir. You have quite a few admirers in that part of Georgia." A tiny smile played across his lips as I frowned, shaking my head. "The little incident along the Withlacoochee River? Your uncle, the judge, made sure that I heard about your conflict. How many did you kill that day? Oh, it doesn't matter. We have other business here, I believe."

He turned back to Wilson, nodding curtly at him and Sturtevant. They had drawn back away from the table and were staring at the famed Mississippi general who had worked his way up through the ranks in the Confederate Army to finish the War as a feared general for whom even Lee expressed admiration.

"I believe pistols were indicated, sir?" he said, addressing Wilson. The gambler gave a terse nod. "Then might I send one of my men to my room? I have a matched pair of LeMat pistols in my cabin. Certainly not the choice of two gentlemen, but in the absence of the appropriate weapons, I believe they will do if you have no objection?"

"I have none," I said and smiled at Wilson, feeling the red rage working along my veins. His eyes were pinpoints of blackness, belching forth hatred. Yet I could see from the muscles working in his cheeks that Forrest's familiarity with me and the suggestion that I might have killed a man disturbed him.

"I will not fight with any of your ruffian armament," he said stiffly. He turned his head slightly to the right. His eyes shifted nervously from me to Forrest. "Sturtevant?"

"I agree. This is to be between gentlemen, according to the *Code Duello.*"

"I'm familiar with it," I said. "Quite familiar, in fact."

Forrest gave me a quick look, a tiny frown line appearing between his eyes, and one eyebrow rose quizzically. "You have blazed, sir?"

"I have," I said, smiling again at Wilson. "And the matter of the pistols is up to the one who has been challenged, I believe? At least that is what I heard when a Union officer cast aspersions upon a lady's honor. A Miss Belle Boyd, sir," I said to Forrest.

He smiled. "A lovely woman. Lovely woman. I trust you were able to accommodate him without mishap?"

"I was. And the LeMats will be fine," I said.

"Then the matter is settled unless"—he turned to Wilson—"unless you wish to apologize, sir?"

"I do not. *And* I protest the choice of weapons as those not becoming a gentleman!"

Forrest's eyes flattened. An impassive mask slipped over his face. Wilson looked away and I knew then how he had been so successful during the war: looking into a face like that was like looking into Achilles' shield and seeing one's own destiny.

"Those are my pistols, sir," he said quietly. "I carried LeMats pistols during the War. Are you inferring that I am not a gentleman?"

Forrest's aides moved up and around his shoulders like dark wings, staring at him, unblinking. Wilson swallowed nervously at the dead look in their eyes.

"No, no," he said hastily. "It's just that, well, they have more than one shot," he finished lamely.

"Tell you what we'll do," I said. I slipped Pinkerton's twin Deringers from my pocket and laid them upon the table. "Perhaps you'll feel better about using these. Shall we say, five paces?"

"Five?"

An incredulous look came over his face. At that distance, neither of us would be able to play with odds. Both of us would undoubtedly be injured.

"You're quite right," I said. I moved both pistols into the center of the table with the handles pointed toward him, giving him the advantage.

"There is a good chance that both of us might miss." I looked at Forrest. "Deringers are so unpredictable at any distance more than a few feet." I glanced back at Wilson.

"Select which one you will and fire upon General Forrest's count. I will take the other," I said offhandedly. A cough bubbled through my chest. I picked up the glass of whiskey from the table and drained it. His eyes bulged in disbelief.

"That is suicide," he whispered. Then the arrogance

returned to his face. "No gentleman would agree to these . . . schoolboy antics."

I shrugged. "Why, Mr. Wilson. Whatever do you mean? It all depends upon how fast you are, I believe."

"You're drunk," Sturtevant said. "That's why you want to keep the distance so short." He nudged Wilson. "At ten paces, he'd be seeing three of you."

"That's all right," I answered, waving my hand in airy dismissal. "I'll shoot the one in the middle."

He moved uneasily at that, the muscles along his jawline clenching and unclenching. He shook his head and said, "A drunkard's answer." But I knew that I had made him uneasy with my nonchalance.

"Then the matter is settled?" Forrest said impatiently.

"Unless the gentleman withdraws his complaint about your pistols, sir." I heaved a great sigh. "Killing is such a formality, isn't it?"

"I'll take the LeMats!" Wilson said furiously.

Forrest nodded at one of his aides. The man disappeared through the crowd. A murmur of excitement rose through the crowd as individuals began making wagers. One man laughed and said, "I'll give odds of three to one on Wilson!"

I turned to him, removing the money from my coat. I tossed it onto the table. "I'll take those odds," I said. "There's about a thousand dollars there, give or take. I'll wager it all that he won't."

The man blanched, licking his lips. He tried to step back away from the table, but the crowd refused to part. The others began to tease him and his face flushed dark red.

"Very well. You're covered," he said tightly.

"I think I would like a little of that too," Forrest said. He took a sack of coins from the side pocket of his coat and tossed it onto the table. "There's another five hundred in gold that Dr. Holliday will emerge the victor from this little fracas. You *do* have the funds to cover that, do you not, sir?"

The man nodded, his lips a thin line. "I'll take your wager, sir." He reached a hand into his pocket and removed a sheet of paper with a fancy letterhead. "I have a letter of credit here on the State Bank of Chicago for fund deposits in Barclay's Bank of New Orleans."

"Then might I suggest that the money be held by a third party?" Forrest said. "I'm sure that you understand? After all there will be, let's see"—he counted the money I had thrown onto the table—"Fifteen hundred plus my five hundred is two thousand at three to one makes it eight thousand all total." He nodded at an aristocratic-looking white-haired man in the crowd. "Will you, sir, look after the stakes?"

The gentleman smiled and nodded. "Colonel Thomas Lee Jackson of Nashville, at your service. I would be most happy to oblige you, General Forrest. And, er, you, too, sir," he added, raising an eyebrow in the direction of our bettor. Forrest handed him the money. He held his hand out to the other man.

"I will give you a draft on Barclay's Bank in New Orleans," the man said.

"The question is, sir, to the validity of the draft," Jackson said without smiling. "A letter of credit is of no use to anyone if the credit has been spent."

"Are you questioning my honesty, sir?" the man said, drawing himself up.

Jackson shrugged expressively. "These are hard times, sir. Sometimes a gentleman overestimates his worth."

"Take the draft in the amount that he is short from his ready cash," Forrest said. "The draft will be good. Or," he added offhandedly, "I will turn your name over to our . . . 'friends' in New Orleans. We have quite a few sympathizers there. Simple."

The man blanched. His lips barely moved as he said, "The draft is good. I give you my word."

Jackson spread his hands, a tiny smile playing at his lips. "Then you have nothing to worry about, do you?"

The temper of the room suddenly charged with tension as the crowd smelled blood. Forrest's man reappeared with a mahogany box. He opened it, displaying the LeMats in the burgundy felt lining the box. Forrest lifted one, broke the cylinder, and loaded it from a box of cartridges in the box.

Quickly, he loaded the other one and laid it, too, back in the box. He looked at both of us.

"They are a presentation set from friends in Tennessee. Neither has been shot by me or another. Therefore, there can have been no tampering with either, nor can I advise Dr. Holliday on a shot pattern. As far as I know, they both hold true. I see no reason to load the shot barrel," he said. "If either of you gentlemen cannot do with six, then buckshot is not the answer, either. I suggest that we adjourn to the hurricane deck to avoid bloodstains upon the carpet."

I nodded and strolled from the room. The crowd parted for me. I heard Wilson stamping angrily after me and smiled. Suddenly, a Chopin nocturne came to me and I whistled the tune softly as I climbed the stairs to the hurricane deck. I walked to the edge and looked down at the black water swirling in the moonlight beneath the boat's hull. Within moments, the others had emerged, followed by as many as the small deck would accommodate.

"I believe the deck is roughly twenty paces, wouldn't you say?" I said.

Forrest glanced at the distance, nodding.

"Then might I suggest that Mr. Wilson take one end and I the other. We can dispense with this most simply. Perhaps Colonel Jackson will simply give us a five count, at which time we'll fire."

"It would be my privilege, Dr. Holliday," Jackson said, giving a short bow.

"Chancy," Forrest murmured. "He has more than one shot."

I shrugged. "Who can live forever?"

He looked sharply at the tinge of bitterness in my voice, started to say something, then shook his head and shook my hand.

"You are a strange young man, Dr. Holliday," he said. "Most strange. But I like your spirit."

"Can we get on with this?" Sturtevant said.

Forrest's eyebrows raised. "If you are in that much of a

hurry to die, then so be it. Do you accept Dr. Holliday's terms?"

"Agreed," Wilson said, white-faced. "I'll take this place."

I shrugged and strolled back to the wheelhouse, standing at a right angle to it.

"Smart," Forrest said sotto voce as he came down to me. "The white boards give him an outline to shoot at in the dark. You've only got the night."

"It's enough," I said, taking one of the LeMats from the case held by Forrest's associate. The pistol felt heavy in my hand. The associate turned and walked down to the other end, letting Wilson take the pistol. I glanced again at the dark water gliding by, a Dante nightmare.

"You won't need a funeral, Mr. Wilson," I called.

He glanced down at the oily, black-looking water and turned set-lipped to present his right side to me. His eyes gleamed white, fire-bright in the night. A thin white line appeared as his lips stretched tightly over his teeth.

"We'll see, Holliday," he said grimly. "Maybe it will be you in the water."

"You might get lucky," I teased. But I didn't believe my words, for I didn't feel Death's breath moving across me in the night, although I felt his shadow standing beside me. A laugh bubbled up within me and I gave release to it in the night. The excited talk died down among the onlookers and I could feel their eyes upon me, watching, wondering.

"Gentlemen. Are you ready?"

"One moment," I said. For pure bad prank, I took the flask Belle had given to me from my pocket and the silver cup. I filled the cup and held it by its handle, replacing the flask.

"Now I'm ready," I said gaily, sipping at the whiskey. A murmur of admiration rose from the crowd. Wilson's face grew taut and white, a pale orb above a black obelisk in the night. I looked up at the moon, full and white glowing in the darkness, cloud streamers filtering across it. A low fog began rolling up to the lower deck from the river. I laughed again, delighted with the night and the damp coldness, and beside me the Dark Spirit laughed, too, my partner.

"You are a cool one, Dr. Holliday," Forrest said, pressing my arm for luck and stepping back and away from me. "I wish I would have had you under my command."

"That would have been just peachy, General," I said, sipping again.

Jackson smoothed his coat down his side and cocked an ivory-handled Colt Model 1849 Pocket. He coughed, cleared his throat, then said, "Gentlemen. Let both know that I will shoot either of you who defiles his honor by breaking this gentleman's agreement."

"Get on with it," Wilson said tightly.

Jackson raised his eyebrows. "I will, Mr. Wilson. But remember what I said. He cleared his throat and began his count. "Ready, gentlemen. One . . ."

Wilson raised his pistol.

"Two . . ."

I heard the hammer ratchet back on Wilson's pistol. A fierce joy spread through me.

"Three . . ."

From Wilson's pistol, an orange tongue of flame spat toward me. I heard the report and felt the breeze of the ball flying past my ear.

"Damn you, Wilson!" Jackson shouted. He raised his pistol.

"No!" I said sharply. "Continue the count!"

He stared down at me. I smiled and shrugged.

"Four . . ."

Wilson fired again. This time his ball tugged at my coat.

"Five!" Jackson shouted.

I raised my hand and fired in one movement, pulling the hammer back on the LeMat with the ball of my thumb and letting it fall again.

Wilson staggered backward from the first shot, then spun around. His pistol fired again into the deck at his feet, then his hand opened and the pistol clattered to the deck as he swayed, then pitched over into the inky darkness of the river. I heard his body splash. Then I raised my cup and finished the whiskey, dropping it back into the capacious side pocket of my coat.

"A bit unbalanced," I said, handing the pistol to Forrest. "But it holds true enough."

"It's missing the shot charge," he said gravely, taking the pistol from me. "When it's fully loaded, then it balances well enough. And it's good to have that big load a time or two."

"Maybe," I said. I grinned. "But we move in different worlds, General. I don't think I'll be doing much raiding or riding at the head of the cavalry."

"I don't know," he said thoughtfully, handing the pistol to one of the bearded men, who silently placed it back in its case. "I have a hunch that you weren't meant to be a doctor." He looked down the length of the boarded deck to where a small group clustered around the edge of the deck, staring down into the dark water. "No, I don't think doctoring is your call."

Jackson crossed the deck, grabbing my hand and pumping it enthusiastically. "That, sir, was one of the greatest exhibitions of courage I have ever seen! Congratulations!"

A cough suddenly struck, shaking my shoulders. I quickly pressed a handkerchief to my lips as a copper taste slicked across my tongue. I glanced at the blotch of blood on the white of my handkerchief before folding it away.

"Are you injured?" Forrest asked, concern frowning from his face.

I shook my head. "Not from Wilson. But I'm right dead enough, for all of that. His bullet would have made everything highly anticlimactic."

"I see," Forrest said. He turned to Jackson. "I believe you have money for us?"

"The man gave us two thousand and a note for four," Jackson said apologetically, handing the bundle to me. "I am not sure of the value of the note, however. Remember, I questioned the validity of it before accepting it."

"You did well and we appreciate it. Thank you, Colonel Jackson," I said. I handed the sack of money to Forrest and took a thousand in bills from the pile and gave him that as well.

"That should take care of your wager, General," I said, pocketing the rest along with the note. "I intend on laying over a day or two in New Orleans and have no objection to collecting the remainder of our bet."

My coat sagged uncomfortably. I shrugged my shoulders, trying to reset the coat. I removed the flask and took a sip and handed it to Colonel Jackson. He drank and handed it to Forrest. Forrest took a small sip and returned the flask to me. His aide came up with Wilson's pistol, and Forrest added it to the one I had used in the box the second aide opened.

"Will you gentlemen join me for an aperitif?" Colonel Jackson asked.

Forrest shook his head. "Thank you, Colonel Jackson, but I will be leaving the boat tomorrow when we take on wood at Pike's Landing. Friends will be meeting us there. It is imperative that I get a little sleep between now and then. So, if you will excuse me, I believe I will retire."

"Of course. I understand," Jackson said, giving him a slight bow. "It has been my pleasure meeting you, sir."

"And mine," Forrest said, shaking hands with him. He turned to me. "This has been a profitable venture, Dr. Holliday. Thank you for the honor of being your second. And," he added, padding the pocket of his coat where he had placed the wager, "thank you for settling in advance. By all rights, we should both take the risk of an uncollectable wager."

"The honor, General, was all mine," I said. "But it is unnecessary. I do not believe the gentleman in question will be so foolish as to give a bogus note to you. If he does . . ." I shrugged.

"Perhaps we'll meet again," he said, stepping away from us.

"I shall look forward to it," I answered. The crowd parted respectfully for him as he left, the two silent men following in his footsteps. I turned toward Jackson.

"As for the aperitif, Colonel Jackson, I would be most appreciative of one. But will you join me in a glass of champagne before?"

"You, sir, are a gentleman," he said, drawing himself up.

He turned to the side, allowing me to leave. We retired to

the salon and drank the night away, and when morning came, I remembered then that it was Christmas, but instead of snow, rain fell, a cold, hard rain that stopped just this side of snow, and I felt no Christmas in the empty part of me where once my soul resided.

2

I swore and hastily leaped back as a carriage rolled down Chartes Street, oblivious to the pedestrians. I narrowly avoided getting splattered with mud, but bumped into a young Creole girl whose dark eyes flashed dangerously at me. Her escort caught her elbow to keep her from falling. I lifted my hat, ruefully smiling through a cough.

"I'm very sorry, mademoiselle, please forgive my rudeness."

She smiled while her escort stepped in front of her, one hand grasping the lapel of his coat. His eyes flashed furiously at me, the bright eyes of a Creole vain enough to take quick offense at the slightest provocation, a young man who felt the need to prove to himself that he had become a man. She flinched and grabbed his arm, tugging on it.

"Philippe! He did nothing!"

"Did he not? We have had enough of men like him over the past few years."

"It is the fault of the young to make too much of a trifling matter," I said, bowing to the young lady. I smiled at her. A dull flush began working its way up his cheeks past the pencil-thin mustache daringly clinging to his upper lip. His black eyes narrowed.

"But I cannot say that this has not been very fortuitous as it has allowed me the opportunity to make the acquaintance of such a charming lady."

"You, sir, are a boor!" he said stiffly.

"And you, sir, are boring," I answered coolly. I nodded at the young lady. "I have already offered my apologies to the young lady, and I can tell by her most delightful smile that she has accepted them."

"Impertinence!" he snapped, raising his hand.

"If you wish to die, sir, I will be obliged to accommodate you," I said before the blow landed. His eyes widened, then narrowed again as he took a small step forward, and I braced myself.

"Philippe!" the young girl said sharply. "Stop it this instant!"

He glanced quickly at her, then reluctantly lowered his arm. The young girl stepped between us, her chin lifted high. Similar lights to his danced in her eyes, but hers were the lights of one with pride in herself.

"Please excuse my brother, monsieur," she said. "He is quick to take offense. Even where none has been offered. We see so few gentlemen from the Américains these days that one naturally assumes all to be alike. You understand, monsieur?"

"Of course. The fault is with their age; the young are always quick to anger, mademoiselle," I said. A brief humor flashed over me; I was not much older than he and only a few years older than herself. Yet I sounded like a man of years. Perhaps I was, I thought. The old are the ones who look death in the face on a daily basis.

He bit his lip and ducked his head away from us for a split second before raising it, staring at me defiantly. A faint grin touched her full lips, and I knew that she, too, knew that only a year or two separated her escort and myself. For a moment I thought he might try to begin a new quarrel, but he maintained his silence, staring hate at me.

"It has been the War, monsieur. Your General Butler has caused much hatred among the people of New Orleans that cannot be so easily dismissed."

I knew what she said was true. Major-General Benjamin F. Butler, who had taken command of the city after the Union forces had captured it during the War, had become incensed at the refusal of the New Orleans population to recognize his authority or to include him within their society. He issued an order against the women of New Orleans, stating that any who should by word, gesture, or movement show contempt for any officer or soldier of the occupying army would be immediately treated as "a woman of the town plying her vocation." In essence, Butler's order immediately called nearly every woman a prostitute, since the majority of the ladies in New Orleans had strong Confederate sympathies. Butler's order had been condemned by all, and the lush green grounds of the dueling oaks where gentlemen had for years settled their differences behind Saint Louis Cathedral took on a decided reddish hue within weeks of the order being issued.

"General Butler was and is a cad, mademoiselle," I said, lengthening my Georgia drawl.

"In fact, I have yet to meet a Yankee with whom I would be willing to pass a moment's pleasure unless, that is, we were to meet with our seconds."

An amused smile dimpled her cheeks as she drew back, appraising me. I knew my words had the ring of a young man's braggadocio, but she did not know if I had meant them that way or if I was sincere. The hate disappeared from her escort's eyes as he began to reappraise me.

"You sound, sir, as if you were accustomed to defending your honor."

"He is an Américain. What would he know about honor?" Philippe said disdainfully, but an uncertainty showed grudgingly from his eyes.

"A couple of times," I said. I smiled at him. He pulled himself upright, trying to stare down at me. His lips tightened beneath the faint hint of a mustache.

"I do not share the hypocrisy of some who give lip service only to the word." I looked back at her. "I'm rather old-fashioned that way, mademoiselle."

I could feel the cough coming and took a large handkerchief from my jacket, pressing it tightly against my lips.

"Are you all right, monsieur?" she asked, frowning.

I shook my head. "A terrible inconvenience, mademoiselle. Please excuse me."

I turned and started to walk away, but she laid her hand on my arm, staying me, much to her escort's disgust.

"My name is Solange Thibideaux," she said. "And this rude individual is my brother, Philippe, who would be happy to assist you."

"Solange!" Philippe complained.

"Hush, Philippe," Solange said. Her eyes twinkled. "Monsieur, I hope that you will not view this as, how you say, 'typical'? of our people here. The War has destroyed much of what we knew, but there are a few who maintain the old ways."

"Tradition is a fine thing," I said, bowing slightly from the waist. "Especially when found in one so young."

"You see, Philippe?" she said delightedly. "He is not a barbarian.

"Vraiment," Philippe muttered. She ignored him.

"Tell me, monsieur, would you be open to a dinner invitation?" she asked.

At first I was inclined to refuse, but then I glanced at her brother's face and the devil rose in me. The thought of eating opposite him and watching him forced to politeness was irresistible.

"Of course, I will be delighted," I said. "If you will send around a card?"

"One must have a name and address, monsieur," she said delicately.

"Dr. John Henry Holliday," I managed, stifling the cough. "Presently residing at the Pontalba Apartments."

"Then until then, monsieur . . ." she bowed her head slightly.

I nodded and walked away, leaving them standing alone.

"Really, Solange! At times you behave like a poule!" Philippe complained. Her laugh tinkled in the air behind me.

"Philippe, you are always taking yourself so seriously. I think he might prove . . . interesting," she said teasingly just before I passed out of hearing. Interesting? Not exactly the word I would use. Her dark eyes and the unmistakable woman's body beneath her cloak and dress appealed to me far more than simply "interesting." Then I coughed and remembered that I could no longer move within the society of ladies and manners; the women I would know from now on were a part of me: whores, who by virtue of their occupation, were for all practical purposes dead with me. Thanks to my sickness, I now lived in a world where polite society might visit but never live.

I tried to force the cough away as I walked down Chartes Street, toward St. Cyr's gambling establishment, which I had proceeded to make my second home after arriving in New Orleans a few weeks ago. I had planned on waiting only until the bank draft I carried had cleared before continuing my move on west, but New Orleans held a strange fascination for me, especially the area known as Vieux Carre, the "French Quarter." At first I had stayed in a small room at an inn near the quay, but then decided to take an apartment in one of the dark red brick buildings built by the Baroness Pontalba on St. Ann Street, fronting the Place d'Armes, which had been renamed Jackson Square, although the older residents still referred to it by its former name. Living here gave me more immediate access to the gaming rooms.

Although the casinos had lost a lot of their luster since the War, the most popular games were still faro, roulette, and vingt-et-un. In smaller rooms specifically set aside at St. Cyr's, draw poker had become immensely popular, as it had at the establishment of Major S. A. Doran on Royal Street, which was my favorite. Doran's place was much newer than St. Cyr's, which had become a bit seedy after the legislature had outlawed gambling halls. But the gentility still had a tendency to visit St. Cyr's, paying a token call upon Doran's place in the early morning. I followed their lead simply because whatever money remained in a battered New Orleans still trying to recover from the War was in their hands, and they still visited St. Cyr's.

It was also the favorite gambling place of Pierre You, the

young Creole who insisted he was the bastard son of Dominique You, one of the pirate Lafitte's men before the pirates were forced to leave Barataria by a suddenly proper government who only months before had begged for their help in repulsing the British. Pierre's notorious father gave him limited access to New Orleans society, and he traded as much as he could on that reputation, even to adopting the dated bottle green forked-tail coat and heavily ruffled lace shirts of his ancestors. Unfortunately, he was not the gambler the old pirate was and when drunk became a reckless player. I held a note against his play from two days ago, and he had missed our appointment at Barclay's Bank for its redemption.

I knocked on the door of St. Cyr's and waited until Black Tom opened the door and verified my identity before letting me in. I had been a frequent visitor to St. Cyr's over the past two weeks, yet Black Tom always looked for my letter of introduction before he would let me enter. In a city as steeped in tradition as New Orleans, the letter would become tattered and illegible before I would be granted automatic entrance as one of the recognized.

"And how are we today, Tom? Is your daughter better?" I asked as I stepped into the entry and handed my hat and cane to him. His face, heavily scarred from the many fights he had fought for his owners before being freed, remained frozen into the black marble mask he displayed toward everyone. His hair was grizzled, but too many had taken that to mean he was sub-servient and useless, finding out otherwise only when they found themselves being escorted firmly and painfully from St. Cyr's.

"Very well, Mr. Holliday," he said politely. "Thank you for asking. She thanks you for the doll that you sent around."

"Oh. Well." For a moment I was embarrassed; on a whimsy, I had arranged for the small doll, quite an expensive one dressed as Marie Antoinette, to be sent anonymously to his young daughter, who was recovering from some mal-odorous illness simply referred to as "the fever." I had not wanted my name associated with the gift, but apparently the young lady with café au lait skin had deliberately ignored my instructions and placed my name on the gift.

"Think nothing of it, Tom," I said. "Young girls need surprises when they are ill. Takes their minds off being sick for a little while. Is young Mr. You playing today?"

"I believe you will find him in one of the back rooms, sir," he said formally, his voice husky and soft from a blow to the throat that had partially crushed his larynx. He turned and made a dignified exit into a side room, where he carefully placed my hat upon a shelf and stood the cane beneath it.

I smoothed my hair and tucked the handkerchief away before I stepped out of the entry into the gaming room. The carpet was worn and thready in places but the green felt on the gaming tables was clean and smooth and the roulette wheel turned soundlessly on a well-oiled spindle. A huge crystal chandelier hung from the ceiling, and along the back of the room, next to the entrance that led to a small hallway where one would find the private gaming rooms, stood a well-burnished oaken bar with a brass foot rail although no one stood at the bar for more than a moment or two, preferring to allow the liveried servants to deliver their drinks to the tables.

The bartender noticed my approach and had a crystal glass filled with Old Williams by the time I arrived at the bar. I picked it up, sipped it, and felt the smooth bite of the bourbon cut through the spasms of my lungs. I sipped again and went to the hallway, looking for Pierre You. I found him playing draw poker with three others in the second room down the hall. He looked up at my entrance, his eyes wary in his thin face. I wrinkled my nose at the acrid smell in the room; he had been playing long enough for his collar to have wilted and for the sweat to have dried upon his shirt. A lock of black hair hung damply over his white forehead. From the chips on the table and the small pile in front of him, I could guess what had been happening.

"Pierre, I was looking for you at the bank today," I said pleasantly. I reached into my vest pocket and removed a small piece of paper, folded twice with St. Cyr's coat of arms on the outside.

"Perhaps I misunderstood our arrangements?"

He glanced involuntarily around at his playing partners. I recognized two of them from games at Doran's place before the doors were closed to them. The other one had been pointed out to me on the streets as one of the maîtres d'armes who specialized in teaching young men how to handle weapons in order that they might defend their honor by carving each other to pieces with swords or shooting holes in each other from the prescribed ten paces. The position maître had once been a proud one, but since the War, the need for such studies had ceased to be as important as they had been when the Creole families had had enough money to allow for such luxuries within their society. Jean Duval was a recent newcomer to the field and a bit hungrier than most. He had already made quite a name for himself on the dueling fields, trying to build up the name of the academy he had established on the Exchange Alley along with the other maîtres.

"I am sorry, Monsieur Holliday," Pierre said. "But circumstances have been, er, 'impossible.' "

He glanced at the others at the table. I felt his helplessness and silent plea. I sipped from the glass and as I took a quick look at the backs of the cards in the deadwood. I recognized the cheap markings on the back that only a raw amateur could miss and felt the familiar recklessness returning. He was being cheated and he knew it, but if he left before his table was clean of chips, the others would claim he had insulted them and Duval would quickly demand satisfaction for the insult to his friends. I had heard of the tactic first being used by professional gamblers in the seedy taverns by the riverfront at Natchez-Under-the-Hill to fleece the young who allowed themselves to be wooed into joining them for a "friendly" game. I had not expected such a situation to be allowed at St. Cyr's, though.

I nodded at the pile of chips in front of him, sliding the promissory note back into my vest pocket.

"It seems as if your luck is running as bad now as it did the other night," I observed.

"Yes, it does," he admitted.

"Sometimes it helps if you change your seat or take a break," I said mildly.

Duval leaned back in his chair and gave me a long, level look.

"I do not think you were invited to this table, monsieur," he said. The others slid warily back in their chairs.

"Now, that is not very friendly, monsieur," I said. "This bothers me very much, for I am a very friendly person. I am sorry to have to break up your game, but I have some business with this young man that is long overdue. I am sure you understand?"

Duval spread his hand and waved languidly. "That is too bad, monsieur, for we are not ready for the game to be broken up."

"This is most distressing. Most distressing," I said. "But I am afraid I must insist."

"And I, too, monsieur, must insist," he said, his eyes cold black dots. His hands rested easily in front of him on the table.

"Well, now. You're quite a daisy, aren't you?" I said. I glanced at Pierre. "Get your coat," I ordered. He glanced at Duval and the others. "Now don't mind them; they're just a bit grouchy. But they'll get over it."

Pierre hastily rose and stepped to the rear of the room and removed his coat from the back of a chair. He shrugged into it and returned to the table, sweeping his chips from the table.

Duval stood up, his hand flickering inside his coat. I palmed one of the Deringers out from my waistband and leveled it at him. He smiled thinly and carefully brought his hand out from beneath his coat.

"My card, monsieur," he said, tossing it contemptuously on the table between us.

I reached down into the deadwood, ran my fingers through them, and selected a pasteboard, flipping it across the table to him. It landed faceup: the ace of spades.

"And mine, monsieur," I said, feeling the rage beginning. I muffled a cough. "I do hope you're not superstitious." His eyebrows lifted in puzzlement.

"La carte morte," one of the others said.

"Ah," Duval said. "But whose death?"

"A very poor job of trimming. The aces stand too clear to be of any use except for those who do not have a suspicious mind," I said. "And the markings, really, messieurs, would not one method of cheating be enough that you had to add another?"

"Are you accusing us of cheating?" one of the others said flatly.

"Of course, I am," I replied carelessly. "And very poor cheats at that."

"I am ready, Dr. Holliday," Pierre said nervously.

"Go ahead," I said. "I will meet you in the entry. Tell Black Tom to get Monsieur St. Cyr. The river is up and rats have been looking for a new home. Three of them seem to have settled here."

He left, slipping warily behind me. One of the others started to rise, then froze as I waved the pistol at him to sit back down. I took another drink from the crystal glass in my hand. The door opened behind me and St. Cyr entered the room. He swiftly took the situation in hand, then stepped carefully to the left. He gave the impression of icy grayness: gray coat and vest, his hair streaked with gray, his eyes slate gray.

"Yes, monsieur," he said, addressing me. "I believe you have a complaint?"

"I do apologize for being such a nuisance, Monsieur St. Cyr, but there is a problem with these three gentlemen. Apparently they have been taking advantage of Pierre You by using cards of their own special manufacture."

He stiffened, his eyes glowing brightly for a moment before settling like agates into the whiteness of his face. "Monsieur?" he said.

"The cards have been trimmed, leaving the aces high," I said, motioning toward the deck open on the table. He stepped to the table, gathered the cards with one practiced motion, and tapped them lightly against the table, running his fingers over the edges. He glanced at the backs of the cards, noticed the markings, then contemptuously tossed the deck onto the table.

"You will, of course, be refused further admittance to these rooms," he said formally to the other three. "The stakes at this table are confiscated. Your names will also be posted to the other houses within the district. You may find a game down along the quay, gentlemen, but not in the Vieux Carre."

He bowed at the table. I pocketed the Deringer and finished my drink, placing my glass upside down on the table. St. Cyr gave me a wintry smile.

"And you, Monsieur Holliday. Will you be staying long in New Orleans?"

I shrugged. "I haven't made any plans as yet, sir. I believe in keeping my options open."

He glanced at Duval. "You may not have as many options as you think. But there will be no trouble in this house. I hope that I have made myself quite clear?"

I nodded and turned to leave. Duval called, stopping me. I turned back, letting my hand rest casually beside the Deringer.

"My seconds will visit with yours at the Absinthe House at two tomorrow afternoon," he said stiffly. "That is, unless you are like other Américains with no honor."

"That is the second time I have heard my countrymen insulted today. The first I will excuse, but in your case, why, I'm your huckleberry," I said, tapping the handle of the Deringer.

"Gentlemen!" St. Cyr exclaimed.

"The Absinthe House at two tomorrow," I said, bowing slightly to the room. I turned and exited. St. Cyr remained as I closed the door behind me. Pierre was waiting for me in the entry.

"Thank you, monsieur Holliday. I am afraid that I was in a most difficult position," he said ruefully.

"I suggest, sir, that you give up your gambling," I said. "You are a very bad gambler. You may be able to trade upon your grandfather's name among the gentry, but when you play with others like Duval and his friends, you are playing with those who do not hold your grandfather in very high regard. You have been lucky this time."

"I appreciate your help, monsieur," he said stiffly, his eyes angry. "But I will make my own way."

"Then let us make your way to your bank before you get into any more games," I said.

His jaw set angrily, tiny knots bulging from under his ears as he turned and left. Black Tom held the door, his face as impassive as ever. I nodded as I passed him.

"Be careful, Dr. Holliday," he said softly. "Watch your back."

I paused and smiled at him. "Thank you, Tom. I believe we are going to try and remedy the situation of the men in back."

He shook his head.

"Ain't them I'm talkin' about what," he said softly. He raised an eyebrow at Pierre, who was waiting impatiently at the wrought=iron gate leading from the courtyard.

"There are them as who has friends who work in the dark, them," he said.

"Pierre?" I said doubtfully, turning to look at him with new interest.

"Honor ain't what it used to be then, Dr. Holliday. The young only they give it lip service, they, I think. You know what I mean?"

"Why are you telling me this?" I asked, taking a bill from my pocket. I tried to hand it to him, but he shook his head, stepping back away from me.

"Naw, sir. I won't takes that from you. You polite to me, treating me like you to others ain't nigras. That enough, me."

He nodded stiffly at me and gently closed the door. I slipped the bill back in my pocket and pursed my lips as I looked at Pierre You impatiently tapping the tip of his walking stick on the flagstone, noticing for the first time the weakness in the soft flesh of his face and the set of his shoulders, slightly hunched forward as if expecting a blow, and instinctively I knew Tom was right: Such a man would not hesitate to hire others to take care of his problems.

A slight chill came across the night as I made my way to Kate Townsend's home at No. 40 Basin Street, a three-story palace of marble and brownstone, the most opulent brothel in the country. Kate reserved a suite of large rooms for herself on the Common Street side of the building on the first floor. It was a handsome suite, equipped in magnificent fashion. The fireplaces and mantels had been carved from white maple and the furniture, upholstered in rep and damask, had been constructed from solid black walnut to match the woodwork and floors.

But it was her bedchamber that Kate had made into a dream world. In one corner, she had placed an étagère covered with tiny statuettes made by renowned artists and small articles of vertu. A marble table separated it from an armoire with a glass door behind which she had stored her linens. A richly upholstered sofa stood in front of the fireplace, while above the fireplace was a French mirror in a gilt frame. A large sideboard held a variety of liquors and silver and tableware. Her bed had been covered with lace, including the mosquito bar while a basket of flowers hung from the tester of the bed. The walls were covered by costly oils from the masters.

A visitor to her private rooms would have been hard put to believe that the owner of these tastefully decorated rooms was a madam of fierce temper who ruled her brothel with an iron fist. Yet with me Kate was always tender and loving, wildly passionate, and totally unafraid of kissing my lips, often times soothing them after a seizure when they were flecked with blood.

I had met Kate my third night in New Orleans when I visited the Absinthe House after a game broke up at St. Cyr's. I was exhilarated with my winnings, and the prospect of going to my room in the St. Charles Hotel seemed most dismal. I

struck up an acquaintance with another gentleman, who tactfully invited me to accompany him to a house of ill repute,
and, after hesitating a moment, I agreed, within minutes finding myself standing on the threshold of No. 40 Basin Street.

Kate Townsend welcomed us to her house after a uni-
formed nigra maid showed us into the drawing room. She
joined us in a glass of wine. I still remember her dress that
evening, a chantilly lace affair that barely contained her
breasts and exposed her arms upon one of which was tat-
tooed A.PIMM. When I asked her the meaning of that, she
laughed and asked if I was from Georgia or Alabama. When
I declared myself from Georgia, she pulled me aside and sat
with me on one of the sofas while my acquaintance disappeared from the drawing room with an elegantly clad lady of
the evening. Suddenly, I was taken with a seizure, flecks of
blood appearing upon my lips. She quickly helped me from
the drawing room and into her private suite, where I stayed
two days, the second day spent in her arms. I don't think she
had planned on that happening: She had assisted me origi-
nally not from the kindness of her heart, but simply because a
gentleman coughing blood in a whorehouse is bad for business. A caller might think the disease had been caught there.

I rang the bell and the maid answered, giving me a polite
smile and stepping aside after recognizing me. I handed her
my hat and cane and asked, "Is madame in the drawing room,
Loisette?"

"Oui, monsieur," she said. "She is entertaining the public
administrator. It is that time of month when payments must
be made. As always."

"I see. Thank you," I answered, suppressing a smile. Cor-
ruption lifts its ugly head whenever men in power have a
chance to exercise the power to satisfy their secret longings.
The officials of the officialdom of New Orleans were no
exception.

She curtsied and took my hat and cané to the cloak room. I
crossed to the drawing room and stepped inside. Kate saw
me and excused herself, hurrying to my side. She stood on

tiptoe to kiss me, her large breasts pushing hard against my chest.

"Are you all right?" she asked in a low voice. Her eyes showed concern. I laughed.

"Why wouldn't I be?"

"Word of your challenge has been brought to me," she said. "Do not laugh. Jean Duval is experienced in duels. He is an expert swordsman."

"Ah, alas, I'm afraid that Mr. Duval will have to forgo his desire to carve me like a Christmas goose. The choice of weapons will be mine."

"And you will choose?"

"Pistols," I said calmly.

"Pistols!" she said with exasperation, slapping my arm. "And what makes you think he is not as good a shot as he is a swordsman?"

"And what makes you think I cannot shoot?" I teased, crossing to a sideboard. I took a crystal glass and filled it with bourbon, sipping it.

"Can you?" she challenged, following me. She unfolded her fan and waved it furiously in front of her, more out of agitation than trying to cool her fevered breasts.

"Why, Kate! You sound a bit upset! Thank you."

"Who will be your second?"

"Do you know Philippe Thibideaux?"

She frowned. "The Thibideauxs on Royal? Of course. Everyone knows them."

"Could you have one of your people deliver a message to him tonight?"

"How do you know them?" she asked suspiciously.

"A bumping acquaintance," I said. I leaned down and kissed her again. "But I'll have him meet me tomorrow morning. Unless . . ." I paused delicately and raised an eyebrow in the direction of the public administrator, who was glaring daggers at us. She glanced over her shoulder, then turned back to me.

"Don't worry about him," she said scornfully. "It is true he desires me, but after a few more glasses of wine, he will go willingly with one of the others and tomorrow convince himself that he was with me."

"Then shall I . . ."

I nodded toward her rooms. She smiled and shrugged elaborately.

"Yes, of course. I will send Louis to get your message when you are ready for him. But John, do not make your appointment with Philippe too early."

I finished my drink and poured another and carried it back to Kate's suite. I pulled a sheet of paper from her desk and quickly penned a note to Philippe, asking him to meet me in my rooms at the Pontalba Apartments at (I smiled, remembering Kate's suggestion) 10 A.M. on a matter of some urgency. Undoubtedly, I thought as I sealed the message and handed it to the waiting Louis, he would have heard about the challenge and would know why I had requested his presence. In New Orleans, I reflected, such news travels fast, as fortunes could be made (or lost) on the outcome. And a strange macabre delight in the possibility of death is also one of the factors of the Creole mind. Philippe would be there; of that, I had no doubt.

As it was, I barely beat Philippe to my rooms. I was finishing changing my clothes when his knock came at my door. I opened it, still shrugging into my coat.

"Well, Philippe, you are prompt, I will give you that," I said.

He entered, removing his hat but hanging onto it stiffly. His eyes flickered over my room, noticing the furnishings, clean and neat, but spartan: two chairs, a desk and chair, and small table in one room. Through an open doorway, he could see my tiny bedroom with its bed, wardrobe, and washstand. His lips twitched, but he kept the sneer under control. He removed my note from a pocket and held it up.

"I received your note, but cannot understand for what reason you would extend such an amenity," he said formally.

I smiled and motioned to a seat across from me. I had

stopped at the Café du Monde on my way across Jackson Square and ordered café au lait and beignets for us. I poured a cup and handed it to him, then one for myself. I offered the tray of beignets to him, but he refused. His left eyebrow raised as I took a bottle of bourbon and laced my cup before settling back against my chair, sipping.

"Well, Philippe, I cannot believe you have not heard as yet. of my little encounter with Jean Duval at St. Cyr's yesterday," I said.

He took a tiny sip of the coffee and made a gesture of dismissal with his free hand.

"And who has not heard of this? You are, unfortunately, unknown so the odds are five to one with Duval as the favorite."

I grinned. Obviously, Duval was not held in high favor by Philippe, who had omitted the polite form of address from his name.

"This seems like an opportunity for us," I said. I removed a sheaf of bills from an inside pocket and tossed them on the small table between us. "Would you mind placing that for me? You might wish to spread it around to get better odds."

He took another sip and placed the cup back in its saucer on the table before us. He put his hands upon his knees and leaned slightly forward.

"Why me, monsieur?" he asked. "You know my feelings toward you. Why ask this of me?"

"Because you're honest, my friend. Despite whatever other kind of pompous ass you may be, you are honest," I said. I drained my cup and put it aside. I coughed gently and smothered it with my handkerchief.

"When we met, you did not pretend to be other than what you were: a man who detested me. Somehow, I believe that means you can be trusted. I trust you." I shrugged.

Slowly, he reached for the sheaf of bills. He fanned them, then caught his breath and slowly worked them apart between thumb and forefinger, his eyes widening as he calculated the amount. Thoughtfully, he stacked them neatly on the table between us.

"You must be very confident, monsieur," he said.

"Well," I laughed, "it will do me no good if I am dead. Why not make it work for me while I'm alive?"

A tiny smile flitted across his lips, then returned. Admiration began to sparkle in his eyes. "You are more than . . ." He groped for words. ". . . de grandeur naturelle. Non, monsieur, un homme magnifique . . . I am sorry; I cannot express what I am feeling."

"You have said enough," I said. "There is one other thing, however."

"Oui, monsieur?"

"I need a second."

His eyes began to shine with excitement.

"Me? Vous êtres très amiable! I would be pleased! Solange will not believe this."

"You must meet with Duval's seconds at the Absinthe House at two P.M."

"And the choice of weapons?"

"Pistols. Twenty paces. Specify that we will furnish the pistols subject to the referee's approval."

An eyebrow lifted over his dark eyes.

"Somehow, monsieur, I feel that you are not new to this affaire d'honneur, no?"

"I have dueled before," I said.

"And?"

"I am alive."

There was no need to say more. The implication was there; I had fought before and there could be only two outcomes: a draw or life.

"I see," he said. He riffled the sheaf of notes again. This time his lips traced a different smile. He rose.

"I shall be happy to do this, monsieur. Forgive me if I depart. One can always get better odds before the terms are announced. When word gets out that you have specified pistols instead of swords, mon dieu, but the odds will drop."

I rose with him.

"I understand. You might try to make the 'appointment'

for seven A.M. instead of the usual. And make sure that my back is to the east."

The smile rode higher on his lips. He gathered his hat and cane.

"A gambler's odds. I like this. Don't worry: I'll get what you want," he said grimly. "Duval's people will be very arrogant and will be, uh, condescending to us. We can use that to our advantage. I will set the field before I do the arms. The other way would make them suspicious and not give us the grounds."

I laughed and rose, clapping him on the shoulder as he followed me to the door.

"I think that I have found the man that I want as my partenaire en crime. Do what you can. It really doesn't matter," I added. He frowned at the bitterness in my voice. He started to say something, then snapped his mouth shut and left. The door clicked shut behind him, and I stood for a moment staring at it, remembering briefly what promises I had made.

I gathered my hat and cane and left my apartment for Kittredge & Folsom's store at 55 St. Charles Street. It was time for me to find the pistols I wanted to use.

Folsom looked up when the bell above the door jangled upon my entrance. His lips spread in a polite smile as he moved toward me. I glanced around the room: The walls were lined with firearms, and I smelled the sharp tang of cleaning solvents and oils, harsh and acrid. Glassed cases created a series of aisles ending against the far wall, where a short staircase led up to a mezzanine where clerks bent over books at their desks.

"May I help you?" he asked. His voice was soft and warm, his eyes blue and moist behind gold-rimmed spectacles, his hand warm and dry to the touch.

"Yes," I said. "I find myself in need of a set of target pistols. I'm looking for a pair of Bailey's, twelve-inch octagon barrels."

His eyebrows rose. He pursed his lips for a moment, considering, then tugged at his cuffs.

"Pardon me for asking," he said tactfully, "but would you be having a 'meeting'?"

"I would," I answered gravely. "Tomorrow, perhaps the day after. But I am anticipating a meeting. Unless, of course," I said with a grin, "the other gentleman apologizes."

"Would that 'gentleman' be Jean Duval? Not," he hastened to add, "that I'm pressing you, sir, but the gentleman's name might assist me in helping you to select the weapons you need."

"I take by your tone, sir, you do not hold Duval in, shall we say, high esteem? Not that I am pressing you, sir, but an answer might assist me in my decision," I said. I gave him an engaging look.

He smiled a wintry smile. "You may take that correctly, sir."

"Then I confess that the gentleman in question is indeed Duval."

"I see." He pursed his lips and hooked his thumbs in his vest, rocking back on his heels. He blew out through the corners of his mouth, lifting the ends of his mustache. His brown eyes considered me.

"The Baileys?" I queried gently.

"I'm thinking, I'm thinking," he said, his eyes set on inner thought. "Simply choosing a pistol by name is not enough. Weight, for example, must be taken into consideration as well as the span of the grips."

At last he inflated his cheeks and turned from me, walking back to a cupboard against the wall next to the staircase. He took a small key from his vest pocket and unlocked it, swinging it wide. The shelves were filled with mahogany boxes, their finished surfaces gleaming dully. He took out a small pile of boxes and set them on the glass case behind him. Then he reached into the cabinet's depths and drew out a box built of ebony, its surface gleaming like enamel. He crossed to me and opened it on the case between us. A pair of pistols lay inside, nestled in cutouts covered with black velvet, the black steel of their barrels gleaming, their walnut handles carved in a checkered cut warm to the touch. A brass powder flask lay between them along with a ball mold and a box of percussion caps for the nipples.

I lifted one from the box. The handle swung naturally to my hand, the barrel balancing to my grip. I rocked the hammer back with the ball of my thumb and swung a sight pattern onto an imaginary target. The blade of the front sight settled on the target. The pistol seemed an extension of my hand, a part of my being.

"Very good," I said, lowering the hammer and reluctantly returning the pistol to its case. My fingers lingered on the pistol, caressing it. It felt warm to my touch, sensual. I breathed shallowly, feeling the excitement race along my veins.

"I'll take these," I said.

He nodded his head. "They are one. Molded from a single mold, bored from a single rod. Even the stocks are taken from the same tree. You may fire them if you wish, back there," he turned to indicate a door beneath the staircase. "But you will find their patterns identical. It is strange that such a pair could be molded. Usually there is a discrepancy in a shot pattern, a minute distribution of weight, a variance in sight. But, strangely, these two have none. You lift one, you lift the other."

He shook his head. "It is a freak, you understand, an accident in the machinations of man that created two precisely identical weapons."

"Or," I said softly, tapping the case lid as I dropped it on the pistols, "the devil's."

His eyes widened. "Or the devil's," he acceded.

My eyes fell upon the case in front of me, focusing upon a Manhattan .31-caliber revolver in a pocket model. Oil gleamed ominously from its black barrel. Vague visions swept in front of my eyes, riders from the clouds, wispy shadows, dark shadows shuffling through a macabre dance. Dimly, I heard strange notes swelling out of the darkness.

"Dr. Holliday?"

I realized my eyes were closed and opened them. He frowned at me. I grinned and pointed at the pistol in the case.

"May I see that?" I asked.

He slid the case open and placed the revolver in front of me. I lifted it, feeling the balance settle decidedly forward. I took one of Pinkerton's Deringers from my pocket and compared it to the Manhattan. The difference in size was slight, but the advantage decidedly belonged to the Manhattan: It offered more than one shot.

"I believe a shoulder holster, cut to fit just above the waist and canted forward, might serve you best if you have occasion to visit the same, er, establishments where you met Mr. Duval," he said suggestively.

"Very tactful," I murmured. "Might I try it?"

"Certainly. And the others?"

"Why not?" I laughed. "Surely Duval would have tried his pistols."

"Oh yes," he said. "I can assure you that he has tried them many times." He gave a wintry smile.

"But in his academy, not on the field. I am most surprised that Duval let himself get angry enough to issue the challenge. Usually he maneuvers others into challenging him so he might have the choice of weapons. And that choice is always foils. They call him le Butcher, but not, of course, to his face."

"Well, we shall see if we can accommodate Jean Duval in another field," I said. "I use a knife to carve my meat, not to settle affairs of honor."

He opened the door beneath the staircase, and we entered into a small courtyard that had been set up as a target range for gentlemen to try the wares before purchasing. He carefully loaded the target pistols and nodded at the opposite end of the courtyard, where targets had been placed in front of a sloping iron wall that would direct the shot down.

"If you would care, monsieur," he said.

I lifted the pistol smoothly and sighted, squeezing the trigger as the front blade settled just beneath the tiny black dot. A puff of white smoke momentarily obscured my vision, then it cleared. I shifted pistols and raised the other one, sighting rapidly and firing.

We walked down the range together and looked at the target. Both shots had lodged in the center of the black, touching each other. I nodded admiringly.

"They do hold a true sight, Mr. Folsom," I said.

"They only shoot where they are aimed, monsieur," he said. "And now the Manhattan?"

We returned to the firing line. I took the proffered Manhattan and sighted, thumbing the hammer as rapidly as I could. Again we walked down to the target. Not all were in the black this time, but they were certainly close enough to score highly. He nodded with satisfaction.

"Very good," he said. "If you would allow a bit more time to allow the smoke to clear before firing your second shot, I believe all of them would have been in the black."

"That might prove a bit costly; the other man might not be willing to wait to give me a second shot."

"That is true," he said. He nodded at the pistol in my hand. "Will you be taking that as well?"

"Yes," I said. "I'll take the set and this."

Rain began to fall as I left Kittredge & Folsom's, the Manhattan firmly snugged under my left arm just above my waist in a half-cut shoulder holster, the handle canted toward the front of my coat. Beneath my arm I carried the ebony box. I felt ready for my confrontation with Jean Duval.

The sun promised to be no factor as a gray drizzle soaked the ground around us. The old oaks formed a canopy over the clearing, gray moss hanging in shrouds from their limbs. The doctor remained in his carriage under the oaks out of the rain. Two other carriages stood next to him. I had been surprised to see Pierre You and a friend in one. The two gamblers who had been with Duval at St. Cyr's were in the other.

Our seconds held umbrellas over us as the referee gave us our warnings, but the cold and dampness were enough to make me cough intermittently and I sipped from a pocket flask filled with Armagnac to quiet the threat of a spasm in my chest as I listened to the referee Philippe and Duval's seconds had agreed upon. Duval, dressed in aniline black, smiled tightly as he made his selection from the box Philippe proffered, but a tiny shadow of doubt lingered in his eyes as he hefted it experimentally. I reached in the box and lifted the mate from it, casually letting the pistol hang by my side. I smiled gaily at him.

"Well, are we ready now? Are you satisfied, Duval?"

"Let's get on with it," he said tightly.

"My, are we grumpy this morning? Did you breakfast? That makes all the difference in the world, they say. Would you care for a drink?"

I offered the flask to him. Philippe looked on with misgivings. Duval lifted his lip in a sneer.

"I do not need to bolster my courage," he said.

"Oh?" I raised my eyebrows. "What do you need?"

He flushed angrily, and I smiled at him, casually turning my back as I handed the flask to Philippe.

"Well then, if I cannot offer you anything, let us indeed get on with it, as you so succinctly put it. Referee?"

"Please place your back against Dr. Holliday's, Monsieur Duval," he said. "I shall count the paces. If either of you turns before I reach ten, it shall be my unpleasant duty to shoot him. Do you understand?"

We nodded and he began the count in a funereal tone. I began humming a death march in time to his count. *dum-dum-dumdum-de-dumdumdumdumdum*. He hesitated for a moment, then continued. I felt like dancing over the green, my steps jaunty and confident. I pictured his broad forehead in my mind, concentrating on that as my target.

"Ten."

I spun in a three-quarter circle instead of turning to my right. His shot split the air where I would have been had I not made the amateur's turn. I smiled as I raised my pistol. His second started to protest, but my shot broke through his words. Duval's head snapped back as the bullet took him in the forehead. He fell on his back, his arms flying out, forming a cruciform, the pistol landing on the wet grass below his right hand. The doctor stepped from his carriage and hurried, bag in hand, to Duval's side. He took a quick glance, hesitated, then shook his head.

Philippe stepped forward to take the pistol from my hand. I took my flask back from his and took another sip of its contents as a cough ripped through my chest. I shrugged into my coat and patted my right-hand pocket, feeling the comforting weight of the Manhattan as I walked toward the referee.

"Tricheur! Coup de déshonneur!" his second snarled at me. He turned to the referee. "I protest this . . . outrage!"

"It is most unusual," the referee said. "But there is nothing in the Code Duello to prohibit Dr. Holliday's behavior. He was quite within the rules. If anything, he was careless. And lucky," he added, nodding at me.

"I would not, monsieur, use that technique again if the occasion should arise during your stay in New Orleans. It will be remembered in the city after this." He glanced at Duval's body. "Although it was most effective today."

"I agree," I said, adding, "Philippe and I were going for breakfast. If you would care to join us?"

"I would be honored, sir," he said, nodding.

"You will have little time for dining!" the second snarled.

His hand darted inside his coat. I slid the Manhattan out of my pocket, raising it and cocking it in one smooth movement. He froze as the bore centered on his forehead, his hand half out of his coat, the pistol evident in his palm. Duval's other second took a hasty step away, lifting his hands waist high to show them empty.

"Do you really wish to join your friend?" I asked, feeling my smile tighten on my lips. He hesitated, then his face hardened. His hand swept out of his coat, the pistol cocking as he tried to bring it up. I waited until he had nearly leveled it, then shot him where his throat emerged above his collar. Out of the corner of my eye, I saw his friend's hand snake beneath his coat. I turned, thumbing the Manhattan's hammer back and letting it fall in one motion, then fired again, holding deliberately lower. The first ball caught him in his chest, staggering him. The second struck just above the waistband of his trousers. The pistol spilled from his hand as he grabbed himself and fell in a fetal position to the ground. A scream slipped past his lips. His legs convulsed.

"Mon dieu!" the referee whispered.

"If you believe in Him," I said dryly. I replaced the pistol as the doctor hurried to the man's side and knelt beside him, prying his hands away from his stomach. His jaw tightened as he ripped the man's vest open and pulled up his shirt, exposing the ugly wound. Blood and a clear fluid seeped from it. He took a bandage from his bag and pressed it hard against the wound, trying to stop the bleeding. The man's legs convulsed once more. He coughed. A froth of blood appeared on his lips. His eyes suddenly stared at nothing. The doctor felt for a pulse in the man's neck, then rose, shaking his head.

"He is dead," he said. He looked at me. "You are very quick. Very quick."

"No, they were not quick enough," I said. I slid the pistol back in my pocket and looked at the referee.

"Shall we say Antoine's in two hours? All this activity has given me quite an appetite."

His eyebrow quirked. "You are obviously not as much an amateur as you would have us believe, Dr. Holliday. False colors?"

"I am what you see, sir. But I cannot control what it is you are seeing," I answered.

"Antoine's. In two hours," he said. He moved off to his carriage, shaking his head.

The doctor motioned to the gamblers to come and help him load the bodies in Duval's carriage. Philippe bent and retrieved the pistol Duval had used, wiped the moisture from it with a handkerchief, and replaced it in the case with the other. He gave me a strange look.

"You were very lucky," he said.

I laughed. "Lucky? Yes, I suppose so."

I coughed. *Lucky to die another day by inches.* I moved toward our carriage. I capped the flask and dropped it in my left-hand pocket. I turned and looked back at the prostrate forms on the dueling green. *Perhaps with a bit more luck, I could have been one of them.*

I climbed into the carriage and settled back against the cushions as Philippe joined me. He placed the pistol case carefully on the seat between us, then bent to a basket by his feet and removed a bottle of champagne and two glasses. With a practiced twist of his wrist, he removed the cork and filled our glasses.

"To life," he toasted. I shook my head.

"Let us drink instead to death," I said. "He seems to be more evident today."

We drank and Philippe refilled our glasses, then leaned back against the cushions with a sigh.

"We have done very well today, my friend," he said.

"Oh? You did get good odds, then?"

He smirked. "Five to two. That will make you a wealthy man, I believe."

"And you?"

"As well," he laughed and drank again. He glanced over at Pierre's coach. The young man must have sensed Philippe's attention, for he gave us a dark look, then leaned forward and spoke to his driver. The driver shook the reins and turned the horses in a tight circle and gigged them to a trot.

"Our friend does not look very well, does he?" Philippe said airily, waving his hand in the direction of the disappearing carriage.

"What do you mean?" I asked, sipping.

"It is he who offered the odds," Philippe explained.

"Pierre?"

Philippe nodded. "Yes. And he seemed to relish the chance. It was almost . . ." he hesitated, glancing at me.

"Almost?" I said gently.

"He acted like a man's enemy would act if given such a chance. Do you know what I mean?"

"I think so," I said. I took another sip of the wine. "But be sure that you collect as quickly as possible from him."

He shrugged and drained his glass. "He is coming over to the house tonight. As are you. For dinner. We will collect from him then."

"To your house?"

His eyebrows raised in surprise. "Why, yes. To see Solange. Did you not know?"

"Know what?"

"He is one of her . . ." he groped for the word. "Il est toujours là l'après-midi. You understand?"

"At your house? A caller?"

A frown crossed his face. "Yes, but more than that. A marriage to Solange would mean much to his family. The Yous have been trying for years to be . . . respectable."

"I think I understand," I said slowly. A thought suddenly occurred to me. "Did Duval call upon your sister?"

"Duval?" He gave a short laugh. "No, not him. He would not have been allowed in the door."

"Strange," I said, slouching down against the cushion.

"I do not understand."

"Why would Pierre bet on Duval against me when I saved him from Duval?"

"Ah! You think . . . what do you think?" he asked, suddenly perplexed.

I shrugged. "Probably nothing. I only wonder why one man would bet on his enemy. Did you tell him that I had been invited for dinner tonight?"

"Solange did."

I nodded and finished my wine. He took the glass from my hand and replaced it in the basket. A cough rumbled from my chest. I hastily pressed my handkerchief to my lips to smother it, wondering about the strange turn of events beginning to unfold like a Greek play in front of me. Aeschylus, I thought. But which one of us was Agamemnon?

Kate was mad. I had no doubt about that and if I did, the broken crystal lying on the floor beside the wall where she had flung the vase was proof enough. I smiled at her.

"Don't you think you are overreacting," I said.

"Overreacting?" Her words had the thick Cockney of her background to them. "You stupid asshole! You know she's playing a game with you!"

"I know nothing of the sort," I said calmly.

"The Thibideauxs of this world don't open their doors to people like you or me."

"Thank you for including me in your austere company," I said dryly. I knew the truth of her words, but I did not like to hear them. Deep inside, I think I still held tightly to the hope that my consumption would reverse itself, although common sense and the bloody streaks in my washbasin in the morning told me otherwise.

"Listen to me! Your fine plantation manners may mean something in Georgia around the cockchafers and quims in your cotton fields, but here in New Orleans, they don't mean nothing! Oh, you may get in the door, but only as a curiosity. You don't belong. Not any more than me. You're only a curiosity, mate, nothing more!"

I finished knotting my tie around my neck, then shrugged into the harness of my shoulder holster, carefully positioning the butt of the Manhattan where it would be hidden by the fall of my coat yet available if I needed it. I picked up my coat and slid my arms through the sleeves, correcting the set around the pistol.

"You see?" she said, nodding at the pistol. "That don't exist in their world. Only in ours. Doc," she said, coming forward and pressing against me, "don't do this to yourself. Stay here with me where you belong."

I gently pushed her away. "I'm sorry. But I have an invitation to dinner. Besides, there is the matter of a debt to clear up. A gentlemen's wager."

"Go ahead, then," she sighed sullenly, falling back onto her bed. "Find out for yourself!"

"Oh, I will," I said. I leaned forward and bent to kiss her cheek. She drew away from me.

"Don't," she said. Her eyes flashed up at mine. "And if you leave, don't be draggin' yourself back to this bed!"

I laughed.

"I mean it! Don't come back! The door will be closed. You can go down to Twenty-one and see Hattie Strauss! You're probably more used to niggers anyway!"

"Tch, tch. Such style, Kate," I said, clucking my tongue over her tirade. I picked up my hat, carefully set it at an angle. I took my cane and winked at her.

"Ah, you bastard!" she yelled and grabbed another vase. I stepped out, hurriedly closing the door behind me as the vase crashed against the wall beside it.

I walked from the house and turned down the street, looking for a carriage. The rain had quit and stars were shining coldly down onto the damp streets. The temperature had fallen. I was surprised to see my breath in a tiny cloud in front of me. I could feel something moving thickly through my chest, and suddenly I was coughing, leaning weakly against a colonnade of wrought iron, dragging my life up in flecks of flesh through my windpipe until a bloodred thing writhed out and I spat it onto the stones of the street and gasped the heavy air, drawing breath by shuddering breath. I reached into an inside pocket of my coat, my wrist brushing against the handle of the Manhattan, and withdrew the flask with Belle's flowery inscription engraved into its silver finish. I opened it and drank deeply, wincing and swallowing against the gorge threatening to spew from my mouth. I leaned my forehead against the damp metal, letting its coldness soothe my fevered flesh.

A carriage paused near me. The driver leaned down, frowning at me.

"Bien, qu'est-ce que vous avez?"

"The world," I said. I drew another deep breath and felt the evil in my chest fly out into the night. "Do you know the Thibideaux house?"

"Oui, monsieur."

"Then take me there," I said, climbing into the carriage.

I leaned back against the damp cushions and drank again from the flask in my hand as the fog pushed hard against me. I shuddered and pulled the soiled blanket tossed on the seat for the passengers' protection about me, shivering in the warmth of its folds.

Yvon Thibideaux leaned against the brocade upholstered back of his Louis IV chair and lifted his glass of champagne.

Bright lights sparkled from the liquid like diamonds, patterning after the lights shining through the crystal chandelier hanging over the heavily laden table. I glanced down the length of soft damask tablecloth upon which rested platters of roast fowl, slices of apple-roasted pig, silver plates with broiled fish in respect of those who observed their Friday's edict, bowls of fruit and vegetables, bowls of gumbo, a calf's head, collard greens (untouched by the Creoles, who considered them beneath their dignity), and French delicacies that I had heard of but never tasted until then, and now obscured by the fog of years and . . . bourbon. Light glinted from the monocle in his eye.

"To our new friend, Dr. John H. Holliday," he said.

The others at the table—Creoles from the finest families whose lineage went back before the Lewis and Clark expedition—lifted their glasses, in solemn obedience to his proclamation:

"To Dr. Holliday!"

And they drank and set their glasses with a solid *thump!* beside their finely cast porcelain plates, wiping their clean chins with softly glowing clean damask napkins before looking expectantly at me. All, that is, save Pierre You, sitting next to Solange, whose lips had barely touched the wine in the toast, enough to earn no hard words from Philippe although a sharp glance had been directed at him. I smiled at him and rose, bearing my wineglass aloft with me. I glanced at Solange sitting at his right across from me, her shoulders, the color of old ivory, gleaming softly in the light from the candles on the table and crystal chandelier overhead. She wore a green velvet dress that bore a vague resemblance to a Trafalgar gown. Her hair had been piled up on her head and secured with a ruby clip. Her full lips curved into a smile, widening into deep dimples on either side of her cheeks as she waited, knowing with a Manx's wisdom what I would propose.

"Thank you, monsieur. You have been most gracious to invite me into your home. And to you, madame," I continued, bowing slightly to the opposite end of the table where his wife, in severe black, sat looking from beneath lowered lids down the length of snowy damask to where I had been placed close by her husband's left hand. "You have been most charming."

She nodded graciously. I turned back to Solange. Her smile had widened, and devilish lights glinted in the depths of her black eyes.

"And to you, mademoiselle, I give you my honor if you should ever need it."

She demurely lowered her eyes, gazing up at me from beneath long lashes. I felt a foolish grin spreading across my lips as the others lifted their glasses to my toast.

"Thank you, Dr. Holliday. I shall remember your words if I ever find myself in a situation where I need a champion," she said teasingly. "But to how many young women have you given your honor? Quite a few, I would venture."

"To only one," I said. "My cousin." A twinge of betrayal of her tugged. I took a large swallow of wine to wash it away, but it still hung at the edges of thought.

"Your cousin?" Her eyebrows shot up in becoming question marks. "I would think that others would have been, ah, more appropriate."

"Enough of this, Solange," Philippe said. He looked pointedly at his father. "One may be fashionably late, but to be too late is to be only ill mannered."

I had forgotten that following dinner we were to appear at the Bal de Bouquet at the home of one of Philippe's friends. Only a few short blocks from us, the summoning of needed carriages to transport all of us and the readying of the household for the trip would take at least a half hour. His father nodded and motioned expansively with a languid hand.

"By all means, Philippe, we would not wish to miss the crowning of the new queen. And I wonder, would you be anticipating a wreath of flowers upon your own brow this evening?"

He smiled as Philippe blushed furiously. I looked over at Solange. She caught the question in my eyes.

"Philippe has been paying a shocking amount of attention to Louise Cabanel this year. It is she who will select the next king, and Father will have to hold the next Bal de Bouquet in Philippe's honor should he be selected. Tell me, Philippe, will you return the favor of Louise should you be chosen?"

Laughter rang around the table as we rose. Philippe's face blushed scarlet above his white collar. He shook a finger at her in mock anger.

"Mon dieu! But someone should be spanking your bottom yet," he said. She laughed at him and looked archly at me.

"And you, Dr. Holliday, do you agree with my brother?"

I bowed to her and shook my head. "No, mademoiselle, I do not. One should always return jest with graciousness. That is the secret of attraction."

"Actually," Pierre said from beside her, "I think that is the mark of a weak man, don't you? It strikes me that often when one is trying to be charming, one is trying to conceal one's dependence upon another."

"I see," I said coolly. "Tell me, then: Are you charming to your valet? Or, do you treat him with disdain? Perhaps that would explain your jacket."

"And what do you see wrong with my jacket?" He glanced involuntarily at its impeccable fall, the pearl gray beautifully offset by black velvet at the collar and lapels.

"It reminds me of a peacock's feathers," I said calmly. "Charming, but the animal beneath is still a fowl."

His jaws clenched tightly as the others within hearing distance laughed at him. Philippe stepped between us, clapping Pierre upon his shoulder.

"One must be quicker of wit these days, Pierre!" he said. "Come! Let us go into the library and settle our business."

"And what business might that be?" Solange asked curiously.

"A small matter of a wager," Philippe said vaguely.

"A wager? Upon what?"

"Upon my life," I said dryly. "It seems as if Pierre cannot accustom himself to selecting a winner."

His anger blazed across at me as Philippe hastily took his

arm, drawing him off in the direction of the library. I started to follow them, but Solange halted me by placing her hand upon my arm. Concern edged her eyes as she leaned in close to me. I could smell the spice of her perfume and remembered that I was a man. I breathed gently, cautiously, but deeply of its scent.

"He lost a great deal of money?" she asked.

"Yes. Quite a bit," I said evasively. "It seems he puts too much credit upon his grandfather. He needs to be himself, not pretending a reincarnation of the old one."

She opened her mouth to speak but her mother summoned her from the doorway.

"Solange! Come! We must go!"

"Coming, Mother," she said. She looked thoughtfully at me, then tapped my forearm with her fan.

"Please help him," she said. "For me?"

"Solange!"

"Yes, Mother!"

She turned and left. I watched her slip between the doors in front of her mother and disappear. Her mother gave me a disapproving look, then shook her head and crossed over to me.

"Dr. Holliday," she began.

"Yes, madame?"

She hesitated, then defiantly lifted her chin. A long hair curled from a mole beside her nose. Her skin had a parchment dryness about it and a faint scent of funereal lily lifted like dust from her.

"About Solange, there can never be anything for you there. Do you understand what I am trying to say?"

"Yes, madame, I do. But do you not think that that decision should rest with her?"

"No, I do not. That is a decision for her parents. Her father, to be precise. Solange is a foolish girl who thinks she is a woman. I trust you will remember that during your association with Philippe? Do not take these silly flirtations any further with Solange. Please."

"Flirtations are harmless," I said haltingly, trying to keep from giving my promise, for I knew once my promise was given, there would be an end to something pleasant between me and this family. I did not want that. I felt a certain . . . homeliness about it even if the politeness was artificial.

"Not always, Dr. Holliday. It is flirtations that lead most times to marriage. For a young girl like Solange, marriage must be correctly made, a wise decision that will prove most beneficial to her."

"And you do not think such a relationship is possible with me?"

"You are a gambler, sir," she said apologetically.

"So is Pierre."

"Yes, but with him it is an occupation, not a vocation. And there is the question of his family."

"And mine?"

"Yes, there is the question of yours as well. You are an American. That is enough."

"I see," I said slowly. A slow anger began to glow within my stomach. The flesh around my eyes tightened. I forced a smile.

"I am afraid that I am ill made for marriage, madame. Indeed, I find little use for the institution. I believe that although most marriages are made in heaven with the father's consent, they are too often repented in hell."

"You, sir, are impertinent!" Her eyes flashed angrily at me. I bowed.

"Of course, madame. But I am American. As you have reminded me. That is my excuse. What is yours?"

She turned and walked regally from the room without a backward glance, making an outcast of me with the coldness of her shoulder. I laughed and made my way to the library, but I did not feel the laughter: a coldness had settled over me, a bitter, solitary coldness.

Philippe looked up angrily as I entered the library. His nostrils were pinched and white, his eyes furious. Pierre stood quietly by the fireplace, a sneer playing around his lips. Tiny notes of alarm played dimly.

"What's wrong?" I asked, quietly closing the door behind me.

"Pierre does not wish to pay his debt," Philippe said. He spread his hands. "But what can one expect from one who has a buccaneer's blood in his veins?"

"Insulting me won't change my decision," Pierre said. He crossed to a small side table and helped himself to a glass of brandy from a decanter standing there. "Besides, there is no proof of the wager."

"No proof?"

I looked at Philippe. He took a handkerchief from an inside pocket and dabbed at the perspiration suddenly appearing on his forehead.

"It was a private settlement between what I thought were two gentlemen," he said. "Of course, I will make appropriate restitution to you, Dr. Holliday," he added formally.

"No need for that," I said casually. "Pierre will pay."

"And why will I pay you?" Pierre said, his eyes laughing at me over his glass. "What will you do? Lodge a suit against me? There is no provision for that in our courts and even if there were, there is the matter, as I said, of proof."

"You will, of course, be barred from this house," Philippe said.

"Will I? I wonder what Solange will say to that?"

"You will stay away from my sister!" Philippe said, taking a step forward.

Pierre gave him a smirk, finished his glass of brandy, and placed it on the mantle. He bowed to both and swaggered from the room. The door closed behind him. Philippe used his handkerchief to wipe the perspiration from his face.

"I am sorry, my friend. There is no honor in that man, and where honor is missing, well, there is nothing I can do. I will, however, make arrangements for you to be reimbursed for your losses. I can do no less through my carelessness."

"It is only money, Philippe," I said. "Nothing more. Do not worry yourself over it."

"But my honor! . . ."

I shook my head. "There is no road or ready way to honor. Pierre will discover that when he finds what this has cost him in reliability. Once word of this gets around—"

"You do not understand New Orleans, my friend," Philippe said, interrupting me. "It is not Philippe who will appear the fool, but you. Everyone will see this as a plaisanterie of Pierre's. They will say il 'a fait par plaisanterie when they speak of it. You forget that the American soldiers did not make themselves very popular with the people of New Orleans when they were here. No, my friend, it is you who will be the object of insult and ridicule, not Pierre. Mark my words!"

And so it went for the next two weeks as I made my way around New Orleans. Ares came down the river no worse for the wear after the days aboard the flatboat, but he was restless and nudged me hard in the chest with his nose when I came to greet him. I rubbed his velvet nose affectionately and he grumbled grudgingly deep in his chest, moving his feet restlessly. I made arrangements for keeping him at Pierre Lafitte's old blacksmith shop, now a stable on Royal Street. I made a rule of riding every day out southwest of the town or up Old Plantation Road, where the old oaks festooned with sheets of hanging Spanish moss grew, twining their arms overhead to form a shaded canopy. I was beginning to enjoy myself. Solange and I began to spend more and more time together at dances and balls, sitting quietly in the courtyard beneath a palmetto tree when the weather was nice, or in the music room of their house.

One evening, Solange played Mozart as I sat with a glass of claret beside me. Her mother nodded, then frowned as Solange faltered in one place, but recovered and finished with a flourish. She turned on the stool, smiling at me. I grinned back.

"Very good," I said. "Especially the 'Little Minuet.' "

"But a little practice is needed, I believe," her mother said. "Perhaps you need to begin your lessons again?"

Solange pouted. "I am tired of the lessons. Besides, Monsieur Coulard's breath smells of absinthe."

"Maybe I could be of help?" I asked.

Solange's eyes widened slightly. Her mother gave me a wintry smile.

"We are speaking of the piano, Monsieur Holliday. And how to teach one to play. Not how to listen."

I smiled and placed my glass on a small table beside my chair and rose. I crossed to Solange and gave her my hand, helping her from the stool. She rose and tapped my forearm with a long, manicured finger.

"Please forgive Mama," she said lowly. "She does not mean to insult you."

"May I?" I said, gesturing toward the piano.

Her eyebrows rose, and she canted her head to the side, gesturing toward it.

"Of course. But you do not have to do this."

"Of course I do," I said. "My honor. You understand?" I smiled at her mother, who watched impassively as I sat behind the piano. I ran my fingers over the keys, feeling their tension. Then I slipped into Chopin's "Opus No. 1 in B-Flat Minor," and a pang of loneliness struck me as I remembered Mother patiently tapping the time on a small chair beside me as she gently corrected my tempo, the curve of my hands over the keys. When I finished, I sat quietly for a long second, then turned on the stool to face the room.

Solange's eyes were moist. She rose and came to me, pressing my shoulder.

"That was beautiful, John," she whispered. "Beautiful. And so sad."

Her mother rose and started from the room, then paused and looked back at us, her eyes veiled.

"Perhaps you could help Solange, Dr. Holliday," she said, then turned and left the room.

The next few days were happy. I wondered if I was beginning to fall in love with her, then pushed that thought away. I still was too close to Mattie and the memory of what we had together. And there was the matter of my sickness, the conquering worm in my chest that threatened to curl and strangle me in the damp nights. I began to spend more and more time with her, though, taking more and more time away from the tables at St. Cyr's and other places in Old Town. It was just as well: The story of my encounter with Pierre had begun to make the rounds.

No one commented on it to my face, for word had traveled as quickly that I was dangerous with a pistol, but I could hear the sniggers and jests made behind my back as I passed in the street or sat at the gaming tables. I knew it would only be a matter of time before someone would assume that I did nothing to Pierre You because I was afraid. A man's reputation as a blazer lasts only as long as his next confrontation. I did not expect, however, that that confrontation would be with Pierre You.

I remember well that night, as it was the night when Rex, the King of the Carnival, made his appearance, the night before Ash Wednesday. I had taken a table at Doran's Place on Royal Street and opened it to four members of the ancien régime when Pierre You pulled out the chair across from me and sat, arrogantly tossing a marker at me for chips. A quiet immediately spread over the other tables near mine as gaming halted and the players leaned back to watch my reaction. He glanced around at the others.

"Ah, Holliday," he said. "Make it a thousand, if you will."

I quietly picked up his marker and tossed it back to him, saying, "This game is table stakes only. Your marker's no good here."

He flushed. Someone sniggered. He leaned forward in his chair, his eyes bold and demanding.

"What is wrong with my marker?" he asked.

"It won't be honored when you lose," I said. The tightness of the room felt like a band around me. I leaned back in my chair, regarding him, toying with a stack of coins on the table in front of me.

"What do you mean?" he demanded, lowering his voice threateningly.

"Precisely what I said," I said. I idly tapped my watch, my fingers scant inches from the holstered Manhattan at my waist. I looked at him levelly.

"You have a reputation as a man who does not pay his

debts, sir, and that is not the man with whom I prefer to gamble. This is, after all, a gentlemen's game."

The others discreetly pushed their chairs back from the table, distancing themselves from any ruckus that might erupt. Pierre's face blanched, then tiny red spots began to glow just beneath his earlobes.

"Are you saying that I am not a gentleman?" he demanded angrily.

"Yes," I answered calmly. "Gentlemen are not born; they are made each generation by those who wish to have themselves called 'gentlemen.' It is a title given to men who have earned respect and with that respect, honor. You have earned neither."

He leaped to his feet, his chair overturning with a crash. His hands trembled and the blood vessels bulged in his forehead.

"Do you know who I am?" he said thickly.

"Dear me, yes. You are being rather tiresome. Everyone knows who you are: You have traded on your grandfather's name and honor for so long that one would be hard pressed not to know who you are. But as to what you are, why, if you wish, I will give you a name: how about: *intrigant,* for when you give your word, you are really giving   "—here I switched to French so all would understand—"des promesses qui ne sont qu'un trompe-l'oeil!"

A gasp came from the room, then a slight twitter of laughter. For a moment, I thought he would deny me pleasure, as his face turned a mottled purple, but he quickly recovered and, in a strangled voice, offered, "You will answer for this . . . this . . ."

"Outrage?" I offered. "Why, of course. Forgive me if I wasn't paying enough attention to you."

I turned to the others in mock despair. "Please forgive me for my ill manners. One simply has a hard time these days distinguishing between cambrioleurs et messieurs."

I used the vulgar way of speaking, and the room erupted in laughter. The mottled purple in Pierre's face became one dark shade. His hands began to shake with tension on the table as he hunched forward, straining toward me.

"Sacré! Illégitime . . ."

And his words froze in his throat as the Manhattan appeared in my hand.

"How do you do? I am Dr. John Henry Holliday," I said mildly.

"La magie noire!" someone whispered, the words suddenly loud in the room. The wildness spread up into my throat, and I laughed and placed the pistol down at the edge of the table where I could quickly grasp it if I needed.

"There! Now, let's begin over. You want to play; it is simple: Give me what you owe for preferring Jean Duval to me."

The room began to buzz. I realized, then, that few knew the entire story. But others in the room who did quickly began whispering in the ears of those who did not. Scornful glances began to be directed toward Pierre. Beads of perspiration broke out on his forehead as he felt the change in the atmosphere toward him: from admiration to contempt.

"You cannot live with those words," he whispered.

"And you cannot live by challenging them," I said. "Do not become a larger fool than you are by pretending to be something you are not: your grandfather's reincarnation."

"The choice is yours!" he said angrily, swallowing heavily.

"I do not wish to do this," I said slowly. "You may still withdraw if you wish."

"Then you are a coward! Or else, make the choice!"

"Why, that should be obvious!" I exclaimed. "Pistols."

"I expected no less," he sneered, glancing around, trying to regain the stature that he had lost among those present. "A barbarian would never select the weapons of a gentleman!"

"Ah, yes. Swords. Long knives, aren't they? Such as those used to carve beef or fowl. Tch, tch. Frankly, I have never thought of myself on that level: with the beasts of the field."

Laughter erupted at my words, at first spontaneous, then rueful, as those present recognized the irony of my words. A deeper flush stained Pierre's face. He glanced down at the pistol near my hand. I shrugged apologetically and carelessly nudged it next to the small Matterhorn of chips by my right hand.

"Well, I suppose that I must appear uncivilized, but really, I doubt if we can find a set of pistols here."

A look of relief appeared over his face although he tried to mask it from the others present. He didn't succeed, as was evident from the snickers that accompanied his change of expression. But then everyone knew that was the reason why Pierre was so unsuccessful as a gambler: He could not control his emotions.

"But," I continued, a recklessness building within me, "we should certainly be able to make some sort of arrangements here. Surely some gentleman has a pistol that you can use."

"I use a strange pistol while you use one with which you are familiar? That is hardly within the *Code Duello*," he said scornfully.

I sighed and made an expansive gesture.

"Well, in the hope of preserving what little remains of New Orleans gentility, I would be more than happy to let you use mine while I use the stranger's pistol. It matters little to me, you see. Either way, I win."

"I do not understand," he said.

"You never would," I answered. I stood and surveyed the crowd.

"Will not someone here lend me a pistol with which to oblige a poltroon?"

"By God! This bears playing to its full conclusion," a voice said from the back of the room. The crowd parted as a man dressed in a coat of sea blue, lace spilling from his cuffs and throat, strode to my table. Whispers followed his steps.

" 'Tis John Allard."

"Allard?"

"You know: Allard Plantation. Where the dueling oaks are?"

He paused and slipped a Colt M1855 Root Model pocket revolver with an ivory handle from an inside vest holster. He presented it, butt first, to me.

"Will this do?" he asked.

I took it and tried its balance: He obviously had had a gunsmith work balancing plugs into the handle to place the weight back into the palm. Although the butt was a bit small, my hand fit comfortably around it.

"This will do nicely," I said. "And the shots are equal."

I glanced at Pierre, whose face had grown white at Allard's appearance and now had a slight tinge of green to it.

"Well, Pierre? Are you ready? Do you have your seconds?"

"What do you mean?" he asked.

"Why, a duel, of course."

I waved my hand around the room.

"This is roughly twenty paces across and if a bit more or less, it won't really matter, will it?"

I looked at Allard.

"Will you, sir, referee?"

He grinned, his teeth flashing white in his sallow face. He took a snuffbox from an inside pocket and opened it, taking a pinch from its contents and bringing it delicately to his nostrils. He inhaled sharply, waited a second, then sneezed gently into a perfumed handkerchief he took from his sleeve. His manners were decidedly old-fashioned, but none there dared give him any cheek about them: The Allards were famous for their willingness and ability to accommodate detractors.

"I would be honored, sir," he said. He looked over at Pierre.

"This should prove most interesting. Your grandfather was a great lover of affaires d'honneur, I believe. Wasn't there a time when he refereed such a matter between someone and a certain James Bowie?"

"A long time ago," Pierre said. He smiled weakly. "Of course, he would hardly have approved of this."

Allard frowned. "Really? I would think he would have found it highly interesting. Was there not an affair in which there were knives in the dark? Bowie's knife against a maître's—if I'm not mistaken, a Contrecourt?—sword. A most interesting situation. I don't suppose . . ."

He frowned for a moment, looking from me to Pierre and back, then shook his head.

"No, I suppose not." He heaved a sigh. "Proprieties must

be observed as we try to regain our . . . heritage. Well, gentlemen, I believe that we are ready?"

He looked expectantly at Pierre, who nodded, then at me. I shrugged and smiled, spreading my hands expansively. I looked across the table at Pierre.

"Good luck, Pierre," I said. I picked up the Manhattan and handed it to Allard along with his own pistol. "I believe we are ready."

"There is the question of seconds," he said, frowning. "That is, if we are to follow gentlemen's rules."

"Oh, I think there are enough here who will be willing to serve in that capacity," I said, shrugging.

He weighed the pistols in his hand a moment as he looked around at the crowd, then a knowing smile split his lips.

"Yes, I think I know what you mean. Tomorrow, all here can claim to have been the second for the winner of the duel between . . ."

"A gentleman and a barbarian?" I broke in.

A short laugh escaped from his lips. His eyes glinted with pleasure.

"Yes. But the question is, which is which? Still, I suppose we should have an official designee for each."

Pierre's eyes flickered over the crowd, searching. I knew instinctively he was looking for Philippe. A smile tugged at my lips.

"Philippe!" I called. "Will you oblige me?"

He became an island as the crowd turned to him, their faces suddenly grave with that impassivity reserved with those deemed contemptuous. His face flushed for a moment, then a reckless grin spread across his face. He gave Pierre a long, level look, then smiled a dangerous smile and nodded.

"I would be honored, monsieur," he said. He moved defiantly to my side as the crowd buzzed with his support of me instead of Pierre, perhaps not one of them, but closer to their society than I.

"And I will take . . ." Pierre's eyes studied the crowd and settled. "Monsieur Ragnieux. Will you honor me?"

I recognized one of those who had been fleecing Pierre

when I had "rescued" him at St. Cyr's. A dangerous recklessness began to build inside me as he moved to stand beside
Pierre. I wondered how he had escaped St. Cyr's posting of
him to the other houses.

"Good!" Allard said, smiling and clapping his hands in
approval. "Then let us begin. Dr. Holliday, if you will take
the south end of the room, and Monsieur You, the north?"

The crowd buzzed as we stepped to our places. Wagers
were shouted frantically across the room, were met and
agreed upon as we slipped from our coats and released our
ties. Impulsively, I took a swarthy gentleman's offer of nine
to five. He blinked, and I gestured toward the chips on my
table. He nodded, scribbled on a piece of paper, and handed
it to Philippe as Philippe appeared by my side, Allard's pistol presented toward me, lights sparkling from its ivory grip.

"Gentlemen!" Allard called.

The room fell silent as the crowd split between us, creating
a comfortable margin in the event that a ball went awry.

"Ready!"

We moved to our places, pistols held by our sides.

"On the count. At five, you will be free to fire until one
falls. Is that understood?"

I glanced at him: He held a mate to my Manhattan. A grin
tugged at my lips. I nodded, and Pierre followed suit.

"One."

The crowd grew silent.

"Two."

Breaths involuntarily drew in and were held.

"Three!"

Pierre began firing. I smiled and waited until two bullets
buzzed by my ear, then coolly leveled my pistol and fired
once. The ball slapped him above his eyebrows. His head
snapped back and a fine spray of bloody mist flew behind
him as he fell to the floor, the pistol falling from his grasp.

For a long moment, the crowd fell silent as death walked
among them, then excited voices broke the silence as wagers
were claimed. Philippe gently took the pistol from my hand
as Allard came toward me. He gave it to Allard.

"I am sorry, my friend," he said.

I laughed, coughed, and nodded. "Yes, it might have been better if he had won."

"I do not understand what you mean," he said. "But this will mean that you must leave New Orleans. Solange . . . Well"—he looked at Pierre crumbled on the floor opposite us—"there was something between them," he finished delicately.

"I see," I said slowly.

"No," Allard said. "I don't think you do." He nodded at Philippe. "Your friend is right."

I looked at him.

"Pierre comes from an old family with many friends in the 'old trade.' They will all be looking for you."

"Then let them find me," I said, laughing. "No man ever got out of this life alive. We all owe someone a death."

"Yes, but what honor is there in that?" Allard asked quietly. "It would be best for you, Dr. Holliday, if you would leave. I regret this, for I feel that you would be a lively addition to this pathetic society that insists on clinging to its antebellum ways. But, well . . ."

"I understand," I said quietly, taking the Manhattan from his hand. I gave him the Root. "I understand."

And I did.

The night brought with it a damp coldness that drew the warmth from my body, biting through my cloak and coat with a vengeance. I tried twice to hail a cab, then gave it up and plodded through the rain-swept streets to the Thibideaux house with Philippe beside me, grim and silent, understanding my need for silence. Dark despair deepened my mood as I repeatedly raised my handkerchief to my lips, coughing, coughing, feeling the great worm move in my chest. I tasted brass in the back of my mouth and spat dark sputum onto the pavement.

Philippe cleared his throat apologetically. "Are you all right?"

I laughed.

"I do not find this a laughing matter, my friend," he said. "I can tell that you are not well. And I do not think this will endear you to Solange. Solange was, well, Solange was interested in Pierre. Do you understand? Far beyond what one might call infatuation. I do not think it was love, no, that I do not think. More, I would say the romance of his grandfather, old Dominique, Jean Lafitte's man, and those friends of Pierre's who are the grandsons of old Dominique's friends. The buccaneers have stayed together, mainly because no other will have them other than as the odd curiosity at a party or two throughout the year, which they are sure to attend because they want to become a part of New Orleans.

"Maybe," he mused, frowning, "they have more right than others. After all, it is they who brought powder and guns for your General Jackson when the British tried to take New Orleans. But"—he gave a Gallic shrug—"they are still not acceptable. There is bravery, my friend, then there is foolishness."

"Thank you, Philippe, but this is something I must do myself."

"Why?" he asked, perplexed.

"Because there is not that much difference between Pierre and myself," I answered. "We are both outcasts." I smiled at him to take the sting out of my words: "Both are oddities at parties."

He flushed and bit his lip, looking away. "Believe me, my friend, when I say that you are more welcome than Pierre in our house."

"Perhaps, but would you want me to marry your sister? Oh, don't worry." I laughed at the startled look on his face. "I would do anything for your sister except make her a young widow."

"Monsieur?"

"Never mind," I said, as we came to the wrought-iron lattice fence surrounding the Thibideaux home. "It was a poor attempt at humor."

Despite my attempt to remain alone with Solange in the library, Philippe insisted on remaining with us. I stood as close to the fire as possible, trying to warm myself from its heat and the heat of the brandy Philippe had pressed upon me as we waited for Solange to join us.

She wore a high-necked dress, dark blue, and carried a shawl of Chantilly lace around her shoulders. A slight smile attended her lips, and her eyes danced with sardonic humor.

"Philippe!" she exclaimed upon entering. "Ever the brother! Do you not think that I will be well protected in my own house without you in attendance? Are you now to be my gouvernante?"

"You would be safer with Dr. Holliday than you would with any other," he retorted.

"Why?" She looked boldly at me. "Do you not think he is a man? Like other men?"

"No, Solange. Not like other men. Not like Pierre."

Her eyebrows rose. "Pierre? What does he have to do with this?"

"He is dead," I replied.

Shock spread over her face. She groped for the back of a chair to steady herself. Philippe stepped close to her, but she waved him away.

"Dead? But how?" she exclaimed.

"An affair of honor," I replied.

"Of which he had none," Philippe muttered, moving to the side table where he had placed the brandy decanter after pouring a glass for me. He poured two more, and handed one to Solange. She took a tiny sip, shuddered, then held the glass between both hands.

"What happened?" she asked quietly.

"He played an insult that I could no longer ignore," I said.

"You!" she exclaimed. Her lips tightened. Twin spots of color appeared high in her cheeks.

"I am sorry," I answered gently.

"You killed Pierre!"

"He left John little choice, Solange," Philippe said.

"For what reason? Honor? What is there about that that is worth Pierre's life?" she asked scornfully. She rose and flung the contents of her glass at me, but the brandy fell short, splattering on the carpet at my feet.

I looked quickly at Philippe, who frowned and shook his head as she rushed from the room, slamming the door behind her. He sighed and took a long swallow, finishing his brandy, then poured another.

"Perhaps I underestimated her feelings," he said apologetically.

I laughed and drained my glass, handing it to him for a refill. He poured a generous dram and handed it back.

"Either her feelings or her sense of drama," I said. "She holds her role clear in this drama and plays her part well."

"You take this very lightly," he said.

"There is little else I can do," I said, sipping. "What is done is done and cannot be undone."

"Yes," he said, studying his glass. He sighed and placed it on the table, clasping his hands behind him. He studied me for a long moment, then said, "You will have to leave New Orleans."

"And why is that?" I asked, straightening from beside the fire.

"There will be others; Pierre's friends who will be ready to challenge you on his behalf. Allard explained that. Had you forgotten?"

"Let them," I said gaily. "I will be happy to oblige them." I laughed again. "Perhaps they will bless me and get lucky."

"No. You are making honor a game. That is not what you want," he said.

"You have no idea what I want," I retorted.

"Don't I?" he said quietly. "I have seen you cough, my friend. And I have seen what is left after you cough. Oh, I have not told anyone," he said as I quietly placed my drink on the mantle above the fire and turned squarely to face him. "That is your business. I know what you wish: a death at once and not in pieces of you scattered over the ground. What honor is there in that? What honor is there in knowing that you can kill those who come against you or that if they do kill you, it does not matter? Does that not give you an unfair advantage, knowing that your life is worth nothing? Make a bully?" He shook his head. "No, my friend, that is not for you. Despite what you think now, that is not for you. And I will not let you do that."

"And what will you do to stop it?" I asked.

"I will tell everyone about your condition," he said, staring calmly into my eyes. "Which would be worse? To leave, or suffer the sympathy of others who deem it unnecessary to battle with you?"

"And if they follow? That will still be a game, won't it? I cannot help it if I am followed."

"Yes. But the rules will be reinvented and in that, you may find a certain sense of honor, for I will be silent if you leave. You have my word." He nodded toward the door. "And more deaths won't make Solange like you any more than now. Perhaps in time . . ." He spread his hands in dismissal.

Laughter bubbled up inside me, and I turned, taking my glass back from the mantle and draining its contents. I tossed the glass into the fireplace, breaking it.

"Ah, yes. Honor. Well, honor pricks me on until it pricks me off."

I gave him a small bow and turned to leave, then paused and looked back at him.

"Should you . . . or Solange . . . need my help, you may reach me through my father in Valdosta."

"I will remember," he said solemnly.

He crossed and held out his hand. I took it, feeling the friendship in his grip, and knew then that his words had not been given lightly. A sadness broke over me. I released his hand and left.

Outside, the rain had begun again, mixing with its coldness tiny flakes of snow. I shivered and wrapped my cloak around me. Light glinted through the windows of the houses down the street from the Thibideaux home. Somewhere, a pianoforte tinkled tinnily, but the gaiety it made was not for me. The night had become my prison. I turned and walked alone back to my rooms through the darkness.

3

All stood reverently aside on the sidewalk of Market Street, removing their hats and bowing their heads as the hearse rolled somberly past, drawn by a pair of pampered matched blacks, arching their necks and nodding their heads beneath the black plumes rising like a potentate's crown over their noble heads. Their coats shone like wiped satin. Black bunting draped the windows of the enameled black hearse to frame the polished mahogany casket with burnished gold handles. A mound of lilies and hyacinth lay on the casket top.

The undertaker sat stiffly beside the driver, his face stern and unapproachable, lips drawn fine as if spoiled prunes had slipped down his gullet. He wore a black cutaway, striped trousers, and a high silk hat like Lincoln wore when he became president two styles in the past. The driver wore a somber black suit with a bowler clamped down to his ears, which stuck out from the sides of his face like jug handles.

Behind the hearse came a row of carriages. In the first, an emaciated preacher with fervent eyes clasped a heavy Bible tightly to his breast with one hand while the other rested condescendingly across the shoulders of a dumpy woman weeping behind a black veil. Behind them came another carriage with two young ladies escorted by men who were obviously their husbands: They wore the same look I had seen on the faces of slaves before the War.

A man standing beside me nudged me. I looked down at him. He nodded and raised his eyes to my hat.

"Your hat, sir," he whispered.

"Yes, you're right," I said.

I smiled pleasantly at him and moved away, strolling down Market Street, studying the displays in the windows of the various stores I passed. The dead did not interest me; I felt too closely akin to them to be in awe of the mystery to which others paid homage with elaborate funerals. I had been in Dallas on the Trinity almost a week now, wandering around, trying to decide what I wanted to do, trying to forget New Orleans, trying to forget Solange. I took a short train ride across the peninsula to the *Morgan Line,* an iron steamer that crossed the corner of the gulf to Galveston. From there, I took the Houston & Texas Central into Dallas, my clothes smelling of wood smoke and honeycombed by tiny holes made from hot cinders flying back from the small steam engine that rattled and bubbled and gurgled like a coffeepot. Ares was moody and pensive after stepping nervously from the box car in which he traveled. But once he felt the ground under his hooves, he snorted and danced, showing his eagerness to gallop. I arranged quarters for him at a livery stable a short walk from my hotel standing on the outskirts of town away from the main thoroughfare.

The walk from my hotel to the livery was not the five miles that physicians were recommending for people with my sickness, nor did I follow my walk with a cold bath. Neither the walk nor the bath made sense to me as a "cure" for consumption, despite the assurances of doctors, and the patent medicines that physicians alternately prescribed were heavily laced with laudanum. I ignored them, as I had found whiskey to do as much for me as the patent prescriptions, and it did not leave me groggy for hours. The whiskey seemed to hold the cough at bay if I took it in small quantities over the course of the day.

A cough worked its way up from my chest. I stepped out of the flow of traffic and covered my mouth with a handkerchief I took from an inside pocket. A man paused down the street from me and turned deliberately to look into a store window. I frowned and wiped my lips. Why would a man who wore a New Orleans suit be staring into a window display of farming tools? His face was dark and lean, his hair carefully barbered.

A smile moved across my face. One of Pierre's friends? I

spat in the gutter. Perhaps he would be the one. He glanced furtively toward me, his face narrow and pinched like a rat's, eyes close-set and shifting rapidly away from me. I grinned recklessly at him when he looked back. He turned away and hurried down the street, following in the hearse's wake. I sighed. No, he would not be the one.

I turned and walked down the street, now *my* street, for I had gained position of it with my failure to follow the sheep and pay obeisance to a man I never knew simply because he was dead and in death I found no mystery. I turned onto Elm Street, walked a block, then doubled back on Austin Street and made my way along the walk, checking my back in the store windows I passed. The man in the suit reappeared behind me after a block. I grinned, then stepped into an alley and quickly slipped behind a stack of packing cases. I heard the sound of running footsteps, then the man appeared in the alley, hurrying toward the other end. I stepped behind him as he passed, and drew the Manhattan.

"Now would you be looking for me?" I asked.

He whirled, his hand dropping inside his coat pocket, then stopped as he caught sight of the Manhattan.

"Ah, ah," I said warningly, shaking a finger at him. I slipped up to his side and reached into his pocket, removing a small pistol. I dropped it into my pocket. "This wasn't very friendly of you," I said conversationally. "Who are you?"

"Jean Dupres," he said in a surly voice.

"New Orleans?" I asked. He hesitated, then nodded quickly, his head making one short motion. I sighed and stepped back and away from him.

"Go back home," I said. "And tell your friends to leave me alone."

"There is the matter of honor," he began.

"And the matter of money from the You family, right?"

He flushed and did not answer, but I could tell from his eyes that I had hit upon the truth.

"Tell them that I will kill the next person they send after me," I said. "What happened was an affair d'honneur. They have no reason to be pursuing this any further."

"The Yous have many friends," he began.

"And," I continued, "tell them that I will return to New Orleans if I must. There will be no further warnings. Do you understand?"

He nodded. I gestured with the Manhattan at the end of the alley behind him.

"Now, go. If I see you in Dallas after tomorrow, I'll kill you. Do you understand?"

He stared with hate-filled eyes into mine for a long moment, then spun on his heels and walked briskly down the alley, disappearing into the bright sunlight at the end. I sighed and put away the Manhattan and left the alley. I walked down to Julian Bogel's saloon for "swells," as he called his clientele. I opened the door, kept shut against the dust of the day, and stepped into cool darkness. I hesitated for a moment, letting my eyes adjust to the dark.

"Hey, Doc!" a man called from the depths.

I squinted through the smoke and recognized Cole Younger from a poker game a few days previously when I felt obligated to stake him to a meal after he lost his proverbial shirt to me by holding two pair to four eights. Obviously, his fortunes had turned again, and I smiled and gave him a small wave, turning toward the mahogany bar gleaming darkly in the depths of the saloon. Behind it, tiny stars flickered from the surfaces of bottles. Frank, Bogel's bartender, dressed in a snow-white shirt and black bow tie with a starched, white apron over his black trousers with knife-like creases down the front, watched me approach, his eyebrow raising a half inch when I rested my elbow on the bar and my foot on the gleaming brass rail running down the length of the bar. I looked into the dusted mirror behind the bar and took stock of myself: my gray suit folding correctly across my frame, face ivory white despite the Texas sun, the hint of a mustache making itself known over my upper lip. A diamond glinted from my gray cravat. I lifted two fingers to him and turned half-around on my elbow to study the room.

"Mr. Holliday?" a voice asked from my left.

I turned, my hand sliding automatically inside my coat and slipping across the cold, gutta-percha handle of the Manhattan. Frank slid my drink to the bar tactfully away from my elbow.

"Yes?" I answered. I faced a slim, older man dressed in a black suit that folded nicely over a small paunch. He wore a black derby slanted over one highly arched eyebrow. Black eyes stared steadily into mine from the middle of folds of tiny wrinkles. His nose was thin, his cheeks slightly hollowed, not quite having caught up to his run at obesity. A tiny mustache clung like two chips of coal dust above his lips.

"John Henry Holliday? Of Georgia?"

"You have the advantage of me, sir," I said.

"I'm John Seegar. Dr. John Seegar," he emphasized, holding out his hand. I touched it with my fingers, quickly pulling back before his hand could close around them. He looked startled for a moment, then gave a thin smile.

"From Georgia," he added almost apologetically.

I lifted the glass Frank had silently slid in front of me, sipping it, rolling the Old Williams around on my tongue, savoring its flavor and after bite, for, despite the calming effect it had upon my consumption, I had become quite fond of its flavor, the hint of charcoaled maple, the . . .

"Would you care for a drink?" I asked, gesturing with my glass. He glanced at it and shook his head.

"Thank you, no. I find it a bit early for my taste, but please proceed without me," he added so quaintly that I could not take offense. I laughed and gestured to Frank for a refill. He moved down the bar, sliding the bottle in front of him, then poured with a practiced twist of his wrist, then pointedly left the bottle in front of me, a tight smile accompanying his move. I frowned at his back as he moved away from me down the bar to serve another customer. I have never liked bartenders who belong on the Methodist or Baptist holy-roller circuit. I firmly believe that one who works in a saloon should be neutral, ambivalent toward his customers, yet sympathetic, even if only artificially so.

I took another look at Seegar. He appeared to be about twenty years older than I, and I wondered what he wanted with someone like me, a newly made dentist. Was his practice that large that he desperately needed a partner? I didn't think so, but there weren't that many dentists in Dallas at the time. Perhaps I was wrong. I smiled and took another tiny sip of Old Williams.

"So, Doctor," I said. "And what can I do for you?"

He smiled quietly and smoothed his finger along the tiny mustache. "I have been looking for you for quite some time now. Your father made me believe that you would be in Dallas in January."

"Sorry. I stopped over for a while in New Orleans. But you said Father contacted you?"

"Yes. I was with your father in Mexico. He found out from a mutual friend of ours in Atlanta that I was in Dallas. Actually, our paths did cross briefly during the War in Virginia when Hood met up with your father's unit after the big summit conference with Pickett and Johnston and others. That was just before Lee made his sweep north through Gettysburg. I never knew what happened to the major after that. We were good friends in Mexico. For a while, well, that's a story for another time."

His eyes were sharp and intense, but I could feel the warmth behind them. For a moment, a lump formed in my throat. Father had gone to a lot of trouble to run Seegar down for me and to make sure that I would not be friendless in a faraway place. I felt ashamed of the way I had treated him. Although I remembered his harsh standards at home, I began to see a reason behind them. He had been trying to prepare me for the world he had known. Even though that world had not been mine at the time, it appeared to be the world I was entering, a world where friendship was at a premium.

"It was good of you to be so persistent," I said. "I'm sorry that I wasn't on time."

"That doesn't matter," he said, waving off my apology.

"Did Father tell you . . ." I toyed with the glass, dotting wet circles on the bar.

"Yes," he said quietly. "I'm sorry."

"Fate," I said. I laughed, but the laughter sounded false, even to my ears. I quickly drank the whiskey in my glass and poured another from the bottle Frank had set in front of us. I took a cautious breath, breathing in deeply until I felt the familiar tickle begin, then quickly let it out. I took a tiny sip and placed the glass back in front of me.

"Well, Dr. Seegar—" I began.

"Please," he interrupted. "Make it John."

"Two Johns in one room. Sounds obscene," I said. He laughed, and I felt myself drawing closer to him.

"Very well, John it is," I said. "Did Father give you any message for me?"

"Oh yes," he said. A mischievous sparkle came into his eyes. "He sent along a letter for you. As did someone else?"

He reached into an inside pocket and removed a long, thin letter and passed it over to me. My heart quickened as I recognized Mattie's handwriting, a fine copperplate with whorls under the "y" in my name. A pang struck deep within me. I took the letter from him.

"Pardon me," I said. He nodded and I took a small step away, eagerly opening the flap with my forefinger. I read briefly, my eyes burning:

Dearest John,

I have missed you terribly and have waited long for you to write. I understand that times are difficult for you, but, John, I will understand if you have found another. If it is only your sickness, why, that does not matter. How can I . . .

I read on to the end about how Father's crop was good, yet the country was still poor. But my eyes kept roaming to the top of the page where she wondered if I had found another. I had tried to tell her that another had found me, that my sickness had become my bride. Mixed emotions ran through me. I folded the letter and slipped it into my breast pocket. My fingers brushed across the cold butt of the Manhattan in its shoulder holster.

"Thank you," I said quietly. I picked up my glass, draining it.

A heavy eyebrow arched questioningly at me, but when I made no attempt to respond, he quickly changed the subject, clapping his hands together and glancing up at the repeater on the wall above the bar mirror.

"Well, maybe it *is* close enough to evening for me to join you. May I?"

He gestured at the glass in front of him. I reached for the bottle and filled it. He took it, sipping, as I watched critically. He rolled the few drops he had taken around in his mouth, then swallowed in installments, his Adam's apple working familiarly in his throat. He nodded appreciatively.

"Good. *Good.* I had better be careful; this could become habit forming."

I laughed.

"Somehow I don't think that will ever become a problem with you," I said.

"I hope not," he said. "But one is never very sure about what lies on the morrow."

"Perhaps," I said dryly, draining my drink. "But for some of us, that does not seem to be a problem."

"I'm sorry," he said quickly. "I . . ."

"Don't be silly," I answered. "It is there between us and that is all there is to it."

"Have you made plans for dinner?" he asked, abruptly changing the subject.

"That is good," I said. "Very good. No, I haven't made any plans for dinner. Are you free?"

"Does Standish's sound good?" he asked, naming one of the better eating places far enough away from the stockyards to be fashionable.

"It does," I said, adding magnanimously, "and the dinner is on me."

"I won't argue," he said, draining his glass. "And I think if we time it right, we might have enough time for another before making our way across town."

"You're the doctor," I said, pouring.

He grimaced. "Please. Dispense with the puns."

Standish's had been carefully planned by Leslie Standish, a black sheep from an old English family. He brought with him to Dallas not only a vast appetite for the life that he had known in England, but also a love for the freedom that the West gave him to exercise his enormous appetite for danger and intrigue. His restaurant was ebullient, lavish, and opulent, almost too much for taste, but it had rapidly become de rigueur among the social scions of Dallas: plump, bustled dowagers with hard lines etched deeply in their faces, their hair drawn back tightly in buns that screeched, feathers molting in the high humidity and floating into one's soup from the mahogany fans turning sluggishly overhead. The men bore their servitude to their wives' social expectancy with dour expressions, their powdered, red necks chafing under the pressure of tight, starched collars. A piano player, who moonlighted in Bogel's saloon after the dinner crowd closed out, wore tails and a frilled shirt while he played, rather poorly if I'm any judge, selections from Mozart designed in his estimation to ease digestion of the overdone steak that the majority selected from their somewhat limited taste. Few availed themselves of the various meals Standish's cook produced in his kitchen, but the select few who did partake of steak au poivre with its green peppercorn sauce or the duck à lòrange were admitted into Standish's inner circle and had automatic seating in the back rooms—an envied arrangement that was hungrily watched by the starched and powdered set in the front room.

Seegar had backroom privileges, not so much from a sensitive palate, but because Standish had been one of his patients and Seegar had made a painless extraction that had pulled him close to Standish's heart. Bogel, beefy and red-faced, a dark glass of wine in front of him, was seated there as well when we entered, and called heartily to us as we were shown to our seats by the maître d'. Seegar winced and nodded politely at him. Across from him, Tom Austin turned in his chair to see who had drawn Bogel's attention from him. He was dark and saturnine with black and thick eyebrows meeting over sharp eyes. He, too, owned a saloon, but on the lower side of town, where the railroad workers would frequent and the cowboys roaming through the city, looking for work. It was a sad, evilly run place where the thick sawdust on the floor remained dark with black blood spilled almost nightly over women and cards despite the frequent raking. I didn't like him and hadn't since I had witnessed a time when he had coolly drawn a pistol and shot a cowboy who complained about the tab his bartender had laid upon him after he had dropped his year's salary in a crooked faro game.

"I see you have made the dubious acquaintance of one of our more, ah, 'colorful' characters," he said. He glanced at the wine list the steward tactfully held in front of him and pointed at a Rothschild. The steward took the list and disappeared in the back.

"Bogel or Austin?"

"Does it matter?"

"Yes," I answered. "Bogel is a man of honor. Or," I amended, "as much honor as a man like Bogel can have. There are lines that he won't cross."

"And Austin?"

I smiled. "Austin is a man who rewrites the rules as he plays. I take it you don't care for him?"

"I think both are men of color."

"I take it you don't like Bogel, then?"

He made a face. "Don't turn your back on him. He's highly opportunistic. You're only as important as the one who is standing next to you."

"He does keep a nice saloon, though," I said.

He smiled. "Oh yes. That he can handle. But he wants more."

He leaned back in his chair as the steward poured a small

measure of the wine into his glass. He tasted and nodded. The steward quickly poured a glass for each of us, then placed the bottle on the table. I tasted the wine: dry.

"He wants," Seegar continued, then stopped, thinking. "He wants . . . respectability."

"Don't we all." I grinned. "There is a certain demand in most of us, isn't there? We want the freedom of the lower classes, yet we want the sanctity of our own. Where do we find the satisfaction of belonging?"

An eyebrow arched high above his dark eyes. He absently touched his mustache with a forefinger.

"A philosopher. Well. This promises to be interesting," he said.

"In what way?" I asked, toying with my wineglass.

He leaned back and studied me from under lowered brows. His lips drew down into a thin line, then he gave a quick nod and leaned forward, resting his forearms on the snowy tablecloth.

"I could use a partner," he said. "Would you be interested?"

"I might," I said casually. "What type of partner are you looking for?"

"A full partner," he said seriously. "I have more patients than I can handle and Dallas is growing rapidly. The city holds roughly seven thousand now, but by the end of the year, that figure will probably grow another thousand. I have it on good authority that the railroad is thinking of making Dallas a major terminus here, and if that happens, why, we'll easily be as large as St. Louis and Denver in ten years. I think the time is right for a major commitment."

"What type of commitment?"

"There's a good building available on Elm Street between Market and Austin. That, I think, will be the major business district in a few years. It already is a highly lucrative area and will be, I am sure, the place to do business in a few years. Now, I propose that we go in fifty-fifty on the building and offices. I can handle the major surgery while you take care of the immediate practice—the daily trade, so to speak. This would leave me open for the more difficult work. Of course," he continued, leaning back again in his chair, "I do not propose to leave you holding the damp end alone. I would work those patients also, but this sort of arrangement would free me from the daily routine."

"I see," I said slowly. I tapped my fingers on the table and frowned slightly at my wine. "How much do you anticipate this to cost?"

"About two thousand apiece," he said. "That would provide us not only the building, but would also allow us to set up and give us a working capital."

"Two thousand. A tidy sum," I said. "And guarantees?"

"None, but I currently have between twenty and thirty patients a day. The other dentists in town see about half that many."

"Why don't you ask one of them to go in with you?" I asked. "They would at least bring part of a practice with them. I can bring you nothing."

"I know," he said. "I planned something like that a little later, but when I heard from the major . . ." He shrugged. "Carpe diem."

"The others don't have the two thousand?" I asked innocently.

He laughed. "Well, a couple do, but they are not the ones with whom I would like to associate. Besides, I owe the major a favor."

"You mentioned that before," I said. "Mind telling me what favor?"

"Yes," he said. "At least for now. Perhaps later. We'll see. What do you think about my proposition?"

"It sounds good for me, but I don't see what you are getting out of it. Why would you want a lunger for a partner? You know that the partnership will be decidedly limited in time."

"It is not given to man to know his future."

"Isn't it? Perhaps not for some, but others have the future thrust upon them whether they want it or not."

"Then shall we say that I'm easing my conscience while doing a favor owed a friend? That should be enough."

"All right," I said. "I hope we don't come to regret it, but I'm game."

He stretched his hand across the table. I took it and we sealed our partnership with a handshake and a glass of wine. But I should have knocked on wood at the time to keep temptation from the minds of the gods. And plenty of wood was around us.

Things were a lot different back then before the railroad pushed on south to El Paso. Most people today see things only firsthand since the time the railroad pushed on. Yes, things were a lot different then.

For a year, our partnership seemed blessed. Father sold another of my properties and promptly sent the money I needed for my share of the partnership. Our offices were constantly filled with patients, and Seegar even took special pains to introduce me to his circle of friends. I met Fanny Perkins, the daughter of one of the more prominent bankers in Dallas, and we became fast friends.

Unfortunately, the richness of her father brought several fortune hunters to her door. Austin was one of the worst, driving the other would-be suitors away with brute force. But Austin was a saloon-keeper and not of the social state that endeared him to Fanny's father, who made no bones about how he was unsuitable for his daughter. But Fanny had, shall we say, a "curiosity" about Austin that led her into flirtatious behavior whenever Austin was near her, and this led Austin to believe that he was socially acceptable.

I daresay that Doc Holliday would have been received with that same curiosity as Austin—that fascination one holds for a rattlesnake—but Doc Holliday had not yet emerged from the cocoon of Dr. John Henry Holliday of the gracious manners and the correct background that earned him the sobriquet of "gentleman."

Fanny and I became the social item that made tongues wag in delicious anticipation as we appeared at parties and dances or at the church socials.

I kept my illness a secret as long as I could. I think Seegar was tempted a time or two to broach the subject when he thought Fanny and I were becoming too close. But he refrained from speaking the thoughts I saw at times behind his eyes. I was the perfect escort: one who could put no claim upon her for the future.

But this could not last. Slowly, the sickness returned, coughing spells appearing suddenly at the most awkward times when I was bent over a patient's gaping mouth, hard, wrenching, wracking coughs that brought my life up in bright red droplets of blood.

Seegar was forced to take on more and more of my patients in addition to his own as the railhead began to move southwest toward El Paso and more and more people flooded into Dallas in search of work. But he did not reproach me for this although the strain upon him became more and more evident as the summer came with its intense heat that lifted the water from the Trinity River in humid clouds that rolled over the city.

Seegar was right; our practice grew and grew, but I was the one the gods elevated to near glory only to cast down after teasing me with hope. I became a respected businessman for a while, but the nights became filled with pain. I tossed and turned during the nights, imagining the horrors creeping up on me through the blackness, trying to convince myself that the sickness was not returning with a vengeance, hoping that the signs were wrong: that the spots and blemishes upon my handkerchiefs were only temporary. Later, when the attacks came more frequently, I began to spend more and more time away from the office, playing cards through the night, stilling the spasms in my lungs with generous draughts of Old Williams. Seegar still never reproached me. I think he resigned himself to the man I was making in the various dens of iniquity available to me, believing that I would eventually die before thoroughly degrading myself. But he did not take into account my determination.

I welcomed the bright sunlight with relief and embarrassment for what I had imagined lurking in the blackness of the night, and I hated what I had become, and I hated those who gave me piteous looks, and I hated the life in them.

Whiskey helped ease the pain, and with whiskey I found that I could be amiable toward people, greeting their pity with smiles instead of snarls, turning my sickness into a joke, the joke that was upon me for being human, for being born.

I found relief from life in the gambling halls and burlesque shows and the plays at Field's Opera House, where life, even if only an imitation of life, was constantly evident. Slowly, my life began to change. By day, I was reminded of what I was; at night, a playful facade draped comfortingly over me. I discovered that life at night was preferable to sleep; at least sleeping during the day removed the uncertainty of the blackness. But that reduced my effectiveness at our practice. I found the scrape of sandpaper on a broken tooth grating on my nerves, which were tightly strung from the previous night's drinking.

Surprisingly, Fanny became closer and closer to me, nestling tighter in my arms during our waltzes, flirting with me during our walks, her eyes suggesting promises of . . . I refused to dwell upon the possibilities because I knew that I was becoming like Austin in her eyes as well.

I began to slip from Seegar's world, from the world of the socially acceptable, sinking deeper and deeper into the frantic make-believe world not meant for everyone, but only those few whom life had rejected. Doors formerly open to me began to close, apologetically at first with feigned regrets and flimsy excuses. Then they did not open at all.

Fall came and went and, although Fanny and I still frequented some of the same parties, the invitations became fewer and the stares more hostile. But their hostility I could deal with; it was their pity that I could not accept.

Pity.

I hated the very sound of the word. I hated those who offered it to me because the pity was offered with secret looks that confirmed their own life while reminding me of the rapid end drawing to mine.

Damn them!

And damn the gods that molded my fate!

And then one morning I realized that although the gods

could take life from me, strip my dignity from me, my honor was mine and mine alone to surrender, and I chose never to surrender.

I began to practice with the Manhattan for two hours every morning, riding Ares to a hidden bend of the Trinity where I would draw and shoot at old tomato and peach cans, whiskey bottles, rocks, anything that would provide a suggestion of a target, concentrating on speed and accuracy; draw and shoot, draw and shoot until my hands stung from the recoil of the Manhattan and my ears rang from the deafening echo of the cartridges.

Slowly, my metamorphosis began to take shape, as the gentle man Mother had hoped for began to disappear. Oh, I still retained the manners and mannerisms of the southern gentleman—those were too far ingrained within me to be removed by anything—but sincerity became replaced with caustic cynicism, which I used to lampoon myself.

In the fall, bad news reached me in a letter from Mattie. Father's experiment with Sea Island cotton had proven so profitable that others had changed to growing it in place of other crops. Then the boll weevil came and destroyed the crops and what little had been rebuilt of Georgia. Once again, planters faced bankruptcy and ruin with no money crop in sight. Yet I felt no sympathy for them; I felt the loss of Mattie even more. And fall passed into winter and Christmas, but I spent Christmas in Bogel's saloon, clearing nearly ten thousand dollars in an all-night poker game with other dissolutes.

On New Year's Day when I called upon Fanny, I found her in tears, sitting in a darkened parlor, clutching a handkerchief to her eyes. The day had been a good one for me, no coughing and plenty of patients who had celebrated more than they should have, breaking teeth in fights, cavities suddenly appearing while eating the rich fare at dinner tables. I placed my doctor's bag on the floor and turned to her. She refused to look at me until I grasped her chin in my hand and gently raised her face. An angry red blotch covered one cheek.

"What happened?" I asked quietly.

She shook her head, refusing to answer.

"Fanny?" I pressed. "What happened?"

"Tom," she sobbed.

"Austin struck you?" She nodded. "Why?"

"He asked me to marry him," she said. "And . . ."

"You refused."

"Yes."

"Then he struck you."

She nodded again. The old, familiar recklessness began to surge through me, the red darkness, and I patted her hand, rising.

"John!" She grasped wildly for my hands. "Don't do anything! He is . . ."

"Now, now," I said soothingly, gently pulling my hands free. "You had better put cold compresses upon your cheek before it swells. You know what your father will do if he discovers that Austin struck you."

"I know," she said softly, miserably, and began to weep. "Oh, John! What shall I do? Father is no match for him!"

"You know you are responsible, don't you? You made him believe that he was welcome; that his attentions had a chance of succeeding," I added as she lifted her tear-stained face to mine.

"Yes, I know," she said bitterly. "But you don't know what it is like to be blessed with . . . with . . ."

She rose and ran to the door, threw it open, and stormed inside the next room. I followed, pausing inside the foyer as she stood in front of the full-length mirror affixed to the wall. She glared at her features.

"You don't know what it is like to be stared at because you have the face of a horse," she said. "I know why the men come around and it isn't because of my beauty."

She turned and stared defiantly at me, but I could see the depth of the hurt she felt deep within her eyes.

"The men come around because of my father's money. Not because of me!"

Tears brimmed in her eyes. She tried to smile, but the smile did not rise to the twin dimples in her cheeks.

She turned and fled up the stairs.

I stood alone in the foyer, listening to the ticking of the clock on the mantle, regular and muffled like the beating of a heart in the darkness that seemed to fall around me. The darkness deepened. Horned shapes stirred in the shadows of the room around me. I left, closing the door softly behind me, gathered my bag from the porch, and walked from her house, bending my steps toward Austin's saloon.

Smoke hung like a dense blue-white cloud over the room when I pushed through the doors of Austin's saloon in the southwestern corner of Dallas. I knew the piano player in the corner and waved to him when he lifted his chin in my direction upon my entrance. Stinky Porter shook a tired forefinger in my direction from the faro table and immediately turned his attention back to the game before one of the players could move his chips to a corner of the cards on the table, covering two bets for the price of one, or placing a copper after the card was pulled from the dealing box. Jimmy, the bartender, flinched when I walked to the bar and placed my doctor's bag upon it, and hurriedly slid a smudged glass and bottle of whiskey down to me. I considered the glass critically, then nonchalantly tossed it behind the bar and took the engraved silver cup Belle had given me from the bag, pouring it full from the whiskey bottle. I drained it, refilled it, then turned, sipping, to consider the room.

Every table was filled with cowboys frantically wagering their month's wages in hopes of momentarily escaping their humdrum existence. In the corner, the roulette wheel turned with a monotonous rattle of the roulette ball every minute, the dispassionate voice of the wheeler calling the number and color and sweeping the losing bets off the green felt.

Austin sidled up next to me and glanced over the bar to where I had tossed the glass his bartender had offered. His upper lip curled.

"Something not to your liking, Holliday?" he asked.

I took another sip of the whiskey, then shook my head and tossed the whiskey onto the floor. His eyes narrowed. I took a handkerchief from an inside pocket and mopped the inside of the cup before dropping it back into my bag. I grinned at him, feeling the old recklessness let loose inside.

"Your whiskey, Austin," I replied coolly.

"What's wrong with it, Doc?" he asked.

"Doctor," I corrected.

His eyebrow lifted. "Doctor," he repeated. "Well. Please forgive me."

Those within hearing distance paused and laughed, turning their attention in our directions to watch the growing challenge between us. I grinned, loosening my coat.

"It tastes as if you had made it yourself." I lifted the bottle from the bar and sniffed it, grimaced, and dropped it to the floor. Heads swung toward us as the bottle shattered against the floor, splashing whiskey over the sawdust. "And made it from rattlesnake heads and tobacco juice you culled from your cuspidors."

His eyes narrowed. He slid back away from the bar. A figure moved into the edge of my vision. My eyes flicked toward him; a burly figure, ill-dressed in a suit, grinned at me: Jim Daniels, a former pug who had earned a meager reputation with his fists and gun at Austin's direction. I edged my coat back away from the Manhattan. The smile faded on his face. I looked back at Austin.

"But what should one expect from someone like you?"

"And what kind am I, Doc?" he asked dangerously.

"You'd sell your mother for a handful of trade beads," I answered.

His eyes narrowed, and his hand slipped beneath his coat. I'd stepped clear of the bar, my hand starting toward the Manhattan, when an iron band dropped down over me, clamping my arms to my body. I twisted my head and Daniels grinned at me, his breath reeking of spoiled meat. A gunshot roared, and glass tinkled behind me. Austin grinned balefully at me, his gun smoking in his hand. I twisted away from Austin, presenting Daniel's back to Austin. Another shot rang out.

"Don't, boss!" Daniels shouted. The arms slipped away from me as Daniels dived beneath a table. A mad screeching of chair legs against the scarred wooden floor clawed at my nerves as gamblers and drunks dived down to the floor, hugging the planks for security.

Daniels fell to the floor and scrambled awkwardly, like an injured crab, behind the bar. Another bullet ripped through the air by my ear, then the Manhattan was in my hand. Austin's eyes widened. He snapped a wild shot at me as he moved down away from me.

I squeezed a shot at him. The bullet blasted splinters into his face as he dropped behind the bar. Curses flew at me. I fired again. Splinters again flew, this time into the air. Curses flew at me. Austin peeped over the bar, hugging it closely. He fired at me twice in rapid succession. I heard the bullets and grinned at their passing. I fired back. A bottle burst next to Austin's head, showering him with glass and whiskey as he quickly ducked back down behind the bar. I laughed.

From behind me, a quiet voice commanded, "All right, boys, put down your pistols."

I twisted my head, looking back at the saloon doors. Caleb Fisher stood there, a double-barreled shotgun lifted cautiously between both of us.

"Put it down, Dr. Holliday," he said.

I shrugged and placed the Manhattan on the bar, taking the flask Belle had given me from an inside pocket. He stiffened as the metal flashed in the saloon light. I grinned and toasted him. He shifted his attention to the other end of the bar.

"All right, Austin," he said quietly. "You're next."

"Not until Holliday throws his pistol in!" he yelled.

Fisher glanced at me. I shrugged, toasting him with the flask.

"Done," he said quietly.

Austin rose from behind the bar, a malevolent smile splitting his face. He leveled his revolver at me, then hesitated, his eyes slipping over toward Fisher.

"Drop it, Austin," Fisher ordered calmly. "I mean it, now."

Muscles bunched along Austin's jaw. Indecision flickered in his eyes. I winked at him and he flushed, raising his pistol toward me. Fisher rocked back the hammers on the shotgun, the ratcheting loud in the room, the only other noise a man coughing softly in the smoky air.

"I can't miss, Austin," Fisher said softly. "And this here's loaded with ten buck a barrel. That's a lot of holes to put in a man, and I'll give you both barrels."

Austin slid his pistol onto the bar and rose to his full height, his hands sliding over his suit, brushing splinters away. "Arrest that man, then. He—"

"I saw it, Austin," Fisher said, lowering the hammers on the shotgun. He draped it negligently over the crook of his arm and collected my Manhattan from the bar before walking down to get Austin's ivory-handled pistol. He glanced at it and shook his head.

"Smith and Wesson Second Issue." He looked at me and dropped the pistol in a sidepocket of his coat. "I don't think you had much to worry about, Holliday."

"I wasn't," I murmured, lifting my flask and sipping.

"Holliday?" A figure dressed in a worn suit stirred from one of the tables and rose, coming forward. He peered closely at me. His eyes were bloodshot, a day's whiskers showing on his chin, the flesh beneath it soft and pliable. "John Henry?"

Memory stirred within me, then sunny days on the banks of the Withlacoochee slipped to the forefront of my mind. I held out my hand. "Ben Hawkins?"

"It's been a while," he said, gripping it warmly. "I heard you were in Dallas."

I shrugged. "For a while, anyway."

"Yeah, I heard about that, too," he said, dropping my hand. His lips twisted in a sour smile. "Father does send a letter when he mails my, ah, allowance."

"I hate to break in on this reunion, but let's go, Dr. Holliday," Fisher said, motioning to the door. "You too, Austin."

"Where?" Austin answered, frowning. "I was just defending myself against this—"

"Careful, Austin. You're about to go too far," I said, smiling at him. The frown disappeared from his face.

"Go to hell, Holliday! I'm not afraid of you," he said stiffly.

"You should be," Hawkins said, breaking in. "John's one of the best hands with a pistol I've ever seen." His eyes warmed as he looked back at me. "They're still talking about that time you shot that nigra when he tried to raise his rifle on you."

Curious eyes turned in my direction, new interest showing in their depths. I shook my head, walking toward the door.

"You do go on about the old days, Ben Hawkins," I said, trying to pass his words off with a laugh. "This shouldn't take long, and I'll buy you dinner."

"That will be good, John," he said ruefully. "Father's letter isn't due until tomorrow and I seem to find myself in, ah, financial difficulties. I'll wait for you at Bogel's!" he added, raising his voice as the doors slipped shut behind us. Austin vehemently protested his arrest all the while as we marched down the street in the direction of the jail.

> *Dr. Holliday and Mr. Austin, a saloon-keeper, relieved the monotony of the noise of fire-crackers by taking a couple of shots at each other yesterday afternoon. The cheerful note of the peaceful six-shooter is heard once more among us. Both shooters were arrested.*

I folded the *Dallas Herald* and laid it beside my plate, an advertisement for Colt .45 Model 1873's on top. I lifted my coffee cup, sipping in the late morning sunlight streaming in through the window at my back, musing on the advertisement. The *Herald* had not reported the entire story about the peace bond that had been levied on both Austin and myself, but it was enough, I was afraid, to damage my partnership with Seegar permanently. I couldn't blame him: My reputation had slipped steadily downhill the past year since my sickness had decided to take control of my life once again. I smiled, remembering with irony the prediction of the doctors in Atlanta. Two years had passed since their death sentence. I was living on time borrowed from the gods now.

A chair scraped as it was pulled away from my table. I looked up as Fanny's father slipped into it across from me.

His eyes were sunk deeply into the pouchy folds of his banker's face. He folded his hands on the table.

"I read about your escapade yesterday in the paper," he said without preamble.

"Coffee?" I asked, motioning toward a waiter.

He shook his head. "I also have a pretty good idea of why you did that."

I shrugged. "There's something inside of each man that makes him want to tilt at windmills a time or two in his life."

"I don't believe that for a moment," he said quietly. "Your windmills, I think, would have to be the real giants. Why did you do it, John?"

I remained silent, sipping my coffee, feeling the ugliness of the day beginning to move inside my chest. I willed myself not to cough. After a long moment, he sighed and took a cigar case from an inside pocket. He offered one to me, but I shook my head. He selected one, then leaned back in his chair to avail himself of the gold cigar clip he took from a vest pocket.

"I had a little talk with your friend Hawkins. He came to see me this morning about a temporary loan," he said. He shook his head. "I cannot condone what you have done, but I can understand what you have done. The rashness of youth . . ." He made a vague gesture with his free hand as he shook out the match, blowing blue-gray smoke at the ceiling between us. A small cloud floated across the table, tickling my nostrils. I coughed gently.

"But," I said, "you no longer want me to call upon your daughter, is that it?"

He looked startled for a moment, then a sheepish smile spread across his face.

"Yes," he said quietly. "That is it, John. I thank you for your chivalrous nature—I could expect nothing else from a gentleman—but I do have Fanny's reputation to think of. I wish . . ." A dark look clouded across his face. He shook his head. "Damn it, John, I wish—"

"I know," I interrupted, sighing. "I know. But fate has her own ideas about what we are to be. Don't worry. After yesterday afternoon, I think I have worn out my welcome in Dallas. If not then, then surely this afternoon."

"What do you—" he started, then stopped as I smiled at him. He looked down at the glowing end of his cigar and frowned.

"Yes," I said. I put my hands on the table. "Now, if you'll excuse me, I must see my partner and make . . . arrangements."

He rose with me, staring at me. He shook his head and held out his hand. "Good luck, John. I hope you find what you are looking for somewhere down the line. If there is anything I can do for you—"

"I know," I interrupted, taking his hand. It was soft but firm with its grasp. "I'll let you know where to forward my accounts after I'm settled."

He nodded and left, leaving fragrant cigar smoke in his wake. I took a deep breath, then coughed, tasting brass in my mouth. I took a handkerchief from an inside pocket and gently blotted my lips, glancing at the crimson splotch before refolding the handkerchief and placing it back inside my pocket. My fingers touched the handle of the Manhattan tucked under my arm. I smiled and left the café, turning my footsteps down Market Street to Havermann's Gun Shop.

The bell tinkled as I opened the door and stepped inside. Havermann came from the back room, wiping his hands on an oily rag. He gave me a sunny smile.

"*Güt morgan,*" he said in a thick German accent. "Vat may I help you vith?"

"I saw in the paper you had Colt .45 Model 1873's for sale. I would like to look at one," I said.

"Certainly," he replied, beaming. He led the way to a glass case tucked in the far corner of his store. Light gleamed from the blue-black and nickel-plated revolvers in the case. He opened the glass and reached in, lifting out an ivory-handled, nickel-plated revolver, handing it to me.

"Dis vun I haf vorked on," he said proudly. "It has a five-inch barrel to suit a gentleman. Unless," he added apologetically, catching himself, "you vould vant one bigger barreled for outside of town?"

"No," I laughed, weighing the pistol in my hand. "No, I do not think so. The shorter barrel will better suit my purposes."

I hefted the pistol: It felt butt-heavy, but I knew that when cartridges had been placed in the cylinder it would balance well. I tried the hammer: drop-heavy but firm. I took the Manhattan from its holster and slid the Colt into it. The pistol lay awkwardly in it. Havermann's eyes blinked.

"I haf something dat vill vork like dat," he said. He disappeared into the back room only to emerge within seconds with a soft leather holster in a double shoulder harness. I slipped off my coat, handing it to him, and took off the shoulder holster, laying it in the case. I slipped into the harness and turned my back so he could adjust the straps. I slid the Colt into the holster. It rested, butt canted forward, the bottom of the barrel just at belt level. I drew it; it slipped naturally into my hand.

"Yes," I said. "May I try it?"

He nodded and led the way through the back of his shop, cluttered with saws and drills and lathes, to the rear. We stepped outside onto a tiny board platform. Silhouette targets had been placed about twenty-five feet away. He reached out and gave me a handful of cartridges. I loaded the Colt and placed it back in its holster and turned, facing the targets. With one smooth motion, the pistol slid into my hand. I thumbed the first shot as I raised it, the second when it reached eye level, then quickly emptied the revolver. We walked down to the target. The first shot had landed in the middle of the chest. The other five were loosely grouped in the area designating a man's heart.

"I think you haf found your pistol," he said quietly. He looked at me. "I am not a superstitious man, but I tink you and this pistol vere intended for each odder. I also tink dat dis is not a good thing."

"It is only a pistol," I said.

"True," he murmured. "But together, you and dis pistol are . . ." He shook his head. "But I am only a foolish old man. Vat you vant to do vith the Manhattan?"

"I would like you to add a holster on the right side of the

harness," I said, slipping out of it and handing it to him. "I want the barrel of the revolver to fit just above my belt line."

"Higher than the odder vun?"

I nodded, and followed him back into his shop. He picked up a measure from a bench and made a few rapid calculations, then stepped back, nodding.

"It vill be ready by tomorrow," he said.

I shook my head. "I'll give you an extra ten dollars if you'll have it ready by four o'clock this afternoon."

He blinked owlishly behind his glasses, then slowly nodded. "Yes, I vill dat. I tink," he added as I paid him, "dat I vas right: Dere is evil at vork here."

I smiled and left his shop. I walked down three blocks and over one, and opened the door to our offices on Elm Street. A high-pitched whirring stopped as the bell above the door tinkled. Moments later, Seegar emerged from his room opposite mine.

"Morning, John," he said quietly.

"Good morning," I said. I waved at the empty waiting room. "I see that we are not exactly overrun with business today."

"No," he said, closing the door behind him. "I have a cowboy in the chair who lost a tooth in a brawl last night, but that's it." He paused. "I see by the paper that you were busy last night."

"Oh, just a little disagreement," I said. A tickle made itself known at the back of my throat. I slid the flask out of my pocket and opened it, sipping. His eyes followed my movement, then he bit his lip and stared at the floor.

"John," he said. "We need to talk."

"Yes," I said quietly. "I know."

"I think that I've been more than patient with you—" he began, then stopped as I held up my hand.

"And I'm grateful," I said. "But, well, I think it would be better for both if we just dissolved our partnership."

He nodded, his lips pressing tightly together. "I'll have to arrange a loan to buy you out."

"No," I said. "I have arranged for my accounts to be transferred once I've relocated elsewhere. I'll carry the note myself. Say fifteen thousand over three years?"

"That's pretty steep," he said.

I shrugged. "But that's what it's worth right now. And I'm not charging you interest. That's only five thousand a year you have to come up with. Say yearly payments on this date. That gives you interest over the year on the money you'll have to pay out."

He nodded slowly. "Yes, it's more than fair. Especially considering . . ." His voice faltered. I grinned. He had the grace to blush. "All right. I'll take it."

I held out my hand. "You can have the furnishings in my office as well. All I need is my bag and instruments."

He shook my hand. "John, I'm sorry."

"So am I," I answered. I replaced the flask and nonchalantly touched my hat. "I'll keep in touch."

"Do that," he said. He motioned toward the closed door apologetically. "I'm sorry, but I have to get back."

"I understand," I said.

"Good luck, John," he said, opening the door and closing it behind him. The drill started again, and I smiled and looked over the office. It had been a good idea at the time, and I was grateful for Seegar taking me in as he had, although I knew that my entering into partnership with him had been mutually beneficial to each: He had gained the money he needed to make the move that would eventually make him rich; I had gained a year in which I had been able to live a normal life.

I entered my office, pausing for a moment as my eye touched briefly on my instruments laid out in a neat row on a table next to the leather-backed chair and foot-operated drill. I quickly packed the tools I intended to take with me, then quickly left, closing the door firmly and finally on my old life.

Ares moved restlessly as I snubbed him to the hitching post in front of Austin's saloon. His feet shifted in the dust, eager to be on the road out of town. I smiled and rubbed his velvet nose affectionately.

"Soon, old boy," I whispered. "I have some brief business to attend."

I checked the saddlebags packed and tied behind my saddle and my bag with my dental instruments firmly tied on top of the saddlebags behind the cantle. I turned away, settling my coat carefully on my shoulders. I touched the Colt .45 under my arm and the Manhattan on my right hip, then pushed open the doors and entered the saloon.

Talk stopped as if cut off by a knife as heads swiveled to stare at me. I smiled thinly and crossed to the bar. Austin looked at me, then stepped back away from the bar where he had been standing.

"Well, well," he said. "You're breaking the law, Holliday. We're not supposed to be within fifty feet of each other."

The judge had placed a peace bond on both of us, but that was of little consequence. In a land where one went where one wished, such things as "peace bonds" amounted to minor inconvenience.

"Why, Austin, I didn't know you cared so much for my welfare. That's very touching indeed."

"You want I should throw him out, boss?" Daniels said, stepping next to Austin's side.

"That would seem to be the best," Austin said, adding, "And I don't think you need to be gentle about it, Daniels."

Daniels grinned and started for me, then froze as I slipped the tail of my gray coat back, exposing the Colt, its ivory handle gleaming threateningly.

"I believe we have some unfinished business, Austin," I said. "Your bully boy doesn't figure in this unless he wants to die."

"Are you threatening me, Holliday?" Austin said. His fingers played along the lapel of his coat.

I grinned. "No, just preparing you."

"For what, Holliday?"

"For your master," I said. "I understand it's hot there. I do hope you're not overdressed."

"Tell me, Holliday," he said conversationally. "Do you remember the Yous? I believe you encountered them in New Orleans?"

Startled, I frowned, and he took the moment to slip his hand inside his coat. Metal flashed. I drew the Colt, thumbing back the hammer and snapping a shot. The bullet took him high in the shoulder, spinning him back and away, his pistol flying away from him.

An angry shout followed my shot. A bullet buzzed by my ear. Without thinking, I turned to my left, lifting my pistol like a duelist as a second shot cut through the air beside my head. Daniels's red face settled in my sights. Coolly, I squeezed the trigger. The Colt bucked in my hand. Daniels's head flew violently up as the back of his head disintegrated, showering bits of flesh in a bright red spray over the shoulders of the customers diving to the floor. I swung back to Austin, staggering through a door at the opposite end of the bar. I snapped a shot at him, the bullet clipping the wood beside his head. The door slammed behind him. I fired twice more through the door, then turned and walked rapidly from the saloon.

Ares shied as he smelled the gunsmoke on me, then danced away from the hitching post as I swung up on his back. I touched my heels to his sides, and he broke into a long, ground-gaining lope away toward the outskirts of town. Within minutes, his heels were kicking Dallas dust behind him where it hung in the air, turning the sun to copper. Ahead, the road stretched in a long, twisting, lonely line toward Jack County, a hundred miles west.

4

Ah, Jacksboro!

Glassy dust swirled around us as we rode into Jacksboro. Surging billows of grit. Filthy beyond comparison, streets either a quagmire of mud that added pounds to each step or streets of deep ruts that broke axles on Conestogas that hap-

pened to slide off into them. At one end of the street stood
maguey and a dried pile of cactus that gave no fruit. Dead
stores and bars lined the street, gray-wooded sides cracking
and warping, colorless, people walking listlessly in the baking sun, faces leathery and seamed, eyes dead and listless,
waiting for night when for one brief, ecstatic moment life
came to them in the music of guitars and pianos, of clicking
chips and snapping cards, the clink of bottle against glass, the
burn of whiskey and mescal seeping down their throats, the
gunshots and screams of the dying that assert the living their
lives and their envy of the dead.

A dry wind kicked a tumbleweed down the street, causing
Ares to shy, his hoof slipping into a rut, staggering him. I
soothed him as he pranced sideways. Dry laughter floated up
on the dry air. I glanced under the wooden awning of a store
advertising dry goods on a cracked, wooden sign. A young
woman with a porcellana face stared back boldly, her eyes
the bold bright black buttons of a doll, her red lips curving
into deep dimples.

And this, I discovered was Lotte Deno. Cultured, attractive, a redhead who knew her own beauty and used it wisely
against those who sought to take advantage of it, Lotte could
deal seconds and bottom-cut a deck with the best. Of course,
her white shoulders and deep breast line helped hold attention away from her long, limber fingers, which curved gracefully around the deck. I didn't know this at the time, for Lotte
was two people: a night person, brazen and open, yet demure
and withheld, an enigma; and a day person whom one might
confuse with a clear soprano in the church choir, a paragon of
virtue.

"You have a lively one there," she said. Lights danced in
her blue eyes, lending her a boldness not in keeping with the
austerity of her black bonnet and severe black dress. She held
a brown paper-wrapped package under one arm and carried a
parasol unfolded against the sun. I grinned back, steadying
Ares with one hand upon the reins while I tipped my wide-
brimmed hat with my free hand. A cough ripped through my
chest, robbing me of the gesture.

"A handful," I gasped.

"May I help?"

I looked sharply at her, searching for the pity normally inherent behind those words. But her face was open and concerned, not pitying. I shook my head.

"Well, you could tell me the best place to stay," I said, wryly looking up and down the one street, blinking against a sudden dust devil flinging sandy quartz granules against my eyes.

In the far distance, Fort Richardson loomed on Lost Creek, along with the mud huts of the Tonkawas, hereditary enemies of the Comanches, who viewed them as cannibals and who were nominally employed as trackers when a Comanche raid came close enough for the Richardson commander to send out a halfhearted patrol, demanding their quick return, for the same patrol might be needed as escort for a mail stage trekking southward to El Paso or for cattle herds moving northward along the Chisholm Trail to the Kansas railhead.

"In Jacksboro?" she laughed quietly, then tilted her head back and gazed up at me coolly. "Well, if I were you, I would try Kelly's." She pointed at a building a few feet away. "He's a bit more expensive than the others, but there are no bugs in the mattress or sheets."

"What about the pillows?" I asked.

She laughed. "None there, either. That I know of," she added mischievously. She nodded and tilted her parasol to shield her face, walking away from me.

I nudged Ares with my knee and slackened the reins, allowing him to pick his way over the deeply rutted street. I turned him into a stable at the end of the block and gave the hostler a dollar to feed and grain Ares and rub him down and another dollar for clean straw in his stall. The hostler raised his eyebrows at this needless expense, then shrugged and turned Ares loose in the back corral while he took a pitchfork and began to clean out the box I had selected for Ares.

I took my saddlebags and doctor's bag and turned to go,

and bumped into a cavalry lieutenant and sergeant. I stepped back, muttering an apology, and started around them.

"That is a nice-looking horse," the lieutenant said admiringly. "What would you take for him?"

"He's not for sale," I said. "But thanks the same for your offer."

The lieutenant grinned. "Come now, everything's got a price. What would you take for him?"

"I told you: He's not for sale." I nodded and started to go, but the sergeant stepped in front of me, his beefy face wreathed in a smile.

"Now there's some that would be taking that badly," he said, the brogue deep in his voice. "And the lieutenant's good at getting what he wants."

"With you to help him?" I asked, raising my eyebrows. He grinned and placed his hands on his hips above his holstered gun, the flap snapped down.

"Sergeant O'Malley, at your service. Aye, that it is," he said. "When he doesn't get what he wants, why then he treats the rest of us sorely. So you see, it's in me own favor if I help him out with his little problems now and then."

I glanced at the lieutenant; a small smile played upon his lips. Blue eyes mocked mine. He raised a gauntleted finger and smoothed a blond wisp of mustache clinging to his weak upper lip.

"O'Malley?" He nodded. "Of course. It would be, wouldn't it?"

"Now what would you be wishing with that remark?" he asked, his eyes narrowing suspiciously.

"Oh, that? Nothing. Just words," I said, waving my hand negligently. "But the answer is still the same; Ares is not for sale."

"Ares? The god of war," the lieutenant said. "A strange name for a gambler to give a horse."

"Dentist," I said, lifting the black bag in my right hand. "Dr. John Henry Holliday." A cough rumbled in my throat. I draped the saddlebags across a shoulder and transferred the black bag to my left, taking a handkerchief from my right pocket to press against my lips.

"I really do fancy that horse," the lieutenant said. "I'll give you a hundred dollars for him."

"Sorry," I said, stepping around him. "Like I said: He's not for sale."

"I'll go a hundred twenty-five," he said.

I shook my head and walked away stiffly. I felt tired and dirty after my long ride and crossing of the Red River, and wanted a clean room and a bath and something to eat.

I entered Kelly's Hotel, and stood blinking for a moment, waiting for my eyes to adjust from the coppery sunlight outside to the cool dimness of the narrow lobby. A black leather sofa and matching chairs stood to my left, their surfaces gritty and cracked, but the spittoon was polished and I took the dust to be a daily accumulation. To my right, a small shunted staircase led to the second floor.

"May I help you, sir?" the clerk asked from behind the desk. A ledger and pen and bottle of ink rested on the desk. Behind the clerk, a nest of pigeonholes hung on the wall.

I crossed to the desk and wearily dropped my saddlebags on the floor, resting my bag of instruments on the desk beside the register. The clerk was thin and myopic, his eyes huge behind the thick lenses of his glasses. A string tie, the ends carefully matched, draped over a snowy white shirtfront from beneath a celluloid collar. Sleeve protectors ran halfway up his forearms.

"Yes, you may," I said. "I would like a room, preferably one in front, and a bath. And can you recommend a place to eat?"

"Rooms are two dollars a night, ten dollars a week. Baths are fifty cents, but you can get one for a quarter at the barbershop if you don't mind using second water," he said, sliding the register around and handing the pen to me.

"I prefer my own water," I said. "And I would like to make daily arrangements. Say at four o'clock in the afternoon?"

"Would five o'clock be all right, sir? Miss Deno has prior arrangements for four."

"Five will be all right," I said.

"Very well . . ." He turned the register around, reading. "Dr. Holliday. I shall add the cost of the baths to your weekly bill, if that is all right with you."

"That will be fine. Would you prefer payment in advance?"

He took a key from one of the pigeonholes behind him, laying it on the desk. "A gentleman's word is good enough," he said a bit stiffly. "I shall prepare a weekly bill and leave it with your mail, sir." He nudged the key with a thin forefinger. "The President Grant room, sir, is at the top of the stairs and fronts the street."

"Grant?" I took the key, weighing it in my hand. "Isn't there a General Lee room?"

"Lee lost the war," he said. He smiled thinly. "People are superstitious about staying in rooms named after losers. Especially gamblers," he added.

"Indeed," I murmured. I turned and started up the stairs. "Arrange for a bath immediately, will you please?"

"Yes sir," he called as I reached the head of the stairs and turned to my left. "The bathroom is at the end of the hall on your right."

President Grant's room was spartan: a double bed with a brass headboard, a chair with brocade cushions beside a small chest of drawers that doubled as a nightstand, and a washstand. A coal oil lantern with a tasseled shade had been placed upon the table. I dropped my bags on the bed and crossed to the window, opening it. I stared down into the street for a moment, watching the soldiers swagger along the street and the citizens step aside for them.

I dropped the curtains back into place and returned to the bed and began to unpack, wondering how long it would be before my trunk would arrive from Dallas.

The smell of sour beer struck me as I pushed open the batwing doors to the Silver Slipper and walked inside. It was a narrow bar, but long. A plank bar with a cracked planked top ran down one side of the room nearly to the end before squaring off in front of a roulette wheel. A piano player played drunkenly at a piano badly out of tune. I barely recognized "Buffalo Gals." The tables were busy with soldiers. A professional gambler sat at one, dealing poker. The faro table had an empty chair. O'Malley stood behind his lieutenant. He raised his head and grinned at me. He nudged the lieutenant. The lieutenant glanced up and nodded. I ignored them and moved toward the bar. A tired-looking whore in a stained yellow satin dress looked up with interest as I paused beside the bar. I shook my head, and the smile slipped from her lips as she turned back to stare into the half-filled glass in front of her.

"Old Williams?" I asked as the bartender moved in front of me, wiping his scarred hands on a stained apron.

"What's that?" he asked. "Whiskey? I gots Jim Crow and Old Hickory. But it don't matter none which you chooses 'cause they both come from the same barrel."

"And where does the barrel come from?" I asked.

He grinned, exposing stained teeth and a black gap where three had been knocked out. "Out back. But it's straight whiskey from Indian corn. Ain't no rattlesnake heads in our'n or anything else to give it kick. Other bars in town you don't know what they gots in their'n. Ten cents a shot, two dollars a bottle."

"Doesn't matter much, does it?" I asked.

He shrugged. "Depends on whether you wanna look at a bird or ol' Jackson hisself."

"I'll take Old Hickory," I said. "At least I can pretend it's Tennessee sippin' whiskey that way."

"That you can," he said, slipping a hand under the bar and bringing up a dark brown bottle. The glass he spun in front of me was clean, and he filled the glass with an economy of motion. I tossed two dollars on the bar and he left the bottle as he stepped back to the cash drawer and tossed the money into it, sliding it shut with his hip.

I sipped; not as smooth as I liked, but palatable. I glanced over at the faro table, considering. I watched the dealer fit a deck into the shoe and slide out soda, the top card. He quickly slid out two more, the loser and the winner, and flipped them up. The casekeeper slid the beads, marking the cards played. The dealer didn't catch it, but I watched the lieutenant nudge his bet to the corner, playing two cards instead of one, the winner being included in his bet. A tin-horn move. I took another sip of whiskey and glanced at the table where the gambler sat. A soldier tossed his chips down in disgust and rose, freeing a chair.

"Tough deal?" I asked as he came to the bar.

He shook his head and clapped his hat onto the bar. "The worst," he grumbled. "I haven't won a hand in ten sets. Gimme a beer," he said to the bartender, sliding a dime onto the scarred surface.

The bartender pulled a pint from a barrel behind the bar and knifed off the thin foam before sliding the glass in front of the trooper and collecting the dime. The soldier took a long swallow and placed the mug back on the bar.

"I reckon I'm done for the night," he said. "I've got 'nough to haul my ashes down at Melanie's and that's gonna have to do it for this pass." He shook his head. "I hoped I'd pick up enough to ride out the month, but. . . ." He laughed ruefully. "I'm not a professional, but I can usually pick up a hand in five. Odds should gimme that. Not today, though. Nope. Not a drop."

He drained his glass and moved away to stand next to O'Malley, behind the lieutenant.

I finished my glass of whiskey and picked up the bottle, moving to the seat vacated by the soldier. I placed my glass and the bottle on the left side and dropped into the seat. The gambler glanced over me, taking in my gray suit, studying my hands. I took a sheaf of bills from an inside pocket and dropped them on the table.

"Name's Holliday. Dr. John Henry Holliday," I announced to the table. "Mind if I sit in?"

Two buffalo hunters next to each other across from me shook their heads. A cowboy next to them shrugged while the man dressed in the black suit next to him held out his hand.

"Nice to have a fellow professional in the game," he said. "Dr. Farnsworth."

I shook his hand and looked at the gambler. He gave me a thin smile as his long, thin fingers neatly stacked his chips and money from the last pot he'd pulled in.

"Suit yourself," he said carelessly. His eyes watched as I filled my glass from the bottle. "Straight poker."

I nodded and tossed in a dollar for ante. His hands swept up the deck, expertly splitting it and riffling a shuffle, the faces of the cards snapping against the felt of the table. His fingers flashed whitely as they skated the pasteboards to the players. I took a sip of whiskey and replaced the glass at my left before picking up my cards. I ran my fingers around the edges of the cards, feeling no nicks or pinpricks. I glanced at them: two eights, a three, jack, and five. I folded them neatly, waiting as the buffalo hunters squinted at their cards.

"Pass," the first one grumbled. The second tossed in his cards while the cowboy shoved out five dollars from the small pile in front of him. Farnsworth called. I hesitated.

"Your play," the gambler said. I smiled.

"Why, I do believe you are in quite a rush," I said. I took another drink and glanced again at my cards, stalling. "Well, this isn't the best, but I'll stay for five dollars."

The gambler took a quick glance at his and tossed in a twenty-dollar gold piece. "Raise fifteen," he said.

The buffalo hunter folded, the cowboy took a long, careful look, then sighed deeply and folded his cards.

"Too steep for what I got," he mumbled.

Farnsworth shook his head, and the pot was left for the gambler and myself. I grinned, and tossed in twenty dollars.

"I guess I can go five more," I said.

"It'll cost you ten more," he said promptly.

"Why, you must have a stand-down hand," I said.

"What do you mean by that?" he asked suspiciously.

"Why, nothing," I said. I tossed in a ten-dollar piece. "But against a hand like that, I can only call."

He stared suspiciously at me. I smiled disarmingly. He

took a cigar from an inside pocket and took his time lighting
it. He blew a cloud of blue smoke at me. I coughed gently
and reached for my handkerchief. I blotted my lips, revealing
a tiny splotch of blood. I sensed a presence at my shoulder
and looked up. Lotte Deno smiled down, her ivory shoulders
gleaming in the dull light.

"Looks bad," she said solicitously.

"We are all found wanting," I replied, tucking the handkerchief back into my pocket. I tossed in three cards. "I'll
take three."

The gambler smiled thinly and swiftly passed three cards
to me. But I heard the tiny *snick!* made by a card pulled from
beneath the one on top. He dropped two cards on top of his
hand. "Dealer takes two." He swept up his cards, studying
them.

A sudden rush swept through me. I picked up my glass,
draining it. I replaced it, smiling at him. He sensed my stare
and looked up from his hand.

"Your bet," he said.

"Check," I answered. My cards still lay untouched in front
of me. He glanced at my eyes. Uncertainty flickered behind
his. A tiny muscle jumped in his jaw. He reached out his fingers and tossed a twenty-dollar gold piece onto the table.

"It'll cost you twenty," he said.

I smiled and tossed a twenty on top of it, still without looking at my cards. The buffalo hunters edged back from the
table. Farnsworth muttered, "Dear God," and slid away from
the table. Lotte squeezed my shoulder, then moved away to
my left. The gambler frowned, then lay his cards fanlike on
the table in front of him.

"Four tens," he said. The muscle ticked again in his jaw.

"Now isn't that a peach of a hand?" I said, not revealing
my own. "Why, I'll bet you a hundred that it'll beat mine.
And I haven't looked."

Silence pressed down heavily upon the room. The gambler
stared at me, tiny beads of perspiration suddenly dotting his
upper lip.

"What are you saying," he said lowly.

"Why, you're second-dealing," I said. "And not very well, either," I added. "Back in Georgia, there ain't a nigra boy around who would be that clumsy."

The table cleared as the buffalo hunters and cowboy and Farnsworth suddenly slid their chairs back and melted away.

"You calling me a cheat?" the gambler said, stalling for time. I grinned contemptuously at him.

"Stupid, too," I said. "That isn't a good combination in your business. Your mistake was trying it on the first round without checking the newcomer at the table. Too bad. Now back away."

His hands slipped up from the table, wavering gently in front of his fancy vest. I leaned back in my chair, letting my coat fall open to reveal the Colt .45 in its shoulder holster. I tapped the ivory handle with the index finger of my right hand.

"Now, are you going to let foolishness compound your mistake?" I asked. He hesitated, and I reached out with my left hand to pick up my glass of whiskey. It was a sudden smile slipped over his thin lips as he took advantage of the moment to draw his pistol from beneath his coat. But I was already pulling my pistol, anticipating his move. My bullet took him in the center of his chest. For a moment, my vision was obscured by a cloud of gray-white smoke, then it cleared and the small pistol slipped from his nerveless fingers and fell on the table as he slumped to his left out of his chair.

"Jesus," someone breathed. "I didn't even see his hand move."

I grinned, suppressing a cough from the smoke. I had started to draw even as I reached for the glass of whiskey. A bit of misdirection that wouldn't have fooled even the most amateur of magicians. A hand pressed my shoulder. I looked up into Lotte Deno's eyes.

"Swift," she murmured. Her eyes sparkled. "And clever."

"You're too kind, ma'am," I said modestly.

"Yes," she said, then bent over to whisper, "I am."

Her perfume was heady, her red lips close to mine. She hesitated for a minute, and I took the opportunity to brush

hers with mine. She drew back instantly, pressing her fingertips to her lips.

"Why, Dr. Holliday!" she exclaimed.

"Paris had his Helen, Achilles his Briseis," I said.

A tiny smile quivered on her lips. "And which am I?"

"Dulcinea," I said firmly. "The ideal woman."

"You are too kind, sir. But I could expect more from a
southern gentleman."

"And that?"

"Permission before going too far, sir."

I could not tell if she was being a coquette or not; she was
that good a gambler at maintaining an act. But that did not
matter at all; I had behaved in a boorish fashion and owed her
an apology and made it. From that moment on, we became
fast friends, sharing meals together, walking and talking. She
was an able horsewoman, which made me suspect that she
came from a family every bit as good as mine, but on that
subject she remained secretive, enigmatic.

She was highly successful at the tables. Men flocked to
her, waiting to be fleeced, begging to be fleeced. Occasionally I sat in a game or two with her and admired her manipu-
lative ways with cards and the fact that the others did not
seem to care if she short-carded them or not. I suppose we
were so close because we were both outcasts; neither of us
belonged to either social set in Jacksboro: the small, elite
class who ran the stores and faithfully attended Sunday services in John Lowden's general store where Lowden, a self-
styled preacher, did his best to imitate the fire-and-brimstone
preachers from the Baptist South, or to the saloon and gambling dens where the owners and dealers and trade girls slept
until late afternoon and gathered occasionally for a late lunch
before hitting their stride when the sun set.

Perhaps we might have become comfortable enough with
each other that something romantic would have evolved, but
there were too many hands against us: most notably, the lieutenant who kept pressing for me to sell Ares, and O'Malley,
his Irish lapdog, awkward and vulgar but willing to do anything for his officer. By the time autumn came, wagers were

being made on the time when the lieutenant would throw his McClellan saddle over Ares and ride him back to Fort Richardson.

One night in late October, I awoke with my chest burning, a racking cough pulling my lungs up from my chest with hard claws. I reached for the bottle of whiskey sitting on the table and poured a large tumbler full, drinking it. My mouth tasted brassy, my breath raking my lungs with steel nails. I sat up and leaned back against the brass headboard. I poured another glass and sipped it, waiting for the spasms to cease.

Finally, I rose and walked around the room, pulling back the curtains to stare out onto the street. At last, I dressed and went downstairs and outside, breathing the dry, cold air tentatively. I turned and walked down to the stable to visit Ares. I slowed as I neared the stable, frowning at the open door. A low groan came from inside, and I drew the Colt .45 from beneath my arm as I slipped inside.

They stood cursing down at Ares's stall, a bull's-eye lantern giving them needed light. Ares snorted indignantly, his hooves thudding against the sides of his stall.

"Goddamn it, O'Malley! Hold him!" the lieutenant said.

"I'm trying, sir, but . . . sweet Jaysus, look out!"

Ares backed from his stall and reared, lashing out with his front hooves at the lieutenant. The lieutenant swore and his hand lashed out at Ares, the quirt taking him across his nose. Ares squealed in pain and reared again.

"You sonuvabitch!" the lieutenant swore. "I'll teach you respect!"

"And then I'll kill you," I said coldly.

They froze for an instant, then O'Malley reached for his pistol. I cocked the Colt, and his hands raised shoulder high. Ares stood nervously at the sound of my voice.

"I should kill you now," I said. "Turn around."

They obeyed, the light shining on the pistol in my hand. I walked down to the lieutenant and took the quirt from his hand. I lashed him across the face. He gasped and raised his hand automatically to his face. I jammed the pistol in his belly.

"Get your hands back down!" I ordered. "And O'Malley, you move and I'll kill you right after I blow a hole in your lieutenant's belly big enough for a hound dog to go through!"

I lashed the lieutenant across the face again, then again, hitting as hard as I could. At last, I stood back, gasping from my exertions. The lieutenant snuffled, trying to keep his dignity and failing.

"Take this . . . white trash out of here, O'Malley," I gasped. "And if I find either of you around my horse or this stable again, I'll kill you."

"Ah, Jaysus! Lieutenant . . ." O'Malley took the lieutenant by the hand, leading him from the stable. They paused at the door.

"Holliday, this isn't the end," the lieutenant choked.

"Why, I'm your huckleberry," I said.

They left and I turned to Ares, soothing him. At last he quieted and I returned him to his stall. I turned to the moaning in the corner and found the stable hand laying behind a bale of straw. A small trickle of blood ran down from a lump on the back of his head. I took a bucket of water and poured half of it over his head. He rolled onto his back, sputtering. His eyes flickered open.

"Wha—What happened?" he choked.

"O'Malley and that lieutenant of his tried to steal my horse," I answered.

"Sonuvabitch!" he said. He sat up, swearing again, grasping his head between his hands. "I'll kill those bastards!"

"I suggest that you place a guard on your stable. This isn't the first time he's tried to get my horse. He tried to buy him before, but I wouldn't sell. I guess he thought that this way, he'd save himself a few dollars," I said.

"I'll do better than that," he said angrily. "I'll tell the post commander what the hell they did."

I left him swearing vengeance upon the pair, listing the different ways each would die if he could get his hands upon them.

The next evening, O'Malley and the lieutenant entered the Silver Slipper before the evening crowd. Lotte and I were bumping heads in a two-handed game of poker, each trying to outcheat the other. O'Malley wandered over to the bar and noted the tote sheet listing the days and odds against me.

"What's the odds on the thirty-first?" O'Malley asked the bartender.

The bartender glanced up at O'Malley then at the lieutenant.

"Christ, Lieutenant! You look like some husband came home too late," he said and laughed.

"Tend to your own business," the lieutenant said coldly. "Just pour the whiskey."

"Touchy, aren't we," the bartender said, pouring a glass of whiskey for the lieutenant. He took it down to the end of the bar, where he stood, quietly sipping, the scars on his face crisscrossed like a map carved out of flesh.

"Now, would you be looking at your sheet and be leaving the poor man to his whiskey?" O'Malley said.

"I wonder what happened to him," Lotte said, nodding at the lieutenant.

"False face shows what false heart hides," I said. She looked at me. "He tried to steal Ares. I caught him."

"He's lucky," she murmured. "Anyone else would have killed him."

The lieutenant looked up and caught us staring at him. He flushed and lifted his glass, draining it.

The bartender frowned and checked the sheet. "Day after tomorrow? You wouldn't be trying to past-post me, now, would you, Sergeant?"

O'Malley laughed and spun a twenty-dollar gold piece on the bar. "I'll take five to one," he said.

The bartender shook his head, glancing down at the lieutenant. "You'll take eight to five or nothing. I don't mind taking a chance on being past-posted," he added gruffly, "but I'll be damned if I'll make it too profitable."

"There must be a bit of the English in you," O'Malley complained. "But I'll take it, thieving scoundrel that you are."

The bartender swept the gold piece off the bar and jotted the odds and the bet on a scrap of paper and slid it over to him. O'Malley picked it up and carelessly thrust it into his pocket. He swaggered over to the table and pulled out a chair, sitting.

"Now, what are we playing?" he asked, dropping a handful of coins on the table. .

Lotte cast a swift look at me, then slid the cards together, cut them, and placed them in the exact center of the table.

"Draw," she said. "Dollar ante, table stakes." She raised an eyebrow in my direction. I nodded and filled the glass beside my left hand from the bottle I had bought earlier.

"Well, now," O'Malley said, leering at her. " 'Twas hopin' I was that we could be makin' this a private game, if you catch my drift?" He raised his huge hands and draped them over the deck.

Twin spots of color appeared high in Lotte's cheeks. She shook her head. "The stakes are too high for you, soldier. Stay with the cards; at least you have a chance with them."

His eyes flickered over his shoulder to the lieutenant, then over to me. Suddenly, I knew that Lotte was just the wild card; what was going to be played would be among the three of us.

"I'm thinking that maybe the two of us should be alone, bucko. Move along."

Lotte flushed and started to rise, but he reached out and pulled her back into her seat.

"Now, dahlin', would that be any way to be treatin' the man you love?" he said.

"All right, O'Malley," I said quietly. "Let her go."

He frowned, pretending ignorance. "Now what was that you said?"

"We both know what you are after," I said calmly. "Let her go."

"Now, why would I be wantin' to do that?"

"Because you're just a bog-trotting paddy and a lady such as Miss Deno is out of your grasp," I said quietly. I leaned back in my chair as a satisfied look crossed his face. "Now, take your filthy hands off her," I added, slipping my coat open.

He stood up, kicking his chair away from him. His hand unbuttoned the flap on his holster, folding it under his belt. "Now, those are words I take from no man. Not even a wee boy such as yerself."

Lotte quietly rose and slid away, carefully keeping the distance between O'Malley and myself open. She stepped to the bar, standing just wide of the lieutenant.

"Leave it alone, O'Malley," I said. "You're probably a good man with your fists, but you've no chance with that pistol."

"Well, now, laddie," he began, then jerked the pistol from its holster. I waited until he started to bring it up, then drew and shot him in the shoulder. He cried out, the pistol flying from his hand as he grasped his shoulder and spun away from the table. I shifted my aim as a bullet flew by my cheek. I fired once instinctively, then rose and turned sideways, leveling the pistol, and fired again. My second bullet took the lieutenant in his face, splattering his doughy features across Lotte. She reacted instinctively, her hands flinching to her face, scrubbing down it. Twin streaks of red ran down her face. Her creamy shoulders were splattered with red like freckles. I took a clean handkerchief from a side pocket of my coat and handed it to her. She took it automatically, wiping at herself ineffectually.

"John," Lotte began, then fell silent. I looked at her questioningly. She glanced from me to the sergeant, then to the lieutenant, shaking her head.

"Jesus," the bartender said. He came from around the bar and knelt by the lieutenant. He glanced up at me. "Well, it was certainly self-defense, Doc, but that ain't gonna make any difference to the military. Least, not when he gets done with his story," he said, nodding at the sergeant.

The sergeant stared at me, his face white like suet, blood dripping from his fingers to the floor. He stared back, his lips thin, pain making his eyes dark and threatening.

"You can't run far enough," he said thickly. "Not near far enough."

"Well," I said. "We could resolve this now."

I raised the pistol, rocking the hammer back. His eyes grew round, then Lotte's hand pressed against my forearm.

"Don't, John," she said. "It'd be murder now."

"She's right, Doc," the bartender said. "You should have taken the shot when you could have." He shook his head. "Best if you leave while we get him back to the fort. There'll be hell to pay over this, being the dead one's an officer and all."

"A pig," Lotte said. "All this over John's horse."

"No," I said. "Ares was only part of it."

She looked uncomprehendingly at me, then slowly nodded as she realized what I was suggesting. "It was because you said no to him, wasn't it?"

"Will someone be gettin' the doctor before I bleed to death standing here and listening to yuh jabber an' all?" O'Malley complained. The bartender strode over and pulled O'Malley's blouse back to look at his wound. O'Malley groaned and flinched away from the bartender's probing fingers. The bartender took a dirty handkerchief from a back pocket and bunched it over the wound, pulling the blouse back to secure it.

"You'll live," he said roughly, adding, "Unfortunately."

"Hey, now," O'Malley complained. " 'Twasn't me who murdered the lieutenant here."

"No," the bartender said, "but it was you and the lieutenant who set Doc up to be murdered. And that's the way I'll tell it to the captain after we drop you off."

"You do that and there won't be another trooper from the Sixth Cavalry Regiment in here," he said warningly.

"Tell it to someone who'll care," the bartender said. "You'll be lucky if we don't post you from town as it is. That was low, even for you, O'Malley."

He spun O'Malley around by his good shoulder and pushed him toward the door. He glanced over at me. "I don't know what else I can do, Doc, but it'll be at least an hour before anyone will be mounting after yuh. I can give you that much, no more."

"It's enough," I said wryly. I glanced at Lotte, white-faced beside me.

"Maybe I'll see you . . . somewhere," I said.

"Yes, John," she said. She stood on her tiptoes and kissed my cheek. "Watch yourself, now."

"Why, I'm your huckleberry," I said. I winked at her. "If you need me, send a message to my father, Henry Holliday, in Valdosta. He'll know where I am. Maybe," I added ruefully, walking away.

Within the hour, I was packed and on Ares, pointing his nose north toward the Red River and Colorado, seeking an honorable end, the creak of leather and the steady beat of Ares's hooves easing tension from my muscles. Dust trickled up, making me sneeze, then cough. I took Belle's flask from an inside pocket and drank.

I had little other choice: I didn't know if the state of Texas wanted me for the shooting in Dallas, but the United States Government would definitely want me for killing the lieutenant. Yankees were the new elite: Southerners were only white trash thrown outside the law. Although I would have welcomed death, death at the end of a rope was repugnant. It was a question of honor.

5

Across the Red River, the land turned from brown sand and grit to grama grass burnt honey brown and white, bending to the breath of the wind as it blew across the softly rolling hills that break the horizon of endless prairie.

Ares loved the prairie; those long distances gave him the chance to unlimber his long legs, gathering the distance within them and casting it behind.

Distance.

God, the distance.

At times I thought I would never see another human being. Campfires built, cold nights. Six days out of Jacksboro I ran out of whiskey. Two nights later, I hemorrhaged, coughing my life up in great gouts of blood. Ares hovered close around me, nickering softly, nudging me with his velvet nose, uneasy, pacing back and forth in front of my bedroll, trying to lift me to my feet with the strength of his will, leaving me only to sip from a nearby creek, to nuzzle a few blades of grass.

I healed slowly, crawling weakly from my bedroll to the creek to ease the thirst that rose within me, crawling back, finally dragging my bedroll with me because it took too much strength to crawl back and forth over the prairie grasses to get water that now had the importance whiskey had had in my life.

At night, the spirits of long-dead warriors rose from their world beneath the earth to ride around me on their ghost horses, their painted faces stretched in a grotesque mask of horror, frozen for eternity in a rictus of horror that they had seen from the time the soldiers of Coronado had ridden arrogantly over the plains in search of Cibola to the time when U.S. soldiers had ridden arrogantly over the plains in search of more savages to kill. Coyotes moved around my camp, scenting the weakness of a dying human, mortal enemy, yellow eyes gleaming in the darkness.

During the day I lay on my back, watching the birds fly overhead, listening to the sounds of the prairie coming to life, the drumming of prairie chickens searching for mates, the bark of coyotes, the scurry of mice in the tall grasses. With contempt, I stared at my hands, cursing them for their weakness, at last fighting for strength to return to them, willing them to be strong.

At last I began to heal, fighting the night demons, driving them back down into the earth from whence they had sprung, by sheer force of will, clinging to reality outside my dreams. And within them, I saw ancient soldiers rising from the earth, wearing breastplates, bearing the colors of Spain, truncated dreams of naked, painted, golden men riding ghost horses against the armored warriors, shrieking death chants to Manitou, riding endlessly against the flashing blasts of gunpowder. I felt the shock of lead balls striking chests, the throbbing rhythms of the locomotive riding across steel rails stretched over the graves of even older warriors, driving the animals from their land, driving the spirits and souls of the ancient warriors from their lands, the protests. I sensed the anxiousness of spirits wondering if the life they had would be remembered among the cactus and grasses and flowers of the prairies among which they roamed free. I felt my spirit merge with them, and I rode endlessly toward an abyss.

When at last I could rise and move slowly around the prairie, gathering buffalo chips for fuel, Ares constantly at my shoulder, rumbling and grumbling his concern for me in his deep throat. I fed the fire of my soul and slowly I emerged from my dream world into the bleak and brown prairie where I had fallen.

Ares nickered softly. I glanced up, looking for what had drawn his attention, and spied an Indian sitting on a painted pony watching me in the near distance. I nudged the Manhattan belted at my waist and the Colt in the shoulder harness, loosening both. I picked up my canteen and shook it, gauging its contents, then sipped. I stoppered the canteen, then rose and gently ran my hand over Ares's neck. He nuzzled me affectionately, then looked out at the Indian again, ears pricked suspiciously.

"I know," I said softly. "I see him."

He grumbled again. I picked up my saddle blanket and gently smoothed it across his back, then lifted the saddle. It took two tries in my weakened condition to settle it on his broad back. I rested for a long moment, then tightened the girth. Ares lowered his head to take the bridle, gumming the bit to warm it. He shuffled his hooves impatiently as I slowly gathered my belongings and stowed them in my saddlebags.

I glanced again at the Indian. He began moving in toward me, carrying a rifle high on his right hip, hand over the hammer. It looked like an old Spencer, but I couldn't be sure. I rose and tied my saddlebags behind the saddle, taking the time to loosen the Colt under my arm again. I wondered if he was alone and how long he had been watching. Long enough, I decided, to know my weakened condition.

He halted again. I turned and took a step away from Ares to face him. I didn't want to chance Ares being struck by a stray shot. The Indian stared silently at me, then lowered his rifle and placed it crossways in front of him. He raised his right hand. I followed suit, and when my hand reached my shoulder, he suddenly kicked the paint, screamed, and galloped toward me, guiding the pony with his knees.

He raised his rifle and tried a shot, but the bullet went wide. I drew both pistols and fired with the Colt as he entered my camp. A dark blue hole appeared in the middle of his chest. He fell backwards off the pony. The pony wheeled at a right angle and galloped away, leaving its rider upon the ground. I crossed to the Indian. He looked up, eyes glazed with pain and puzzlement. He reached weakly for a belted knife. I lifted the Manhattan. He hesitated, then his lips twisted in a smile and he brought the knife out of its scabbard. I shot him between the eyes with the Manhattan. His head jerked against the ground from the force of the bullet.

I holstered my pistols and took my first good look at an Indian. He was clean, not dirty as I had expected from listening to the stories told about Indians by the saloon stalwarts in Dallas and the soldiers at Jacksboro. Worn moccasins covered his feet. An old buffalo robe lay bunched under him. I picked up his knife, studying it: blue Spanish steel honed to a fine edge, the handle horn topped with a small steel ball to give it weight. I wondered briefly about the former owner, then took the leather sheath from the thong holding his breechcloth in place, placed the knife in it, and slid it behind my belt. A small, unadorned leather bag hung around his neck, now lying limply on the ground. I opened it and took out a handful of jerky. I tentatively tasted it, then chewed rapidly, glorying in the mastication of it, feeling the strength seep back into my muscles.

Ares snorted, and I rose from the dead Indian. I glanced at his rifle; it was an old Spencer, broken with his fall. I left it where it lay and strode to Ares, mounting. I took one last look around the prairie: We were still alone, but I knew others could not be far. Maybe they had heard the shots, maybe not. I touched my heels to Ares's flanks and pointed his nose to the north, settling back in the saddle as his stride lengthened, feeling the power of Ares creeping up through my legs, strengthening me.

I found Pueblo recovering from the depression that had swept across the country, the poker tables jammed with gamblers frantic with sudden life and the wealth to enjoy it. I rested there, calling myself by my Uncle Thomas's name in case the damn army had placed John Henry Holliday on wanted posters for killing the lieutenant.

And there was Mattie. I wanted nothing to hurt her. Ah yes, I was romantically noble, for I was still young enough to be romantically noble then, feeling the kindred spirits of Achilles and Ulysses, Don Quixote, riding beside me. Mattie became my Penelope, my Guinevere, my amour courtois who filled my thoughts with nobility, letting me dream and invent my own chansons de geste in moments of idleness.

I rested in Pueblo for a short time to replenish myself and enlarge my bankroll. But soon I again took Ares north, pointing toward Denver, feeling the magnetic draw of the large city built over an ugly bunch of hills where Cherry Creek and South Platte merged beneath Mt. Evans. To the east, homesteaders and a few ranchers had planted fields of tall timothy grass that waved gently in the fall breezes that blew steadily across the plains to the mountains.

A steady stream of gamblers poured into the saloons along Larimer Street—Little Casino, the Mint, among others— from the gold fields of Black Hawk and Central City, up a narrow canyon behind the bordering mountains. Bawdy houses, gunshops, even a daily newspaper—the *Rocky Mountain News*—and several Chinese laundries filled the back streets.

I found a stable for Ares who grumbled sourly as he was

led again into the building and back corral after enjoying the freedom of the open prairie, but I promised him daily rides, cupping his velvet muzzle, and he appeared mollified as I searched for rooms. I found a hotel on Blake Street and began to make my rounds of the gambling houses, searching for one where I would be comfortable.

One day, I walked into Babbitt's House down the street from my hotel and ordered a drink, turning to watch the action at the gaming tables. A man, wearing a long-tailed gray coat with a black velvet collar and a gold-embroidered waistcoat, stood watching the deal at a table near the bar. He lit a cigar and absently blew a blue cloud of smoke in my direction. I coughed and he turned black eyes in my direction, nodding.

"Sorry," he said. "Didn't realize you were there."

"No matter," I said, taking the glass of whiskey from the bartender and taking a large swallow to keep the tickle from building into a convulsion.

"You're new," he said, his eyes flickering back to the table. The gambler laid down three treys and pulled in a medium-sized pot.

"Here, yes, but I've been in Denver a couple of weeks now," I said.

His eyes flicked back to me, quickly taking in my gray, blocked suit and blue shirt with its soft, white collar. I wore a cravat with a pearl stickpin. His eyes strayed over my hands. A tight smile slid across his narrow lips as he recognized a fellow gambler. He switched his cigar to his left hand and held out his right.

"Charley Foster," he said. He raised his eyebrows, glancing around the room. "I own this, such as it is." He glanced back at the game. "But I may not tomorrow."

"Tom McKey," I murmured, touching his hand briefly with my fingers. I nodded at the table. "Trouble?"

"Yeah," he growled, his heavy eyebrows nearly coming together in a frown. "He's been winning steadily ever since he sat down. Can't figure out how he's doing it. But if I can't break him soon, Charlie Ward will own this place along with the Mint."

"I see," I said, sipping. "This Ward is making a move toward collecting the gambling in Denver?"

A sour smile flashed ruefully at me. "Yeah. We go through this periodically, where one owner or another makes a run at the rest of us. Ward is the latest."

"You ever try?" I asked.

He shook his head. "No, I'm satisfied with what I got. People who get too ambitious end up cannon fodder for the newspaper and Justice Sayer's court. Sayer wants to keep everyone small and his hand in everyone's pockets. If one owner gets too big, he may make a run at Sayer's office." He shrugged. "This way, he can keep a grip on everything."

"I see," I said slowly. I sipped thoughtfully for a moment. "Who's the gambler?"

"Budd Ryan," he said. "Normally he deals faro over at the Mint. He's damn good. Killed a man over at Moses's Home down on Larimer when the man accused him of cheating. He was lucky even then; the man's pistol hit the table coming up and that gave Ryan a chance to use his knife. Since then, he's been the cock of the walk."

"Interesting," I murmured.

He gave me a sharp look. A muscle moved at the corner of his jaw. He chewed reflectively for a moment on his cigar, then shrugged and turned to face me squarely.

"Would you be a man of chance?" he asked.

"By chance," I said. The pun missed him.

"How would you like to take a hand in the game?" he said.

"You don't know me."

"I'm impulsive," he said. "Besides, I don't seem to be having any luck with what I've got now."

"How much?" I asked.

His eyes sharpened. He glanced again at my hands, running his eyes over my clothes, noting the immaculate fit of the coat, the chain fitting over my waistcoat.

"All right," he said. "I'll stake you until the money runs out. You keep a fourth of the winnings."

"Three-fourths," I said casually.

"That's robbery!" he complained, shaking his head.

"You're losing now," I observed. "Something's better than nothing, isn't it?"

He suddenly grinned and held out his hand. This time I took it. "You've got nerve, I'll give you that. And a seat in the game. Fifty percent?"

"Sixty," I said.

"Done."

He moved briskly to the side of the sweating dealer wearing an eyeshade and tapped him on the shoulder.

"Take a break, Johnny," he said. "I've got a relief dealer for you." He nodded at me.

"Yes sir. Thank you," Johnny said gratefully, sliding back his chair. He shook his head as he passed me on his way to the jakes. "I can't figure him," he whispered. "He's good. Too good."

I motioned to the bartender and pointed at a bottle of Old Williams on the shelf below the mirror behind the bar.

"The bottle," I said. "And a clean glass."

He slid the bottle onto the bar in front of me and placed a chipped glass beside it. I glanced at it and shook my head.

"Another," I said.

The bartender frowned. "Drink with that one, or none."

I shrugged and took the small silver cup Belle had given me from the side pocket of my coat, hooked my finger through the handle, and picked up the bottle with the same hand and walked to the table. Foster glanced at the bottle and started to say something, then decided against it and stepped back away from the table.

"Mr. McKey will be the new houseman," he said to the table.

Ryan glanced up lazily, his brown eyes taking in the bottle and silver cup in my hand, the set of my coat. A tiny smile played along his lips.

"Giving up, Charley?" he said.

"Everyone needs a break now and then," Foster said.

I slid into the chair and glanced at the others. All wore suits; it was not a game for cowboys or drovers.

"Mike Wilson." The man on my left grinned. A glass half-filled with whiskey sat beside his right hand. A small pile of red and blue chips rested on the green felt in front of him. "I scribble now and then."

"And very badly," the man next to him said. "John Madding. Doctor."

"If you're very unlucky," Wilson answered.

They grinned at each other, and I felt their fondness for each other across the table.

The next man was Ryan, who shrugged when I glanced at him. On his left sat a nervous little man with a tic in his cheek. "Arnold Bowles." He shrugged. He wore a flashy diamond on his right hand.

"Well then," I said. "Let us begin, shall we?" I moved the copper in front of Ryan to Bowles. "Your choice, Mr. Bowles."

He glanced quickly at Ryan, whose eyes flickered momentarily. "Draw," he said, tossing in a white chip to ante.

"Draw it is," I said.

I divided the back and snapped the two halves hard together against the felt, riffling them together. I repeated the movement, then slid the deck in front of Ryan for a cut. His hands slid over the deck, dividing and slipping the pack together again. I half smiled to myself. He was good; I had barely caught the double-fold as he tucked the cards with his left hand. I picked up the cards, double-cutting without looking as I drew attention to my right hand by pouring a measure of Old Williams into the silver cup. I took a sip, glancing as I did into Ryan's eyes. They stared back blankly. I couldn't tell if he had caught the cut or not.

I dealt the cards around, swiftly dropping the second card from beneath the top card in front of me. I didn't know what it was, but it was the card that Ryan had tried to stack for himself. I followed the movement with the second and third card for myself, then dealt straight for the last two cards. It didn't matter how good a dealer was, to set up a full hand on one cut was impossible.

I glanced at my cards: three tens, a four, and a trey. Not the best of hands, but I knew where the fourth ten was: on the

bottom of the deck. I waited. Wilson checked. Madding bet
five dollars. Ryan bumped him ten. Bowles frowned, then
hesitantly pushed out fifteen to call. I tossed in the fifteen
then picked up two blues and negligently tossed them into
the pot.

"Another twenty," I said.

Wilson threw his cards in with a rueful grimace. Madding
studied his hand, then sighed and folded. Ryan gave me a
faint grin.

"A bit flashy," he said.

"New dealer, new luck," I answered, taking another sip
from Belle's cup.

"Your twenty and fifty more," he answered, tossing in the
chips.

Bowles folded his cards together tidily and placed them in
front of him, dropping his hands to his lap.

"Too rich for me," he said regretfully.

I gave him a smile, then matched Ryan's fifty and added
another hundred. Dimly, I became aware of a stillness in the
room. Wilson's chair scratched back from the table. Ryan
stared into my eyes for a long moment.

"The question," he said, clearing his throat, "is, what you
are doing?"

"Why, Mr. Ryan," I answered. "I thought that was obvious: I'm betting I can beat you."

A tiny laugh rippled through the room. Dark red began to
climb up the column of his throat, spreading out into his
cheeks.

"Let's see how strong you are," he said. He added two
hundred to the bet. The room grew extremely quiet. Foster
muttered "Jesus" from behind my chair.

"Well," I said. "You must have a honey of a hand." He
smiled faintly. "But I'm your huckleberry." I tossed in five
hundred dollars. "The question is, are you mine?"

He called. I held up the cards questioningly. He shook his
head, dropping his hands to his lap.

"I'll play these," he said mockingly.

I knew at the time that I probably had the winning hand on

the board. I slid the top two cards off my hand and tossed them away, not taking my eyes off Ryan. A tiny frown line appeared between his eyebrows as I slid two cards in front of me, including the ten off the bottom of the deck. I didn't know what the top card was because I had used it to disguise the removal of the ten from the bottom, but I did know that I had four tens to play with.

"A heavy bettor for drawing two," he said. His hands remained in his lap.

"Is it? I hadn't noticed," I said carelessly. "Your bet."

"Check," he answered.

I tossed in a hundred, still keeping my eyes on him. I had yet to look at my hand, and I could see that was bothering him.

"You know," he said. "A man could get suspicious of play like that."

I leaned back in my chair, letting my coat fall open. I tapped the ivory handle of the Colt. "Why, Mr. Ryan. Whatever do you mean?" I asked.

"You have a mighty strange way of playing," he said.

"And you have yet to play," I observed gently.

His hands came up from the table and hovered over his cards before picking them up. I saw the card drop onto the pile before he gathered them to him. I immediately rose and leaned forward, pressing my left hand down on top of his, pinning them to the table. With my right hand, I slipped out the Colt, cocking it.

"I'm betting," I said, "that you have a daisy of a hand. Six petals instead of five. What do you think? Five hundred?"

He turned white as the blood drained from his face. His eyes burned angrily, but he stayed still, his hands between mine.

"Turn your hands faceup. Slowly," I added.

He obeyed, and I picked up his cards, fanning them. Three kings, a four and a deuce, and another king, the one passed to him by Bowles.

"My, my, Mr. Ryan. You do seem to have more cards than I," I said.

He said nothing, his eyes glittering at me, at my pistol, then looking back to me.

"Now, I think the pot belongs to me," I said. I used the pistol to pull the pile of chips in front of him to my side of the table. "And these, for the insult. No wonder you have been so successful: hard to beat a man with six cards while you have only five."

He jerked his hands off the table. They hovered by his lapel as I steadied the pistol on him.

"Why, Mr. Ryan! You look as if you're all horns and rattles! Surely you don't want to go wakin' snakes!"

I could see the desire in his eyes, dark and ugly, his lips quivering with desire to pull his pistol. I smiled at him, then suddenly lowered the hammer on the Colt and laid it on the table, straightening.

"Well, then," I said softly. "Let us proceed like gentlemen."

I pulled the edge of my coat back slightly with my right hand, exposing the handle of the Manhattan. His lips tightened; his fingers touched his coat, then fell away.

"No?" I said softly. I shook my head. "I didn't think so. You'd better go now." I looked at Bowles, who sat white-faced beside me. "You, too."

He nodded and rose, scurrying through the crowd like a rodent for the door. I smiled at Ryan, raising my eyebrow.

"You might get lucky," I said softly.

He wanted to; oh, God, how he wanted to. But even if he beat me, he would still be the loser among the crowd in Babbitt's House. He rose, settled his coat on his shoulders, then walked out. The air spilled out of the saloon with a rush as the crowd headed for the bar. Charley Foster clapped me on the shoulder.

"Well, you certainly don't waste any time, Tom. I thought you would play it a little closer to your vest, but God!"

"Why stretch things out?" I said. "I knew how he was doing it."

He shook his head. "You've got a part here as long as you want it. Pick a table. Twenty percent." I looked at him. "For the house," he added. "For the house."

"Seems like I've found a new home," I said, draining the

cup. I immediately refilled it from the bottle. "For the time," I added. "Until the deck runs cold."

Foster clapped his hands together and called for a bottle of champagne to seal our new partnership. I drained the cup and dropped it back into my pocket after drying it with my handkerchief. I took a sip of the wine from the glass Foster handed me. The wine was good and cold. I wondered how long I would be able to enjoy it.

How long did I enjoy it? Perhaps six months?

I no longer remember. I had stopped counting the days and weeks and months. Time had become immaterial to me. I practiced with my pistols daily when I took Ares for a gallop out in the country, preferring the ride up the forbidding mountain looming over the city. Up there I felt closer to freedom, although I dared not stay long, for the high altitude forced me to labor for breath. But there was a peacefulness and a contentment there that I had not felt for a long, long time.

The rest of the time I practiced with a deck of cards, refining my riffle shuffle, a reverse cut that would break up a deck someone had stacked, and trying to deal seconds without the telltale *whiff!* that the card made when it slipped out from beneath the top card.

During the evening, I spent most of my time at Babbitt's House, although I did have occasion to visit the other gambling houses along Larimer and Blake Streets: the Little Casino, the Mint, Ed Chase's place. Denver was the Mecca for people like me: ripe with confidence men, gamblers, cattlemen, and I fit in comfortably, earning my living and making Charley happy whenever Chase or another saloon owner tried to run the house by sending a cardsharp to play against him. Most of the time, lady luck ran well with me. I suppose that was some compensation the gods made for the hand they had dealt to me with my life. Or maybe money had ceased to become important to me. If one's life is no longer of any importance, then what else is there?

Except honor. In spite of becoming one of fortune's minions, I clung to my honor, refusing to sacrifice that for anything. Occasionally someone would take me for a frail misfit and try to run over me, but a quick look at one of my pistols was usually enough to settle him into his proper place.

I did like the German beer gardens where there was an enjoyment of life all around me: plump blond ladies playing full-bodied German songs that filled the room with happy music upon the piano and concertina while hefty waiters with no necks passed around pitchers of beer and fat pretzels with hot mustard with which to season them. Then there was the Turnverein Society, which gave an unsophisticated form of entertainment in the manner of a circus with tumblers and acrobats at Turner Hall. At the theatre, I ran into Eddie Foy again when he appeared with his troupe of players. Foy made me laugh with his comic rendition of "Over the Hill to the Poorhouse" and we spent many a fine night together after the show drinking our way across the city and back. I found out that Belle had left her husband and gone to Texas to find me, but strangely, I felt only a little sadness that I missed her. Already her face was dimming within my memory.

At night I would sit in an overstuffed chair in my room, reading the latest offering. I remember T. B. Whitman's *Wild Oats Sown Abroad,* but my favorite at that time was Ouida's *Sigma.* Of course, I kept my own little library handy—a book of poems by Tennyson, Dickens's *A Tale of Two Cities,* Shakespeare's *Hamlet* and *Macbeth* (I no longer found his comedies amusing), and, of course *Richard III,* for I, too, often felt the winter of my discontent. I have always carried books with me, devouring them when alone in the belly of the tiger of night, pushing away the loneliness and despair by immersing myself deeply in imaginary worlds, finding myself in Quixote and Hamlet more than those swashbuckling heroes of Buntline and others.

It was a fine time, the best of times that I would know for quite a spell. I did not have an attack until late December, after Christmas, when snow fell for the first time. I awoke, feeling the worm moving turgidly within my chest. I poured a glass of whiskey and drank it, then another, but still the worm moved, eating at the raw nerves of my lungs. My cough worsened, making my chest feel like hot glass, tiny granules grinding away inside. My chest tightened as my lungs heaved to bring in a thin, cold breath of air that torturously twisted and turned its way over and around the mass of phlegm, irritation, and blood clotting in my chest. Despairing, I rose and quickly dressed, then went out in search of a doctor and laudanum, swearing as each movement brought perspiration to my brow, wilting the shirt just back from the Chinese laundry.

Halfway down the street, I found a sign labeled M. WALKER, M.D. with an arrow pointing up a staircase attached to the side of Richards & Co. I climbed up the stairs and knocked. A young woman dressed in men's clothes opened the door. I paused, taken back at the sight. She smiled faintly at my reaction.

"Yes?" she said. "May I help you?"

She would have been pretty except for the tightness of her lips, which caused twin lines to break the natural curve of her cheek. Her eyes were cold mirrors sealing the private person from the world. Her auburn hair had been cropped close in an attempt to make her appear mannish, but accented, instead, the graceful curve of her alabaster neck, a sensual white column.

I coughed and tasted blood in my mouth. I turned away from her and spat over the side of the landing.

"I'm looking for Dr. Walker," I said.

She pushed the door wide and stood back. I entered, dabbing at my lips with my handkerchief. Tiny blots of blood appeared on its white surface. She glanced at the handkerchief.

"How long have you been hemorrhaging?" she asked.

"A little over two years," I answered. I looked around the room. A desk stood in the corner next to a glass-faced cabinet filled with pharmaceutical supplies, a mortar and pestle on a marble counter in front of the cabinet. A wooden filing cabinet was separated from a small surgery by a white screen. I could see no other doors; we were alone in the room. I glanced at her. Challenging lights danced defiantly behind the mirrors of her eyes.

"Yes, I am Dr. Walker. Dr. *Mary* Walker," she added.

"I see," I said slowly.

"Does that bother you?"

"No," I answered. "Should it?"

Her eyes tightened. "Most people turn around and walk out as soon as they find out that Dr. Walker is a woman."

"I'm not most people," I said mildly. The cough bubbled up in my throat again. I swallowed.

"Then you're not bothered being examined by a woman?"

"Does it bother you?" I asked.

She frowned. "I'm afraid I don't understand."

"Why don't you put Dr. Mary Walker on your sign instead of Dr. M. Walker?" I said.

"Because you probably wouldn't have climbed the stairs if I had," she said. "Most people seem to think that women cannot be doctors. Oh, it's all right if we change their bandages and empty their bedpans, but to confide their sicknesses to us is something not done. When I took anatomy, I had to sit behind a screen that separated me from the rest of my class and the professor." She grimaced. "The professor claimed that he was afraid my sensibilities would be offended by the graphic subject matter, but I believe it was *his* sensibilities that would have been offended."

"Maybe you sell people a bit short," I answered. I suppressed another cough.

"*Would* you have climbed the stairs if the sign read Dr. Mary Walker?" she challenged.

"Do you always speak in italics like dialogue written by E.D.E.N. Southworth?" I answered.

She stepped back a half step, her eyebrow arching in a pleasing manner.

"Well," she murmured. "An educated man as well. At least a reading man. Somewhat unusual."

"That I read or that I'm a man?" I said, smiling, then coughing violently into my handkerchief as a spasm shook me.

She took my arm and gently led me to a chair hidden

behind the screen. I collapsed gratefully into it. She pressed her wrist against my forehead, then ran her fingers gently, but firmly, beneath my jawline, probing my throat.

"What are you taking?" she asked.

"Whiskey," I answered.

She shook her head. "And when the attacks come?"

"More whiskey," I answered.

She frowned. "Whiskey is only temporary. It may cauterize for the moment, but whiskey's not the answer."

"Neither is laudanum," I answered. I shrugged. "At least I can think with the whiskey. Laudanum dulls the senses too much."

"And that is death for a gambler," she said ironically.

Her words stung, but why they stung I had no idea. Perhaps it was the certainty by which she labeled me, or maybe it was that I found the white column of her neck attractive and her breasts pushing against the man's vest and her hips rounding the seat of her man's trousers suggestive, but for some strange reason, it suddenly became extremely important to me that I not be labeled a simple gambler and be shelved away with the rest of the riff-raff in her mind.

"Actually, I'm a dentist. Dr. John Henry Holliday. From Georgia. Valdosta," I added.

She glanced down at the Manhattan holstered on my right side and touched the slight bulge the Colt made on my left.

"And these are a dentist's tools," she said acidly.

"They are the tools left to me when my patients took exception to my cough," I answered. "Much the same argument that is made about a woman doctor who dresses in men's clothes, I would think," I added.

Her eyes widened, then narrowed as she pursed her lips, considering. Suddenly, I tasted copper, then coughed and a gout of blood exploded from my mouth, spattering against her vest. I tried to speak, but another flood of blood flew up and my knees sagged. I felt her arm, thin but muscular, wrap around me, supporting me as we staggered like two drunk dancers to the surgery table. I fell upon it and rolled to my side, vomiting blood and mucus onto the floor. My senses swam and a dark veil slipped over my eyes.

So this is death, I thought, then nothing.

I awoke in a bed, but it wasn't my bed. My mouth tasted gummy with the familiar smoky taste of an opiate. A dim light burned from a kerosene lamp on a small Hepplewhite table next to a washbasin and a towel with dried bloodstains showing upon it. A framed pencil drawing of a young woman dressed in a flowing Grecian garment hung above the table. A serpentine-back sofa sat in front of a window that apparently looked out onto the street, although I could see only a small part of a balcony through the nearly pulled blind. She sat in a spindle-backed Boston rocking chair with cyma-curved arms near the bed, her eyes closed, breathing gently. Dark circles made the flesh beneath her eyes seem bruised. A damp curl lay over her white forehead. A vein beat faintly in the white column of her neck. Her thin hands loosely held a book in her lap, her place marked by a forefinger. I tried to read the title but couldn't. She stirred and her eyes flickered open. Brown, with flecks of gold.

"You're awake," she said matter-of-factly.

I tried to speak, but couldn't. She slipped a ribbon into the book at the place marked by her finger, then rose and poured a glass of water. She took an eyedropper from a bottle of milk-white liquid and carefully counted out five drops. She mixed the liquid in with the tablespoon, then raised my head and held the glass to my lips as I greedily drank. I winced as the water hit the parched area in my throat.

"Easy," she murmured. "Take tiny sips."

I obeyed, holding the water in my mouth for a moment before swallowing in stages. I nodded, and she lay my head back on the pillow. I felt gritty and stale. She filled a tablespoon from a bottle of Hale's Honey of Horehound and Tar and held it to my lips. I opened my mouth and swallowed the sickly-sweet mixture.

"How long has it been?" I asked.

"Two days," she said. "It was bad. For a while I was afraid

you wouldn't stop hemorrhaging. You lost a lot of blood. And lung tissue," she added.

"And your prognosis, Doctor?" I asked.

"You know that as well as I," she said. "You should go to a sanitarium. But you won't."

"And how do you know that?" I asked.

"Because you would already be there."

"Would it make any difference if I did go?"

"Probably not," she said. "The consumption's too far advanced. But you would be more comfortable. And," she added, shrugging, "who knows? There is always chance. As a gambler, you should appreciate that."

"I really have no intention of dying in bed," I said.

"That's why the pistols," she said. It wasn't a question, but I nodded. "I thought so. That's why I kept you here instead of having you taken to your own room. It would have been bad if you had been caught in your condition by your enemies."

"Perhaps," I said indifferently. "At least it would be over then."

"That seems self-defeating."

"The suspense is killing me." I tried to lighten the mood in the room, but she ignored my attempt at humor, the flecks of gold glowing softly in her brown eyes.

"Then why don't you end it all yourself?"

"Why make it easier on the gods?" I said.

"So you'll kill other men until one manages to kill you. I don't see the rationale of that."

"The ones who will fall into either category are the ones who should die anyway," I said. "They will be no loss to humanity. Nor will I. Maybe I'll do some good before someone outdraws me or shoots me in the back."

"At least stay out of those stinking cigar-smoke-filled saloons," she said.

"Saloons are where I'll find those men," I said. "May I have a glass of whiskey?"

"No," she said. "I've given you too much laudanum. They shouldn't be mixed." I smiled at her. A tiny smile appeared on her face.

"I know. But humor me. Please?"

I shrugged. "If it will make you feel better. What else do you prescribe, Doctor?"

"Bed rest for at least a week," she said firmly. "A steady diet. We need to rebuild your strength."

"We'll see," I said drowsily, feeling the narcotic begin to take effect. I yawned.

"Sleep now," she said softly. I felt a cold cloth wipe my face, refreshing me. I tried to thank her, but I slid once more into darkness. But this time, I knew it wouldn't be permanent, and for once I was thankful.

I gave her a week, but rebeled against the soft diet she tried to feed me. At last she gave up and brought a small steak to me. I devoured it hungrily and asked for a glass of whiskey. Reluctantly, she gave me a glass filled with Old Williams. I restrained myself from gulping it, sipping instead.

"I'll move your clothes and belongings in here, if you want," she said.

"Thank you, my dear doctor, but I am a bit weak yet," I answered.

"You're incorrigible," she laughed, twin bright spots appearing high in her cheeks.

"But faithful," I said.

"It might prove interesting," she said archly. "But the truth of the matter is I have to go to Cheyenne. There's been an outbreak of diphtheria up there and the doctor—Jason Fields—sent a telegraph asking me to come up and help."

"You're leaving me here alone?" I asked, pretending to be hurt.

She remained silent for a long moment, staring at me, then slowly shook her head. "There would be nothing there for either of us."

"Sometimes a few moments are all we are allowed," I said.

She slowly shook her head. "No, no. I want more than moments. And"—she hesitated, then lifted her chin defiantly—"I have had enough of men."

I waited, knowing she would tell me if it was time, and knowing it would be time if she had thought about it before.

At last she sighed and raised her hand to her mouth for a long moment, then dropped it resignedly to her side.

"I was in love once," she said. "Back east. He taught at St. John's Hospital, where I interned. We became lovers and he promised . . ." She hesitated. "It was to be forever. We promised each other that it would be forever." A grin twisted her lips. "But forever for him lasted only six months, and then there was a nurse, and a patient, and . . . his wife. He had been so secretive that I didn't even know he had been married."

"And for that you punish yourself?" I asked quietly.

She turned and walked from the room. I listened to her heels cross the floor of her surgery, then the door open and shut. I lay back against my pillow and stared at the ceiling, thinking of Mattie.

I lasted four days after Mary left before the restlessness within me forced me from my bed, much to the consternation of Mrs. Upjohn, who had been left assigned to me. She was a good woman, but dedicated to the good doctor's orders: barley soup, fresh bread, and liberal applications of Hale's cloying concoction. Since the good doctor had not prescribed whiskey for my diet, then I would have none, she told me sternly, and when I swore at her, she smiled grimly, slapped a beefy arm across my chest, and poured an extra dose of that damnable Hale's down my throat.

I waited until midafternoon, when I knew she would be making her rounds down at the far end of Blume Street, where a tired widow maintained a home for orphans, before pulling myself from my bed. I clung weakly to the iron foot of the bed until the dizziness passed, then took my black, blocked suit from the wardrobe where it had been hung and slowly dressed myself. I dressed in a highly starched white shirt, then tied a tie carefully around my neck. I sat down to pull on a pair of black half-Wellingtons, brightly polished, and rested for a moment before rising and packing a carpetbag I found in the bottom of the wardrobe with an extra suit, gray, several blue shirts (a color to which I had taken a fancy), and a couple of extra ties. I found a cane—a slim shaft of ebony with a gold head—standing in the back of the wardrobe and thankfully took it. I tried to slip into the shoulder harness bearing my pistols but almost fell from the effort and reluctantly dropped them in the carpetbag on top of my clothes. I slid the Spanish dagger I had taken from the Indian into an inside pocket, dropping one of Pinkerton's Deringers into a side pocket of my coat. It was the best I could do in my weakened condition.

I hobbled out of the room and across the surgery and office and opened the door. I stepped out onto the landing. A group of boys were playing mumblety-peg in the dirt of the alley beneath me. For a moment, a brief memory flashed painfully across my mind, then was gone.

"You there!" I called. They looked up. I pointed at one. He pointed at his chest. "Yes, you. Come here. I want you to carry a bag to the depot for me." He hesitated. "I'll give you a dollar," I added.

His eyes leaped, and he jumped from the dirt to scamper up the steps to my side.

"Whassa matter, mister?" he asked. "Why don' yuh kery it yersef?"

I motioned at the cane, upon which I was leaning heavily. "I am afraid I can't manage with this," I said. "You'll find it back in there in the bedroom."

He nodded and disappeared into the room, appearing within minutes, lugging the carpetbag with both hands. It was heavy for him, but he pretended not to show the difficulty he was having with it.

He followed me as I moved slowly down the steps, resting the carpetbag on the step behind him as he paused on the next step and waited for me. Together we made it down the steps. We stopped at the stable where I boarded Ares. I made arrangements with the owner's helper, an old-timer with a wooden leg who had ridden with Longstreet in the War, to lead Ares daily into the country, not ridden; no one could have ridden Ares.

The young boy and I continued on to the Mint, where I

ordered him to wait outside while I went inside to buy a bottle of Old Williams and to have Belle's flask filled. I slid the flask inside my right pocket and left, placing the bottle inside my carpetbag. Slowly, we made our way to the depot. I gave the boy a dollar and bought a ticket for Cheyenne on the Denver Pacific Express. The man at the ticket window gave me a concerned look.

"Are you all right?" he asked solicitously. I nodded. He sucked his lips into a tight line, then said, "There is a later train if you need one. Heard about the sickness up there, I s'pose?"

"Yes," I answered. I took a handkerchief from a pocket and gently dabbed the perspiration from my face. I coughed gently into it, but there was no blood. A good sign, I thought.

"I appreciate your concern, sir," I said, "but this train will do just as nicely as the next."

He shrugged. "Suit yourself. It's leaving in fifteen minutes, though. I'll have Sandy take your bag aboard for you. If I were you, I'd take the back seat by the left window," he added. "Dust will blow quicker away from there as you go through the pass."

"Thank you," I murmured. I turned and moved out onto the loading platform and paused before climbing into the passenger car. I could see that I was going to be the only passenger from Denver: Word of the sickness in Cheyenne was apparently keeping people away for the moment, although that wouldn't last long. Cheyenne was the beginning of the stage line for the run into the Black Hills in Dakota Territory, where gold fever was still running heavily. Fortune seekers would eventually get over their fear of the Cheyenne sickness as the gold fever mounted.

"Well, well. Tom McKey," a voice said from beside me. I turned and faced Budd Ryan. He was dressed in a pinstriped suit, gray with blue threads, a bowler cocked to the right on his head. A short, nervous man wearing a black suit stood beside him. He gave a nasty smile. "Leaving us so soon?"

I ignored him and turned back to the train. Out of the corner of my eye, I saw the flush run up into his beefy face.

"Not very civil today? Just as well," he said. He nodded at the passenger coach. "I wouldn't come back if I were you."

The conductor appeared, carrying my carpetbag. He lifted it up into the car and carried it on. I watched as he stopped by the seat by the back window and lifted it up into the rack above the seat. He leaned over, eyeing us curiously for a moment before coming back outside, waiting for me. I placed my foot on the step, pulling myself up into the car with an effort that brought the perspiration again to my face. I removed the handkerchief and wiped it away.

"Are you listening to me, McKey?" Ryan said loudly. The nervous man pulled on his arm. Annoyed, Ryan glanced down at him.

"What'd you call him?" the nervous man asked.

"Tom McKey. A tinhorn gambler. A cheat," Ryan said loudly for the benefit of those around him.

"I don't think so," the nervous man said, sidling away. "I think that's Doc Holliday."

Ryan frowned, then shrugged and looked back at me. "That true? Are you Doc Holliday?"

I turned my head and stared into his eyes. They shifted, tried to hold, then glanced away as the conductor called "Board!" and the train jerked, then began to roll away from the loading platform.

"Doesn't matter a goddamn to me!" Ryan yelled. "Don't come back no matter what your real name is, you flashdancer!"

I leaned back against the swaying seat of the coach, bracing myself by placing my feet against the seat opposite. I reached into my pocket and removed the flask and opened it, sipping. The whiskey bit against the back of my throat, then slid warmly down to my stomach. I slid down, slouching in my seat, making myself comfortable, as I could not have had there been other passengers. I leaned my head back against the cushion, watching the train gather speed as it chugged north away from Denver, heading across the brown and bleak prairie toward Cheyenne. I thought dispassionately about Ryan. Someday I would probably have to deal with him, I thought tiredly. But not today. Not today. I took another sip from the flask, then placed it back into my pocket and tiredly closed my eyes, relaxing to the lulling rocking of the coach.

The train pulled into Cheyenne at 12:15 P.M., and the sun had slipped behind a gray bank of clouds, heavy with threatening snow in a late winter storm. I stood on the docking platform for fifteen minutes, looking for someone to carry my bag to the hotel, but the streets were nearly empty, the passersby avoiding eye contact with each other. A section gang at the far end of the spur track running off from the main line was loading a flatcar with steel rails and heavy timbers prior to making a run down the line, checking for line breaks or other repair work.

"Can I help you?"

Thankfully, I turned, leaning heavily on my cane and found myself staring at a tall man, thick through the body, a badge pinned to his split cowhide short coat, cut around the black handle of a Colt riding in a holster just below his hip. A wide-brimmed hat shaded a pair of bright blue eyes staring hard into mine. His lips smiled beneath a tobacco-stained mustache, but the smile never reached his eyes. He held out his hand.

"Jeff Carr. Town marshal," he said. His eyes raked over me, noting the cane, upon which I leaned heavily.

"Holliday," I said, taking his hand. "Dr. John Henry Holliday," I added, thinking the title would ease his thoughts somewhat. I looked down at the cane and smiled ruefully. "Yes, you can help me, if you would be so kind. I'm afraid that it would be a bit awkward trying to handle my bag with this. Could you find a boy for me?"

"No need," he said, easily lifting my bag in a large, callused hand. "I'll help you along. Hotel?"

I nodded, and we turned, leaving the loading platform. A cold wind blew bitingly down the muddy street, gnawing at my face, numbing it, as we moved out from the protection of the train depot. My eyes watered and I lowered my head, gasping as I leaned heavily upon my cane against the force of the wind.

"Takes some getting used to," Carr said solicitously from beside me. "We're not long from the first snow. Mud froze a couple of days ago and that's always the first sign. Over at the Excelsior, Janson always runs a sheet on when it'll come. The snow, I mean. You a gambling man?"

His eyes had already noted the cut of my clothes, the pearl stickpin, the ruby on my left ring finger, so the words were only an amenity, giving me a chance to deny the appearance if I wished. I coughed gently.

"Dentist," I said. "Although I've been known to sport a little on the turn of a card or two."

"I've heard about a dentist turned gambler from down Texas way," he said, casting a sidelong look at me. "S'posed to be a fair hand with his pistols."

"I've heard that too," I answered coolly. I had little trouble keeping a tone of neutrality in my voice with that cold wind blowing straight into me. "I also heard he's pretty peaceable if left alone."

"That so?" He frowned. "Hope so, anyway. This job's hard enough without a gunny runnin' around shootin' holes in folks that upset him a mite. Cheyenne's growin'; ain't got much use for gunnies around here anymore. Quiet. Sort of," he amended. "We gotta couple of tongs at war with each other, but that don't count none. They police themselves mainly. Inter-Ocean Hotel's just down in the next block. You get any time for it, the Bella Union Variety Theatre's just down the way. Kinda quiet just now, but usually has a pretty good show."

He lifted his free hand, pointing, finishing the gesture by tugging his hat brim lower over his bronzed, seamed face. His bright blue eyes blinked back the tears. He shortened his stride to match my limp.

"Hope there's room," I ventured.

"We don't get many travelers stopping over on account of the diphtheria epidemic," he said. "Fact is, the last one was a drummer yesterday, an' 'fore that, a female doctor up from Denver to give ol' Doc Fields a hand."

"She staying at the hotel too?" I asked casually. His eyes snapped back at me, considering.

"Friend of yours?"

"You could say that," I panted. Working against the wind was beginning to tire me. "She's my doctor."

"Uh-huh. Thought you looked a bit peaked. You got the sickness, too? Don't mind me askin'. Just trying to do my job."

"Consumption," I answered shortly.

"Aw, that's a hell of a thing. Sorry to hear that," he said as if the news pained him.

I believed him. Some people give lip service to their words, then shy away as if I would contaminate the air they breathed. Others laugh and try to joke away the news while a few humanely grieve for anyone with a lingering sickness, with death gnawing at his lungs. Yet I also sensed that he knew a man like me had little to live for and that knowledge made me a dangerous person. Strange how all this can make one more aware of the fallacies of the man. Carr struck me as being above all this.

"Here we are," he said, opening the door and holding it firmly to keep it from slamming back against the wall and shattering the glass.

I stepped into the narrow lobby. An old Hepplewhite sofa and armchair stood separated by a sturdy table, reminiscent of Renaissance Victorian, holding a kerosene lamp with an ornate shade like a glass bowl with tiny red flowers painted upon its surface. A small potbellied stove in the corner glowed with heat; the room smelled of damp heat, and perspiration broke out on my face.

A tall desk stood at the end of the room with a small rack of pigeonholes behind it. A clerk stood behind the desk, reading a newspaper, wearing a green eyeshade and a black suit. His tie had been carefully knotted in a Windsor knot, quickly coming into fashion, thanks to Prince Albert, below a celluloid collar. He looked up from his paper, interest quickening in his eyes as he saw my bag in Carr's hand.

"May I help you?" he asked in a high, reedy voice. His hands fluttered like tiny sparrows across his desk, touching the pen and inkwell, the register, neatly squaring them to the desk edge.

"Got a customer for you, Jerry," Carr said cheerfully. He placed my bag beside the desk. "Just came in on the train."

"I see," the clerk said, pursing his lips beneath a small mustache that clung precariously to his upper lip. "From Denver?"

"Yes," I added, coughing. The damp heat made the air feel heavy in the small room.

The clerk frowned. A tic began high in one cheek. I coughed again and took my flask from an inside coat pocket and opened it, draining the little left from my journey on the train. He flushed and turned, pretending to study the pigeon-holes behind him.

"Well," he said doubtfully, "if you don't have a reservation . . ."

"Cut it out, Jerry," Carr said roughly. "You haven't had enough lodgers to keep a quail in birdseed in two weeks. You gotta room. Stop trying to jack up the price." He winked at me. The clerk flushed.

"If you are ill, sir, might I recommend Mrs. Watkins's boardinghouse on the outskirts of town?" he said nervously.

"You can," I answered, taking the pen and dipping the nib into the ink. "I would like a room facing the street. Preferably a suite, if you have one." I scratched *Dr. J. H. Holliday* in bold strokes across the page.

"Sir," the clerk began, but Carr cut him short.

"It ain't that kind of sickness, Jerry," he said pointedly. The clerk flushed.

"I beg your pardon." He glanced at the ledger, his eyebrows rising to his high widow's peak. *"Doctor* Holliday?" he said, raising an eyebrow.

"Yes," I said, taking a cautious breath. The worm moved nervously in my chest. "And I would like a bath drawn. Hot water," I added.

"Yes sir," he said, taking a key from a slot in the pigeon-holes behind him. "Room Six at the top of the stairs to your left. The Presidential Suite."

"Does Jefferson Davis visit often?" I asked, taking the key from his fingers.

Confusion slipped across his face. "I beg your pardon?"

"Have my bath drawn immediately, please," I said. I bent

and picked up my carpetbag, staggering with the sudden weight. I turned toward the stairs. Painfully, I made my way slowly up the stairs, pausing every fourth or fifth step to take a slow, deep breath.

"I'll see you around, Doc," Carr said, respectfully touching his hat. I waved weakly at him. "You take care," he added. He nodded at the clerk, then left.

I reached the second floor and turned to the left, finding an iron number 6 on a plain wooden door three down the narrow hallway. I opened the door and stepped inside. The room had a causeuse upholstered in mauve with a matching medallion-back sofa and Sleepy Hollow armchair, separated by a wide, oval table carved from mahogany. A reading lamp with a green shade rested upon it. A small mahogany bar stood against the wall to my left with a writing desk opposite beneath a peg lamp. The walls were covered with gold-flecked paper. A door opened onto the balcony in front of me, heavy green velvet curtains pulled back and tied with brocade sashes to brass tie-backs. Another door opened on my left into a small room that held a large bed with a heavy mahogany head and footboard, a matching wardrobe, with twin night tables on either side, and an ewer and basin on a stand beside a dressing table with a large, gilt-edged mirror over it. Brussels carpets with large red roses woven into them covered the floor in both rooms. The rooms were cool but not cold, and I drew a thankful breath, feeling a calm begin to settle within me.

I sighed contentedly and pushed the door closed behind me. I tossed my hat and overcoat on the sofa and hobbled to the bar and examined the decanters, selecting one that promised whiskey and filled a cut-glass tumbler full, sipping it. Outside, the wind picked up in force, and I crossed to the door with French windows and watched as fat flakes of snow began to fall. Across the street, yellow lights beckoned from the Excelsior in the gloaming, but I was in no hurry. The saloon would still be there later, even tomorrow. I took another drink, feeling the warmth spread through me.

* * *

My fourth drink—or was it the fifth or sixth? I no longer counted drinks and seldom remembered bottles as a count to my life any more than I remembered days—warmed me as snow rattled against the windows. I felt better than I had for days, refreshed by my bath, a fresh shave, my cheeks laved with bay rum, the room cool enough for my dark blue lounging jacket with black piping on the sleeves and along the collar. I languidly turned the pages of Charles Dickens's *Bleak House,* reading

"It was a cold, wild night, and the trees shuddered in the wind. . . ."

when there came a knock upon my door. I reached over to the table by my elbow and removed the Colt, placing it in my lap beneath the fold of my book.

"Come in," I called.

The door opened and she walked in, pausing just inside the door, tiredly rubbing her eyes, her narrow waist accented by the cut of her mannish suit, full around solid hips. Her face was worn and white, revealing the faded chiaroscuro of her entire body in her wide forehead and cheeks. Her lips tightened as she glanced at the glass on the table beside me.

"What are you doing here?" she asked. She placed her black bag on the bar and leaned against it. Smudged half-moons curled around her eyes like smoke.

"Good evening, Dr. Walker," I said. "I thought Cheyenne might be more restful. Would you care for a drink?" I rose, sliding the gun onto the table, carefully marking my spot in *Bleak House* before resting it beside the Colt.

"Prepared, I see," she said, looking at the pistol. "Yes, I would like a drink. And you aren't supposed to be here. You're supposed to be in Denver."

"Bourbon?" I said.

"Brandy?" She dropped in the chair and sighed, stretching her legs out in front of her. I nodded and poured a large dollop into a snifter and handed it to her. She took a large swallow and closed her eyes, rocking her head back and forth. I stepped behind her, massaging the muscles in her neck, pressing deeply with the balls of my thumbs.

"Nice," she murmured. "You should have stayed in Denver. You're not well enough to be gallivanting around the country."

"Your concern for my health is touching," I said.

"I hate losing patients."

"Where is it written that you were destined to be the soul and conscience of the world?" I asked.

"Perhaps the world needs one, nevertheless," she answered.

"Does it deserve it?"

"You cannot judge others by yourself. There is love in the world, you know."

"Oh yes. There is love in the world," I said bitterly. "That is one of the demons. There is no more detestable creature in nature than a man who refuses to acknowledge his demons."

"Or embraces them," she said quietly. We stared at each other for a long moment, then I forced a laugh.

"Lose many here?" I asked. She grimaced and drained the brandy, handing the glass to me.

"A few. But it's about over." She yawned. "At least it's under control, I think."

She scrubbed her free hand over her face. Her hair lay lank over her forehead, curling damply over the collar of her shirt. A sour odor rose from her shirt.

"You need a bath," I said.

"I need some sleep," she corrected.

"Not until you've had a bath."

She opened her eyes, staring at me. "What difference does it make to you?"

"I have clean sheets on my bed," I answered.

"You took a lot for granted, coming all this way."

"Faint heart, fair lady," I said. I poured another glass of bourbon, sipping. "Did you think that I would wilt away like a hot-house flower?"

She looked away, then back. Her eyes met mine. "I don't want complications."

"Neither do I," I answered. I grinned and coughed once,

gently. "But Christmas is not far off and who wants to stand alone under the mistletoe?"

"Christmas is nearly two months off," she said.

"Yes, but one mustn't rush into things. Practice, my dear. Practice. We must learn first if we are, uh, compatible?"

"We're not," she said flatly.

"Aren't we?" I made an exaggerated bow. "What more can we lose? We've already lost everything, haven't we?"

A haunted look appeared in her eyes. They grew larger as they stared into mine, slowly becoming more vulnerable. "Perhaps."

"Then we can only gain?"

"Your logic—" She fumbled a moment and I interrupted.

"—is impeccable. Perhaps not the best of syllogisms, but faultless, nevertheless."

She shook her head. "I'm sorry, John. I truly am. But I can't. There is something about you . . . something . . ."

"We call it 'consumption,' ma'am," I drawled.

"No, that's not it. I wish it were that simple, but it isn't. I sense something not quite . . . real about you." She pursed her lips, looking thoughtfully at me. "You seem not of this world, and that frightens me, John. I can't put my finger on it. Please don't ask." A faint hint of red rose up from her throat. "I know it sounds bizarre, but could we not just be friends? Good friends, I mean, but friends nevertheless? Lovers are easy to find, but friends? I don't have that many. And friends are much more important than lovers. With a friend, we can be true with each other. But with a lover, well, one must lie on occasion. Lovers cannot afford hurt feelings. Friends rise above that."

"We can be whatever you want," I said. "Friends. Lovers. Friends and lovers. We don't have to make a choice, either. We can simply wait and see what happens."

She rose and put her arms around me, hugging me close.

"Thank you, John," she said huskily.

"Ah, my sweet magnolia blossom," I drawled.

Her tired face broke into a full smile. "Doctor Holliday, you are a gentleman."

"And so are you, my dear," I said, looking at her clothing. "So are you."

She glanced down at herself and broke into laughter.

The long-awaited blizzard struck in the middle of the night like an angry beast bellowing in pain. For three days and four nights it raged and howled around the eaves of the hotel, driving huge drifts down the street before it like dust. I rested, quietly gathering my strength, sometimes reading aloud to Mary from *Bleak House* when she returned half-frozen from making her appointed rounds.

But all things must end—the good, that is; the bad things are only postponed. And so it was on the fourth day when I decided to return to my labors as a sporting gentleman. I did not venture far, only across the street to the Excelsior, an experiment in opulence that stopped just this side of bad taste: crystal chandeliers, whiskey served in cut-glass tumblers, a piano player with a repertoire of Chopin and Mozart instead of the common fare of the day: "Where Was Moses When the Lights Went Out," "Are You There, Moriarity," "Brannigan's Band," or "I'll Take You Home Again, Kathleen." The Irish, still the Judas goats for society, requested the maudlin songs so often that they became as much a part of saloon ambience as the mirror and the pink-and-white Rubenesque nudes behind the bar.

The man behind the bar looked up from his copy of the *Wyoming Weekly Leader* at my approach, an eyebrow quirking in query.

"Bourbon," I said, adding as his hand closed automatically around the neck of a bottle of Amazon whiskey, "Old Williams, if you will."

He shrugged and changed grips, pouring a large measure into a tumbler and sliding it in front of me. I took it, sipping as I turned to survey the room. A dealer sat alone at a table dealing patience to himself; two other tables were empty, their green felt surfaces freshly brushed, a deck of cards sealed and waiting in the center. The roulette wheel stood empty in the corner next to a dice table. A lone customer bucked the tiger at the faro table. Not wishing to break in on the man's game of patience, I carried my drink to the faro table and took a chair. I looked at the casekeeper on my left: a thin, sallow-faced man riding the hearse. I glanced at the case: two queens had been played, along with a trey and ten. The deck was fairly fresh.

"Mind another player?" I asked the dealer.

"It's your money," he said. "I'm Jack Bowden." He nodded at the casekeeper. "Billy Newman."

"Tom McKey," I said. The casekeeper nodded at me.

"Place your bets, please," the dealer said in a soft voice hoarse from whiskey. He wore a black suit with a string tie knotted neatly around his throat. His long and pale fingers fluttered nervously around the shoe where the cards were kept with a tight spring holding them to the top. I glanced at the board, a strip of green felt upon which the thirteen spades had been pasted: the lone bettor, a drummer by his attire, was placing his bets to get the maximum coverage, using one bet to cover two or three cards simultaneously. I reached over and dropped ten dollars on the ace. The dealer raised an eyebrow; I shook my head. He pulled a ten for the loser and an ace for the winner.

I slid the twenty dollars over to the jack and won again. Then I sat out, waiting for the cat-hop: the last three cards. When they came up, the dealer waited on us, his eyes flickering back and forth between us. I took another sip of bourbon.

"Five to one?" I asked. He shook his head.

"House will only go three to one," he said.

"Anything on the side?" I asked.

He hesitated, glancing around at the room: We were still the only players. He shrugged. "I'll give four on a hundred or better," he said.

I dropped two hundred on the table, picking my order: seven, deuce, king. The drummer gave me a sour smile.

"That's a fool's bet," he said.

"Maybe," I answered, sipping again.

The drummer played the seven to win, the deuce to lose.

The dealer slapped the shoe hard with his hand and fed the cards onto the table king-deuce-seven.

"Sorry, gents," he said, scooping our bets from the table. "The house wins everything."

The drummer swore. I picked up my glass, sipped, then placed it down on my left instead of my right.

"I think," I said quietly, "that I would like to examine the shoe."

The drummer slumped back in his chair, his eyebrows drawing together in a frown as he turned toward me. The casekeeper's hands slipped from the table into his lap while the dealer quietly slid his right hand into his cupped left hand, his fingers close to his sleeve.

"What the hell?" the drummer murmured. "What the hell?"

"I don't think I'll allow that," the dealer said softly. I took another sip of the bourbon, feeling the rage beginning to build in my stomach, spreading throughout my frame. I grinned at him.

"Well, now, aren't you the daisy, Jack Bowden?" I said. I twisted in my chair to keep the casekeeper in view, freeing myself from the edge of the table. The Manhattan rode just above my right hip, my left hand resting casually on the edge of the table above it. I placed the glass of bourbon in front of it, letting my right hand fall lightly upon my left forearm. I glanced at the faro shoe.

"If I'm not mistaken, that's a Frisco Box. Slap the top of it and you release a spring that slides a lever against the top card, holding it against the lid and freeing the second card," I said.

The dealer sat silently for a moment, his black eyes burning coals staring into mine.

"Well, well, Billy," he said softly to the casekeeper. "I believe we have a man of the trade among us."

"Sounds like it, Jack," Billy said. His voice was high and reedy, his nervousness apparent. His hands twitched and rose to his lapels.

"I wouldn't," I said softly.

He hesitated, staring into my eyes. I heard cloth rasp

across the table felt. I slipped the Colt free and thumbed back the hammer, firing as I turned to the dealer. A fine spray of blood fountained from his throat where the bullet caught him. He tipped backward in his chair, the derringer he'd pulled from his sleeve clattering onto the table. At the same time, I pulled the Manhattan and leveled it at the case-keeper, but he was staring at the dealer on the floor behind the table. He held a small Smith & Wesson .22-caliber First Model revolver half-drawn from his shoulder holster. I reached over and plucked it free, dropping it into my pocket. A high, mewling sound came from his throat. He rose from his seat and scurried around the table, falling to his knees beside the dealer. He took him tenderly in his arm, trying to wipe away the blood, which had slowed to a dribble from the dealer's throat.

"Jack! Oh, Jack!" he said, tears streaming down his eyes. He bent over, pressing his lips to the man's forehead. His shoulders heaved as he sobbed.

"Mr. McKey, that was the damnedest thing I ever saw!" the drummer exclaimed from beside me.

The door opened and closed behind me. I twisted in my seat and watched as Carr moved into the room, a shotgun held in one hand, the barrels pointing toward me. I placed the Colt and Manhattan on the table beside me and slowly stood away from them, taking my glass of bourbon with me. I coughed from the black powder smoke and took a sip, waiting.

"Well, Ben?" Carr said to the bartender. His eyes never left mine.

"He"—he nodded at me—"asked to see Jack's box. Called him fair, Marshal. Jack and Billy tried to work it between them like they did a couple of months ago with that cowboy, remember?"

Carr nodded, his eyes still steady on mine. "I remember. Go on."

"Jack drew. Even had his pistol leveled before that fellow pulled and shot him. Billy never even had a chance to get his pistol out."

"It was self-defense, Marshal," the drummer stuttered from next to me. "I saw it all. Except his hands." He pointed at me. "Mr. McKey drew before the dealer could shoot. Fact is, he had to or the other would've killed him."

"McKey?" Carr smiled thinly.

"I didn't want any trouble," I said apologetically. "Staying incognito seemed the best thing to do under the circumstances." I grinned and gestured at my pistols. "May I secure my firearms?"

He hesitated, then eased the hammers down on the shotgun and tucked it under his arm. "Reckon so. Seems like you're gonna come out of it with only a twenty-five-dollar fine."

"Fine?" I asked, tucking the pistols back into their respective holsters. I coughed again and dabbed at my lips with a lace handkerchief I took from an inside pocket. I emptied the tumbler and carried it over to the bartender, placing it in front of him. He quickly filled it and placed the bottle beside the glass.

"Disturbing the peace," he said. "Discharging a firearm in the town limits. Wish I could make it more, but I can't." He crossed over to the bar, laying the shotgun on top of it. He took a glass and poured a generous drink from the bottle. He glanced over at me.

"No offense, but I'd appreciate it if you would be making Cheyenne your former home," he said. He took a drink and shuddered from the bite of the bourbon.

"Are you running me out of town, Marshal?" I asked, idly tapping my fingers on my glass. He glanced down at the Colt's ivory handle jutting forward from its holster.

"No, don't reckon I could make it stick if I did," he said. "But I'm askin' you to take your business somewheres else. Deadwood Gulch would probably be more up your line. Be more action there than here, that's for sure. At least until the epidemic is over," he added. He gestured at the room. "The only action you'll get 'round here is what you see. Nickels and dimes to a dealer like you, Holliday."

"Holliday?"

I turned. The drummer stood open-mouthed beside us. His widened eyes stared into mine. *"Doc* Holliday?"

I sighed and turned away, looking back at the marshal. He shook his head.

"Doc Holliday? I've heard about you. They say you've killed ten men," he said reverently.

"You see what I mean?" Carr said. He took another drink of bourbon, not wincing this time from its bite. "By the time this makes it back to Denver, you'll have killed five more, shootin' with each hand, fifteen shots at least without reloading. You know what they've done with Bill Cody?"

"Man would rather have legends than reality," I murmured. I emptied my glass, refilling it from the bottle. "Legends tell him what he wants to be. Reality makes him what he is."

"My wife ain't gonna believe this!" the drummer said. "Damn! Doc Holliday! I'll buy his drinks!"

"My friend," I said, wearily turning to him, "you could not afford to buy my drinks." I tossed another down and refilled my glass from the bottle. My hand was still steady. The heaviness in my chest was beginning to lift. The room seemed like crystal, bright and lucid. I smiled carelessly at him. "But for the sake of your fair wife, who no doubt pines for tales of your western adventures, I will buy *you* a drink. And you," I said, turning to the marshal.

He shook his head. "That's my limit," he said.

"Nonsense. Not even a farewell drink?" I lifted the bottle, poising it over his glass, quirking my eyebrow in question.

He studied me for a long moment, then nodded. "All right. If you mean that. Then, yes, I'll drink a farewell drink with you."

"Good." I filled all the glasses and held mine aloft. "Then shall we drink to life? Or for what passes for life?"

"Doc," he said, shaking his head, "you're gonna have to stop this. You won't last long at this pace."

"The gods have already written that," I murmured. I tilted my head back, swallowing deeply.

6

The lead gray sky loomed ominously over us and large puffy flakes of snow began to fall as we entered the canyon leading to Deadwood. I huddled deeper into my chesterfield, wondering if I had made the right decision in trading Cheyenne for Deadwood, but I knew that I always would have made the same decision: There was something romantic about the name "Deadwood" that drew me: Maybe it was the ambience created by the name; maybe it was wishful thinking. It didn't matter; I was here, I reflected sourly, and the die was cast; all that remained was for me to read the spots.

The Black Hills Stage Company prided itself on never having been stopped from making the run from Custer to Deadwood. From the antics of our driver, Johnny Slaughter, I could little doubt that advertisement. The Indian problem had settled down after the massacre of Custer and his men of the Seventh Cavalry in June, but the trip through Red Canyon was still eerie enough to put everyone on edge. Tall black pines stood silently, resentfully, beside the road. Crumbling shale runs fell from the canyon walls. Rumor had it, my fellow passenger confided, that no animals were ever seen in Red Canyon despite the lush grass along the creek bottom.

Silence.

Except for the cracking of Slaughter's whip and the curses dropping frequently from his lips as we crested a hill, exhorting the animals to pull harder.

"Pull in, driver!" a loud voice commanded.

Slaughter cursed loudly, but obeyed, easing the panting team to a stop.

"Passengers out," the same voice commanded.

The miner and myself stepped down from the Concord. A tall man wearing a blue mask pulled tightly against his eyes confronted us. He held a pair of Allen & Wheelock .44-caliber revolvers, one centered midway between the miner and myself, the other on the driver and guard.

"I don't know what the hell you're doing stopping us going to Deadwood." Slaughter swore. "Anyone with a lick of sense knows that we carry freight going in and money comin' out. Ain't nothing here but passenger pickins'."

"Shut up and toss me down the mail sack," the holdup man said. Slaughter swore and reached down between his feet and tossed the canvas bag on the ground.

"You," the holdup man said, pointing at me with one of his revolvers. "Toss your weapons into the coach and stand clear." He looked up at Slaughter. "Toss down the shotty and your sidearm."

I slid the Colt and Manhattan from their holsters and tossed them inside the coach onto the seat and stepped away from the coach as Slaughter's pistol and shotgun landed in the road.

"All right," the masked man said. "Now empty your pockets. Yours, too, driver!" He tossed a pair of saddlebags on the ground. "Put everything in there."

The miner resignedly took a small sack of coins from an inside pocket of his buffalo coat and picked up the saddlebags, dropping the sack inside. I took a wallet from an inside pocket and gave it to the miner.

"That watch, too, fancy man," he said to me.

"This has sentimental value to me," I said quietly.

He rocked back the hammer on his pistol. "It has sentimental value to me, too. Gotta be worth twenty-five dollars at least."

"My mother—" I began, then lapsed into quiet as he rocked back the hammer on his other pistol.

"Makes no difference to me. I can take it off your dead body if I have to."

"I'd do what he says, mister," the miner said nervously. "I think he means it."

"I do mean it!" the holdup man said loudly. "I'll blow your fuckin' head off just as soon as look at you."

Silently, I unhooked the chain from my vest and dropped the watch into the bag. The holdup man nodded in satisfaction.

"Good. Now hand it up to me. Careful," he warned as the miner stood forward and lifted the bag to him. "Now, driver, pull that team forward about a hundred feet or so. You two follow on foot."

He gigged his horse, turning him and galloped away as we obeyed. Slaughter halted the coach and set the brake before climbing down and scurrying back to collect his shotgun and pistol.

"Close one," the miner mumbled, taking off his hat and wiping the sweat from his forehead despite the coolness of the day. "Last holdup through here left two people dead." He glanced at me. "Sure ain't a good way of welcomin' you to Deadwood, young man. Sorry about your money and watch."

"The money doesn't matter," I said, feeling the rage beginning to build within me. "But that watch does."

"Ain't nothin' to be done about it now, I reckon," he said as we reached the stage. He opened the door for me. I climbed in and took my pistols, settling them back into their holsters. He climbed in after me and shut the door as Slaughter hurried up.

"Hang on," he said as he climbed into the driver's box. "We gotta make up some time or we might get caught out here. That storm's abrewing bad now."

I glanced at the clouds building around the edge of the cliffs. The flakes had grown bigger and were beginning to fall faster. Slaughter's whip snaked out and cracked and the team leaped forward, jerking the stage into motion.

"Yep, I'd say we were pretty lucky, given everything," the miner said.

"You said that once before," I answered pointedly.

He gave me a strange look, started to say something, then fell into silence as the stage jerked and rattled its way over the deep-rutted road. About an hour later we arrived at Deadwood. It was my first experience with a mining town, and I was both taken aback and amused at what I saw. The town had been built up around a stream with houses like cracker boxes planted wherever the builder's whim suited him. The main street weaved around the houses, following the creek and was jammed with mule and oxen teams, horses, jacks, wagons, and humanity. Con men in soiled garb, tired-looking women in homespun or calico dresses, miners wearing mule-eared boots and canvas trousers, their hands rough and cracked from working the flumes where placer mining could be gouged from the creek banks, gunmen, ex-soldiers, tramps, frontiersmen, bullwhackers, grub-line riders looking for a quick dollar or two, coopers, cordwainers, farriers, knackers, peddlers, runners, sawyers, vendors, tailors, teamsters, wheelwrights, all jammed together, pushing and shoving against each other while they made their way up and down the narrow street.

At the far end of the gulch, tents had been strung over a framework of rough lumber while what passed for the main street was lined with saloons, gambling houses, honky-tonks, cribs, general stores, and a couple of hotels. The miner hurriedly stepped down from the coach when we pulled to a stop in front of the stage office with Slaughter bellowing that we had been robbed eight miles back and where the hell was the goddamned sheriff?

I stepped down from the stage, bringing my black bag with my dentist's tools with me, and collected my carpetbag, which Slaughter had carelessly tossed onto the ground. I looked around, trying to get my bearings. I bumped into a slim young man, staggering him. Angry eyes turned to mine and I took a deep breath, recognizing in the thrust of breath and hip not a young man but a young woman wearing man's clothes.

"I beg your pardon," I said.

"Why don't you watch where you're going?" she demanded, her hand dropping menacingly to a .36-caliber Colt M1851 revolver in a cavalry holster, the flap cut off, riding high on her hip on a large black belt. She wore a tan-and-green-checked shirt under a fringed buckskin jacket, a blue bandanna looped in a wide circle around her neck, and a wide-brimmed Spanish hat broken to shade her face, but her raven curls escaped from the hat and her eyes were bright and dancing and daring in her long, thin face.

"My, my, aren't we testy," I said.

She stared at me suspiciously. "Are you making fun of me? 'Cause if you are then we can settle things right here."

"Frankly, my dear, all I want is a clean hotel room and a bath," I said wearily. I shivered as a wind kicked a small dust of snow down the street. "And the sooner the better," I added.

"I don't like being shoved around. You damn men are always trying to shove me around!"

I gave her a faint grin. It seemed that it was my fate to run into women who were sorry they were born women.

"Then why do you compete with them?" I asked. "You want to dress like men and play men's games, then expect to be treated like a man."

She stared for a long moment, then burst into a long, loud laugh and thrust a callused hand out to me. I took it gingerly, wincing at its dirt and roughness.

"Martha Jane Canary," she said. "Folks call me Calamity Jane, though," she added, boasting.

"I can understand that," I said, then hastily added as her eyes narrowed threateningly, "Pleased to meet you. I'm Dr. John Henry Holliday. A dentist." I noticed a familiar look coming over her eyes as she contemplated various hurts and aches.

"Well," she said. "Pleased to meet you." She frowned. "Holliday? Heard about a Holliday who is pretty handy with a pistol. But that was down Texas way. I think," she added with another loud laugh. "I was pretty liquored up down that way. Fact is, I'm pretty liquored up most times. When I can afford it," she said pointedly.

I sighed. "I'll trade you a drink for the name of the best hotel."

"Deal!" she said, clapping me firmly on the shoulder, staggering me. She lifted my carpetbag from my hand. "Come on! Drink first!"

She led the way to a building built out of rough-hewn planks. Snow was falling more heavily, now, but I could still smell the whiskey and sour beer and the stench of unwashed bodies rolling out of the door. Shouts and laughter greeted us as my guide pushed her way inside and, using the carpetbag. as a ram, forged her way through the crowd with me in her trail. She reached the bar, rough planks supported on empty kegs. Inside, heat poured across the room from a potbellied stove glowing cherry red in the corner and bodies jammed tightly together. She slammed the carpetbag down on top of the bar, drawing the bartender's attention.

"Eddie! Give us a couple of whiskeys down here!"

Eddie shook his head. "Money first, Jane! You've drunk enough on credit!"

She made an impatient gesture, jerking her thumb at me. "This here's the man with the money." A rat-faced man wearing cast-off boots and pants stiff with dirt tried to shove in between us at her words. She elbowed him away. "Get your own benefactor, McCall!" He stumbled away, snarling at her through blackened teeth.

The bartender lifted an eyebrow at me. I nodded. He shrugged as if to say something about a man's choice, then slid a couple of glasses in front of us and slopped whiskey from a bar bottle into them. Jane took hers and tossed it off, shuddering, then whooping, "God!" and wheezing, "That's good!" She arched her eyebrows at me. I lifted my glass and took a tiny sip, shuddering. I handed my glass to her. She took it greedily as I motioned to the bartender. He slid down, lifting the bottle. I placed my hand over her glass.

"I would like some whiskey," I said.

He snorted and lifted the bottle to show me the label: a snake coiled around the label proclaiming it to be Diamond-back Whiskey. "Whaddya think this is? Mouthwash?"

"Which might be better," I answered. "That tarantula juice you're passing off as whiskey will blind a person before long."

He set the bottle carefully on the makeshift bar in between

us. "Are you saying my whiskey is pizen?" he asked in a dangerous voice.

I smiled and nudged my coat open with my left hand, exposing the ivory handle of my Colt. "Lye, alcohol, tobacco juice, and probably a couple heads of rattlesnakes tossed in for added kick. That's usually the recipe."

The people at the bar glanced down at their drinks, then pushed them back and slid away. The bartender flushed and dropped his hands under his apron.

"Don't make that mistake," I warned him softly, leveling the Colt at him. I rocked back the hammer, the ratchet loud in the quiet area around us. Beads of perspiration formed on my face. I muffled a cough. The skin tightened over the deep pits in his cheeks. He stared at the black bore of the Colt for a long second, then forced a smile beneath his heavy handlebar mustache.

"Hell, mister, if you wanted special whiskey, you kin have it. Costs extra," he warned, reaching behind him to the bar. He pulled a bottle off and held it up for me to inspect. "Monongahela all right?"

"No Old Williams?" I asked, lowering the hammer on the Colt and sliding it back into its holster. The miners around us breathed a sigh of relief and stepped back to the bar, reaching again for their drinks. The noise level picked up again.

"Sorry, mister," he said. "It's this or gin. I kin make a couple of drinks for you. How about a Tip and Ty? Or a Deacon or Stone Wall? Got a bit of applejack handy, too."

"The Monongahela will do," I said. He nodded, hesitated, then took the first glass Jane had used, gave it a perfunctory wipe with his soiled apron, then filled it and placed it in front of me. He hesitated, then placed the bottle beside it.

"Help yourself," he said, and moved off back down the bar.

Jane breathed a deep sigh and shoved the glass she had been holding out onto the bar.

"Goddamn! John, but that was the damnedest thing!" She motioned at her glass. I obliged, filling it. She took it and tossed it off in one quick draught, smacking her lips over the aftertaste, then frowned. "Ain't got much kick to it. Think I like the other better." She nodded after the bartender, who was busily filling glasses down at the other end. "Eddie killed a man in here couple days ago for saying things like that about his booze. Favors a razor. Good with it, too."

I drank the Monongahela. Not as good as Old Williams, but it would do. I poured another glass. "I do my own shaving or use a barber."

She sputtered in her drink, coughing behind her laughter. "Damn! But yer gonna kill me, John." She straightened, wiping her eyes with the back of her hand. She reached for her glass again.

"I really would like my room," I said gently, pushing the bottle away from her eager fingers.

"Refusin' a lady a drink?" she said. She shook her head. "Ain't very gentlemanlike, John. I thought you'd be a gentleman, given the cut of yer clothes and the way you talk, nice and slow, like molasses would roll in yer mouth."

"All right," I said resignedly. "One more." I poured us each a drink, then opened my small dentist's satchel and took out a leather wallet that I had secreted inside. I motioned to the bartender. He came down and I handed him the bottle along with five dollars. He turned for the cash drawer. "Keep the change. For your troubles," I added when he looked back in surprise. He nodded and grinned.

"Anytime, Mr. . . ."

"Holliday," I answered. "John Henry Holliday. Dentist."

"Got one of them. Fact is, we got two if you count Tom, the barber." He leaned on the bar as I continued to sip from my glass. "But I reckon we allus got room for one more. Especially one who's good with those." He nodded at the pistols beneath my coat. "Some folks get a bit cantankerous after visiting a dentist and getting a molar yanked. Best if one can take care of himself."

"Ol' John kin take care of hisself," Jane said, slurring her words. "Done it before down Texas way. Killed a coupla men thought they could ride him."

Apprehension showed in Eddie's eyes. He shook his head. "Holliday. Thought the name sounded familiar."

"Actually, I believe he killed a man in Cheyenne, too," a soft voice said. I glanced over my shoulder at a man with long blond hair curling in long ringlets down over his broad shoulders. His lips, thin and compressed, were partially hidden by a straw-colored mustache.

"Bill!" Jane exclaimed and threw herself at him, trying to clasp her arms around his neck. He sidestepped neatly, taking her firmly with his left hand and pulling her away from him.

"Aw, Bill! Don't be that way," she said, staggering and righting herself when she caught up next to a poker table. She came away from the table and stood, gently swaying beside him.

"You pick strange friends, Jane," he said softly.

"Oh, Pah-don me," she said, rolling the words around in her mouth before releasing them. "Bill, this is Dr. John Holliday. John, this is Wild Bill Hickok."

He grimaced at the introduction and stepped forward, holding out his right hand. He was tall, about six-two.

"Bill, please," he said, extending his hand. I took it, marveling at the strength beneath its softness and thinking that it belied the legend expounded on in the ten-cent novels one could find lying around the tables in hotel lobbies. In fact, he looked far from the colorful figure one came to expect from the legend. He wore a striped shirt, open necked, with a red silk neckerchief knotted like a cravat and tucked inside. Around his waist he wore a matching red sash with two pistols tucked inside, handles facing each other across his flat stomach: engraved ivory-handled .36-caliber Colt 1851 Navy revolvers. Later I would discover these were his "working" pistols; he carried a pair of single-action .44 Colt revolvers with pearl handles, tastefully engraved, given to him by Bill Cody when he was back East playing in *Scouts of the Plains*. Salt-and-pepper trousers were tucked inside of flat-heeled boots with half-moons stitched on the sides. His eyes were covered with spectacles filled with blue glass, which had become popular when a doctor proclaimed that the glasses and blue windowpanes were a cure-all for everything from headaches to gonorrhea.

"My pleasure, sir," I said courteously. A tiny smile lifted the corners of his mustache.

"And your friend?" he asked, nodding at my side. Jane frowned and stood close to him, placing her hand on his arm.

"There ain't no one there, Bill," she said nervously. "Just him."

His lips compressed again into a tight line. A flush moved up behind the tan of his face, darkening it. He half turned to his side, then said, "Ah, I see now. Just a shadow."

"As is yours," I said. "Kindred spirits," I added lightly.

He glanced sharply at me. I grinned and lifted my glass, toasting him, then draining it. I thought I saw a shadow of sadness flick over his face, then it was gone and the slight, mocking grin back.

"Maybe we can play a hand or two later," he said.

"I've been known to turn a card or two in a friendly game," I said. I placed my glass back on the bar upside down. With the same movement, I collected my bags from off the bar and turned toward Jane. "You promised the hotel in exchange for a drink?"

"Hotel?" Bill said sharply. He peered at Jane. "You promised him a hotel?"

She stirred nervously, tipping her hat back from her wide forehead with a dirty forefinger. "Aw, Bill! You know how it is!"

"Is there a problem?" I asked, looking from Jane to Bill. He nodded.

"A small one. There's not a room to be had in all of Deadwood. I'm camped up the creek in a stand of aspen with Colorado Charley Utter. Deadwood's growing. Nearly fifteen thousand people here and more coming each day. 'Course, that'll taper off with the snow blowing, but I don't think it will do you much good."

"I see. And your suggestion?"

He shook his head. "Ain't got one. Leastways, not one for

you. I don't mind you tossing in with Charley and myself, but . . ." He cast a quick look up and down my clothes. "I don't think you're made for it. No offense."

"None taken," I said. "What would you say is the best hotel in town?"

He shrugged. "The Pioneer, probably. Next to the China Palace, probably the best eatin' place in town. Leastways, for Chink food. A good steak can sometimes be had down at the Longhorn, but only if a couple cattle stray in. Most of the time it's buffalo, and that's a bit hard if not cooked right." He shook his head. "Most people can't cook buffalo steak. They wanna fry the damn thing. And then there's Irish Johnny's down next to the tinsmith's. He makes the best stew."

"Thank you," I said. "Deadwood sounds very cosmopolitan. But I believe the first order of business is to find lodging. And if the Pioneer is the best hotel, I think I'll start there."

He shrugged. "Good luck. You want a game later, I'm usually here at old Number 10."

"Number 10?" I said, glancing at Eddie. He grinned.

"Deadwood's growing so fast we plumb ran out of names. Took to numbering them. I'm in the tenth one after the Bucket of Blood."

"A bit melodramatic," I said. He took a cigar from his shirt pocket and placed it in his left cheek, chewing it with stumpy, yellow teeth.

"A bit," he grinned. "But it draws. By the way, if you really want that Old Williams, you might try Herminne and Treber's place down the street. They're the liquor dealers around here."

I nodded. "Thanks," I said, hefting my bags to get a better grip. I coughed again, shuddering. I placed my dentist's bag back on the counter and motioned at the Monongahela. I spun a coin onto the bar. "Meanwhile, I'll take that."

He reached beneath the bar and removed a full bottle and set it beside my bag. I opened the bag and placed the bottle inside. A cough exploded again from my lungs. I turned and spat a bright red gobbet of blood onto the floor. Fresh perspiration spotted my face. I picked up my bag. Suddenly, its weight doubled.

"I guess I'd better get down to the Pioneer and see about that room," I said past the coppery taste in my mouth. Hickok reached out and took one of my bags, leaving his right hand free.

"Reckon I can give you a hand," he said. He nodded at Jane. "Take his other one."

"You got two hands," she objected. He turned his head, staring at her through the blue lens of his glasses. She defiantly returned his stare for a moment, then her face dropped and she reached for the other bag. "All right, Bill," she mumbled. "All right. I guess I owe him."

We left the saloon, turning into the biting wind blowing down the main street. Snow fell in earnest now, beginning drifts in the alleys and spreading out onto the frozen mud of Main Street. Teamsters were hustling their horses off the street and into the various liveries. A couple of tarts hurried by, turning into the Green Front, giggling as they cast bold glances at us in passing. I looked at Bill. He sighed.

"Past me now," he said ruefully. "Long past. You?"

I shook my head, taking a cautious breath. The cold air cut deep into my lungs, nearly causing a paroxysm of coughing. Cautiously, I took several short breaths, feeling better as oxygen flooded my lungs.

"Not many want a man like me for any money," I said.

He nodded. "I know what you mean. Men like you and me, why there ain't nothin' left inside to attract the good ones. Just one big empty hole. The only ones I get now are those who want to sleep with Wild Bill. But there ain't nothin' to that for me." He glanced back at Jane and leaned close, whispering. " 'Sides, I'm married now. Agnes Lake. Circus rider. Ever hear of her?"

The pride in his voice made me want to nod, but I hadn't and knew that if he pushed the conversation farther along those lines my lie would become obvious and somehow, I didn't think he would take kindly to the lie. Jane saved my dilemna.

"What's that, Bill?" she asked suspiciously, coming up behind us.

"Just askin' Doc if he was feelin' better," he said quickly, winking at me and wagging his eyebrows frantically. I smiled and nodded, feeling the humor of the situation: a man with his reputation afraid of a woman in man's clothing?

"Very philosophical," I managed.

"Just good sense," he said. "No sense starting fights when you don't have to."

"What the hell are you two talkin' about?" she demanded, trying to push between us with my bag.

"Philosophy," he said, turning into a doorway. "Here we are: the Pioneer. Such as it is."

At least the floor was covered. Bare boards laid flat together. A small desk held a ledger and inkstand in front of a set of pigeonholes that held twenty keys. A small stove in the corner cast wet warmth into the room, making it seem like a steam room. A small table stood beside two moth-eaten overstuffed chairs in green brocade that made me wistfully remember New Orleans. I glanced at the book on the table and smiled: *De Witt's Ten Cent Romances: Wild Bill, the Indian Slayer.* I glanced at my companion. He blushed.

"You can't help what some people print," he said defensively.

"You read it?"

He shook his head. "Ain't no truth in it. I've killed a few Injuns, but by the time you'd get to page five of that thing you'd have racked up my entire account and still have fifty pages or so to go."

A nervous clerk watched as we approached. I could see he knew who Bill was, and the distasteful look he gave Jane said he knew her as well. He wore a black suit like a preacher with a tight cardboard collar, around which he had tightly knotted a bow tie in an attempt to fill the distance between his chin and chest, but his neck was as scrawny as a banty rooster and his tightly compressed lips made him look as if he had been sucking on alum or lemons. I would have bet ten dollars that he purged himself every morning with a hefty dose of Dr. Powers's Radical Pills guaranteed to cure a young man of constipation and "secret habits."

"We're all full," he said in a nasal whine. "You might try the livery stable. I hear Wilson's letting people sleep in his loft for two dollars a night."

"This man's sick," Bill said, dropping my carpetbag at the edge of the desk. Jane deposited my dentist's bag beside it, sneered at the desk clerk, then plopped herself down in one of the two chairs.

"I am truly sorry for your misfortune, sir," the clerk said, noting the perspiration beaded on my face, the hollows beneath my eyes. "But I am still full. Ain't nothing I can do about that. Sleeping two to a room in shifts, now."

Bill shrugged, turning to me. "It's as I told you, Doc. No room at the inn."

"I'll give you ten dollars a night," I said to the clerk. "Double your rate." His eyes wavered, fell to the ledger, then he looked up, the muscles working greedily at the corners of his jaws. Regretfully he shook his head.

"I'd like to accommodate you, but I would have to displace someone and that would cause trouble," he said.

"I'll handle the trouble," I said. "Just give me the room." I spun the ledger around and took the pen, dipping the nib in the ink, scribbling my name in bold strokes in the ledger.

He sighed. "Well, seeing as how you're sick and all, I guess I can put you in number six. You'll be sharing that room with two miners and a faro dealer over at the Bucket of Blood." He frowned. "Mr. Tanner will simply have to put up at the stable. But he's a teamster, so that seems to be the logical way of handling things."

"I beg your pardon, but I have no intention of sharing the room with anyone," I said coldly.

"Now, look here!" he said hotly. "I'm obliging you the best I can!"

"And you're still making two dollars more than you were by the eight dollars you were collecting from the four," I said. "I'll need clean sheets and blankets as well. I do not sleep in others' leavings. Is there a bath?"

"I—" the clerk began, but Bill leaned forward, looking harshly at him through his blue lenses.

"I don't mind a four-flusher, but I hate a two-bit chiseler," he said softly.

"That's tellin' 'im, Bill!" Jane said loudly from her chair. She struggled upright, pulling her pistol around from behind her, snugging it around her hip. "Let's just plug this weasel in the liver and see what leaks out! The son of a bitch wouldn't let me inta the building when Tanner an' me was gonna tumble a while back. Cost me two dollars, he did!"

"Now, just a minute!" the clerk said, trying for bravery, but he blinked rapidly and swallowed against the fear building inside him, and I knew the room was mine.

Bill stretched his six-two frame across the desk and plucked the key to room six from the pigeonhole behind the clerk. He handed it to me, the same tight smile spreading across his lips. He bent down and picked up my two bags.

"Come on," he said. "I'll help you set up your room. Then you can buy me dinner at the Chink's place."

"Hey! Wad about me?" Jane said thickly. Her head nodded loosely and her eyes drooped heavily. She flopped back down on the chair. Within seconds, she was snoring, the sound loud and reverberating throughout the room. Bill shook his head.

"Never could hold her liquor," he said sadly. "No matter how much she tries to be a man, her womanhood keeps gettin' in the way."

"I don't think it's that," I said.

"No?" His eyebrows rose questioningly as we climbed the stairs.

"I think she just tries too hard to belong somewhere."

"You could have something there," he said seriously.

He led the way up the stairs to number six. I opened the door and threw it wide, gagging on the man-stench that rolled out of the room, then leaned back against the wall, coughing and coughing. Bill wrinkled his nose in disgust and shoved his way past me into the room. He dumped my bags in the middle of the floor and strode across the bare pine planks to the window, shoving it wide. Fresh air, followed by flakes of snow swept into the room. The room was plain: an iron bedstead, wardrobe, straight-backed wooden chair, a pitcher and ewer on a stand beneath a small shaving mirror, chamber pot under the bed. Four distinct piles of clothes were carelessly tossed into the four corners of the room.

Bill grabbed the piles of clothes and heaved them out into the hallway as the clerk came up the stairs with fresh linen in his arm. Bill fixed him with a stern eye.

"Don't you ever check your rooms?" he demanded.

The clerk glanced at the pile of mismatched clothing in the hallway. His nose twitched. He coughed apologetically and slipped into the room.

"You may find this hard to believe, but the linen is changed weekly," he said, tossing the bedclothes onto the chair. He stripped the blanket and sheets from the bed, shook his head at the black streaks upon the sheets, and proceeded to remake the bed with the clean linen with quick, economical movements, neatly tucking the corners of the sheets and blankets.

"You're right," Bill grunted, watching him at work. "I find that hard to believe. I find it harder to believe that a man would come up out of the mines and be content to go to bed smelling like skunk's puke."

"Air it out," I instructed the clerk. "I'll be back in an hour or two. Maybe it'll be ready for humans by then. Though I'm having my doubts," I added. "Come on, Bill. Let's get Jane and I'll buy us all something at the Chinaman's."

We trooped downstairs, where Bill grabbed Jane by the arm and lifted her from the chair. She protested crossly and swung a backhand at him, but he dodged with the ease of long practice and pushed her toward the door ahead of him. The shock of cold air quickly woke her, and she shivered and pulled her fringed coat tighter around her.

"Goddamn, Bill," she said. "Coldern' a witch's teat out here. Whyn't yuh leave me where it was warm?"

"Doc's buying us supper," he said, nodding at me.

She brightened at the prospect. "The Chinaman's?"

I nodded, turning my head away from the wind tearing my

eyes. I pulled my wide-brimmed Stetson tighter on my head, and shrugged deeper into my chesterfield.

The cold bit through, chilling me to the bone. Yet I felt comfortable, lucid in the winter setting in to the Black Hills. I glanced up at the cliffs surrounding Deadwood, at the top of the mountain the miners were already calling Mount Moriah. A strange feeling swept through me and I knew then why the Sioux fought so hard to keep the white man from their *Paha Sapa:* a spiritual life flowed through these hills. Whether it was the great Manitou or the Wankan Tonka of the Sioux, I did not know, but I did know that a more powerful force than we knew was there, and we were disturbing it. An ancient power, moving reluctantly from its old home. I felt sad, then, knowing that that power was giving way to a newer god, a more powerful god that was rewriting the destiny of the people: Mammon.

I wintered in the Black Hills, making my way from saloon to saloon, slowly building a small fortune at the tables, usually with Bill sitting in on the game as well, his back against the wall more for appearance's sake than from a fear of being shot in the back for anything past the table was little more than a blur. His eyes were going bad quickly despite his belief that the blue glasses were helping him. I think his belief in that blue glass was based more out of desperation than on reality. He kept his ailment as secret as he could. If word leaked out, he would have been dead long before Jack McCall killed him, for his enemies were legion.

Once when he sat with me when my sickness was in full stride and I was trying to assuage the hunger of the worm turning in my chest, gnawing at my flesh, with liberal quaffs of Old Williams, we visited about fornication, with Bill at last confiding that he no longer thought about the act with the zestfulness of youth.

"Ah, but I remember fine times, fine times," he said, shaking that great leonine head of his. His eyes saddened. "I remember *the* time that changed me as well."

"Changed you?" I asked.

He nodded. "Yes, I remember the woman who changed me."

"Your wife?"

He shook his head. "Oh no. She was the result of the change. The change was a pretty little whore in Buffalo."

"What happened?"

He laughed. "Forget it."

And that was the end of that subject. I don't know what happened, but I have strong feelings. I believe Bill's encounter with his little whore in Buffalo was much like Marlowe's Barabas: fornication better refused. More than Bill's eyesight was deteriorating: His mind was slipping away from the reality of the moment at odd times, slipping back into the past or, what was worse, leaving him staring blankly into space for long periods, almost as if his thoughts had suddenly become scrambled and were slowly being sorted.

Still, winter passed for me in Deadwood and summer brought rains that turned the street into a quagmire that bogged down heavily laden wagons, leaving the tempers of teamsters and bullwhackers stretched thin. Fights broke out and Eddie's Saloon No. 10 was nearly destroyed twice by whaling rioters desperately trying to kill each other with their fists. But the gold fields flourished and the tables in the saloons were never empty of men desperately looking for relief from the tedious labor of pulling the golden calf from the veins of the mountains.

And so passed summer days and nights. I remember little about them, for one day pretty much was the next and the one following that had little to distinguish it from its predecessor. Twice I shipped boxes of dust and nuggets to my bank in Denver and twice the shipments got through, although many did not. Talk began among the tradesmen of a need for law in the mining camp. Vigilante committees began to meet, but little was accomplished save the hanging of two men in what turned out to be a case of mistaken identity.

In July, a man tossed a watch into the pot to call a raise I had made. I glanced at the watch and recognized it as my own. I looked up at him and reached for the watch, opening it. The first notes of Chopin's nocturne tinkled in the saloon. I opened the back and saw the lock of Mother's hair still there.

"That there's my mother's hair," the man said. "Should bring me luck."

I looked up at him and looped the watch over my vest, carefully slipping the hook on the chain over my vest button. A puzzled look came over his face.

"Now, wait just a minute there," he sputtered. "You ain't won the pot yet! Put my watch back on the table."

"My watch, you mean, sir," I said mildly. "You stole it from me when you held up the stage a few months ago. And don't insult my mother by claiming her as yours. I don't think you even know who your mother was, you lying son of a bitch."

The other players scrambled away from the table as he leaped to his feet, tugging at the two Allen & Wheelocks sheathed at his hip. I waited until the barrels cleared their holsters, then slipped the Colt from its holster and shot him twice in the belly. He flew backwards, the big Wheelock flying away from him, clattering against the wall as he fell to the floor. His legs twisted briefly in agony. He screamed. Then he lay quietly in a gathering pool of blood.

The bartender came over and knelt beside him, feeling for a pulse in his neck. He shook his head and stood, beckoning to his swamper to carry the body out. He glanced at me.

"Heard what you said," he said. His eyes glanced at the watch in my pocket. "Can you prove that?"

I took the watch out of my vest pocket and pressed the spring to open the lid. Chopin's nocturne again danced in the air.

"The inside has my uncle's name engraved on it and my mother's," I said. "It was a gift from her to him. He gave it to me when she died. The name inside is Thomas McKey."

He bent over the watch, peering at the fine, copperplate engraving for a second, then stood.

"It's as you said. Reckon this was meant to be." He glanced at the man being dragged out of the saloon. "Doesn't matter no how, I reckon. Clearly self-defense. Hell, you even gave 'em time to kill you. Not many'd do that." He glanced at the money on the table. "Reckon that's yours as well. Case closed."

He turned and stumped back behind the bar, loudly calling for the others to do the same. I sheathed my pistol and pulled the money to me, carefully separating the bills and coins. The others retook their seats and someone spun a dollar onto the center of the table and announced the game as draw poker, and the game continued as if nothing had happened while the holdup man's blood slowly congealed among the sawdust and used tobacoo plugs and cigar butts on the floor. The case had been heard by the saloonkeeper and the decision made as to justice being served, and that was the way of the mining camp. Each saloonkeeper was his own judge and jury, the house rules being the law of the moment, for there was no law in Deadwood, a fact that a disgruntled few lamented.

Some of the townspeople approached Bill and asked him if he would be willing to wear a marshal's badge once again. He declined politely, preferring to spend the majority of his time with cards in the various saloons while his partner, Colorado Charley Utter, moved around the gold fields, buying up claims that showed promise, speculating on possible growth and worth. But no one believed him—especially after he walked into a saloon filled with gunfighters who had been bragging about town what they were going to do to him. I was there when Bill walked through the door and faced them.

"I understand that some of you two-by-four gladiators have been making remarks about me," he said quietly. "So I decided to come by and warn you that if any of you try something, this camp is going to have a lot of cheap funerals to contend with."

And he left after collecting their guns. That was enough for the underworld. They began talking up the need to get rid of Bill before he cut himself in on their "deal."

I did not see Bill's death, for I was playing in the Bucket of Blood at the time, but I believe that it was brought on by the townsfolk constantly pestering Bill to take the marshal's badge. The lawless element in Deadwood did not want a man of Bill's caliber wearing that badge, even if he no longer was the man who had walked the streets of Hays City. He was still more man than most could contend with. With that in mind, I believe a certain number found the most worthless individual they could find and talked him into killing Bill, making him believe that Bill's reputation would transmute itself onto his shoulders.

On August 2, Bill was playing poker with some of his friends in Eddie's saloon when Broken-Nose Jack McCall slipped up behind him with a rusty pistol and fired a round into the back of Hickok's head. It was the only bullet that could have been fired from that pistol, the others proving worthless. A lot has been written about Bill's death, and I see no reason to add more. Deadwood buried him the next day with Bill Hillman, John Oyster, Charlie Rich, Jerry Lewis, Charlie Young, and Tom Dosier as pallbearers. McCall was freed by a miner's court stacked with Bill's enemies.

But those who had talked McCall into killing Bill—everyone knew it was Tim Brady and Johnny Varnes for they were seen drinking with McCall shortly before McCall killed Bill—did their own disservice. Talk began in earnest about secret committees meeting with an eye toward rectifying the lawless problem in the hills. Jane attached herself to me for a while, crying at the drop of a dollar about being Bill's wife, cadging drinks with her story of their affair. Bill may have been one of the many who slept with her; I don't know. I don't care. The legend of their affair is much better than any reality could possibly be, and that is all that is important.

I returned to Denver, where everything was pretty much the same except for the damn blue-glass fad that had made its way here as well and new ordinances made the carrying of firearms illegal. Denver seemed as if it was trying to convince itself that it had indeed joined the more cosmopolitan

centers with Colorado's new statehood. I took to wearing the
Spanish dagger I had taken from the Indian so many months
before in a sheath sleeve under my left forearm. I had money
and decided to enjoy myself, spending most of my time with
my good friend Charley Foster in Babbitt's House when I
wasn't escorting Mary Walker to one of the shows. With her
short hair and insistence upon wearing men's clothes, she
was often mistaken as my brother, which caused her much
secret merriment. I wrote a letter to Mattie and quickly
received one back in which she told me that the cotton crop
had failed again at home thanks to the boll weevil, but Father
was making ends meet with his pecan groves. Yes, I was
happy in Denver, but happiness is short and the gods dislike
contentment. I had three months.

In November, Budd Ryan found me in Babbitt's, where I
was playing poker with four others. He swaggered through
the door of the saloon, fresh snow dusting his shoulders. He
ordered a drink in a loud voice, then caught sight of me dealing a game of draw to my friends at a corner table. He
brought his drink over with him, dropping into one of the
vacant chairs.

"Well, well," he said, his lips curling in scorn. "If it isn't
the lunger. Still trying to play poker, lunger?"

"My name is McKey," I said quietly. "Tom McKey."

"That's not what I heard." He paused, looking around to
see if he had an audience. The others edged back from the
table, tensing to fall to the floor or jump away if things went
wrong. Others paused in their gaming to cast curious glances
our way.

"I heard your name is Holliday. *Doctor* John Henry Holliday," he said. "Now, why would you not use your real name,
Holliday?"

I sat back in my chair, gently spreading the lapels of my
coat wide. "I'm not armed, Ryan," I said. "There's a law
against carrying pistols in Denver now. One of the by-
products of civilization."

"Is that right?" he said. He carelessly let his coat fall open, revealing a small pistol tucked in a shoulder holster. It looked like a Root, but I couldn't be certain.

"I guess it's all in who you know. And I know you, Holliday," he said, leaning forward, glaring at me. He picked up his drink, tossing it off. "You're a cheap bottom-dealer."

"Now, Budd, is that any way to talk," I said, feeling the rage build through me. I picked up my glass of Old Williams, sipping. "I thought we'd come to an understanding the last time we played cards together. You don't sit at the table with me, and I won't go into the mah-jongg parlors where you try to cheat little old ladies out of their nickels and dimes."

A vein began to beat heavily in the center of his forehead. His eyes grew ugly.

"You know what I think, Holliday? I think you're afraid," he said. "I think you're nothing more than a lonely lunger that no one will have anything at all to do with." He snapped his fingers. "Oh, 'cept one." He winked at the others around us. "That female doctor who can't make up her mind if she's a woman or a man. That what attracts you to her, Holliday? Fact that you might fuck a woman and pretend you're fucking a man? That your turn-on?"

Nervous laughter ran around the room. A red haze settled over the room, the crystal chandelier, the scarred wooden floor, the green eyeshades of the dealers, the white shirts, ties, coats and suits, glinting off bottles behind the bar that seemed filled with blood, reflecting off the mirror, shading the large painting of a nude above the bar. Suddenly I saw Ryan's face in clear, lucid detail: the tiny nicks where he had slipped with his razor, the deep pits beneath his eyes filled with blackheads, the march of tiny hairs like caterpillars above his eyes. I felt my lips stretch in a grin.

"You are a slimy, gonorrhea-dripping, pig-fucker," I said softly.

His face whitened, then his eyes tightened with anger. His hand darted beneath his coat, reaching for the pistol under his arm. I reached into my left sleeve and seized the Spanish dagger. I lunged across the table, flipping the dagger with my wrist across his face, slicing a thin line from his right ear down to his chin. He threw his head back and away from me as I followed the back slash with a thrust to his neck. I missed his jugular, but a tiny red line appeared along the side of his throat, then blood flowed heavily as he fell away from me onto the floor. The pistol clattered on the floor beside him as he clutched at his throat with both hands.

"Don't kill me!" he squawked. "Oh, God! You have! You have killed me, Holliday! Oh damn! The blood! The blood!"

He screamed as a thin young man darted forward and fell on his knees beside him. He quickly took a handkerchief from his pocket and pressed it against Ryan's face, then pulled another from an inside pocket and pressed it hard against Ryan's throat. Ryan struggled for a moment, then lay quietly and sobbed.

"Someone give me something to tie these on with!" the thin young man snapped in a familiar voice. I looked closer at him and recognized Mary.

"Sorry, gentlemen," I said to the white-faced players at my table. "I'm afraid that the game is temporarily curtailed."

They mumbled their apologies and gathered their money, quickly exiting the table. Someone handed Mary two rawhide laces. Quickly, she tied them on, staunching the flow of blood. She stood and gestured at two men standing in the crowd.

"Clem! You and Harry take him up to my office! He'll need some sewing after this. Although," she added, looking down at him, "I'm damned if I know why I'm helping him."

Clem spat and said, "Should just leave him bleed to death after what he said about you, Doctor Mary. Wasn't any call for that. Just being mean, trying to push this man into a fight. He got what he deserved."

"That may be so, but now he needs attention. Please take him to my office," she said tiredly, running her hand across her forehead.

Clem shrugged and unceremoniously pulled Ryan to his feet. Harry took the other arm and together they shuffled Ryan off through the crowd.

"All right, folks!" Charley said loudly. "This is all over now. Let's get back to our games."

The crowd slowly dispersed, with several looking over their shoulders at me. I took a lace handkerchief from an inside pocket and wiped the dagger clean. I tossed the handkerchief onto the table, where someone immediately seized it for a souvenir. I slid the dagger back into its sheath then picked up my tumbler of whiskey, finishing it.

"Sorry, Mary," I said lamely.

She shook her head. "You can't help being what you are, John. But . . ."

"But," I prompted.

"Violence seems to be the answer to all of your problems," she said.

"It's a violent world we live in, Mary," I said lamely. I could see where she was heading and knew the truth behind her words. I also knew the truth about myself, but, like everyone, I did not want to hear the truth.

"But you don't seem to care about life!" she cried. The agony in her voice startled me, and I felt an emotion I thought long dead begin to stir in me, the same emotion I had first felt with Mattie when we had first walked as adults with adult feelings among the pecan trees in Valdosta instead of children playing children's games.

"Perhaps I don't," I said quietly. "But I can only play the cards that I've been dealt."

She shook her head. "No, John. That's not true. You're not playing the cards that you've been dealt. You're playing the cards you want to be dealt." She reached up and touched my cheek. "And you are a good man," she whispered. "I can sense that in you. But there is too much bitterness there for love."

A slow blush turned her cheeks rosy. She started to say something else, then stopped and turned, hurrying from the room after Clem and Harry, but not before I caught a glint of tears in her eyes. I started to follow, but Charley caught me by the arm, pulling me to the end of the bar.

"So, you're Holliday, not McKey," he said in a low voice,

signaling to the bartender for a bottle and two glasses. The bartender slid them down to us and Charley filled two glasses.

"I thought it better to be so," I murmured, picking up my glass. I touched his with mine and drank.

"Too bad you couldn't stay that way," he said. "But right now you've got pressing business somewhere else."

"Where?"

"I don't know. It doesn't matter," he said. He drank and poured each of us another. "But what I do know is that Charley's brother is on the police force. How long do you think you're going to last in this town once he hears what you did to his brother?"

I shrugged. "Doesn't matter."

"I think you want to die," he said.

"We all have to go sometime," I said.

"Maybe, but I sure wouldn't want to go beaten into a bloody pulp in the back room of the jail," he said. I slowly nodded.

"You got a point there," I said. "Perhaps it would be best if I visited elsewhere. Maybe take the waters in Arkansas for my health."

"Visit anywhere and it's for your health," he said. He stepped away from the bar, clapping me gently on my shoulder. "But you've been fair with me, Holliday, and if there's anything I can do, let me know."

"There is one thing," I said, finishing my drink and turning the glass upside down on the bar.

"What's that?"

"Arrange to have Ares saddled and brought to my hotel while I pack," I said.

He nodded, and I stepped away from the bar. The crowd parted, and I could hear the whispers as I walked through, wagering how long I would last as soon as Ryan's brother found out what had happened.

The old recklessness I had first felt when I took Father's pistol and money and set forth to find Uncle Thomas swept through me. I felt young and happy, and I laughed as I

pushed my way through the door into the cold Denver night.
Light snow was falling, making a nimbus around the streetlamps. I breathed deeply, feeling life surge through my
scarred lungs.

7

Fort Griffin, Texas.

The smell rolled up from it like a fetid cloud.

Ares snorted and shied away, trying to turn back toward
Pueblo as we topped the rise leading down to Fort Griffin,
where the heavy stench of rotting meat and buffalo hides
reached him. His nostrils quivered indignantly as I soothed
him, running my hand down the glossy black of his neck.
After a moment he quieted, but I let him stand, quivering with
rage, on the grama grass of the prairie for a while to calm
himself before moving down the gentle slope into the town
beneath Government Hill upon which stood Fort Griffin,
west of the village set up by the Tonkawa Indians, the cavalry
used as scouts against the Comanche. The town was gener-
ally referred to as the Flat, but I was in no hurry to ride to it.
Besides, Ares had earned the right to voice his discontent.

After I had sliced Budd Ryan and made my way back to
my hotel and made arrangements for most of my belongings
to be shipped to the Palmer House in Pueblo for holding
pending my arrival, I packed a second gray box-coated suit, a
few colored and white shirts and white collars, and a couple
of thousand dollars (in greenbacks, to lighten the load) into a
pair of overlarge canvas saddlebags. When I carried my load
outside, staggering a bit under its weight, Ares nickered
softly, tossing his head against the reins held by a stable boy.
I paid for the week's lodging that I still owed, tipping the boy
a dollar over for his work, and tied my bags across the back

of my saddle. Ares turned his head, impatiently nudging me, eager to be off, and when I stepped into the stirrups and gave him his head, he hunched his shoulders as if gratefully stretching from the release of the stable confines and broke into an eager, ground-gaining lope. Over the two weeks it took us to make our way south to Fort Griffin, we had become reacquainted. At night he continually nudged me, assuring himself that I had not deserted him again. I had no heart after his devotion to force him into Fort Griffin before he was ready.

Meanwhile, I took the opportunity to consider my new temporary home. I took Belle's flask from an inside pocket of my coat and drank, trying to drive the memory of the stench from my nostrils; although I knew that I would be fighting a losing battle. I had chosen Fort Griffin for numerous reasons, primary of which was its location, where the McKenzie Trail lay on the flat plain eroded by the waters of Collins Creek and the Clear Fork of the Brazos, a river that carved its way with surgical precision from the high plains of Texas to the gulf. The government had established a military post on top of a hill to protect the anticipated settlers from raiding Comanche parties. But the settlers didn't come; instead, buffalo hunters by the thousands invaded the area. A railroad spur was built to accommodate the thousands of hides the buyers shipped out from hunters trailing the southern herd of the great bison, dropping off the stragglers with well-placed rounds from Sharps .50-calibers at ranges from a hundred yards to five hundred, depending upon the hunter telling the story.

Now, however, the stench of piles of thousands of hides stored in ricks that from a distance resembled the buildings of a miniature city rolled over the plains in a fetid cloud of spoiled meat and blowflies. But gamblers and purveyors of sin knew that those who slew the buffalo, peeling their hides off them with teams of horses hooked to special draglines, needed something to drive the brassy taste of death from their lips and had thrown up ramshackle buildings of split pine that rapidly turned gray under the hard sun and grains of sand blown across the buildings by harsh, dry winds and filled those buildings with games of chance and cheap whiskey. Whores had followed them and taken up residence in cheap rooms with half-doors, across which they would lean in good weather, displaying the bulging white of their bosoms to prospective buyers looking for seven minutes of love.

In the summer, the Clear Fork rolled and twisted its way through the valley like a silver serpent. Stands of cotton-woods followed the path of the river. The big bend of the river gathered huge, white, twisted trunks of trees the spring floods uprooted on their way south toward the gulf. The trees lay like the bones of prehistoric carcasses on the bright green grama grass.

I had chosen Fort Griffin for no less a reason than that here I felt I could lose the persona that had become Doc Holliday, for among the names of those who had made Fort Griffin their temporary home were people such as Mike O'Brien, Hurricane Bill, John Selman, Monte Bill and Smoky Joe, and others whose names were synonomous with death. The town was a crossroads as well for cattle moving up the Goodnight-Loving Trail, and was the closest town for supplies for cattle-men up to two hundred miles west. Here I could rest and recuperate. And think. I needed to think. Mary had proven to be a platonic friend, but a friend whose platonism was built around sexual prejudices.

I spurred Ares down into the town, bypassing the fort. He danced his way into the town, preening himself through the main street, past the ramshackle stores and saloons and sad-dlers and gunsmiths with their gray siding, to the livery sta-ble at the end with its gray siding. I turned and looked back down the dirt street and saw no swatches of color. The whole town seemed draped in gray mourning. And no churches. I felt at home.

I took a room in the only hotel in Fort Griffin. It had no name, but it made all the pretensions to the better hotels in what the owner perceived to be the correct cosmopolitan style, but with an eye toward economy as well. The hotel had a dining room attached to it, but the dining room had only six tables, each covered with gravy-stained white cloths, the meals served on blue-flowered, chipped china with coffee in thick-lipped mugs and no saucers. The rooms were spartan, with iron bedsteads and feathered mattresses on coiled springs that shrieked in protest at every movement a sleeper made and proclaimed across the hotel through thin walls the lust of male and female who racked and groaned their ways to respective climaxes. A washstand and mirror, stained chamber pot, and nails hammered in the walls in place of wardrobes completed the furnishings. The ambience was no different from cowtowns up and down the Chisholm or Goodnight-Loving Trails despite the pretensions.

I found a place for Ares in the cleanest of the two livery stables in town. He looked piteously at me when I handed his reins to the keeper, and grudgingly followed him to the back corral, where he danced restlessly around the peeled-bark railings. I patted his velvet nose and promised him daily ridings out onto the clean prairie away from the stench of the buffalo hides. He grumbled deep in his chest and nudged me affectionately with his nose. On an impulse, I threw my arms around his neck and gave him a kiss that drew raised eyebrows from the stablehand. I didn't care; I had had more affection from Ares, more love, than I had found in anyone since leaving Mattie in Atlanta.

I settled in quickly, paying two dollars more a week since I had no luggage other than my canvas saddlebags, bathed, and went out to contemplate my surroundings after dressing in my gray suit and mauve shirt with black tie. There wasn't much other than saloons: a tanner, gunsmith, my hotel and a rooming house, two general stores, and telegraph next to the sheriff's office. The sheriff was a sober, hard-bearing young man named Bill Cruger, although he liked to be called "the Kid," a sobriquet that he did not deserve being fully thirty years old at the time. I called him "Billy," which irritated him and did nothing toward solidifying our relationship, but he had nothing that would contribute to a mutual relationship: He used to have the livery boy read his telegrams to him.

I walked into the largest of the saloons and made my way to the bar and ordered bourbon, breathing deeply the yeasty smell of stale beer and cigar smoke. To my surprise, the bartender pulled a bottle of Old Williams from under the bar and filled a tumbler, shoving it to me. I drank appreciatively, then bought another drink and sipped while I surveyed the saloon. It was larger than most, with a restaurant and dance hall adjoining it through double doorways on either side. The saloon itself had several tables for gambling, including two faro layouts, a dice table, and a roulette wheel.

"It's early yet," a voice said.

I glanced over my shoulder at a tall, beefy man with a red face. Bay rum wafted to me. He wore a wine-colored long coat over a lace shirt whose cuffs extended a good inch beyond the sleeves of his coat. He wore black-and-gray striped trousers and ankle-jacks. A diamond ring glittered on his left pinkie, and his nails were polished and square-cut. Heavy scar tissue over his eyes spoke of some time in the ring.

"John Shanssey. I own the place," he said, extending his hand. I took it, carefully folding my thumb inside in case he was a bone-crusher as most men of the ring are, but I was surprised at the gentleness of his touch.

"Holliday," I said. "John Henry Holliday. Dentist."

His eyes narrowed slightly. "Heard about a Holliday from over Jacksboro way."

"Oh? What have you heard?" I asked, taking a slight step to my right, freeing my right arm from the bar. He noticed my movement and gave a slight smile.

"That he dealt a fair game," he said dryly. "If you're the man, you're welcome here. I could use an honest dealer. Interested?"

"Maybe," I said casually. "It would depend upon the terms."

"Eighty-twenty," he said. "Eighty for the house, and I supply the funds."

"Pretty generous for an unknown," I said. I relaxed back against the bar and took my glass, sipping.

He laughed and gestured and the bartender promptly

placed a glass of wine in front of him. He sipped and replaced the glass.

"Oh, you're not that unknown, my friend," he said. "Your name has been bandied about a bit around the circuit. Tell me, then, are you interested? Or would you be thinkin' about setting up in your dentist trade?"

I shrugged. "My tools haven't arrived yet. And, I must confess, I really haven't made up my mind."

"Well, when you do, let me know. I'll put you up next to Lotte."

My ears pricked at the name. I gave him a sharp look. "Lotte? Lotte Deno?"

He nodded, a bushy eyebrow pushing the mass of scar tissue toward his hairline. "Would you be knowing her, then?"

"Could be," I said. "Redhead?"

"From Jacksboro way," he said. "She starts play about eight at the table in the back." He nodded to one covered in green felt. Two unopened decks of cards had been neatly placed in the center of the table. A rack of chips neatly stacked stood at what would be the dealer's left. "She's very good. Always quits a winner." He frowned. "Wish I could say that about my other dealer."

"Losing?" I asked casually.

"More than he should, I think. Or else he's not as good as he thinks. But he's popular. Name's Ed Bailey."

"Maybe he's skimming," I said.

"I've watched for that," Shanssey said. He shook his head, sighing. "But I can't catch him."

"A ringer in the game with him?" I suggested.

"Maybe." He sighed again. "I don't know. I'm about ready to cut him loose, but I need a good reason, you know what I mean?" His eyes suddenly glinted. "Look here: How about you setting in on a game with him this evening and see if you can spot something? I'll stand your losses."

"Not a good way to start in a new town," I murmured, finishing my drink and motioning the bartender away as he made to refill my glass. "Especially if the man is as popular as you say. I'd hate to set up here with the reputation of a rat killer."

"A thousand dollars if you catch him cheating," he said. "If not, then you've lost nothing. Anything you win is yours, and I'll still stand the losses."

"We'll see," I said. His face fell. I carefully placed my wide-brimmed hat over my hair, checked its angle in the mirror, then nodded in satisfaction. I muffled a cough. "Right now, though, I think I'll take a closer look at the rest of the town. Get my bearings."

"There's not all that much to see," he laughed. "But you do that. The offer still stands."

He turned and left, making his way through the tables to his office in the back of the saloon. I glanced at the plain mirror, the beefy nude hanging over the bar, the shining glasses on a ledge behind the gleaming mahogany bar. The floor had been clean-swept and the brass spittoons polished. It wouldn't be a bad saloon to work in, I mused as I walked toward the door.

That's where I made the major mistake of my life. I should have continued walking back to my hotel room, slept, and left the next day, disappearing into the oblivion of the West. Instead, I met Kate.

It didn't take long to make a tour of the town. At Beeker's General Store, I was delighted to discover that he had books for sale, and after some consideration, I bought *Twenty Thousand Leagues Under the Sea* by Jules Verne and took it back to my room to occupy my time until evening.

After supper, I strolled back to Shanssey's place and peeked in the saloon, but Lotte had not shown. A burly man in an ill-fitting shirt sat at the table next to hers, dealing poker to four other men dressed in range clothes. He wore a derby pushed back on his head, exposing his receding hairline. A scraggly salt-and-pepper beard covered his face but could not conceal the weak chin. He glanced up, his rat's eyes catching mine and holding them boldly before returning to the play. His lips moved, and the players laughed and glanced up to where I stood in the doorway.

I ignored their stares and crossed the room to the dance hall and glanced inside. Two blondes, one wearing a red satin dress cut low over her breasts, the other in blue, looked up from the table where they sat. I could see their lives stamped in tired lines on their faces. A dark woman I took to be a half-breed with long, glossy black hair and a white dress pulled so low over her breasts that I could see the beginnings of the dark areolae sat alone at a table in the center of the room. She looked up, her black eyes daring. The fourth, a dark redhead, stood beside the piano, a glass of wine in her hand. Gray eyes stared boldly across the room into mine from beneath a broad forehead. An aquiline nose gave her a haughty look above a wide, generous mouth that curved up into deep dimples when she smiled. She wore a bottle green dress that pushed up hard against magnificent breasts and curved down over generous hips.

I stepped down onto the dance floor and crossed to the piano, seating myself at the keyboard. She smiled down at me, bold and challenging.

"Do you think you can play?" she asked in a husky voice, her eyes giving double meaning to her words. For a moment I couldn't place her accent, then I recognized it as Hungarian. She leaned closer, her breasts threatening to burst free from her dress. I smelled the musk of her perfume and felt the thrust of her sexuality immediately in my groin. I grinned at her and ran my hands over the keys of the piano, playing scales and feeling the tension of the keys, hearing the notes tinkle harmoniously against each other. Surprisingly, the piano was in tune.

"That the extent of your repertoire?" she taunted, her full lips curling in derision. She drained her glass of wine and placed it with a challenging thump on top of the piano.

I grinned and moved slowly into Chopin's "Opus No. 1 in B-Flat Minor." Her eyes widened, and she straightened, looking down at me in surprise. Her long, shapely fingers touched her throat, fingering a small necklace with an amethyst stone.

"Chopin?" she said. "Strange to find a man in here playing Chopin."

"Strange finding a young woman in here knowing him," I answered.

Her eyes flared, then she laughed deeply and gently touched the back of my neck with her fingers, cool, yet my flesh burned from where her fingers caressed it.

"And what would you expect me to know?" she said softly, teasingly.

I segued into "You Naughty, Naughty Men" and she giggled and playfully slapped me on the shoulder.

"You are a tease, you know that? You are a tease," she said.

I rolled off an F-sharp into "I'll Take You Home Again, Kathleen" and she sobered, her face softening from her whore's mask, showing the vulnerability of the woman.

"And what made you take that one?" she asked.

"You seemed to be a Kathleen. Are you?" I asked.

"Kate," she said. "Kate. I'm Kate. Kate Elder."

"Not a Kathleen?"

"No. Not now, not ever."

"Sorry," I said and slipped back into the nocturne.

"But I liked your gesture," she said, touching me again. "It was very nice. What's your name?"

"John Henry Holliday," a voice said from behind us. A woman dressed in ivory moved into view on my left. "Dr. John Henry Holliday."

"Hello, Lotte," I said, grinning. "How are you?"

"As you can see: a desperate woman," she said. She looked closely at me, then smiled. "Why, John! When did you grow a mustache?" I smiled back, slipping again into the nocturne.

"Here now," Kate said, annoyance plain in her voice. "Find your own man."

Lotte smiled faintly at her, then dropped her hand affectionately on my shoulder. "I haven't seen you since Jacksboro. I've heard about you, though. You've been busy."

"Look," Kate said, anger making her husky voice rise. "I told you to leave us alone."

"We're good friends," I said to her, hoping to avert any trouble. But Kate always seemed to find trouble, even search for it.

"And we're about to become better friends," she said, starting for Lotte around the chair upon which I was sitting. She pulled up short as Lotte's hand slipped from a fold in her dress, carrying a small derringer. The hammer clicked back loudly in the room above the quiet notes of the nocturne.

"Now," Lotte breathed, "if you don't want a third eye, back off."

"Whore!" Kate spat, moving slowly back around to my right.

"We all are, dearie, in our own way," Lotte said. "But I do my business at the tables."

"Now, ladies," I said, finishing the nocturne and leaning back to face both. "Let us all be friends here. Kate, Lotte is merely a business acquaintance. Not that kind of business," I hastily added as her eyes narrowed dangerously. "We occasionally indulge in games of chance together."

She slowly nodded. "Gambler, huh? Thought she called you Doctor."

"I am that. Actually, I am a dentist," I said, beginning to wonder why I was explaining myself to a dance hall whore. I began to feel annoyed with myself and the way things were progressing among the three of us.

"Then what are you doing here?" she said, a puzzled look coming into her eyes. Lotte slipped down the hammer on the derringer and restored it to its hiding place among the folds of her dress.

"Cum dignitate otium," I said.

A blank look fell over her face while Lotte smiled gently and said, "But do you think you will ever find it?"

"No," I answered, standing. "Man's dignity is written in water."

I patted Kate's shoulder. A light brightened for a moment

in her eyes, then faded as I shook my head and turned to walk with Lotte back into the saloon and the tables.

"I think, John, that you are looking for the impossibility," she said. "There is no dignity in man, only the rattling of sabers in scabbards and endless tales told by idiots."

"I fear you are right, my dear, but still I have hope," I answered as we took a step up into the saloon. I glanced over at the men still sitting at the table next to Lotte's. The complexion hadn't changed; the same man dealt, the same others played to his hand.

"Who is that?" I asked.

Lotte followed the direction of my gaze. Her face twisted with disgust. "Ed Bailey. Fancies himself a flashdancer, but he's a poor imitation of a player. He uses shiners and shaved aces. Once in a while he tries to deal seconds, but his hands are too fat to make the pull. He carries derringers in pockets inside his vest on either side. But his vest is too tight. You can see the outline of the derringers."

I glanced at his chest; Lotte was right. I shook my head. If he had to reach for those in a hurry, he would find himself dead before he could squeeze his sausagelike fingers under the cloth. Lotte nudged me with her elbow. I looked down at her.

"Want to try your luck?" she asked, nodding toward her table. "I'll save you a chair."

"No, I think I'm going to try Bailey," I said, patting her hand, which she had tucked into the crook of my elbow.

Her left eyebrow rose fractionally. "For Shanssey?"

"You know?" Warning bells began to tinkle carefully.

"He asked the same of me," she laughed. "I wouldn't do it because he has too many friends here. Watch yourself; his friends make him cocky."

"I'll be careful," I said. I kissed her cheek. She smiled and withdrew her hand, walking to her table. She arranged her shoulder wrap along the back of her chair and sat. Within minutes, her table was filled. She smiled faintly at me, then her face settled into its poker mask, and she reached for a deck of cards, slicing the seal with her thumbnail.

"Well, gentlemen, the name of the game is draw," she said. She made three quick riff shuffles and slid the deck to the man on her right for a cut. He double-cut, and she smiled at him as she brought the sections of the deck together, deftly sliding the second cut back to where the original had been. Her hands moved smoothly with an economy of motion, and not one man at the table realized that she had stacked the deck. Or maybe they didn't care. Lotte's beauty made it worthwhile for some simply to sit at her table.

I winked at her and turned to the bar, nodding at the bartender. He slid a tumbler full of bourbon in front of me. I sipped and nodded as the familiar bite of Old Williams rolled down my throat. I coughed gently and patted my lips with a linen handkerchief I took from a side pocket of my coat. A figure moved next to me. I looked at Kate.

"Then buy me a drink," she said.

"Pardon?" I asked. She nodded at Lotte.

"If she is only that to you, then buy me a drink," she challenged. She leaned forward and again I caught a whiff of the musk of her perfume and felt nearly forgotten stirrings in my groin.

"Why not?" I murmured. I motioned to the bartender. He slid down, looking narrowly at Kate.

"You know the rules," he said. "Mr. Shanssey wants you women to stay in the dance hall. This is for serious gamblers. Women aren't allowed here."

"And what about her?" Kate asked belligerently, pointing at Lotte with her chin. Her nose lifted, registering her disdain.

"She has John's permission to deal," he said.

"Maybe I should deal too!" she exclaimed loftily.

"Maybe you should. But until then . . ." He pointed to the dance hall.

Twin spots of color appeared high in her cheeks. Her eyes flashed dangerously once, then grew luminescent with tears as she moved away from the bar and started for the other room. Impulsively, I stayed her, placing my hand upon her arm. She paused, looking up at me. I glanced at the bartender.

"Perhaps we can make an exception again," I said.

He frowned. "I'm sorry, sir. But Mr. Shanssey is pretty set about that. I only work here. I gotta follow the rules too."

"What's the problem?" Shanssey asked, moving up next to me.

"I've decided I want Miss Elder to accompany me this evening," I said. "I understand you have a house rule forbidding it?"

"I do," he said. "We make one exception, we have to make another. Sorry."

Kate sighed and started to pull away. I tightened my grip, feeling the old recklessness beginning to race through me. I smiled at him.

"A strange way to request a favor from a gentleman," I said. I touched my mustache, smoothing it with the ball of my thumb. "Or did I misunderstand our previous conversation."

He hesitated, his eyes flickering back and forth between Kate and myself. He took a cigar from an inside pocket and bit the end off it, spitting the severed piece into a spittoon.

"Another condition?" he asked, lighting it. He blew a stream of dirty gray smoke up at the reflector lights hung around a wagon wheel.

"Shall we say a compromise? That sounds so much better," I said.

He mulled my words over for a moment, then nodded. "Okay. Same terms as before. Eighty-twenty."

"And you supply the funding," I said.

"Be back in a minute," he said. He walked back to his office. I turned to the bartender.

"Give Miss Elder a glass of wine, please, and put it on my account."

"You did it. I'll be damned," she said under her breath as the bartender nodded and moved away from us.

"Probably," I answered, taking my glass from the bar. "We all are, in one way or another. I am ravished by sweet analytics, for this is hell and I am in it. As are you."

"Huh?" she asked, perplexed.

"A paraphrase, my dear. Marlowe. We shall talk about this

later. As for now, why, dear sweet Kate, Kate of the Kate-Hall, the game beckons." I nodded at Bailey's table.

"I don't understand half of what you're saying," she said, shaking her head and reaching for her glass of wine. "But I dearly love the way you say it."

"And I, my dear, understand completely what I am saying and abhor the way I say it. Wait for me where you will," I said, moving toward the table.

Shanssey came out of his office and met me halfway across the room, slipping a sheaf of bills into my pocket. I grinned and patted him on the shoulder. He glanced past me at Kate, who was standing at the bar, sipping her wine.

"Doc, she's just a whore, nothing more," he whispered. "Ain't nothing you can do to change that, 'cause she likes her work. The others do it because their husbands talk them into it or because they got trapped in it when they were kids. But Kate, well, she's just a whore, plain and simple."

I smiled at him and nodded at the table. "And who is not, in this world?"

I stepped to the table and grinned at Bailey. "I see there is an empty chair. Would you gentlemen have an objection to another joining you in your game of chance?"

"I have no objection," a man dressed in drover's clothes said from across me. "One fancy gambler's as good as two in this game. Ain't no one winning 'cept Ed Bailey here no how. I'm Karl Mumford." He nodded around the table at the three other men. "Jim Tate, Bob Whiteman, and Bill Taggert."

"Holliday," I said, sliding into the empty chair directly across from Bailey and placing my glass at my left. "Dr. John Henry Holliday, dentist, at your service, gentlemen."

"A dentist, huh?" Taggert said on my immediate right. He grimaced. "I came across one of them up Abilene way last year. Yanked two of my teeth and charged me two bucks. Thought he was gonna kill me while I was in that chair. Spat blood for two days after thatun. Got another needs to come out, but sure don't like the thought of goin' through all that again."

"Why, sir, I would be more than happy to accommodate you," I said cheerfully. "And I will guarantee satisfaction."

"You will?" he looked closely, suspiciously at me. "Sure don't sound like no dentist to me."

"There are dentists, then there are dentists," I said, taking a sip of my bourbon. "Just as there are gamblers"—I glanced at Bailey—"and gamblers."

"And this deck is getting cold," Bailey said. "Let's play cards." He moved a brass coin in front of me. "Since you're the newcomer, you get first call. Ante's a dollar now. Table stakes." He fingered the rack of chips on his left. "How much you want?"

I took the sheaf of bills from my pocket, thumbed them, counting, then tossed them across the table to him. They knocked over one of his stacks, and he restacked them, annoyance showing on his face. "Twenty-five hundred in there."

He slid the pile in front of him, moistened a finger, and began counting. Annoyed, I watched him.

"Trust is a marvelous creature. It suggests the trappings of a gentleman despite the stable of his breeding," I said. I drained my bourbon and lifted it, drawing the bartender's attention. He walked from behind the bar with a bottle of Old Williams, filled my glass, then corked the bottle and placed it beside my glass.

"Thank you, my friend," I said as Bailey finished counting and looked up. "Twenty-five hundred. As I said."

He slid over stacks of blue and white chips. I reached for them, counting them one by one, my eyes holding his. His lips tightened as he watched.

"You will pardon my counting," I said. "But since there is a dearth of gentlemen here, one cannot be too sure." I coughed and interrupted my counting to take a sip of whiskey.

"Pretty cocky for a dentist," Bailey said arrogantly. He stacked the money beside the rack of chips. "Hope you can play as well as you can talk."

"Why, Mr. Bailey! You are a most impatient man. Shall we all try our hand at a game of draw?"

"Jesus, you do talk," Whiteman complained. "Deal, Ed. Let's get on with it before that deck freezes from disuse."

Tate cut and Bailey drew the cards together, his fingers fumbling with them, rearranging the cut. I smiled and took another sip of the bourbon, feeling its warmth ooze through me as Bailey flipped the cards around the table. He was terrible, and I wondered how he had escaped being shot for so long. Fort Griffin was not the fanciest place on the circuit of gamblers at the time, but a good share of them waltzed through the place from time to time, and Bailey surely had had to come up against someone who recognized his fumblings and bumblings and called him on it. Yet here he was, still dealing, and still cheating. I wondered.

I glanced at my cards: a pair of eights with no chance for a make. I waited as Mumford bet five dollars and Whiteman bumped another five. I tossed in my cards and Bailey sneered as Taggert and Tate called.

"A bit too steep for your blood? Thought you were a gambling man," he taunted. "Your five and ten more."

I ignored him and sat back through that hand and four or five others, playing cautiously, collecting one small pot with three jacks caught on the deal, watching the play, watching the tells of the players as they played their hands, trying not to tip off the others as to their feelings about their hands. But none were seasoned gamblers. Mumford rubbed his upper lip with his forefinger, Tate tugged his earlobe, Taggert drummed the fingers of his left hand, Whiteman couldn't control a tic in his right cheek. And Bailey, Bailey licked his lips like a coyote over a fresh kill. The devil moved within me and laughter bubbled up inside. I waited, knowing that Bailey would be making his move at the twenty-five hundred since I had shown myself to be a cautious player in the game. Bailey might not have been much of a gambler, but I knew he was enough of one to hold the cautious player in contempt. A gambler needs to pursue Lady Luck, and once he finds her, ride her for every orgasm he can get. I was playing certains, and he had to give me a hand that would come close to being certain, but not quite, before a certain player would release the tiger inside him and bet high and footloose.

The hand came about two and a half hours into play. Mumford had called for draw poker. I cut and Bailey did his usual sloppy stack, trying to find the aces to tuck on top, fumbling when he couldn't find them on his first run through the deck. A frown settled over his face, then a smile tried to filter over his face when he found them on the bottom. Or what he thought were the aces. We had been into the second deck for thirty minutes and Bailey had varied his technique, using the ring with a tiny spur forged into the palm side to place pin pricks around the edges of the cards. What he thought to be aces were kings; I had the aces in the sleeve of my right hand, waiting for Bailey's move.

I picked up my cards: three queens. I felt a smile building and forced it away. Mumford checked, Whiteman bet five, I let the smile show and raised ten dollars. Taggert raised another ten and Tate followed suit. Bailey called everyone and raised fifty dollars. Mumford and Whiteman called and I raised another fifty. Taggert hesitated, then folded and Tate called. Bailey's lips flexed as he stifled a grin.

"Three hundred," he said, tossing in a stack of chips. He looked challengingly, boldly across the table at me. Mumford folded, as did Whiteman, leaving myself, Taggert and Tate. I picked up my cards, frowning at them a moment for effect, then folded them and placed them on the table in front of me, sighing. I reached for my chips.

"Your three hundred and two more," I said, tossing in the chips. Taggert folded. Tate hesitated, made to throw in his chips, then shook his head and tossed his cards onto the deadwood.

"No, too steep for me. With these," he added.

Bailey looked at me. "Coming on pretty strong. You must have a stand-down hand."

"You know it," I said. He frowned, not quite knowing how

to take my words. A muscle worked in the corner of his jaw.
His fingers twitched on the table. Then he decided my words
were innocent enough and tossed in two hundred, calling me.

"Cards?" he asked. I tossed in two. He passed two more
over to me. I didn't look; I knew the fourth queen was one of
them. He picked up his cards, glanced at them, then smiled
over at me.

"Figured to bluff you," he said. "But I reckon you don't
bluff, do you?"

"It's happened," I said. He shook his head.

"Nope, I've been a fool. Reckon I'd better try to better
myself with a draw if I'm to salvage anything. Dealer takes
four cards."

"Jesus, Ed," Mumford complained. "Thought you knew
what the hell you were doing. That's a beginner's play, bet-
tin' that high then drawing four."

"We all make mistakes," Bailey said. "I guess I'm as enti-
tled to make one as the next. Besides"—he nodded at me—
"I don't think I could run a bluff on him. Just a hunch, but I
think he's sittin' on the nest."

He pulled four cards and placed the deck to his left. He
scooped up the cards, tapped them once on the table to set
them, then spread them like a tiny fan, staring at them. A tiny
frown line appeared between his eyebrows. He glanced
sharply, suspiciously, at me. I took a drink, then tossed in a
stack of chips.

"Well, we're playing for hundreds. Might as well begin
with two," I said, pretending to act nonchalantly. "Drawing
four when I hold three, well, I think I can risk it."

Bailey shook his head. "Well, I don't know." He peered at
his cards again. A tiny muscle moved in his jaw. An
admirable act, but I knew it was more than an act: He was
wondering where those aces had gone and whether he had
marked the cards correctly. Still, four kings was nothing to
discount: Only one hand could beat it. I read his mind as he
glanced toward the deadwood: What were the chances that I
had that one hand?

"Well, sir," he said, determination suddenly shining from

his eyes. "I think I'll be able to accommodate you. Yes sir, I think I'll be able to accommodate you. And raise you five hundred."

He tossed in his chips, then looked mockingly at me. "The trouble is, you don't know what I drew."

I shook my head. "You're right about that," I said. "Well, I don't know. . . ." I let my voice trail off doubtfully, then suddenly shook my head and tossed in a thousand. "But I don't think that you were that lucky. So it'll cost you another thousand to see if you could have beaten me or not."

"And another five hundred," he said promptly, tossing in his chips.

That would leave me with a few paltry dollars if I called. If I didn't, well, he'd cut my stake down to nearly the twenty-five hundred he had cashed at the start. A good night's work. I clenched my jaws, chewing on my cheek. I drained my glass of bourbon and poured another, looking agonizingly from my hand to the ceiling as if seeking deistic inspiration, playing the scene to the hilt. Booth would have been proud of me, Foy tickled.

"Well," I drawled out the word, then tossed in my stack of chips. "I guess I'll call. It all has to end somehow."

"Reckon it does, Doc," he said, gleefully turning over his cards, exposing the four kings. "Luck is with those who wait patiently."

"And those who make their own luck," I said pointedly, turning over the four aces. "Will you look at that? Now isn't that a honey of a hand?"

He caught his breath, then strangled, coughing harshly. He turned, gagged, then coughed as I raked in the pot, carefully separating the chips and stacking them in front of me.

"Whew!" Mumford said. "Don't that beat all. I been playing this game for fifteen some-odd years and never saw those two hands come up together in the same round."

"Gotta admit it's unusual," Taggert added. "Reckon I can stand drinks on that." He motioned to the bartender and circled his hand around the table.

"You . . . you . . ." Bailey gasped. His eyes bugged like

blowfly eyes. His face grew a deep crimson. For a moment I thought he would collapse from the apoplexy. Then he leaned back in his chair and drew three deep breaths, calming himself.

"I what?" I asked softly, leaning back in my chair and tapping the ivory handle of my Colt.

His eyes narrowed, and he drew a last, deep, shuddering breath. "I reckon you euchered me. Ain't many can make that claim."

A deep weariness settled over me. I lifted my glass, sipping, then placed it back on the table at my elbow. "I'm surprised; I thought there would be a lot that could make that claim."

The room fell silent. I laughed. "This is becoming a dead metaphor," I said.

"What do you mean?" Bailey said.

I gestured around the room. "Oh, that? Nothing. Nothing. It's just the matter of old romances."

A frown settled over his face. "Huh? What the hell are you talkin' about?"

I sighed. "Too much for a tinhorn to understand. Perhaps more time with books and less with cards would enlighten you."

"I don't need your preachin'," he snarled, his hand sweeping the cards and chips from in front of him. A fat forefinger pointed across the table at my nose. "You cheated!"

"Ed," Taggert said nervously, "let it be. He beat you. That's all."

I eased back from the table, letting the lapels of my coat fall open. The Manhattan's black handle gleamed ominously from my right side, the Colt's ivory handle from my left. I dallied my fingers across the handle of the Colt. His eyes strayed to my fingers, then back to my face. Suddenly, a cough arched its way through me, my shoulders heaving with the effort.

"I . . ." I started to speak, then the room turned red, bright red, as if the carmine shade of blood swept through it. Then I slipped sideways from my chair, blood spewing from my mouth. Bailey grinned and slowly drew a pistol, aiming at my forehead.

"Toss it, you peckerhead!" a voice exclaimed. I rolled my head and saw Kate standing over me, a Root pocket pistol in her hand, her long, shapely ivory limbs gleaming beneath the hem of her dress. Bailey grinned as he stared at Kate.

"Damn short time I'll live if I listen to a whore," he said.

"We can arrange that," Lotte said. She stepped next to him, cocking the derringer she took from her dress, pressing it against his temple. The blood rushed from his face, leaving it a dirty white. I laughed, hearing the laughter as if coming from a distance. Then a darkness slowly settled over my eyes like a thundercloud, and I fainted.

Slowly the room swam back into focus. For a moment I stared in confusion at the rough ceiling boards, feeling damp sheets around me, trying to sort out the strange sensation of the bed upon which I lay, remembering last the hard oak chair I had sat upon at Shanssey's place. My mouth tasted brassy, of familiar death, and I remembered then what had happened and marveled that I was still alive.

"Good morning," a husky voice called from beside my bed. I tried to rise, but I was too weak. She leaned over, and I stared at Kate, her face devoid of makeup, now soft and vulnerable. She wore an ivory wrapper with lilies embroidered in black upon it that did little to hide her lush figure. I heard water dripping into a pan, and then a cool, damp cloth wiped my face.

"Good morning," I croaked, swallowed, and tried again, but the raven voice was still there. She lifted my head and held a glass to my lips. I drank, tasting water that did little to hide the brassy taste, but I felt better as the liquid cooled my throat and esophagus, spreading coolness in my belly. I tried again.

"Good morning," I said, and although a roughness still tinged my words, the raven voice was gone. "How long have I been out this time?"

"Two days," she said. She wiped my face again and pulled

back the covers. Cold air prickled my flesh. I looked down: I was naked, my ribs standing out starkly, my belly falling into a hollow. She rinsed out a washcloth and began wiping my body. I tried to feel embarrassed, but couldn't.

"We thought you were dying for sure," she said.

"We?"

"Miss Lotte and me. We brought you here. She is all right, that woman," she added roughly, and I knew the effort it must have taken her to admit that another woman was not an enemy or competitor.

"She kept that man Bailey from killing you," she said. "Took her pistol from her dress and held it to his head." She gave a short laugh. "I thought that man would pee his pants when she cocked the hammer back of that little pistol and stuck it on his head. He shook like he had Saint Vitus's dance. Sweated like a pig."

"He tried to shoot me when I was unconscious?"

She nodded, her eyes narrowing into mine. "He is not a good man. Mr. Shanssey told him to get out, that you would have his table when you were well enough to take it. He didn't like that. He shouted at Mr. Shanssey, cussed him like a bullwhacker, but Mr. Shanssey just reached across the table, plucked that pistol out of his hand, and threw him out of his saloon. Thought he was too fat, but Mr. Shanssey picked him up and threw him through the door. Broke his nose when he landed in the street. Almost as much blood as you left on Mr. Shanssey's floor."

"That was nice of him. He didn't have to do that," I said. I shifted my shoulders, trying to lift my head and look around the room. "What about the money?"

A hurt look came into her eyes. She straightened from the bed, her large breasts moving under the wrapper. She pointed to a small table and student lamp and Belter chair that had been added to the room while I was unconscious. I could see the money stacked beside the Jules Verne book I had purchased.

"It's all there," she said. "Each shinplaster and dime. I

took nothing. Mr. Shanssey, he made the split, so if something's missing, it's him you have to see."

I reached up and took her hand, startling her. I smiled. "I believe you, my winsome Kate. If you had taken the money, you wouldn't be here now. The question is, why are you here?"

She sniffed and wiped her nose along the sleeve of her wrapper. She pushed a strand of hennaed hair back from her broad forehead. Her eyes were red-rimmed and puffy from lack of sleep, yet an earthy beauty clung to her: mother and whore, that which most men desire most. I raised her hand to my lips and kissed it.

She jerked back, startled. A smile softened her full lips. Her eyes misted. "Can't remember when a man last did that. They've done a lot of other things, but not that."

"Then they should have," I replied. "Ladies need to expect such things."

"And been a long time since I was called 'lady,' " she said.

She bent down, and her lips brushed my forehead. I smelled cinnamon on her breath. I reached for her, but she slipped away.

"No," she said. "You're too weak."

"I'm also dying," I said. "Dying faster than usual. There's no cure of consumption. You know what that means."

She shrugged. "Nothing's certain. I'll get you some beef broth. That should help put you on the road."

"I'd prefer whiskey," I said, trying to struggle upright and failing.

"I'll bet you would. But for now, broth," she said sternly. A strange look came over her face. "I'll dress and leave after I get something into you."

An awkward silence feel between us, then she gave a rueful smile and started toward the door. I hesitated, thinking, remembering the lonely nights in the lonely rooms in the lonely towns that had been my world since leaving Dallas.

Loneliness.

November. Always November. Melancholy. Raw and cold afternoons alone in gloomy rooms.

"Why don't you swing by your rooms and bring your things here?" I asked. Instantly I regretted the words, but forced my face to remain closed to my thoughts.

She halted at the door, staring at it for a moment, then turned, her face tense, eyes sharp.

"You know what you are asking?" she said.

"No, I know what I am offering," I said. I waved around the room. "There isn't much here, but then I'm not much, myself. I have no heirs. And I'm lonely. I think you're lonely, too."

"All right," she said lowly. "But this ain't permanent."

I shrugged. "We've all got our own lives to lead. If you want to lead part of it together with me, then I would like to live a part of it with you, too."

"We can try," she said, turning back to the door. She opened it and paused. "I hope it works, Doc, but I don't think it will." A rueful smile twisted her lips. "You'll get tired of people calling me Doc's whore."

"Ah, but you are called Plain Kate. And bonny Kate, and sometimes Kate the Cursed. But Kate, the prettiest Kate in Christendom; Kate of Kate-Hall, my superdainty Kate . . ."

She roared with laughter. "Dainty Kate? I've been called a lot of things, but never dainty. I do like the way of your talk, Doc. Okay. Okay."

She left, calling down the stairs for a bowl of beef soup. I looked up at the ceiling, feeling my weakness, knowing that I had not been entirely truthful with her, but knowing my need for her as well, as both whore and mother. I still felt the needs of man, but I also felt the needs for a mother. My sickness had worsened, my mornings being spent clinging to the sides of the dry sinks in nameless hotel rooms. The time had come for me to have a companion, and Kate had already proven she knew how to take care of me when my sickness laid me low.

For a moment I felt a twinge of regret, then the feeling passed, and the familiar emptiness returned.

And we became lovers. No, not lovers; madcaps sealed to the Devil, seizing what life we could find by the cockles and shaking it free from the dictates of convention. We fought; we made up; we fought; we loved—ah, yes, we loved as if we had invented the act and, realizing the nakedness of each other, found a purpose for our flesh.

And Kate was perfect for me, robust, rolling, and bursting with health that I couldn't have, but sharing that health with me, making me feel . . . feel . . . feel like—a man. Perhaps we would have remained longer together than we did had it not been for Wyatt.

We had sunk into a routine by the time Wyatt rode into the Flat. Our day would begin sometime around five in the afternoon, when we would appear at Shanssey's, where we'd eat dinner and I'd play poker while Kate danced on the floor with the drovers and soldiers who came down from Government Hill on a brief pass, looking to shake the humdrum duties the fort had pushed upon their shoulders. Sometimes she'd take a fancy to one of the soldiers and they would disappear for a couple of hours, Kate returning flushed, her clothes in disarray, the musky scent of her stronger. But I felt no jealousy, no betrayal. Kate was Kate and she had become that Kate before I rode into the Flat. And I was Doc, the consumptive who took what love he could get even if that love came on the installment plan.

In late October, Wyatt rode into the Flat, looking for Dave Rudabaugh, who had robbed a train in Kansas. Wyatt was working for the railroad at the time as a private consultant. Rudabaugh had ridden south into Indian Territory after robbing the train and Wyatt followed him to Fort Griffin before losing the trail. Rudabaugh sneaked out one night before Wyatt arrived, after dropping three hundred dollars to me in a poker game. When Wyatt arrived, he went immediately to see Shanssey, knowing him from a time in Cheyenne when Wyatt had refereed a fight between Shanssey and Mike Donovan, when Shanssey was younger and thought he had the makings of a pugilist. He hadn't. Donovan had beaten him to a pulp before Wyatt stopped the fight. Yet the two remained fast friends.

I had no intention of helping a peace officer, private or

public, but Shanssey had treated me fairly when I went down with my sickness and had not reneged on our deal after I got rid of Bailey for him, so when Shanssey asked me to help Wyatt to get a lead on Rudabaugh, I decided to square our accounts.

I was dealing solitaire after a bad night spent coughing my lungs out. Kate was still sleeping in our bed, grumpy after nursing me through the night. I took a drink of bourbon, the sharp barley fumes rinsing the brass taste from my mouth, cauterizing my throat and lungs as it rolled down to my stomach. A cold gust of wind blew through the door of his restaurant as Shanssey came in through the street entrance with a tall, brooding dark-blond man dressed in a black frock coat, a black-handled, long-barreled Remington holstered on his right side, the handle riding just above his hip. His tie was neatly tied, and his white shirt was clean and his collar stiff with starch. I glanced down at his low-heeled boots: Wellingtons, highly polished. But it was his eyes that drew mine: gray-looking in the light inside, but alive with tiny lights flashing in their depths.

"Doc," Shanssey said. "I want you to meet Wyatt Earp. Wyatt's a good friend of mine."

"Lawman?" I asked.

"Why do you say that?" Wyatt asked, his voice flat and curious.

I felt a smile twisting across my lips. "You look like a lawman," I said.

"You don't like lawmen, I take it," he said.

"I don't think one way or the other about it," I said, playing a black ten on a red one-eyed jack.

"They say you've killed a couple of men," he said, taking a seat across from me and removing a cigar from an inside pocket of his coat. His glance flickered at the half-full glass of bourbon in front of me and the half-empty bottle beside it.

"Drink?" I asked, picking up the bottle. He shook his head, lighting his cigar. I replaced the bottle and took a mouthful of bourbon, rolling it around in my mouth before swallowing it in stages.

"Actually, I believe they say I've killed a lot of men. Whoever 'they' may be," I added. I played another card as he blew a cloud of smoke away from me. I smiled.

"And as for lawmen, well, most want to see me out of their towns. Fact is, you're right: I don't have much use for them," I said.

"Dr. Holliday, I need a favor," he said gravely. "I need information about Dave Rudabaugh. I understand you played a game or two with him the night before he left. Would you have any information about which way he went?"

"I think I've heard about you, too," I said, taking another drink. "From Wichita, right?" He nodded. "I thought so. You're the one who likes to beat up drunks." His lips tightened. "Speaking as a drunk myself, I take offense at that, Mr. Earp. We have as much right to be drunk as you to be sober."

"Yes, you do," he said quietly. "But when you are drunk, you do not have the right to tread on my toes. Being drunk is no excuse for rude behavior, Dr. Holliday."

"That's the second time you've called me Dr. Holliday," I mused. "Most people just call me Doc as if it were a nickname."

"I understand that you are a doctor," Wyatt said. "That makes it a title, not a nickname."

I laughed, and the laugh turned into a cough. I took my glass and drained it. He watched as I refilled the glass, but there were no disapproving grimaces or recriminations for my actions. He nodded at the bottle.

"That help?"

"All that does," I said. "Except laudanum. I have less use for that than I do bourbon."

"Man has to do what he must," Wyatt said stolidly.

"I told Wyatt that you'd help him, Doc," Shanssey said. "I figure you owe me a bit for that time with Bailey."

I felt a smile tug at my lips. "All right," I said suddenly, surprising even myself. "I'll see what I can find out for you. I won't guarantee anything, but I'll see what I can do."

"I appreciate that, Dr. Holliday," he said, rising. He stuck out his hand. I looked at it in surprise for a long moment, then looked up into his eyes. They stared into mine unchanging, showing no pity, accepting me as I was. I reached up and tentatively shook his hand. His grip was firm, the grip of a man to his friends.

"You may call me John. Or Doc," I added.

"We'll see, Dr. Holliday," he said. "We'll see."

He left with Shanssey. I watched carefully to see if he would wipe his hand after touching mine, but he didn't. He simply sauntered from the restaurant as if he had just eaten a full breakfast and had little on his mind except a stroll around the town to settle his stomach. I turned over another card: the ace of spades. I laughed and rose, finishing my glass of bourbon before settling my coat around my shoulders and strolling out the door, looking for Nosey Nell. She couldn't stand not knowing everything about everyone. If anyone knew where Rudabaugh would have gone, it would be her. Besides, she was pretty and blond and nearly as knowledgeable about men as Kate, and she had been hanging over Rudabaugh every chance she got.

I walked out to the edge of town where Nell had a small cabin and knocked repeatedly on her door, finally drawing the Manhattan and banging with its handle upon the door.

"Who is it?" she called crossly.

"Holliday," I answered.

"Go away."

"Open up, Nell. I need some information on Dave Rudabaugh," I said.

"He ain't here," she said. "Goddamnit, Doc, but it ain't even three! Go away!"

I knocked again on the door. "Rudabaugh?"

"Last I heard he was going over to New Mexico. Now go away, Doc, and let me sleep!"

I chuckled and turned away from the plain wooden door and walked back to town, feeling the cold wind bite deeply in my lungs. I considered going to Shanssey's place, but it was too early except for maybe a nickel-and-dime game, and I didn't feel like that. I walked to Beeker's Store, past the bolt goods and stacks of tins and cracker barrel to the shelf in the back where Mr. Beeker kept his books. Mr. Beeker greeted me with a smile, for I had proven to be a steady customer for his books.

"Good afternoon, Dr. Holliday," he said. "Looking for a new book?"

"Yes sir, Mr. Beeker," I answered. "I finished *Silas Marner*. I liked it very much."

"A kindred match, I believe," Beeker said. His eyes twinkled over the tops of his wire-rimmed spectacles. "There's a lot of Silas in you, too, I believe."

I laughed. "I'm afraid, sir, that I'm far from being a miser."

"No," he said, "but there is a hidden goodness in you, too, I believe, Dr. Holliday."

"I would like to think you were right, sir, but I think any goodness has deteriorated with my health," I answered. I motioned at the books. "I see you have some new titles."

"Oh yes," he said, coming from behind the counter to join me. "Have you read Dickens's *The Old Curiosity Shop*? It's quite good, if a bit melodramatic. Then there's *Little Women* by Louisa May Alcott. That's fairly new. And I have a copy of Herman Melville's *Moby Dick*. If you haven't read it, I think that should be something that would contribute toward your education. Besides, it's a good story about a man seeking to destroy evil, only to become evil himself."

"Ah, yes. Perhaps a metaphor for life?" I said. "All right. You were right on the last one. I'll take it. And a can of peaches," I added, "if you'll open them for me. I can't get those at the restaurant."

He opened the peaches and gave me the book. I paid him and left, tucking the book in a side pocket and using the Spanish dagger to fish the peach halves out of their syrup as I strolled back to Shanssey's place. The peaches bit hard at my teeth, making them ache, and I remembered that I was nearly out of baking soda which I used to clean my teeth. I made a mental note to purchase some the next time I went back to Beeker's.

I entered Shanssey's and finished the peaches, setting the can on the bar for the bartender to throw away. Lotte was already at her table with three soldiers, playing draw poker. She glanced up at me and smiled.

"How are things going, Lotte?" I asked, sliding into my chair. The bartender crossed with a full bottle of Old Williams and a glass and placed them by my left elbow.

"Sixes and eights, John," she said. "Sixes and eights. With you?"

"I'm alive," I said. I muffled a cough with a handkerchief and made a mental note to buy another dozen from Beeker as well as the baking soda. "At least I'm up for another day."

"Let's play a little poker," one of the soldiers, growled, rapping a coin against the top of the table. "I wanted talk, I'da stayed back in the barracks." He glanced over at me. "Do your chinin' on your own time, mister." His hair showed salt-and-pepper beneath his cavalry hat, and I could see where his sergeant stripes had been sewn on and removed from his sleeves. His face was lumpy and scarred.

"That's right," another chimed in. His face was flushed from drink beneath his short blond hair. He looked as if he had been off the farm only a year or two, but his eyes danced with devilment and I knew he was "out to see the elephant."

"This is my table," Lotte said to them, "and I'll speak to whom I damned well please. Now if you don't like that, you can just check out of the game."

Angry sparks danced in her eyes. I chuckled, and the soldiers swiveled to glare at me. I poured a drink and gave them a lazy look, sipping the whiskey.

"I'd say you boys are a bit short on manners," I said. I coughed and took a larger drink.

"Is that right?" the young one said. "Well, maybe we don't need a skinny asshole like you to tell us what to do." He glanced at the older man beside him for approval. "Do we,

Lon, huh? We don't need any ad-vice comin' from someone like him, do we?"

Lon looked over at me, his eyes taking in my sunken cheeks, the hollows beneath my eyes. My size appealed to the bully within him. He nodded to himself. "You might have something there, Billy. Yes sir, you might have something there." He pushed himself back from the table and stood, his belly struggling against his belt, his huge scarred hands hitching his pants higher.

"Now, why don't you just go away like a good little man and leave us to our game?" he asked, nudging my table with his boot. The young man rose and stood beside him, hands on hips, his head thrown back to look down his nose disdainfully at me.

"I say we teach this bugger to mind his own business. What do you say, Lon?"

"Well, now," Lon said, wiping the back of his hand across his lips. "Maybe we should do just that. Maybe we should take down his pants and teach him a little lesson."

"That does it," Lotte snapped. She reached across, pulling in their cards. "This game is over. Take your money and get out."

Lon leered at her, his eyes insolent. "And sure, if we don't mind a little quim provided she don't have the French pox."

"John!" she said loudly. "John!" Her eyes snapped angrily, her lips drawn down into a thin, fine line. She sat back in her chair, her right hand disappearing into the folds of her dress at her waist.

I grinned, leaning back in my chair, and touched my pistols with the tips of my fingers. Lon caught the movement and grinned, leaning forward on the table with his hands splayed out to hold his weight.

"Now, you just draw one of those little things, boy, and I'll ram 'em down your throat before you can whistle 'Dixie,' you southern trash."

"What's going on here?" Shanssey demanded, coming up to the table.

"These soldiers are causing a bit of trouble, John," Lotte said, pointing at the two standing in front of my table. "They've been threatening John and me."

"That the way of things, Doc?" Shanssey demanded, looking from Lon to Billy.

"We're after a little relaxation and this southern trash broke in on our fun," Billy said. "I reckon we're going to teach him a little manners that he should've been taught by his mammy. If he knew her," he added insolently.

I rose from my chair, stepping to the left, feeling the band tighten around my head, the room rapidly becoming rosy red. "All right, you Yankee pecker-head! Whenever you're ready to teach this Georgia boy some manners, you unleash that pistol and have at it."

"Now, we'll be having none of that," Shanssey said. "You soldiers get your money and get out. Now!"

Lon gave him a slow, level look, noticing the scars above Shanssey's eyes, the breadth of his shoulders, the thickening of his waist. He smiled.

"Looks as if you're a man handy with his fists. Maybe you'd like to throw us out. Or try!" he said, then his breath exploded from his lungs as Shanssey stepped forward, pivoting on the balls of his feet and planting a huge fist deep into Lon's stomach. The air exploded from his lungs as he sank to his knees, his mouth opening and closing like a catfish as he tried to gulp down air. Shanssey reached down and grabbed hold of his collar and dragged him across the floor. The other two soldiers leaped to their feet, protesting, then froze as a quiet voice spoke from behind them.

"Follow him out quietly now, boys," Wyatt said. They craned their heads and stared at Wyatt, standing beside the bar, his Remington dangling loosely by his side.

"We'll be back!" one of them said, gathering their money from the table. The two of them followed Shanssey to the door, where he heaved Lon through into the street. The two soldiers followed.

I looked at Billy, grinning. "Your turn," I said softly. He flushed and unbuttoned the holster of his pistol. I reached down and picked up my glass of bourbon and took a large drink.

"Now, if you're quite ready, you Yankee trash?" I said.

"Don't, John. It would be murder," Lotte said. The young boy's eyes darted toward her and back. He swallowed, his tongue slipping out to moisten his lips. Lotte looked at him. "Back off, kid. You don't stand a chance."

"You're awful sure of yourself," he mumbled indecisively.

"You've been drinking. That's the liquor talking," she said. "Now button your flap and leave with your friends. And don't come back," she added.

He stiffened, glaring at her and me. "I ain't afraid of you!"

"She's right, boy," Wyatt said quietly. Billy's head jerked toward him. "You don't stand a chance. That's Doc Holliday you're trying to brace."

"Never heard of you," he blustered.

"That makes us even," I said. "I never heard of you, either." I took another drink. "But you're playing my game in my house. Listen to what they're trying to tell you. All you have to do is apologize and leave."

"John," Lotte began.

"No, Lotte. He can go. But first he'll apologize. I will not be misabused; even by a snot still wet behind the ears." I grinned, but knew there was no humor in the smile I was giving him.

His eyes widened with the anger of youth, then he glanced down at the ivory handle of the Colt showing beneath my coat. A tic began high in his cheek and perspiration suddenly broke out on his forehead. His hand wavered indecisively over his pistol butt, then fell away as his eyes drew away from mine and centered on the floor.

"I'm sorry, ma'am," he said to Lotte. "Sir." He nodded at me. "I reckon I got to drinking a bit too much."

"And . . ." I prompted gently. His face flushed beet red, and for a moment I thought he would try to draw again, but Lotte broke through the challenging air between us.

"John, let it go. It's all over now," she said. "You act as if you want to kill this boy." She looked at the young soldier.

"You'd best run on now, before things get any worse than they already are."

"Go on, boy," Wyatt spoke from behind him. "You don't need this."

"Come on, son," Kate said loudly, stepping forward and tugging at the young boy's gun arm. "Let's you and me take a little walk and put that fire in your blood to better use."

"Stay away from this, Kate," I said.

"Drop it, Doc," she answered. "You're messing with my business."

She rubbed the boy's arm between her breasts and trailed her cool fingers across the back of his neck. "Let's go chase the tiger, whadda you say?"

The boy turned thankfully to her, and let himself be pulled out of the saloon into the dark night.

I took a handkerchief from an inside pocket and wiped the perspiration from my face. I glanced at Lotte; she was staring strangely at me. Wyatt walked over and pulled out a chair, seating himself.

"What's the matter?" I asked. Lotte started to speak, then shook her head and picked up her wrap.

"I need a cup of coffee," she said, heading through the door to the restaurant.

"I say something?" I asked Wyatt.

He shook his head and reached for the deck of cards on the table, turning them over in his thick, blunt fingers. "No, it's what you almost did," he said. "You almost killed that boy over nothing. He was just a young kid letting off a little steam, that's all."

"I will not be addressed in that fashion by anybody," I said calmly, seating myself. I took the fresh deck of cards from his hands and split the seal.

"It's things like that, though, that make a person very unpopular," Wyatt answered. "People remember killings in the respect of who needed to be killed. That boy didn't need to be killed."

I gave him a twisted grin. "Maybe."

"Holliday." I looked up as Bill Cruger approached our table. "What was that all about?"

"A bit of an insult," I said. I indicated Wyatt sitting across from me. "May I introduce Wyatt Earp. Sheriff Bill Cruger."

"Sheriff." Wyatt nodded.

"You are running in bad company, Mr. Earp," Cruger said. "I'd suggest that you remember a man is known by the friends he keeps."

"I'll remember that," Wyatt said coolly.

"Holliday, consider this as a warning," Cruger said. "Fort Griffin may not be Chicago or Saint Louis or Dallas, but we do have law."

"They were pushing pretty hard," I said, holding his stare. "I will not be pushed by anyone."

He sighed, sliding his hat back on his head. He hooked his thumbs in his wide leather belt, which held his pistol scabbard with the big Army Colt perched prominently by his hip.

"Holliday, we need the military here more than we need you," he said. "That's the pure economics of the situation. When those soldiers come into town, they leave a lot of their money behind. People like you just take."

"Sounds as if there's a bit of a double standard at work here," I said, leaning back in my chair. "I always thought the Union stood for equality. Leastways, that's the reason you damn Yankees gave for marching through Georgia. Seems to me like the only law is for people like me, while the soldiers can do pretty much what they want."

"In a way, Holliday, that's what I'm telling you. Like I said: economics. Any more trouble from you and I'll arrest you." He nodded at Wyatt and walked away, his spurs jangling against the hard floor.

"I think he means it," Wyatt said.

"Maybe." I looked up and caught Mr. Beeker standing at the bar. "I guess this proves you wrong, Mr. Beeker."

He picked up his beer and brought it over to the table. "No, it doesn't. That good is still there; it's just buried deeper than I thought."

"It's nice to be certain," I said.

"Tell me, Dr. Holliday, would you have killed that boy?"

"Yes," I said. "Yes, I would have. Unless he killed me first."

He finished his beer and nodded, leaving the saloon. Wyatt watched him go, puzzlement showing upon his face. "Now what was that all about?"

"Mr. Beeker thinks I have the making of a saint," I said, dealing a hand of draw poker to the two of us.

"Optimistic," Wyatt said, drawing his cards to him. "His glass is always half full."

"Just call me Saint John of the Miseries," I said.

Kate showed up about three hours later, staggering, her dress awry, her lipstick smeared, eyes bright from drink. She strolled up to the table where I was playing with four other gentlemen, two cattlemen, a drummer, and Tim Oates, a gunsmith in town. Wyatt had left earlier after I told him what I had learned about Rudabaugh. She watched the game for a moment, swaying belligerently behind my chair. Finally she leaned over, propping her breasts on my shoulder.

"You 'bout done, Doc?" she said, her words slurring.

I could smell the soldier upon her and felt disgusted. "You're drunk, Kate," I said, shrugging her off. She staggered, steadying herself with a hand on the back of my chair.

"Goddamnit, Doc," she complained.

"Go home and sleep it off," I said, sliding a small stack of chips forward, calling Oates. He showed two pair, and I pulled in the pile with three sixes.

"I don't wanna sleep," she said. "I wanna drink. And I wanna fuck."

"You're being crude now, Kate."

"Yes, I'm being crude. I wanna be crude. I wanna take my clothes off and have someone chase me around the room. If it ain't you, I'll go find someone else."

"Looks like you've been chased around enough for tonight," I said calmly. "Go get a drink and tell the bartender to put it on my tab."

"Aw, shit!" she said, weaving drunkenly. "Come on, Doc! I'm feelin' horny as hell."

I rose and turned to face her, feeling a coldness slipping over me. "Kate, I'm not telling you again: that's enough."

"Looks like you can't handle your women, either, Holliday."

"Why, hello, Bailey," I said, turning. "Still trying to shoot men in the back?"

"Take it easy, boys," Shanssey said, moving over to the side of my table. "Doc, you stick to playing, and Bailey, I told you to stay out of my place. You're not wanted here."

"Afraid of the competition, Holliday?" Bailey sneered, looking at the men at my table.

A recklessness swept through me. I laughed. "Why, I'll take your money, Bailey," I said. I looked at Shanssey. "Let him play, John."

Shanssey looked from Bailey to me, shaking his head. "I dunno. I gotta bad feeling about this, Doc. A real bad feeling."

"I'm just a lamb," I said, grinning at Bailey. "And Bailey, why, just look at him. He's a right jolly old fat man. Nothing more. Right, Bailey?"

Bailey grinned at Shanssey, but I could see that my words stung him by the tightening of his jaw muscles.

"All right," Shanssey said grudgingly. "But I want no trouble, Doc. You leave your pistols holstered, you hear? And you, Bailey. I don't want no trouble. You keep your fat mouth shut, you hear?"

Bailey spread his hands and laughed, taking a seat on my right next to Oates. "All I want is a little game. How yuh doing, Tim?"

"Fine, Ed. Just fine," Oates said, shaking his hand. "Maybe you'll bring me a bit of luck."

Bailey laughed and clapped him on the shoulder. He looked at the others. "Don't think I made your acquaintance. I'm Ed Bailey."

"I'm Don Perry," the man on my immediate left said.

"Jim Stalker," the next one said, "and this is Bob Hollinger."

"Pleased to meet you all," Bailey said. He took a sheaf of bills from a pocket and tossed them on the table. He glanced at me, smirking. "Table stakes, I presume."

"You presume correctly," I said, taking my seat.

"Aw, Doc!" Kate wailed. "Goddamnit, Doc!" She stalked over to the bar. "Gimme a whiskey," she demanded. The bartender raised his eyebrows and looked over at me. I nodded. He shrugged and reached beneath the bar for a bottle of my whiskey. I turned my attention back to the game.

"Well, gentlemen. We'll let Mr. Bailey make the choice, as he is the newcomer to the game." I pushed the copper in front of him. Bailey grinned and tossed in a dollar for an ante.

"Let's try a little draw," he said, rubbing his hands.

"Draw it is," I said. I slid the cards to him for a cut. He gave a straight cut, and I smiled as I picked them up. "Surprised me, Bailey. You're playing straight."

His lips tightened, and he started to say something, then glanced over at Shanssey and held his tongue. But I could tell he was seething by the way he snapped his cards in his hands, squeezing them tightly in his hand. He tried to cover up his annoyance by laughing and sliding into a vulgar joke about a cowboy and a proper woman who objected to the smell of manure in the dining room. I ignored him, concentrating on the game. The others laughed, and tension eased around the table.

Oates won the first hand, then Stalker won a small pot of fifty dollars and Oates came back with a twenty-five-dollar pot. Then I hit a streak of luck and pulled in four straight hands, the last one with three tens and a pair of treys. Bailey's money had shrunk considerably as he tried to be in on every hand to the end despite his cards. When I gathered the cards from the last hand, he glanced over his shoulder: Shanssey had left. Something flickered in his eyes, and he turned to glower at me.

"What is that, Holliday? Four in a row? Pretty lucky, you ask me."

"Nobody asked you, Ed, but since you brought it up, why, yes, lady luck seems to be smiling on me."

"Let's try draw again," he said, tossing in his ante. "And this time, let's have the cards right."

The other players slid back their chairs, poised on the edges, watching. I smiled at him, taking the cut and flicking the cards around the table.

"I always play straight, Bailey," I said. "Unlike yourself."

I picked up my cards and spread them. Two queens, a six, eight, and nine. Not the best of hands, but I had had worse. "I believe it is your bet, Mr. Oates?"

Oates checked to Bailey, who promptly bet twenty dollars. I raised him twenty. Stalker was the only other one to stay. Bailey threw in another twenty. I called and Stalker stayed. I picked up the deck, looking at Stalker.

"Three cards," he said, tossing his discards onto the deadwood. I handed him three and looked at Bailey.

"Two," he said, dropping two on the pile. He picked up Stalker's discards, glancing at them.

"Play poker, Bailey. Leave the deadwood alone," I warned. "Once more, you forfeit the hand."

He sneered at me, but I ignored him and dropped three cards onto the pile. "Dealer takes three."

I spread my cards, looking. I had four queens with a ten kicker. I looked over at Stalker.

"It'll cost you twenty," he said, tossing his chips onto the pile. Bailey upped the bet another twenty and I promptly raised fifty.

"Must've had a good draw," Stalker said. "Or you're trying to buy the pot."

I shrugged. "It's going to cost you to find out," I said. He smiled and tossed in fifty and another twenty.

"That's seventy to you, Bailey," I said.

"And another twenty to you, Holliday," he said, tossing in his chips.

"Let's make it another fifty," I answered, looking at Stalker. "It'll cost you another seventy."

He shook his head, tossing his cards onto the deadwood. "Too steep for me. I don't think you're bluffing after all."

Bailey lifted the edges of Stalker's cards, peeking. I tossed my cards on top of the pile and reached, pulling in the pot.

"What the hell," Bailey snarled.

"I warned you about looking at the deadwood, Bailey. I'm claiming the pot."

"He's right, Ed," Oates said next to him. "That's a cheap trick."

"Not any more cheap than those bottom-dealing stunts of his," Bailey said hotly, jerking his thumb at me.

"That's a lie," I said quietly.

"Are you calling me a liar?" Bailey said.

"Why, yes, I am," I said, stretching across the table to collect the last of the cards.

Bailey leaped to his feet, his fingers stabbing inside his vest for one of his derringers.

"Look out!" Stalker yelled, diving out of his chair.

"Doc!" Kate called.

I was caught out of position for my pistols. I slipped the Spanish dagger out of my inside breast pocket and swiped it across the table, stabbing for Bailey's midriff. Blood spurted out of his belly.

"Ahhh!" he cried, stumbling back.

I took a quick sidestep to my right. Bailey tried to bring the derringer around to bear on me. I stepped forward, swiping my arm through his, knocking his arm away, and slipped the dagger up inside his belly again, ripping up, through layers of fat and cloth. The derringer dropped from his fingers as he stumbled back again, trying to hold his intestines from curling out like fat blue worms, and failing. He gagged and sank to his knees, trying to stuff them back inside, then his eyes rolled up inside his head and he fell to his side. A heavy stench lifted up to pervade the room.

"Jesus," Stalker gulped, then turned his head and vomited onto the floor.

"Damn it, Doc!" Shanssey said, running from his office. "I told you—"

"Sorry, John. I didn't have a choice," I said. "Bailey tried to cold-deck me again."

"I'll take your guns, Holliday," Cruger said, stepping up to my side. I glanced at him; his pistols were still in their scabbards. I smiled lazily at him, stepping back and away. He shook his head. "Don't do it, Holliday! You may beat me, but you'll hang for sure if you do."

"He's right, Doc," Shanssey said lowly. "Ed had a lot of friends here. One more killing will set them off for sure. Give the sheriff your pistols."

I slipped the Colt and Manhattan free and reversed them, handing them to Cruger, butts forward. He took them and shook his head.

"I told you to play it easy, Holliday," he said. "Now, let's go; you're under arrest."

"It was self-defense," I protested. "Since when does a person go to jail for self-defense?"

"He's right, Bill," Shanssey said. "You can take his pistols, but putting him under arrest, well, that's just not right."

"Hell with that," someone said from the gathering crowd. "Someone get a rope! Let's hang him! Ed was an okay guy."

"Anybody got a rope?" someone shouted.

"There'll be no hanging here," Cruger said loudly, sticking my pistols in his belt and drawing his own. "There's been enough killing for the night, but I'll shoot the first one who tries to take Holliday." He waved his pistols threateningly. "Let's go, Holliday," he said under his breath. "You wanna get out of this alive, let's go. Now."

"Take care of my chips, John," I said to Shanssey, picking up my hat. I settled it on my head and sauntered through the crowd, feeling their hatred stretching out to touch me with heated fingers.

Outside, I turned toward the stable, but Cruger reached out to stop me.

"To your hotel," he said, jerking his head. I looked at him in surprise: the county seat was Albany. "I don't want to be caught on the road by any of these yahoos," he explained.

I gave him a long, level look. He met my eyes for a moment, then his eyes fell and he turned, pushing me gently toward the hotel. I turned, following him along the boardwalk, listening to our heels echo hollowly in the cold night. I glanced at his profile.

"Tell me, Cruger," I said softly. "How good a friend was Bailey to you?"

His eyes shifted over to me, anger stirring in their depths. "Are you accusing me of something, Holliday?"

"Not yet," I said.

"I don't need any lip from a man like you," he said angrily.

"Then don't give me any reason to give it to you," I responded. "Why are we going to the hotel? That doesn't seem to be very safe to me."

"You let me do my job, Holliday," he said roughly as we reached the hotel. He opened the door, motioning me inside. I stepped in and walked to the desk, calling for my key. Cruger reached in front of me, claiming it. "Send someone for Charley Travers," he said to the clerk. "I need someone on Holliday's door. He's just killed Ed Bailey."

"Yes sir, Sheriff," the clerk said, slipping out from behind the desk. "I'll go myself." He left in a hurry, closing the door behind him. Cruger motioned up the stairs. I turned and climbed slowly up the stairs. A door opened at the top and Wyatt appeared.

"What's going on?" he asked, looking from the sheriff to me.

"Holliday's killed a man. Ed Bailey. Gutted him," Cruger said.

"He drew first," I said. "Tried to shoot me across the table. I had no choice."

"Sounds like self-defense," Wyatt said. Cruger stepped in front of him, his eyes snapping.

"I'm ordering you to get back in your room, Earp!" he

snapped. "You may be the cock of the walk up in Wichita, but this ain't even Kansas."

Hot lights flickered for a moment deep in Wyatt's eyes, then he shook his head and stepped back into his room.

"Good luck, Holliday," he called, shutting his door behind him.

"Asshole," Cruger muttered, unlocking my door. He grabbed my shoulder, pushing me inside. I stumbled, catching myself by the bedstead.

"Keep your hands to yourself, Cruger," I said icily, straightening. He took a step toward me, raising his pistol.

"Mind your mouth, Holliday," he said menacingly.

"Watch your manners, Cruger," I said.

He started to say something else, then changed his mind and stepped outside, slamming my door shut and locking it. I listened to his footsteps disappear down the hall and crossed to my window, looking down the street toward Shanssey's place. A crowd was gathering on the boardwalk and the street outside. I listened to them clamoring for my head, working themselves up into a frenzy. Kate slipped outside the door and looked up at the window, her face white and tight, lips compressed. She lifted her skirts, pulled off her shoes, and ran down the street, her long legs, naked save for net stockings and garters, stretching and flexing whitely in the dark toward the abyss. I turned away from the window and poured a drink from the bottle on the table by the window, sipping it. I wondered how long it would be before the crowd would find enough courage to storm the hotel. I picked up *Moby Dick* and settled myself in the chair to read, my glass and the bottle on the table beside me.

About an hour later, a loud commotion rose from the streets. I frowned, marked my place, and rose, taking my glass to the window.

"Fire! Malkie's barn!"

I looked down the street and saw flames flickering from the loft of the barn at the far end of the street. The crowd broke, men sprinting for the barn, buckets magically appearing in their hands. I finished my drink and placed the glass back on the table. I took my canvas saddlebags from the nail upon which I had hung them and quickly stuffed shirts and my spare suit into one, then stuffed as many of Kate's clothes in the other side as I could. I stripped the sheets from the bed and tied them together and to the bed, trying to drag the bed over to the window. But the bed was too heavy and I was too weak. I shrugged, knowing that this would be my one chance, and tossed the length of my homemade rope out the window. I leaned out, looking down: I still had a good eighteen-foot drop. I sighed and went back to pick up my saddlebags. Suddenly a slight commotion stirred outside my door, then the door opened and Wyatt stepped inside.

"Hurry," he said. "Kate's got your horse down at the bosky along Collins Creek."

I shouldered my bags, staggering a bit then catching myself. I held out my hand to Wyatt. He looked at it, then quickly took it and pulled me out the door, shoving me down the hall. Travers lay unconscious on the floor, a large knot forming behind his ear.

"I owe you one, Wyatt," I said solemnly.

"You owe Kate one, Doc," he said. "She's the one who's set everything up. She even set the fire." He patted my shoulder and gave me a gentle push for the stairs. "Good luck!"

I slipped down the stairs and cautiously opened the front door, peering out. The street was clear; all hands were down at the fire. I slipped out the door and ran as fast as I could down the street, cutting through the alley by Beeker's Store to the bosky.

"Kate!" I whispered in the darkness.

"Over here," she said. I saw her pale form in the darkness under a cottonwood and hurried to her. She thrust a flour sack in my hands and took the saddlebags, tossing them over Ares's back, cinching them to the saddle while I bent over, coughing, trying to clear the phlegm from my lungs, working

hard to drag in air. I fumbled open the flour sack and withdrew two nickel-plated, ivory-handled pistols: my Colt .45
and a new double-action Colt Lightning, also nickel-plated
and ivory-butted. I held them up, amazed.

"How?" I asked.

"I stole your pistol but couldn't find the other one. I think
the sheriff had it in his pocket. So I bought the Lightning
from Oates. A hundred for the pistol and another five for
boxes of bullets. They're in there too." I slid the Colt into the
left holster and the Lightning where the Manhattan had formerly rested, then reached in and removed a box of cartridges for each of the pistols and dropped them into the side
pockets of my coat.

"Your money's in the saddlebags along with some food,
thanks to Shanssey, but it cost us a thousand for it and the
extra horse and saddle. Goddamnit!" she swore and turned to
me. "I can't ride in this dress; it's too tight and the damn bustle's too big!" She fumbled behind her and swore again.

"Help me, Doc," she panted. "I can't get the goddamn
buttons."

I reached up and ripped the buttons from the fabric. She
stepped out of her dress, kicking it away from her, standing
naked in the moonlight except for stockings and garters: her
flesh pebbling from the cold, her legs long, shapely columns,
her breasts full but held proudly high, a heavy, dark triangle
between her legs. She shoved Ares's reins into my hand, then
climbed up on the other horse. I glanced at her, naked, her
hair flying free and wild in the moonlight. She looked like a
Valkyrie.

"Let's go, Doc!" she said urgently.

I stepped into the stirrups and swung up on Ares's back.
He danced a bit, then pointed his head across toward the
hills, black knobs in the moonlight. Kate flashed past, her
naked legs clenched tightly around her horse's flanks, her
bare breasts brushing the flying mane. I touched Ares with
my heels, and he galloped off into the night, heading north
toward the border.

8

Here, nothing. The great nothing-nothing land of the Great Plains. Land flat, arid, treeless except where the buffalo had rolled springs free from the loamy ground, and where cotton-wood seeds, roaming the prairies on the endless winds, had taken root where there was nothing but blue skies and prairie, an immense stage upon which we are destined to stand, small and shameful pawns within the majesty of the theatre.

Kate dressed herself as soon as we had put a fair amount of distance between our horses' hooves and Fort Griffin, borrowing a pair of pants and two shirts from me. I was surprised that I had shrunk so much in the throes of my sickness; Kate fit my trousers better than I, and her breasts strained the buttons on my shirts to bursting. We took an extra blanket and sliced a hole in the center for her to wear as a serape in place of a coat. Instead of shoes, she wore four pairs of my stockings, lacing them tightly about her ankles with strips of rawhide cut from the ends of my saddlebag straps. When I saw her in her tramp's reach-me-downs, I felt a bewildering series of complex, erotic feelings: tenderness and strong sexual urgings; there is something about a woman-tramp that brings out earthy desire in a man. For a while our trip across the Indian Nations was taken slowly, with many stops for lovemaking at the fords of various creeks we crossed, in hollows where wildflowers bloomed and bumblebees and butterflies flitted and danced from blossom to blossom, and sparrows and wrens sang, quail whistled "bob-white" tunes, and mourning doves shocked the interim silences with "who-goosed-me-how-dare-you-dare-you" songs.

Surprisingly, during that long, long ride over the Nations, we slipped past roaming Indian bands and outlaws, and I never once suffered a hemorrhage, thanks, I am sure, in part, to Kate's thoughtful hand quickly grabbing four bottles of Old Williams and secreting them in the saddlebags she had hurriedly packed upon my arrest. Yet I found little need for the bourbon other than the small, steady sips I constantly need when slight tickles in my throat herald a coming convulsion or turnings of the deadly worm in my chest threaten to eat away the lining of my lungs. Once Kate and I fairly used the contents of one bottle when we took shelter from a "blue norther" streaking down from Canada, holding up in a deep hollow.

We heard the sound of the train long before we saw Dodge City on the Arkansas. The long, lonely wail echoed eerily over the plain, flying over the grama grass and prickly pear cactus and the yucca that the Indians used for needle and thread and soap, like the cry of the banshee or Valkyries swooping down from the heavens on their winged horses, black as night, to carry fallen heroes back to Valhalla. But there was no Valhalla here; only the empty prairie, and the bones and dust of forgotten warriors whose civilization and society and land had been rudely wrested from them by the members of a stronger civilization and society. But the sound was still enough to raise the hackles on the back of the neck. Whether it was from the sound itself or from what the sound meant I do not know; I only know that I felt a wave of annoyance, then anger, even though I also knew that our trip was nearly over, the hardship endured, and our mettle thoroughly tested.

Ares felt the same irritation as I, for when we topped the final rise of the hill that opened Dodge City to us, he danced sideways, angrily pawing the earth and trying to turn away from the town. At the edge of the town stood huge, white boulders through which the railroad tracks ran in a straight line toward a gathering of frame buildings after crossing the iron bridge over the Arkansas River. For a moment I felt an urge to let Ares have his way, to let him take us where the wind blew, letting random direction direct our destiny. The wind blew into our faces, bringing with it a strange smell: brassy and earthy, sour—death. But the town had things that we needed; that Kate needed, and I owed her much. I nudged Ares toward the town with my heels, firmly reining his head around when he tried to resist.

As we drew closer to the town, I could see what I had mistaken for white boulders were piles of white-bleached buffalo bones, what was left of the magnificent herds that once roamed the prairies from north to south and back again, multiplying themselves until the herds stretched for miles, changing the prairies into a sea of black and brown masses moving like waves, the livelihood of the Indians who hunted them with religious awe and with the blessings of their deity who had graciously given the buffalo to them. But that god had given way to a newer and more powerful god whose benevolence had yet to be shown.

We circled the town to approach down Front Street, past blocks of ramshackle shacks built across a mud-bogged street away from the tracks. People stared at us curiously as we rode slowly through the thick mud of the street, Ares shying away from the stench that caused even Kate to turn pale and cup her hand over her mouth and nose, which had been scoured clean from the smell of saloons and people by the prairie winds. No trees graced the boulevard; no paint graced the buildings except for rough-lettered signs.

After three blocks, however, we moved into a separate section of town and to Deacon Cox's Dodge House at the corner of Front Street and Central, which, although not the Inter-Ocean in Cheyenne or the St. James in Denver, was, nevertheless, a vast improvement. I tethered our horses at the rail in front and helped Kate down. She staggered, swearing as her foot slipped out of the stirrup, nearly tumbling her into the street.

"Goddamn, Doc," she complained, pulling her (my) shirt tight against her breasts.

"Sorry, Kate," I said. "I wasn't ready, I guess. Or," I added lamely, "maybe the horse shied?"

"Maybe my ass, too," she said, climbing the step to the boardwalk. She removed the scarf she wore in place of a hat, sighed, and wiped her forehead with her forearm. "Goddamn! Will a hot bath ever feel good!" She looked roguishly at me. "Maybe we could share one? Ever done it in water, Doc?" A passer-by stopped and stared curiously at us.

"You forget the Red River, my dear," I said dryly. "We spent a couple of days there, if you recall."

"That was a couple weeks ago, I think," she said. "Hell, it could have been a couple years ago, for all I remember. I'm talking about now, Doc. That's all that's important for you and me. Just now."

"Indeed," I murmured, taking her arm and steering her toward the hotel entrance. "What else is there but the present?"

The clerk glanced with disdain at us as we crossed the lobby to him. The lobby was typical of what I had encountered in other "immediate" towns that had sprung up in the West, but more pretensions at elegance had been made here than in the others: green velvet, tied-back curtains; two cartouche-shaped medallion-backed sofas with upholstery matching the curtains along with heavy armchairs also bearing the green velvet upholstery; kerosene lamps with ornate hand-painted shades; a walnut table with magazines and newspapers neatly stacked upon it. But the addition of brass spittoons made a tawdry intrusion into the quest for elegance.

"Yes?" the clerk asked, and I knew immediately the extent of pretension to which the Dodge House had fallen, for in every other hotel I had entered, the clerk had always said "May I help you?" even if in a sonorous manner through his nose. This clerk obviously disdained all proprieties.

"We would like a room," I said, staring hard into his eyes. He tried to hold mine, but he was not that strong in character despite his desire to appear proper and sophisticated upon the entrance of two tired, dirty travelers in frayed garments.

A Good Samaritan our clerk was not, despite all his pretensions otherwise and his avowance to be so in the church he hypocritically attended with religious regularity on Sundays. Mind, I didn't know all this at once: It took a while before I knew him for the Baptist hypocrite he was, damning the whores and bartenders during the day and sneaking full draughts of elderberry and dandelion wine at night with an occasional bracer of brandy thrown in when the "spell" (or mood) was upon him and visiting the back door of Miss Frankie Bell's house when the "season" was upon him or the establishment of Timberline if he was in the mood for the more "exotic."

"I trust you are willing to pay. In advance," he added, his voice rising to a high squeak despite his attempt to hold it in check.

"Mrs. Holliday and I will have two rooms," I said, spinning the register around and reaching for the pen. I disdainfully flicked the excessive ink from it, splattering his shirt with droplets, I signed my name with a flourish and spun the register back to him.

"Really! This is most unacceptable!" he complained, snatching a handkerchief from the breast pocket of his coat and dabbing ineffectually at the spots.

"As are your manners," I said, tapping the handle of my Colt .45 significantly. His eyes widened. He swallowed heavily, his prominent Adam's apple moving convulsively up and down in his scrawny throat. His hands froze at the spots in his shirt. I nodded at the pigeonholes behind him.

"Two rooms?" I reminded.

He turned and fumbled at the keys, grasping, selecting at random two keys and sliding them over the table to me. I lifted the keys from the desk and held them for a moment, clicking their brass tags together, drawing the clerk's attention to their presence in my hand, letting the silence between us stretch out uncomfortably. A dull red moved up his face. He nervously licked his lips. When I decided that he had learned his lesson sufficiently, I turned away and led Kate to the stairs, her hand tucked regally into the crook of my elbow.

"Don't forget to draw the bath, my good man," I said as we took the stairs one at a time. "Clean water. Clean hot water twice. The first immediately."

"Yes sir," he said, reaching for the bell. "It will be carried up immediately."

"Sometimes, my dear, it pays to be an asshole," I murmured to Kate. She giggled and squeezed my elbow.

"It must come natural to you," she whispered back to me. "Tell me, did you mean that about Mrs. Holliday?"

"Of course," I said magnanimously. I could afford to be magnanimous: propriety meant little to me anymore, but I owed something to Kate. If being known as Mrs. Holliday would give her pleasure, why, I had no objection. It was only a small thing as far as I was concerned.

"Doc, you're too good to me," she said. A tear sparkled in her eye and trickled down through the fine sift of trail dust on her cheek. She stepped up on her tiptoes and kissed my cheek. "Thank you."

"You're welcome," I said. I opened the door and stepped aside as a wave of dry, musty air rushed out. Wrinkling her nose, Kate crossed the room to the window and threw open the sash. She turned and began dropping her dusty clothes to the floor, careless as to where they fell. Her Rubenesque figure emerged slowly, teasingly, tantalizingly: white, pink flesh; her breasts rosy-tipped, proudly full; her hips full and tapering into shapely legs . . .

We tried. Oh yes, we tried to be respectable. I gave up gambling and tried to set up a dental office in the Dodge House in the spare room I had rented. I placed an advertisement in the *Times*:

DENTISTRY

J. H. Holliday, Dentist, very respectfully offers his professional services to the citizens of Dodge City and surrounding country during the summer. Office at room No. 24, Dodge House. Where satisfaction is not given money will be refunded.

And wrote a letter to Shanssey, asking him to send my trunks and dental tools to me. Kate outfitted herself in respectable gowns straight from *Godey's Lady's Book:* two velvet dresses, lace flounces, robes princesse of lace, and assorted other dresses in pongee, velour, piqué, and an evening robe in Swiss muslin below which she wore black lace and net stockings for our private moments. I removed myself from gambling, not even tempting myself by entering a saloon. Wyatt helped out there, taking time from his duties to bring my daily ration of Old Williams to me from the Long Branch Saloon. For a while, I thought the respectability I had sought with Mattie would again be mine. Oh, I had no illusions of the perfect life: I could have had only one of those, and that with Mattie. I knew Kate for what she was, and she knew me. That was undoubtedly the chink in the armor that we drew around our relationship. We knew each other all too well. I knew her for a whore; she knew me for an adherent of Diogenes.

Then I made the mistake of telling her about Mattie.

Hell hath no fury as a woman who learns about other women in a man's life especially if that life had a distinct flavoring of the dolce vita. From the moment Kate learned about what I had been and that my fall from grace was not limited to a character flaw, she was determined that she would share that life with me other than the life we had together. In short, Kate wanted to belong to the society that the members of her Hungarian royal lineage lived. Yet she repeatedly found herself drawn to taking occasional walks on the wild side.

We couldn't blame those who lived north of the Deadline for making us outcasts; we did that ourselves. Or rather Kate did, when the old restlessness set in after days of playing the proper wife waiting at home.

The final downfall, my final slide to oblivion, took place after a most vehement argument when I returned exhausted to our room, trying to strangle tiny coughs without resorting to the whiskey. At last I gave in and took a tumbler of whiskey, slowly sipping it until the spasms in my chest ceased.

"And what," she slowly asked, "do you think I should be doing while you sit in your easy chair sipping your whiskey?" Bright lights sparkled dangerously in her eyes. I glanced involuntarily at the bottle of whiskey, wondering if the level was the same as I had left it. She caught my glance and straightened, stabbing her hands onto her hips and arching her back, thrusting her breasts at me.

"I haven't touched your precious supply," she snapped.

"I didn't think you had," I said, lying lamely. I took another sip and rubbed my eyes tiredly. My back ached and tiredness had long swept over me, leaving me drained and empty. My chest felt heavy, making it an effort to breathe.

"You're a liar!" she snapped. "I saw you look at the bottle."

"Then I'm a liar," I said wearily. "Please, Kate, let's not have this tonight."

"Have what?" she said scornfully. "We haven't had anything since you opened your practice. Not," she added with a vengeance, "that I see you having that many patients."

"I thought that's what you wanted," I said, feeling a tiny spot of anger begin to glow deep inside. "Respectability. You know, that thing that has eluded you so far in your travels through the fleshpots of the West."

"Oh no! Not that plantation-and-wisteria crap! You're no different than me, Doc, for all your plantation talk! Look at you, sucking on that whiskey bottle like it was a milch cow's teat! Your family would be proud to know you!" she sneered.

The hot spot within me glowed and burst into flame. I rose and took two quick steps to her side, striking her hard across the face with the flat of my hand. She staggered backwards, her hand clutching the bright red spot that flamed in her cheek. She stared at me for a long moment, then crossed to the washbasin, took a towel from the rack beside the stand, dipped it into the ewer standing beside the bowl, and held it close against the welt bulging beneath her eye, staunching the swelling. Her gray eyes stared emptily through the mirror to me. I felt their emptiness in my soul and immediately regretted striking her.

"I'm sorry," I said, shame shunting through me.

She laughed, the sound brittle in the room. Her eyes shone with diamond hardness. "Why? Isn't that what whores are for? Besides, that's the first time you've paid attention to me in weeks."

She stared hard. Then she laughed again and crossed to the door, picking a shawl off a chair and draping it around her shoulders over her green velvet dress as she left. The gold tassels around the lampshade danced from the impact of the door slamming hard behind her. I sighed and finished the glass of whiskey, pouring another from the bottle on the side table. I returned to my chair, pausing to pick up a copy of Eliot's *The Mill on the Floss*. I raised the wick on the lamp and relaxed back into the deeply cushioned walnut chair. She would return in a few hours, I told myself as I opened the book and began to read.

June bugs bumped the light shade and fell onto their backs, squirming to right themselves. A gunshot echoed down the street followed by a cowboy's rebel yell. Dimly, I heard the sound of a piano hammering out "The Flying Trapeze," the piano player trying to improvise a bass rhythm. I took out my watch and opened it, glancing at the time: nearly ten. I pressed the repeater and listened as "Opus No. 1 in B-Flat Minor" tinkled, the notes lonely in the room. Kate had been gone four hours. Enough time to walk the entire length and breadth of Dodge City five times easily. I sighed, marked my place in my book, and rose. I crossed to the wardrobe where I kept my gun harness and slipped into it, checking the loads in both revolvers before seating them. I hesitated, then took Belle's gift from a shelf: my silver flask and matchng cup. I dropped them into my pocket, took my hat, and left, closing the door softly behind me. I stood for a long moment, staring at the raw wooden planks. It seemed as if a part of my life remained behind that door. I wondered if I could ever open it again.

I turned right on Front Street as I emerged from the Dodge House, passing Mueller and Straeter's boot shop, Andy Johnson's saloon, and C. M. Hoover's liquor dealership. But I didn't find Kate. I crossed First Street and walked slowly past Koch and Kolly's barbershop, Beatty and Kelley's restaurant, and the Alhambra saloon. I paused for a moment to look at the gun display in Zimmerman's store window and turned, pausing, wondering where Kate had gone. I glanced down at the Long Branch Saloon. I hesitated, then suddenly grew angry at her temper tantrum. I stepped down off the boardwalk and crossed over to the saloon, pushing the doors open gently and pausing before entering. Kate wasn't there. I pushed past a cowboy clumsily dancing with a tired-looking saloon girl with hennaed hair.

The bar was handsome, with attractive hanging lamps, a large plate-glass mirror, and green felt-covered gambling tables scattered in the back past the scarred upright piano. I motioned to the bartender, who smiled at me like an old friend.

"Old Williams?" I asked.

He raised an eyebrow. "Ain't bar whiskey," he said amiably, then reached to the shelf behind the bar and removed a bottle, spinning a clean, sparkling glass in front of me. He poured deftly, then stepped back and watched as I lifted the glass, sampling. I nodded, and he beamed, capping the bottle and replacing it.

"A discerning drinker," he said. He raised his eyes and nodded at someone in the back. I turned and watched as a small, intelligent-looking man with a neat mustache and carefully combed hair rose from a table and walked on well-polished half-boots up to me. He wore a long-tailed coat, and a small diamond ring flashed from the pinky of his left hand. A pearl stickpin had been precisely centered in his tie.

"My name is Luke Short," he said, extending a well-manicured hand. "We are just beginning a gentleman's game in the back. Would you care to join us, Mr. . . . ?"

"Holliday. Doctor John Henry Holliday," I said, taking his hand. His palm was soft, but I could feel the strength held in check beneath the softness.

"The dentist?" I nodded. He smiled, his teeth flashing whitely at me. "We would be honored, sir."

I glanced at the door and again at the room. I knew then that Kate was gone and what we had tried to build, what we had tried to change in our lives, was gone as well. I felt the recklessness building up inside. I had tried to keep it in check, had tried to be what Mother had wanted for me, what Father had wanted when he sent me north to Philadelphia to dental school. But the gods had ruled otherwise. My fate had already been decided, but my destiny was still my own. I could walk away from Short's offer and return to my hotel room and my books and quiet nights filled with pain and sips of whiskey and loneliness, bleak loneliness, living in the silence of the night until the final hemorrhage when I would drown in my own blood and sputum. Or I could spend the rest of the time I had left surrounded by cheap thrills and the moving vibrance of life.

"Why not?" I said. I reached in my pocket and removed my flask and silver cup. I poured the whiskey from my glass into the cup and placed the glass back on the bar. I handed the flask to the bartender.

"Fill that with Old Williams, please, and bring it to the table in back," I said. He took it from my fingers, nodded, and turned back to the shelf, busying himself.

"I'm at your service, sir," I said to Short. He nodded and turned, leading me back to the table.

And so my hypocrisy ended as I pulled out the empty chair at the table and slid onto it, my fingers lightly brushing the green felt, feeling the familiar nap. At the piano, a young woman, her face heavily caked with pancake makeup to hide the wrinkles that would make her look forty if she were to appear honest before the world, broke into a local favorite:

> ". . . In gambling hells de-laying . . .
> ten thou-sand cattle stray-ing . . ."

I smiled at the others around the table and pulled a deck of cards to me, slitting the seal with my thumbnail.

"The name of the game, gentlemen, is poker," I said. I fanned the cards out on the table, slipping the jokers from the deck and tossing them aside.

So it began again. My dental business, such as it was, died an ignoble death in room 24, and I moved from my rooms at the Dodge House to a little hotel *du dive* in Tin Pot Alley, a small, one-room shanty between Second and Third Streets with an attached lean-to kitchen and outhouse a discreet distance behind. When Kate visited, she cleaned with a vengeance and she returned frequently enough that I had no need for a housekeeper. Meanwhile, I spent my evenings in saloons, away from the solitary darkness in which my demon flourished. My fortunes rose and fell but mainly flourished as Dodge waited for the summer and fall trail herds to make their way up from Texas and New Mexico and cross the ford at the Arkansas River, five miles west. The end of the depression that had haunted 1874 and '75 was almost in sight with the burgeoning demand for beef in the East. Wyatt occasionally settled in with a hand or two at my table, but Ed Masterson, the city marshal, and his brother Bat, did not. Although I got along well enough with Ed, Bat was a bit aloof, having little to do with me. I sensed that he was a bit of a phony, with his derby and Havana cigars and the affectation of his gold-headed cane.

The trail herds came, and with them came the cowboys who enjoyed little more than "treeing" a town. Jack Wagner and Alf Walker murdered Ed Masterson. The town tried to get Wyatt to take the job, but Wyatt was enjoying a fantastic run of luck at the faro table and turned down the offer. Charley Bassett took the post and, after much pressure, Wyatt agreed to be his assistant as long as the job didn't cut too much into his turn at the tables. As for Kate, well, she made the rounds when the mood struck her, returning when sated, apologizing, trying again for respectability. I always took her back. I owed her a lot. Kate and Wyatt—a matter of honor.

"John Henry Holliday!"

I turned toward the voice, slipping sideways to my right to present my left to the speaker, my hand slipping the button on my gray frock coat, my fingers lightly touching the ivory handle of the Colt .45. I relaxed as I recognized the green-and-ivory-checkered suit, the bowler cocked jauntily over one eye, spat-covered feet spread wide.

"Eddie Foy!" I exclaimed. He advanced toward me in his swaggering Fifth Avenue strut, holding out his hand. "What are you doing in Dodge?"

He took my hand, enthusiastically shaking it. "Well, my

good man, I am appearing at the Comique," he said, nodding down the street at the theatre cum saloon, dance hall, and gambling house. "I trust that you will be in attendance?"

"Of course," I said. I withdrew my hand. "And Belle? What do you hear about Belle?"

"She's back on the circuit," he said, looking away.

"Still doing Mazeppa?"

"On occasion."

"What's the matter?" I asked.

"I don't know what you mean," he said defensively, trying to meet my eyes.

"Sure you do," I answered. "Something's wrong?"

He shook his head, sighing. "Well, John, she's left that worthless husband of hers, but now she's with another equally as worthless. The last I heard from her, she was down in Texas."

"She never did have luck with her men, did she?" I asked.

"I wouldn't say that, John," he said, placing a hand affectionately on my shoulder. "You did all right by her. And she knows it. You were just . . ."

"Consumptive?" I asked.

A faint red touched his cheeks past his sweeping mustache. "No, not that. As strange as it may sound, there is honor in Belle. Oh, she may flirt and . . . but her word is her word. The vow is sacred if the act isn't. Such an attitude lifts one from the dregs of society who believe there is nothing sacred, including their own souls."

I laughed. "Eddie, you do have a way with words even if your logic is faulty."

"It isn't my logic," he said smugly. "It's Belle's. I am simply a purveyor of words. I lend thought to action."

"And justification where none is needed," I said.

"Forgive me," he said soberly. "I thought that you and Belle . . ." He delicately let his voice trail off, implying only what I chose to think instead of being didactic.

"Only friends," I finished. "Perhaps there could have been more had the time been different, but it wasn't."

"And now you play the part of the stoic," he said. "It is not a part that you play well. It's not a part that anyone plays well. It is a part that one plays only when one is thrust into it."

"As I have been," I said. "But enough of this street-walk philosophy. I trust that there are a few seats left?"

He drew himself up proudly, looking down scornfully in imitation of Edwin Booth. "Eddie plays to full houses."

"Ah yes. Booth is quite a talent," I said. "What a disappointment that must be for the rest of you."

He laughed and patted my arm. "I've missed your wit, John. Or what passes for wit. I'll leave word for you to be given the best seats. And after, perhaps we'll be able to share a split?" His nose wrinkled. "I trust that there is something closely resembling civilized fare in this ever-expanding metropolis?"

"I'll see what I can find," I said, taking his hand again in farewell.

He tapped his bowler and continued his strut down the walk, his heels drumming a refrain to the anonymous song in his head.

I sighed and turned, continuing on my way, thoughts of Belle and remembrances of past delights—and the life I once had—again running through my mind, reminding me of mortality.

I do not remember when the first herds hit Dodge; it doesn't matter. Time meant little then, for there were only the cards and money and hand after hand that merged into a blur, that helped me pass the time. Kate disappeared frequently to satisfy her own devils, which constantly worked their will upon her.

I believe it was in August—yes, it was August; I remember the summer had been hot and dry with dust fogging up and drifting into every nook and cranny of every room, sifting even into our food and drink. Whenever a freak thunderstorm roared down upon us, I felt as if my chest would collapse under a tremendous weight and would take to my bed, suffering from hideous spells of malaise and chronic indigestion that prohibited my taking even the most minuscule amounts of whiskey to prevent my hacking cough, which was getting steadily worse. When the siege lifted, I felt empty, a vacuum inside.

At night, the voices of ancient warriors spoke to me from the dust beneath my shack: chanting ancient spells, singing ancient songs, wooing ancient maidens, teaching ancient lore. A long-dead world and a world that was rapidly disappearing came through the shadows to my fevered bedside. Warriors naked save for flowing, many-feathered headdresses rode wild on the backs of horses through visions of blue-green grama grass bending gracefully in the wind like gentle waves across an undulating sea. I heard the ghostly cries of warriors echoing like hollow owl calls across the prairie, ghosts rising through misty fermentation of morning, ghosts of humidity embracing reverberating sunlight that cut through the fractured skein of my dreams, wild-eyed horses, nostrils flaring blood red in the dimness, keening wind drams whipping their manes into wild array, shimmering air lending mirages, specters, then the turbid beat of drums, redolent, making the earth echo with their drum, drum, drumming beat that worked its way into the senses, bouncing off the earth, the sky, tombstone-shaped crags, the Black Hills.

All this visited me in the night when the cold sweat fell upon me, only to be followed by hot flashes of fever when ghostly memories of my New Orleans Kate and Lotte—and Mattie—moved slowly on wisps of fog to me, lying helpless on sweat-soaked sheets. . . .

Where was I?

Oh yes.

Shanghai Pierce, who once offered to pay Nebraska's debt if they would allow him to have the faro concession on trains running across its prairies, brought his trail herds up from Texas and, in his over-bearing and pompous manner, decided that his territory extended up from Texas, across the Nations, and into Dodge. And, in the pompous certainty of people like him, he reckoned himself to be above the law.

Wyatt gently reminded him that he was only mortal.

Pierce had led his men into Dodge, six-guns blazing,

yelling like denizens of Dante's inferno. Wyatt and Bat stopped them at Front Street. Pierce tried to bluff his way through, but Wyatt's greener held him fast until, at last, he turned his horse's head, the silver bridle flashing in the streetlights, and headed back out of Dodge. A couple of herders who had been toasting the end of the trail earlier with a little Who-Hit-John decided that Wyatt and Bat could be intimidated with a few well-placed shots. Wyatt returned fire, wounding one of the cowboys, while the other made good his escape. The wounded man tried to ride out of town but fell just before he reached the bridge. He died after Dr. McCarty amputated his arm.

Wyatt came under attack by several citizens of Dodge who had decided that Wyatt's idea of law enforcement was hurting business in town by keeping the cowboys so well in line that they were drawing their wages and heading over to Wichita or Ellsworth or someplace else. Pierce took advantage of the split feelings about Wyatt to offer a thousand-dollar bounty for Wyatt's head.

One night in the Long Branch, Wyatt was playing poker with a group of citizens who still stepped with awe into the light of Wyatt's flame when a shot rang out in the street. Wyatt sighed, tossed his cards onto the deadwood, and walked unhurriedly from the saloon, settling his coat over his shoulders as he pushed his way through the doors.

"I dunno, Doc," Skunk Curley, one of the players at my game, said. "I think that's a big mistake."

"What is?" I asked. Curley jerked a dirty thumb toward the doorway.

"Him. Going out that way." He tossed five dollars on the pot, calling me. I showed three kings and pulled in the small pot as he disgustedly threw an ace-high away. "Thought you were bluffin'."

"You mean the marshal?" I asked.

"About what?" Curley asked, surprise on his face. He had already dismissed the event from his mind. I shook my head, gathering the cards and sliding them together, stacking them almost self-consciously.

"About Wyatt," I said. "Why do you think he's made a big mistake?"

"Oh that. I heard a bunch of Pierce's men along with Tobe Driskell and Ed Morrison were going to come into Dodge tonight to get him. You know"—Curley explained as I raised an eyebrow at his words, "get 'im"—"They plan on roughing him up and riding him out of town on a rail. Or something like that. He makes a move for his gun, they'll kill him. 'Sides, Driskell and Morrison are ready for that. The marshal and them had some trouble together back a few years ago in Wichita.

"Say," Curley said, his eyes brightening, "you think he'd be that crazy? To draw against a mob that has the drop on 'im?"

I didn't answer as I shuffled a coin back and forth across my knuckles, contemplating the odds. Wyatt wasn't crazy, but I knew he would not compromise his honor for anything or anyone—even if it meant his death.

"You will pardon me for a few minutes, gentlemen?" I said, suddenly making up my mind. I motioned for the bouncer and indicated my winnings. I stood while he came and dutifully gathered them, taking them to the bar for holding until I returned.

"I guess we can all use a break," Curley said, rising. He glanced over at the free lunch counter containing Limburger and Swiss cheese, pickled herring and caviar, liverwurst and rye bread and crackers. The others made faces and rose, following.

I settled my pistols comfortably in their holsters and made my way toward the doors. I caught up short just before pushing my way through the doors. Wyatt stood facing ten or twelve cowboys. One held a blacksnake—I recognized Ed Morrison—another a coil of rope. Two others held pistols on Wyatt, taunting him as the others grinned their anticipated pleasure.

"Well, Earp," the bearded one in dusty clothes and stained chaps said. I recognized Tobe Driskell. Morrison stood to his left. "We can do this easy or hard, whichever way you want."

"Do it hard," a lean, hard-eyed youth with one of the pistols on Driskell's other side said. "I ain't killed no one since breakfast."

"You ain't killed no one no how," Driskell, a grizzled veteran of several cattle drives, said, holding his pistol steadily on Wyatt.

"Don't mean I won't kill him," the young one taunted. "Come on, hotshot. I've heard you were good against drunks and others who turned their backs on you. Let's see you jerk that hogleg now."

Morrison snapped his whip at Wyatt's foot, popping the dust up onto the toe of his polished boot. "Yer choice, gunny. What's it gonna be? Come on, you white-livered northern son of a bitch! Yer such a fighter, here's yer chance to do some more!"

I stepped out through the doors, slipping the Colt .45 from its holster. I held it negligently, pointing it in the general direction of the two pistol-bearers but making sure the others knew they were included in its watchful eye.

"Evening, Wyatt," I drawled. I coughed and spat a pink-tinged gobbet of sputum into the dust at their feet.

The cowboys stiffened, half turning in my direction.

"This is no concern of yours, Holliday," the one with the rope warned. "It's only him we want."

"Shit, if that lunger wants to be a part of this, I reckon we can accommodate him," the younger one gloated. He started to lift his pistol toward me. I thumbed back the hammer and put a bullet into his belly. The charge knocked him flat on his back, his pistol spinning from his hand.

The red rage fell hard over me, a red mist spreading before my eyes to encircle the group of cowboys. The old recklessness moved upon me as an older cowboy who had stood behind the young man tried to jerk his pistol from its holster. I felt my lips stretching into a grin as I pulled the Lightning from its holster and put a bullet into the knee of the older man, crippling him. He screamed and dropped his pistol, falling to his side, hugging his knee. The crowd fell into shocked silence.

"Any more of you cow-swyving sons a bitches want to buy into this?" I demanded softly, feeling the craziness moving upon me. Wyatt jerked his Smith & Wesson American from its holster and stepped forward, slamming it against Morrison's brainpan. He folded and fell as if poleaxed to the ground.

"The rest of you unbuckle your gun belts and let them fall to the ground," he said quietly. His eyes glinted dangerously. "Now," he added as a few in the back shuffled undecidedly. He cocked his pistol. "You first, Driskell."

Slowly, one by one, gunbelts fell into the dust at their feet. When the last pistol raised a puff of dust, he motioned with his pistol. "Down to the jail. All of you."

"On the other hand, Tobe, if you would care to make this a gentleman's game, why, I'm your huckleberry," I said cheerfully.

His eyes locked with mine. Slowly, his hand went to his gun belt. He slipped the leather through the buckle and let it fall behind him into the dust.

"Aw hell," one started to object. I laughed. His eyes jerked toward me, widening.

"To hell or jail. Your choice," I said, the recklessness full upon me. I felt alive, vibrant. Night voices sang to me.

"Anybody else care for some?" Wyatt asked in a quiet, dangerous tone. "Move, if you want."

"By all means, please," I said, sweeping my pistols back and forth across the ground.

Reluctantly, they turned and walked slowly toward the jail. "We'll get you for this, Holliday!" someone yelled from the group. I laughed and slipped my pistols back into their holsters.

"Thanks," Wyatt said shortly, looking up at me.

I touched my hat brim politely. "I owed you one," I said.

"I think this was more than one," he said. "This was quite a few."

"The risk, though, was the same. If caught," I added airily.

He looked strangely at me for a long moment, started to speak, then a tight look came over his face and he reached out a long forefinger and touched the back of my wrist. It was a gesture of intimacy, and for one eerie moment, I felt a kinship with him that far transcended the bounds of brotherly ties. A lump formed in my throat. His eyes flickered away, toward the cowboys marching desolately down the street. He nodded without looking at me and slipped the American back into its holster at the back of his hip and, turning, walked after them.

A deep satisfaction suddenly filled the black emptiness inside me, and I felt a sense of belonging sweep over me, a satisfaction of being once again among the living. I watched until he disappeared into the jail.

I turned and walked away from the saloon and away from Front Street. Away from Dodge, for that matter, making my way down to the banks of the Arkansas River, where I found a patch of willows and, disdaining the damp ground, sat within the clump of willows, staring at the gray surface of the water, stark moonlight glinting off its leaden waters slowly flowing to the sea. An owl swooped silently overhead, its shadow flickering over the trembling surface of the waters as its yellow eyes stabbed through the darkness looking for its supper.

I stayed there for hours, staring at the surface of the waters, thinking over the years since I had left Georgia, had left Mattie.

Mattie.

I tried to bring her face to mind, but the picture I held within me blurred around the edges.

Later, I rose stiffly from the cold ground and pushed my way through the damp, silvery-bottomed leaves of the willows to the curling, brown grass of the banks. Lights still winked at the dark in Dodge as I made my way over the dry clods of prairie earth to the town.

A drunken, painted lady of the evening shrieked with delight as she and her equally drunk customer staggered out of a saloon. Her breasts suddenly leaped free from her dress, and she laughed and pointed to them as the lips of her customer dipped eagerly to the taut nipples standing tightly from her dark areolae.

But tonight, I did not feel the simmering anger that usually burned inside the emptiness inside me when Kate was gone and Mattie's memory had worked its way to the back of my memory and I found myself alone.

The next day I was a celebrity. I read the account of my exploits in the Dodge City *Times* as I ate breakfast, warming my coffee with a nudge of Old Williams as I worked half-heartedly at a steak smothered with eggs. Ben Haskill, the *Times* reporter, portrayed me as Galahad, the dashing and daring Holliday. But even though I was a hero, I was still an undesirable in his eyes, my lips "spewing curses as he swung through the door with the bartender's greener belligerently thrust out like Galahad's lance at the black knights threatening our Dodge City's Arthur."

I laughed at the picture, then sobered and studied the picture of myself as others saw me. Ruefully, I recognized that I was being made into Hagen, not Galahad. I was the black knight whose momentary gesture of goodwill did not hide the blackness of his heart, the anarchy of his spirit, the absence of his soul. I felt alone, empty, the object of fear and loathing.

I looked around the dining room, realizing that I sat alone in the corner, the other diners sitting as far from me as possible. Even Ella, my waitress, watched from the other side of the room. Loneliness swept over me, and I pushed my breakfast away half-eaten and picked up my coffee, sipping it. I thought about Kate, but she had been gone for two days, since our last fight. Probably held up somewhere with a young, healthy cowboy who had attracted her passing fancy.

I drained my coffee and reached inside my pocket and removed Belle's flask. I filled half my cup and lifted it to my lips, bracing myself for the first bite. Someone snaked the chair out from the table across from me and sat. My fingers reached automatically for the pistol on my left hip, then relaxed.

"And how is our young Lochinvar this morning?" Eddie Foy said, beaming brightly. He wore a houndstooth suit of green and brown, his hair heavily pomaded and slicked back, large mustaches dramatically curled. He motioned toward Ella and crooked his finger.

"Bad night," I said, taking a large swallow of the whiskey. I let it slide down my throat in installments, then took another sip, swishing it around in my mouth to clean my teeth.

He leaned back as Ella set a cup of coffee in front of him. He tasted the coffee, nodded, and placed the cup back in front of him. "Yes, I read about it in the paper." He closed his eyes and recited from memory: "Snarling with rage, the gunman 'Doc' Holliday stormed through the doors of the Long Branch Saloon preceded by the 'greener' shotgun that he had taken from behind the bar. Less than eloquent phrases dripped from his thin lips as he leveled the shotgun at the cowboys who had accosted Marshal Earp en masse and were threatening to lynch him for shooting one of their own."

He shook his head. "Quite a colorful picture. 'Less than eloquent phrases,' John? Come, now. Such behavior is quite demeaning to a gentleman, don't you think?"

"Not today, Eddie," I said wearily, shutting my eyes and rubbing them.

"I'm sorry," he said quickly. "That wasn't the bad part of the night, I take it?"

I shook my head and took another sip of the whiskey. "No. The arms of Morpheus did not welcome me into salubrious slumber, I am afraid."

He laughed. "Now that is the John I remember! So, what is bothering you?"

I shrugged. "My curse. We are all children of fate, servants to the gods who play their games with us. We only pretend to be sophisticates who direct our own destinies."

"You need to go to Colorado," he said softly, his eyes intent upon mine. "There's a place in the mountains."

"So I hear," I said. "But that's not for me. I prefer to defy the gods."

"Could be a short life," he answered. I laughed.

"If I'm lucky. I prefer being Achilles to Methuselah," I answered, toasting him mockingly with my cup and draining the contents. I poured another whiskey. "Our sainted biblical friend may have lived a long life, but I believe it must have been a rather boring one as well. One can make love only so many times and ways, experience only so many dishes, before everything becomes passé. I do not intend going to my grave with my tastes stultified or eroded. Familiarity breeds contempt, you know. Besides, the gesture is everything. The gesture."

"Gesture?" A puzzled look moved slowly behind his level gaze. I grinned.

"Oh yes, the gesture," I said softly. "One must live life with a certain panache, carrying with him his honor in his deeds, not the feathered plumage of his dress."

"Wasn't there a fellow like that in a book long ago? Something about windmills?" Eddie asked, his eyes twinkling.

"Ah, yes. Don Quixote. A fellow sophisticate who determined that honor was missing in his world and went out in search of it, carrying a rusty sword and broken lance with which to tilt at the world of unbelievers. *My* sword and lance, however, are not blunted or rusted," I said, touching the ivory handles of my pistols.

"Very dramatic," Eddie said slowly. "Quite melodramatic, in fact. And the critics accuse me of overacting when I try something serious. Tch, tch. You were born for the stage, John Holliday. The stage is your medium, not the dusty plains and trails of the West. Although," he added, "you are quite good within its limitations. I can understand your willingness to thrust your life recklessly in the way of the denizens, rescuing the fair damsels and all that."

"I am afraid that my followers are not that popular," I said dryly. "In fact, I believe that I am alone among them."

"Nonsense," he said, taking a sip of his coffee and wincing. I offered him the flask. He shook his head. "Egad, if I had your sickness I do not think that I could bear it. You are quite a brave man, John, to cast yourself upon a society that looks upon someone like you as leprous. I am surprised that some towns don't make you wear your own shroud and stumble through town, ringing a bell and crying, 'Beware! Beware!' I can understand you and I admire you for it."

"Then you are the first," I answered curtly, looking around the room as anger coursed through me. "Do you know what I see when I look at the world?" He shook his head. "A world peopled by hypocrites enjoying themselves without thinking about the end. Consequently, they are never prepared and greet death like . . ."

"Like," he prompted gently.

"A tyrant," I answered.

"And you don't?"

"No, it's an adversary, but not a tyrant. Besides," I added, tasting the whiskey, "I am well accustomed to his presence. He's an old friend instead of the recent acquaintance others will make of him. We have made a pact, and I thoroughly intend to honor my part of it, and," I added, "I have it on good authority that he will honor his as well. But I do not intend on making it easy for him, either. My problem is that I am afraid that the times will end before my time does. I do believe that civilization is beginning to rear its ugly head. When it finally grasps the ambience of Dodge, then people like me will become dinosaurs, a whimsical part of the not-so-romantic near past that they would just as soon forget in the spirit of their newly found sophistication."

"You have a point," Eddie said, finishing his coffee. "As the railhead pushes farther and farther west, the people here will be demanding finer and finer refinements to their newly acquired Eden. As rapidly as it began, I am afraid that the West, despite its romantic attractions, is dying a quick death."

"As am I," I said. I could not keep the bitterness out of my voice although I tried. I did not want self-pity or pity of any kind. For some reason, however, I seemed to draw pity from people like a dowsing rod.

His eyes softened and looked sadly into mine. "Yes, John. And people like you will not be remembered for what you have done, but only the nature of your doing. You will achieve immortality, my friend, but it will not be the immortality sainted by poets. Yours will be the product of dime-hackers who will paint you as that"—he reached across and tapped the *Times* with a well-manicured fingernail—"has painted you: daubed with streaks of red."

"Ah yes. Who could forget that hour? One of my finest moments, I believe," I said. I took another sip of whiskey, debated on refilling my cup, then decided against it.

"Well, I must go," he said, rising. "We have a rehearsal for a new number tonight. 'Out of Work.' Will you be there this evening?"

"Why not?" I said, shrugging expansively. "My notorious pursuit of the tiger can wait one night. Or two or three. I am not one pressed for time." I smiled sourly.

He tilted his hat forward, splayed his feet on the floor, arched his back and, thrusting his thumbs into the pockets of his vest, began declaiming,

> "The Moving Finger writes; and having writ
> Moves on: not all your Piety nor Wit
> Shall lure it back to cancel half a Line,
> Nor all your Tears wash out a Word of it."

I laughed and leaned back in my chair.

> "Let fame, that all hunt after in their lives,
> Live registered upon our brazen tombs,
> And then grace us in the disgrace of death;
> When, spite of cormorant devouring Time,
> The endeavor of this present breath may buy
> That honor which shall bate his scythe's keen edge,
> And make us heirs of all eternity."

He made an exaggerated bow and, turning, strutted from the dining room. I glanced around: the others were watching curiously, but when my eyes caught theirs, they quickly turned away and pretended to be busy with their meals. I laughed and rose, tossing a dollar on the table to pay for my meal, and left.

The September sun was bright, but there was a coolness to the air that suggested Indian summer. I breathed deeply and decided to walk along the river for a brief constitutional. I turned left and rapidly made my way to the bridge. A large cottonwood stood downriver, its leaves beginning to turn golden with the change of seasons. I walked toward it, listening to the birds singing in the willows.

A gun cracked. I flinched and twisted to my left, turning my right side in the direction of the gunshot. Another came. Cautiously, I made my way to the cottonwood and snuggled next to it, carefully sliding my head around the corner.

Wyatt stood, relaxed, his arms dangling casually at his side. Suddenly his right arm lifted and snapped forward, the American firing as it came level with his chin. A tin can leaped in the air twenty feet in front of him. He let it fall, then thumbed the hammer, spraying the can with dirt.

"Tch, tch." I said, sliding around the cottonwood. He whirled, the pistol steady in his hand, the bore straight at me. I nodded down at the tin can. "Now if that had been Driskell or Morrison, you might not have had a chance for a second shot."

"Think you can do better?" he said, turning back to the can. He slid the pistol back into its holster.

"I don't know. Pretty small target," I said, stepping up next to him. I caught the movement of his arm out of the corner of my eye and drew and fired in one smooth motion. My bullet was a fraction sooner, kicking the can away from his bullet. I fired again, catching it in midair and spinning it off into the river.

"Not bad. For a gambler," he added grudgingly.

I laughed and pointed with the pistol at the ground where the can had once stood. "Not very good for a lawman. Especially one whose life seems to suddenly be worth a thousand dollars."

"You thinking about collecting, Doc?" he asked, a small smile lifting the corners of his lips.

"Not me," I said. "You might get lucky."

"Yeah, I can see where that might worry you," he said. "Doc, about last night . . ."

"Forget it," I said, slipping the Colt back into its holster.

"Just wanted to say I'm grateful," Wyatt said.

"Nonsense," I said generously. I could afford to be generous; my feats had already been well recorded by a rather romantically inclined member of the fourth estate, the facts well hidden, but the heroism duly noted. "Those waddies would have backed down once you unlimbered that American of yours."

He shook his head. "No, you're wrong, Doc. They would have killed me; it was in their nature. I could see it in their eyes. Like a cat worrying a mouse: teasing it because it knows it can kill it any moment it chooses. That's the way they were playing with me before you came through the saloon doors. I want you to know that I appreciate that, Doc. I really do."

"Well," I said, feeling a bit embarrassed. "Let's not get maudlin about it, shall we, Wyatt?"

He grunted, nodded at me, tugged the brim of his hat lower over the tanned span of his forehead, and walked away. I felt less alone for the first time in years. A rosy feeling began to burn in the pit of my stomach.

I had no few challengers willing to wager their lives to destroy my honor. Yes, even that very night when I attended Eddie's show I ran afoul of one of those gunnies eager to add my name to the two notches he had already carved in the walnut handle of his pistol.

A goodly crowd had filled the theatre, or what passed for a theatre, when I entered and made my way to the box that Eddie had set aside for me. Kate and I had made one of our temporary peaces, and she followed, her hand upon my arm, regal and proper, wearing one of the powder blue dresses that we had purchased when we first came to Dodge City, one that displayed the creamy white of her deep bosom, thrusting out proudly in front of her, a formidable bulwark brazenly challenging all to breech its defenses.

A narrow-hipped cowboy, blond hair cascading in loose curls around his gaunt cheeks, stepped in front of us, blocking our path. He leaned forward, looking boldly into the valley between Kate's breasts.

"Now, there is a wonder through which the Brazos could

flow," he said. He glanced up at her, a slow smile spreading over his thin lips. "And if you're not a passel of woman who could give a man a ride, I'm a poor judge."

Bright lights began to dance in her eyes as she leaned back to look coolly at him. I recognized the signs as twin spots of color began to flow down from her high cheeks.

"You will pardon my rudeness, cowboy, but the show is about to start," I said, stepping between them. I took Kate's arm, steering her around away from him.

He glanced at me and his lips twisted in a derisive smile. Deliberately, he stepped forward, bumping me with his shoulder. I stepped back away from Kate, swinging my coat open and away from my pistol.

"Please do not crowd my revolver lest its bite prove fatal," I said. His eyes narrowed, then he laughed. I felt my lips tug into a smile, but from the silence of the crowd watching, I knew it was a smile that none would care to see in the darkness of their dreams.

"Big words for a skinny runt," he drawled, his hand hovering above the walnut handle of his pistol holstered low at his side. His fingers twitched. I tapped the handle of my pistol and grinned at him.

"I have my equalizer, sir," I said, matching his drawl with my own. "But this is not the time nor the place."

His eyes flickered around the room. "What's wrong with it?"

"One simply does not interrupt the curtain," I said. "It is not civilized."

"I've never been accused of that," he said, looking around at his friends, who dutifully laughed at him.

"That, I can believe," I answered. "But I'm your huckleberry. I would be pleased to accommodate you in the street, if you insist. Although," I added, nodding at the stage, "I'm afraid that would deprive you of what I anticipate to be an excellent performance."

"Huh?" he said, frowning.

"He means you'll have a hard time seeing anything if you press it," a man said from beside him. "That's Doc Holliday."

His left eyebrow rose a fraction. "I've heard about you," he said. "They say you're one of the fastest men around with a pistol."

"You have the advantage, sir," I said.

"Ben Tully," he said. "Some call me the Kid."

"A rather common sobriquet," I said.

"I'm pretty fast, too," he said, his lips thinning into a wolfish leer.

"Indeed?" I murmured. "Perhaps we can get together after the show and compare our acquaintances."

"What's wrong with right now?" he asked, his fingers twitching with nervous anticipation.

"I never miss the curtain. If I can help it," I added. I removed my watch and opened it. Chopin's notes tinkled in the silence. "And I see that we have barely a minute to reach our seats. Might I suggest that you do so?"

"Sounds like good advice to me," a voice spoke quietly from my shoulder.

"Hello, Wyatt," I said without turning. "Have you come to watch Eddie's new number?"

He ignored my question and moved a step forward, sliding in front of me. I took a quick step to the right to put Tully back in view. "Better give me your pistol, cowboy," he said.

Tully frowned, his eyes flickering toward me. "What about him?" he asked, pointing his chin in my direction. "You gonna take his pistols too?"

"What I do with him is none of your business," Wyatt said quietly. He took another step forward, his eyes cold and gray, intent upon Tully's own. "Now, give me your pistol."

"Not until you take Holliday's," Tully said, trying to take a step backwards. He bumped into the crowd behind him, half turned, and Wyatt took the opportunity, sliding quickly to the cowboy's right and plucking the pistol from its holster.

"Hey!" Tully yelped, his hand slapping at the now-empty holster. "Gimme my iron!"

"After the show," Wyatt said. "Now take your seat before I run you in for disturbing the peace."

"Come on, Billy," one of his friends said, tugging at the

young man's arm. "Yer buckin' a stacked house here. Let it go."

"I'll be seeing you," Tully said sullenly, his face flaming red with anger. He pointed a finger at me. "I'll be seeing you!"

"If you insist," I said, inclining my head mockingly. I took Kate's arm gently above the elbow and nudged her toward the steps leading to our box. I could feel the angry heat of the crowd as Wyatt followed us as we threaded our way through their mass. I paused at the first step and turned. "Will you be joining us, Wyatt?"

"Thanks, Doc," he said, "but I've got rounds to make. Perhaps another time?"

"My pleasure," I said magnanimously.

"Doc, I'm going to have to ask you for your pistol, too," he said, leaning close so his words didn't carry out to the crowd. "It won't look right if I take just that waddy's pistol and let you walk away totin' your own. You see how it is. Good form and fairness."

A quick retort leaped to my lips, but I hesitated, then shrugged and slipped the pistol from its holster, handing it to him. He took it and half turned so that the others could see it, then reached to place it in his coat pocket, concealing his movement with his body as he slipped it through a hole in the pocket of his coat, into his left hand. He nudged it in my belly. I slipped it away and into its holster, pulling the fold of my coat over it to conceal it.

"Thanks, Wyatt," I murmured.

He made a tiny movement with his hand, then shrugged, tipped his hat to Kate, and made his way out of the theatre.

I stepped after Kate to our box. The lights dimmed as we took our places, and the small orchestra whipped into a lively rendition of "The Daring Young Man on the Flying Trapeze." I took Kate's shawl from her and hung it beside my hat on the rack leading into the box and took my place beside her. I took out my silver cup and poured a dollop of whiskey into it from the matching flask. I sipped.

"I hope this is good," Kate whispered. I could barely

understand her words through her thick Hungarian accent. She leaned close, her breath warm against my ear. "I haven't been to a show in a long time, John. Thank you."

"You're welcome," I said. I looked at the stage, remembering the night Dickie and I had abandoned our studies and taken in Belle's show during happier times when hope existed. I finished the whiskey in my cup with a practiced twist of my wrist, reaching automatically for the flask to refill it. Kate's hand came softly onto mine, staying it.

"Please don't, John," she said softly. "That is, unless you need it," she hastily added. I hesitated, listening to the warmth, the lure of her voice, debating. Then her hand came down hard upon my thigh.

"Goddamn it, John! I'm horny, and if you drink too much you'll be worthless in bed!" she complained, her voice bit louder.

I laughed and put the flask and cup back in my coat pockets and leaned back in my chair as Eddie strutted out to center stage with that trademark peculiar stiff-legged gait of his that he used just before breaking into song.

"Oh, he flies through the air with the greatest of ease . . ."

I glanced down into the audience and caught Tully's eyes glaring up at me. I smiled and waggled my fingers at him. Even in the dim light of the theatre I could see his face darken with rage. He turned to the man sitting next to him and whispered into his ear. The man looked up automatically, our eyes meeting. He hastily turned his attention back to the stage.

Strange, I thought. Why would a man deliberately want to start something like that? Then I shrugged and leaned back to enjoy the show as Eddie mugged for the audience and pranced around the stage, slipping into a quick soft-shoe shuffle, the white spats on his shoes a blur that brought a roar of approval from the audience. I tried to concentrate on both the show and Tully and his friends below, but Eddie's stage presence was such that soon I was lost in the show, my foot tapping to familiar tunes sung with a fresh style far eclipsing the whiskey-hoarse voices of the saloon girls who pretended a sophistication that was only a dim memory.

All too soon, Eddie took his final bow, and I led Kate backstage to meet him. Laughter echoed from his dressing room. A young woman nearly spilling from her costume pushed past us, leaving a trace of makeup on the sleeve of my jacket. A fiddle played from somewhere, and it took me a moment to recognize "The Fox and the Hounds." We pushed our way through the crowd of congratulators. Eddie's face lit up when he saw us.

"John!" he exclaimed. He wore a blue brocade dressing jacket with a white silk scarf carelessly knotted around his neck. He grabbed my hand, enthusiastically pumping it. "Did you see the show? What did you think?"

I winced from his grip and gently removed my hand. "Very good. Very good. I liked the new number."

He beamed. "Just as I thought. Well. Let me change, and we'll go to Dog Kelly's place to celebrate. Champagne's on me." A frown line instantly appeared between his eyebrows as he realized what he had just said. But he made little shooing gestures with his hands, pushing everyone out of his dressing room. I draped Kate's shawl around her shoulders while we waited outside his door. The stage manager bumped into us as he passed, muttering imprecations against a Jack-somebody who had left a cigar burning by a bucket of turpentine.

"He seems nice, your friend," Kate ventured. "Have you known him long?"

"A lifetime," I said. In the stage lights she looked vaguely like Belle. I reached into my pocket and removed the flask, opening it.

"Doc," she began, then fell silent, looking away from me. I sipped, waiting. She sighed deeply and turned back, reaching for the flask. "Well, might as well join you. Lot more fun than standing by and watching you get drunk."

I gave her the flask. "I warned you about trying to change me."

"Yeah, but I didn't give up hope. 'Til now," she said, tipping the flask back, sipping. She lowered the flask and gave me a sad look. "I tried, though. You have to give me credit for that, Doc."

"Maybe," I said.

"No maybe about it," she said in a tight voice. "I loved you, you son of a bitch, but you didn't love me back, did you?"

I shrugged and said nothing. I could see where the argument was going: In a few minutes she would storm away from me and begin making the rounds of the saloons below the Deadline. Fortunately, Eddie threw his door open and strutted out in all his glory—tails, gray waistcoat, gray cravat with pearl stickpin, striped pants and gray spats—before Kate and I had passed that moment where I became proper and she became a harridan and we began clawing at each other's spirits.

"Am I suitably attired for our self-indulging soirée?" he asked, preening.

I laughed and reclaimed my flask from Kate, placing it in my pocket. "You look . . ."

"Like a peacock," Kate said. She laughed, and he took her hand, bowing low over it, kissing it. She roared with laughter. "I feel like the Queen. Nobody 'sides Doc here has treated me that way since . . ."

A cloud fell over her face, and she withdrew her hand, turning away.

"Since?" Eddie prompted.

But she shook her head and refused to look at him. Eddie raised his eyebrows at me. I shook my head and stepped forward, taking her arm. She stiffened and pulled away.

"What is it, Kate?" I asked gently. I reached and took her chin, turning her face. Tears trickled through her makeup, leaving black runnels down her high cheeks. She lifted her head away from mine and stepped back, eyes flashing angrily at me.

"I am not a whore!" she said.

"Of course you are," I said without thinking. "We are

both whores, you and I. Yours just happens to be more pleasurable."

A stunned look came over her face. She moved faster than I had thought her capable of, and her hand slapped me across my face, stinging, staggering me with the force of its blow. I reeled, caught myself, and felt the anger beginning to burn and mold itself deep inside. I took a step toward her, but Eddie quickly moved in front of me, placing his hands on my shoulders then quickly jerking them away as he looked into my eyes.

"John!" he exclaimed. "Don't!"

I blinked, pulling myself back from the inner rage beginning to boil up through me. I drew a deep, ragged breath, then another, turning away and fumbling for the flask in my coat pocket. I drank deeply, finishing it, then turned back.

"Go ahead," she taunted, stepping back and posing like a tart with one hand on her hip, her breasts thrust hard toward me. "Go ahead! You sons a bitches are all alike. All of you!"

I swallowed hard past the lump in my throat, feeling the whiskey slowly work the anger away, leaving me at the center of an inner core of warm peace. The world became softened around the edges, stark reality being replaced by a maudlin serenity. I touched my mustache, the imperial I had recently grown, and considered Kate's challenge. I decided I didn't care.

"Kate," I began.

"Go to hell," she snapped, her eyes blazing arrogantly, angrily at me. Tears suddenly glistened in them, and she turned and walked away, pulling her shawl tightly around her shoulders.

"What the hell?" I muttered, turning to Eddie.

He shrugged. "I don't know, John. I don't know. I thought you . . . never mind."

"Never mind what?" I asked.

He looked embarrassed as he turned away, flicking at imaginary dust on the sleeve of his coat. He cleared his throat. "Well, I thought that maybe you . . . and . . . her . . . that is . . . You've changed, John. Changed greatly from

Philadelphia. There's a . . . hardness about you that wasn't there before. A . . . blackness around you . . . shadows . . . Am I making any sense at all?"

"No."

"I was afraid of that." He rubbed his nose with the palm of his hand. "I really do not know what *kind* of relationship you and Miss Elder have together."

I burst out laughing. "No, my friend, we are not of that mind. At least," I added, "I prefer a more 'traditional' role in our relationship. Whatever made you come to that conclusion?"

"Her actions," he said. "But what the hell do I know? I'm a song-and-dance man. Not God. I made a pact with Him long ago: He stays out of theatre and I stay out of creations."

A darkness began to fall over me despite his attempt at humor. I forced myself to grin at him, but I could tell from the sadness that glowed from his spaniel eyes that he knew it for a false grin. I clapped him on the shoulder and turned toward the stage door.

"Come on," I said roughly. "Your audience anxiously awaits your entrance."

"Ah! Come, my friend! One must not be late for one's entrance! It simply is not good form!"

He tucked his arm through mine and began a fast shuffle, forcing me to follow his lead, as we tripped gaily to the door. But gaiety did not touch my soul. I wondered where Kate had gone.

We took our way down Centre Street to Dog Kelly's place, the Alhambra, Eddie nodding and making eloquent bows to those we passed who complimented him on his show. The night was balmy, an Indian summer night, full with a harvest moon that suggested cold winter was not far off. Shadows danced in alleyways from light spilling out saloon windows. A few drunken individuals staggered along the boardwalk, stepping aside, one nearly falling into a watering trough when his heels slipped off the edge of the walk.

We turned into the Alhambra. Eddie paused dramatically inside the door as the saloon broke into applause at his entrance. He beamed at the audience. I slipped off to the side and made my way to the bar, coughing from the thick cigar and cigarette smoke. I motioned at Timmy, the bartender. He grinned and spun a shot glass in front of me, filling it with Old Williams. I paused to cough again while I tossed it down, then motioned to a cocktail glass on the ledge behind him.

"Sitting in for the night, Doc?" he said, filling the glass with the whiskey. I sipped and nodded.

"As good a place as any," I said. I took the glass and headed for the back where Bat Masterson and four men I didn't know were in a game of poker. I paused beside it and grinned at Masterson.

"Got room for another?" I asked.

A look of distaste came over his face and for a moment I thought he was going to refuse, but he shrugged and nodded at a chair across from his left.

"I have no objections if the others don't," he said.

I almost laughed. Masterson and I didn't care for each other. I objected to his dandified mannerisms while he objected to my "excesses," as he called them. But he was a friend of Wyatt's and for that I tolerated him even if at times I couldn't help baiting him. I raised an eyebrow at the others. They exchanged glances then shrugged, and I moved around the table and pulled out the chair, sitting.

"We're playing draw," Masterson said. He shuffled the cards with a quick downward motion, pressing the lips of the cards together, and slid the deck across to me for a cut. I pressed my fingers around the edges of the cards, feeling for trimmed edges, then cut the cards in the middle, placing the top half toward Masterson. He had caught my movement and smiled thinly as he gathered the cards.

"We're running honest here, Holliday," he said, dealing the cards around with a quick flick of his fingers. "There's no need to doubt the cards."

"I beg your pardon, Masterson," I said. "I forgot that I was in the presence of an honest man. One meets so few of them these days that one simply isn't sure anymore. Why, you could be as honest as my Aunt Beulah and I probably would still check the cards. Of course," I added carelessly, picking up my cards and studying them, "my Aunt Beulah was one of the better stackers around. The tricks she could do with those cards would make your heart swell with admiration and just plain burst. Did you by any chance—No, that would be too coincidental, wouldn't it? Where *did* you learn your tricks, anyway?"

He flushed and started to say something, but the man next to me quickly shoved out a dollar, betting. I grinned at Masterson and raised the man five dollars. His eyes dropped back to his cards, studying them as the bet worked its way around to him.

"Give us the call, Eddie!" someone cried.

I twisted my head to watch Eddie grin and leap up onto the bar and begin strutting down its gleaming, mahogany surface. I glanced at Dog Kelly: His face became mottled, and I thought for a moment he was going to choke on his cigar as he watched Eddie's shoes click on the bar's surface, scarring it. The piano player quickly began pounding out "Turkey in the Straw" as the cowboys present grabbed the bar girls and began to dance around the room, swinging them high, each trying to outdo the others by twirling them until their short dresses rode high to their waists. Shrill laughter leaped from the girls' lips as their red and black undergarments and net-stockinged legs were exposed to the room. I froze for a moment as Kate swept by in the arms of the young man who had accosted us earlier at the theatre. She lifted her chin and laughed, but I could tell from the hard planes on her face that she was doing what she was doing to spite me. My stomach tightened with anger and—something, I don't know what. I kept my face immobile and turned my attention away from her and back to Eddie, prancing in pristine pleasure. He rocked back on his heels, tucked his thumbs into the pockets of his waistcoat, and began to chant.

"Here we go with the old chuck wagon
Hind wheel's broke and the axel's draggin'

Meet your honey and pat her on the head.
Do-si-do, folks, do-si-do!"

I laughed, wondering where he had picked up on the chuck
wagon: Philadelphia and New York, even Chicago, were
noticeably short of chuck wagons. Masterson cleared his
throat, saying, "Your bet, Holliday. Ten dollars to you."

I dropped my hand to the table and tossed in twenty dollars, smiling at him. "And another ten."

He frowned as the man on my left threw in his hand. I
turned my attention back to Eddie, thoroughly enjoying
himself, prancing like a barnyard rooster in front of hens
from his place on the bar. I laughed as he did a quick shuffle,
then movement near the piano drew my attention. I swiveled
my head in time to see Tully and his friend leveling a pistol
at me. A satisfied grin stretched across Tully's face as he
stared at me. I threw myself away onto the floor, cursing as I
landed in a litter of mud, manure, old cigars and cigarettes.
Bullets splintered the chair where I had been sitting.
Screams and shouts echoed through the saloon. The crowd
rushed for the exit or else jumped behind the bar or fell flat
on the floor. The next instant, Masterson was on the floor
beside me.

"What the hell?" he swore. "Goddamnit, Holliday!" He
opened his coat, reaching automatically for a pistol, and
swore again when his hand came away empty.

I palmed the Colt from its holster, slipped the Colt Lightning free, and rolled and tossed the Colt Lightning to him.
"You can shoot back if you want to. Careful," I added, "it's
loaded."

He swore again and spun around to his knees, cautiously
raising his head. Bullets struck the table, splattering him with
splinters. He involuntarily ducked, again flattening himself
on the floor. I laughed and came to my knees, bobbed up and
fired twice rapidly, dropping quickly to the floor beside him,
but not before I caught a glimpse of the man beside Tully
slamming against the wall, the pistol flying from his hands as

he grabbed his stomach and fell to his knees. I peered through the legs of the table and chairs: He leaned forward, resting his forehead on the floor, and I knew I had hit him.

"Got mine," I whispered to Masterson. "How you doing?"

"You son of a bitch, Holliday!" he snarled. "What the hell have you dragged me into?"

"Why do you always think it's my fault?" I asked in an injured tone. He popped up, fired twice, and dropped back down.

"Missed," he said disgustedly. He glanced at the pistol. "Damn self-cockers. A thirty-eight at that!" He looked at me from under thick eyebrows. "Well, is it?"

"Yes," I said.

"That's why I always think it's your fault. Because it is." He jerked his head toward the shooter. "On three?"

I nodded.

"Three," he said abruptly. He rolled to the right of the table as I rose and took a quick step to the left. Tully's eyes flickered uncertainly between the two of us. I fired at the same time as Masterson and watched as Tully jerked, bending forward only to have a bullet strike him in the forehead, straightening him. Blood sprayed the wall behind him. He fell to the floor; his legs twitched twice, then lay still.

Masterson rose cautiously to his feet. Together we crossed to the pair. Both were dead. Masterson shook his head in disgust.

"You know you aren't supposed to be carrying guns in the city limits," he said. "I'll have to arrest you."

"Self-defense," I protested. "This cockleburr would have put me down if I wouldn't have been armed. Maybe you, too. And," I said pointedly "where was your pistol?"

He turned beet red. "I'm off duty," he said defensively. "And obeying the law. Which is more than I can say for some people here. Oh, don't worry," he said as I started to protest. "I know it was self-defense. But there's still the fine for carrying pistols in the city limits and a fine for discharging firearms and disturbing the peace."

"How much?" I asked suspiciously.

"The judge usually fines the cowboys twenty dollars. Fifty if they destroy private property."

"I didn't miss," I said, pointing to the holes in the wall beside the piano. "Those are your bullets."

"From your gun. Oh, forget it. Say twenty dollars."

"Take it out of the pot you lost," I said, turning back to the table. The game was broken up, the other players gone. I holstered the Colt and took the Lightning from him, slipping it into place under my left arm.

"Make sure you leave those pistols in your room, Holliday," he said warningly. "By rights I should claim them, but seeing how it's you. . . . What do you mean take it out of the pot? I got three jacks."

"Three kings," I answered.

He reached out and flipped my cards over. "Damn!"

"Oh yes," I said, picking up the pot. I slid a twenty-dollar piece to him. "All magnolia and lilacs."

"Huh?"

"It means you lost," I said. I touched the brim of my hat and turned toward the bar, motioning to Timmy as Wyatt came through the crowd. He glanced at the bodies, then at Masterson.

"What happened, Bat?" he asked quietly.

Bat pointed at the bodies. "Those two came shooting for Holliday. We killed them in self-defense."

"We?" Wyatt said.

"The two of us," Bat said. "With Holliday's guns. I fined him twenty dollars."

"I see," he said. He looked at me. "Did you know them, Doc?"

I took the glass from Timmy and drank before answering. "The one from the theatre," I said. "Called himself Ben Tully. Remember? I figure he was out after a reputation."

"Probably," Wyatt said. His eyes flickered over at Kate, standing at the bar down at the other end, then back to the figures on the floor. "You sure that's all there was to it?"

"Wyatt," I said, putting an injured tone in my voice. "On my word as a southern gentleman." I held my glass out toward Timmy. He hurriedly stepped forward and filled it. I took a large drink and swallowed it in installments.

"You forgot that the South lost the War," he said. He nodded at Kate. "Better take her home, Doc. I'll let you know if we need anything more."

"All right," I said. I finished my drink and placed it on the bar. "I take it that I may keep my weaponry?"

He hesitated, glanced at the crowd, then said, "Since you were acting in the public defense, you may. But leave them in your hotel room from now on."

I smiled and tipped my hat in their direction. "I will be more than happy to accommodate the wishes of the law. By the way, Masterson has already collected my fine. Twenty dollars. I trust that will suffice?"

Wyatt turned and gave Masterson a long look. Masterson turned beet red and said, "I've got it, Wyatt. Just thought that we'd take care of it ahead of time."

Wyatt sighed and turned back to me. "Keep your guns in your room, Doc."

"Lucky I had them this time. Otherwise you might be short one deputy as well as a dissipated gambling man. Besides, you have to justify your salary somehow, don't you?"

"I should be so lucky," he grunted. He waved me away. "Go on, now. We'll clean up here. And don't be doing me any more favors. Leave your guns in your room."

"Yes, massa," I said, drawing out my drawl. I touched the brim of my hat to the two and left the saloon.

A large crowd had gathered outside. I stepped down from the boardwalk and they parted reluctantly for me. I felt the heat of their hatred as I moved through them and a joyful laugh bubbled up inside me.

"That's Holliday," one whispered as I passed. "He's just done for two more cowboys."

"What's he got agin us?"

"Dunno unless it's 'cause he can't keep his woman in line. She's always goin' out huntin' up a cowboy, seems like."

"Must want someone who can stay in the saddle a little

longer 'stead of that lunger," another replied. "Scrawny little runt like that probably ain't got a pecker bigger'n a pea pod."

The crowd broke into laughter at that. I halted and turned to face my detractor. He glanced into my eyes and took a reflex step backward. Then, the muscles tightened in his jawline and he stared defiantly into my eyes. I smiled, but the smile never touched my eyes and the crowd fell silent.

"So," I said softly, "you are the big man with a dick the size of a bull? That makes you a man? Prove it."

His fists balled at his side. His eyes challenged mine from under bushy eyebrows clinging beneath massive scar tissue. "I ain't gotta gun, Holliday. Why don't you take yours off and meet me like a man?"

A grumble of assent went around the crowd. I laughed. "That would really make it fair, wouldn't it? Did you ever give anyone an equal chance?"

"No balls, Holliday?" he sneered. The crowd gasped as I stepped forward and slapped his face. His head jerked back, his hat nearly falling off his head. He flushed and took a step forward, raising his hands, then froze as I leveled the Colt .45 at his nose.

"Come on, you wilted daisy, let's see what size your balls are," I said. The air around me turned bright and lucid, a red haze moving within it. "No?" I spun the .45 forward on my forefinger, catching it with the ball of my thumb and directing it into its holster. In the same movement, I slapped his face again. "Perhaps I can entice you, sir." I backhanded him, catching his nose with my knuckles. His eyes watered and a slight trickle of blood began to slide down to his lips.

"I told you, I don't have a gun," he said, the words nearly strangling in his throat. I laughed again and drew the Lightning from beneath my arm, flipped it and caught it by the barrel, extending it to him.

"That's sure no problem, buttercup," I said. "I have two: one for you and one for me. Take it."

His eyes jerked from mine to the pistol and back. I could see how badly he wanted to reach for it. His eyes glittered with hatred, the skin of his face pulling back hard against high cheekbones, making his face skeletal in the night. His lips drew into a thin line.

"No?" I said mockingly. "Not enough of a chance? Why, you're no daisy, that's for sure."

I flipped the Lightning, catching it by its grip, and slid it back into its holster. I gave him a contemptuous look and said, "Get a pair of ballocks of your own before you accuse your betters of having none."

I deliberately turned my back on him and faced the crowd. I took a step forward: they didn't move. Their faces were frozen in anger. Laughter bubbled up inside me. I let it explode into the night air, feeling the spirit of Lucifer moving upon me.

"All right," I said. I drew both pistols, cocking the .45. "Let's get on with it. Who's first?"

"He can't git us all," someone shouted from the back of the crowd.

"That's for sure," I agreed. "I can't get all of you. But I'll take twelve of you with me. Question is, which twelve will it be?"

Uncertainty spread over the faces of those in front as they stared into the bores of my pistols. The cowboys behind moved their feet restlessly, beginning to push the front line forward.

"And those he don't get, we will," a voice called from the boardwalk behind me. I took a quick look: Wyatt stood there with his American leveled at them, Masterson at his side with a greener he had taken from behind the bar.

"I didn't think you cared," I said to Masterson. A tight grin spread over his face.

"You've got some of my money," he said. "I want a chance to get it back."

"Good a reason as any," I said gaily. I turned back to the crowd. "Well? What's it going to be, boys? The world's your oyster: Step up and collect your pearls or back off."

"Cut it out, Doc," Wyatt said softly, but there was a hint of steel in his voice that cut through the air around us. "Break it up. All of you, or I'll run you in for distrubing the peace."

They stared sullenly up at him, holding their places defiantly long enough to show him that they weren't afraid of his threat, then, like petulant children, they slowly moved away, opening a lane for me. I holstered my pistols and turned back to Wyatt and Masterson.

"Gentlemen," I said, tipping my hat to them. "I trust you'll have a good night."

"We will as soon as we get you tucked in," Wyatt said, stepping down off the boardwalk. Masterson nodded and lowered the hammers of the greener before turning back inside the saloon.

"I thought I told you not to cause any more trouble," Wyatt said, falling in beside me.

"Now, Wyatt, it was a gentleman's honor that was being sullied by this riffraff. Surely you wouldn't want me to let that go by," I said.

"Yes, I would, if it would keep the peace," he said bluntly. "You think that was worth a man's life?"

"Life is a highly overrated commodity," I said, smoothing my mustache. "It is only a temporary inconvenience at best."

"Some may not think that way, Doc. Some people may have a fondness for what they've got."

"Then they're fools," I said curtly.

He shook his head and placed his hand on my shoulder. "Doc, the whole world ain't hell," he admonished.

"Isn't it?" I muttered, shrugging his hand free. I coughed. "Obviously, we live in different worlds. Mine has no meaning at all, since the world is devoid of reason."

He sighed. "Have it as you would, Doc. But do me a favor, will you? No more killings in Dodge. There's a lot of feeling against you."

"By the better half?" I asked sardonically. He looked away. I looked into the black hole deep inside me, feeling the emptiness that I felt all too often in the middle of the night, awakening cold and perspiring, the sheets wrapped damply around my body like winding sheets, my mouth musty with the taste of the grave in it.

"I told you, Wyatt, that it wouldn't be long before the good people of Dodge would feel the first nudgings of sophistication," I said softly. "Remember?" I reached out and patted his shoulder. "Don't let it bother you, Wyatt. I won't be around much longer." He looked up at me, frowning.

"Doc," he began, then fell quiet and shook his head. His hand pressed my arm for a second, then he turned and stepped down off the boardwalk into the dust of the street. He looked back up at me. "I'm about out of options," he said.

"I know," I answered quietly. "I know."

He nodded and left. I coughed again and looked up at the star-filled night, wondering briefly which were my own crossed stars of destiny.

Kate was waiting in our small house when I opened the door and stepped inside. The light from a single lantern formed a golden nimbus around her. She stared at me for a long moment, then looked down at her hands clasped in the folds of her dress. I sighed and removed my hat, hanging it on a peg beside the door. I crossed to a cupboard, opened it, and removed a bottle of Old Williams. I picked up a pair of glasses and carried them back to the table.

"I'm sorry, Doc," she said lowly. I placed a glass in front of her, tipped the bottle and filled the glass half full. I repeated the gesture with mine and drank. She left hers untouched on the table.

"I know," I said. "We are all sorry for what we do to each other. But that doesn't keep us from doing what hurts others, does it?"

"You don't understand, Doc," she said.

"I think I do," I said, pouring another glass. A slight cough bubbled up inside. I suppressed it with a swallow of the whiskey. "We give meaning to our life by hurting the one we love. That's called human nature, darling."

She shook her head, staring into the glow of the lantern, her eyes glazing as if she were hypnotized. Her face looked waxen. "My father's name was Dr. Michael Haroney. I was born in the Pest section of Budapest, Hungary, and named after my mother. She was a Baldizar. That means nothing to you, but in Hungary, that name belongs to royalty."

"Please. It's a little late for theatricals, Kate. I don't mind playing stage games with you, but not tonight. This night belongs to . . . the devil," I said, finishing my whiskey.

She ignored me. "We moved to the United States in eighteen sixty-three and settled in Davenport on the Mississippi River. It was nice there. My sister and I used to go down to the river and watch the riverboats and play games about where they were going and where they would take us. We were happy there. For a time. But the next year, when I turned fourteen, I became a woman. And Daddy . . ." She shuddered and reached for the glass of whiskey, draining it. She coughed, and bright spots of red appeared in her cheeks. She took a deep breath and let it out slowly.

"Daddy used to take me on his lap and rock me and tell me stories. My favorite was about the hedgehog. Have you heard it?" She looked up at me. I shook my head. She returned her stare into the hot center of the lantern. "It doesn't matter. The story is only a children's story."

"Kate—" I began, but stopped when she shook her head.

"When I grew older, he still took me on his lap, but the stories stopped. Instead, he would . . ."

She reached for the glass, but it was empty. I quickly refilled it. She took it and drank. "Mommy died of cholera the next year. We buried her, and Daddy cried and cried. Our house was so empty without her. Then, one night, Daddy came to my room. My sister was asleep in her own room. We were alone. He pulled my nightgown up and . . . he hurt me. He hurt me bad."

Tears began to stream down her face. "I thought I was dying, Doc. You know? Blood all over. But I didn't die. And he came back the next night and hurt me again. I burnt my sheets and didn't say nothing because I was afraid of what else he might do, you know? Soon it didn't matter. He kept coming to my room, and I knew he was coming to my room and there wasn't anything I could do about it but wait for him to come to my room. Then, one night, he didn't come, and the next day I saw how he looked at my little sister and I knew what he was thinking. That night, I took my sister from the house and told her that we were going on the riverboat like we had pretended we would. She wanted to know why Daddy wasn't coming too, but I told her it was part of the game we were playing. We were going to surprise Daddy.

"I took her down to the river and put her on a boat. I didn't have enough money for both of us, so I lied and pretended that I had made a mistake. I told the captain of the boat that she was to go to the convent in St. Louis and he promised to look after her. I could see he wanted me to go along with him. His eyes kept straying to my breasts." She looked up at me, her lips twisting with mockery. "Men have always wanted me that way, you know? I told him that I would be back. That I had to go get something I had forgotten. But I didn't go back. Instead, I went back to the house and . . . I poured kerosene all around the house and set it on fire. Daddy was asleep.

"I found a man, Tom Elder, who was going to Wichita with a wagon train and convinced him to let me go along in exchange for certain 'favors.' He told the others that we were married, but we weren't. He was a good man, and I told myself that he would probably marry me sometime, but he didn't. I took his name anyway when I went to work in Jim and Bessie Earp's whorehouse. You know the rest of the story," she said. "Pretty much, anyway."

"So you see, Doc, it ain't got nothin' to do with you. Us fighting and all, I mean. It's just that . . . I don't know. Sometimes, when I see you, I see Daddy, and things get all mixed up inside and I don't know what I'm saying or doing. I don't suppose you'll wanna have anything to do with me now. But I felt like I just had to tell you. It ain't you, Doc, that's causing all the trouble between us. Do you think you can take me back?"

I sighed and reached for the bottle of whiskey, pouring.

"Kate—" I said, but she interrupted me, her wide eyes staring beseechingly into mine.

"Please, Doc," she said desperately. "You've gotta take me back. I said I was sorry."

"It isn't your fault, Kate. It isn't my fault, either. The two of us really don't matter at all." I took a deep drink. "People like you and me are the Judas goats of a world that needs a conscience and no longer has one. That's all we are and all we'll ever be."

"Doc," she said, biting her lips. "Doc, you owe me." I looked up at her. She stepped quickly forward and knelt on the floor beside me, her hands grabbing mine around the whiskey glass.

"I'm begging you, Doc. You know you owe me. Fort Griffin. Remember? You would have been dead by now if not for me."

"I'm not sure you did me any favor there," I said. I tried to free my hands, but she clung desperately to them and I marveled at my own weakness that kept me from pulling free from her. A black melancholy settled over me. I shrugged.

"Yes, Kate," I said wearily. "Yes, you're right: I owe you."

She bent forward and kissed my hands. I pulled one free and raised the glass to my lips, finishing it. But the whiskey tasted like gall on the back of my throat. For a moment I thought I would choke, but I willed the sensation away: I couldn't give her that much of a hold over me—the knowledge that I needed her.

For a long time, we existed together in a kind of limbo, each treading warily around the other. I tried to avoid Kate whenever possible and she did her equal best to keep me beside her, compounding my hypocrisy with kindness. I began to feel closed in, suffocating from her attention, wondering if the rest of whatever short life I had left would be spent leashed to her wrist. But I didn't have to worry for long: Masterson got a telegram from a friend of his with the Atchison, Topeka, & Santa Fe Railroad down at Carson City asking for help against the Denver & Rio Grande Railroad.

He found me in the Long Branch, pulled up in a small table in the back, dealing a game of patience and hoping that Kate would not find me there. He pulled out a chair and plopped down in it, sighing. He placed his bowler on the table and pulled a long white handkerchief from it to mop his brow. The day was warm and the room hotter, and his long black coat, vest, shirt and tie warmed his bulk until perspiration popped out along his fine eyebrows and carefully trimmed mustache.

"Go away," I grunted. "I'm in no mood for pretentious lawmen."

He ignored me and reached for the bottle of whiskey, looked critically at the smudged glass, and called for another. Wilke, the bartender, silently brought over another, giving it a perfunctory wipe with his soiled apron. Masterson sighed, poured.

"Reckon this has enough bite to kill whatever might be clinging to the glass," he said.

I played a red ten on a black jack and did a clean second sweep to catch a black nine below the top card. He shook his head.

"Christ, you can't even play patience fair," he complained.

"A hard habit to break when I'm forced to play with hypocrites," I answered. I did an undercut, flawlessly, smoothly, flipped out four aces, folded them, placed them in the middle, did a riffle shuffle, and dealt them off the top.

"Christ, and I play with you?" he said. "I've gotta be crazy."

"I won't argue with that," I said laconically. I drained my glass and reclaimed the Old Williams, pouring another.

Masterson looked around the room and shook his head. "You know why you're sick all the time?"

"I've got a pretty good idea," I said dryly. He ignored my sarcasm.

"You spend all your time in this dump and others like it," he said. "What you need is good clean mountain air to drive all those bugs out of your lungs."

"I'm not going to a sanitarium," I said. I looked at him suspiciously. "Kate put you up to this?"

"Not a sanitarium. The Royal Gorge," he said.

"What the hell are you talking about? Where's this Royal Gorge and why would I want to go there?"

"Clean air. *And*," he added emphatically, gesturing like a carnival barker, "you'll get paid as well for going there. Philanthropic work."

I shook my head and leaned away from him, squinting through the smoke of the room. "Let me understand this correctly. A philanthropist has taken a certain interest in me and wants to pay me to get healed. That it?"

"Well, not exactly," he confessed. "A friend of mine has a little problem and—"

"Forget it," I interrupted, coming forward and sweeping the cards into a pile. I formed the deck and did another riffle shuffle. "I got enough problems without inheriting another's."

"Yeah, I can see all your problems," he said dryly. "You got such a loving household and everything."

"Easy, Bat," I murmured. "We're not that good of friends."

"I'm offering you a bit of a vacation," he said. "Hell, you probably won't even have to use your gun."

"Guns?"

"Ben Thompson's going. And Captain Webb."

"Lay it out, for Christ's sakes, will you?" I said.

He sighed. "All right. You know that the Denver and Rio Grande went bellyup and were taken over by the Atchison, Topeka and Santa Fe." I nodded. "Well, General Palmer went into court and got the railroad reassigned to him. He then snuck surveyors in ahead of our railroad out of Atchison—"

"By 'ours' you are waxing metaphoric, I presume?"

"Christ, Doc! Will you let me tell this my own way?"

"Sorry."

"It's just that you are so damn hard to talk to!"

"I promise to be good," I said solemnly, placing my hand on the cards like a Bible and raising my right.

"The Atchison is Kansas. We are Kansas. It's a matter of pride," he said patiently.

"I understand."

"You're sure."

"I said I did. Get on with it."

"All right. Palmer sent surveyors out ahead of the Atchison and they've managed to grab land along the Atchison's right-of-way. J. H. Phillips has asked a bunch of us to go out along the way and help the Atchison get its right-of-way back."

"Bunch? Who else you got?"

"I just told you," he complained.

"So tell me again. Thompson and Webb don't make a 'bunch.' "

"Well, there's Luke Short, and . . . Damnit, Doc, are you the least bit interested in this or not?"

I coughed and considered, remembering Kate back in our little house. "Yes, I guess I'm interested. At least I'll get a chance to see some new country."

"And it will be healthy," he said. "You can tell Kate that you're going to the mountains for our health. She'll be ecstatic."

"Ecstatic?" I gave him a shrewd look. "Bat, have you been reading Buntline again?"

He flushed and muttered something about ". . . wild gulch . . ."

"You have. Well, I'll be damned!"

"It's better than being ignorant," he said defensively. "But that's not the question."

"I'm not sure I remember what it was," I answered. "But I'll go."

"Good." He drained his glass and rose, settling his bowler firmly above his eyebrows, carefully cocking it at a rakish angle I recognized as Foy's. I smiled as he flicked his fingers against its brim and disappeared, his walk a shadow of Foy's strut.

I dreaded telling Kate, but it had to be done. I waited until the last minute before putting together a few necessaries and packing them in saddlebags. I know she didn't believe me, but she *wanted* to believe me so much that she put up only a token resistance and demand that she come along.

I had tried to get Eddie to go along because his run was over in Dodge, but he refused, saying that he would just as likely shoot himself in the foot as hit the side of a hill. I tried to talk him into going along and taking a shotgun. He would have made a good week's salary in a couple of days, but Eddie refused, preferring to take the train back to Chicago.

Ares was just as happy as I to leave Dodge. I had known that he would be for a long time. For weeks, when I would take him out for his morning ride, he would fight the bit each time I turned back to Dodge. I guess he knew before I did that our time was up in that town. Strange how animals seem to have that sixth sense that tells them what humans should know.

Within three days of getting the telegram, Masterson led us out of Dodge, heading toward the Colorado Territory. John Joshua Webb was with us, along with Ben Thompson. We arrived on a Saturday, looking for a fight, but found only a skeleton camp at the Royal Gorge. At that time, Masterson came up with a plan that was, I must confess, a bit Machiavellian.

"Look," he said to a small group of us. "If we make a grand show of trying to stop the Denver in Pueblo, then everyone will be concentrated there. A small group of us could lead our surveyors through the Gorge and keep Denver's men prisoners until we get the right-of-ways secured. Then we've got the Denver where we want 'em."

"Sounds rough to me," Thompson said, nervously fingering the thick gold chain that crossed his middle. He took his watch out and wound it with a small key he wore as a fob. "They might bring in the soldiers."

Webb snorted, his thin face twisting in a ridiculing smirk. "You afraid of a few bluebellies?" he taunted. "Guess the English ain't as brave as they pretend."

Thompson flushed, his eyes becoming pinpoints of bright light. He placed his watch back in his pocket and pulled his jacket back with the other hand, exposing the black gutta-percha handle of his Smith & Wesson.

"We can solve all that right now, if you wish, sir," Thompson said softly.

Webb's eyes narrowed and he stepped back, squaring his shoulders. Masterson stepped hastily between them, his hands spreading out.

"Now knock that off!" he said. "We didn't come down here to start squabbling between ourselves!"

"All right," Webb said, pulling his hand away from his gun handle. "I reckon we can settle this later."

"Shut up, both of you," Masterson said. They glared at each other for a second while he continued. "I figure if we take the Denver roundhouse in Pueblo, that'll keep them from going up the line to the Gorge. They can't wait forever for supplies and men. While they are trying to get our people out of the roundhouse, our surveyors will be working their way up the valley and into the Gorge," he finished.

"It might be kind of hard on those men in the roundhouse," Thompson said. "But I'll go if we can get others to come along."

"I'll go," I said diffidently. I coughed and spat a brown stain upon the ground. I took Belle's flask from an inside pocket and drank deeply. "I might get lucky," I added, replacing the flask.

"Damn, now I have a martyr with me," Thompson said. He looked belligerently at Masterson. "I need more than Holliday, that's for sure."

"Why, Ben! I thought we were kindred spirits!" I said in mild protest.

"To a point, Holliday," Thompson said. "But this is no lark."

"Au contraire, mon ami," I said. "I find it to be quite invigorating! Another chance to tilt at windmills."

"Aw, shit," Webb said disgustedly. "Look, we'll send twenty men over with you. Including Holliday," he added. "Maybe they'll take pity on you for having him along."

I laughed. "It is so hard having so many friends forcing

me to make a choice," I said. "But I'm for Pueblo and the roundhouse."

And so it was settled. The next day, Thompson led twenty of us over to the roundhouse. They weren't expecting us, so we had an easy time taking control of the building. We kept the switchman and the section foreman with us as hostages. It wasn't long before the regional director hurried to the roundhouse, his fat face red with anger, heavy jowls waggling like a turkey's wattles.

"Just what the hell do you think you're doing!" he demanded.

"Just who the hell is asking?" Thompson countered.

He drew himself up, his belly almost splitting the gold brocade vest beneath his pearl gray suit. A huge purple vein in his bulbous nose threatened to explode. His thin lips sprayed the air in front of him as he spoke.

"I'm Mr. J. P. Perelman and this is my section! You've got just ten goddamned minutes to get out of my goddamned roundhouse before I call in the goddamned soldiers!" he exploded.

"Call in your goddamned soldiers, then," Thompson said mildly. "I don't give a goddamn if you don't give a goddamn."

For a minute I thought Mr. J. P. Perelman would keel over with apoplexy, but he turned on his heel and stormed back across the way from the roundhouse, his patent leather shoes kicking tiny puffs of dust ahead of him. Thompson slid the door shut to a crack and told Kinch Riley to keep his eye on the happenings across the street. Somewhere Jerry Converse found a stool and took it over to keep Kinch company while he stood watch. Thompson saw me smiling and jerked his head. I followed him back to a corner out of earshot of the others.

"What do you think?" he asked lowly. "That little pecker-head going to call in the army?"

"Sure as a coon likes corn," I said. "People like him have a habit of throwing their weight around. Thinks it impresses people if they can order the army around. Prestige and stature."

Thompson frowned and pulled worriedly at his mustache. "Think they'll come?"

I raised my head and glanced out a window. "Oh yes. They'll come. The army needs the railroad across the company. That'll give them a quick way to transport troops from one end to the other. Besides, there's a lot of money to be made out of this for anyone with half a brain. Election year's coming up, and it takes money to run elections. Yes, they'll come."

"You don't have to sound so damn happy about it!" he snapped. He took a deep breath and blew it out the sides of his mouth, ruffling the ends of his mustache. "Sorry. What do you think we should do?"

"I'd get supplies in here if it was up to me," I said mildly. I shook my flask; it was half full, but I had two quarts of Old Williams carefully wrapped in extra shirts in my saddlebags. "Won't be long and the men will start getting hungry. And thirsty. Frankly, I don't give a damn. I don't have much of an appetite anyway. But others in here, like Kinch"—he turned and looked at the huge Irishman standing patiently by the door crack—"well, old Kinch can eat a steer all by himself. Along with a dozen spuds and half a dozen eggs," I added. "You don't feed your men, they'll leave. And I'd get the supplies now before Perelman gets everyone worked up."

"Kinch!" Thompson yelled. The big man turned, blinking heavily as he stared through the gloom to us. "Take Converse and get us some supplies." He took a small leather bag of money from an inside pocket of his spencer coat and tossed it to him. The bag struck Kinch in the chest and fell to the ground. Converse quickly picked it up, shrewdly weighing it in his Scotsman's hand.

"But you told me to keep watch, Ben," Kinch said, his heavy brow furrowing, trying to understand. "I can't do both."

"That's all right, Kinch," Thompson said patiently. "We'll put Pony Tom on it." A big, burly man looked up at mention of his name and rose, taking his Henry with him as he lumbered over to the door.

"All right, Ben," Kinch said. Converse slid the door open and slipped out. Kinch followed, his broad shoulders shoving the door open farther.

"Think he's an oar shy of the canoe," Thompson said softly. "Well? What else?"

" 'Bout it," I said. "The rest is up to Perelman and whoever he gets here. But until then, the Denver isn't going anywhere."

He nodded and moved out, pacing nervously around the roundhouse, checking the shooting ports, chewing nervously on the ends of his mustache. I sighed and took Ares to a corner and took the saddle off and slipped the bit from his mouth, leaving the bridle hanging. He shoved his nose against my chest and grunted deep in his belly.

"I know, boy," I said. "I'm not crazy about this either." I took an apple from my saddlebag and held it while he munched at it. "Hope we don't end up wrong here."

We didn't have long to wait; Kinch and Converse came back in a couple of hours, Kinch carrying four gunnysacks, two in each of his huge hands, while Converse staggered behind him, bent double with eight canvas water bags over his shoulder.

"Hey, Ben!" Kinch said excitedly. "I got a lot of food and even brought back some of your money!"

"Did you get any whiskey?" I asked. His face fell.

"No, but you didn't say to, either!" he said truculently. He dropped the gunnysacks at Thompson's feet and stepped back. "But if'n you want me to go back and get you some, Doc, I'll do it."

"I don't think that would be a good idea right now," Pony Tom called softly from the doorway. "Ben, you'd better see this. You too, Doc."

We pushed our way through the others who quickly crowded around the doorway. I stumbled over a rail and swore, not so much from the pain, but from the scuff mark I knew it put on my boot. I stepped up next to Thompson and peered through the door.

Across the street, a small troop of cavalry stood in the street in double column. A captain with enough gray on his head to qualify him as a general stepped down stiffly from a sorrel gelding and slapped the dust from his tunic. The troop behind him slumped in their saddles, patiently waiting with that lethargic easiness that marked veteran troops. Perelman stepped down off the boardwalk in front of the hotel and began talking and gesturing wildly at the roundhouse. The captain nodded patiently and then straightened his tunic and the gold scarf around his neck before marching toward us. Perelman followed, doing a short hop and skip every third step to keep up with the captain's long strides. They paused about twenty feet outside the door.

"You in there! Get out here where we can talk with you!" Perelman shouted authoritatively.

"Well now," Thompson murmured, his English accent deepening. I knew he was getting angry at Perelman's officiousness. "Will you check the little bastard?"

"Take it easy," I cautioned.

He looked up in surprise at me. *"You* are cautioning me to take it easy?"

I shrugged. "For the moment. Let's hear what he has to say. You can still call him a little bastard if you want."

"Thanks," he said dryly and pushed the door open. I followed him outside.

"Well now," Thompson said. "Isn't this grand?"

The captain smiled faintly. "Captain John Saint Sinclair, at your service, suh."

I grinned delightedly at him. "Why, I do declare, a Georgia man, or I miss the peach in your voice."

His smile broadened at my accent. "And you must be a son of the South or I miss my guess."

"Dr. John Henry Holliday, sir, of Griffin and Valdosta," I said, thrusting out my hand. He grinned and took it, giving it a friendly clasp.

"And I'm from Macon," he said. "I've heard about you, sir, if you are the son of Major Henry Holliday who served with General Beauregard at Richmond?"

"I am," I said. "I take it you were with Beauregard?"

"A fine man," he said. "Both the general and your father. I was the general's adjutant, sir."

"Then it is indeed a pleasure," I said. We shook hands again and I offered him Belle's flask. He took a quick drink and handed it back while Perelman watched, outraged at our amenities.

"Goddamnit, Captain," he complained. "I don't want a social with these assholes! I just want them out of there! Now do your duty!"

St. Sinclair stiffened at this, his eyebrow quirking at Perelman's words. "I will do my job, sir. I do not need you to tell me what to do," he said stiffly. Perelman swelled up like a cock ready to attack, but St. Sinclair pointed a gauntleted finger behind him and ordered, "Remove yourself to the boardwalk, sir. This is now army business."

"Why you . . ." Perelman sputtered.

"I declare this area now under martial law," St. Sinclair said calmly, interrupting. "Now get back there or I'll place you under arrest for interfering with the U.S. Army's duty." His lips twisted at the end of the last, and he glanced ruefully at me. Perelman started to say something, but St. Sinclair lifted his hand and the railroader turned hastily away, furiously kicking dust ahead of him as he waddled back to the boardwalk. St. Sinclair sighed and turned back to us.

"I apologize, sirs," he said. "Now, is there a possibility that we can solve this amicably? Or . . ." he hesitated, looking from Thompson to me.

Thompson shrugged and looked at me, saying with his glance that I had the opportunity and to run with it as far as I could.

"Well, Captain Saint Sinclair," I began.

"John, please," he said.

"John and John." I grinned. "It's good doing business with a countryman. This is a long way from Beauregard."

He nodded. "Yes. I was an instructor in English at the Point with Lee when Georgia seceded. My profession had already been declared. You understand?"

I did. Many of the South's best officers had been educated at West Point before the War. After the South seceded from the Union, those officers elected to stay with their people, their land, because their roots were there; something the North, whose people jumped around the country like crickets, didn't understand. St. Sinclair and I knew the link that tied one to his birthplace, to the people.

"They only gave you a captaincy?" I asked. He nodded, smiling ruefully.

"I was lucky; some of the others were lucky to come out in the officers' corps," he said. He glanced over his shoulder. "But I think we've talked enough about this, John." The informal use of my name warmed me. "What do you propose doing?"

"Well," Thompson said, clearing his throat, but I placed my hand on his shoulder and gently squeezed. He quickly lapsed into a coughing spell.

"Actually, John, this is really a game," I said.

He frowned. "A game? I don't understand."

I proceeded to explain the situation to him about how the Denver & Rio Grande was trying to take advantage of the Atchison, Topeka, & Santa Fe's right-of-ways to cut the Atchison out of the railroad picture. I leaned heavily on General Palmer's name, and St. Sinclair's eyes flared for a moment, then his jaw tightened.

"I see," he said. "That, of course, was not explained to me. I apologize, but what can I do? I have to evict you from the roundhouse. You see how it is?"

"Oh yes, we understand," I said hurriedly. "But who is to say how *long* the negotiations have to take?"

"A delaying action. How interesting." He laughed. "I swear, sir, that you are a reader of Tacitus. Very well. You wish to delay until . . ."

I glanced at Thompson. He shrugged.

"Oh, perhaps ten days?" I suggested.

He shook his head. "No, I can give you no more than five days. After that I'm afraid my superiors would be questioning my ability as an officer." He gestured apologetically. "I do have a family, sir."

"May we send messengers out?" I asked. He nodded.

"Of course. In the interest of maintaining peace, I would be more than happy to accommodate your messengers."

"Very well," I agreed. "Five days. But how will you explain it to Perelman?"

He glanced over his shoulder and shrugged. "I won't. But then, I don't have to, either. Shall we agree to keep negotiations between us?"

"Agreed," Thompson said quickly.

"I do not envy your conference with him," I said. "But thank you."

"Oh, you are quite welcome," he said. He stepped back, then paused. "Lee's surrender at Appomatox did not surrender all of us; it just put us on reserve for a while." He nodded pleasantly and turned and marched back to the boardwalk.

Thompson looked up at me. "Shit and a rose," he said. "Christ, Holliday, if I had your luck, I'd be a millionaire right now."

"Doesn't interest me," I said, turning back toward the roundhouse. He put his hand on my arm, staying me.

"What does interest you?"

"Death," I said. His eyes widened. I smiled faintly. "I live with it every day and still I don't know anything about it."

St. Sinclair was as good as his word; he delayed things until the Atchison had gathered all the titles to its right-of-ways, which they managed to do within the five days that he allotted us, then we arranged to ride out of the round-house with all our dignity and arms with no warrants issued for our arrest. Perelman, I heard, had a fit and was confined to his bed for ten days by his doctor, during which time he consumed a full quart of peppermint to quiet his upset stomach.

Dodge City was a bit upset at the easy settlement, or at least the paper was, because an editorial suggested that we were less than men for not wiping out the Denver people at the time and solving the problem forever. I ignored the editorial damning us. Somehow, I thought Dodge City was behind me. I don't know why; perhaps it was St. Sinclair's reminding me of my roots, perhaps it was because I had tired of the nouveaux sophisticates of Dodge, perhaps it really doesn't matter; the restlessness within me triggered a sense of "new discovery." I wanted to move on.

After the "battle," I saddled Ares and drifted down to Trinidad, where I heard they were in desperate need of a dentist. I wired Kate to meet me there. I played a little poker in Ben Howell's saloon while waiting for Kate to join me. The second day she was there, I was playing cards in Howell's saloon and making quite a few friends when this young gunny calling himself Kid Colton came in, spoiling for a fight.

"I hear yer pretty good with a gun," he said.

I ignored him, and he went to the bar and got a drink and brought it back to the table. I remember I was sitting pretty with jacks over nines and the pot was worth the taking. He drank his drink and continued to say how he heard also that I had made my reputation against drunks. He laughed and said he apparently wasn't drunk enough for me and reached for my bottle of whiskey. The undertaker was playing with us—can't remember his name . . . George, something, like earth, I think, but that's not it, either—and he told the kid to go home before he got into trouble.

I took the bottle of whiskey away from him, and the kid got all red in the face and started yelling that I'd insulted him. He tried to pull his pistol. I killed him with the Lightning—two bullets, each hitting him in the face. It was a fair fight, but Trinidad was going the same way as Dodge was with its new found respectability, and I decided that Kate and I would be better off if we found someplace else to try and put down roots. But I knew in my heart as I lifted Ares into a trot out of Trinidad, leaving Kate to follow later, that there would never be a place for Dr. John Henry Holliday. To think dif-

from the bar. He poured himself a large tot and downed it, licking the last drops from his lips. He raised his eyebrow. I nodded. He poured another glass and handed it to me.

"I'm afraid that I allowed whiskey to make a fool of me," he said. "I came here for a new start."

"It seems as if your start has been a bit postponed," I murmured.

"Yes, it has, for the moment," he said. The humor slipped from his face. He glanced out the window. "I intend to establish a practice here. If I can," he added.

"What's keeping you from it?" I asked.

"Money," he said. He jerked his thumb toward the East. "A group of men have staked out a new townsite on the other side of the Gallinas River around where the new depot has been built." He shook his head. "A lot of people have been hurt by that."

"What do you mean?" I asked.

"We thought the Atchison, Topeka and Santa Fe Railroad would be coming through Las Vegas. This town," he amended. "But someone managed to convince them to go on the other side of the river. Over ground that several speculators took options on."

"Sounds to me as if there's a nigra in the woodpile somewhere," I said.

"Precisely," he said dryly. He shrugged. "There's nothing more we can do. If we want to be a part of the new town, we'll have to pay their price. And it's a grim one."

"I see. Someone's surely a daisy for putting this one together," I said.

"Yes. Well, I have to get back to work." He pointed a long forefinger at me. "And you, sir, would do well to remember my admonitions: Stay away from the mining camps. What you need is the dry air, not the thin air."

"I'll bear it in mind," I said.

He patted my shoulder and turned back to the bar, where several individuals were waiting impatiently for libations.

I met Jordan L. Webb in the Buffalo Hall of the hotel over a poker game, and when he complained of an impacted molar, took him back to my rooms and removed it with the aid of a pair of pliers and a bottle of Old Williams that we shared in lieu of a fee.

"You know," Webb said, "there isn't a future for you here in Old Town. But there's money to be made in the New Town once the Santa Fe line comes through this summer."

"Speculation?" I said, sipping from Belle's cup. He shook his head, a smile lighting up his saturnine features.

"No, well, in a way, I suppose," he said. "I'm talking about going in partners in a saloon."

I shook my head. "I don't mind gambling, but I really do not have any desire to go into business, my good man. I tried that once: in Dallas, a couple of years ago. A miserable failure, I'm afraid." I coughed. A faint brassy taste lingered in the back of my throat. "Besides, the odds of me living to realize anything from such an investment are odds on which only the most desperate gambler would be willing to wager a shinplaster or two."

"I'll go for seventy percent of the building," Webb insisted stubbornly. "Your share can be the other thirty percent and a working partnership for a fifty-fifty split."

"Why so generous?" I asked, curiosity needling me.

He shrugged. "You're a better-than-average gambler and should be able to keep a faro table from becoming bankrupt."

"That's it?" I asked, raising an eyebrow in disbelief. "That seems very tenuous for a man to wager such a sum." A small grin flitted across his lips.

"No," he said. "I'm buying your reputation with the other twenty percent. I'm no gunman," he explained. "I might be able to hit someone across a table from me, but I'd just as soon not try even that. As to a gunfight, well, I couldn't hit a hill if I was standing on top of it."

"I take it you are expecting some trouble," I said.

He nodded. "You put your finger directly on it: Hoodoo Brown. Oh, that ain't his right name. He just calls himself that. Guess he thinks Hyman G. Neill is a bit washy for this part of the country."

"What's his game?"

"A piece of everything," he said grimly. "To the tune of twenty percent. His bodyguard is his collector as well. John 'Dutchy' Schunderberger. Big-shouldered man with granite fists. Brown sends him around for weekly collections. Comes right off the top, too."

"Who else?"

"What do you mean?" he asked.

I smiled faintly. "There must be a gunny around to back up the fist man. Otherwise he'd get his head blown off the first time he tried to put the rail on some of the barmen I know. Fact is," I continued, thinking back to Fort Griffin, "I know a barman who was pretty good with his fists, too."

"He's got a few on his police force," Webb said grudgingly. "Some Dodge City boys he brought down and a couple of drifters who've made a name for themselves here and there."

"Who from Dodge City?" I asked

"Dave Mather. They call him Mysterious 'cause he don't say much. But you look into those gray eyes and you'll have second thoughts about pulling any pistol. You know him?"

"I've sat with him for a hand or two," I said casually. "He's not bad."

"Well, you can see what I mean," he said. "He's got a couple of others, too. Dave Rudabaugh, a hard case who came down with Mather, but I don't know how good he is with a gun. I've got to have someone who can keep them off us. Somebody has to stand up to Brown or he'll end up owning the entire town. Unless," he continued, gesturing at the bloody pair of pliers in the bottom of the washbasin, "you want to try and make a living with those."

I glanced at the pliers and thought about the times in the past when I had tried to set up in practice, of the time in Philadelphia, of the disappointments. I looked down at my hands, noticing the blue veins stark under the translucent skin. My fingers trembled. All the whiskey I had drunk over the past few years was beginning to take its toll on the nerves. How much longer would it be? Not long now. Maybe Mather would be the one. A deep melancholy began to settle over me. My lips twisted in a bitter, self-mocking smile.

"All right," I said at last. "We'll give it a try."

He stretched his hand over the table between us and I shook it gingerly, folding my thumb inside my palm to keep it from being crushed. I didn't have to worry: His hand was soft and pliable, like dough.

We didn't have to wait long after opening before Brown's men made their first appearance. Schunderberger swaggered through the door as if he owned the saloon, Mather trailing in his steps. Webb blanched and pretended to be engrossed in studying his cards. Schunderberger stepped up to the bar and snapped his fingers at Hoyt, who had left his place at the Exchange to work at our bar on Centre Street. Hoyt glanced toward me at the faro table. I grinned and shook my head.

"Yes sir?" he asked.

"A bottle of champagne," Schunderberger said arrogantly, his words rasping in his throat. Mather stepped to the end of the bar, where he could watch the entire room. It wasn't that large: six tables, a faro layout, a chuck-a-luck birdcage, and dice romp. The gandy-dancer in front of me coppered the king. I slid a deuce out of the box and followed it with a king winner. The railroad man swore and stepped away from the table, swinging toward the bar, his huge shoulders bunching angrily beneath his work shirt, straining the seams.

Hoyt shook his head at Schunderberger's request. "I'm sorry, sir, but we don't serve champagne."

"No champagne?" Schunderberger said, pretending to be angry. Tiny lights danced in his eyes. Hoyt shook his head. "What kind of a cheap dump is this?" he demanded.

"Is there something else I can get for you, sir?" Hoyt said patiently. His eyes flickered at me.

"Give me a beer," Schunderberger said, turning and leaning his elbows on the bar.

"Fresh out, sir," Hoyt said. Schunderberger glanced over his shoulder. Hoyt gave him a slight smile. Schunderberger's face turned beet red.

"I don't believe you," he said flatly. Hoyt shrugged. "Whiskey, then."

"Sorry," Hoyt said.

Schunderberger's hands gripped the edge of the bar hard, his knuckles white. I stepped up beside him and grinned down at Mather. Mather's lips lifted in a faint smile beneath his full mustache. He nodded.

"Holliday," he said softly.

"It's been a while, Dave," I answered. I coughed and motioned at Hoyt. He poured a glass of Old Williams and placed it in front of me. I took it, sipping.

"Thought you said no whiskey," Schunderberger said.

"None for you," Hoyt said, his eyes suddenly burning bright. Schunderberger stared open-mouthed at him for a second, then his shoulders bunched and he tried to reach across the bar for Hoyt, only to pull up short when I stuck the Lightning in his ear.

"Now, I wonder, Dave. If I pull the trigger, will the bullet pass through or shatter against the block of granite this gentleman wears between his ears?" I said easily.

Schunderberger glared sideways at me, then down at Mather. "Well? What the hell you gonna do about this?" he demanded. "Blow this asshole away!"

"Well, now," Mather said, his eyes expressionless upon mine. "I can do that. But while I'm doing that, what do you think he'd be doing?"

"What the hell are we paying you for, anyway?" Schunderberger said thickly.

"To protect you and to keep you from getting your fool head blown off," Mather answered. "Which is what will happen if I try to shoot Holliday. Unless that bullet goes through without hitting the pea you got stuck between your ears. Could happen, I suppose. How you been, Holliday?"

"Fair to middlin', Dave," I answered easily. "What are you doing with this riffraff?" Schunderberger tensed his shoulders, the back of his neck glowing red with anger. I ground the pistol harder into his ear to make sure he hadn't forgotten its presence.

Mather shrugged. "It's a living, I s'pose. Beats eating dust behind a bunch of mangy cows. Yourself?"

"Sixes and eights," I answered casually. I grinned and nodded toward Schunderberger. "Are we all right on this? My hand is getting tired. I'm either going to have to shoot him or let him go."

"Let him go," Mather said. "It's over."

I nodded and stepped back, dropping my hand with the pistol. Schunderberger turned and took a step toward me.

"That's enough!" Mather snapped.

"You know what we're supposed to do," Schunderberger said. "Whose side you on?"

"It's not a question of side," Mather said. "It's a question of common sense. And I gave my word. It's over."

"Next time will be different," Schunderberger said thickly, glaring at me.

"You're right as rain about that," I said easily. "Next time I'll pull the trigger." I slid the pistol back into its holster, then aimed my finger at him and dropped my thumb down like a pistol hammer. "Bang. Problem solved. Am I clear on that? Even for a thick-headed Dutchman?"

He whirled and stormed out, the door swinging shut hard behind him. Mather smiled and pushed his hat to the back of his head and smoothed his mustache.

"Well," he said, "I reckon we'll have a bit of trouble over that."

"Drink?" I asked. He nodded, and I turned to Hoyt. "The Old Williams." Hoyt slid the bottle and a glass down to Mather.

"Sorry, Dave," I said.

"It had to happen sometime," he said, giving me a twisted grin as he lifted his glass, tasting it. "Brown's been stepping high and wide. Sooner or later someone was going to push back. If not you, someone else."

"Will he push again?"

"You can make book on it," he said, finishing his drink and declining another. "Oh, yes. He'll push back. Next time it'll be a bit harder."

"Dave," I said, idily making half-moons with my glass on the bar's surface. "You going to be the huckleberry?"

"No," he said. He smiled faintly. "No percentage in it. Might be kind of interesting, though, from a professional point of view."

"Only if you're still alive after," I said. "Otherwise it might be as boring as Aunt Matilda's tea party."

"Same could be said for you," he answered.

I laughed. "That would be a blessing." I coughed again and took a quick sip of the whiskey. Mather shook his head.

"You could be right," he said. "When a man's got nothing to lose, he's got the edge on the world."

"Or," I said past the tight constriction of my throat, "he's fortune's fool."

Sputum flew from my mouth as a fit of coughing convulsed me. I leaned weakly against the bar, sipping the whiskey, waiting for its artificial strength to shore me up again. Mather waited until I had finished coughing and then took his leave. I didn't think we'd have any problem from him; Dave was a gunfighter, but he was also one who carefully considered the percentages. Although he didn't have a fearful bone in his body, he was not a foolishly brave man. He would walk away from a fight if he didn't feel he had the edge and he knew that he didn't have the edge with me. Oh, he might have been quicker with his pistol, but he was not as good a shot. And he cared about living.

Brown finally made his move one day in July, the nineteenth, one month almost to the day when Charlie White and I had a little altercation in one of Brown's own saloons.

White was a son of a bitch Brown brought down from Dodge City. Actually, he didn't bring him down; I had told White to get out of town or I'd kill him after he started bragging that he had faced me down when I came to him for money after he slept with Kate. I sent word to him to meet me below the Deadline, but he never showed up; he left town instead.

I didn't know that he was in the Magnolia in Old Town when I walked in looking for a four-flusher who had stiffed

Webb with an IOU at the table. As soon as the door swung to behind me, I knew that I had been set up.

"Holliday! You goddamned drunk!" White yelled from across the room. I remember his eyes gleaming with satisfaction when I turned toward him. He leveled his pistol and fired. The bullet snapped through the air beside my ear. I pulled the Colt and fired twice back at him. I saw his arms throw up into the air, and then he twisted and fell facedown into the sawdust. I crossed to him and saw the blood on his neck and figured I'd killed him. I backed out of there and went back to New Town and didn't find out until two days later that I had only creased him with my bullet. He had left town again by that time, so I thought nothing more about it.

But Brown did. He spent a lot of time among the citizenry of Las Vegas, spreading the rumor that I was a cold-blooded killer who had tried to shoot White without provocation. Unfriendly faces stared stolidly at me whenever I walked through the town, and the clerk at the Exchange Hotel where I had my rooms began to drop hints about how the management would appreciate my taking my business elsewhere. I found the whole affair amusing.

On the nineteenth of July, however, Brown made another move against me. At the time, I had hired Monte Holman to work a table in our saloon. Monte was a beautiful, dark-eyed brunette who immediately raised Kate's hackles when she discovered Miss Holman working for us, but I refused to fire her despite Kate's demands, as the men would always flock to her table, hoping to get lucky. None did. She hated all men and despised all women and kept peace at her table with a small revolver that she placed next to her right hand while dealing. I could understand the men wanting to get close to her: She wore red velvet dresses with brooches of diamonds and rubies with gold and diamond clasps intricately wound into her hair.

The nineteenth of July was hot and dry. Not a breath of air stirred. Miss Holman was dealing poker at one of the back tables when Mike Gordon came in and went to the bar. He had a couple of drinks, then went back to Miss Holman's table, where he stood behind her, watching the play for a while. I lost interest in him, paying close attention to the faro table, where I had been relieved by Jim Harper. The fact is, I didn't think that we would have any trouble from Gordon. He had been with the Fifth Cavalry and had taken part in several hostage exchanges with the Indians, rescuing young children who had been captured in Indian raids, but ever since someone bit off the end of his nose in a brawl, he had taken to the bottle, sinking deeper and deeper into oblivion. I was wrong, though. Suddenly Miss Holman stood up and slapped Gordon's face.

"You cheap bastard!" she said.

Gordon's face went white, then he laughed and grabbed her, pulling her to him. I don't know why Miss Holman didn't pick up her pistol when she stood, but she didn't. Gordon held her tightly and was trying to kiss her when I came up beside him and hit him with my pistol. He fell, stunned, to the floor. I gestured to Hoyt, who picked him up and threw him out the door. I followed.

"You bastard, Holliday!" he yelled, picking himself up from the dirt of Centre Street.

"You are not welcome here, Gordon," I said coolly. "Take your business elsewhere."

"You can't treat me like this!" he yelped, his voice climbing higher through his fury.

I ignored him and went back inside. I turned toward the bar and had taken a couple of steps when two bullets passed through the doorway where I had been standing. People fell to the floor. I turned and went back out, drawing my pistol. Gordon laughed when he saw me.

"Well, Holliday," he said. He grinned.

"What's this all about, Mike?" I asked.

"Nothing personal," he said. He waved his pistol between us. "But, well, you should have listened to Hoodoo."

"You're making a mistake, Mike," I cautioned.

"Maybe." He grinned. Suddenly his hand flashed up. A bullet tugged at my coat. I turned sideways and raised my pistol, firing as it leveled in front of me. The bullet took him high in the chest. He spun around, falling facedown in the dust. I glanced down, noticing the blood seeping out from beneath his shoulder blade. I sighed, holstered my pistol, and went back inside the saloon, crossing to the bar. Wordlessly, Hoyt slid a glass of whiskey in front of me. I picked it up, drained it, and set it in front of him. He filled it immediately.

"Is he dead?" a low voice asked from beside my shoulder.

I looked down at Miss Holman. Close up I could see the marks of dissipation, tiny cracks marring the smooth porcelain of her face. Her eyes were expressionless, her full lips drawn down.

"Yes," I said. She placed a hand on my arm, gently pressing.

"Thank you," she said softly.

"It wasn't you," I said.

A tiny smile lifted the corners of her lips. She removed her hand. "I know. But thank you anyway. It's been a long time since a man behaved like a gentleman for me. Regardless of the reason." The tiny smile turned into a self-mocking grin. "Still, it's nice to know that someone still thinks enough of me to use me in that way. As—"

"A reason?" I interjected.

"You're very good," she said. "Gallant. The southern gentleman still is the perfect gallant."

"At your service, ma'am," I said, bowing before her. She smiled, ran the tips of her fingers along my jawline, then made her way back to her table.

I heaved a sigh and turned to the piano in the corner. I sat down and began playing my Chopin nocturne.

I probably should have paid closer attention to the political happenings in Las Vegas, but I never have cared much for politics, and local politics are more boring than any. Usually, those who go into politics do so out of a certain vendetta rather than civic-mindedness. Brown was into politics, but the only civic duty he cared about was filling his own coffers.

Wyatt and his Mattie came to Las Vegas along with his brother James and his wife in October, I think. Yes, it was October. Fall. That's when disgruntled citizens start thinking about reform. Always in the fall. Perhaps they feel a need to conform to those preconceived ideas of gentility, those omnium-gatherums, they mistake for the earmarks of civilization: music halls instead of saloons, streetlamps, omnibuses, police forces, magistrates, and other cosmopolitan trappings for the new sophisticates.

For a while, Wyatt dealt faro in my saloon, but Brown continued undermining Webb and me. He no longer sent his gunnies to try and extort money from us. It was good that he didn't, as Wyatt would have been a formidable foe for them to face. They might have dealt with James: He was little more than a drunk; the War had taken everything from him, leaving him a dry husk of a man, the juices sucked from him. Wyatt tolerated his drunken bumblings because he was his brother. He never would have suffered the antics of James in another man.

Kate greeted their arrival coldly. I found out later that she had briefly worked for James but had left him to strike out on her own. But that wasn't the real reason she disliked the Earps so much: it was our relationship together. Wyatt's and mine, that is. That was a part of my life that she couldn't enter. Kate was my Anti-Christ. She wanted to own me body and soul, partly, I believe, because she saw in me her father. I'm not sure how much of our relationship truly was love, how much was a convenience (sexual and economical), and how much was a gratification of her anger toward her father. When I did resist her attempts at running my life, anger would spill from her lips with vinegary vengeance and she would run away, burying herself in decadence, punishing me through herself.

J. H. Koogler began to draw public attention to what he referred to as the riffraff in town through the pages of his *Gazette*, hinting that my shooting of Gordon was murder instead of self-defense. I recognized the hand of Brown in Koogler's writing and knew it was only a matter of time before a citizen's committe was formed—a polite euphemism for a group of vigilantes—I knew that I had little time left in Las

Vegas. Brown had discovered that subterfuge could succeed where force could not.

Meanwhile, Wyatt had heard from Virgil, another brother, about the silver strike in Tombstone and, after Brown began to suggest that Wyatt's reputation was highly inflated and that he was little more than a rogue in a black frock coat, Wyatt decided that Tombstone offered more opportunities than Las Vegas.

Some have said that Wyatt left because of Brown's manipulations of his (and my) reputation through the press, but that simply isn't true. Wyatt could see that there was no longer any room for him in Las Vegas. Although there had been a time for him and those like him, that time was rapidly disappearing. The West was shrinking. The last event that decided Wyatt to move on happened in January.

A cowboy by the name of Tom Henry and three of his friends, John Dorsey, James West, and William Randall, came into town and swaggered into the Close and Patterson Dance Hall, their pistols prominently displayed. Joe Carson, the town marshal, asked them to check their guns, but they laughed at him and began to insult him. Suddenly, Randall drew his pistol and shot Carson. Carson fell to the floor but managed to pull his gun and shoot twice before the cowboys put nine bullets into him.

Mather, who had been appointed to the position of assistant town marshal through Brown's manipulations, drew his revolver and opened fire on the cowboys, killing Randall and putting a bullet into West's middle. Henry made it out the back, but the newspapers the next day began an outcry against the lawlessness in the town. Brown was interviewed as an indignant citizen and took the time to launch into a tirade against those individuals who had a singular disregard for human life and less of a regard for decency.

It was the beginning of the end for Las Vegas as many knew it. At least I could tell that civilization was on its way. I think Wyatt knew it too, although he didn't say much, just stared off into the distance, his eyes vacant and his thoughts turned in, thinking. I wasn't surprised when, the next day, Wyatt told me that he had decided to go to Prescott in Arizona to meet Virgil. Morgan, his brother who had been marshaling in Butte, Montana, would join them there and together they would caravan to Tombstone.

"It's the future, Doc," Wyatt said to me, a glass of whiskey barely tasted in front of him. "It's all over here just as it's all over in Dodge and Denver and other towns. You make a place right for good people to live in and when the good people arrive, they don't want you around anymore."

He stared gloomily out at the roof of the depot, visible over the buildings lining Centre Street to the railroad tracks. "The railroad's a good thing, Doc. I ain't saying it isn't. But it closes things in, you know? Oh, people sure cry hard enough for law and order and for those that can tame things down, but once things get civilized, why, they want to get rid of those that brought it."

"Understandable," I said. He looked up, his brow furrowing in question. I laughed and drained my glass of whiskey. "People like you and me, why we remind them of the briar patch they once lived in. They don't want that. They want to be able to point with civic pride to the future, not remember the past. In time of danger, not before, we are valued people. Well, you are, anyway," I amended. "When danger's over, then people like you are forgotten."

"Words of wisdom, Doc," he said. "Words of wisdom. Well, Mattie and me are going to Prescott to meet up with the rest of the family. When you come right down to it, that's all that matters: blood. What about you?"

I shrugged and tossed off another glass of whiskey with a flourish. "I'm another dinosaur," I said. "I think I'll travel along with you."

"And Kate?" he frowned.

"That's up to her," I said.

"She's no good for you, Doc," he warned. "She'll be trouble."

"We all have to have someone," I said.

10

Kate elected to stay in Las Vegas for a while. She raised a ruckus when she heard that I was planning on going with Wyatt to Prescott, and stormed out of the Exchange like her bustle was on fire. In a way, I was rather relieved: She had become a bit too demanding. I heard later she took up with Dave Rudabaugh who had come in with Brown. I didn't think that would last long, but who knew?

Ares was happy to go, settling into a canter beside Wyatt and Mattie's buckboard. At times, I'd give him his head and let him gallop over the hills, exploring side canyons, feeling the spirit of the spaces. A bit dangerous, I know, given that the Apaches had fled the reservation again. Nana and Geronimo were around somewhere, but we never saw them, although we ran across some of their handiwork. Enough to make a skunk gag. Mattie was in near-hysterics a time or two, I tell you. When we got to Prescott, Wyatt took over the top floor of the hotel. I found a spartan room next door to the *Weekly Miner,* but I wanted something more than a simple cot and a couple of nails as a clothesrack.

"I'll be damned!" Wyatt said, a broad grin spreading across his lanternlike face. I turned to follow his gaze and noticed a well-dressed middle-aged man hurrying down the walk toward us, his hand outstretched in greeting.

"Wyatt!" he exclaimed, coming up to us. "How are you?"

"Fine, Richard. Just fine," Wyatt answered, pumping the man's hand. He clasped him on the shoulder, turning to me. "Doc, I'd like you to meet Richard E. Elliott. He and Virgil go back quite a few years. Richard, Dr. John Henry Holliday."

"More years than we'd like to admit," Elliott said, his hand stretched out to mine. His eyes narrowed fractionally. "Holliday. From Fort Griffin?"

"I've been there," I said easily, waiting for him to withdraw his hand. He didn't, and my respect for him went up a couple notches. I took his hand; he gripped it firmly. Two bankers meeting on the street.

"Been to Dodge, too, Richard," Wyatt said. "A mighty lucky thing for me."

"Oh?" His eyebrows raised as his eyes probed mine, looking for the story. I smiled instead.

"Wildflowers, not a daisy among them," I said. I muffled a cough.

"I see," he said, but I could tell from his eyes that he was far from satisfied. *You'll have to find that out from Wyatt,* I thought. As if reading my mind, he turned back to Wyatt.

"Your brother in town too?" he asked.

Wyatt shook his head. "No, not yet. But he'll be coming down tomorrow or the day after. I've got rooms for them over at the hotel." He pointed at me. "Doc here is still looking, though. He's got a place at the paper, but it ain't the best for him. Kinda rough."

Elliott grinned and shook his head. "Things are hopping in Prescott. I don't think you'll have much luck. But I'm staying at a boardinghouse on North Montezuma Street with John J. Gosper, the secretary of state. There is a room available there if you're interested. Clean and respectable. Ten dollars a week and board. Nice place. And, it's better than the *Weekly Miner.* I can guarantee that."

"You're a daisy," I said. "I'll just pop on over and settle up. May I use your name by way of introduction?"

He waved my request away. "Any friend of Wyatt's can use my name. John should be in later tonight. Fremont's over at Santa Fe so John's been filling in as governor." He shook his head. "Sure will be glad when the President appoints someone else to be governor. Fremont spends more time away than he does in. We need leaders, not figureheads."

"I thought Fremont would be a decent governor," Wyatt

said. "I was thinking of asking for a commission for the Tombstone area."

Elliott gave a grim laugh. "Not unless you've got the price for it. You've heard of the spoils system?"

Wyatt shook his head.

"A Yankee invention," I said. "It means legalized theft and power where the nigras can lord it over the white folk."

"Well, maybe not quite like that," Elliott said. "But the intent is there. Jobs are open to whoever scratches the right back."

"I see," Wyatt said slowly. "So what do you advise?"

Elliott shrugged. "Your guess is as good as mine. Let me talk with Gosper and I'll see what I can do."

"Thanks, Richard," Wyatt said.

"You're a peach," I said. I touched my hat brim in farewell. "I'll just leave you two to reminisce while I tend to this lodging business." I glanced at Elliott. "I would be obliged, sir, if you could join us for dinner?"

"I'd be honored," he said, shaking my hand again.

I nodded and left, making my way along the boardwalk, far enough in to avoid being splattered by wagons and horses moving down the muddy street. I took a deep breath, feeling the sharp bite of the cold air, tasting the pine needles from the tall pines on the outskirts of the town. Prescott was cleaner than Las Vegas and quieter. And friendlier, I thought as a man nodded politely to me in passing. I paused to study my reflection in a store window: thin, too thin, perhaps, but there was nothing to be done for that: my appetite had not been good lately; hollow-cheeked, a thin mustache, carefully clipped; freshly barbered; my gray suit (I had taken to wearing gray instead of black; black made me look cadaverous) impeccably cut and falling well from the shoulders and cut wide enough to accommodate my revolvers; my wide-brimmed hat shadowed my eyes, but took away from the narrowness of my features. All in all, not too bad. I looked more like a gentleman than a gambler. I turned, stepping away from the window, bearing my weight on the cane in my right hand, taking the strain off my right foot, which had been giving me trouble lately. I suspected gout.

It didn't take long to rent the room Elliott had mentioned. In fact, I was just in time; two others came in while I was registering, asking if a room was available. I counted myself lucky. Linen would be changed twice a week and breakfast would be served, but not lunch and dinner. An unusual arrangement, as usually all meals went with rooms, but I didn't argue. I was happy to have it even if the price was a bit steep.

I made arrangements with Mrs. Wilson to send her son over to the spartan room I had above the *Weekly Miner* to pick up my luggage. The two men quickly left with him, arguing over which one would get the room, trying to talk themselves into sharing. I silently wished them luck; the room was little bigger than a closet, barely large enough for me, let alone two.

I left right behind the others and strolled down the street, enjoying the crisp air. I breathed deeply and coughed, then coughed again, and took a quick look around to make sure that no ladies were present before spitting into the street. I noticed the tinge of blood in my sputum and turned into a saloon on the corner for a glass of whiskey.

A warm, yeasty smell greeted me as I stepped into the interior. I glanced around the room, recognizing no one. I walked over to the bar and ordered Old Williams. The bartender shook his head.

"Sorry, friend, but I can't help you," he said.

"What have you got?" I asked.

He reached automatically to a brown bottle on the ledge behind the bar. I shook my head.

"Not that swill," I said. "Bourbon?"

He frowned. "A liquor salesman came through town the other day and left some samples. Let me see." He bent over and brought up a bottle of Paddy's. "Will this do?"

I pointed to a glass. He poured a sample. I tasted, nodded. "How many bottles did he leave?"

"Near a case," he said, counting.

"I'll take them," I answered, dropping a twenty-dollar gold piece on the bar. Keep them for me."

"All of them?" he said. I nodded. He frowned. "That good, is it?"

"Not the best, but it'll do," I said. I took the bottle from the bar and the glass and turned toward a table in the back. Four men were playing poker. I approached them, smiling.

"Gentlemen," I said. "Would there be room for a fifth in your game?"

"Don't see why not," one of them said, half standing to stretch forth his hand. "I'm Billy Leonard. Jeweler. And these other rascals are Jesse Everhart, Jack Braden, and Al King. A most disreputable bunch . . ."

". . . but willing to play with a low jack like you," Everhart said. "Sit in with us, if you care to. I run the livery and Jack has the stage office. Al's our local banker. Watch him. Money squeaks before he lets it go."

"Off with you, now," King said, standing. He nodded at the bottle in my hand. "I see the man comes prepared."

"Would you care for a touch?" I asked, motioning for the bartender to bring glasses.

"We've been known to have a jot," Leonard said, his eyes twinkling.

I laughed and slid into a chair. I felt easy and relaxed, almost as if I had come home.

I enjoyed being in Prescott, for a few months, anyway—ten, I believe. The air was crisp and cold, smelling fresh and clean, like pine, in the early morning when I would take Ares for his daily ride. Ares enjoyed it too.

Other entertainment came often to the town. A theatrical group calling itself Pinafore on Wheels came through. I dined several times with the owner, Pauline Markham, whose daring costumes, although not as daring as Belle's had been, brought a lot of stage-door Johnnies waiting with bouquets of wildflowers in hand for the end of her performances. It was a bit of a toss-up as to whether she or Josephine Sarah Marcus, an eighteen-year-old Jewish beauty from San Francisco, would have the most suitors, but there was something about Josephine that made me feel, well, wary around her. She was wild and careless with her affections. Eventually she took up with a two-bit womanizer named Johnny Behan. That pretty much set her apart from the other members of the troupe, for although many members of the Pinafores were a bit careless with their charms, all recognized the worthlessness of men like Behan, balding, carefully groomed with a mustache he kept waxed with a tiny tin he kept in his vest pocket. He had a weak chin and quickly departed the area if a suggestion of an altercation between two men arose. Pauline and I were lovers, after a fashion. I prefer platonic lovers, though, for each of us knew that what we had was only temporary and because of that, we enjoyed each other's company immensely.

I made friends there—Elliott, Gosper, Leonard, Everhart, King, Braden, and others. I rode with Gosper, a good-looking man who had the women staring with undisguised lust when he took his evening constitutional down Montezuma Street and over to the saloon, where I usually held a table for two. Together we explored the pine glades and mountain meadows, the sylvan streams where fish would jump in quiet pools.

I had friends.

For the first time, I felt I belonged somewhere. I think that I could have been happy there. I mean I could have been. I won a lot of money—nearly forty thousand dollars—before Wyatt's brothers joined him and, together, they traveled to Tombstone. I stayed behind. I told Wyatt that I would join him later when my luck ran out. I don't know if I would have if Kate hadn't shown up, but that was in the hands of the gods. I suppose that is why I elected to go to Tombstone.

She came in through the front door of the saloon, wearing a light green dress that plunged down to her hips and a bunch of feathers wrapped around a small piece of cloth for a hat. I recognized the throes of a hangover: her eyes were puffy and bloodshot and her hands trembled a bit. She smiled tentatively at me, the smile wavering and almost disappearing when I frowned.

"Hello, Doc," she said, crossing to stand beside my chair. "How've you been?"

"As usual, Kate," I said. I took a quick look at my cards: Something might have been made from them, but I could feel my luck slipping away. On a hunch I threw them onto the deadwood and pushed back from the table.

"Quitting already, Doc?" Leonard asked, looking up. I shook my head and pulled my money off the table, shoving it into the deep pockets of my coat.

"You're too good for me, today, Billy," I said.

He laughed, his voice going soprano like a young girl. The others laughed along with him, then turned their attention back to the game. I took Kate by the arm and led her to the bar, motioning to the bartender for my bottle and two glasses. Silently, he slid the bottle down along with the glasses. I could tell from the way his eyes flicked over Kate that he knew her for what she was. I poured two drinks. Kate picked hers up, nearly spilling it, and tossed it off, quick and neat, shuddering.

"Christ," she said. "I needed that." The color began to come back into her face. She looked questioningly at the bottle and I poured her another. She sipped at it.

"Well, Kate," I said, then stopped. I didn't know what to say to her. She grinned.

"Well, I caught you out, didn't I, Doc?" she said. She gave a short laugh. "You look like you weren't expecting me. Ain't you happy to see me?"

"Of course," I said hurriedly, taking a large drink from my glass.

"No you're not," she said. "But here I am anyway."

"What do you want from me, Kate?" I said quietly.

"You know," she said, looking away. She focused on the glass of whiskey in front of her as if staring into a gypsy's ball. I sighed.

"Kate," I began, then stopped.

"You trying to get rid of me, Doc?" she asked.

Yes, I wanted to say, but I knew I couldn't. I still remembered Fort Griffin. *You will always remember Fort Griffin,* I thought. *Always.*

"No, Kate," I said resignedly. "I'm not trying to get rid of you."

"You sure?" she asked suspiciously.

"Yes, I'm sure."

"Well." She brightened and stood closer to me, slinging her hip into mine. "Where are we staying? How's the action here?"

"Not good," I said, making a face. "It's been tapering off for the past couple of weeks. I was thinking of going down to Tombstone." I lied, yes, but I had found peace at Prescott and I suppose there was something inside of me that suggested I might be able to return to it. I knew I didn't want to share it with Kate. I wanted it to be something private for just myself.

She made a face. "Ain't that where the Earps are?"

"Yes," I said. "But there's also a lot of money down there. They're finding new veins every day. It's as if the damn town is sitting on a hill of silver."

"It ain't gold, Doc," she said.

I shrugged. "No, but it'll do until another gold strike comes along."

"All right," she said arrogantly. She grabbed the bottle and poured herself another drink. "Let's go make our fortunes."

I think a small something died there between us, although I wasn't aware of it at the time. Perhaps I should have been. Often I wonder what would have happened had I stayed in Prescott and not gone to Tombstone. I couldn't have stayed, however, not with Kate. And so, two weeks after Kate came back into my life, I left my Eden and traveled to hell.

Tombstone was a sense of false sophistication, holding to an aura of pseudo-gentility upon a flat plain surrounded by an arroyo and heavy yucca and spears of ocotillo. Elaborate oil lamps had been placed at the intersections of the streets, yet the streets were dust, the buildings showing gaudy facades that new sophisticates thought to be cosmopolitan. Dry and dusty, Tombstone held a giddy sense of madcap enjoyment that made the senses reel with delight. Chinatown provided whatever vices one couldn't find in the various saloons and "houses" run by whites. Chinatown really wasn't a town as much as it was a series of tents snugged against each other. But opium was in plentiful supply there, as could be attested by the glaze-eyed miners strolling the streets with moronic grins upon their faces.

Wyatt and his brothers had taken a couple of adobe houses across from one another on Allen Street while waiting for their own to be built. James had taken a temporary job as a bartender at Vogans while Virgil had finagled his way into the position of U.S. Deputy Marshal. Wyatt had refused the marshal badge offered him and settled instead for a job as Wells Fargo messenger guard for a hundred twenty-five dollars a month.

I took a couple of rooms with Kate in Fly's boarding-house, which was next to his photography studio. The rooms were not as spacious or as nice as the ones I had shared with Gosper and Elliott in Prescott, but they were adequate: a desk and chair, two more upholstered medallion-backed chairs for company, a brass bed large enough for active lovers, lamps with globes painted with twining peonies, and plain pine wardrobes. Both rooms had a balcony upon which we could sit in the cool of the evening and enjoy the sunset.

I took a game in the Alhambra saloon. My nights usually started around eight unless Kate and I took in a performance at Schieffelin Hall, a large building that had been made into a theatre. Several acts came through there on a regular enough basis that boredom was seldom encountered.

The Oriental, however, was the best saloon in town. Milt Joyce, the owner, used to brag that it was the finest place of its kind east of San Francisco. I don't know how far east Joyce had been or how many other saloons Joyce had seen in order to make such a comparison for the Oriental, but it was, at least, the finest of its kind in town. The bar was well-polished mahogany with a well-polished brass foot rail running down the front and side to keep cowboy boots and spurs from scratching the gleaming front. The sideboards had been made for the Baldwin Hotel, but Joyce had bribed the right man to have them "lost" in shipment. The gaming room had Brussels hangings and wallpaper. The lights shone through clear crystal, and a piano and violin provided soothing back= ground music in high contrast to the ragtime music pounded out on pianos badly out of tune in the other bars. Sometimes Joyce held dances for everyone, but respectable women were hesitant about attending, although the time I consented to give a brief recital in Chopin did bring them out in their east- ern dress with high-button shoes and tiny parasols that did little to protect them from the brutal desert sun that sucked the juices from the fairest of the fair and left them old with leathery skin far before their times.

For those who didn't yearn for the finer things in life, those who had no dreams of becoming cosmopolites, Dutch Annie's place was very popular along with Big Minnie's girls in the Bird Cage Theatre. Lizette, billed as The Flying Nymph when she came through town with the Monarch Car- nival Company, found that quicker money could be obtained in the set of the demimonde than flying high over the stage on trapezes.

The Bird Cage Theatre, however, offered not only a wild and wicked time (the best since my stay in New Orleans in Basin Street), but the entertainment was also varied. It never closed its doors in twenty-four hours. I remember it well: a hand-painted stage where not only cancan dancers appeared, but even my old friend Eddie Foy.

Eddie and I wasted little time renewing our acquaintance. At the end of his first performance, I had to rescue him from some cowboys who thought he had insulted them with his lines about their masculinity and took exception with what John Clum called his "Fifth Avenue swaggering strut." They roped him and dunked him into a horse trough and were in the process of readying a branding iron for him when I made an appearance.

"Ah, John!" Eddie exclaimed, his face wreathing in relief. "It is so good to see you. Have you met my new, er, friends?"

"Hello, boys," I said easily. "I see you are making a friend of mine welcome."

."Stay out of this, Holliday," a burly cowboy with scraggly whiskers said. A lump of tobacco tightened one cheek to near bursting. "This dude has been treading on our reputations."

"Now, I know he couldn't have damaged your reputations any, being the shiftless lowlifes that you are," I said pleasantly. "Turn him loose."

"I'll be damned if I will!" the cowboy exploded. "This little shit—"

He stopped as I pulled my cloak back and away, exposing the Colt to their view. I smiled, enjoying the uneasy silence that spread through them.

"Why, Jim Philby!" I exclaimed. His eyes widened as I called him by name. "Are you treading upon our friendship? I certainly would hate to lose you to a misunderstanding."

He flushed and his hands tightened on the branding iron, but another cowboy pulled on his arm, turning him away from me. Reluctantly, he turned, tossing the branding iron into the water trough. It sizzled and Eddie clambered out and away, his checkered suit dripping water, his spats wilting around his shoes.

"Thanks, John," he said. He ran his hands over his hair, smoothing it back, and picked up his wide-brimmed hat from where it had fallen in the dust. "Things were getting a bit testy there."

"Oh, don't worry too much about it, Eddie," I said, clasping his hand. "How have you been?"

"Just fine, just fine," he said. His lips spread in a shaky grin. "Belle's down in Texas now. She was up in Denver at the Tabor Grand Opera House. But she isn't well, John," he added, his face saddened. "She's not holding her age very well. You knew her husband turned out to be bad, didn't you?"

"Bad for her," I said. "But not how bad."

"He ran out on her, taking her jewelry and all, leaving her without a dollar. She's been trying to get back into theatre, but she's too old for some of her roles. Now she's lecturing. Telling her story about the War."

"I see," I said.

"She asks about you," he continued. "But she's remarried that man from Texas. . . . I can't remember his name."

"It doesn't matter," I answered. I waved my hand to indicate the town. "Well now, how do you like Tombstone?"

"It's not bad," he said, his eyes lighting up. "The theatre's a bit cramped and it's not Philadelphia or New York, but it pays the rent. You know that Booth is coming soon."

"No! Really?" I exclaimed. "Not doing his Hamlet."

Eddie nodded. "Oh, yes. He'll be here in a couple of months. Then we'll see how these cowboys handle the Bard."

And Booth did come, playing to a silent audience that broke into wild applause after he finished. Funny thing about cowboys: You'd think that they had no appreciation for the arts, but many of them had read all of Shakespeare and most had read the Bible. During the cold winters, that's what many did to occupy their time when they were in the line camps high in the mountains.

Booth was a success. We had a fine reunion. I hosted a champagne party for him, and the three of us, Eddie, Edwin, and myself, spent many fine nights talking into the early morning hours, irritating Kate to no end. They asked me to go with them to California but, well, the air was good for people with my condition. But my condition wasn't cooperating at all. I constantly felt feverish and cold, perspiration dotting my face, my lungs twisting and burning, forcing me to drink more and more whiskey in order to quiet the spasms. Morgan, one of Wyatt's younger brothers who had come down from Butte with his common-law wife Lou, rode with me in the late afternoons when I took Ares from his stall at Gray & McLane's Stables next to P. W. Smith's Store and exercised him. Morgan usually rode Wyatt's thoroughbred, Dick Naylor.

One afternoon in September, Wyatt and I were sitting on

the balcony of my room when a messenger came from Joyce, asking Wyatt to come around at five. Wyatt grinned at me as he flicked the note with his thumbnail.

"What do you say, Doc? Want a drink at the Oriental?" he asked.

"What's it about?" I asked, pushing myself up from my chair. He stood in one lithe movement, smoothing his coat over his shoulders.

"A gambler's been trying to get Joyce to take him into partnership in the gaming room," he answered. "There's bad blood between him and Lou Rickabough, who already owns the gaming room. He's been throwing his weight around, scaring off Joyce's customers. I think Joyce wants to get rid of him."

"Why doesn't Lou get Fred White to throw him out?" I asked. "Seems the job for the town marshal, not a private concern." I frowned. "Better be careful, Wyatt. Might be a nigra job there somewhere."

"Well," he said, tugging at an earlobe, "I sorta thought you'd watch my back. According to Rickabough, this Johnny Tyler's there now with some of his friends and they've taken over one of the faro tables and ain't stepping back from it."

I shrugged. "I could use a drink," I said, stepping through my room to collect my hat. Kate relaxed back on one of the medallion-backed chairs, her dress hiked up enough to show her garters, fanning herself against the heat. She watched as I shrugged into my pistol harness.

"A bit early, ain't it?" she asked petulantly, glaring at Wyatt.

"Just going for a drink with Wyatt," I answered. I checked the loads in the Colt .45 and Lightning, settling them easily in their holsters. She pushed herself up on the chair and sighed.

"Give me a minute," she said.

"You can catch up to us," I answered. "We'll be at the Oriental."

"Goddamn you, John! You can just wait for me to change my clothes!"

Wyatt turned politely away as she began undressing, her breasts springing free from the bodice of her dress. Contempt stirred with me. I coughed.

"I'll wait outside, Doc," Wyatt said, opening the door and stepping through it. He tactfully closed the door behind him. I turned to Kate.

"What is your problem?" I asked.

"My problem? What is my problem? You. You're my problem. I've tried to make a sea change in you, Doc—"

I interrupted her. "I told you that was a useless thing to attempt."

She sighed. "You have another woman," she said dully.

"Kate . . ."

"No, you do. Who is it? That slut claiming to be Wyatt's wife? She was a two dollar hooker!"

"I wouldn't cast stones if I were you," I said.

"Never for that, Doc. Never that low."

"Why do you persist in behaving like a slut?" I asked.

"Watch your mouth!" she snapped. "You're no better than me."

"Than I," I corrected. "And that's debatable."

"Oh yes, the southern gentleman," she sneered. "Wisteria vines and pecan trees and those nappy-headed niggers walking and running around saying, Yes, massuh and no, massuh and those dances beneath the magnolia trees with that woman you're mooning about—your cousin, whatever the hell her name is."

"What brings this on?" I asked, a cold anger settling in behind my words.

"When you wrap her letters in a black velvet ribbon and pack them carefully away, what the hell did you expect me to do?"

"Perhaps try being a lady," I said. "But I can see that's an impossibility."

"Wyatt Earp's little errand boy. If you're so goddamned good, why are you constantly hanging around an asshole like him?"

I sighed. "He's my friend. And I haven't many."

"And what am I?" she demanded.

"I don't know," I said, opening the door. "I really don't know."

I pulled the door shut behind me. A glass shattered against its surface. Wyatt raised an eyebrow. I shook my head.

"The heat, I think," I said.

"She's been gettin' worse," Wyatt said gravely. "She cussed out Virgil the other day when he suggested that she go home and stop staggering around the street. He thought she might be trying to pick up a trick or two. She's lucky Virgil didn't jail her."

I shook my head; Virgil was the city marshal and had been bending over backwards trying to maintain peace between Kate and the citizens of Tombstone, not so much for my sake, but Wyatt had quietly asked him to give her a little rein. I was beginning to wonder if things wouldn't be better if Virgil ordered her out of town.

"Maybe she was," I said. I took a deep breath. "But that's my cross to bear. At least she isn't sucking constantly on a bottle of laudanum."

A deep flush darkened Wyatt's face; it was no secret, although Wyatt pretended not to know, that Mattie, the woman who claimed to be his wife, had a penchant for laudanum, a habit that drained a quarter bottle a day. He turned without another word and clumped down the hall and down the stairs. I followed.

The inside of the Oriental was cool but bright, despite the shades pulled three-quarters down the windows against the late afternoon sun. Joyce looked up from his place behind the door as we entered. His eyes brightened at the sight of Wyatt, then narrowed fractionally as he recognized me beside him.

"Hello, Wyatt," he said. "Drink?"

Wyatt shook his head. "I might take a cigar."

"Sure thing," Joyce said quickly. He pulled a Havana from a glass on the bar and handed it to Wyatt with a small flourish and popped a match, holding it until the sulphur smell had disappeared before lighting Wyatt's cigar. Wyatt looked sideways at me from under bushy eyebrows as he sucked gently on the Havana, inhaling the cigar smoke. At last, when the cigar was lighted to his satisfaction, he leaned one elbow comfortably on the bar and looked at Joyce.

"So, Milt, how's business?" he said easily.

"I'm glad you asked that, Wyatt," said Joyce, leaning confidentially over the bar close to Wyatt, ignoring me. I felt annoyed.

"I'd like a glass of whiskey, please," I said. Joyce looked at me with thinly disguised contempt.

"What?" he said, his tone implying he really didn't want to know what I wanted.

"I prefer Old Williams," I said mildly. I reached into the glass and removed a cigar for myself. I bit the end off it and spat it into a cuspidor beside my foot, then placed the cigar into my mouth and waited patiently.

Joyce glanced at Wyatt. He raised his eyebrow, watching. Joyce's lips drew down tightly. He struck another match, lighting my cigar.

"Now, as I was saying—" he began, but I interrupted him.

"Old Williams?" I said gently.

"What?" he snapped again, this time making no pretense at his displeasure.

I tapped the bar gently with my fingernail. "You forgot my drink. Old Williams."

He stepped down the bar and picked up the black-labeled bottle of Old Williams and a glass and placed them in front of me. He stepped back away from the bar and glared at me.

"Now, was there anything else?" he asked, his face red with the effort of maintaining civility.

"Not at the moment," I said sunnily, smiling at him. "But I'll let you know if there is. You're a peach. A real peach."

"Uh-huh," he grunted.

From the back of the gaming room, Tyler's voice filtered out. "Jesus Christ! Don't none of you know how to play this game?"

Wyatt smiled at Joyce. "Having a bit of trouble, Milt?"

"You could say that," Joyce grumbled. He glanced back at

the gaming room, then leaned forward to speak conspiratorily with Wyatt. "Johnny Tyler's back there with some of his friends. They came in yesterday and drove Teddy Daniels off his table. Since then they've refused to leave."

"Sounds like a job for the marshal," Wyatt said softly.

"Right," Joyce said, his voice dripping sarcasm. "Oh, I'm saying nothing against Fred—he's a good old boy, but that's just it—he's old."

"Sure glad you said nothing against him," I said.

"It's still his job," Wyatt said, ignoring Joyce's glare. "I don't think Fred would shirk his duty."

Joyce didn't like what Wyatt was suggesting and cut to the chase. "I'll make it worth your while, Wyatt," he said.

Wyatt covered his grin by drawing deeply upon his cigar. "You will?"

"An eighth of the gaming room," Joyce said.

"A quarter," Wyatt said. "And a faro table."

"Jesus, Wyatt," Joyce complained. "That's Lou's bread and butter. I can't go that steeply."

"Sure you can," Wyatt answered genially. "Why don't you just step back there and ask old Lou if he'd be willing to give up a piece of the action?"

Tyler's voice came on the end of Wyatt's words. "I told you sons of bitches you didn't know how to play poker! Now you all can just kiss my ass!"

Joyce threw up his hands, shaking his head. "All right. You've got it."

"Well, let's see if we can't just reason with Johnny Tyler a bit," Wyatt said easily, pushing off from the bar. He glanced at me. I nodded and finished my drink and walked to the end of the bar, where I would have a clear view of the gaming room.

"Talk with him!" Joyce complained. "Good Lord, I can talk with him! I want him out of there."

"You probably just don't know how to reason with a fellow, being Yankee and all, Milt," I said, leaning casually upon the bar. I kept my eyes upon the room as Wyatt approached the table where Tyler held forth.

"When I want your advice, Holliday, I'll ask for it," he said, watching Wyatt move into the gaming room.

"Oh yes," I said. "Yes, I know you will. And I can't tell you how long I've been waiting for that distinct pleasure," I said.

Wyatt walked over and stood beside the faro table where Tyler was holding court. A couple of his friends lolled on the felt of the table, watching intently as Tyler slid two cards from the deck he held in his hand and passed them over to the man on his left. He glanced up at Wyatt, who was watching.

"Something on your mind?" he asked toughly.

Wyatt gave him a small smile and blew a cloud of smoke over the table toward him. "I'd appreciate it if you would get out of my seat," he said.

Tyler's eyes bulged. His face mottled as one of the men leaning on the table laughed.

"You hear that, Johnny? He thinks this is his table," the man said.

"I heard him, Ike," Tyler said. "What makes you think this is your table?"

"I just got it from Milt," Wyatt said, pointing with his cigar toward the bar.

"Trouble is, the table's already taken," the second man said.

"I see that, too," Wyatt said. "You can stay and play if you want, Brocius; but the dealer's going to change."

"The hell you say," Tyler said thickly, leaping to his feet. His hand reached down, clawing for his pistol, but froze as Wyatt took two steps forward, bringing himself within inches of Tyler.

"I just did," Wyatt said. His hand flashed, cutting across Tyler's face, the slap loud in the room. He backhanded him on the other cheek. Tyler stumbled back against his chair, trying to get distance between him and Wyatt as he tried to drag his pistol from its holster, but Wyatt stepped forward, keeping inches between them.

"Well?" Wyatt demanded, his voice suddenly harsh in the room. His hand slapped Tyler again, bringing a small trickle of blood to the corner of Tyler's mouth then dropped down

and snaked Tyler's pistol from his holster when his hand
went up to protect his face.

"We don't have to take that shit!" Ike said hotly.

"Of course you don't, gentlemen," I said, taking a step into
the room. Their heads swiveled around to face me. I smiled.
"I don't think we've been properly introduced."

"The chubby one's Ike Clanton," Wyatt intoned. "The
other's Curly Bill Brocius."

"Gentlemen," I said, easing my coat back.

Clanton's eyes drew magnetically to the ivory handle of the
Colt on my left side. Muscles moved in his suety cheeks as he
clenched his teeth together. Brocius gave a big grin and
stepped back away from the table, his hands dropping down to
the two big Colts holstered at his side. I drew the Colt and held
it negligently in front of me, the barrel canted toward his feet.

"Now I don't think it would be very gentlemanly to interfere in a business argument, do you?" I said mildly.

"Fucking goddamn pimp!" Clanton said, his eyes wild.
"Fucking goddamn pimp!"

"Tch, tch. Such manners," I said. "I really don't think you
want to start dancing, do you?"

Brocius laughed and shook his head. Tiny lights sparkled
with amusement in his eyes. "You're on your own, Johnny,"
he said.

"But . . ." Ike spluttered

"Be quiet," Brocius ordered.

"Enough talk," Wyatt said. He grabbed Tyler's nose
between thumb and forefinger, pulling him forward. Tyler
jerked his head away, but Wyatt had reached from in back
between his legs and grabbed his belt, lifting.

"Ow! Ow!" yelled Tyler, going up on tiptoes as Wyatt
lifted harder. "Leggo! Damn you!"

Wyatt turned and propelled Tyler out of the gaming room
and to the front door of the Oriental. He opened the door and
gave a final lift and heaved Tyler through the door, sending
him sprawling in the street. His hands cupped his groin as he
rose painfully to his feet.

"Now, stay out until you develop some manners," Wyatt

ordered. He brushed imaginary dust from his coat and turned back to look at us.

I grinned and swung my head toward the door. "Will you be staying?"

"Not this time, I think," Brocius said. He grabbed Clanton's arm and tugged him with him.

"Curly—" Clanton began to complain.

"Let's go," Brocius said. "We've got cattle to attend."

"Aw, Curly! Goddamnit!"

The smile never disappeared from Brocius's face, but the lights began a new and different dance. Ike stared at them for a moment, then shuddered and, turning, walked quickly from the saloon. Brocius grinned and shook his head.

"You gotta excuse him," he said. "He thinks he's more grown-up than he really is. At heart, he's just a big softy."

"Seems more a pansy than a daisy," I said.

"No, that's more Billy Breckenridge," he said, adding when he saw no sign of recognition in my face, "the jailer. Likes to think he's a deputy, but he's nothing but a turnkey. Don't back up to him."

"I'll remember that," I said. "What about yourself?"

"Me?" He acted surprised. "Why, I'm just the ramrod of the Clanton outfit." He grinned and pointed at the door. "I'm supposed to keep him out of trouble."

"You do your job well," I said. "But it doesn't look like it's very hard."

"Depends on how much Ike's drunk," he said. "He gets a bit braver with a little Dutch courage inside him."

He settled his hat on his head, snapping the brim with a forefinger, which he quickly lowered and pointed at me as if it were a pistol. "I'll be seeing you around."

"I have no doubt of that," I said. "Just as sure as goober peas."

He laughed and swaggered from the saloon. Wyatt stepped aside as he neared, watching him intently. The door swung shut and Joyce let out a huge sigh of relief.

"Whew! I thought for a minute we were going to have a lot of trouble there," he said.

"Not with Ike," Wyatt said. He glanced over at me, his eyes still flinty. "Ike is a bit of a blowhard unless he's been drinking. Even then he'll back off if someone presses him immediately."

"Yeah, but you never just know for sure," Joyce said.

"I do," Wyatt said seriously.

Joyce started to laugh, then glanced at Wyatt's face and lapsed into silence. Nervously, he wiped a towel across the bar's already gleaming surface. Wyatt watched him for a long moment. Finally, he said, "Look, Wyatt, about that twenty-five percent."

"You wouldn't be going to welsh on me, now, would you, Milt?" Wyatt asked softly.

"No, no. Of course not," Joyce said hastily. "It's just that, well, I don't know how I'm going to tell Lou when he comes back from Tucson."

I grinned and shook my head. I took the bottle from the bar and poured myself another drink. Joyce gave me a look of distaste, then took the bottle back, firmly corking it and placing it behind the bar out of my reach.

"That's something you're going to have to solve, Milt," Wyatt said mildly. "Morgan and I will start tonight."

"Morgan?"

"He'll be my casekeeper," Wyatt said.

Joyce gave him a sour look. "You won't be using the room's man?"

Wyatt shook his head. "No, I prefer keeping it within the family."

"What about Holliday?" Joyce said, jerking his head at me.

"What about him?" Wyatt asked quietly. His eyes bored deeply into Joyce's. I wanted to laugh at the bartender's nervous gestures, but drew deeply upon my cigar instead.

"How does he fit into your plans?" Joyce said at last, his voice betraying his nervousness.

"Any way he wants to," Wyatt said.

"Thanks, but I'm privately employed," I said, draining the glass of whiskey. I set it back on the bar and nodded at Joyce. "Be seeing you around, Wyatt. Maybe I'll stop in tonight and initiate you into the wiles of poker."

"Faro, Doc. Faro," Wyatt said.

"A sucker's game," I said. "The odds are all with the house."

"I always did like sure bets," he answered. A small grin lifted the corners of his mustache. "Be seeing you around."

"As sure as little green apples," I answered. I looked at Joyce and pointed a finger at the bottle of Old Williams. "Sure hope you don't run out."

I stepped outside into the dusty street, wincing against the brightness of the sun. I walked across the street and stepped up under the board awning shielding walkers from the afternoon sun. I breathed deeply and walked into the store, looking at the titles of new books that had just been unloaded, while I watched the front door of the Oriental. I could be wrong, but I didn't think Wyatt was done with Johnny Tyler. Not quite yet. I picked up a copy of George Eliot's *Daniel Deronda* and took it to the clerk, paying for it.

The door opened and Wyatt stepped out, drawing deeply upon his cigar. He spied Virgil and Morgan walking down the street and stepped out to greet them. I dropped the book into my pocket and stepped out from the store. From an alley, Tyler appeared, walking toward them, a greener held ready as if he were hunting grouse. I stepped forward, back into the sun.

"Why, Johnny Tyler! What do you think you're doing with that shotgun?" I called.

He whirled toward me, the greener coming down level. I grinned at him. "Don't, Johnny. That is, unless you think you're the daisy to get it done."

Indecision wavered in his eyes, then he lowered the greener. "Doc! I didn't expect . . . that is, I didn't . . ."

"I know, Johnny. I know. Now put that shotgun down and be off like a good boy."

His eyes flared, and for a moment, I thought he would raise it again. I grinned and tapped the nail of a forefinger against the ivory handle of the Colt. The tiny ticking drew his eyes. His lips tightened, then he bent forward at the waist and carefully laid the shotgun in the dust. He straightened, staring into my eyes with twin coals of hatred.

"Off with you now," I said and made shooing flutters with my fingers. He turned and started away.

"Just a minute," Wyatt called, a hard edge to his voice.

Tyler took a look at Wyatt, then flashed a glance at me and began sprinting back down into the alley. A small crowd of cowboys standing in front of the Alhambra, taking in the confrontation, broke out into laughter.

"Run, Johnny! Run!" one of them cried out.

"Er-er-er-er-oooo!" another crowed, flapping his arms.

Wyatt crossed over to me. His eyes held mine. "You knew that was going to happen, didn't you?"

"Let's just say I suspected as much," I said easily. I bent and picked up the shotgun, handing it to him. "Here. I don't have much use for these things."

He took it, checking the loads automatically, then closed it and dropped his arm to his side.

"I owe you again, Doc," he said quietly.

"Fort Griffin," I murmured.

"That's a while back. You made good on that in Dodge."

"Did I? I don't remember," I said.

I turned and walked away, heading down the street into the afternoon dust.

That evening, Kate came with me to the Oriental. We had quarreled again earlier and were putting on those tight smiles that couples use when they do not want the world to know that relations are temporarily strained between them. But Kate began to drink heavily, and soon, was singing bawdily in that husky voice of hers to the accompaniment of the piano player.

> "He was an old cow haaand
> With more in his haaaand. . . ."

Wyatt winced and looked up at me from his seat at the faro table. "Not exactly subtle, Doc."

I shrugged and took a sip from Belle's cup. "No, she's no

Philomela, I grant you. But neither is the piano player worthy of her talents, such as they are." I took a handkerchief from my pocket and mopped my face ineffectually: I could feel the perspiration begin again, dotting my forehead and cheeks. I coughed and took another sip.

"As a favor, Doc. Do something, please. That song's a bit raw. Even for here."

"Wyatt Earp."

We looked up. Brocius stood across the table from us with a group of cowboys. He grinned down at Wyatt. "Heard you might be willing to take a little bet."

"Place it," Wyatt said laconically.

"A thousand on the king. To win," Brocius added.

"That's a lot of money," Wyatt said quietly. Morgan moved a step to his right, freeing him from the table. Brocius grinned.

"You must be Holliday," the man beside him said softly. Murky shadows moved in the depths of his eyes. Smudged shadows hung below the marcasite eyes, and a full mustache covered his upper lip. His face was pouchy from dissipation, but he was thin, with twin holsters holding Colt .45's hanging from his narrow hips. He wore a short, braided Mexican jacket and his hat hung from a rawhide strap off the back of his head. His hair had been combed back from a high forehead. He was dusty, but his pistols had been wiped and oiled despite the carelessness with the rest of his appearance.

"That's what they tell me on occasion," I said, bending my lips to my cup.

"Careful, Johnny," Brocius said sardonically. "He's as fast as lickety-split with those pistols of his."

I felt Kate move up beside me and glanced down. Interest shone in her eyes as she studied the man across from me. His eyes traveled down to her full breasts bulging above the bottle green velvet dress with a deep décolleté.

"You just have to be Johnny Ringo," I said. I turned to Kate, gesturing with my cup. "Darling, I'd like you to meet Johnny Ringo. They say he's the fastest man on the draw since Wild Bill. Do you think it's true?"

"Does it matter?" she said, her Hungarian accent grown thicker with man-interest. Her pink tongue slipped out between her full lips, wetting them.

"You know," I said, "he reminds me of someone, but I just can't place who." And then I knew: I was looking at my doppelgänger . . . my twin . . . me.

He glanced into my eyes and a tiny, knowing smile wrapped itself around his lips. He took a small step to his left, giving him a better angle for a draw. I grinned.

"Don't mind him," Morgan said, taking a step to the right of Wyatt, clearing him from the table. "He's been drinking."

"In vino veritas," I said raising my cup to my lips.

"Age quod agis," Ringo answered softly.

I slowly lowered the cup from my lips, staring at him. "Asinus asinum fricat."

"Stet pro ratione voluntas," he answered, touching the handle of his pistol with his right hand.

"Insanus omnis furere credit ceteros," I said.

"Plures crapula quam gladius," he said, his eyes mocking me.

"Incidis in Scyllam cupiens vitare Charybdim," I said.

His eyes narrowed, and I pulled my coat back with the thumb of my left hand, which was holding my cup. The air around us became charged with tension. A red haze began to drop slowly over everything, and I felt a sudden joy leap up from the pit of my stomach.

"That's enough," Fred White said, taking care that his intentions wouldn't be misunderstood as he moved between us. "Let's have things a little easier now, boys. We don't want to get anyone killed."

"That's Latin, darling," I said, half turning to Kate. I felt the muscles of my face tighten as I turned my head back to Ringo. "Mr. Ringo would like us to believe he is an educated man."

His hand darted down for his pistol. I slipped the Colt from its holster and brought it up, my arm outstretched. Our hammers clicked open together as one.

"That's enough!" Wyatt snapped.

"Stay out of this, Wyatt," I answered. "This is between Johnny and me."

"No, it's me they want," he said softly. "And, Ringo, if that pistol goes off, I'll cut you and Brocius in two."

I heard the double click of hammers being cocked on a shotgun and glanced quickly at Wyatt. He had Tyler's greener leveled over the table, centered between Brocius and Ringo. The touch of one trigger would cut them both in two at that range. I lowered the hammer on my pistol and returned it to its holster. Ringo followed suit.

"One day, Holliday, your nursemaid won't be around," he said.

"We can step outside now, if you wish," I answered. I drained my cup and twirled it around my forefinger, pointing it at him for emphasis.

"Now, boys," White said, spreading his hands. "Let's have a little peace here, okay? No one got hurt. Where's that damn piano player?"

"My pleasure," I said, moving toward the piano. "Kate." I handed her my cup and gestured toward the bar. She hesitated, giving Ringo a long, slow, smoky look, then sauntered toward the bar, swishing her hips, a cat in heat. I seated myself at the piano, flexed my fingers, then began playing Chopin.

"We still gotta bet, Earp," I heard Brocius say.

"So we have," Wyatt answered. A card snicked out of the shoe. A king. A loser.

"Goddamn!" Brocius said, slapping the table in front of him. I smiled as I caught his movement to the bar out of the corner of my eye. He gestured at Joyce and held up two fingers.

Kate slid onto the bench beside me and placed my cup on the piano in front of me. I held a run while I took a sip, then replaced it. I felt Kate begin pressing against me, moving herself sensuously against my side in time to the music.

A figure detached itself from the bar and came over, resting his elbow on the top of the piano. His spurs jangled. I smelled the perspiration on him and cows. He wore a blue work shirt with a large grease stain on the right breast, his legs encased in leather chaps. A single pistol hung heavily from his hip, a Smith & Wesson Russian. He took a sip of beer from the glass in his hand and looked back at the crowd. I glanced over at Brocius out of the corner of my eye, recognizing Ike beside him. Ringo was at the far end of the bar, drinking alone, a bottle of whiskey at his elbow.

"Hey!"

I looked up; he was young, barely eighteen, his jaw long and thin, nose slightly hooked. His eyes flickered arrogantly over mine.

"What?" I said softly.

"Is that 'I Dream of Jeannie With the Light Brown Hair'?" he leered at me, then ran his eyes boldly over Kate.

"I beg your pardon?"

He snickered. "You know: Stephen Foster."

"No, it's a nocturne."

He frowned, wondering for a moment if he was being insulted. Then curiosity got the better of him. "Whatja say?"

"You know: Frederic Chopin. It's a shame you never finished school. Of course, then you would have picked up some manners and learned not to wipe your hands upon your shirt." I nodded at the grease stains.

His lips tightened and he stepped quickly away from the bar. "I don't have to take that from anyone!"

"Let it go, Billy," Brocius said.

"But he—"

"I said, let it go," Brocius repeated, the words soft, but threat hanging onto each syllable.

I kept playing, watching the boy's face move indecisively, then his eyes wavered and fell and he turned, storming from the Oriental. Brocius caught my stare and smiled, raised his glass and drained it, then placed it on the bar and, turning, walked slowly from the bar.

"Holliday, you're going to be the death of me one of these days."

I looked up at Fred White and smiled. "I reckon you better protect me, then."

He shook his head. "The law's the law. I'm going to have to take a peace bond out on each of you and the cowboys if you keep this up."

"Be a bit expensive, wouldn't it?" I asked, moving into a series of runs on the piano.

"I was sort of hoping that I could talk you into leaving Tombstone," he said.

I shook my head. "I kind of like it here. The air's good for my affliction."

"Yeah, but it could be killing others," he said.

Shots came from the street followed by a long coyote wail. More shots were fired. White glanced over at Wyatt.

"Leave it alone," Wyatt said quietly, pulling another card from the shoe and collecting the bets that had lost. "It's just Brocius blowing off steam. You knew he'd do that."

"Is that what you would do?" White asked.

"No," Wyatt said. He gave White a bleak smile. "But you ain't me."

White flushed. "No, I can't be you, but I still gotta do something."

He hitched his gun belt a little higher, wiped his mouth with the back of his hand, and left. I rolled into the end of the nocturne, then began another, playing the runs low and sensual. Kate began to move faster against my side.

"Doc," she began, but a shot exploded from outside, followed by a cry:

"Jesus Christ! Curly Bill just killed the marshal!"

I glanced over at Wyatt. He reacted swiftly, rising from his chair and hooking the Smith & Wesson American from Morgan's holster as he ran from the saloon. I stood abruptly, toppling Kate onto the floor. She swore long and fluently as I took my whiskey cup from the top of the piano and hurried after him.

When I reached the street, I saw White lying on the ground off to the right, his hands cupped around his groin, blood seeping out through his fingers. Brocius lay on the ground at Wyatt's feet. Wyatt bent down and pulled him to his feet. He rocked drunkenly, his hands pressed against the sides of his head, and I knew that Wyatt had buffaloed him, whacking him over the head with the barrel of his pistol.

A group of cowboys moved up slowly, surrounding Wyatt. Ike Clanton stepped forward, glanced at the cowboys backing him, and said, "Let 'im go!"

"No," Wyatt said softly. He gestured at White, who was now being attended to by a couple of men, including H. M. Matthews, the coroner. "He shot a lawman. He'll go to trial for that."

"Go to hell!" Ike said loudly, swaggering forward. Suddenly, he staggered, as Wyatt's pistol rose, stabbing him in the face. Blood streamed from his nose and his face drained white as Wyatt's pistol steadied scant inches from his face.

"Probably," Wyatt said, his voice rasping like steel across a file. "But you'll meet me when I do!"

"Aw, shit! Let's get 'im. He ain't going to do nuthin' with all of us around," Billy said, stepping forward.

"Stay back, Billy!" Ike said desperately. He pulled a dirty handkerchief from a pocket of his pants and pressed it to his nose, trying to staunch the bleeding.

"He's bluffing," Billy said, continuing forward.

"Billy!" Ike said desperately. "He'll kill me, damnit!"

Reluctantly, Billy slowed to a stop. I grinned and drew my two pistols.

"And you, my friend, will be next," I said.

Billy turned to face me, his face tight with tension, wanting to strike out at someone. "Well, I'll be damned! The piano player's trying to be pistoleer! What the hell. You're as good as the next man." He pointed at the pistols in my hand. "Think you can hit anything with those? I'll bet you're seeing double right now."

"That's all right, pumpkin," I said. I cocked the Colt and took up the slack in the Lightning's trigger. "I have two pistols. One for each of you."

A shotgun exploded in the air and Virgil and Morgan pushed through the mob of cowboys surrounding Wyatt. Each was armed with a shotgun. Even though they outnumbered the Earps, no cowboy was willing to step up in front of a greener at that distance.

"It's all over, boys," Virgil said. "Go home. Curly Bill goes to jail like Wyatt says."

"They can't get all of us," someone said.

"No," another answered. "But those greeners ain't picky about which one they get, either."

"What they don't get, Holliday will," someone else said.

"He's only got twelve shots. . . ."

"Yeah, but that's a probable twelve dead men. You wanna be one?"

"He ain't that good. . . ."

"You wanna die proving he ain't? 'Sides, it's enough that he thinks he's that good. . . ."

Slowly the crowd dispersed as the cowboys continued to argue among them. Virgil turned and took Curly Bill from Wyatt and marched him off toward jail, with Morgan following watchfully in his trail. Wyatt crossed over to me.

"This is getting to be a habit for you," he said.

"You want me to stop?" I asked.

"No." He pressed his lips together, then reached out to touch me gently on the shoulder as I replaced my pistols. "But you're making a lot of enemies on our behalf, Doc. Watch yourself."

"Pallida Mors aequo pulsat pede pauperum tabernas regumque turres," I said. I had tipped my hat and turned to go back into the Oriental when Kate walked by, arm-in-arm with Ringo. She looked at me boldly, then laughed, the sound brittle like icicles in the air. Ringo gave me a mocking grin and turned to swagger down the street with her. For a brief moment, anger flared inside me. Then I felt Wyatt's hand on my arm.

"Maybe it's better this way, Doc," he said lowly. "She's been a millstone around your neck for a long time."

"Varium et mutabile semper femina? Perhaps," I answered, then sighed and shook my head. "It would be easy if I could dismiss her that easily, Wyatt. But it's far more than the fickleness of a woman. This is between Ringo and myself."

He waited for me to continue, but I didn't. I couldn't explain it to him then. I'm not sure that I would have even if I could. The truth always gets lost among big lies and little lies, and those who try to separate them to get at the truth only create bigger lies. I knew what Ringo was doing; we were kindred spirits, and since we hated ourselves so much, we hated each other even more.

11

Shifting sands of time constantly upset our plans. So it was with me and Milt Joyce. I suppose it had to do with me being drunk—drunker than usual, perhaps, would be a better description—but all of that is inconsequential. The only thing is that it happened.

It? Well, *it* happened in October when I walked into the Oriental for a drink and found that Johnny Tyler was again making inroads with Lou in an attempt to regain the table he had lost when Wyatt had so ignominiously thrown him from the premises with a twist of Tyler's ear. Tyler was standing at the bar drinking some nefarious cocktail while visiting with Joyce when I walked in.

"Well," he said, "here's the little drunk." He laughed. "Still chasing Earp's coattails?"

I ignored him and stepped up to the bar and pointed a finger at the bottle of Old Williams behind Joyce. I coughed and spat pinkish phlegm into the cuspidor between Tyler and myself.

"A glass of your best, if you please," I said.

Joyce turned and poured the drink, setting it on the bar between us. I took a large drink, swallowing it in installments to ease the tickle, trying to keep the beast in my chest at bay. Tyler laughed.

"Planning on playing today, Holliday?" he asked. He nodded toward the gaming room. "I might accommodate you at the table."

I sighed and turned to him. I gave him a long, level look. "Trying to be a daisy instead of a petunia, Johnny Tyler? You know the table belongs to Wyatt."

"Maybe not for much longer," he said arrogantly, nodding at Joyce. "We are in the process of negotiations."

I gave my attention to Joyce. "What gives, Milt?"

He ignored me for a moment, busying himself with a towel across the bar. Finally, when he saw that I wasn't going away, he shrugged and said, "Johnny's offering to take the table alone without a percentage. Just business, Holliday."

"Why you ungrateful peckerhead," I said softly. "You came running to Wyatt to pull this piece of shit out of your saloon when he was driving away the customers and now you're going back to him?" I shook my head. "I don't think I would want to be in your shoes when Wyatt finds out."

"Who you calling a piece of shit?" Tyler blustered.

"Getting your nerve back, Johnny?" I asked, turning to him. Gleeful anger rose within me. "All right," I said recklessly. "I'm your huckleberry. Pull that shooter and let's dance."

I stepped back away from the bar, pulling my coat open around the Colt. "Say when."

His face suddenly went white. His fingers twitched. I smiled at him, tapping the ivory handle of my Colt.

"Time to call the tune, Johnny," I said softly.

His lips tightened. I could smell the fear oozing out of him. I laughed. "Come on, Johnny. The day's not gettin' any younger."

"Knock it off, Holliday," Joyce growled. "Everybody knows Johnny can't beat you."

Rage swept through me. Joyce had yet to utter a civil word to me since I came to Tombstone. I could understand a scion of public virtue treating me in this fashion, but Joyce's business depended upon people like me.

"You trying to be a daisy, too, Milt?" I asked icily.

He flushed and raised a thick forefinger, pointing it between my eyes. "Keep a civil tone in your voice when you talk to me, Holliday," he warned.

"Or what, Milt?" I asked softly. "You'll talk me to death? My, my. I don't think I could take it."

"You son of a bitch!" he snapped. His face went beet-red. A large vein began to pulse in his forehead. I grinned and looked back at Tyler.

"Why, Johnny! You still here?" I said. "Very well. Let's do it."

Johnny's tongue came out, licking his lips. He raised tentative fingers to touch his mustache, then suddenly turned around and ran out of the Oriental. Laughter followed him from those watching. I sighed and turned back to Joyce.

"Well, now, Milt, my huckleberry friend, are you willing to dance with the devil?" I asked.

"Get out, Holliday! Get out!" He threw up his hand, pointing toward the door.

I gave him a mock smile and moved easily to the door. Just as the door closed behind me, he said to someone at the bar, "A worthless lunger. Thinks his gun will make him a man. Ain't nothin' but a goddamn killer. Hangin' around Earp, hopin' some of the glory will rub off. Southern bastard. Nothin' for him but someone should shoot the bastard."

Laughter erupted. I whirled and thrust the door open, stepping back inside. The crowd fell instantly silent, watching me warily. Red mist tinged the outline of the room. Laughter bubbled up inside me and I let it escape, feeling the excitement rush through my veins.

"All right, you cowdancers, make your plays! All of you," I added. Laughter bubbled from me again. No one moved, and they all kept their hands in plain sight. "No?" I said. "No one? Not one brave lad among you willing to trade shots with a lunger? Pray, do. No? I shall let you all draw first. Then I will."

"Shit," someone muttered. "The son of a bitch wants to die. It's a fool's bet against that."

"Think of the glory. Think of the honor. We shall all die exquisitely."

"That's enough, Holliday," Joyce said, coming from around the bar toward me. "You're out of here."

I drew the Lightning with my left hand and turned toward Joyce. Out of the corner of my eye, I caught a flicker of movement from the bar and swung my head toward it. Joyce took two steps and swung a bung-stopper at my head, I jerked back, but I was too slow. The mallet glanced off my skull, stunning me. I fell backwards against a table. The table tilted and I landed on the floor. I pulled the trigger reflexively, then Joyce fell on top of me, pinning me to the floor. I felt hands tearing the Lightning from my grasp. I fumbled for the Colt, but then Joyce jerked it from its holster, striking me again with it. Darkness fell.

The room swam back into focus and I recognized my own lodgings. A blinding stab of pain shot across my temples and I winced.

"Back to the living, Doc?"

I squinted across the room to where Wyatt sat patiently in the chair by the window. I struggled to push myself up on my bed against the headboard. He rose and poured a glass of whiskey and brought it to me. I drank thirstily.

"What the hell happened?" I asked. I held my breath, squeezing my eyes tightly together, then opening them. Slowly the pain disappeared.

"You tried to shoot it out with the entire Oriental Saloon," he said. "An overly romantic gesture even for you."

"Ah, but the gesture was everything!" I said. "I know that! What happened after? Ah, Joyce."

"What brought it on?" Wyatt said.

"A bit of defiled honor," I said. "Joyce took your table and gave it to Tyler, did you know that?"

His eyes narrowed sharply and I knew it was news to him. "And you thought you would kill my snakes for me?"

"No, this had nothing to do with you," I said. "At least not directly. Not everything does, you know. The world doesn't revolve around the Earps."

His lips tightened, then he smiled. "Yeah, I know. It's going to the dogs."

"Except we call it civilization," I said. I shook my head. "You know, Wyatt, we have already outlived our time. We're relics, shadows of the past, ghosts that people want to lock in closets and forget about."

"Perhaps. But right now you've got a court date."

I was taken before Jim Reilly, the justice of the peace, who gave me a nominal fine for drunken misbehavior. It was just a token fine, but not done to please me so much as to warn me that behavior such as mine would no longer be tolerated. I think Reilly decided to try and use me for an example because he knew about my friendship with Wyatt. An example had to be made as a warning to all. To pick on one of the cowboys was to pick on all. But me, well, there was safety there because of my friendship.

Ben Sippy had been appointed to replace White after White was killed by Brocius. Sippy's appointment was only temporary. An election was held with Sippy running on the Democratic ticket against Virgil on the Republican. Bob Paul, one of our friends, ran against Charlie Shibell for Pima County sheriff. Wyatt had been a deputy to Shibell, but resigned in order to support Paul. Shibell was a Democrat while Paul was Republican. That's when that asshole Johnny Behan was appointed to replace Wyatt. I didn't pay much attention to that, thinking that Paul was a shoo-in, but the election was rigged. The San Simon cowboys supported Shibell with Johnny Ringo as the precinct judge and Ike Clanton the voting inspector. Two scurvier bastards you will never find. Well, the Republicans lost. Election fraud was proven when Wyatt made a deal with Brocius to tell who stuffed the boxes. It was Ike Clanton. Wyatt testified at Brocius's trial for killing White that the shooting was accidental, and Brocius was let off. But the Democrats still held the strength in the town.

A short time later, Wyatt's thoroughbred, Dick Naylor,

disappeared. Sherm McMasters, one of Wyatt's friends, let me know that Billy Clanton had the horse over on the San Pedro. Wyatt asked me to go along, and together we rode over to the small mill town. We didn't have far to look; Dick Naylor was tied to a post in front of the saloon when we rode down the street.

Wyatt went over to his horse and uncinched the saddle, throwing it in the dust. From the doorway of the saloon, Billy Clanton yelled out loudly, "Hey! What do you think you're doing?"

Wyatt ignored him, and Clanton stepped down off the boardwalk, trying to grab the reins from Wyatt's hands. Wyatt backhanded him. Clanton staggered, then tried to draw his pistol, but I stepped forward and shoved my Colt in his stomach.

"What, Billy Clanton," I murmured to him. "Would you be shooting a man in the back? They hang people for that, you know. Even in Arizona."

"Holliday," he said angrily. "You and this—"

"Let it go, boy," Wyatt said quietly, turning his terrible eyes upon Clanton. Billy raised his chin, staring hotly at Wyatt.

"I ain't afraid of you!" he said.

"Fear has nothing to do with it, boy," Wyatt answered. "Common sense does." He nodded at me. "Do you really think you can take the two of us?"

I grimaced from those words, yet the gay fire of battle was beginning to burn within my veins. I felt an impulse to giggle, then stifled that impulse as I reached for Belle's flask, one-handedly opening it. I took a long drink, then coughed and put it away. It was the wrong thing to say to a young man like Billy Clanton. It was the wrong thing to say to any young man sure of his own immortality and the vulnerability of the world.

"Wanna back off and gimme a try?" he demanded, a malignant glint to his eye.

Two young children ran by, pushing a wheel-hoop with a stick, a yellow dog barking at their heels. They ignored us, intent upon their own play. I grimaced and shook my head. Suddenly I didn't want to kill him; I was looking at myself the day I went after Uncle Thomas.

"No guts?" he said. He grinned tightly, recklessly. "I thought not."

I sighed and reached down to his holster, pulling out his Smith & Wesson Russian. I tossed it into the water trough at Dick Naylor's knees. Clanton's face went livid.

"I'll kill you for that," he said.

"I don't think so, boy," Wyatt said. "Not with that pistol anyway."

He gathered Dick Naylor's reins in his fist and mounted the horse he had ridden in on. I snapped my fingers, and Ares grunted and stepped to my side, shuffling his feet in the dust. Clanton's eyes opened as he took in Ares.

"A good-looking horse," he commented.

"And mine," I said. I waved my pistol under his nose for emphasis. "And he'll stay mine, do you hear me, lad? If I find him missing, I'll give you your chance to be a daisy. I'll blow your knees away and leave you hobbling on stumps. Not a good end for a cowboy."

"I ain't scared of you," he said.

"I know," I answered.

I replaced the Colt and took the reins, climbing into the saddle. "But you should be," I said to Clanton before turning Ares' head and following Wyatt out of town.

And that was the beginning of our apocalyptic meeting with the Clantons and McLaury's in the OK Corral. I know you have read about that. For some reason it seems to have captured the romantic minds. In reality it was only a settlement of old grudges and hot blood. Who was at fault? All of us, none of us—it was a series of misunderstandings.

"Hiya, Doc!" a happy voice cried out.

I turned and Billy Leonard stepped up, stretching forth his hand. I gripped it, feeling a smile spread across my face. "What are you doing here? I haven't seen you since Prescott."

He coughed and spat a pinkish blob into the street. "Thought it might be good for my lungs. Yeah," he continued as he noticed the look on my face, "I know."

"Sorry to hear that," I said. "You going to open up a jewelry store here?"

He shook his head. "No, there's no future in that. The time I have left and all, well, I'm working for a couple of people over on the San Simon."

"The San Simon?" I said slowly. "The cowboys? What are you doing for them? Not punching cows, that's for sure. Not with that." I tapped him on the chest.

He glanced around, then lowered his voice. "Well, I'm melting down some old things that they picked up in Mexico. You know."

"Uh-huh," I said sarcastically. "I believe I do know what you're doing. Billy, that isn't a smart thing to do. Who you with?"

"Luther King, Harry Head, and Jim Crane. It was Crane who brought me down here."

"Good God almighty! Billy, those are some of the biggest crooks around."

His face tightened defensively. "They're my friends," he said stoutly.

"Friends don't ask friends to do what they're asking you to do," I said.

"Leave it alone, Doc," he said. His lips tightened. "Just leave it alone."

He turned and left. I watched him make his way down the street toward the stables. He was thin, ascetic-looking. Innocence radiated from him. And loyalty. I sighed and turned in to the Alhambra, a feeling of dread dropping over me like the curtain on a bad show.

Things went from bad to worse. Wyatt wired Bat Masterson and Luke Short to come down from Dodge City, and within three or four days of their arrival, Luke shot and killed Charlie Storms in front of the Oriental when Storms thought it would be fun to pick on the little man. That did nothing to help the relations between Milt Joyce and myself. Shortly

after that, Jim McAllister killed One-Armed Kelly in the
saloon—a single bullet square between the eyes and blood
everywhere. Joyce used that as an excuse to close down the
gaming room and throw Wyatt out of business.

Wyatt became a detective for Wells Fargo. Of course that
isn't wellknown; everyone just assumed that one of the mining claims he had won at the faro table was finally producing.
He even hinted that the Mattie Blalock Mine, the one that
he'd named after the woman who claimed they were married,
was the one, but we knew better. Poor Mattie! She killed herself a couple of years later. That was about the time that
Wyatt stopped going to her and took up with Josie—
Josephine Sarah Marcus—a little whore who had the airs of
a lady and the morals of an alley cat. She came down with
Pauline Markham's Pinafore On Wheels dance troupe and
promptly took up with Johnny Behan. But once she found
out that Johnny had no intention of marrying her, she booted
him out and sank her claws into Wyatt. Mattie was heavy
into laudanum at the time so Wyatt was out on the look and
ripe for the plucking, a regular pecan.

I suppose things could have been better between Kate and
myself, but when she took up with Johnny Ringo, I had had
enough. I knew it wouldn't last, but, well, it is hard for men
like me to have a companionable relationship.

Pauline Markham and I became lovers. There's the short
and long of it. As strange as it may seem, that curly-haired
vixen with shapely legs that drove the miners wild in her wee
costume took a liking to me despite my affliction. She was
nearly as deeply bosomed as Kate, but prettier. Yes, much
prettier. What she lacked in expertise in bed she more than
made up with enthusiasm. She was a joy for me, but she was
also my Eve.

The door flew open and Kate stormed in, drunk and bran-
dishing a self-cocker. Pauline screamed and rolled off the
bed, crawling under it. I swung my skinny shanks to the
floor, taking a large step toward Kate.

"You asshole!" she yelled. She pointed the pistol at me and squeezed the trigger. Pauline screamed from beneath the bed. For a moment I was blinded by smoke, then I reached out, grappling with Kate. I swung my fist, smacking her jaw. She staggered and fell. I pulled the pistol from her and tossed it behind me onto the bed.

"Get out," I said, pulling her to her feet. She tried to swing around behind me to the pistol, but I shoved her out through the door, closing it in her face. She began kicking the door, yelling obscenities. I coughed and made my way to the dry sink and spat the bloody phlegm into it.

"Is she gone?" Pauline asked, peering out from beneath the bed.

"Yes," I gasped. I coughed again and motioned to the bottle of whiskey sitting on the table by the window. Pauline crawled out and brought the bottle to me. I took a long drink, holding it in my mouth and swallowing in installments. I gripped the iron bedstead with my hand, steadying myself.

"Who was that?" she asked as she pulled on her clothes.

"Kate Elder," I said, rinsing out my mouth. "We used to be together, until she decided Johnny Ringo was a far more interesting person."

"It doesn't look like she intends on taking her hooks out of you," she said.

"She lost that when she went with Ringo," I answered.

"I see." She nodded. "Are you sure?"

"What do you mean?"

"It appears that there's still something between you," she said.

"Maybe there is," I said. "Do you lose everything when you stop being lovers?"

"I don't know," she said. A tiny grin dimpled her cheeks. "What do you think we can expect now?"

"Oh, Christ!" I said. "Well, I'm afraid Kate will make certain that your reputation is gone."

"Pot calling the kettle black," she said.

"You don't know Kate," I groaned.

She laughed and came over, giving me a long, deep kiss, an affectionate kiss that is a kiss between sexual partners, not lovers.

And so it became known that we were having an affair. Wyatt took Josie away from Behan about the same time. Kate and Mattie became friends after that; I suppose they had something in common. Peace reigned briefly and, like a fool, I thought things were going to be different. But that wasn't the end of my trouble with Kate.

Not long after Kate's dramatic entrance, I ran into Billy Leonard on the street. He told me about a high-stakes poker game that had been going on for two days and nights in Charleston, about twenty miles away.

"Honest, Doc," he said. "I think you might be able to pick up a few bucks there."

"Who's playing?" I asked.

"Nobody you heard of," he said. "At least there ain't any ringers that I know about."

I thanked him for his information and since Ares needed a workout, decided to ride over to Charleston and see for myself. By the time I got there, though, the game had broken up. I decided to return to Tombstone, letting Ares have his head the last few miles, enjoying the rippling muscles stretching out beneath my legs. About a mile outside of Tombstone, I met Old Man Fuller driving his water wagon back to town. He did a good business supplying the town with water from The Wells ten miles out on the Charleston Road.

"Hey, Doc!" he shouted. "Get down and sit a spell."

I tied Ares off behind the wagon and rode the rest of the way in with him. He dropped me off at the Alhambra. I debated about taking Ares back to the stable, then decided to get a drink first.

"Hey, Doc! You hear the news?" Tom Cleary asked when I walked in. "Budd Philpot was shot and killed on his run last night."

"No," I said. "What happened?" I motioned at the bottle of

Old Williams on the shelf behind the bar. He turned and gathered the bottle, filling a glass in front of me.

"Seems like him and Bob Paul traded places on the seat 'cause ol' Philpot had the shits, and his stomach was aching something fierce from some Mex grub he ate before they left. They got to that long crawl up the pass—you know the one I mean?" I nodded and he continued. "And someone rode out from behind the rock and told him to pull up. Bob couldn't see who it was so he whipped the horses up and the guy unloaded a shotgun into Philpot. Killed a passenger on the dickey seat, too. Some drummer. Anyway, Johnny Behan got together a posse and they're out looking for the bandits right now."

"Wyatt and Morgan go with them?" I asked.

He nodded. "And Virgil and Bat Masterson. Behan wasn't too happy about that, but Wells Fargo said that they wanted Wyatt along. Behan's got Billy Breckenridge with him." He grinned and winked. "Think Behan'll share his roll with Billy?"

I laughed. Breckenridge's sexual preferences were common knowledge and the butt of many jokes. He tried to be tough, but there was a softness about him that made no one except a few Mexicans take him seriously.

"I don't know," I answered, sipping. "Maybe they'll do a little flower gatherin' when the sun drops down. I'll bet Wyatt and Morg are having a good time with that."

"I imagine," he said. He glanced behind me, raising his eyebrows. I turned and found Stumpy Bracken.

"Would you care for a little drink, Stumpy?" I asked, motioning to Cleary.

"Thanks, Doc. Believe I will." He motioned for a beer. Cleary pulled a glass and placed it before him. He took a long swallow that knocked the contents down by half, then slapped his tattered hat upon the bar and mopped his bald pate with a dirty bandanna.

"Whew!" he said. "Hotter'n the hinges of hell. Heard anything about the posse?"

"No," Cleary said, leaning meaty forearms upon the bar. "Don't 'spect to either until tomorrow."

Stumpy shook his head. "I reckon we'll have some problem if they catch the shooter and bring 'im here. Budd had a lot of friends."

"That he did," Cleary said. "That he did. What've you been up to, Doc?"

"Rode over to Charleston to play a little poker but the game broke up before I got there," I said.

"See you got a Henry on your saddle," Stumpy said. "Looking for someone?"

"No," I said. "I thought I might run into a renegade Indian or two but I didn't. Better to be safe than sorry."

"That it is," Stumpy said. He turned to Cleary. "Remember the Watkins family over in Red Rock Canyon?"

"Do I!" Cleary shuddered, then looked at me. "Found pieces of them all over the place. Butchered like hogs." His eyes grew thoughtful. "Never did find the little girl, though. What was her name?"

"Susan," Stumpy said finishing his beer and wiping his mouth with the back of his hand. "Like as not she's at some renegade's wickiup across the border." He looked regretfully at the empty glass of beer.

"Another?" I asked.

He shook his head. "No, got too much work to do. Mucking out is hard work but leaving it makes it harder." He glanced toward the door. "You want me to take that stallion down for you, Doc?"

"Might as well," I said, shrugging. I tossed off the glass of whiskey and shoved it across to Cleary. "Don't think it'll get cool enough for riding this evening. 'Sides," I added casually, "I think I'll take in the show at Schieffelin Hall."

Stumpy winked at Cleary. "I'd be careful 'bout that I were you, Doc. Kate's drinking again down in Mex town."

"Damn!" I said. "She'll be rolling again. Yes, take Ares down to the stable and brush him and give him a nosebag of oats."

"Take care," Stumpy said, hitching his pants higher. He

turned and walked out. I reached for the glass of whiskey, draining it.

"What are you gonna do, Doc?" Cleary asked. I waved away the bottle.

"Move," I said. "Seems the smarter thing to do. It'll take Kate a while to find me and I'll have a little peace."

"Fly's got a room, I think," Cleary said, mentioning the town photographer, who had a rooming house next to his studio. "You want, I'll send the boy over to move you. That way no one will see you carrying your bags over to Fly's."

"Thanks, Tom," I said. I glanced toward the rear of the saloon. A game was just getting started. "I'll take a few hands while you tend to that."

The boys didn't return for a little over two weeks. They caught Luther King, who was apparently one of the bandits, and sent him back with Behan and Billy Breckenridge and Marshall Williams, the Wells Fargo agent. They left King with Under-sheriff Harry Woods, but Woods was King's friend and let him walk out while he pretended to be busy in a horse trade with John Dunbar, the county treasurer, who was partners with Behan in the Dexter Corral and Livery Stable. Behan claimed he had bought King's horse from him while on the way into Tombstone and while the bill of sale was being drawn up, King walked out the back door and got away. Wyatt was furious about this, but not as mad as I was.

Pauline and I were in bed when the knock came on the door. She grumbled and nudged me with her elbow until I gave up and rolled out of bed, pattering to the door in my bare feet. I picked up the Lightning and stood to the right of the door, calling out, "Who's there?"

"Johnny Behan. Open the door, Holliday," he said.

"Go to hell, Behan," I said, yawning. I glanced at the window: light shone in through the crack in the blind. I coughed and started automatically to the bottle of whiskey next to the dry sink.

"Holliday, you open this door right now or I'm going to kick it in," Behan demanded.

"You kick that door in, you son of a bitch, and I'll put a

bullet in your ugly head!" I shouted back. I took the bottle, poured a glass, and drank, shuddering from the first bit of whiskey. I could hear murmurings out in the hall. I crossed back to the door, carrying the glass of whiskey in one hand, the Lightning in the other. My flesh pebbled from the cool morning air.

"What is it?" Pauline asked sleepily from the bed.

"Behan," I said.

"What's he doing?"

"Being a horse's ass," I said. I stopped beside the door again.

"Holliday, this is Sheriff John Behan and I'm ordering you to open this door."

"Got a warrant?" I challenged.

"Yes."

At first, I couldn't believe what I heard. I frowned, trying to make sense of it. "A warrant? For what?"

"I'm arresting you for the murder of Budd Philpot and Peter Roerig and attempted stage robbery," he said pompously through the door.

"Who the hell is Peter Roerig?"

"He was the drummer on the dickey seat. When you cut loose you killed him, too," Behan said. Then his voice changed to a whine. "Come on, Holliday, open the door."

"You have nothing, Behan," I said. "I was in Charleston or Tombstone."

"Your woman says otherwise," he said. "She signed a statement swearing she heard you bragging about doing the job with Leonard and his pals. Now, are you gonna open the door?"

"Wait a minute," I said. I crossed to the wardrobe and pulled on a clean pair of longhandles. I took my pants from a hook and pulled them on.

"Damn it, Holliday!" Behan called.

"Who's with you, Johnny?" I called back.

"Ringo and a couple of others," he said.

"Uh-huh," I replied, knotting a tie around my neck. I picked up a small Remington derringer that Kate had given me back in happier days and dropped it into a side pocket of the coat. I took the Lightning and opened the door, standing back as Behan stepped in. He glanced quickly at the bed, his eyes raking over the tousled Pauline, who stared back defiantly. Ringo grinned, half-drunk and hollow-eyed, his lips spreading, making his face look like a death's head.

"Nemo malus felix. Reckon you've been plowing a bit of ground, Doc," he said, staring boldly at Pauline then back to me.

I raised the pistol, pointing it between his eyes. The smile never left his lips, his eyes lazy, challenging.

"You keep a civil tongue in your head, you peckerwood, or I'll put one there for you," I said.

"Doc," Behan said nervously. "Let's all be friends here, now."

"You shanty Irishman! You goddamned piece of goat shit!" I said hotly. "You come into my room in the middle of the goddamned morning and you expect me to be goddamned friends with you? For ten cents, you four-flushing mother-swyving bastard, I'd put a hole where it would do the world the most good: between your legs so the world would see the end of the Behans!"

His eyes darted nervously between Ringo and myself. Ringo lazed against the doorjamb. He ignored Behan's nervousness and pulled a sack of Bull Durham from a vest pocket and began building a cigarette. His eyes mocked mine as his tongue slipped out like a snake's, wetting the tissue.

"You through?" he said softly. He stuck the cigarette in the corner of his mouth, lighting it. He blew a cloud of gray smoke toward me. My eyes watered. I coughed. He laughed.

"Facta non verba," he said. He nodded at the Lightning. "You have the solution in your hands. Why not use it?"

"It'd be murder, Holliday," Behan whispered. "Murder."

"It would be euthanasia, Behan," I said curtly. I turned and tossed the pistol onto the bed. "Let's go."

I didn't stay in jail for long. Wyatt bailed me out, posting a five-thousand- dollar bond. Together we found Kate, drunk, in a shack in Chinatown where Behan had stashed her. Morgan loaded up a pot of coffee with about a pound of salt and poured it down her throat until she puked up enough to make her sober. We took Kate back to Judge Wells Spicer and she admitted she didn't recall signing any paper. The last thing she remembered was that she had been drinking with Behan and Milt Joyce and other friends of theirs. Old Man Fuller came in and testified that I had ridden back to Tombstone with him on the Charleston Road. Spicer put it all together and realized that I couldn't have killed Budd Philpot or the drummer or shot at Bob Paul. Spicer tongue-lashed Behan and threw the case out of court. As we left, I told Wyatt I knew I had been an embarrassment to him and suggested that I leave Tombstone. Wyatt said everything would be all right if I would send that fool woman away—meaning Kate. I handed her a thousand dollars, then I told her to get out of town.

"Doc," she said, standing beside the stage to Prescott. "Doc, we can still be together. I promise that it won't happen again. Really."

I sighed. "It isn't that so much, Kate, as you taking up with Ringo. You know how I feel about that."

"The others you didn't seem to mind," she flared momentarily.

"The others weren't Ringo," I said.

"Doc—" she began, but I interrupted her.

"It's over, Kate. I can't be a surrogate father to you anymore."

Her eyes widened. A tear trickled down through the fine dust on her cheek. She shook her head. "It wasn't like that, Doc."

"Wasn't it?" I said softly. "Then why do you persist in calling me Doc—the same name as your father?"

She bit her lip and shook her head. Her eyes went blank, haunted, and turned away from me. "I don't know. I don't know."

"Kate," I said, putting my hand on her arm. She flinched and drew back. I didn't follow. "Kate, I know what your father did to you. It wasn't right, but you can't go on punishing him for it. He's dead."

She began to cry silently then, her shoulders shaking, tears making muddy streaks down her cheeks.

"Time to go," Paul said roughly.

She turned, and I handed her into the coach, shutting the door behind her while Paul climbed up on the seat and gathered the reins.

"So long, Kate. We've had a good run," I said. I reached up and patted her shoulder through the door. She jerked back, then lashed out, her nails clawing for my face. I leaned back away from her.

. "You son of a bitch, this ain't over! You can throw me out for that . . . whore! But I'll be back! I'll be back!" she said thickly, tiny bubbles of spittle appearing in the corners of her lips.

"Good-bye, Kate," I said and stepped back up on the boardwalk as Paul shouted to the team, uncurling his long whip over their backs. The stage jerked, then pulled away, Kate glaring wild-eyed at me through the window.

I sighed and turned to go, bumping into Wyatt. I hadn't heard him come up beside me.

"Well, that's over," he said, taking a cigar from an inside pocket. He bit the end off and spat it into the street. "Good riddance, you ask me."

"I wonder," I said, watching the coach disappear down the street.

"She's gone, Doc," he said. "What can happen now?"

"Coelum non animum mutant qui trans mare currunt," I said. His eyes narrowed in puzzlement. I shook my head, clapping him on the shoulder. "Never mind, my friend. I'm simply not as confident as you. Let's drink."

Turning, we walked together down Allen Street to the Alhambra, falsely gay with each other. But a dark cloud had already begun settling over me. I could feel it, even if I couldn't see it. Perhaps I couldn't blame Kate for everything. We are all villains by necessity. Consequently, we make ourselves guilty of the disasters that befall us. The sun, the moon, the stars, we blame them for assuming the roles of villain we are born to play. Fortune's minions, all of us.

12

Time passes.

I remember little, little.

Not much, but enough.

And I find myself growing weaker and weaker by the day.

I know the time is not long, but Wyatt needs me. I cannot give in to the worm coiling around my lungs, my heart.

Pauline tries to help. And sometimes Josie, but not often, for Josie knows that I know her whore's heart all too well!

Let copulation thrive!

I tried to maintain a low profile after what transpired between Behan and myself, but Harry Woods, the editor of the Nugget, *the paper that supported the cowboys just as John Clum's Epitaph supported the Earps, kept printing editorials, constantly bringing up my name as the "assassin of Philpot."*

At last I lost my patience and issued a public advertisement through the pages of the *Epitaph* as well as by mouth along the saloons and bars of Allen Street:

> *The next man who accuses me of complicity in the stage robbery that resulted in the death of one Budd Philpot will be obliged to meet me in an affaire du'honneur or will be shot forthwith if he refuses.*
>
> *Yrs. truly,*
> *Dr. John Henry Holliday*

After that, subtleties disappeared and all smiles stopped. People stepped warily around me when I chanced to take a constitutional along Allen Street in the twilight before attending to business in the Alhambra.

Meanwhile, the rough-and-tumble political rivalry between Wyatt and Johnny Behan was rapidly racing toward its peak. Wyatt made a temporarily insane announcement that he would solve the mystery of Philpot's murder, but no leads appeared. Eventually people began snickering at Wyatt's rash brag, which prompted him to deal with the devil, Ike Clanton.

I knew absolutely nothing about this deal until Ike began to nose it around that I was the one who betrayed him to the cowboys being led, at the time, by Curly Bill Brocius and Johnny Ringo. I was mystified about Ike's charge because Wyatt had not told me about his arrangement with Ike.

Apparently, Wyatt had gotten Ike drunk, then met alone with him behind the billard parlor and made a deal with him to turn in the murderers of Budd Philpot. Wyatt arranged with Marshall Williams, the Wells Fargo agent, to give Ike the reward money for Philpot's murder and the attempted stage robbery if Ike would finger the murderers. Clanton had agreed, being the cowardly scag that he was. But as he sobered up, demons began to plague him about what he had done. If Ringo found out what he had agreed to, he would roast Ike alive over a gridiron like that sainted man of the moneybags, whatever his name should be.

I supposed I can't blame Wyatt for dealing with a thief like Ike Clanton. He wanted to beat Johnny Behan for the sheriff's position bad enough to deal with the devil himself. Who could blame him? A lot of money was at stake; the sheriff was also the tax collector and received a portion of all taxes he collected in addition to his salary. That could amount to as much as thirty or forty thousand dollars a year if the sheriff was crooked enough. I'm not saying that Wyatt was crooked, but Wyatt could see that days for men like him were numbered, and no honest sheriff or peace officer received enough money to save up for the future. Those who did usually provided little "extras" for certain clientele such as looking the other way instead of closing down houses of prostitution for a little remuneration, usually money and his pick of whores when he wanted one. Some even met women who became their wives in such places; that's where Wyatt met Mattie Blalock, the woman who claimed to be his wife, although I don't think they ever marched before a preacher or justice of the peace. I think that was an honorific title she took to convince herself that Wyatt really loved her.

I really don't think Ike would have given Wyatt the men he wanted, but I could be wrong. Cowards are unpredictable: just when you think they'll run, they'll turn like a rabid dog and attack. But I *think* little would have come from all this folderol if Marshall Williams had not gotten drunk one night and loudly assured Ike that Wells Fargo would indeed stand to the agreement Ike had made with Wyatt.

It was a bad time for Ike to be reminded of his conspiracy. His father, Old Man Clanton, along with Dixie Gray and Jim Crane, had been ambushed and killed in Skeleton Canyon by some Mexicans while they were trying to bring a stolen herd across the border. Ike was undoubtedly strung tighter than Jack Kemp's rope, for the poor man had no one left to do his thinking for him. He was rather duncey, you know, barely more intelligent than the horses he brutalized on his rides back and forth from the ranch to Tombstone.

Finally, Ike could stand it no longer and cornered Wyatt in the street and demanded to know if Wyatt had told me about their arrangement. I suppose he picked on me because Wyatt and myself were so close at the time, but I don't know. Ike became more and more paranoid, and finally Morgan brought me to a meeting with Ike and Wyatt.

"Doc," Wyatt said, "did I ever tell you about an arrangement I made with Ike?"

"Arrangement? About what?" I asked, frowning.

Wyatt turned to Ike. "See there? I told you he knows nothing about it. Someone's just shooting at the moon and jerking your chain. You're a fool, Ike, to be blabbing about town that Doc did you a disservice."

Ike scowled between Wyatt and myself. "Well, it's around that we did it, and someone had to scag. I don't know which one of you did it, but one of you is a liar."

"Think careful before you say anything, Clanton," I

warned. "I'd just as lief take care of you now as hear you've been bandying about accusations about me."

"Leave it alone, Doc," Wyatt said, putting his hand on my arm.

And out of deference for him, I did. But later that evening, John Clum found me eating at the Chink's and told me that Sherm MacMasters had just told him that Ike had been shooting his mouth off in the Alhambra that I'd sold him out. I immediately rose and made my way to the Alhambra.

Ike was sitting at a table working his way through a bottle of who-flung-John when I found him. I walked up to the table and grinned at him.

"Ike, I hear you're bandying words around about me again. I told you about that," I said.

"Doc, I don't know where yer hearin' things like that, but it just ain't true," he said. But perspiration began to bead on his greasy forehead, and I knew from the way his eyes shifted from mine that he was lying.

"I've had about enough of your little intrigues, Clanton. Stand up," I demanded.

"I ain't armed, Doc. For God's sakes, I wouldn't lie to you."

"Oh? Why not? You lie to everyone else. And now you try to cover your ass by complaining that I'm lying about you. You can't have it both ways, Ike. Let's dance."

Ike swallowed heavily and spread his dirty hands apart in front of him. "Honest, Doc. I didn't do no such a thing."

Morgan appeared at my side and gently pushed my shoulder with his forefinger. "Come on, Doc. Leave him alone. The greasy little son of a bitch ain't worth your time."

"No? Anything that damages honor is worth time," I said. "This son of a bitch has been bragging it about that he's going to kill me." I turned back to Clanton. "Well, peckerwood, this is your chance. Pull and let's get dancing."

"I told you I ain't got a gun!" he said, his voice climbing noticeably up the register. "Please, Doc. You wouldn't shoot an unarmed man, would you? That'd be murder!"

"In your case, it would be performing a public service.

And I'm feeling public spirited, Clanton. Get on your heels and find one."

"Come on," Morgan coaxed. "You can see that he ain't got a gun. Come on, I'll buy you a drink at the Oriental and you can rail at Joyce some more."

I turned reluctantly and walked out ahead of Morgan, leaving Clanton sitting, puddling his breeches for all I know.

I don't remember much about that night except that Morgan and I became involved in a poker game at Jim Earp's Sampling Room. I remember playing a pot close to my vest, letting it build and build, knowing that I had it with four nines. Then, without warning, my chest constricted, and a spout of bright red blood flew from my mouth. I leaned over my chair, coughing and coughing, watching the blood string from my mouth to the dirty floor, then . . .

Nothing.

"Damn you, Doc!"

"Wake up!"

Someone pressed a damp cloth to my eyes, wiping gumminess away. I opened then, blinking in the bright sunlight streaming in through my window. Louisa, Morgan's wife, his file de joie, bent over me, her lovely face frowning with concern. I reached up and touched a curl of golden hair that had escaped from the bun into which she had pulled it.

"Lou," I whispered. "God, you're lovely."

"Stop it, Doc!" she exclaimed, pushing my hands away. She lifted my head, pressing a glass against my lips. I drank. I gagged. I sputtered. She persisted. I drank the glass dry and fell back against my pillow, gasping.

"What happened?" I managed.

"You passed out at James's place. Morgan and James brought you here. We thought you were dying and . . . Oh God! There isn't time for this now, Doc! All hell's about to break loose!"

I blinked, trying to bring her back into focus. She shook her head and stretched her arm past my sight. I heard glass chink against glass, the gurgle of whiskey pouring into a glass, felt the glass pressed against my lips.

"Ike Clanton, Tom and Frank McLaury, Billy Clanton, and Billy Claiborne are in town, gunning for Wyatt and Virg and Morgan. Ringo and others are supposed to be on their way in, too. Doc, we need you!" she said, her face tight with concern.

"Dying . . ."

"No, you're not dying!" She shook my shoulders hard. "Not yet, you bastard! Don't you dare die yet!"

Tears fell down her cheeks, spattering against mine. I blinked.

"Please, Doc!"

Her image swam out of focus behind falling darkness. Then lips pressed against mine and air filled my lungs. I coughed, felt flesh rip in my chest, felt tissue burning. A cool cloth pressed again against my eyes, my forehead. I drew a shaky, ragged breath.

. . . Ike Clanton, Tom and Frank McLaury, Billy Clanton, Billy Claiborne . . .

. . . Ringo . . .

"Doc," she said from a distance.

I pushed her hand away and fought my way up out of the covers, pressing my back against the cold iron of the bedstead. Her face swam in and out of focus.

"My clothes," I muttered.

four

DEATH

1

Time grows short. . . . Darkness. . . . approaches. . . .
. . . I must be brief. . . . Father. . . .

The day was hot—hotter than ever I can remember in Tombstone. Fires licked at my flesh. I stumbled on the boardwalk, catching myself by planting my cane firmly on the ground and drawing a deep breath before continuing.

"Hi, Doc!" someone said. I stared at him, but it took a while for me to recognize Billy Clanton and Frank McLaury. Clanton smirked and held out his hand. "Maybe I'll see you soon and we can settle things between us."

"I'm your huckleberry," I said, but my voice sounded like a frog's croak. I shook his hand and pulled away. I stumbled over the walk again and heard him laugh, but I ignored him and shambled my way down the street toward Hafford's Saloon, where three black figures stood, staring up the street at me. Light gleamed from them like sunlight on ravens' wings. Perspiration began to flow over my body, soaking the clean shirt, dampening the gray suit I wore. I smelled the stench of myself, harsh and bitter. I glanced down at my suit, checking its fall, the knife-edged creases in the pant legs. The pistols weighed heavily from my shoulders, but I knew they were ready.

"What's the matter with Holliday?" someone muttered as I hobbled past.

"Shh. He might hear you. God, he looks like death."

I stepped up into the shade of the wooden awning over the boardwalk and stared at Wyatt. He wore a high-peaked black hat with black pants drawn down outside highly polished black boots and a long-skirted, square-cut black coat. A black string tie trickled down the front of a soft, white shirt. I glanced over at Virgil and Morgan: three dark angels, three dark shadows. All metaphor.

"What's the matter?" I asked.

"You should be in bed," Wyatt said.

"I should be dead, but I'm not," I retorted. "Well?"

Wyatt looked away, leaving it to Morgan to answer.

"Things have been falling apart over the past two days, Doc."

"Two days?"

"You been out two days," Morgan said. "From the looks of you, you should be out more."

"Go on." I took Belle's flask from my coat pocket and opened it, sipping. The whiskey spread inside me, burning, cauterizing, washing the stink from my nostrils. The weariness began to ooze from my bones.

"Ike Clanton got to drinking over at the Occidental. He finally got drunk enough to lose what little sense he had and got his rifle and pistol and started staggering up and down the street hollering he was gonna kill someone. Think he meant you, but he could've meant Wyatt. Don't really know. Anyway, Virg tried to calm him down, and he called Virg a pimp. Virg buffaloed him—whacked him over the head with his Remington—and arrested him for being drunk and threw him in jail. Frank and Tom McLaury came in to get him out and Spicer fined him twenty-seven fifty. The McLaurys took him over to Doc Gillingham to get his head fixed and then Tom McLaury threatened Wyatt. Damn fool tried to draw a hideout pistol and Wyatt took his gun away and busted him over the head with it. The McLaurys and Clanton went on over to Hafford's place and got to drinking some more. Hafford tried to get Clanton to get out of town and forget everything, but he wouldn't. We got word a minute ago that they're waiting for us down at Fly's place."

"That ain't the real reason," Wyatt said softly. "You know that, Doc."

"This goes back to Philpot, doesn't it?" I asked. "When Behan and his crew tried to set me up?"

"Looks like it," Wyatt said. "This is just a schoolyard

ruckus. Ain't nothing that couldn't be solved without someone sitting down and going over things politely together. But that ain't going to happen. Other things have gone too far."

"Yes, I can see that," I said. "It's really about power, isn't it?" Wyatt turned his level gaze into mine. I shook my head. "No, that's what it's about, Wyatt, and you know it. It's over who will run Tombstone and the county: the Earps or the cowboys. Behan's nothing more than a corrupt puppet dancing whichever way his strings are pulled.'"

I pointed at the pistols they were carrying. "Those aren't the answer, I'm afraid. All they'll do is mark you for the same thing that you claim you're trying to rid Tombstone of: shooters. You ran a campaign for law and order, Virg, Wyatt. You claimed that you wanted to bring civilization to Tombstone. Well, you were right about one thing: civilization is on its way. But when it gets here, you don't want to be the ones holding the guns, because guns and civilization don't mix. You saw that up in Dodge. It's true down here. The old ways are gone, my friends. Gone."

A coughing spasm shook me and I leaned up against a porch post, clinging to it to keep from falling down.

"They've got guns," Virgil said dryly. "That's why we got ours, Doc."

"That's a misdemeanor, Virg," Wyatt answered quietly. "Doc may be right. You want to start something like this over a misdemeanor?"

"It's the law, Wyatt," Virg said stubbornly. "It's my job."

"Behan went down to get their guns," Wyatt pointed out.

"Behan." Virgil spat into the street and shifted the shotgun he was holding to his left side.

"Maybe they're just getting their horses," Morgan opined with misgivings.

Virgil stared at him. "That doesn't make any difference. You know that."

Wyatt heaved a sigh and looked at me. "I reckon it's gone too far for anything else. You don't have to get involved in this, Doc."

Anger flushed through me. I took another sip of whiskey

and put the flask in my side pocket. "That's a hell of a thing to say to me. I guess I'll go along with you. What else is there for me? Maybe I'll get lucky."

"All right," Wyatt said, trying to be casual, but I could see gratitude flicker behind the veil he dropped over his eyes. I wondered briefly if I heard resignation in his voice, but dismissed the thought. He looked at Virg. "Give Doc your shotgun. They might not get too nervy if they think he's an on-the-street officer."

"Why?"

"It'd be better. Make it look more official," Wyatt said meaningfully.

"I don't follow that at all," Virgil said uncertainly, but he gave the shotgun to me and took my cane. The weight of the 10-gauge Richard's was almost too much for me. I turned away from them to draw another deep breath.

"Let's go," Wyatt said quietly. He took his Smith & Wesson Russian from his holster and placed it in the pocket of his long black coat.

Together we stepped out into the street. Immediately, the heat began to drum against my head. I opened my watch: Chopin's music tinkled in the dusty silence. I replaced it and continued down the street, placing myself to Morgan's right. My leg cramped. I swore under my breath and began whistling to take my mind off the pain, forcing myself to lift foot after foot down that dusty, dusty street.

We turned down Fremont, paralleling Allen Street, heading toward Fly's studio. Patches of boardwalk alternated with footpaths running along the side of the road. An alley ran through the block.

Johnny Behan rushed up, his face florid, red with fear, shiny with sweat.

"Hold up, boys! Don't go down there or there'll be trouble!" Behan said desperately.

"Those men are carrying guns and I mean to disarm them," Virgil said without breaking stride. Behan backpedaled desperately to keep out of his way.

"I've already disarmed them!" he squeaked.

But we all knew he lied. I took advantage of the pause to take my flask out of my pocket and take a long drink. I placed it in my right-hand coat pocket. A cough rumbled in my chest. I forced it down. Around me, everything seemed etched in crystal clarity and I became aware of

. . . Addie Bourland's millinery shop . . .

. . . courthouse . . .

. . . the *Epitaph* . . .

. . . Aztec House . . .

. . . Bauer's Butcher Shop. . . .

In the near distance, the rear entrance to the OK Corral with its stable on the north side of Allen Street and open yard backed with stalls extending across the alley to Fremont . . .

I fumble a handkerchief from my pocket and mop my face . . . cough, spit . . . bright red blood . . . I am hollow . . . void of heart, liver, stomach . . .

"Let 'em have it," Morgan said.

"All right," someone said distantly.

. . . Me? . . .

We moved slowly, dreamlike, down to the front of Fly's place. Ike Clanton stared at us with red eyes. Frank McLaury crouched, Tom McLaury held a horse, watching us intently. Billy Clanton smiled and stepped out, his movement a swagger. Billy Claiborne's eyes suddenly widened with fear and he backed away, dodging behind the Harwood House.

. . . A drop of perspiration hangs on the tip of my nose . . . falls away. . . . I hear it strike the dust, a wet plop! . . .

"Boys, throw up your hands. I want your guns," Virgil said.

"Sure we will," Frank said. A hard grin touched his lips.

Tom McLaury suddenly dropped the reins to his horse, his hands reaching up toward the Winchester in the saddle scabbard tied next to the pommel of his saddle.

I pulled the shotgun from beneath my coat. I felt the grin starting. He raised his hands and rested them on the saddle of the horse, pretending innocence, but the Winchester was now only inches away in the saddle scabbard.

"Hold on! I don't want that!" Virg yelled.

Frank smiled, his hand lifting the pistol from his holster.

Billy grinned.

I grinned at him.

. . . Pure mad prank from the wildness building up within me . . .

His eyes widened in madness. He lifted his pistol. I registered the Colt .44-40 and wondered what happened to his Russian.

His finger tightened on the trigger. Flame and smoke poured from the bore of his pistol.

Virgil's foot flew up as if he were kicking a tin can.

I heard another shot.

Tom's hand slapped the stock of the Winchester, drawing it from its saddle scabbard.

He fired.

"I'm hit!" Morgan yelled.

I pulled the trigger of the Richard's. Its discharge staggered me. I dropped it, snaking the Lightning from its holster.

Tom staggered.

Ike screamed and ran to Wyatt, throwing his arms around Wyatt, blubbering, saying something.

Wyatt spun him away, roaring, "This fight's commenced. Get to fighting or get out!"

Ike sprinted toward the back of Fly's. I snapped a shot at him.

Missed.

Morgan staggered. Fired.

Billy Clanton reeled back. Firing. He turned. His face grinned at me like a death's mask.

I shot twice at Billy. But he was already falling.

Frank shot.

I felt the bullet strike, staggering me.

Another bullet snapped past my ear.

And then I felt Billy's words nudging my thoughts:

. . . Damn you, stand still . . .

. . . Oh, Billy . . . Billy . . . Your life is only one fine flicker-flash of light in dull eternity . . . For this you die. . . . Time is only an illusion. . . . This you learn now, but it is too late . . .

*too late . . . The beginning, the present, the end . . . all
wrapped up now in one consignment for eternity . . . Once
passionate vision, now only darkness . . . Your piddling free
will has brought you to this, the* sine qua non *of your
achievement . . . Is it worth it, boy? . . .*

. . . You . . . lunger . . .

I shook my head sadly and put a bullet into his chest.
Blood bubbled from his lips. He howled in fury.

. . . Nothing interests you but excitement and violence . . .

Frank fired again at me.

I absentmindedly put a bullet into him as he fired once
more.

Billy lifted his pistol. I fired twice, the bullets slamming
him against the wall.

*. . . Billy . . . you confine yourself to the Dark Ages . . . or
the Ageless Dark . . . Life's essence is found in the frustra-
tions of established order . . . did you not know that?*

Frank fell. Pushed himself up.

I walked toward him.

"I've got you now, you son of a bitch!" he said thickly,
raising his .45.

I smiled at him and spread my arms to give him a good shot.

"You're a daisy if you do," I said gaily.

His eyes blazed with hate. His finger tightened on the
trigger.

I waited no longer and raised the Lightning, firing into his
chest. Simultaneously a bullet struck him under the right ear,
knocking him back into shapeless dust.

I turned.

Morgan grinned painfully from his place on the ground. I
hurried to his side. I became conscious of a crowd of people
rushing to us: Fly, Clum, others.

"Thought he had you, Doc," he whispered.

"Not quite," I said. Then I remembered that I'd been shot.
But I felt no pain and for one brief moment I thought, *It's
over.* Then realization struck:

"Where is that son of a bitch Frank?" I demanded furiously, looking around. "He tried to kill me."

"You killed him, Doc," Wyatt said soothingly. "Easy, now. It's over."

I glanced over at Billy.

He grinned back, blood staining his teeth.

He tried to raise his pistol, but Fly pulled the pistol from his hand. A group of men raised him from the ground and carried him and Tom McLaury into someone's house on the corner. I turned and looked back up the street at Frank McLaury, still lying in the dust while a group bent over him. I glanced back at Wyatt and his brothers, but they were gone, and I was alone with Wyatt. He nodded at me and followed a wagon carrying Morgan and Virg. John Clum walked beside him, gesticulating and speaking urgently. Behan rushed up.

"All right. You're under arrest," he blustered.

Wyatt stared coldly at him. "I don't think I'll let you do that."

He pushed Behan out of the way and passed with Clum. Behan looked over at me. I grinned and raised an eyebrow. He turned white, bit his lips, then scurried away into the house where Tom and Billy had been carried.

I turned slowly in the street.

I was alone.

2

In my room, I examined myself, wondering why I didn't die. I reached into the pocket of my coat and removed Belle's flask. Its side was dented. I removed my coat and dropped my trousers, tracing with gentle fingers a burn along the back of my bony hip, feeling the rawness of the wound. I took a linen handkerchief and spilled whiskey on it, gently daubing at the burn, cleansing it.

A sadness fell upon me as I realized I was still alive. I

poured myself a large drink and pushed up the window in my room as far as it would go and sat in the chair, watching, letting the warm breeze dry the perspiration on my body. I took my pistols from their holsters and looked at them: ivory-handled, chrome, gleaming like death's smile in the dimness of my room.

I rose and took a small case from a wardrobe and opened it, took out oil, a small brush, and a rag. Methodically, I began cleaning my pistols. The metal felt warm in my hands. Alive.

H. M. Matthews, the county coroner, decided that we were justified in killing Billy Clanton and Frank and Tom McLaury, and we were free.

But that didn't last long.

Ike Clanton swore out complaints for our arrest in an attempt to justify his own cowardice.

There was a trial.

Virgil and Morgan stayed under house arrest because of their wounds, while Wyatt and I faced the jury together in Judge Wells Spicer's court. Thomas Fitch served as Wyatt's lawyer while I retained Thomas J. Drum. Lyttleton Price should have been the prosecutor, but Brocius and Ringo, along with W. R. McLaury, the older brother of Frank and Tom, brought in Ben Goodrich because they didn't trust Wyatt's association with Price.

The trial lasted about a month. Fitch and Drum decided that they would let Wyatt be the sole witness for us. I volunteered to take the stand, but both the lawyers talked me into remaining silent.

"No offense, Doc," Drum said, "but your reputation might work against us."

"Besides," Fitch added, "you're a Southerner."

"And?" I asked.

"Most of those here are Northerners," he said.

"Goodrich is from Texas," I pointed out.

"Yes, but that isn't Georgia," Drum said. "No, you sit quietly and let Wyatt carry the load."

And I did.

Sit quietly.

Like a shadow at the defense table. Sipping whiskey from Belle's battered flask, which had saved my life, to keep me from coughing and taking attention from Wyatt's testimony.

Behan lied about everything in an attempt to take the light away from his own connections with the cowboys. He claimed that the cowboys had thrown up their hands and tried to surrender. But Addie Bourland said she didn't see anyone holding up their hands. They were firing.

We were set free.

But for some strange reason, we became pariahs in the town. Oh, people still respected us, but they respected us as killers, not as gentlemen.

One day we stepped into the Oriental for a drink, both Virgil and myself hobbling on canes. Milt Joyce stared me in the eye and said, "Well, well. Looky who's here. I expect there will be another stage robbed before morning."

I backed away from the bar, but Virgil acted quickly, stepping up and slapping Joyce hard across the face while Wyatt grabbed hold of my arm, keeping me from drawing the Lightning while I leaned with my right hand on my cane.

"You're a lucky swartwouter," I said.

He backed away, his hand holding his cheek. "You won't get a chance to shoot me in the back and I don't think you have the nerve to shoot me when I'm looking at you."

I shrugged free from Wyatt and stepped aside. "I'm looking at you, Milt. Why don't you shoot me now?"

"Let it go, Doc," Wyatt said lowly. "It's over. We don't need any more trouble now. Let it die down and be forgotten."

Milt backed out of the door and disappeared. I turned to Wyatt and shook my head. "You may think this is over, Wyatt, but there's a lot more left to it. Act Three has yet to be played."

I didn't know how prophetic I was.

A short time later, Joyce tried to pick a fight with the Earps in the back of Jim Earp's sipping palace, but Behan saved his life by arresting him. I remember looking at Wyatt and saying, "I told you that dough-roller wasn't through. There'll be others."

He shook his head and turned away, not saying anything. But he and his brothers moved with their wives—and Josie, an enchanted moment that, when Mattie Blalock found out her Wyatt was sharing his bed with both of them—into the Cosmopolitan Hotel, where they could be protected by the citizen's committee led by George W. Parsons, one of the Council of Ten of the Citizen's Safety Committee. Wyatt's room was on one side of his brothers' room, and I took the room on the other side. A couple of days later, the youngest Earp, Warren, showed up and took a room on the floor below. The Cosmopolitan had become as impregnable as the Bastille. The cowboys, led by Brocius and Ringo with Ike hanging around them like a puppy dog, took rooms directly across the street in the Grand Hotel.

One afternoon I was returning to the hotel after going to the Alhambra to replenish my supply of Old Williams when Johnny Ringo stepped out of the shadows to face me. A smile lifted his lips into a diabolic grin. He wore a heavy ulster despite the burning afternoon sun, his hands thrust into the slit pockets.

"Well, if it isn't the Earps' little messenger boy. I hear you've been saying some things about me, Holliday."

"That I have, Johnny," I said pleasantly, shifting the bottle from my right hand to my left.

"Mind telling me what you've been saying?" he challenged.

"Not at all," I replied. "I said that I was sorry to see an educated renegade rider like you hanging around cheap, salt-limned mulelickers. You should be a schoolmarm."

"You're quite an auger, Holliday."

"Why, Johnny Ringo! You do carry on so. I'll bet you're

quite a hit with the gents at the church social. Been hanging around Billy Breckenridge? Visiting the lambs? Gettin' your britches paddled by a buck nigra?"

"Why, maybe it was your whore," he said, his lips stretching wide in a tight grin that didn't carry to his eyes. "She has kisses sweeter than wine."

"I can see why you liked them, Ringo. She blew me. That makes you a cocksucker by proxy, doesn't it?"

A dark flush mottled his face. "You cheap, four-flushing, lunger. Lunger!"

I stepped close to him, smiling.

"Let's step out in the street, Johnny," I whispered. "No sense in hurting anyone else. Ten feet is all we need, wouldn't you say?"

Wyatt pushed between us, Virgil and Morgan taking a position on each side, facing Ringo. Wyatt looked disdainfully at Ringo, then turned to me.

"Quit this foolishness, Doc," he said quietly. "We got enough trouble without adding to it."

"Well, if it isn't the three little sister-boys," he sneered. "Come to play with the big boys?"

Wyatt looked over his shoulder at Ringo, saying, "I'm not going to fight you, Ringo. There's no money in it."

"Well, I'm going to fight you. I want your blood," he hissed.

I stepped away from Wyatt, smiling at Ringo. "Why, Johnny Ringo. That's just my game. I'm your huckleberry."

"All right, lunger. I'll send you to hell."

"I'll meet you there. Say when," I said, casually twirling the bottle by its neck.

His hands started out of the ulster's pockets, but Flynn—I never knew his first name; he was a burly, young man Virgil had appointed to the police force—stepped up behind him and caught him in a bear hug.

"Turn him loose, Flynn," I said. "When he does, Ringo, start your dance."

"Let me go, goddamn you!" Ringo yelled furiously. He

tried to spin away, but Flynn held him fast. Morgan stepped forward and took his pistols from the pockets of the ulster.

"Take him to jail," Virgil ordered. Flynn nodded and tossed Ringo in the general direction of the jail, taking the pistols from Morgan's hands.

"We're not finished, Holliday!" Ringo said angrily.

"Only a temporary postponement. The curtain will rise again," I called.

"That was foolish, Doc," Wyatt said. His eyes flickered up at the second floor of the Grand Hotel. I glanced up in time to see a rifle being pulled back through a window. It was a stacked deal.

"Oh well," I murmured. "Lady Luck must've been looking the other way."

"We need to be careful," Wyatt warned.

"Why, yes. By all means," I said.

He stared into my eyes for a long moment, then shook his head and turned with me to enter the hotel. Virgil and Morgan followed.

A week later, Virgil was shotgunned in a thunderstorm.

Virgil and Wyatt, along with Morgan, had been counting the take during a respite in their faro game in the Oriental. It was to be one of their last nights; Joyce claimed to have a new partner but would not name him. Virgil decided he wanted a quiet stroll before he turned in for the night, and left. Wyatt told him to wait until the rain passed, but Virgil laughed and said how he had promised Allie, his wife, that he would be home by midnight for a change.

Moments later, Virgil stepped from the Oriental and crossed Fifth Street. He was silhouetted against the Eagle Brewery's lighted windows. Five shotguns roared, riddling the windows and corner post of the saloon with buckshot. One load caught Virgil in the left side. Another shattered his left arm above the elbow.

Virgil caught the shadows of five men running out of the

alley. They split up, three going down toward Toughnut Street, the other two running over toward Allen Street. He turned and staggered back into the saloon, meeting Wyatt on his way out.

Wyatt helped him to a chair and sent for Doc Goodfellow. When the doctor started to work on him, Wyatt went into the building beside the alley and found a hat with Ike Clanton's name in it. He went out and followed in the direction the men had run. He ran into the watchman from an icehouse on Toughnut Street who told him that Ike Clanton, Frank Stilwell, and Hank Swilling had just run past him, carrying shotguns. Another person recognized Ringo as one of the other two, while the fifth man remained anonymous.

We thought Virgil would die after Doctor Goodfellow removed four inches of bone from his left arm and dug some twenty-odd buckshot from his body. But he didn't.

It was Morgan who died.

Wyatt and Morgan had decided to attend a show by the Lingard Opera Company—*Stolen Kisses*, I believe—instead of trying to set up a new faro game over at the Occidental after Joyce cut them free from the Oriental. Sort of a last night before beginning business again.

I was playing poker at the Alhambra when a shotgun blast shattered the night. *Wyatt*, I thought immediately, and a dreadful feeling washed over me. I reached over for Belle's cup, draining it, tossing in my cards as I rose. A miner broke in through the door, yelling,

"They just shotgunned the Earps over at Campbell and Hatch's!"

I pushed my way through the crowd and ran over to the saloon. Morgan lay on the billiard table he loved so much, blood pouring from his back. Doc Goodfellow, his arms covered with Morgan's blood, probed deeply for buckshot while Wyatt tried to hold the screaming Morgan on the table. A dog howled somewhere.

"Hold him still!" Goodfellow roared.

"I'm trying! I'm trying!" Wyatt yelled back. "Someone shut that goddamned dog up!"

"It's no use," Goodfellow said resignedly, stepping back from the table.

Wyatt gave him a look of disbelief, then rolled Morgan onto his back. Morgan grinned weakly at him and whispered. Wyatt bent down. Morgan's lips moved, then his eyes set fixedly upon a spot in space, and he died.

I turned and pushed through the crowd. Lou grabbed my sleeve as I tried to pass.

"Doc," she began, her eyes staring desperately into mine, asking to be told a lie that would become truth.

I shook my head. She pulled away, her hands going to her lips as tears began to fall down her cheeks. A red rage shook me like a warp-spasm. I shook so hard I felt as if I were turning around in my skin. My calves seemed to swell to twice their size and I felt my temple sinews knot tightly.

"Good God!" someone whispered, and the crowd fell away from me, leaving me alone. I reeled out into the night. I stormed down Allen Street, feeling the fires of hell smoking behind me from my heels. I kicked open the door of one saloon, looking for Johnny Ringo. Or Curly Bill Brocius. Or Ike Clanton. Or all three. It didn't matter; I would have killed them all. Faces turned in protest, then turned away after looking into my face as I moved on down the street, past the saloons, kicking in crib doors, hauling cowboys off whores, smelling sweat and anger and fear and cheap powder and perfume, looking, looking, but finding nothing.

At last I stood on a small hill on the outskirts of town, looking up at the silver, crescent-shaped moon. Around me I felt the dark emptiness of night, but the rage still wouldn't go away. I pulled the Lightning and the .45 from their holsters and fired into the darkness of the night again and again, trying to kill the savageness of the night, venting my rage on the Unknown in the dark. I could feel His smile stretch across pointed teeth, feel the warm caress of His arms, His warm, moist breath, and hear His quiet, contemptuous laughter as His whispers tickled my ears.

3

Wyatt and Virgil took Morgan's body from Tombstone to Tucson to ship it on home with Virgil and Allie and Lou.

Ah, Lou!

I held her in my arms, kissed those full lips ripe with promise, felt the clutch of her hands tight upon my back— and I knew that but for the circumstances, we would have been soul mates, lovers.

We left Josie behind, walking silently from our lives forever—and Pauline.

Wyatt left us in Contention—Warren, Sherm McMasters, Turkey Creek Jack Johnson, Texas Jack Vermillion, and me—to guard Virgil and the ladies, while he sent a telegram to Deputy United States Marshal Joe Evans. Evans joined us a little before Tucson and handed Wyatt his commission as a United States deputy marshal. Wyatt immediately deputized the others, while I demurred.

"I have certain principles that I will not compromise," I said, and went to sit with Lou, taking comfort from her grief.

"Frank Stilwell, Pete Spence, Ike Clanton, and a half-breed are in town," Evans said to Wyatt. "They've been getting telegrams all day long from Tombstone. Watch yourself."

Wyatt nodded absently, looking at the tired face of Virgil, who was showing the strain of the long ride from Tombstone and the train ride to Tucson. I watched him carefully, trying to read his intentions, but his face was granite, hard, unyielding.

Dusk was falling when we reached the Tucson station. Wyatt and I watched Virgil and Allie and Lou while they ate, then escorted them back to the train. When we got back, Warren came up to us, carrying a greener.

"I've seen some men back there in the shadows," he said.

Wyatt nodded and gestured toward Virgil and the ladies. "You stay with them. Doc and I'll check it out." He took the shotgun from Warren and checked its loads.

Warren pouted. "This is a family matter. I should go with you."

"Do as you're told," Wyatt said tersely.

"Wyatt," Warren said hotly.

"Doc's better with a gun than you," Wyatt said bluntly. His brother turned away petulantly. "I've lost one brother. Damn near lost another. I don't want to lose a third. Besides, like you said, this is family."

"He ain't family," Warren said hotly, mounting the steps to the train.

Wyatt looked at me but said nothing. I smiled. I knew why he had chosen me; even the most expert shot can be killed by a lucky bullet in the dark. I was already dead. There was nothing to lose. I felt no animosity toward him; rather I felt relief for being the one chosen. It was a matter of honor.

"Take no mind," I said. "We are all among the brotherly Immortals."

"You take the other side," he said.

I nodded and stepped around the train car, moving into the shadows away from the light spilling from the windows of the car. On the adjoining track, parallel to the train, a string of flatcars waited for hookup. I thought I caught a glimmer of light from the blued barrel of a rifle and gave a little bluebird whistle. Wyatt paused, looking toward me. I pointed toward the flatcars. He turned and moved like a cat on the balls of his feet down the track, disappearing behind a loaded wagon waiting for a freight car. I walked toward the flatcars. My feet crunched on the gravel of the track bed. Metal clanked against metal, and two figures darted out from the shadows of the flatcars. Wyatt ran forward after them. I started running, then suddenly drew up as my lungs convulsed.

"God!" I gasped, coughing. "Not now! Not *now!*"

A shotgun roared. I drew the Colt .45 and tried to muffle my coughing as I forced myself forward. The shotgun roared again. I turned around a train car and came upon Wyatt standing over a figure stretched out on its back in a pool of light coming from the station office. His chest had been blown away by the twin shotgun blasts. Wyatt raised his eyes, staring bleakly into mine. I recognized the look: I saw it each morning in my shaving mirror.

"Stilwell," he said in a monotone.

The train pulled away and Wyatt took a step away from the body, raising a finger toward the heavens. I looked over my shoulder: Virgil's face was pressed against the window of the car. He raised a clenched fist in acknowledgment. Wyatt watched the train go out of sight, then turned back to me.

"Let's do it," he said quietly.

"And thus the Muse will sing of us, of arms and men," I said, following him through the night. I felt like Achilles. Alive. The fires of heaven burning through my veins, touching me briefly with immortality.

Ares snorted with pleasure when I swung up into the saddle on him and turned him next to Wyatt aboard Dick Naylor. We rode up into the Dragoon Mountains, working our way to Pete Spence's ranch by a water hole on the western slope where Wyatt had heard Florentino Cruz, better known as Indian Charlie, had taken refuge. Cruz had been identified as one of the men who had killed Morgan, along with Spence, Stilwell, Fries, and Hank Swilling.

Cruz saw us coming and made a run for the scrub timber on the upper slope of a mountain above Spence's place, hoping to lose himself in the forest.

"Stop him," Wyatt said emotionlessly to McMasters. "But don't kill him. I want to talk to him."

McMasters cocked a leg over his saddlehorn and raised his Henry, sighting carefully. He pulled the trigger and Cruz yelped and grabbed his left leg, rolling around on the ground in agony. We rode slowly over to him. McMasters took a look and shook his head in disgust.

"Hardly hit him at all," he said, spitting. "Way he's yelling, you'd think I blowed his whole leg off."

"Are you Florentino Cruz?" Wyatt asked.

"No habla Inglish," he said sullenly.

Wyatt climbed down off Dick Naylor. He walked over to Cruz, pulled his pistol, and pressed it against Cruz's forehead, cocking it. "Ask him, Sherm."

"I understand," Cruz said, his eyes crossing as he stared down the barrel of Wyatt's pistol. "Don't kill me! It was Curly Bill and Ringo and Claiborne and Swilling and Phin and Ike Clanton! I didn't do nothing! Nothing!"

"He's lying," I said casually, sipping from my flask. The morning chill in the mountains was a bit too crisp yet for my lungs.

"No!" he said frantically. "No! Ringo, him and Stilwell and Ike tried to kill you, Señor Holliday. Twice in Tombstone. Twice! Spence, he had a woman who let him use her house! We watched you move for days! For days!"

"And Morgan," Wyatt asked.

"Sí. With him, it was the same."

"You helped watch my brother?"

"Sí. But I did not shoot. I just watch. Curly Bill, he gave me twenty-five dollars to watch."

"Watch for what?" I asked.

Cruz shrugged. "For anybody. You know."

"To kill me or any other who came around?" Wyatt pressed. Cruz shrugged sullenly.

"Who planned this?" Wyatt asked softly. Cruz looked up at him. "Someone had to come up with this plan. Who?"

"Ringo," Cruz said. A thrill swept through me. Somehow, I knew Ringo had been the one for this plot. It had been too Machiavellian for any of the others to put together; too many details, too many subtle maneuverings.

Ringo. His name burned like a phosphorescent flash. I recognized myself in his name, my other self—fugitive, vagabond, forced to roam, like me, but with no curse branded upon him by the unfeeling god who had branded me.

"Well," Wyatt said, holstering his pistol. "You have another chance to win another twenty-five dollars from Curly Bill. Tell him, Sherm. In the plainest language you know.

Tell him that he's got a pair of guns and he can pull them anytime he wants when I start counting. I won't go for mine until I hit three. If he kills me, he can go free back to Curly Bill for another twenty-five dollars. You and the others, that includes you, Doc, will ride away without harming him."

"Wyatt—" McMasters began.

"Tell him," Wyatt said gently, his voice soft, almost melodious. "Make sure he understands."

A sudden glint came into Cruz's eye. He nodded and stood away from Wyatt, facing him.

"Uno," Wyatt said.

Cruz's hand fumbled at his holster.

"Dos."

Perspiration broke out on his swarthy face as he raised his pistol, trying desperately to thumb back the hammer.

"Tres."

Wyatt's hand flashed up with his pistol. The American roared three times in rapid succession, slamming Cruz back. The first bullet caught him in the abdomen, spinning him around in sudden agony. The second caught him between the shoulders, the third smashing into his temples.

"Two," Wyatt whispered as he punched the bullets from his pistol and reloaded. A brief picture of Wyatt standing over Stilwell's body, his finger raised in the air as the train pulled away, flashed into my mind.

A scorpion darted out from under a rock. Casually, Wyatt stepped on it, grinding it down with the toe of his boot. He stepped into Dick Naylor's stirrups and looked down dispassionately upon the dead Cruz. Overhead, turkey buzzards began to spiral lazily in the still, blue sky. Wordlessly, he kneed Dick Naylor and led us away from Spence's ranch.

We continued looking for the others. Behan took advantage of the situation and swore in Curly Bill and Johnny Ringo as special deputies, along with a bevy of others such as Billy Claiborne, and set them on our trail. We played a game of dodge with them for a couple of days in the Dragoons, then decided to cut over to Iron Springs for water and to rest our horses. We left Warren to watch for Charlie

Smith, a vigilante messenger who was to bring us word about Behan's movements, and Wyatt, McMasters, Johnson, and Texas Jack and myself rode over to Iron Springs.

The trail to Iron Springs climbs up a narrow, rocky canyon into the Whetstones, a dry furnace. About a hundred yards from the Springs, the trail rounds a rocky outbreak and cuts across a flat shelf of deep sand. Iron Springs lies in a hollow beyond the sandy shelf behind which a grove of cottonwoods climbs up the slope. The sun broiled us. I took off my coat and tied it behind my saddle. Wyatt loosened his gun belt and took off his hat, mopping the sweat band with a bandanna.

Suddenly, Dick Naylor threw up his head, snorting. Ares pulled up and looked forward, nickering uneasily, his feet dancing in the sand, his huge jaw mouthing the bit, the muscles in his neck pulling urgently at the reins in my fingers.

"Easy, boy," I said, leaning forward, running my hand down his glossy black neck. "Easy, now."

Wyatt swung out of the saddle, looping the reins over his arm. He reached up, taking a greener from his saddle. Slowly, he started forward.

"Wyatt," I said, then swore as Ares danced sideways, trying to turn away. "What the hell's wrong with you?"

"Curly Bill! Ambush!" McMasters yelled in astonishment. He turned his horse and galloped back for cover. Vermillion hastily followed. I tried to quiet Ares, reaching simultaneously for my pistol.

I took a quick look as Brocius and another leaped to their feet. Brocius grinned as he swung a shotgun to his shoulder. He fired, and Vermillion's horse screamed and collapsed in the sand, pinning Texas Jack beneath him. Ares roared and whirled around, ripping the reins from my hand as he raced after McMasters.

I swung forward, trying to grab the dancing reins. Behind me, I heard the roar of another shotgun, then a man screamed. I made a sudden lunge and grabbed, frantically gathering the reins with my left hand. Finally, I managed to turn Ares. He fought the bit, then I struck him with both heels, and he lifted his head, reared, then raced forward toward Wyatt.

Wyatt was trying desperately to pull his gun belt back up from where it had fallen to his knees. Bullets kicked up the sand around him. Dick Naylor tugged, trying to get away from Wyatt's grip on the reins. Finally, Wyatt managed to pull up his gun belt. He drew a pistol and fired again into the cottonwoods. Then I was close enough to see the shadows of the men in the trees. I pulled the Colt .45 and fired. Someone threw up his hands and fell. Then Wyatt crawled back up on Dick Naylor and grabbed his Winchester, levering shots into the cottonwoods as Dick Naylor backed away.

"Get Jack outta here!" Wyatt yelled at me.

I fired another shot as Vermillion ripped off the cinches of his saddle and threw the saddle—rifle scabbard, shotgun, ammunition belt, everything—onto his back and began sprinting for cover. I holstered my pistol and turned Ares to him, bending to take the saddle from him. It nearly pulled me off Ares. I kicked a stirrup free for Vermillion and he stepped into it, crouching and holding onto the pommel of my saddle as I whipped Ares away from the fight.

Moments later, Wyatt, pale and shaken, joined us. We dismounted to check the damage. Miraculously, he was unharmed. His coat had been shot to shreds, three bullet holes in the legs of his pants, five holes through the crown of his hat, and three through the brim.

"I've gotta be hit!" he exclaimed. "My whole left leg is numb!"

I looked down: A bullet had lodged in the heel of his boot.

"Let's go after them," McMasters suggested.

He shook his head. "We wouldn't last a minute over that flat. They'll have themselves settled down now."

"Miracles ran out even for Christ," I said.

"Precisely," Wyatt said. "No sense in pressing our luck."

He might have said something after that, but I never knew. A dark shadow dropped down in front of my eyes as a gout of blood rushed from my mouth. I fell senseless from my horse. The last thing I remembered was Wyatt's arms catching me, his voice, harsh with concern, crying, "Doc! Doc!"

Sun shone in through heavily starched curtains stretched over a window. I felt a feather mattress beneath me, sheets— I raised my head and looked down at a heavy signature quilt covering me, but the effort was too much and I let my head fall back into the softness of a down pillow. Wyatt's face swam into focus over me.

"How you feeling, Doc?" he asked.

I tried to speak, but my throat hurt from dryness and only a croak emerged. Wyatt nodded and lifted my head, holding a glass of water to my lips. I tasted it, swallowed painfully, then croaked, "Whiskey."

"Water, Doc," he said firmly. He held the glass to my lips again. I shook my head, trying to avoid it, but water spilled down onto my neck and I opened my mouth, swallowing.

"Whiskey," I said again, clearer, after he lowered my head back to the pillow. He ignored me, placing my glass on a mahogany table beside my bed.

"It was a bad one, Doc," he said quietly. Mattress springs squeaked as he rested a hip on the mattress beside me. "You need to get out of Arizona right now. Another one like that will kill you."

"Ringo," I managed. He shook his head.

"He wasn't there. Leastways I don't think he was. Sherm never recognized any tracks of that pinto he rides. You know, twisted shoe on off-hoof? We got three, maybe four, and shot a couple of others," he said. "Ringo will come sooner or later. Right now, there's you."

"No," I whispered. "Morgan."

He picked up a towel and gently wiped the perspiration from my forehead. He shook his head. "No, I think not."

"Wyatt . . ."

"I need you, Doc," he said quietly. I heard a click deep in his throat. "I've lost Morgan, and Virg might as well be lost. Warren, well, he tries hard, but there's a weakness to him that will kill him if I let him go on this way. You're all that's left, Doc." I heard that click again.

I reached out, groping for his hand. He took mine, pressing

it gently between his. I looked at it, stark white, thin, bony, against his brown, meaty grip. A skeleton shaking hands with Antaeus.

"Where are we?"

"Hooker's ranch," he said, then as if embarrassed with the show of affection, he rose and went to the window, drawing back the curtains. Outside, the sun shone brightly, but it could not dispel the darkness I felt inside me.

"You know," he said, "I've had a lot of time to think about this while waiting on you, not knowing if you were living or dying."

"How long?" I whispered.

"Four days," he said. "The spells are getting longer, aren't they?" I nodded. His fingers worked automatically at his mustache. Suddenly, he sighed and turned away from the window. His eyes brooded, staring at me. "I can't take him, can I?"

"Ringo?"

He nodded.

I swallowed heavily. "No. Whiskey."

He started to refuse, then hesitated, shrugged and crossed and filled a glass, bringing it to me. Again he raised my head and pressed the glass to my lips. I drank thirstily. Not a drop spilled. I sighed in relief as I felt the whiskey sear the pain in my chest, the raw wounds from coughing. He rose and replaced the glass, toying with it a second. Suddenly, he filled the glass again with whiskey and drained it.

"What makes a man like Ringo?" he asked.

"Bitterness. There's an emptiness deep inside him," I said. "An emptiness that can never be filled by anything or anyone. He can never forgive the world."

"What? I don't understand," he said, frowning.

"For his birth," I answered.

"Strange words," he said.

"But true," I said. I gestured at the whiskey. He refilled the glass, bringing it to me. "I know him well. When I look at him, I see myself."

4

The story had grown old, but I told it again from my hotel room in Trinidad. Bat Masterson lounged on the chair opposite me, an open bottle of whiskey on the table between us. Outside, rain trickled noisily down a drainpipe and slashed against a windowpane. I grinned at Masterson and refilled my glass, sipping the Old Williams. I pointed to the bottle. He shook his head.

Things had happened since Wyatt brought me into Colorado, slipping us past Behan's posse of cowboys. We settled in Gunnison. Wyatt tried to make us better, to bring us together, but I began drinking more and more, black depression setting heavier and heavier upon me. Moodily, I began to withdraw from Wyatt. McMasters and Johnson and Vermillion had split away from us, leaving the two of us alone.

No, not quite alone. Josie joined us.

And slowly, patiently, she began to develop a rift between us. Nothing has a stronger scent in the nostrils of a man than the scent of a wanting woman. Especially if that scent is accompanied by a sense of guilt. And Wyatt had both.

Finally, we argued about Josie, Wyatt accusing me of having slept with her when she was living with Behan. I argued that I had been far too busy with Pauline. But Wyatt wanted to be rid of me, for I reminded him of what he wanted to forget, of Morgan's death and his revenge, still unfulfilled. It was easier to believe that lying wench than me.

At last, in frustration, I boarded Ares in Gunnison and took a train for Denver, hoping that a few miles between us would help heal the rift.

Denver had changed. Places I knew and had been familiar

with no longer existed. Big brick buildings had doubled the size of the business section, and stone sidewalks had replaced the boardwalks. Horsecar lines ran the length of the streets, along which electric lights had been installed. Telephones, too, had arrived. A certain sadness filled me for the loss of what I had known, but I knew that the future had arrived even if some—like Wyatt—continued to deny the old West was no more. Tourist business was booming in Denver, and gentility and manners had arrived.

I found Mary Walker again, and we quickly picked up where we had left off. But after a short, frantic time together, we became like old married couples, comfortable in each other's presence but nothing more.

And then, one day, Perry Mallen, a short man with a florid face and red beard and eyes like a ferret, walked up to me on the streets, announced himself as a deputy sheriff from Los Angeles, and arrested me for the murder of his partner, Harry White, seven years previously. Of course, the whole thing was a hoax. I had been nowhere near California seven years before. In fact, Denver itself could attest to that, as there was the affair of honor with Budd Ryan about the same time.

The truth of the matter was that Mallen wanted the reward that Arizona had offered for my return for trial of murder. It seems that I had been accused of being an accessory in the murder of Frank Stilwell in Tucson, the murder of a railroad conductor on the Southern Pacific, the murder of a ranchman named Clanton near Tombstone, the attempted murder of his brother, the murder of Curly Bill, a noted cowboy, and a half dozen other crimes of a minor nature.

Charley Foster and some others interceded on my behalf with Governor Pitkin, who lodged a protest with Gowper, at the time still governor of Arizona. Gowper sent a message back that he would be happy to reconsider the Tucson demand for extradition, enclosing a private message for me that he would delay things as long as possible until something could be done on my end to forestall extradition, which he would, eventually, if reluctantly, be forced to press.

Wyatt got together with Bat, and together they filed a complaint with Pitkin, complaining that Colorado had a prior demand for my soul—I was guilty of a bunco scam on one of the citizens of Pueblo, having cheated him out of a hundred dollars. They chose Pueblo instead of Trinidad to keep Bat's name clear of any scandal, pulling a few strings there with a justice of the peace Bat knew from a long way back.

With great relief, Pitkin turned down the demands of Arizona, privately taking great delight in binding me over for trial, then suggesting to district court that due to a backlog of cases, mine be given the lowest priority. In the meantime I was placed under three hundred dollars' bond.

And so, I finally came to Trinidad to thank my benefactor. Only he wasn't in the mood for thanks.

"You came at a bad time, Holliday," he said, refusing the bottle of whiskey. I shrugged and refilled my glass. "Why did you come?"

"To thank you," I said mockingly.

"Cut it out," he said impatiently. "Why did you come?"

I placed the bottle back on the table, corking it, and walked to the window, pulling back the curtains to stare down into the darkness of the street. Lights began flickering up and down the street.

"There is the matter of Johnny Ringo," I said.

He sighed and picked imaginary lint from the lapel of his immaculate black suit. His badge of office gleamed in the soft light of my room. "Holliday—"

"Wyatt's going after him. You know that," I said, interrupting him. "I can feel it. A type of breath like air, dank and dead, moving across the earth, brushing across me. I feel it, Bat. And Wyatt doesn't stand a chance against him. You know that," I said quietly. "Yet he will try. Sometime, and sometime soon. It's eating badly on him. Ringo's the last one connected with Morgan's death, as far as he is concerned. The big one. Ringo planned the whole affair." He looked up in surprise. "Oh yes. I was there when Cruz told him just before Wyatt shot him. He's killed most of the others. You know he'll go back. To his death."

He rose and went to the whiskey, pouring a drink. He downed half of it, then coughed from its bite and nodded. "And what do you want me to do?"

"Arrest me. Put me in isolation. And leave the back door open," I said. "I'll take care of the rest."

His eyes held mine long and hard. Finally, they dropped away. He sighed, removed his derby, ran his hand through his carefully combed and waved hair. His eyes wavered, then fell away from mine. He replaced his hat, then stood and in a formal voice said, "John Henry Holliday, it is my duty as marshal of Trinidad to arrest you for . . ." He thought a moment, then his lips quirked in dry humor. " . . . bilking one of our citizens out of a hundred dollars and for the carrying of firearms within the city limits. Will you please come with me?"

I smiled, enjoying the formality of theatre. "There are those who would like to have me defenseless in your jail," I said.

"We will arrange for private sequestering elsewhere," he said. "I'll suggest your trial be"—he smiled—"ex camera because of your, ah, 'condition,' which seems to be worsening."

"There is truth in that," I murmured, collecting my hat.

He rose, stretching out his hand. I removed my pistols, placing them in it. He nodded, cleared his throat, and said, "Doc, I've never really cared for you. But I sure as hell wish I had a friend like you."

"I'll need those," I said, nodding at the pistols in his hand.

"I know," he said, and crossed to the small black doctor's bag that still held my dental tools. Sentimental value only, now. He opened it and dropped the pistols in, shutting it firmly. "Shall we go?"

Bat found a good attorney for me, one who owed him a favor, which Bat pointedly said he was calling in. The attorney arranged for my case to be placed upon the docket, and on the morning my hearing was scheduled, I left through the back door of the hotel while my attorney appeared on my behalf, telling the court that I had been confined to bed with my sickness.

Ares stretched forth his long legs, eagerly grasping for the horizon. Ahead lay Contention and Kate, to whom I had sent a letter, suggesting a reconciliation. She was more than eager to agree.

"Doc," she said, rising from the table in her room as I entered after bathing and having a quiet whiskey to steady my nerves. Rain rattled against the wooden sides of the hotel, and I knew when I left that the sky would be so blue that it would hurt my eyes and the trees would be fat with leaves and birds would sing. But no birds sang in the room. Not then.

"Kate," I said. I removed my hat and stood quiet, studying her.

She crossed and placed her hands tentatively on mine. Her hands were puffy and her face appeared bloated from her hard drinking. New lines radiated from the corners of her eyes, and puffy pouches sagged the flesh along her jawline. Yet she still held that Hungarian beauty that still drew men to her, an earthiness that boldly suggested itself in nights of pleasure. I smiled and leaned down, kissing her cheek. She had bathed and doused herself with perfume. Her hair had been carefully combed and pinned. She wore one of the dresses I had bought her in Dodge, a red affair with the bodice extremely low cut, showing her breasts, huge and inviting, bubbling up against it, her white shoulders gleaming invitingly from the flame-colored taffeta gown. Her breath quickened. Gently, I pushed her away and walked to the table, where she had thoughtfully placed a bottle of Old Williams and two crystal glasses. I filled both, handing her one. I glanced into a mirror over the high bureau and turned quickly away, not liking what I saw there. I moved my lips into a smile as I turned back to face her.

"Doc, did you mean what you said in your letter? About us

getting together again?" she asked in a voice made girlish with anxiety.

"I thought it might be worth a try," I said. I sipped the whiskey. "We had something once together."

"Yes," she said eagerly, her eyes shining hopefully. A certain frantic need moved restlessly in the backs of them. "Yes, we did: Doc, I—"

"But there is the case of Ringo," I continued. I drank, holding her eyes with mine. "I find that hard to dismiss, my dear. Very hard."

"Doc, it was all that stuff with the Earps and such. You left me for them," she said.

"No," I said. "You drove me to them after you took up with Ringo."

She shook her head and drank her whiskey, trying to bring the memory back. Finally, she said, "Maybe you're right. I don't remember. I remember that I asked you . . . something." She raised her head and stared back into my eyes, hers large and hurt and vulnerable.

"And you said that you could no longer be my father," she said in a little-girl voice. Her face transformed itself into girlish doubtfulness, and I saw her as the innocent she must have been so many years before. "But, you could never be that. My father has been dead a long, long time. He . . ."

Tears came to her eyes. She bit her lip, closing her eyes tightly against the unwanted memory that was trying to come back, the memory I wanted back.

"He hurt me. Bad. There was blood everywhere. He said he would beat me if I told anybody what he had done. And he did it again. And again. And again."

I took her in my arms, stroking her hair softly. She collapsed against me, her hands gripping my shirtfront convulsively, like a tiny girl's hands.

"It's over, Kate," I whispered. "Over."

"Doc," she said. Her eyes looked deep into mine, wanting to trust, begging to be allowed to trust.

"Yes. And things can be once again as they were before

all that. But we have to make things right. They won't right themselves."

"Yes," she said eagerly, clinging harder to me.

"Where is Ringo?" I asked gently.

"Who?"

"Ringo," I said patiently. "It is he, not I, who hurt you. Who pushed Doc away from you. Remember?"

She raised tear-blurred eyes. A tiny frown pinched her brows together. I gently smoothed it away with a forefinger.

"Oh yes," she said gratefully. "Now I remember. It was him all along. Yes, I remember. Him."

"Where is he, Kate?"

She placed her face on my chest, breathing deeply, standing motionless within my arms as if afraid that I would push her away. I rubbed her shoulders gently, looking over the top of her head again into the mirror and hating the man looking back.

"Over in Myers Cienega," she said, her voice muffled against my shirtfront.

I smiled and gently patted her shoulder. Her hands grasped urgently at my coat.

"Things will be all right, won't they, Doc?" she asked hopefully.

"Of course," I said, lying smoothly to soothe her before leaving her forever.

It wasn't hard. I sent a telegram to Ringo to meet me in Morse's Canyon in the Chiricahua Mountains, but I signed Wyatt's name to it. It was necessary, you see; I owed a debt. Buckskin Frank Leslie went with me but left me alone on the road leading up to the grove of trees.

He was waiting for me when I stepped down from Ares and walked toward him. His eyes lit with surprise in his whiskey-bloated face. It was like looking into a somber and immense mirror. He grinned.

"Well, I didn't think you would come," he said.

"I'm your huckleberry," I said, coughing and stepping closer.

"Well then," he said. His eyes moved beyond me, looking down the road for the person he had expected to see. "I was expecting your dog-man. I don't have a fight with you."

"I beg to differ, sir," I said politely. "But there is a small thing to settle between us. A game of blood. Remember."

"Oh, that." He made a deprecating gesture with the flat of his hand. "That's over. It almost worked, but Earp broke it up. I wonder if things would have been better." He looked at me, smiled, and shook his head. "Yes, I expect they would have. You were the one holding them all together. Death." He grinned. "And the other three horsemen: Conquest, Pestilence, and War. But none of them would have been survivors if it hadn't been for you, Holliday."

"The same could be said about the cowboys," I answered. His eyebrows rose. "You were the one making decisions and letting Curly Bill think he was bossing the outfit, weren't you? Especially after Old Man Clanton died."

"How did you figure that?" he said, grinning, enjoying himself.

"Wasn't hard," I said. "We're two of the same coin: heads and tails. Ike and Curly Bill were too dumb to make any plans that called for finesse. Ike was a coward and Curly Bill a killer. That left you."

"Two of a coin?" He shook his head. "You are a walking cliché, Holliday. Surely you could think of a different analogy."

"It works. And we are both clichés, you know. There's nothing left for people like us."

"Except to go out in a blaze of glory, right?" He grinned. "Homeric, but wonderful. Too bad it had to end. I was having a lot of fun with it all."

"I wasn't," I said. His eyes bored into mine, concentrated, meditative. He caught his lower lip in his yellowed teeth, then sudden lights glimmered with delight deep in his eyes, like burning brimstone.

"All right. Let's do it. Like I said: Homeric." His thumb lifted the thong off the hammer of his Colt.

"Say when," I said.

The words hardly made it to the air before his hand flashed down to his holstered pistol. I slipped the Colt .45 from its holster, firing in the same movement. The bullet took him high in the forehead. The top of his head exploded outward. He staggered, then fell backwards. His hand twitched, still trying from nervous memory to raise his pistol.

"Come on, Ringo," I begged.

But he heard no more. I looked down sadly at his body and replaced my pistol. "You're no daisy, Johnny Ringo. None at all."

With a great effort, I dragged his body into the middle of a clump of oaks springing from a single stem and laid him in the hand of the parent oak on top of a large, stone pedestal. I paused, panting from the effort, then pulled his boots from him, and for pure prank, removed his holsters, rebuckling them upside down.

I returned to Ares, smiling at the comic picture Ringo made lying under the tree. I had created a nice mystery that would leave a smokescreen over what had actually happened here. I didn't want anyone to know or even guess that it had been Doc Holliday who had killed Johnny Ringo. If word got out that I had been in Arizona while I was supposedly on trial in Colorado, there would be a public outcry against those who had helped me. Honor dictated that I keep my presence here a secret. I owed Masterson that. As far as the rest of the world was concerned, I was in Trinidad, recovering from sickness while my attorney argued my case in court. And Wyatt was safe. I mounted and looked down at Ringo's body, envying him briefly.

"Silent leges enim inter arma," I intoned. I sketched a hasty cross in the air with my forefinger.

Then I turned Ares and rode slowly away.

It is finished, I thought wearily.

And a great emptiness filled me—the black hole that I had told Wyatt about so many months before.

5

I went back to Trinidad, where I was fined fifty dollars for carrying firearms in the city limits. The bunco charge was dismissed when the "citizen" failed to come forth to testify. Masterson never asked what had happened; the fact that I was still alive was enough for him. Two weeks later, the news of Johnny Ringo's death made the newspapers, but I was in Denver at the time with Mary, trying a new "cure" for consumption with no hope of success. Still, it was worth a try.

One day, a reporter from the Denver *Republican* found me as I was making my way home from dinner. At first I refused to speak with him, but he persisted, and finally I brought him to my room. He was clever, I'll admit that. He took me through the OK Corral incident and at last asked me point-blank: "Who killed Johnny Ringo?"

I took a long sip of whiskey and waited until he began to fidget from nervousness. I debated telling him the truth, but I remembered Masterson and the others who had helped me in the affair. I couldn't betray them; it was a question of honor.

"Wyatt did," I said quietly. His eyes bugged out and he began scribbling faster and faster in his notebook, taking down everything I said in an abbreviated shorthand—too short, as I was to discover later when his article came out, but since the last part of it was a lie, I really didn't care.

"He had to keep it real quiet because he didn't want anyone to know. I was on trial in Pueblo for that drummed-up bunco charge (some people will do anything to get their name in the papers, you know?) and I heard that Wyatt had taken his horse and rode over from Gunnison. He still had quite a few friends in the area, notably Buckskin Frank

Leslie. Leslie owed Wyatt a couple of favors and was willing to help Wyatt on the quiet.

"It was Leslie who found where Ringo was off on a toot. Leslie sent word to him in Wyatt's name to meet him at Turkey Creek. Wyatt killed him up there."

"But why was Ringo not wearing his boots?" the reporter asked. "And why had his guns been buckled on upside down?"

"I don't know," I said, shaking my head. "I think Wyatt caught him as he was making himself ready to ambush Wyatt. He had taken his boots off and wrapped his undershirt around his feet like moccasins. I think Wyatt surprised him before he could put his gun belt back on, they fought, and Wyatt just snugged it around him afterward. Probably an accident that it went on upside down, or maybe Leslie did it when he was drunk. I guess we'll never know, will we?"

The reporter had his story and Wyatt received credit for killing Johnny Ringo. I don't feel bad about that at all; the world likes a hero who avenges the death of his brother.

That was the last interview I gave. A couple of days later, I received a telegram from Father, asking me to meet him in New Orleans. I hadn't heard from him in years. At first I was tempted to throw the telegram away, but suddenly a pang of homesickness struck me. I *needed* to see him one more time. I didn't know if I could make it to New Orleans, but I had to try.

I loaded Ares into a boxcar, and together we traveled to Kansas City and from there to St. Louis and down to New Orleans. Several times I thought I would die along the way, but Old Williams kept me going. The trouble was that I had to drink more and more of it in order for the cauterizing effect to take place.

Father appeared shocked when he met me. At first I thought it had been a mistake, but he hugged me gently as if I were a fragile porcelain doll that would break—maybe I would have, I was that weak—and we went out to dinner together. We ended up back in his hotel, where he asked me to fill in what had happened to me since leaving Dallas. I was surprised for I thought that Mattie would have kept him informed from my letters to her. When I mentioned this, he nodded and said that he wanted to hear the whole story, not the abridged one that I had given her.

So I gave him the story. Piece by piece.

"I came to New Orleans," I finished, looking at Father across from me. "You understand, I hope, why I couldn't take credit for Ringo's death. It really didn't mean that much to me; the credit, I mean. The fact that he was dead was enough. It was a matter of honor. Twice," I amended, "the matter of honor. The first, because I couldn't betray those who had helped me; the second, because . . . well, because it makes Wyatt a knight of the purple sage." I grinned at him. "The world needs some heroes; people like me can never be heroes."

"I see," he said, leaning back in his chair. His face was tired, lined, but he had been celebrating with other members of his regiment at their first reunion and a flushed freshness gleamed faintly from it.

He reached with steady fingers for the glass of Old Williams I had placed in front of him and sipped appreciatively.

"I am sorry for you," he said suddenly, looking up from his glass.

I shrugged. "I am quite a few years past the due date. I still owe God a death."

"Yes." Tears glinted in his eyes. He wiped them away.

An awkward silence grew between us as we avoided looking at each other, each feeling the sadness of the other.

"And Mattie," I said eagerly, changing the subject. "What about Mattie? It's been a long time since I heard from her. Is she all right?"

"She's entered a convent, John," he said gently. "Saint Vincent's in Savannah. She's taken the name Sister Mary Melanie."

I sat back, stunned. The black hole inside widened. Mattie. Gone. Finally. I had always assumed that everything was over between us, yet I had clung to hope, hope that the world would not continue without me, not survive me, and that Mattie and I . . .

My fingers shook as I reached for the glass of whiskey and drained it. I poured another. Drank. And another.

And then the sobs came.

And my father's arms folded around my shoulders. I cried into his chest. I smelled his cigars and the whiskey and the cologne he had sprinkled over his shirt.

I cried.

From the final rejection.

I went back to Denver. I left Ares with Father. He hated to see me go, tugging at the reins, trying to follow me as I walked away from him and down to the levee to catch a steamer up to St. Louis and the train to Omaha and Denver.

Before I left, I paid a visit to Solange and her brother, Philippe. Solange had become, well, a tramp after I killed Pierre You and left, chasing after one man then another. Philippe had tried to rescue her reputation, but had been severely wounded in a duel that left him a cripple and her reputation the laugh of New Orleans.

Out of a sense of friendship and trying to rebuild Solange's reputation or preserving what little remained of it (and perhaps a hope that my pain might finally be ended), I found the man, a card player, down at the levee. It was an easy matter to accuse him of cheating, for I caught him at it in the third hand we played together. We never went to the oaks; we settled the affaire d'honneur there, in the room, in the midst of sweating bodies and foul stenches and swirling cigar smoke. I challenged fate again by shooting for his forehead, but I was too quick, too quick. My bullet beat his a shade before his finger reflexively pulled the trigger of his pistol, sending his bullet harmlessly into the ceiling high overhead.

I served warning that I would be ready for the next would-be suitor for Solange's affections. It was an empty threat, but none there knew it.

* * *

Denver had too many memories, and the vision of Mattie in veil haunted me in the night when my cough did not drive me into the arms of Morpheus and the nightmares. Word came about a new strike at Leadville, high in the mountains. Against Mary's advice, I took a stage there and went to work as a faro dealer for Cy Allen at the Monarch saloon. One of my first clients was Johnny Tyler, an old nemesis from Tombstone, the same Johnny Tyler Wyatt had thrown out of the Oriental for that bastard Milt Joyce. I warned him to stay away from me, but he had many friends who were more than willing to help him. Taunts began, until one day I had enough and challenged Tyler in front of others.

"All right, Johnny Tyler," I said quietly in Allen's saloon. "You've been after me for quite a while. Let's settle this."

"Why I don't know what you mean, Holliday," he said, stepping back in feigned amazement.

"Yes, you do," I said. "Where are you going? Still running, Johnny?"

Hatred flickered in his eyes, momentarily, then disappeared as he put on his smooth, bland gambler's face in the presence of others.

"I have no intention of fighting you, Holliday," he said, pulling open his coat to show himself without arms. "I am not a fool."

"No?" I challenged. I stepped forward, slapping him across the face as Wyatt had years before. But my slap was weak, ineffectual, lacking the strength of Wyatt's. The high altitude of Leadville had begun its slow drain of my life. I coughed and felt the strength of the worm growing in my chest. I stepped back, determined not to humiliate myself by slapping him like a woman again.

"Let's dance, Johnny," I begged.

I could tell by his face that he had heard the pleading note in my voice. He laughed and turned with scorn away from me, leaving me with the choice of shooting him in the back or leaving. I had no intention of ending my days with the ignominy of a loop around my neck. With as much dignity as

I could muster, I spat on his back and turned, waiting deliberately for him to make a move, but he didn't and I slowly walked from the saloon.

Allen had little choice but to fire me.

And Lady Luck turned her back on me as well.

I began to lose hand after hand, finally breaking myself at the poker table in Mannie Hyman's Board of Trade Saloon. Billy Allen loaned me five dollars, and slowly I built up my stake again.

And then one day Billy Allen swaggered up to me while I stood at the bar in the Board of Trade, drinking a glass of whiskey, and said, "Holliday, you owe me five dollars."

"All right," I answered, reaching for my pocket but he stopped me.

"If I don't get it by noon, I'm going to beat the hell out of you."

I frowned, then heard the guffaws from the small crowd around us as he turned and swaggered away.

Red rage nearly buckled me. I coughed and coughed and held frantically to the mahogany bar until the spell passed. I took a shallow breath and gestured for Mannie to pour me another whiskey.

"Are you all right, Doc?" Mannie asked in concern.

"Whiskey," I whispered.

He quickly poured one and placed it in front of me. I drank it and shuddered. The cauterizing effect came slow, and I drank another. And another, losing track of time.

The door to the saloon burst open and Billy Allen entered. I saw his reflection in the glass of the cigar counter and turned as he swaggered toward me.

"Well, Holliday," he sneered. "Tired of running?"

Weakly, I turned to face him, holding on to the edge of the bar with my left hand.

"This is for Johnny Tyler," he said, coming up to me.

He raised his hand to slap me. I slipped my hand inside my coat and pulled the Colt .45. His eyes widened and he turned, trying to flee. I snapped a shot at him, but he twisted away and my bullet slapped into the wall.

"God! No, Holliday! No! Don't kill me!" he begged. He stumbled backwards, away from me.

I grinned at him. His face whitened. I cocked the pistol again with effort, my strength nearly gone. He flinched and tried to run again, but I fired and this time hit him in the right arm. He fell to his back, grabbing his arm and howling. The front of his pants darkened where his bladder released itself. I stepped forward to finish him, caring little about the consequences, but suddenly a brawny hand reached in front of me and jerked the Colt from my grasp.

I whirled weakly and stared into the eyes of Captain Bradbury of the City Police. He shook his head. For a moment I was tempted to draw the Colt Lightning, but I recognized the futility of it all and slumped back against the bar as the blubbering Allen rose from the floor and staggered out.

At my trial, the judge listened to both sides. Allen spun his fabrication, but another there piped up and said that I had tried to pay him the money but Allen wouldn't take it. I explained about my trouble with Johnny Tyler, about Wyatt dragging him from the Oriental, and the courtroom erupted with laughter. The judge freed me but ordered me out of Leadville. I boarded the stage for Denver.

For a while Denver revived me, but then the sickness returned with a vengeance. Mary moved in with me, and we tried to become what both of us wanted. We were happy, but beneath that happiness was a desperation that both of us knew and kept trying to push down instead of letting it become a shadow covering our attempt at happiness.

I knew it was over the night that we went dancing at Charpiot's. Mary was beautiful, her long hair collected in ringlets, and her magnificent body that she had kept hidden so long in men's clothes was on full display in a gown she had made for the evening. Many ladies appeared scandalized when we entered.

"John," she said softly, pressing my arm across the table we had been shown to, "this isn't going to work. Let's go."

I glanced around at the stiff lips and hostile eyes staring at us from the dowagers present. I grinned and leaned back, smothering a cough with my hand.

"Nonsense, my dear," I said. "We don't need them. Pretend that they are not there."

"But they are," she said. Her eyes glittered with tears held in check. "Please?"

"A moment," I said, rising. I walked across to the orchestra and motioned for the conductor. He came down.

"A waltz, if you please," I said.

He hesitated, but I grinned at him and repeated my request. Hastily, he nodded and turned back to the orchestra.

The timing was perfect: the orchestra broke into "The Blue Danube" as I bowed over her hand.

"Madame," I said. "Will you do me the honor?"

"John . . ."

But I pulled her to her feet, and within moments we were gliding around the floor. We merged together as one, our bodies gracefully complementing each other as we circled the floor, one agile figure molded at the hands. A sensuality pulsed through both of us, and we lost track of time and the people enviously watching from their tables.

The room was silent when we finished. Then the musicians broke into spontaneous applause as I led her regally from the floor. We gathered her wrap from the chair and made our exit, our night completed. The stars shone with a cold brilliance, and the full moon heaved high overhead as Mary paused to kiss me gently before we took a carriage home. And I, foolishly, challenged the gods with my happiness.

At last Mary sadly told me that my one hope was to go to Glenwood Springs and take the waters at the hot springs there.

"Will it make a difference? Do you really think it would help me?" I asked from my place on the sofa. Dickens's *Bleak House* lay open on my lap. I reached a trembling hand for the glass of whiskey on the small table beside my shoulder.

"No," she said. She knelt beside me and kissed me gently. "But it would me. At least I'll be able to say that I tried."

"It's that important to you?"

"Yes."

"Will you come with me?"

"No. I want to remember you alive, not dead."

And so I took the train, but when I arrived, I was too weak to get off and two men carried me off like a little baby mewling and puking in his nurse's arms. They put me up at the Glenwood Hotel. I took the baths prescribed by my doctor.

I noticed open sores on my body.

I paid the busboy, Art Kendricks, ten cents each day to bring me a bottle of whiskey despite the doctor's orders. For a while, the whiskey helped, but then came the time when there wasn't enough whiskey in the world.

And the horror came in the night, again and again in the night, and with the horror, the fever.

6

. . . and Kate. My nymph du pavé. The woman was a whore, and there's an end on it. At times she wanted what other women had—husband, home, children—but in the end she would always distrust what she had and the need to prove that she was still desirable to men would become too strong and she would prowl the saloons looking for those willing to tell her she was pretty. Even if they lied, the lies were good enough for the spare, clutching moment.

You have come, Father, blessing my hypocrisy with the sprinkling of your holy drops upon the shell soon to be empty. And now, as I told you yesterday, this confession, my first, needs by your God to be a long one. So forbear.

Are you comfortable? Yes?

Then we begin again.

She had a heart too soon made glad, too easily impressed; she liked what men did for her and her looks went every-

where and she thanked them—good, with her favors. In the end, it was all the same to her. She wanted to be wife, mother, and whore. Her passions were not easily satisfied, and there was always some officious fool willing to dally with her—back alleys, closets, the odd crib or two, all were the same to her when the heat was upon her.

Yet she would always return.

He's mad who trusts in the tameness of a wolf, a horse's health, a boy's love, or a whore's oath. I was among the maddest, for I owed her, not only for her favors that she was willing to bestow upon a lunger—although that is enough, for few ladies are willing to embrace one whose lips taste brassy from spent blood—but there was a time when the wildness was upon us both and she defied an entire town for me. I always took her back.

Until Tombstone.

Betrayal can be forgiven; disloyalty cannot.

Yet I miss our fights.

And lovemaking.

Sometimes, when the November wind moans through the eaves and rattles the window above my bed, I hear the groans of that blond wanton and feel her fleshy thighs gripping my waist and smell the stale, whiskey-stink of her breath! Again I hear the mendacious mutterings in my ear professing her love for me and know them for a whore's hypocrisy. Her lips sucked forth my soul and sent it on trembling wings through the blackness of everlasting night. See where it flies!

Now I have but one or two bare hours to live in this, my thirty-sixth year.

Beside me on the small table my watch chimes Chopin's "Opus No. 1 in B-flat Minor"—Mother's favorite. Pressed into the back is a curl of her hair.

Will I meet her soon?

I wonder what shift Heaven will place upon me. What gifts, what forfeits will I find in this last mystery? I have prepared for it, sacrificing the Presbyterianism of my family for the greater certainty offered by the confessional. My family will not care; they never have. And lovely Mattie will be pleased..

. . . Mattie . . .

Perhaps there will be a mystical meeting beyond middle earth.

We can hope.

I can hope. . . .

What I did I did, for I had no choice . . . no choice. . . . It was a task imposed upon me by my own ego and the soul of the West. . . .

It is a debt I have owed, now well paid. Perhaps it provides a unity to life. It certainly provides an end.

In nomine Patri, et spiritus, et fili. . . .

The rest blurs.

I remember only bits and pieces now.

. . . in vino veritas . . .

. . . Inferna tetigit possit ut supera assequi . . .

. . . Meum est propodsitum in taberna mori;

. . . Vinum sit appositum morientis ori. . . .

. . . but plans greater than mine take precedent. I can feel the horseman riding through the nocturnal sky to bear me to my fate. I look upon his face and see his name set upon him, and I know him as an old acquaintance. Yet, strangely, I find myself reluctant to mount behind him. My hypocrisy remains in full bloom.

The music of my watch slows.

O lente, lenti currite, noctis equi!

Again I feel my immortality and curse it, knowing the mark Lucifer has placed upon me that I have borne over the years, living with the malignant adder in my chest squeezing life from me drop by bright red drop. Now, like a foggy mist, the past unfolds before me to give me a full reckoning of my sins, calling me to account for them, reminding me of the rewards I have won and lost, a creature whose soul was forfeit with his birth like some brutish beast, bargained for pleasure by the parents who engendered me.

Ah! There they appear! Old enemies and nameless ones who thought to make a life by taking mine . . .

A bloody head hanging by a sinew. . . .

. . . blood in eye, blood in mouth, calling me down with the dead. . . . the living, the living dead, the hands upraised. . . .

I want to register the very moment how death has reached my hands, my arms, my feet. We see the light, but it is in the shadows where the truth lies. Step by step, I enter the dark, but the movement is the only truth. . . . I haven't died, but I'm already a ghost. . . . and I wonder what will remain once the dirt of legend washes from me. . . .

Ah, Mephistopheles! Are you disappointed that I would turn from you at the last? You who have practiced hypocrisy since your fall should recognize it by now!

. . . The quick and the dead, the unloved and the loved. . . . Oh, Mattie, the time is not long, now . . .

. . . my friends . . . too few, I fear, for lighting the priest's candles: Wyatt, perhaps Bat, Colonel Deweese, Eddie Foy . . .

. . . and Belle . . .

. . . my enemies . . .

. . . they stand before me: Kelly and Allen, Budd Ryan, Ed Bailey, Mike Gordon, Tom and Frank McLaury, Charlie White . . . I thought I killed him, but only stunned him, yet, he is there. . . . Others whose names I have forgotten. . . .

. . . or never knew . . .

. . . Ringo . . .

. . . Wyatt comes . . . and Josephine. . . . I can tell from the distasteful look on her face that she would rather be elsewhere. . . . perhaps curled naked into Wyatt's arms . . . or one who would be willing to risk Wyatt's wrath without peeing his pants, moving his bowels . . . to hold her creamy flesh in his arms, kiss the dark nipples of her breasts, feel her shapely legs wrapping urgently around his waist . . .

. . . there is no love lost between us . . .

. . . Wyatt speaks, his words flickering from the corners of his mouth . . . I try to answer, but my tongue cleaves to the top of my mouth . . .

"Ah, Doc! The times we had!"

He laughs, the sound nervous, shrill in the death room.

"Remember how Billy Claiborne tried to run away from us at Fly's and fell in that pile of fresh horse shit? I damn near die every time I think of him scampering like a spooked rabbit through the back gate, shit dripping off his face. Remember?"

. . . But I cannot answer . . . Speaking wastes what little breath I can drag into my ragged lungs to rattle around clumps of dead tissue . . .

"The whole damned kit and caboodle didn't amount to fly shit."

He sniggers as the pun registers, then he remembers himself, and his face sobers and settles into a mask as a lone tear begins to seep from the corner of his eye. He wipes it away, pretending to be warm, but the room is cool, too cool, and I feel its coldness in my bones.

. . . I feel old . . . tumbling endlessly down through a soundless void . . . turning and turning in a winding gyre. . . .

. . . I know what he is thinking. . . . I feel his thoughts licking at me like chilly fire . . . pity . . . a flicker-flash of images . . .

"And Virgil and Morgan. We were invincible that day, Doc. The four of us."

. . . And we walked through the burning heat of that day, the four horsemen of the apocalypse . . . Virgil, Morgan, Wyatt and me . . . Conquest, Pestilence, War, and Death. . . . I, the fourth horseman . . . isolated even while belonging to the unholy. . . .

. . . Dying is . . . tedious . . . We stare, vague-eyed, into the past . . . remembering mindless trivia . . . smelling the staleness of the earth upon our flesh . . . seeing images placed before us by our Confessers. . . .

. . . nihil ex nihilo . . .

. . . the communion wafer sits upon my stomach like arid dust . . .

"I must drink . . . no, not water . . . give me Old Williams. . . ."

. . . the sainted friend who has eased me through the trials and tribulations of . . .

Someone raises my head and holds a glass to my lips. I drink thirstily the whiskey that warms me, gives me the illusion of life. All too soon, the whiskey is gone and the deadly cold that has begun creeping up my limbs begins again its eternal return. My bare feet stick up from the covers. I laugh at the absurdity.

"I'll be damned. This is funny."

And gently, I am lowered again to my pillow. I feel the water leaking into my shredded lungs and labor to cough, to expel the drowning fluid.

. . . He comes! . . . He comes!

. . . the Destroyer! . . . the lure of our feelings . . .

. . . See where his skeletal arms beckon, gnashing his teeth, chewing the world down by bits . . . a few random specks . . . a cloud . . . dark nightmare-history . . . time . . . as coffin . . . the world burns! . . . Come ahead . . . make your play . . . do your worst. . . . What more can you do to me? . . .

. . . Ah God! . . . The pain! . . . The pain!!! . . .

. . . Dear Father Downey! . . . If you have God's ear, talk to Him! . . . Talk to Him! . . .

. . . You priests make the world by whispers . . . transmogrify life with your confessions . . . making life a grave undertaking. . . . Heroism is more than noble language . . .

. . . Is this joy I feel? . . . The end of an epoch? . . .

. . . And at this moment, this very moment when I feel my soul fleeing from my body into the firmament and listen to the final chimes of my watch, I think of Mattie. . . .

. . . and November . . .

. . . I recognize the season. . . . The air of the room chills me . . . I hear light taps upon the windowpane . . . heavy flakes of snow falling . . . falling . . . Snow is falling all over the country. . . . There cannot be a place where the snow will not soon lie, soft and gentle, falling on the dark plains, the treeless hills . . . the craggy mountains . . . falling softly on the graves of ancient warriors . . . falling upon the dark waters of the Brazos and the Canadian and the dark water of the placid Platte. . . . Falling upon every part of lonely Linwood with its garden of stone above this house and on the *lonely graves of those I placed in the dusty earth. . . . Drifting thickly over the pine-needled ground, gathering against the trunks of the ponderosa pines, the spruce of the mountains . . . drifting against the gate to Father's house and across Mother's grave and barren branches of the lilac bushes, the barren thorns of the roses. . . . Falling faintly through . . . the . . . universe . . . the last descent upon all the living . . .*

AUTHOR'S NOTE

The novelist's job is to enlighten as well as entertain his audience. If hiswork, like that of all artists, does not teach man about himself, then it is worthless. I have tried to do this with the story of John Henry "Doc" Holliday, a Byronic hero who became an image of Romantic sensibility: mysterious, mocking, sinful, and an outcast who deliberately turned his back on the conventions of his society to live a Rabelaisian life, taunting the gods and fate, which had infected his body and hopes and dreams with a deadly sickness, to take his life on his own terms.

The nineteenth-century West was a time of great turmoil—the Manifest Destiny, a young country like a young man feeling the strength and vigor of his youth, testing himself against the challenges of the frontier. Yet the West was tragic as well, for the time that excited men's souls did not last long—about the same time that Holliday's life lasted.

Holliday lived a life similar to Homer's Achilles or Sophocles's Oedipus. His life was short but adventurous and tragic, for the gods who follow the steps of heroes always see to their frailties as well. It would not do to have heroes grow so strong that they have no challenges left to them but to challenge the gods. So it was that the gods made Oedipus a tragic figure with his hubris and Holliday a tragic figure with his sickness.

His tragedy was compounded in that the one love of his life, with his cousin Mattie, could not be fulfilled. Mattie joined St. Vincent's Convent in Savannah, Georgia on October 1, 1883, four years before Doc Holliday's death on November 8, 1887, in Glenwood Springs, Colorado. She took the name of Sister Mary Melanie and became a Sister of Mercy and a teacher at the Sacred Heart Convent in Augusta.

She later became Sister Superior of the Immaculate Conception Convent and died at St. Joseph's Infirmary, April 19, 1939. Among the young people whose lives she touched when she taught in Atlanta was Margaret Mitchell, the author of *Gone With the Wind*, whose devotion to Sister Mary Melanie was so intense that she designed and named the character of Melanie in her famous book after the gentle Mattie.

Alcoholic, condemned to die an early death, Doc Holliday became a metaphor for the West, which was also condemned to die an early death with encroaching civilization. At no other time in the history of the world was a country's life so brief. Yet, like a dying star, its brilliance shone with such a fierce light that it influenced thousands of storytellers and historians alike.

I hasten to add, however, that this is not a historical work nor a roman á clef in so much that it is a novel about the West told through the life of Doc Holliday. Truth and fiction, however, are difficult to separate. Indeed, more truth can often be discovered in fiction than in what passes for fact—especially in this day and age of the revisionist who enjoys playing fast and loose with the truth. I leave it to the reader to separate fact from fiction, but caution the reader, as well, to beware of mislaying the truth in the process.

—Dr. Randy Lee Eickhoff
El Paso, Texas
Autumn, 1997